W9-DAV-834

Hidden Falls

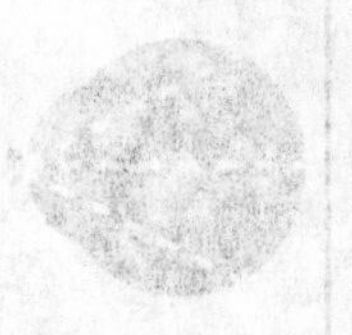

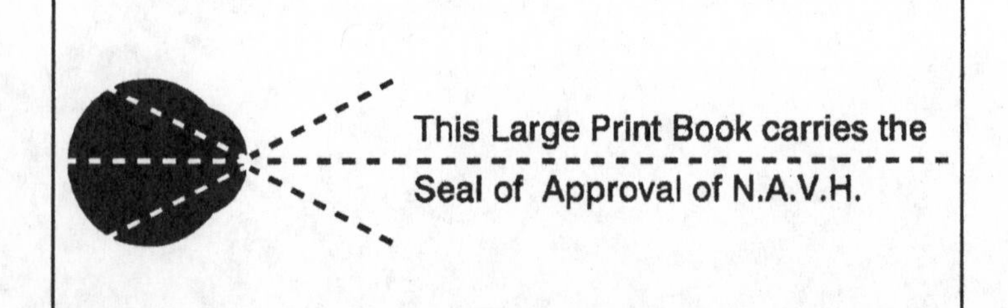
This Large Print Book carries the
Seal of Approval of N.A.V.H.

Hidden Falls

Olivia Newport

THORNDIKE PRESS
A part of Gale, Cengage Learning

Farmington Hills, Mich • San Francisco • New York • Waterville, Maine
Meriden, Conn • Mason, Ohio • Chicago

Thorndike Press, a part of Gale, Cengage Learning.

Thorndike Press® Large Print Christian Fiction.
The text of this Large Print edition is unabridged.
Other aspects of the book may vary from the original edition.
Set in 16 pt. Plantin.

LIBRARY OF CONGRESS CATALOGING-IN-PUBLICATION DATA

Names: Newport, Olivia, author.
Title: Hidden Falls / by Olivia Newport.
Description: Waterville, Maine : Thorndike Press, 2017. | Series: Thorndike Press large print Christian fiction
Identifiers: LCCN 2016046412| ISBN 9781410497017 (hardcover) | ISBN 1410497011 (hardcover)
Subjects: LCSH: Large type books. | GSAFD: Christian fiction.
Classification: LCC PS3614.E686 H57 2017 | DDC 813/.6—dc23
LC record available at https://lccn.loc.gov/2016046412

Published in 2017 by arrangement with Barbour Publishing, Inc.

Printed in Mexico
1 2 3 4 5 6 7 21 20 19 18 17

CAST OF CHARACTERS

Quinn – 55, long-time resident, teacher, and beloved citizen of Hidden Falls.

Sylvia Alexander – 52, Quinn's oldest and dearest friend, mayor of Hidden Falls, daughter of Emma.

Lauren Nock – 28, family ministry director at Our Savior Community Church. Niece of Sylvia Alexander.

Liam Elliott – 38, investment consultant, fiancé to Jessica McCarthy, brother to Cooper, cousin to Dani Roose.

Cooper Elliott – 34, works in law enforcement as a sheriff's deputy. Brother to Liam, cousin to Dani Roose.

Dani Roose – 32, cousin to Liam and Cooper Elliot, makes her living doing odd jobs, handy person, computer nerd. Loves the lake, fishing, solitude.

Nicole Sandquist – 30, investigative reporter in St. Louis, Missouri, who grew up with and dated Ethan Jordan.

Ethan Jordan, MD – 30, neurosurgeon in

Columbus, Ohio, who grew up with and dated Nicole Sandquist.

Jack Parker – 40, lawyer, recently moved his family to Hidden Falls. Wife, Gianna; son, Colin; daughters, Eva and Brooke.

Prologue

Thirty-one years ago

Undeterred by the persistent mist that Hidden Falls cast off, she paced a few feet ahead of him. Reluctantly, he'd released her hand when the path narrowed and they could no longer walk side by side. She paused now, and Quinn knew she was taking care with the abrupt nineteen-inch drop that briefly steepened the stony descent to their destination in another twenty yards.

Sylvia's head turned and she caught Quinn's eye. The core of him went soft at the sight. That smile. The flush of pleasure in this day. The way she embraced the beauty of life, whatever it brought. When he touched her, he sometimes thought his knees were jelly.

He took the deep step off the ledge behind her, and they were side by side again. She reached for his hand, and he gave it. With the other, Quinn patted his jacket pocket, reassuring himself that the small lump he had zipped in was still there. He'd been carrying it around for days, transferring it from one pocket to another. If he was going to remove it, this would be the moment. Neither of them would forget this sunny spring day behind Hidden Falls with full hearts of gratitude for each other.

Quinn dropped Sylvia's hand and put an arm across the back of her shoulders to pull her against him, hip to hip, and walk in step these last few yards. Leaning into his shoulder, Sylvia raised her mouth for a kiss and Quinn obliged.

The spring wind gusted, and the mist felt more like rain as they moved into the hollow of rock behind the tumbling falls. Hidden Falls were not impressively high, but water plunging out Whisper Lake cascaded past this space in a liquid wall before crashing into a bed of rocks below. The winding hike down to the hollow was not one many people bothered with. Tourists were content to hike along the edge of the lake at the top of the falls, and many residents of the town of Hidden Falls were so used to the sight that they barely saw it anymore. With their arms around each other, Quinn and Sylvia tilted their single gaze upward and blinked against the spray that struck their faces from random angles. Sunlight streaming through rushing water danced rainbows around them. Greenery budded with fragrance and promise. Water surged endlessly past them in a vertical river. Though Quinn was only in his second year in the town, he could not imagine tiring of this scene no matter if he lived in Hidden Falls for thirty years. This place had given him a new beginning.

Quinn nudged Sylvia back a few steps, deeper into the hollow, where they could watch the water and remain dry at the same time. They would hear each other better without competing against the collision of moving water and immovable rock. If the words stumbling around his heart passed through his lips, he wanted her to hear them clearly.

At the moment, though, Quinn wanted only to kiss Sylvia. Uninterrupted. Ravenously. Repeatedly. Her form molded against his, as hungry for him as he was for her. If ever he was going to share his life with a woman, Sylvia was that woman. If ever he was going to propose, this was the moment.

"Mmm." Sylvia broke the kiss, trailing hot breath across his face. "This is a perfect day. You . . . here . . ."

The slits of her eyes widened, questioning. This was what Sylvia's face looked like when hope hung before her, present yet intangible, dangling yet beyond her grasp.

Quinn could fulfill that hope. He could give it shape and light. He was certain of the ring in his pocket — they had strolled the shops of downtown Birch Bend together and considered dozens of possibilities. This was the one Sylvia wanted to wear for the rest of her life, eventually with the silver band that would match one on his hand. Had she felt the lump in his jacket during their embrace? Had it stirred her hope of a perfect day? Perhaps it was unkind of him to carry around the velvet box, making her wonder when the moment would rise from ordinariness and lay out her future before her.

It was the nightmares that held him back. *Nightmares* was the wrong word, though. While he did wake in the night, sweating and gasping and scrambling to turn on every light in the room, the days also brimmed with grief and violent distraction.

It still felt fresh and frightening, and Quinn wasn't sure it would ever change. The holes inside him might be bottomless.

One moment could change everything.

Could this exquisite moment on this perfect day, in the safe hollow of Hidden Falls, heal the fracture that ran through him?

Quinn put a hand in his jacket pocket and wrapped his fingers around the box. Then starting with his thumb and uncurling one finger at a time, he forced himself to open his hand and leave the box where it lay.

Sylvia knew Quinn more deeply than anyone else he had ever known. But she didn't know everything. And it wasn't fair to ask her to share a life of shadows.

He stroked her cheek and looked into those stunning, deep eyes before kissing her one last time.

1
Ordinary Secrets

Present Day
Saturday
9:27 a.m.

"It's Saturday morning. Get in the car." Sylvia Alexander gripped the hedge clippers and prepared to forcibly remove them from Ted Quinn's hands.

"And what if I don't want to go?" Quinn eyed Sylvia but released the clippers.

"You said you wanted a normal day. On a normal Saturday, you and I have breakfast on Main Street before I check on the shop."

Quinn tilted his head toward the garage. "You know where those go. Give me a minute to change my ratty sweater." He clomped up the porch steps and into the house.

Sylvia examined the progress Quinn had made since yesterday on trimming overgrown bushes across the front of the house. He must have been working at least two hours already. She crossed to the open detached garage, savoring the crunch of tumbled maple leaves under her feet, and hung the clippers on their hook between the old-as-the-hills hacksaw and the hammer with the longest handle and widest claw.

When Sylvia met Quinn, he hardly knew how to grip a hammer properly. Now he owned the most varied tool collection in Hidden Falls. He bought the old house almost thirty years ago and took odd delight in the discovery that one wall of the garage was pegboard. As Quinn remodeled, one room at a time, he added a hook to the pegboard for each new tool.

Sylvia watched each room take shape, unsure how to interpret Quinn's invitations for her opinions of his taste before he was too far in to turn back from his plan. Gradually she accepted that her opinions were all he wanted. She would never share his home.

Then came the preoccupation with landscaping and another class of tools. Even Dani Roose, who did odd jobs around town, knew Quinn owned any tool she needed.

Sylvia pulled the garage door down, wondering when Quinn was going to give in and install a garage door opener.

By the time Quinn emerged from the house, Sylvia had her engine idling and her hand on the gearshift. He opened the passenger door and slid into the seat. When had his hair receded another half inch toward the back of his skull? And gone another shade whiter?

Sylvia put the ten-year-old red Ford Taurus in gear. "It won't be so bad, you know."

"Of course not. Breakfast is my favorite meal." Quinn turned his head and met her gaze with a smile. "Especially with my oldest and dearest friend."

Wistfulness floated through his expression as it so often did. Even after all these years, some days she couldn't bear what she saw there. Sylvia had stopped asking questions years ago.

"That's not what I'm talking about and you know it," Sylvia said. "Don't change the subject."

As mayor of Hidden Falls, Illinois, Sylvia felt obliged to set an example, so she observed the residential speed limit on the two-mile stretch of road that angled from Quinn's neighborhood of old houses into what everyone called "downtown" — a few square blocks of shops, restaurants, professional businesses, and churches. She eased the car into a parking spot at a right angle to the entrance of the Fall Shadows Café.

Inside, Gavin Owens gave them a wave from behind the counter. "You're late."

"That's my fault," Quinn mumbled.

"I hope your big day isn't getting off to a rough start." Gavin raised a bushy eyebrow.

"He'll be fine." Sylvia pointed toward a

table away from the door and off the path from the kitchen.

Quinn pulled out a chair, and Sylvia situated herself in it.

"He never brings us a menu." Quinn thrummed the tabletop.

"Why should he? You always order eggs Benedict for both of us."

"A person has a right to make a change, doesn't he?"

"If he brought you a menu, you'd need your reading glasses. I'm willing to bet the cost of breakfast that you don't have them with you."

One side of his mouth went up. "If I didn't like you so well, I'd take that personally."

Sylvia put her elbows on the table and leaned toward him. "Quinn, it's going to be a lovely evening. Why don't you just let yourself enjoy it?"

"All the attention. It's silly."

Quinn had been teaching at Hidden Falls High School for more than thirty years. He was the first to volunteer for anything that needed doing around town, and he came up with half the ideas himself. Friendly and approachable almost to a fault, he'd stop and talk to anyone, no matter his own schedule. Traits that normally endeared him to Sylvia at the moment stirred frustration.

"People are fond of you." Sylvia thumped the table edge with two fingers. "Let them appreciate you."

He raised his hands in surrender. "Fine. I'll behave myself."

Gavin arrived with a fist gripping the handle of a coffeepot and two mugs hanging from his fingers of the other hand.

"Thank you, Gavin." Sylvia inhaled the dark roast aroma while the café owner poured. She was due for a booster after the early morning cup in her own kitchen.

"I hear you got a lot of RSVPs from out of town for tonight." Gavin nudged one mug in front of Sylvia and tipped the pot over the second.

"We did," Sylvia said. "We didn't know what to hope for when we sent out invitations, but we shouldn't have been surprised that former students would want to be here."

"I heard Nicole Sandquist is coming." Gavin pulled a rag from his apron pocket and swiped a spot on the table. "And Ethan Jordan. He's some hotshot brain surgeon or something."

"You seem well informed." Sylvia sipped her coffee, feeling the warmth ooze all the way down.

Quinn perked up. "Nicole and Ethan? Both of them?"

Sylvia nodded. "See? I told you it would be nice."

"Your eggs Benedict will be right out." Gavin set the coffee down. "I know, leave the pot."

"I always hoped Nicole and Ethan would be one of the high school sweetheart couples to make it." Quinn scratched the back of his head. "They were together so long. I know they loved each other."

"What are they now, twenty-nine? Thirty?"

"Something like that. I haven't heard from either of them in years. I wonder if one of them found someone else. Or maybe they both did."

Sylvia allowed her eyes to linger on Quinn's pensive face. He still had the strong jawline she first noticed when they were both much younger — younger even than Nicole and Ethan were now — but his forehead had taken on parallel creases that never seemed to smooth anymore. She supposed the tiny cracks running out from the corners of his eyes were no different than her own.

Thirty years.

Some of Quinn's first students had children in his social studies classes now. His tenth grade family history projects had become iconic in town tradition. Children had to interview their parents, and sometimes the parents had to consult grandparents to fill in gaps. Further back than that, it became harder to get reliable information. Every year, Quinn told his students they were one generation away from no one remembering them. Thanks to his efforts, the Hidden Falls Historical Society had copies of essays and family trees that were the subject of an ongoing organizational effort.

And tonight everyone would remember Quinn.

Thirty years.

His hair had been thick and brown, his smile broad and white, his shoulders wide and straight. Teachers came and went through the Hidden Falls school district. It was a good place for a first job out of college, with the ink still wet on a teaching credential. A few stayed as long as five years before moving on to larger school districts with bigger budgets. During Quinn's first semester teaching, Sylvia, fresh out of college herself, went with her mother to a school open house for her younger brother. She melted under the gaze of the new teacher her brother chattered about with unfettered enthusiasm.

Quinn rapped his knuckles on the table. "Where have you drifted off to?"

Sylvia smiled. "Remembering the day I met you. You were quite dashing."

"Have I lost my charm along with my hair and my eyesight?"

She still melted under his gaze. "You find it more every year."

Quinn broke eye contact. "Perhaps if I were less charming, people would not be making such a fuss tonight."

Sylvia rolled her eyes. "Are we back to that? You're going to have a good time. You're going to look as dashing as ever. You're going to see hundreds of people whose lives you've touched. You're going to see Nicole and Ethan and I don't know how many other students you helped launch into terrific futures because you cared about them when they were gawky, nerdy, or in trouble."

"You give quite the pep talk, Mayor Alexander."

"I've learned well from hanging around you all these years."

"I think I might like to meet this teacher you laud so sincerely." Quinn refilled his coffee mug. "Do you happen to have an in with him?"

"We go back a long way."

Once upon a time he held my hand, she thought. *Once upon a time he walked me home from the movies and took me fishing on the lake. Once upon a time he kissed me in the hollow behind the spray of Hidden Falls. Once upon a time we looked at rings.*

Gavin appeared with identical beige ceramic plates and set them down in front of Sylvia and Quinn with precision. "Look around, Quinn. Your gala is good for my business."

"I'd hardly call it a gala." Quinn laid a fork on his plate.

"The ladies have an excuse to wear new dresses, and the men will be in suits. It's a gala." Gavin pivoted and left.

Sylvia glanced around the café. Gavin was right. Nearly all the tables and booths were occupied. Some of the faces she hadn't seen in years. "Look, the Gardners are over by the window. They had six kids go through your classes in ten years before they moved away."

"I remember. We were afraid Number Four was never going to graduate."

"But he did — because of all that tutoring you did before school every morning."

A shadow crossed the table and Sylvia looked up. Quinn's face split in a grin as he scrambled to his feet.

"Cabe Mueller!" Quinn clapped the man on the back. "First-period American history in my first year in Hidden Falls."

"I've been teaching history myself for twenty-five years because of you." Cabe grasped Quinn's hand and pumped it hard.

"Look at us," Quinn said. "I was barely five years older than you when you were in my class. You have no idea how terrified I was. Cabe, this is my good friend, Sylvia Alexander. She's mayor around here now."

Cabe nodded toward Sylvia. "I won't interrupt your breakfast any further. I just couldn't resist coming over to say hello. I'll see you tonight."

After Cabe was gone, Sylvia smiled. "Wasn't that nice?"

Quinn's eyes followed Cabe's path. "He

was a good kid."

"Tonight will be full of moments like that." Sylvia cleared her throat. "Now. Have you got your tux?"

"Check."

"Some shoes other than the loafers you live in?"

"Check. I even have black socks."

"There's hope for you yet." She tilted her head to inspect the hair brushing his collar. "Maybe a stop at the barber?"

"On the list."

"Your speech?"

Quinn picked up his fork and pushed food around on his plate. "Well. About that —"

She cut him off. "Quinn, you must be prepared to say something. Ten or fifteen minutes."

"I have some thoughts rattling around in my head."

Sylvia snapped a paper napkin out of the dispenser in the middle of the table and slapped it in front of him. "Write them down. I've given enough speeches to know not to depend on memory."

"I'm a teacher." Quinn carved off a bite of egg. "I promise to come prepared."

"Shall I pick you up?"

"I'll drive. What time do you want me there?"

"By seven at the latest. That will give you time to greet a few people before everything gets under way."

"Sylvia, you're an excellent mayor."

The statement caught her off guard.

"I mean it," he said, his yellow-brown eyes fastened on her. "You keep this town organized and running like clockwork. We all depend on you. *I* depend on you. Thank you."

Sylvia moistened her lips. "You're welcome."

"You mean a great deal to me. I'm sorry that all those years ago I could not give you what you wanted."

11:18 a.m.

Liam Elliott put his arms around Jessica McCarthy's slender waist and welcomed the deepening, lingering kiss she offered while standing in the middle of his living room.

She moved her lips to the side of his neck. "Do we have to go tonight?"

Liam ran his tongue over his lips and stepped back. "I thought you got a new dress and everything."

"I did." She laid her hands on his chest. "But I don't have to wear it. Or I could wear it, but we don't have to go out. You could come to my place. I'll cook something better than banquet chicken."

"We chose the fish, remember?"

"I don't even know Quinn."

"But I do." Liam recognized the pout forming on Jessica's lips, but he was not going to give in. Not on this. “He was my favorite teacher in high school.”

“That was twenty years ago.”

“I can introduce you. He’s a town legend.”

“I don’t need to meet a town legend. I know who he is. Everybody knows who Quinn is. The crazy eccentric who never leaves the county. Not a single field trip, not even to take history students to visit the state capitol in Springfield. And he calls himself a history teacher.”

“He *is* a history teacher.”

“Why does everyone call him Quinn, anyway? Doesn’t he have a first name?”

“Ted. His name is Ted. Maybe Theodore. He’s just one of those people who goes by one name. That doesn’t make him crazy or eccentric.”

“My point is that you’re the best thing that’s happened to me since I came to this Podunk town.” Jessica expelled a heavy breath, took her hands off his chest, and backed away. “I just want us to have some time together.”

“It’s only a dinner.” Liam paced to the refrigerator and removed two sparkling Perriers. “It won’t be a late evening. Probably two hours tops. We can still do something.”

“We hardly see each other, Liam. You’re always working, and it’s getting worse.”

“I’m only thinking of our future.” He twisted the cap off one bottle and offered it to Jessica across the breakfast bar. "I want us to have a secure financial start when we get married."

She waved away the water. "I mean it, Liam. I have to know you're not going to be one of those maniacs who works all the time. If we're going to have a future at all, we have to see each other."

If? They were engaged. She wore a ring with an impressive stone. It seemed to Liam they were past the *if* stage.

"We see each other," he said. "You're here now, aren't you?"

She gestured toward the corner of his living room that he used as a home office. "And look what I found you doing. Working."

His laptop was open and stacks of papers crisscrossed each other. Six different pens peeked out from beneath the disarray because he could never find the last one he used.

"I'm just taking care of a few things that can't wait." Liam took a swig of water.

"You haven't even showered or shaved. Do you think I can't tell? What time did you go to bed last night? Have you eaten?"

He looked away from her. "Why does any of that matter?"

"Because I asked you to come in after the movie last night, and you said you had to work. And clearly you've been working again all morning. Maybe all night for all I know."

Liam winced. She knew him too well. He

was up most of the night, and he slept — briefly — in the clothes he wore yesterday. "I have a lot on my mind."

"I can see that." Jessica sat on a stool. "So give yourself the night off and relax. With me."

"I explained that my business has had some complications lately."

And if anybody at corporate got wind of Liam's complications, he would never work as a financial consultant again. Or in any career. He would be spending too many years in prison to worry about his career.

He could make the money back. He would find a way to cover that it had gone missing at all. He just needed a few new clients and a little bit of time. Ted Quinn was at the top of the list. Already they had met twice to talk about the services Liam offered, even before Liam realized the extent of his crisis. Quinn was interested, Liam was sure of it. In his fifties, Quinn was of an age where he was thinking about the future more carefully. He needed safe investments that would yield reliably as he moved toward retirement — though Liam had a hard time imagining Quinn would give up teaching anytime soon. Liam reasoned that as a single man with no dependents, even on a small-town teacher's salary, Quinn was doing well. He must have paid for his house by now, and it was worth a considerable sum by Hidden Falls standards.

Quinn said he had several accounts he needed to roll over and was looking for some fresh advice from someone he could trust.

Liam wanted to be that someone. *Several* accounts.

"I think Quinn is going to sign with me soon," he said to Jessica. "It would be bad form if I blew off his big night. Tomorrow we'll do something together. Anything you want."

Jessica rounded the end of the breakfast bar and put her arms around his neck for another kiss. "I promised my friend from work I would go to her baby shower."

"After that, then. You just call me when you're ready, and I'll be right there." Liam cradled her face and kissed her hard.

The doorbell startled them both, and Liam let out his breath. "Come in."

The door opened and his brother stood in its opening.

"Cooper," Jessica said. "What are you doing here?"

"Am I interrupting something?"

Liam glanced at Jessica, who was fidgeting with the ponytail at the back of her head. "It's fine. What do you need?"

Cooper tossed himself into a brown leather recliner. "Do I have to need something in order to come see my big brother?"

Jessica rolled her eyes. "I guess I'd better go cut the tags off that dress and make sure I have shoes to go with it."

"I'll pick you up at seven." Liam leaned over and kissed her cheek. "There won't be another woman there half as beautiful as you."

"Hmm." She picked up her purse from the coffee table. "Flattery is not going to get you out of this. I'll see you later."

The door closed behind her.

"Get you out of what?" Cooper popped out of the chair, scooped up a football from the corner of the couch, and spiraled it across the room.

Liam caught the ball, but instead of returning the pass, he set it on the breakfast bar.

"Ooh," Cooper said, "must be serious."

"She thinks I'm working too much and not paying enough attention to her."

"And?" Cooper plunked back into the chair.

"And what?"

"Are you?"

"None of your business."

"Come on, Liam. Maybe she has a point. You're thirty-eight years old. You guys have been engaged for, what, five years? What woman wants to be engaged for five years? Have you even set a date?"

"Like I said, none of your business."

"I like Jessica just fine," Cooper said. "And I'm pretty sure she doesn't hate me. She gets along with Mom and Dad. What's the deal?"

"There is no deal." Liam picked up his

bottle of water. "Jessica wants a perfect wedding. Her parents can't afford to foot the bill for what she wants, so we both agreed we would wait until we could manage it. I'm just trying to make some money so I can make her happy."

"Does she need a fancy wedding in order to be happy with you?"

"What kind of crack is that?"

"Just a question."

"I thought you said you liked her."

"I do."

"Then enough with the marriage advice. You're thirty-four. When are you going to get a girlfriend?"

"Oh, very smooth. Change the subject to get yourself out of the hot seat."

Liam laughed. "It always worked when we were kids."

"What do I need to wear to this shindig tonight?" Cooper slung his feet over the side of the chair.

"Not your uniform." Liam sat on the couch and eyed his desk in the corner, wishing he had turned some of the papers upside down. At least the laptop screen had gone to sleep. Cooper wouldn't know what any of it meant, anyway.

"I thought women like a man in uniform," Cooper said.

"Not the kind of uniform where the guy can give them a speeding ticket."

"It's true that batting your eyes gets you nowhere with me."

"The sheriff's office can make people nervous." Liam got up to take his empty Perrier bottle to the recycling bin in the kitchen. And to escape looking his brother in the eye.

"We're supposed to make people feel safe and protected," Cooper said. "Isn't that what it says on our squad cars?"

"Every theory has its flaws."

Cooper followed Liam across the apartment and sat on a stool at the breakfast bar. "You all right?"

"Why wouldn't I be?" Liam pulled a bag of black bean tortilla chips from the cupboard just to look busy.

"Fine. Whatever." Cooper made two revolutions on the stool. "I haven't had a suit on in ages. Good thing being a cop keeps me fit and trim so I can wear an old one."

"Keep telling yourself that." Liam crunched a chip between his teeth and wished his brother would leave. His brain was spinning with numbers.

A particular number representing the total of the missing money.

Various combinations that might add up to that particular number.

Account numbers that may or may not be missing funds.

Dates.

Confirmation numbers.

Missing confirmation numbers.

Client telephone numbers.

Reports.

No matter which way Liam added it up, the outcome was trouble. Every time.

He wished he were burning the midnight oil to pay for a wedding or save for his future with Jessica. The truth was, he was hanging by his fingernails just trying to figure a way to stay out of jail. The last person he needed to confide in right now was a brother who worked in the county sheriff's department.

"Can I sit with you tonight?"

"Huh?" Liam made himself look at Cooper.

"Can I sit with you and Jessica tonight?"

Liam shrugged. "I'm not in charge of the seating chart."

"Listen to me, Liam. I don't want to walk in and sit with strangers at a banquet. I'm serious."

"I'm listening, and I seriously hear you saying you can't get a date."

"Maybe I don't want a date."

"Yeah. That's why you're desperate to piggyback on mine. Fine. Wear the black suit."

"Thanks, bro." Cooper gripped the football on the counter in one hand, hustled across the apartment, spun around, and threw a pass.

Liam caught it and automatically tucked it safely against his chest. Once Cooper pulled the door closed behind him, Liam let out his breath and dropped the ball.

He had work to do. He still had six hours before he had to get dressed up, eat dinner, and applaud a man he admired — and whose business might be Liam's best shot at putting his life back together.

1:37 p.m.

Ethan Jordan, MD, swung his car off of Interstate 70 with mild trepidation. With only one stop for coffee midway through the five-hour drive from Columbus, Ohio, he had made good time. Several hours remained before the banquet. After an overnight on-call shift during which he performed two emergency neurological surgeries, he should have slept more before embarking on the drive, but he had been anxious to get out of beeper range and past the point where his surgical chief might decide to revoke the weekend off. He had made do with a two-hour nap, a cold shower, and the black coffee that seemed interchangeable with the blood coursing through his veins.

His chest tightened when he took the exit. He had not been home since Christmas during his junior year of college, and he cut that visit short by claiming he had to get back to work at the part-time job that kept him in books and pocket change during his years as a student. The sleek black Lexus Ethan drove now was a far cry from the banged-up, used blue Chevy that he nursed through college, medical school, and most of his residency. The new vehicle was his one splurge in the face of the educational debt he carried — though the car was also in his possession by debt.

He could have gone home if he wanted to, except that Hidden Falls had stopped feeling like home a long time ago. Each move through his education took Ethan farther from the sleepy central Illinois town. Although he would have said the growing distance was not intentional, he welcomed the relief it brought him.

As Quinn used to say, "Not to decide is to decide."

And Ethan had never decided to come home, so he never had.

Everything that disappointed him in Hidden Falls was behind him. Everything that shamed him dropped off the map of his life. A few things pained him to release, but the relentless rigor of studies and jobs and exams and residency left him little time for regrets.

Ethan wished he regretted not seeing his parents during these years, but in reality he did not. And being within the city limits of Hidden Falls now did not mean he would see them this time either. Quinn was a popular figure in town and had been for decades, but a town population of just over ten thousand people and the price tag attached to the banquet to honor Quinn meant not everyone who lived in Hidden Falls would attend. And his parents would be at the bottom of the list. They had next to no interest in Quinn even when he was a friendly neighbor and a favorite teacher of their son. Why should they care about the banquet now?

Ethan blew out his breath and tried to breathe normally. It was ridiculous to feel like an embarrassed child. He graduated at the top of his college class, the top of his medical school class, and was five years into a six-year neurosurgical residency. In a few more years, his earning power would be beyond his parents' ability to imagine.

It should be enough. So why wasn't it?

Ethan avoided the main highway going into town and instead circled Whisper Lake first. He had his camera — he never went anywhere without it — but he didn't expect to have time to take photos of the lake or the falls it fed into. For now he would settle for soaking up the ring of burnished red and golden leaves shimmering in sunlight and the brilliance bouncing off the gently sloshing water at midday. The lake had been his escape when he was young, a refuge from confusion and discontent. In the intervening years, he had visited countless other lakes and rivers and falls, but no setting ever tugged at his spirit the way Whisper Lake and Hidden Falls had.

Completing his lap around the lake, Ethan

aimed the Lexus toward the high school. From the outside, nothing looked different. It was the same block of unadorned white brick it had always been, with the same worn red sign in front.

Ethan should have been valedictorian. A neck-in-neck race in his final semester surprised him. Ken Lauder had never been bright. He started cheating in the third grade — off of Ethan's papers. Ethan had learned to be more careful to cover his work and more savvy about playground conversations. By the tenth grade, Ken started to lag in the standings to a rank more credible to Ethan's assessment of him. Then in twelfth grade he made a comeback. Ethan never believed Ken was doing it on his own, but he could prove nothing. Even Quinn, who likely believed Ethan's protests, said there had to be proof.

In the end, Ken beat out Ethan by one-tenth of a percent. Ethan never let that happen again.

Ethan drove out to the old neighborhood. Nicole Sandquist's house had been next door to the Jordans, and Quinn's was directly behind. The lots were deep, but Ethan had loosened two boards in the sun-drenched wooden fence, and even in high school he managed to squirm through to use the opening as a shortcut.

He pulled over just up the block from the Jordan home and, in the sanctuary provided by the tinted windows, leaned across the passenger seat, flipped open the glove box, and extracted two envelopes. The first Ethan needed because it contained the details of the evening's event. The second he kept because it contained the reason he had made the trip at all.

Quinn's handwritten note.

Ethan sighed just as he had the day he first opened the envelope. Quinn had the crisp open handwriting that served teachers well. No student could claim to be unable to read the comments on a paper or the assignment list on the blackboard, and parents knew precisely what Quinn intended to communicate in the notes he sent home when he had a concern.

This note, however, confounded Ethan. The script was the same steady presentation as always, but this time Ethan did not understand Quinn's meaning.

Dear Ethan,

Life is not always what we expect. We get caught in its vortex despite our best efforts. It may take generations to discover who we are meant to be. You and I are long overdue for a talk. Please come.

Quinn

Of all the people and places Ethan had walked away from over the years, Quinn was his greatest regret.

No. Second greatest. Nicole would always be first.

Quinn was more than a teacher. He was a neighbor, a friend, a protector, an encourager. Ethan could not imagine surviving his adolescence without Quinn. While he might have tossed the banquet invitation on the pile of junk mail on the corner of his desk because he did not enjoy most formal events, he couldn't do that with Quinn's note. Ethan hoped they could talk before the evening was out, or the next morning at the latest. He needed to get back to Columbus in time to be at the hospital for rounds at seven on Monday morning.

Ethan rubbed his eyes. What he needed right now was food. He hadn't eaten in the last twenty hours. And if he could find a motel bed, he would grab a nap before downing another pot of coffee to keep awake long enough to at least satisfy himself that Quinn was all right physically and did not need Ethan's professional services. He stowed the envelopes back in the glove box, tugged his sunglasses off the top of his head, and pulled the Lexus out into the road. Main Street was two miles away. Ethan's brain was already indexing the choice of small restaurants. If downtown was like everything else in Hidden Falls, the options wouldn't have changed.

He chose the family-style restaurant because he remembered the meat loaf made with a basil pesto. His car did not yet have any scratches on it, and Ethan planned to keep it that way by purposely parking in a manner that would discourage other drivers from squeezing in beside him. With his hand around the clicker, he exited the car, let the door fall closed, and pressed the lock button. When he raised his eyes from the pavement to glance toward the restaurant's front window, Ethan blinked twice at the petite form of a woman whose gait reminded him of the way Nicole used to keep stride with his long legs.

"Ethan?"

He blinked again. It *was* Nicole.

"I didn't know you were coming." She made no move toward him with affection or otherwise.

Nicole was alone as far as Ethan could see. She still had the small mole below the outside corner of her left eye, and she still let her dark hair hang over that side of her face to obscure it. He fumbled for words.

"I suppose nobody knew I was coming except the organizing committee," he said. "I've been out of touch."

She could still make his heart race by doing nothing at all.

"I heard you were in Columbus," she said.

He nodded. "And you?"

"St. Louis. Investigative reporting."

"You had your heart set on journalism ever since junior high."

She laughed. "Thankfully I turned out to be pretty good at it."

"I never doubted you would be." Ethan took a few tenuous steps toward her, relieved that she didn't back away. He wanted to see those emerald-green eyes up close again — he'd taken them for granted all those years living next door to her. Even through five years of officially dating, he passed up too many opportunities to look into them.

"It's been a long time," she said.

"Longer than I ever meant."

"To be honest, Ethan, I never had a clue what you meant. It was sort of a breakup by default, wasn't it? You stopped returning my calls or answering my e-mails. So I guess that was the end."

"I know." Ethan put both hands in his pockets. "I handled things badly."

"I was a big girl by then. We were in college. You could have just told me you decided not to see me anymore."

The flaw in her argument was he never decided any such thing. "I'm sorry."

"Like I said, it's been a long time and I'm a big girl." She glanced down the sidewalk and back at him. "I'm glad you could come, for Quinn's sake, but you don't look so great, Ethan."

"I haven't slept much lately. That happens sometimes in my line of work."

"Mine, too."

"I was just about to get something to eat. Are you hungry?"

"You don't have to do that, Ethan."

"Do what?" Ethan was not sure if the pounding of his heart was from his caffeine consumption or Nicole's presence after ten years.

"Buy me lunch. Chitchat. Any of it."

Her words stung, but Ethan could not blame her. "I'm sure you have other things to do."

"I hope you enjoy your visit to Hidden Falls." Nicole paced away from him and did not look back.

Ethan let out his pent-up breath for the second time in one afternoon.

3:38 p.m.

"So you didn't pick up my dress at the dry cleaner? That's what you're saying?"

Jack Parker's gut burned. "I'm sorry. I forgot."

Gianna's gray eyes clouded. "Jack, sometimes I wonder if you're making an effort at all."

"I forgot *one* errand." He tossed his keys on the table next to the front door in the hall. "I am trying to build a business, after all."

"It's Saturday afternoon." Gianna turned

away. "Why were you even at the office? I hope this won't be Memphis all over again."

"What's that supposed to mean?"

"I'm speaking English. Figure it out."

Jack ran one hand through his wavy brown hair. He was supposed to get a haircut, too, and hadn't done that either. "It's not Memphis. This is going to be different."

"I hope so."

"It will be, Gianna. But we've only been here eight months. We've spent a fortune renovating this old house, and you've still got a long wish list."

Gianna scoffed. "Somehow you've managed to make me responsible for your failure to pick up my dress."

"That's not what I meant. I'm just trying to make a living."

She met his eyes, unblinking. "Were any of the hours you spent at the office today billable?"

Being married to a former paralegal exposed Jack to certain vulnerabilities. She knew too much about the business.

"I don't think it works that way here," he said. "I have to build relationships."

"You bought a practice that is fifty years old. I thought that meant some clients."

"It was a father-and-son practice. Small-fry stuff. You know that, Gianna."

"They were lawyers, weren't they?"

"Yes, but there are other lawyers in the

county. Birch Bend has several nice firms, and it's not that far away. I have to get to know Hidden Falls and prove to people here they can trust me to do right by them."

"You thought you were doing right by that client in Memphis."

"You know it's more complicated than that." Jack loosened his tie and unbuttoned the neck of his shirt. "You used to work at that firm, too."

Jack's transgression had been doing what one of the partners told him to do. Demanded that he do. And when everything was said and done, Jack's name was all over the files with no trace of the partner's bad judgment.

Gianna set her jaw. "They should have given you a much bigger separation package for saving his skin."

"Well, they didn't. You wanted to come here, and we came."

"Before Memphis, it was Atlanta."

"That was completely different, and you know it."

How could Gianna hold him responsible because the practice sold out to a New York firm that let two-thirds of the attorneys go? Jack was weary of having the same conversation in untold iterations.

Gianna yanked a sweater off the coat rack next to the front door. "I do know. What I mean is we can't keep dragging this family through crisis. Our kids are teenagers. Colin will be off to college in a year. Eva and Brooke deserve some stability. I want a home they all want to come back to. Don't you want that?"

Jack swallowed his reply. They went around this same loop at least once a week. It felt like a trap every time. "I'll go get your dress."

"Never mind. I'll do it."

Gianna was out the front door before Jack could make a more convincing offer. He shuffled into the great room, where his seventeen-year-old son slouched in the red leather sofa with the remote in his hand and the big-screen television blaring a sci-fi station. Jack stood there moving his gaze between Colin and the television for a full minute before Colin glanced at him.

"Hey, Dad."

"*Star Trek?*"

Colin rolled his eyes. "*Battlestar Galactica.*"

"Sorry." Jack was tiring of apologizing to his family. Whatever the show was, it was from long before Colin's time. What did he find so interesting about it?

Colin said nothing.

"Do you have homework?" The question seemed like one a conscientious parent would ask.

"It's Saturday."

"So?"

"So I have all day tomorrow. I'm going out in a while."

"What about the girls?"

Colin muted the sound. "Dad, they haven't needed a babysitter in ages. Eva *is* a babysitter."

"I knew that. What about dinner?"

"I guess they can get a pizza. I won't be here." Colin looked up at his father. "I thought Eva wanted to go to the banquet. She has Mr. Quinn and likes him."

Jack wracked his brain. What had Gianna said about this? "I'll let you get back to your show."

He wandered out to the back porch to persuade himself he was not completely oblivious. Jack knew enough about Eva to know she enjoyed sitting out here with a good book. Though, what qualified as a good book in her opinion was a question he couldn't answer under oath.

"Hi," he said.

"Hi, Dad." Eva glanced up but did not close her iPad.

Jack did not remember the pink case around the device and hoped he would not be showing his ignorance by asking, "Did you get a new cover for your iPad?"

She smiled. "The first thing I ever bought from Coach. I saved my babysitting money."

"Good for you." He returned her smile, glad to get something right. "Are you looking forward to tonight?"

"Yep."

He nodded. “Did you get a new dress to wear?”

“I’d look silly in a dress, Dad. It’s a swimming party.”

That’s right. Eva’s new best friend was turning sixteen. Her parents had reserved the pool in Birch Bend long before any invitations went out for the banquet. Melissa didn’t want to change her party even for Quinn, and if she had, her parents would have lost their deposit. It was all coming back to him. Gianna explained it all one night while he only wanted to brush his teeth in peace.

“What time are you leaving?” Jack asked.

“Five thirty.”

“I hope you have a lot of fun.”

“I will.” Eva went back to her book.

Who else will be there? Do you like to go off the diving board? Are there going to be boys there? Do your friends drink? You’re not planning to wear a bikini, are you?

Jack looked at his fifteen-year-old with her legs curled under a quilt and withheld the remainder of his interrogation. Maybe he was already supposed to know the answers to those questions. He was a good enough trial lawyer not to pursue a line of questioning that would expose his disadvantage. Jack did not remember that Eva had ever been a difficult child. Then again, he was rarely home for dinner until a few months ago, when Gianna put her foot down. He had never been to a parent-teacher conference for any of his children. He didn't know what Eva did after school these days or how well his wife knew Melissa's parents.

"Enjoy your book," he said. She already had her eyes glued back to the screen. How much trouble could a bookworm get into?

Jack kicked off his shoes in the mudroom and padded into the kitchen. Thirteen-year-old Brooke had an art project spread across the kitchen table. Paints, butcher paper, brushes, colored pencils. He licked his lips. Was he supposed to know what this was about?

"Hi, Daddy."

She was the only one of his children who still greeted him with a smile.

"Hi, sweetheart." Jack was starting to wonder what Brooke's plans were for the evening if the rest of the family was going to be out. He was pretty sure Gianna would not want to leave her alone after dark. And that meant Gianna had a plan. The corollary of that truth was that she probably had told Jack what it was.

"That's pretty." Jack stood behind Brooke and looked over her shoulders, still not sure if he was supposed to know what she was working on.

"No it's not."

He sighed.

"But it will be!" Brooke's tone brightened.

"I'm making a map of my own fantasyland."

"A fantasyland?"

"You know, like the Shire or Narnia."

He didn't know, but Brooke was no doubt right that he was supposed to.

Rapid clicking across the kitchen tiles reminded him to watch for the puppy. He didn't remember agreeing to a puppy, but the creature had been there for a month now, so he wasn't inclined to start a battle about it.

Brooke pushed her chair back and patted her lap. "Here, Roxie."

The brown-and-black Airedale terrier jumped into the girl's lap.

"When are we going to take Roxie to puppy training?" Brooke asked.

"Can't we train her ourselves? When I was a kid, we did it with a rolled-up newspaper."

"Daddy! How could you hurt an animal?"

"We'll find a trainer."

"When?"

"Soon."

"That's what you always say."

"Soon, Brooke."

When had he promised to find a puppy trainer for a puppy he didn't remember agreeing to own?

Brooke stroked the puppy's right ear, which always seemed to be sticking straight up. Jack turned to the sink and saw assorted lunch dishes piled against the extra-deep blue ceramic that Gianna had chosen. Next to it, the dishwasher's green light announced that the load was clean. He unlatched the door and pulled out the bottom rack. Emptying the dishwasher would be a peace offering. They could still have a nice evening out if he took the edge off his wife's wrath. Gianna would wear the deep purple dress that flattered her figure and the dangling gold earrings. She would turn heads, and he would be proud of the effort she made. He took her two favorite mugs from the rack and set them next to the Keurig.

They both knew the night was important, and not only because Eva was Quinn's student and she liked him better than any of her other teachers.

It was Gianna's idea to come to Hidden Falls. Jack would have started over again in Memphis, but as soon as he started talking about opening his own firm, she jabbered about finding a quiet little town where he could have his own firm and still have a family life. She wouldn't let go. So he came. He found a practice in a town that met her approval, and he spent his separation package to buy it. Jack had a tough time picturing himself happy in a town like Hidden Falls over the long run, but despite their tensions he loved his wife. He loved his children, even if he didn't know them very well. As long as he was here, he might as well give it his best effort. His practice didn't have to remain a quiet, small-town series of dull real estate transactions and unimaginative wills written off a template. Somewhere in this town there had to be something juicy, something that would make Jack glad he went to law school.

It would be good for business to be seen at an event like a banquet honoring this Mr. Quinn. Jack would be sure to meet him, shake his hand, say something clever. If Quinn was as beloved and influential as everyone said he was, and if he liked Jack, he could throw some business Jack's way.

And one of those people would have an interesting problem that Jack could untangle.

He just needed a break. One break. He could still turn this around.

4:49 p.m.

Lauren Nock wished she had put her dark blond hair in a ponytail before she left the house.

She also wished she were taller. And not so nearsighted.

At the moment, she could not change any of those circumstances. She would have to tolerate the hair falling in her line of sight as she studied her clipboard, push her glasses up on her nose, and hope that three-inch heels would give her the look she wanted for the banquet.

No amount of afternoon coffee was going

to make sense of the cryptic entries and empty spaces on the pages on the clipboard. Lauren left a huge tip in the café booth, crossed the street, and ducked into Waterfall Books and Gifts. The bell on the door announced her presence, and the woman behind the counter looked up.

"Hello, Aunt Sylvia." Lauren wove past a display of small ceramic figures to reach Sylvia and kiss her cheek.

Sylvia glanced at the clipboard. "I thought you kept your to-do list on your iPhone."

"This is for the health fair next Saturday." Lauren flashed the clipboard contents toward Sylvia. "The committee made up the list — well, mostly Quinn. I'm the one who proposed a community health fair, and now I feel like I don't know much about what's going on. I've been sitting in the café with this list, and I have no idea what to check off."

"Quinn offered to work on that, didn't he?" Sylvia began to sort a stack of credit card charges.

"Yes. But we haven't had a meeting in two weeks. Now the fair is only seven days away."

"I'm sure Quinn has everything in hand. He always does."

"I know. I just feel responsible. I'm the family ministry director for the church, but I seem to have handed the whole thing off to someone else."

"Not just someone else. Quinn. He won't

let you down." Sylvia looked up. "Do you need something, or did you just come in to chat?"

Lauren tucked the clipboard under one arm and moved toward a jewelry display. "A necklace for tonight." *Something nice but not too expensive.*

"What are you wearing?"

"The sage-green dress. I love the fabric and color, but I never know how to accessorize the square-cut neckline." Lauren spun a rack of thin gold chains and inexpensive arrangements of costume beads.

Sylvia set down her charge receipts and paced to the end of the counter. "I have something here that I haven't put out yet." She pulled a box from a low shelf.

Lauren walked over to see what Sylvia was uncovering. "A Celtic cross. I like that!" Lauren lifted the cross out of its box and ran her fingers over tiny knots engraved in the pewter and the circle that joined the crossing bars. Then she lifted the chain and held it up to her neck. A glance at the price tag revealed no impediment to the purchase. "It will hit perfectly above the neckline. I'll take it."

"Good," Sylvia said. "I am about to close up the shop. I still have a list of things to double-check before the banquet."

"I could come early and help greet people." Lauren swiped her debit card.

Sylvia laid the necklace in its box, slipped it

into a small bag with the receipt, and handed it to Lauren. "Perfect. I told Quinn to be there by seven. I'll pick you up at quarter till."

As soon as Lauren stepped out of the shop, Sylvia turned off the OPEN sign. Lauren pulled her phone from her pocket to look at the time. Just after five. She had plenty of time to walk three blocks down and through the narrow door into the small vestibule that serviced a row of apartments built above adjoining shops on Main Street. Lauren's two-bedroom apartment was above the small barbershop and the town newspaper. Two decades ago someone had carved out enough space for an elevator beside the stairs in her building, but Lauren preferred to take the stairs two at a time. It was only one flight.

As she grabbed the ancient handle on the door to her building, she looked up and recognized the man exiting the barbershop.

"Quinn."

He turned his head. "Hello, Lauren."

"What are you still doing in town? Shouldn't you be home getting ready for your big night?"

He raised his fingers to brush his freshly trimmed hairline. "My haircut is good faith that I will go through with this hoopla."

"You'll look dapper, I'm sure." She sighed in relief. "I'm so glad to run into you. I've been staring at this list of action steps for the health fair, and I'm clueless where everything stands."

Quinn smiled. "Everything stands just as it should."

"Booths? Tables? Vendors?"

He nodded. "All of that and more. Cooking demonstrations of healthy food, immunizations for kids, blood pressure screenings, sign-ups for exercise classes at the community center, a recipe exchange for busy moms, even a book fair — because literacy is healthy for all sorts of reasons."

"I don't remember a recipe exchange."

Quinn shrugged one shoulder. "I may have added a few ideas since we last talked. There's a joke contest, too."

Lauren raised an eyebrow. "A joke contest?"

"Laughter is good medicine."

"Do we need to rent more chairs for the demonstration booths?"

"Done."

"What about electricity for the booths that need it? We can't have extension cords all over the place."

"No, no. Safety hazard. I've already thought of that."

"Trash cans? And do you think we should keep the church building open so we have restrooms?"

"It's all under control, Lauren. Don't let your stress get the best of you. It's not healthy!"

"Are there people I should be calling next week just to reconfirm everything?"

"Lauren, it will be fine." He touched her shoulder. "If it will make you feel better, we can meet Monday after school and I'll go over everything with you."

She took a deep breath. "I don't mean to be freaking out. I just want the fair to go well. It's been a long time since the church reached out to the community with something this big."

"We wouldn't be doing it at all if you hadn't started the ball rolling. But we're in good shape. I promise you."

"Okay, then. I'll come to your classroom on Monday afternoon."

"It will be just like the old days when you stayed after seventh-period geography," he said. "I'll see you there. Now I'd better get going or I'll lose all my spiffing-up time, and what would your aunt think of that?"

Lauren glanced around. "Where's your car?"

"I came into town with Sylvia this morning and just never wandered home."

"You've been here all day?"

"Doing one thing or another, yes."

"You're going to walk now?"

"Two miles is not so far. I do it all the time."

"Aunt Sylvia is just closing the shop," Lauren said. "I'm sure you could catch her and she would take you."

He put a finger to his lips. "*Shh.* Let's keep our meeting a secret. One walker to another."

Lauren didn't own a car and didn't even have a driver's license. When she was younger, she kept putting off learning to drive until eventually she decided she didn't need to. After college she returned to Hidden Falls, started working at the church, and decided to live only a few blocks away. She could walk to any kind of shop she needed. When she had a full day off, she could even hike out to the falls or the lake. She was like Quinn in that way. A few miles on foot were not daunting. Quinn was in good physical shape and could set a vigorous pace. But this time he was cutting it close.

"Tell me you plan to bring your car when you come back to the banquet," Lauren said.

"I am not a complete dolt, now am I?" His eyes twinkled. "I will drive, and I will arrive in time for your aunt to inspect the results of my feeble efforts."

She smiled. If her aunt had married Quinn, as Lauren always suspected she wanted to, he would have been Uncle Quinn to Lauren for her twenty-eight years. Even without the marriage, Lauren could not have been fonder of Quinn.

"All right," she said. "I'll see you at the banquet hall."

She watched him for a moment. There was not much about the way he looked to set him apart. He was middle-aged and balding. Not particularly tall and not particularly short. Not heavy and not thin. His face was one of the blandest Lauren had ever seen.

Yet Quinn was the most remarkable person she knew. He deserved the honor he would receive in two hours.

Lauren glanced in both directions down Main Street. Extra cars with out-of-state plates crawled down the street, and foot traffic was brisk. People had come for Quinn. Lots of people.

With her hand on the door handle for a second time, a rush of denim across the street caught Lauren's gaze. Her eyes widened.

He was here. She had been back in Hidden Falls for six years and not seen him once — and he was not someone she expected would care about coming back for an event like tonight's.

But there he was.

Surely he would not stay long. Probably he would be gone by tomorrow night.

She sure hoped so.

6:02 p.m.

The heft of the fishing reel felt perfect in Dani Roose's hands. The solid brass pinion gearing, the roller to reduce twists in the line, the lightweight spool — it was everything she wanted. While the clerk in the sporting goods shop rang up the sale, Dani tested the spinner for the umpteenth time and imagined the rod she would pair with the reel. Now she could use a heavier line and cast farther out on the lake.

The clerk, Henry, announced the total, and Dani extracted cash from the pocket of her orange quilted North Face vest. For weeks she had researched reels in fishing magazines and catalogs. Once she had made up her mind what she wanted, she checked prices around the county and on the Internet. As much as she dreamed about the reel, it was out of reach until today. Dani ignored her phone most of the time, but that morning she'd picked it up. Sammie Dunavant had a dried and cracking fence post that needed replacing before a stiff fall wind took down twenty feet of unstable slats. Digging postholes was not Dani's favorite task, but she made her erratic income by doing things that were nobody's favorite.

So Dani dug the hole, sank the post, and poured the concrete around it. While it set, she added nails to loose boards. At least she was not building a fence in the high heat of summer, and Sammie's fence would now last at least five more years — longer if she let Dani come back and replace the weakest slats. Then Sammie asked her to fix a window that did not close properly and clean out a bathroom drain.

Sammie did enough business with Dani to

know she liked to be paid in cash. Dani issued receipts for everything she did, whether it was handy work or troubleshooting computers. Nothing was under the table. Dani just thought it was easier not to make unnecessary trips to the bank, and Hidden Falls businesses had stopped taking third-party checks a long time ago.

Henry handed her a few dollars in change. "You going to get out on the lake with that tomorrow?"

"Before dawn."

"Do you still throw everything back?"

"I watch the limits."

Henry shook his head. "I like to eat what I catch."

The store owner was at the door, flipping the sign to Closed. Dani realized she was the final customer. She tossed her long dark braid over her shoulder and carried the reel out to her mud-splattered Jeep.

What Dani did not tell Henry was that she was headed straight out to Whisper Lake. She would be on the water before dawn because she would be at the cabin before dark. The cooler in the back of the Jeep held food for several days. The cabin that had belonged to her grandparents had no plumbing or electricity, but that never bothered Dani. The bed was old, but the quilts were warm. Dani had sealed the doors and windows against drafts, and she could always lay a fire if she got cold.

The rustic conditions were a small price to pay for the thrill of watching the sky blaze toward a new day, surrounded by acres of blue water, the depths teeming with freshwater fish.

With her mind's eye more focused on the lake view than the road out of town, Dani almost didn't see him. She was fifty yards down the road before she realized what her brain had failed to register immediately. Dani gave the wheel a swift turn, pulled to the shoulder, and slowly backed up. When she was certain, she turned off the ignition, got out, and marched toward him.

"Didn't expect to see you here," she said.

Quinn seemed in no hurry.

"Why not?" he said. "I'm on my way home. Practically there."

"You're still a mile away. In an hour you're supposed to be the guest of honor at the town ball."

Quinn laughed. "Town ball. Clever."

"Are they making you wear a penguin suit?"

" 'Fraid so." Quinn looked at his watch. "I have to present myself in forty-seven minutes and fourteen seconds."

"Which is precisely why I didn't expect to find you out here at this hour." Dani scratched under her braid.

"I admit to stopping along the way," Quinn said.

"The ridge overlooking the river?"

Quinn nodded. "The trees are spectacular right now. The reflection of the colors in the river is breathtaking. Tomorrow will be too late for today's view. I wanted one last moment of peace before the onslaught of attention tonight."

Dani and Quinn understood each other on that point.

"Get in the Jeep," she said. "I'll drop you off. That should buy you fifteen minutes."

They got in the car, and Dani started the engine.

Quinn furrowed his brow. "You don't look any closer to being ready than I do."

"I'm completely ready for where I'm going," Dani said. "The cabin is calling my name."

"Oh."

Dani glanced at Quinn, who looked out his window. She pulled out onto the road. If she hadn't stopped, she wouldn't be having a conversation that was rapidly turning awkward.

"Quinn," she said, "you know this kind of event isn't my thing. I don't fit in."

"I thought you told me you sent in your RSVP."

"I did." Dani imagined she was the only person in town to tuck cash into the envelope rather than a check. "Liam and Cooper were after me to do it. I had to get them off my back."

"Listen to your cousins," Quinn said.

"But . . . it's just . . . you know, not *me.* I haven't even had a dress on since my sister's wedding three years ago."

"I'm sure whatever you wore to a wedding would be appropriate tonight."

"My hair."

"Is shiny and striking in a braid. Most women can't carry that off."

"But I'd have to talk to people."

"You talk to me."

"You're different." Dani flashed her eyes at the rearview mirror and then both side mirrors.

They drove in silence. Dani's stomach churned. "You want me to be there, don't you," she finally said.

"Yes, I do."

More silence.

"Will it hurt your feelings if I just can't do it?" Dani asked.

"No." Quinn answered quickly. "It's not about my feelings. I just hate the thought that you don't want to come because you feel out of place. This is your town, too. We're celebrating everything we've done together."

Dani smiled. "They're celebrating *you,* Quinn. You have to accept that."

Quinn squirmed. "That's not how I choose to frame the event in my mind."

"Frame it however you want, but you hold this town together." Dani flipped on her signal and made the right turn onto Quinn's street.

"My speech is going to suggest otherwise."

Dani laughed. "Sylvia is going to love that."

"She said I had to make a speech. She didn't say what it had to be about."

Dani pressed her lips together and turned them to one side.

"I've made you curious, haven't I?" Quinn said.

Dani rolled her eyes. "Yes, you've made me curious."

"Do you want to hear about it secondhand?"

"They'll probably print it in the newspaper."

"Not if they don't have the napkins I've written it on."

Dani slapped one hand against her forehead. "All right. I'll come. But now we're both in danger of being late." She could not even remember if she had the dress cleaned after dropping frosting on it at her sister's reception. Wearing it again never crossed her radar.

"You make an old man happy."

"You're not old and you're not unhappy. You just don't want to be the center of attention."

"On to brighter topics," Quinn said. "My computer is freezing up a lot lately."

"That's probably because it's a dinosaur as

far as laptops go, and you insist on trying to run programs it was never designed to run." Dani turned into Quinn's driveway.

"You always manage to sort things out."

"I can't do that forever, Quinn. But I can help you buy a new one."

"Let's give it one more go, shall we? Come over one night this week and see what you can do."

Dani nodded. "Maybe Tuesday or Wednesday. First I want to go to the lake for a few days."

"I'm jealous."

"Come up tomorrow."

"I just might do that. After church."

Quinn got out, and Dani watched as he let himself in the front door. She backed out of the driveway and turned the Jeep away from the lake and toward town.

Forty minutes later, Dani stood in front of the mirror hanging on the back of her bedroom door. Most of the time she was content to leave a bathrobe dangling from a hook there. A woman who didn't wear dresses didn't need to look in a full-length mirror very often.

She didn't like dresses.

She didn't like crowds.

She didn't like fancy meals.

She didn't like anything about this night except that it was for Quinn.

Dani had long ago made peace with being

a loner. She flunked out of community college because she didn't have enough interest in conforming to do homework that bored her. Two attempts at conventional employment led to two of the most disastrous experiences of her life. No doubt if she organized her efforts she could earn considerably more money than she currently did, whether she took on more odd jobs around town or accepted more computer repair work, but she liked her freedom. Being so tied down that she couldn't decide to spend an afternoon fishing was no way to live.

Dani tugged the gray shift down and straightened the seams along her slender hips. The hem hit just above her knees, which in their exposed state struck her as unreasonably knobby. The dress called for shoes with heels, and Dani had the pair from her sister's wedding, but she refused to put herself through that torture. Rummaging in the back of her closet produced a pair of black flats she wiped clean, and she slipped them on her feet.

The problem with her long, thick hair was that it took forever to dry. Wearing it in a single braid was a practicality more than anything else because she could leave the house with wet hair. In front of the mirror, Dani pulled the braid forward over her right shoulder, flipped it back, and pulled it forward again.

"Who am I kidding?" she said aloud. No one would care. No one would notice. Who was she even going to sit with? Liam and Cooper had dragged her into this. If they didn't also save her a seat, Dani would have a few choice words for them. It was just the kind of thing older boy cousins would have done to her as kids.

A final inspection persuaded Dani she was socially presentable. Only Quinn would appreciate the extreme effort she was making — and Dani suspected he didn't want to be at the banquet any more than she did.

But for Quinn, she would go.

7:11 p.m.

Nicole Sandquist stood in the bathroom where she had first practiced applying makeup. In those days, she saved her babysitting money and hovered in the cosmetics section of the drugstore until she was sure no one in the store knew her before making her purchases. That's what happened to young teenage girls whose mothers had been dead for five years and whose fathers never recovered from grief. They figured out how to grow up without help.

She pressed her lips together to redistribute a blotch of lipstick. Otherwise satisfied, she snapped off the bathroom light and headed downstairs. The house had been empty for the last four years. After two decades in Hidden Falls, Nicole's father accepted a new job in Indianapolis, but the house had belonged to her mother's family, so he held on to it in case Nicole would want it someday.

Nicole brushed her hand against the oak handrail and wondered if Sammie Dunavant still did housecleaning. And what about Dani Roose? Nicole had heard through the Facebook grapevine that Dani was handy at fixing most anything around a house.

This house was a disaster. Well, perhaps not a disaster. *Neglected* was a better word. Nicole had no plans to return to Hidden Falls to live, but even if she decided to sell or rent the house, the list of essential repairs would be discouragingly long. Assembling it was a task for another trip.

At the bottom of the stairs, Nicole wiped dust from a mirror for one last look. The red dress crossed in front and fastened just above the waist on one side. Her mother's pearls, the one nice piece of jewelry she ever owned, followed the curve of the neckline in precision as they lay against Nicole's olive skin. Out of long habit, she deftly arranged a strand of dark hair to cut across the edge of her left eye and cover the mole.

Before her father moved, her trips home for Christmas were in and out. She had not been to her five-year high school reunion or the ten-year event either. Nicole suspected she would see a lot of people tonight from that era of her life. A few she kept up with on Facebook in a casual way, but meeting face-to-face was different. More intimidating.

Any old friends she saw would be pure bonus. The one face she longed for was Quinn's. For years he helped hold together the life of a motherless girl with a distracted, grieving father. Quinn was the person who heard Nicole's own grief, who held her quaking shoulders at the announcement of her mother's sudden passing. Later he was the first teacher to tell her she could write. *Really* write. And for the first time, she had imagined a life outside Hidden Falls.

Nicole picked up the lightweight coat she might like to have later, when temperatures would dip, and walked outside. The passenger seat of her white Hyundai Santa Fe still bore the remains of her sack of snacks for the drive from St. Louis to Hidden Falls. It was ridiculous how much she chomped during a simple two-hour daytime drive. It was not as if she were driving at night and trying to stay awake. Nicole just liked to eat, that's all. With one hand, she swept the wrappers and napkins into a paper sack and rolled it closed.

The banquet hall was not far. Nothing in Hidden Falls was far. By St. Louis standards, *banquet hall* was a generous term for the evening's venue. It was a blockish gray building whose main feature was the large, flexible interior space with a stage. Every large gathering in the county happened here. Nicole pulled into a parking space, grateful that the lot was far from full yet. That increased her chances of greeting Quinn before the festivities began.

The door opened more easily than Nicole remembered — perhaps the building was not as neglected as her house — and she stepped into a softly lit foyer.

"Nicole Sandquist?"

Nicole turned toward the voice. It took her a moment to recognize the round face cradled in a swath of dark blond curls.

"Lauren Nock," Nicole said.

"It's been ages," Lauren said. "Somebody told me you were in St. Louis now."

Nicole nodded. "Investigative reporter for a daily paper."

"You must work on some fascinating stories."

"It beats reporting on the garden club agenda."

Lauren gestured toward a table laden with rows of name tags. "Those might help us know who everybody is, but how can we possibly catch up with everyone?"

Lauren was two years behind Nicole in high school. They never shared classes, but they were on the debate team together. Nicole remembered Lauren as spunky, determined, and talented as an acrobatic cheerleader.

"Are you still throwing yourself in the air

and twisting three times before you land?" Nicole asked.

Lauren laughed softly. "Not much call for that when you work for a church."

"I would think it would impress the youth group." Nicole ran her finger down the *S* row and found her name tag clipped to a card indicating her choice of entrée.

"As I recall," Lauren said, "you used to spend your Saturday mornings grooming horses at a stable in Birch Bend."

Nicole gave a soft sigh. "I haven't done that since high school. Quinn used to give me a ride over. Funny how he always seemed to have something he needed to do in Birch Bend, and always on Saturday."

"What do you suppose he was up to?"

"I never asked," Nicole said. "If I groomed for two hours, I got to ride for one, and that's all I was interested in." She wished she had asked. She wished she had asked Quinn a lot of things. She wished she had been back to Hidden Falls to see him before this.

"It should be a terrific evening," Lauren said. "Are you meeting anyone to sit together?"

Nicole shook her head.

"Then sit with me," Lauren said. "I already put my purse on a chair at a table right up front."

"I'd like that." Nicole glanced into the main banquet area. "Is Quinn here yet?"

Lauren pointed. "Over there against the wall. A few people beat you to it, though. Looks like you'll have to wait your turn."

Nicole clipped her name tag to her dress and looked across the banquet hall. The tight cluster of people was a giveaway that Quinn would be at its core. A broad smile rose from deep within Nicole as her heels clicked against the dated gray-and-green tile in a quickening rhythm. Her eyes were on the man in the tux. Every few seconds the position of someone in the group shifted and Nicole got a glimpse of Quinn.

Gesturing.

Smiling.

Clapping people on the back.

Eyes widening in surprise as he recognized one long-ago face after another.

The people were a mix of generations — from people who might have been in Quinn's classes two or three years ago to those who must have known him in his first year in Hidden Falls.

Nicole's pace slowed abruptly, and the smile on her face faded. Ethan Jordan had his head tilted toward Quinn, listening intently. Nicole drew a deep breath and resumed her pace. Several people drifted away from Quinn as the crowd started to fill in around tables. If Nicole walked away now, she might not get another chance before the evening's program began. Ethan Jordan wasn't going to take this moment from her — or rather, she wasn't going to give it to him. She approached from behind Quinn.

"Promise me we'll finish this conversation," Quinn said to Ethan. "It's important. I'm so glad you came."

"I promise," Ethan said.

"Are you staying with your parents?"

Ethan shook his head. "The motel out by the lake."

The answer didn't surprise Nicole, both that Ethan would choose not to go to the family home and that he would choose the lake.

"I'd love to have you stay with me," Quinn said. "It would give us the time we need. I don't want to rush our conversation."

Nicole's curiosity piqued.

"Can you manage a couple of days?" Quinn asked.

"I'm not sure," Ethan said. "I was planning to drive back tomorrow."

"Please," Quinn said. "I think we need more than one night."

Nicole watched Ethan's face. She knew the moment he spotted her and closed his mouth around his reply to Quinn. She stepped into Quinn's line of sight.

"Nicole!"

His arms surrounded her. She breathed in the same aftershave first embedded in her memory the day her mother died and reinforced at every significant moment through her adolescence.

Quinn. How could she have waited so long? Nicole stepped back. She wanted to see his face.

"What's this I hear about you being a rising star in the world of journalism?" Quinn said.

Nicole laughed. "I have a byline. That's what matters right now." She exhaled relief when Ethan shuffled away.

"I think I might just have to subscribe to a certain St. Louis publication, then. What's your most interesting story?"

"That's easy," Nicole answered quickly. "About three months ago I was working on a story about a doctor with multiple malpractice suits against him because he claimed he could completely remove any kind of birthmark. The truth was, most of the time he turned an innocent birthmark into disfigurement. The lawyer bringing suit found a middle-aged man with a port-wine birthmark on his lower back that looked like a peeling red onion. He was willing to go undercover into the doctor's practice — even let the doctor use a laser on him if that's what it took to prove the doctor didn't know what he was doing. Thankfully it didn't come to that. We were able to prove the doctor didn't have the proper credentials for what he claimed to be qualified to do."

"All this happened in St. Louis?" Quinn's brow creased. "Just two hours from here?"

"Sounds like more of a New York kind of story, doesn't it?" Nicole grinned. "I'm so glad to see you! You deserve this night so much."

Quinn grimaced. "The whole thing makes me a bit nervous, I have to admit."

Nicole responded to a touch on her elbow. "Mr. Devon. Hi. You probably don't remember me, but —"

"Of course I remember you. Nicole Sandquist, star editor of the Hidden Falls High School *Gazette.* You wanted to change the name of the school paper to *The Splash.*"

Nicole laughed. "Are you still the principal?"

"When you have a good gig, why make trouble?" Miles Devon said. "But I'm afraid I must interrupt your reunion with Quinn and steal him away. The mayor is nearly ready to begin."

"Uh-oh," Quinn said.

"Just relax," Miles said. "The mayor will make a few welcoming remarks. You'll come out long enough for her to escort you to your table. Then dinner will be served. The main recognition ceremony will follow the meal."

Quinn took a deep breath and kissed Nicole's cheek. "Thank you for catching me ahead of time. You don't know how glad I am to hear your news."

Nicole watched him stride with the principal to the front of the room and go through a door leading behind the stage curtains.

7:37 p.m.

"There you are." Sylvia's skirt swished as she pivoted toward Principal Miles Devon and Quinn.

"He's all yours," Miles said. "I'll go check in one last time with the caterers. How much time do you need?"

"Ten minutes. Give me the sign when everything is set out there."

Miles retreated back to the main room. Sylvia took Quinn by the elbow.

"This part is very easy," she said. "Everyone else has rehearsed. I just need to make sure you know how it will work."

Quinn glanced around the backstage clutter. "I thought you said I was to speak after dinner."

"You are. This is just an introduction."

"Everybody out there knows me," Quinn pointed out, "or they wouldn't be here in the first place."

"Will you stop analyzing everything and just work with us, please?" Sylvia turned Quinn's shoulders thirty degrees to the left and pointed eight feet in front of them. "Do you see that mark? The silver X?"

"Yes."

"That's where you stand. I'm going to go

out and welcome everyone on behalf of the organizing committee. It won't be a long speech. You should be able to hear everything from back here."

"You haven't gotten to the part about why I'm back here in the first place."

Sylvia sighed. "You stand on the mark. I ask everyone to welcome you. The curtain will open and the spotlight will shift to you. I expect there will be some applause."

He frowned.

"I know," Sylvia said. "Not your favorite. All you have to do is make a gentleman's bow and walk toward me. We'll go down the stairs together and sit at the head table with Miles and some of the town council members."

Quinn was scowling.

"What's wrong?" Sylvia asked.

"It's overdramatized, don't you think?"

"Quinn, a committee planned this event. They had a lot of discussion about the tone they wanted to set. They want to honor you in a memorable way for everything you do for the people of Hidden Falls. This is not a down-home picnic."

He looked her in the eye. "I understand what it is, Sylvia." He paced across the stage and pulled back the center curtain about an inch.

Sylvia stood behind him. "Look how many people wanted to be here."

Members of the town council served as unofficial ushers, helping people find seats. Sylvia was glad to see few openings. For the most part, people who said they were coming actually came. The wait staff, in starched black and white, lined up along one wall with wrists crossed behind their backs.

"Some of those kids getting ready to serve are my students," Quinn said. "I've never seen them look so put together."

Sylvia gasped. "Is that Dani Roose?"

"Where?"

"Over on the left, toward the back, just coming in."

Quinn's shoulders visibly relaxed. "I saw her only a couple of hours ago, headed to the lake. And look, she came. I'm quite persuasive, you know."

"I do know. I see Nicole and Ethan both made it."

"It would warm my heart if they sat together, but that's probably asking too much."

"Ethan looks like he's on the phone." Sylvia watched Ethan walking toward an exit with his phone pushed against his ear.

"I hope it's not a medical emergency," Quinn said. "He needs to stay in town for a bit."

"I'm sure he'll come right back in." Sylvia saw Nicole take a seat next to her niece. "Nicole looks stunning."

"She told me a fascinating story of her work. In fact, I —" He broke off the thought.

Sylvia stepped to one side so she could see Quinn's face. "In fact, you what?"

He shook it off. "Nothing."

She did not believe him. "Quinn, what is it?"

"This is not the time. Just . . . something I need to do."

Sylvia considered his face. He was avoiding her eyes, but she saw an expression that drifted across his features only a few times a year now. When they were younger, she saw it more often.

"Lauren was a nervous wreck this afternoon," she said. "All aflutter about the health fair next week."

"I saw her after my haircut. She has nothing to worry about."

"Lauren was in my shop just before I closed." Sylvia scrunched up her face. "Do you mean you were still in town at that point in the day?"

He shrugged. "I'm here, aren't I?"

Sylvia adjusted her view through the crack in the curtain. "Jack Parker is here."

"I have his older daughter in one of my classes."

"I don't like his attitude. A superiority complex is unbecoming in a community like Hidden Falls."

"Something makes him behave that way," Quinn said. "Everyone has a story. We just don't know what his is yet. When we do, we'll understand him better."

Sylvia softened. Quinn was right.

Through the curtain, she saw Liam put his arm around Jessica's shoulders and lean in to listen to her.

"I've known Liam Elliott all his life," Sylvia said. "His story just seems to get more complicated."

"That reminds me," Quinn said. "I'm supposed to set up another meeting with Liam."

"He has aspirations for managing some town funds, too," Sylvia said. "I'm not so sure."

"He deserves a hearing, but I may have to delay awhile longer."

"Having doubts?"

"No. I have a possible schedule conflict."

Miles stuck his head in and waved a hand.

Quinn blew out his breath. "I guess we should get this show on the road."

Sylvia pointed to the silver mark. "Stand right there and don't move."

Quinn clicked his heels together and stood up straight.

"Just don't move," she repeated.

Sylvia stepped through the curtain and crossed to the left of the stage. A copy of her remarks awaited her on a small podium that had been freshly stained for the occasion. She held her pose while the houselights dimmed and a soft white spotlight encircled her. Gradually conversations hushed and heads turned toward the mayor.

"Good evening," Sylvia said. "Thank you for coming out to spend your Saturday evening as we together honor Ted Quinn, a person who has touched countless lives since he arrived in Hidden Falls more than thirty years ago."

Applause swelled, and Sylvia waited for it to subside.

"Our friend Quinn is a dedicated teacher. Some of you who studied with him in the early years have the joy of seeing your children in his classroom now. He has led one town improvement effort after another through the decades, in his desire to make Hidden Falls a place that feels like home to all who live here and all who visit. As a member of Our Savior Community Church and a deeply caring human being, he looks for every opportunity to speak into suffering with tenderness. His wit and humor keep us all on our toes."

Applause rose again.

"We will hear from Quinn a little later, after we have enjoyed the meal that awaits us. When you picked up —"

A boom thundered behind Sylvia, startled the breath out of her, and launched a surge of adrenaline. She spun toward the scuffling footsteps behind the curtain, but Miles was already out of his seat and taking the side stairs in three long steps before disappearing through the stage door, so she held her position. A nervous mutter rippled across the room. The wait staff along the wall lost their formation. Five hundred faces looked in a dozen different directions.

Sylvia gave what she hoped was a reassuring smile to the eyes fixed on her. "I'm sure Mr. Devon will have things in hand momentarily."

Miles emerged from the stage door and paced across the stage. Sylvia put a hand over the microphone as he leaned in to whisper in her ear.

"Some idiot set the trigger on the theater's air cannon stored back there," he said. "If I didn't know better, I'd say it was Zeke Plainfield, but he's been out here the whole time. Anyway, there's no telling what the cycle time was set for."

Sylvia eased her breath out through upturned lips. "So everything is all right back there?"

"Perfectly fine."

"And Quinn?"

"It wasn't anywhere near him. The cannon was at the back of the stage in a pile of props."

"Good."

"Let's not reward this with attention. Just continue your remarks." Miles casually returned to his seat.

"We've had a mishap," Sylvia said into the microphone, "but nothing to interrupt our celebration. When you picked up your name tags, you also found a card indicating the entrée you selected with your reservation. Please lay this above your place setting, and servers will be sure you receive the meal you ordered. But before we begin the meal, let's welcome our guest of honor."

Sylvia swept one hand in a wide gesture toward the center of the stage. She fell into darkness as the spotlight shifted and the curtains began to draw open. Applause swelled again and the crowd rose to their feet.

The curtains left a wide gap now, and light flooded the stage.

The mark was empty.

Sylvia smiled for the sake of anyone who might be watching her face and walked across the stage to glance around the area out of view from the audience. It would be just like Quinn to get involved in the backstage commotion.

"Quinn," she whispered sharply. "Get out here."

Silence. Not even the shuffle of a step.

Sylvia signaled to a stagehand to turn on the lights behind the curtain. Her eyes swept the area.

Quinn was gone.

2
Losing Quinn

Saturday
7:52 p.m.

Applause thundered. Lauren made sure her clapping was among the most enthusiastic, and her glee for Quinn blotted out the discomfort of her heels when she stood up. Her aunt Sylvia disappeared behind the side curtain to a steady roll of applause. A few seconds later, though, the spotlight dimmed. In response, the ovation tapered off. The standing crowd looked at each other, expressions both expectant and bewildered. Gradually people began to sit down.

"Hey, Lauren, what's going on?"

The pressure on the back of her shoulders could only mean Zeke, an eleventh-grader from church who liked to sneak up on her. Lauren ducked out of his grasp and twisted to see his face. Zeke wore black pants, a white shirt, and a black bow tie.

"I see you're serving dinner tonight." Lauren tweaked his tie.

"That was the plan, but this wasn't in the rehearsal."

"Rehearsal?"

"Yeah. As soon as the mayor walks Mr. Quinn down off the stage, we're supposed to start serving the Caesar salads."

Lauren glanced around the table. Brian and Rachel Gardner looked at her with anticipation. She had been in school with a couple of their kids. An older couple she didn't recognize also seemed to think she would have an explanation.

"You know how it is," Lauren said casually. "You can't predict everything at a rehearsal."

"Mr. Quinn wasn't at the rehearsal." Zeke tapped one foot and jiggled his knee. "Seems like they should've had the star of the show there."

Brian Gardner buzzed his lips. "At least this time I'm not worried that one of my kids was the one not paying attention."

Nervous laughter circled the table.

"All he had to do was stand on an X," Zeke said. "They made it pretty big. I saw it myself."

"One little glitch is not going to ruin the evening." Lauren watched the stage. The curtains were closing.

"It's probably a trick," Zeke said.

Brian Gardner nodded agreement. "Quinn will have the last laugh."

Rachel said, "It's his night. He should enjoy

it however he likes."

While Quinn didn't like being singled out for credit — he believed nothing happened due to the efforts of just one person — his creative humor was legendary. He was the teacher students could count on to ham it up at the faculty talent show or in the skits during pep rallies.

Lauren chuckled. "One time he came out dressed as one of the Trapp Family children in play clothes made out of curtains. I was laughing so hard I nearly fell off the top of the cheerleader pyramid."

Zeke grinned. "Last week he got in one of those human bowling ball cages and let them roll him across the gym."

"Zeke Plainfield, get back in line."

The razor in the caterer's tone made everyone at the table jump. Zeke lurched toward the wall where most of the waitstaff still stood, though they had relaxed their posture considerably.

The curtains took a final tug and sealed the gap between them, plunging the activity behind into mystery. Buzzing murmurs around the banquet room notched up.

"Zeke is probably right," Lauren said. "Quinn has something up his sleeve."

"I don't know," Nicole said, shaking her head. "That doesn't sound right."

"I'm sure it will be dignified." Whatever humor Quinn was going to bring to the evening, he would be in his tux. At most, three minutes had passed since the spotlight showed an empty stage. Considering everything scheduled for the evening, a three-minute delay didn't concern Lauren. A little laughter would relax everyone, and people across the generations would chatter with one another like old friends. It was some sort of an icebreaker, Lauren decided.

"Something's wrong." Nicole spoke softly into the space between her and Lauren. "I don't like the way this smells."

"What do you mean, how it smells?" Lauren said. "It's nothing." They would be laughing about it in another minute.

"Did you see the mayor's face?" Nicole said. "She was not expecting this."

"Of course not," Lauren said. "Quinn never tells anybody when he's going to pull something."

"Why did they turn off the spotlight?"

Lauren shifted in her chair. "Maybe the lights guy is in on it."

"You just said Quinn doesn't tell anybody."

"I didn't mean that *literally.* Obviously sometimes he needs a conspirator."

With her lips pressed together, Nicole shook her head with less hesitancy. "Not tonight. He wouldn't spoil an occasion like this."

"He's not spoiling anything," Lauren said. "He's just being Quinn."

"Quinn will play along with a lot of crazy ideas," Nicole said, "but he's not the class clown. He never let anyone get away with that in class. He doesn't disturb other people's plans."

Lauren had no response. What Nicole said was true.

Nicole nodded toward the stage. "Look at the clues. Your aunt didn't come back out. The light went off. The curtain closed. Now the principal just went up the side steps to the stage and behind the curtain. This is not adding up."

Lauren reached for her water goblet and watched the stage. Miles Devon stuck his head out and glanced around the banquet hall and then quickly withdrew. A stagehand descended the short set of stairs and bounded down the long wall of the room past the wait-staff. Sylvia reappeared, crossing the apron of the stage without pausing at the microphone. The curtains flapped with the continued bustle behind them.

An obnoxious roar from someone in the back of the room stunned Lauren. Her hand trembled, knocking the ice cubes around in her glass.

"What's the matter?" the voice boomed. "Didn't you practice enough?"

Around an entire table, dinner guests guffawed. The rudeness set off a ripple of nervous astonishment that flowed across the banquet hall.

Lauren's breath caught as her head turned along with every other head in the room, like gawkers at the scene of an accident who can't help themselves. She cringed at the way the uncouth disruption would further mar an evening already gone awry. But while most eyes fixed on the ogre who stood and shouted in his own amusement, Lauren's focused on another man at the table. Nevin Morgan passed her on the street just a couple of hours ago, but she'd hoped to get through the evening's festivities without giving him another thought.

"We're going to get our dinner while it's hot, right?" the loudmouth bellowed.

From behind him, Nevin Morgan met Lauren's eyes. Something inside Lauren shriveled; a moan escaped and she snatched back her gaze.

"Are you all right?" Nicole asked.

Unable to speak, Lauren nodded vaguely.

Sylvia came out from behind the heavy stage curtain and stepped to the microphone. "Ladies and gentlemen, please excuse the delay. We ask your patience as we prepare to continue."

Lauren didn't like the color in her aunt's face as she once again pushed the curtain aside and withdrew behind it.

"Sylvia lost Quinn! Sylvia lost Quinn!" The taunter started a chant, and his buddies joined in. Fortunately, his efforts to incite the crowd failed.

Lauren's anticipation of humor dissipated. "I think you might be right," she said to Nicole.

"I'm a reporter," Nicole said. "I can smell a story a mile away. Something happened."

Lauren stood. "I should see if I can help."

Nicole grabbed Lauren's forearm and pulled her back into her seat. "No. That will just make things look more suspicious."

"Maybe Quinn is ill up there. Maybe they found him on the floor with a heart attack." Lauren's imagination raced.

"No. He's not there. That's the issue. He's not there at all."

"How do you know?"

Nicole raked a hand through the hair covering the side of her face. "Because they're still looking for him."

Sylvia crossed the stage again. Lauren watched her aunt's face. It was a mask of control and efficiency, an expression Sylvia put on when she wanted to handle a situation in unruffled calm.

This really was a situation.

7:57 p.m.

Sylvia Alexander was again at the microphone, this time holding up a copy of the evening's program. "Ladies and gentlemen, thank you for bearing with us. You'll notice in tonight's program the invitation to visit the video booth along the side wall at some point in the evening. A videographer will be there to record your personal greetings and remembrances of Ted Quinn. Since it looks like our evening will deviate from the order printed in the program, I invite you to begin availing yourself of this opportunity."

"We might as well sit down." Liam held Jessica's chair.

She seated herself and tucked her long legs under the table. Liam sat beside her. On the other side of him, Cooper's eyes were taking in the scene.

Thinking like a cop, Liam thought. A few people drifted toward the video booth.

"What happened?" Jessica asked.

Liam wondered if anyone else heard the edge in her voice.

"It's fine," Liam said.

"You don't know that," Jessica said.

"I just mean we don't have any reason to be worried," Liam said. "They'll find where Quinn went off to, and we'll get on with the evening. They're probably reorganizing now."

"Don't be too sure." Dani spoke from the other side of Cooper.

"Dani, do you know something?" Liam asked.

She shrugged. "Not really. Except Quinn doesn't like this kind of attention."

"He probably just needed a minute," Cooper said. "Maybe he didn't feel well. He could be in the men's room."

"Is that really what you think?" Dani glared.

"I don't *think* anything," Cooper clarified. "I'm just saying we don't need to rush to conclusions or speculate about what was in Quinn's mind."

"He's not in the men's room," Dani said.

Liam scoffed. "Unless you're in one of your socially inappropriate moods, I don't see how you can verify that, Dani."

She scowled at him.

Cabe Mueller and his wife sat across the table. "Maybe someone needed him. Somebody backstage. Some situation. When I was a student, Quinn was always thinking of someone else before himself."

"He still does that," Cooper said.

"Then I'm sure that's what it is," Cabe said. "Somebody else got sick. It will sort itself out soon enough."

"No doubt," Liam said.

Jessica leaned toward Liam, her hand stroking his knee beneath the table. Her hair brushed against his cheek in that intoxicating way that made him think she did it on purpose.

"I thought you promised this would be a short night," she said, the heat of her breath against his ear.

He touched her face, wondering if her skin tingled as much as his did. "It will be. This is nothing."

Her eyes spoke volumes of doubt.

"Have I told you how fabulous you look tonight?"

She smiled, but not in a persuasive way. "You're going to owe me big-time for this one."

"And I will gladly pay my debt. Every cent I owe."

Liam glanced at Cooper, wishing the subject of debt hadn't entered the conversation. He was doing his best to act normally around his brother. But Liam knew Cooper's face as well as his brother knew his. This wrinkle in events had shifted Cooper's mind into his professional training, and Liam didn't want to be on his radar.

Cabe Mueller scooted his chair back. "Perhaps I'll have a word with Principal Devon. If this were happening at a function associated with the school where I teach, the principal would want reliable assistance."

"I'm sure Miles has it well in hand," Cooper said.

"Still, I'd like to offer assistance." Cabe glanced at his wife. "You'll be all right?"

She nodded, and Cabe left the table.

"I'm sure your husband means well," Dani said, "but he'll find there's nothing to do."

Stubborn as ever. Why did she think she knew more about Quinn than anyone else?

"Did Quinn say something to you?" Liam

tilted his head to get a good look at his cousin's expression.

"Just that he'd like to go fishing," Dani said.

"He couldn't have meant tonight."

"Sure he could."

"People are getting restless." Cooper's gaze slowly arced the room.

"Can you blame them?" Jessica said. "I don't recall anything on the invitation describing a mystery disappearance and a delay of dinner."

"There is no mystery disappearance," Dani said.

"Dani." Liam loaded his tone with as much warning as he could muster.

"People need to stay calm," Cooper said. "There's no reason to worry prematurely."

"Or at all," Dani said.

"Who wants to go to the video booth?" Cooper asked. "Dani? Liam? The three of us can make a message together."

"I'll pass," Dani said.

Liam wasn't surprised. He glanced at Jessica. "Jessica doesn't know Quinn, but I'll go."

"Let's do it." Cooper slapped his palms together.

The brothers scooted around several tables and found clear walking space. The line seemed to move quickly. They stood behind a young couple.

"Hello, Gallaghers." Cooper's bright tone

cut through the subdued waiting. "Do you know my brother, Liam?"

Liam extended a hand. "Pleased to meet you."

"This is Raisa and Bruce Gallagher. They have two adorable little girls you'll have to meet someday."

Raisa visibly flushed with pleasure at the mention of her children.

"I look forward to it," Liam said. He sized up Bruce, whose suit suggested he made a steady but not impressive income.

"Honey, it's our turn." Bruce Gallagher took his wife's elbow, and they entered the booth, an area about six feet by nine feet screened off by a system of PVC pipe and lightweight beige print fabric.

Liam felt a touch on his back and turned toward a member of the waitstaff.

"Excuse me, I need to get through with a message for the kitchen."

Liam knew the teenager firmly pressing his way through the gathering line. He was Dave Plainfield's boy. Liam had met him once on an evening visit to the Plainfield home.

Liam saw the boy's long foot go down in the wrong place, too close to a joint in the PVC frame. He tripped and fell into the booth's frame, knocking apart a support pole. Once one wall of fabric gave way, untethered, a second wall caved in, and a third. Yards of fabric lost their skeleton and fell into a heap.

A sound that could only have been the clattering tripod and tumbling video camera made Liam wince. From inside the toppling mound of pipe and fabric, Raisa Gallagher screamed. Gasps went up from the nearby tables.

Liam and Cooper scrambled to scoop away the remains of the booth and reveal the startled Gallaghers. The videographer probed the yardage until he located the camera.

"Everybody okay?" Liam asked.

"Yes, thank you," Bruce Gallagher said.

"Sorry," Zeke Plainfield mumbled as he sprang to his feet.

"You should be," the photographer snapped. He held up his camera. "It's broken."

"It was an accident." Cooper spread his hands, palms down. "Let's be thankful everyone is all right."

Liam pushed pieces of the booth against the wall, out of the way. Zeke continued his path toward the kitchen. The line for the booth scattered.

Back at the table, Jessica said, "What was all that?"

"An unfortunate mishap." Liam squeezed her hand.

"The evening seems to be full of those," she said.

"Let's relax." Cooper picked up a pitcher of iced tea from the center of the table. "Can

I top anybody off?"

Jessica nudged Liam's elbow. "Does your brother not see that no one has even touched the glasses yet?"

"I'm just trying to help." Cooper reached across Liam and splashed a few drops into Jessica's brimming goblet.

"I don't need your kindly efforts at distraction," Jessica said.

Mrs. Mueller lifted a water glass. "Actually, I've been sipping on this and wouldn't mind a refill."

"Gladly." Cooper exchanged the tea for the water pitcher, rose to circle the table, and filled the glass.

Liam stood as well. "I'll be right back."

"You just got back."

Liam pretended not to hear the warning in Jessica's voice.

"Quinn is not in the men's room," Dani said.

"I didn't say I was going to look for him there." Liam didn't meet his cousin's eye, instead looking at his fiancée. "I'll be right back, sweetheart."

He cut through the line of slouching waitstaff and exited the banquet room into a side hall that ran the length of the building. The restrooms were at the far end, and a handful of people straggled in search of them. Obviously Quinn had left the stage area. The reason didn't matter to Liam. What mattered was finding Quinn, who more than likely had ducked into one of several rooms generally considered to be off-limits to the public but also unlikely to be locked. Liam wanted to find him to get the evening back on track before Jessica lost her patience altogether. And a moment alone with Quinn wouldn't hurt. Liam could drop a hint about his ideas for investments and casually suggest a meeting time to lay out the full plan. Soon.

And then he would have to construct a full, convincing plan and practice his presentation so no vestige of doubt remained about the strength of the plan — for Quinn or for himself. He could give Jessica the attention she wanted tonight and work on the presentation the next day while she was at her friend's baby shower. The papers would be printed and ready for Quinn to sign. Liam took out his phone and entered a note about a fund to suggest to Quinn — one that few at the corporate offices paid attention to. It would only be temporary.

Quinn. Jessica. The money. It would all work out. It had to.

Liam jiggled a door he was fairly certain led to a storage closet. When it opened, he felt along the wall for a light switch before swinging his hand into the middle of the room to catch hold of a string. He pulled it, and the bulb in the ceiling illuminated the cramped space full of folders and records from years gone by and ladders in three sizes. The bottom drawer of a file cabinet hung open.

He moved down the hall to the next door. The identifying tag on the wall next to it said it was the marketing coördinator's office. When, to Liam's surprise, it was locked, he slipped a credit card out of his pocket and easily entered. A few things he'd learned during college proved handy in real life, and Quinn somehow could have trapped himself in this office. Liam left the door cracked for a shaft of hallway light. His eyes adjusted quickly. It was a tidy office with the computer turned off and folders neatly stacked in a silver wire rack. He saw no sign that it had been disturbed. Even the guest chair remained at a precise angle.

Only one item appeared untended, an ordinary business envelope laid at a peculiar slant in a room of right angles, as if left out for particular attention and perhaps forgotten. Liam flipped it over. The printed label was addressed to the marketing coordinator at her business address, but it was the return address that caught Liam's eyes. A Chicago bank with a branch in Birch Bend.

The envelope seemed to burn his fingers as Liam slid it into his inside suit pocket. His heart pounded at the thought that the contents would include an account number — maybe more than one. A random account number with which Liam had no trail of history could be an even better way to buy time than new legitimate accounts. Liam had several clients who used the Birch Bend branch of this Chicago institution. Somewhere in his system he must have routing numbers for moving funds. The account number would complete the equation.

It would be a short-term loan, that's all.

Liam opened several more doors, telling himself Quinn might have needed a quiet place to sit down.

But, of course, he didn't find Quinn. It was like looking for lost keys. Mayor Alexander, Principal Devon, the banquet hall staff, and half the town council would have already scurried through all the obvious places where Quinn might have taken refuge.

Refusing to let himself hurry, Liam shuffled back toward the banquet hall. When he reached the door, he paused and let his eyes settle on the table he had left a few minutes ago. Cabe Mueller was still out of his seat, and now Dani's chair was empty as well. Liam was grateful for an angle from which Jessica could not see him unless she turned halfway around. Nearly twenty minutes had passed since the spotlight turned up empty. Around the room, people had begun to slouch in their seats. Not Jessica. In the six and a half years Liam had known her, he never saw Jessica slouch. She maintained poise under every circumstance, her hair wavy in a controlled yet casual manner and her posture upright with relaxed shoulders.

Beneath her demeanor, irritation simmered. The angle of her neck was slightly off as she listened to conversation. Even from the side and partially behind her, Liam could tell she looked attentive and had a smile on her face, but she had tilted her head in that way that meant she was making no effort to store any information coming through her ears. She was being polite. And could not wait to get out of there.

"Find anything interesting?"

Liam startled and turned. Dani.

"She's a poster child of manners, all right." Dani stared at Jessica.

"You've never made any effort to get to know Jessica."

"Like she would have any interest in knowing me."

"You're being unfair."

"Am I? It's a good thing I'm your cousin and not your sister. If you get married, she won't have to pretend to like me."

"There's no *if.*"

"Whatever."

Liam put his hands in his pants pockets. "Maybe you wouldn't be such a misfit if you tried to get along with people."

"Maybe I wouldn't be such a misfit if people tried to get along with me." Dani slapped his shoulder.

Liam examined Dani from head to toe. "You don't look half bad when you make an effort."

"Wow. Melt my heart." Dani tugged on the braid hanging forward over her shoulder. "This was your idea. I wanted to go to the lake."

8:06 p.m.

Ethan looked up at the night sky, wishing he were doing so in order to admire it rather than to manage his temper.

"I arranged this weekend off two months ago," he said into the phone against his ear.

"I'm standing here in front of the surgical schedule board," Phil Brinkman said, "and I'm telling you, Dressler is out. Flu. They're not letting her near the OR for at least another week. Sutton is in Atlantic City at some family emergency."

"What exactly are you expecting me to do, Brinkman?" Ethan pressed the heel of his free hand to his forehead.

"Get yourself back here and do surgery tomorrow."

"Not gonna happen. Monday morning at seven is the best I'm going to offer."

"What makes you think this is negotiable?"

"What makes you think you're in charge of my surgical schedule?" Heat rose through Ethan's gullet. Brinkman was not the surgical chief or even chief resident. They had begun residency together. Brinkman was another Ken Lauder, trying to get ahead on somebody else's back.

"The chief told me to figure out the schedule and bring him a solution," Brinkman said.

"So figure it out, but I'm not your solution." Ethan punched End on the phone and cut off the call. He depressed the button at the top of the phone and waited for the red bar instructing him to swipe the screen to power it off. With a finger hovering over the screen, Ethan considered his options.

All he really wanted was to hear why Quinn sent that note. What was so urgent that Quinn would extend an invitation for Ethan to stay at his house?

The red bar blinked at him. Ethan hit CANCEL. He would leave the phone on, but when he went back inside to eat bland chicken, he would turn the sound off. No matter how many times Brinkman called back, Ethan would hit IGNORE. He had called in favors and gotten triple signatures just to get two days off. Brinkman puffing his chest and raising his voice was not going to change that.

Ethan eyed the far end of the parking lot. A walk there and back would help him compose himself before he went inside. He was enough of a doctor to know the adrenaline rush Brinkman's call had triggered would take hours to clear his system, but he could at least go into the banquet appearing more placid than he felt. Ethan was not sure what bothered him more — Brinkman's persistent arrogance or the way he let Brinkman get to him.

He paced down the center aisle of the parking lot to burn off steam.

It was more than Brinkman. He handled Brinkman every day, and had for the last five years. It was being in Hidden Falls, seeing Quinn, driving past his family home, circling the lake, running into Nicole — twice — all in the space of a few hours. Everything he separated himself from, intentionally or unintentionally, in the last ten years was here. He had one night in Hidden Falls, and perhaps the morning. He would find out what Quinn wanted. Nothing else mattered. Then he'd go back to Columbus. Ethan doubted he would return to Hidden Falls for another ten years.

At the end of the parking aisle, he pivoted. The gray building lost its shape against the blackness advancing behind it. Light seeping from the windows ringed the hall in a misty halo.

A lone figure came out the front door and lit a cigarette. Ethan followed the tiny point of light as if it were a beacon to find the main door.

"Jordan? Is that you?"

A voice was like a fingerprint or smell from

the past. You just had to hear its timbre scattered over a few syllables, Ethan thought, and every memory it carried rushed toward you. He refused to interrupt his stride, though any ground he had gained reducing the flood of adrenaline was now lost. He walked forward until features emerged from the shadows.

"Hello, Ken." Ethan paused on the wide sidewalk.

"Haven't heard much about you in a long time," Ken said.

"I live in Columbus."

"Got a good job there?"

"Pretty good. Neurosurgeon."

"Whoa. Who would have thought you were *that* smart?"

Ethan let it pass. "What are you up to?"

"Shift supervisor at the screw factory in Birch Bend. Been there since a year after graduation."

"From college?"

"You always were a little slow." Ken puffed on the cigarette. "It only took me one semester at the University of Illinois to know that higher education wasn't everything those high school counselors made it out to be."

Ethan almost choked on the effort to restrain his retort. Instead, he said, "So you came back and started working."

"Nothing wrong with good, honest, hard work."

"Nope. Can't disagree with you there."

Ethan's stomach soured. This man stole Ethan's valedictorian status and did nothing more than flunk out of one semester at the state university.

Ken offered the cigarette.

"No thanks," Ethan said.

"Yeah, I didn't think you would smoke. You never would admit you needed something to help you get by." Ken took a final puff, dropped his cigarette, and crushed it underfoot. "Can you believe what happened in there?"

Ethan shrugged. "I've been out here."

"So you don't know Quinn's gone?"

"What do you mean, gone?" Fresh adrenaline surged.

"The mayor introduced him, they opened the curtain, and he wasn't there. Gone."

Gone.

"If you've been out here," Ken said, "you must have seen something."

"That is not exactly impeccable logic."

"You and your big words."

Ethan wondered what Ken's score had been on the verbal portion of the SAT if he thought *impeccable* was a big word. Maybe he cheated on that test, too.

"The building has multiple exits," Ethan pointed out. "Even if Quinn came out this door, I had my back turned. Being outside doesn't mean I saw anything."

"Yeah, well, tell that to the police."

"Are they involved?"

"They should be. He's been missing almost half an hour now."

Don't you ever watch crime shows on TV? Ethan thought. *Nobody is missing after thirty minutes.*

"And you'd better get your story together," Ken said. "You're sure to be a person of interest. The only possible witness and all that."

"Don't go telling tales. I didn't see anything." The sharpness in his own voice surprised Ethan, but he was glad for it.

"No need to flip out, bro." Ken turned around and paced toward the door. "I'm going to see if they're serving dinner."

Ethan wished he *had* seen something. What kind of nonsense was this about Quinn being gone? Where would he go? And why?

Tasteless chicken was the last thing on Ethan's mind now.

The note. The urgency. The invitation. The promise that they would talk later tonight.

Yes, the promise. Ethan allowed himself a satisfying exhale. Quinn would turn up and they would talk later.

Ethan startled when his phone buzzed, and he fumbled it out of his pocket. Already he was prepared to bark at Brinkman one last time.

GONZALEZ, the caller ID said. Ethan moaned. In ten minutes' time, Brinkman had gone running to their surgical chief. Ethan didn't dare hit IGNORE on this call.

"Hello, Dr. Gonzalez." Ethan wandered out among the parked cars again.

"Hello yourself, Dr. Jordan."

Ethan scrunched up his face, glad Carlos Gonzalez couldn't see him.

"I understand you and Dr. Brinkman are having a difference of opinion about your responsibility to the hospital."

Ethan chewed the inside of his mouth for a couple of seconds before responding. "I merely pointed out, sir, that my absence was properly approved quite some time ago, and I am a considerable distance from Columbus at the moment."

"Valid points, but I need you and Brinkman to be on the same team if you're going to continue on in my service."

Another of Gonzalez's veiled threats. After five years, Ethan was nearly as tired of his chief as he was of Brinkman. If he didn't think Gonzalez was a brilliant surgeon, Ethan would have walked away a long time ago.

"We're on the same team, sir. I assure you."

"Set aside the competitiveness of your residency and focus on being a good doctor."

"I want nothing more than to do just that."

"So I will expect you for rounds Monday morning."

"Yes sir. That's my plan."

"Well, don't change it, and I don't want to

hear excuses. I have five doctors who would jump at the chance to take the spot you're filling."

By the time Ethan's mind formulated his next sentence, he realized Gonzalez had ended the call. Ethan returned the phone to his pocket, leaned against the back of a beige SUV, and squeezed his head between his hands. He couldn't leave now.

He had to know what Quinn's note was about.

He had to be certain Quinn was all right. Surely it would all be cleared up tomorrow.

What Gonzalez saw in Brinkman, Ethan didn't know. Brinkman might one day play hospital politics well enough to land himself an administrator job, but Ethan would be the better surgeon.

He spoke aloud to the blackness. "And whose hands would you rather put your brain in?"

8:14 P.M.

"I need some air." Nicole straightened her dress as she stood.

"You're not leaving, are you?" Lauren tilted her head up with the question.

"No. I just need to think." Nicole fished a pen and small notepad out of her purse, jotted down a number, and slid the sheet beside the set of forks defining Lauren's place setting. "Call me if you hear something. I'll only be outside."

When she reached the exit, before stepping out of the banquet hall, Nicole turned around for a panoramic view of the room. Conversation buzzed, and she didn't think people were reminiscing about the good old days of living in Hidden Falls.

Quinn had been missing for twenty-five minutes, maybe as many as thirty if he stepped off his mark behind the curtain at the same moment Sylvia Alexander began her remarks.

In the last ten years, Nicole had reported enough stories involving crimes to know that twenty-five minutes was a bigger head start than most people realized, precious minutes while people went about their lives unsuspecting that something had gone wrong in one life. Even in a smallish city of 320,000, like St. Louis, it was enough time to be miles away. In Hidden Falls, it was a sufficient interlude to reach the interstate, choose a direction, and enter a web of alternatives. If five people saw you at a rest stop, they would provide five different descriptions to the police — or a reporter.

Nicole scanned the hall, trying to freeze-frame the moment of Saturday at 8:14 p.m. Between four and five hundred people gathered at tables, some sitting and some standing or drifting across the aisles. Dozens had left the room for innocent reasons: a wrap left in the car, a need for the restrooms, a call from the babysitter.

Looking for Quinn.

The room was not secured. Nicole saw not even one uniformed officer on duty for the event.

And why should there be? Hidden Falls was the kind of town where visitors ignoring the speed limit got most of the attention from law enforcement. Occasionally kids took their vandalism too far and faced the consequences. And no doubt in the last ten years drugs had become more available than when Nicole was in high school, as they had everywhere. But if the local newspaper depended on a police blotter for stories to follow up on, the publisher would have been out of business years ago.

Think, Sandquist, Nicole told herself. *You're missing something. What is it?*

She resumed her resolve to seek fresh air. She cared about Quinn, but this was no time to let sentiment cloud a decade of training and experience. If something had gone wrong for him a half hour ago, she needed to be at the top of her game.

High heels stopped hindering Nicole long ago. She crossed the foyer swiftly and pushed out the front door. Cool air wakened the pores of her face. She was glad she'd tossed a coat in her car when she left the house. She would need it by the time the evening ended

— and the way things were going, there was no predicting when that would be.

Nicole hadn't thought beyond getting outside. Maybe there was a bench where she could sit to think. Maybe she would follow the sidewalk that circled the building.

What she hadn't expected was to find Ethan Jordan, feet spread shoulder width apart, a hand pushing his suit jacket back from one hip, and a phone to his ear. In her instant of hesitation, he turned toward her, and Nicole didn't look away quickly enough to pretend she hadn't seen him.

Ethan put his phone away. "I heard about Quinn a couple of minutes ago. Did he turn up?"

Nicole shook her head and shivered. The temperature was cooling but still mild. It was Ethan who caused the tremble of her entire central nervous system. Even after they had been dating for several years, she used to stand behind him and watch his movements when he couldn't see her. In those days, he fought hard for everything he wanted. With the transitory exception of not being valedictorian, Ethan Jordan got what he wanted. When he stopped fighting for her, Nicole didn't have to ask questions to know what it meant.

Memories clanked through her mind. The two of them built a tree house at the back of her yard. She should have looked while she was home to see if it was still there and whether any neighborhood kids squatted in it these days. Ethan and Nicole traded piles of comic books back then. When Nicole got tired of frozen dinners and accepted the fact that her widowed father did not intend to learn to cook, she began collecting cookbooks. Ethan tasted innumerable failed recipes with a smile on his face. As they got older, they realized their friends assumed they were dating. That's how they became a couple for three years of high school and two years of college.

The truth was, not a day went by that Nicole didn't think of Ethan, but she wasn't angry. Not anymore. She just hadn't expected to see him.

"Do you think he's all right?" Ethan asked now.

"I hope so. But I don't know."

"What happened? I've been out here on the phone. Work is a mess."

Ethan gestured with one arm in that familiar way, as if he intended to be sweepingly dramatic and changed his mind midmotion. Nicole could remember Ethan moving that way when they were ten years old. Twenty years ago.

Going into quintessential reporter mode, Nicole gave an account of the facts as she saw them — already arranging them in order of interest and importance, as if she had to find the lead for a story in tomorrow's paper and leave to the end of the article the lines an editor might cut. Ethan listened and nodded, his eyes intent on her. In the dark, it was hard to see the true color of his eyes, but she knew they were brown. She knew one eyebrow rose slightly higher than the other. She had spent years learning to read his moods by the look in his eye and finding her own security there.

"It doesn't make sense," Ethan said. "I spoke to him. He wanted to talk more, later tonight. And then you came along."

"I assure you, I said nothing to frighten him away. I'm hoping to see him again myself before I go back to St. Louis."

"I didn't mean it that way."

"I know." She exhaled. "Sorry."

His shoulders had broadened when he found his full height, and the poor guy looked exhausted, but he was still Ethan. The tilt of his head, the way he plunged his hands in his pockets, his habit of scuffing the ground with one toe like he was nine years old — Nicole couldn't watch these familiar gestures without remembering one moment after another that had bound her to Ethan. This moment, in the shadows outside the banquet hall rather than the sunlight outside the Main Street shops, evoked an intimacy that was hard for her to shirk off.

Go inside, Sandquist. Don't get sucked into

the past. That was a different Ethan.

His phone buzzed. Nicole turned to go, but Ethan held up one finger.

"Just give me a minute, please." His thumbs already tapped the keyboard on his phone.

"Work?" she asked.

He nodded.

Work, not a relationship. She looked away from him. What a ridiculous thought.

The phone buzzed again, and he tackled the message. "Brinkman thinks he can run my life."

"Brinkman?"

"Another resident. What's that line from the dowager of Downton Abbey? Something about giving the little people power and it goes to their heads."

Nicole felt her own eyes widen. "You watch Downton Abbey?"

"Doesn't everybody?" Ethan smiled. "We've come a long way from comic books and cookbooks."

She flushed. He had always been able to read her mind.

"Have you seen Quinn's car?" Ethan asked.

"I don't know what he drives now." Nicole collected herself.

"I'm guessing a 1989 green Oldsmobile."

"Surely not. That old car?"

"He never goes anywhere but Birch Bend, or maybe the town beyond that," Ethan said. "And he thinks nothing of walking five miles except in the worst of weather. I'll bet he doesn't have eighty thousand miles on that old car."

"You don't think he *walked* here tonight, do you? In a tux?"

"The only reason not to would be to avoid the mayor's wrath." Ethan turned toward the parking lot. "Let's look for the car."

"How long have you been out here?" Nicole followed Ethan, who walked toward the parking aisle farthest from the door. "Hasn't anybody been out to check the lot yet?"

"Not that I saw," Ethan said. "I came out to take a call before anything started."

"And you haven't seen anyone?"

"I didn't say that. A few people were arriving late and seemed to be in a hurry to get inside. Ken Lauder came out."

"Ken Lauder is here?"

"Yeah. Just my luck, eh?"

"He doesn't matter, Ethan. Look at you. Look at what you've done with your life." As bewildered as Nicole was by how their relationship had crumbled, she was proud of Ethan.

Her words bounced off him.

"Quinn's car," Ethan said. "The point is, I didn't notice anyone coming out to look for Quinn's car."

Nicole pressed her lips closed. Eyewitnesses missed obvious details all the time. Ethan didn't know who to notice anymore, who might have been significant. And what if Quinn had a new car? They could walk right past it and never know.

"Four out of every five cars out here have Illinois plates," Nicole said. "Any one of them could be Quinn's."

"Strictly speaking, I don't find that to be true."

"Ethan, don't get difficult."

"Too late." He flashed her a smile. "When we lived in Hidden Falls, Quinn drove an American-made sedan, and not a low-end model. We can eliminate all the minivans, and probably the SUVs."

"And the Toyotas and Hondas and my Hyundai. Yeah, yeah. Fine. What are we going to do, break into every Oldsmobile we see to check the registration?"

"Oldsmobiles went out of production ten years ago," Ethan said.

"I knew that," Nicole snapped. "What if he bought one eleven years ago?"

"Unlikely. The old one would not yet have been old enough for him to let go of it."

Nicole sighed. He had an answer for everything. "What are you getting at?"

"Quinn would have bought another General Motors car. That's the only kind of car you can get in Birch Bend."

"And we're supposed to recognize his choice by stumbling upon it in a dark parking lot?" Nicole's earlier sentiment rising out of gentle memories of Ethan was waning. "And, so what if we do? We still won't be able to explain losing Quinn. I say we go inside and see what the mayor has come up with."

Nicole reversed her direction and lengthened her stride toward the banquet hall. The black Lexus with Ohio plates caught her eye.

"This is yours, isn't it?" Nicole waved a hand toward the car without slowing her pace.

"I share custody with the bank." Ethan easily kept stride with her. "I get it three nights a week and every other weekend. Luckily this was my weekend."

"Funny. Not."

"Fine. We'll go in. But somebody with the ability to identify Quinn's car should be out here."

"Who are you sitting with tonight?" Nicole had no idea if the evening would still include a meal.

"Hadn't got that far," Ethan said.

"There's an empty seat at my table. It's right up front where we can see everything the mayor is doing."

8:22 p.m.

"I can't have people see me running around like this." Sylvia smiled blankly over the shoulder of Miles Devon into the dinner crowd. "We have to divide and conquer."

"We've looked in every nook and cranny of

this building." Miles grinned at nothing in particular. "Quinn is not here."

"We can't have mass panic." Sylvia waved a hand as if she were telling a casual story and purposely relaxed her shoulders. Whether she was fooling anyone, she didn't know. "How did he seem when the prop cannon went off? Is that the last anyone saw him?"

Miles blanched.

"What is it, Miles?" She saw his Adam's apple rise and fall and felt fresh adrenaline course through her.

"I don't actually recall looking at him at that moment."

"Surely he was there."

"I ran toward the noise. It wasn't anywhere near where he was standing."

Heartburn flared in Sylvia's chest. "So we don't know if he was already gone."

"Perhaps it's time to involve the sheriff's department." Miles's eyes narrowed.

"Cooper Elliott is here tonight," Sylvia said. "That will be less suspicious than having another officer blare a siren on the way over here."

"Excellent. You think of everything."

"Find a quiet spot and send him a text asking him to meet you."

"Brilliant, Your Honor."

"Now I'm going to smile at you and rattle off Cooper Elliott's cell phone number. Don't write it down. Ready?"

Miles tilted his head in a playful way. "I'm listening."

"You do know how to send a text, don't you?"

"I've learned a thing or two from hanging around teenagers the last forty-five years."

"Here goes." Sylvia gave the number and then gave Miles a friendly pat on the back. She said nothing more, lest even a few words blot out the numbers. Miles shook a few unavoidable hands but didn't stop to talk to anyone before slipping into the hallway.

Sylvia took three calming breaths before turning toward the nearest table. The bread basket was empty. Glancing around, she saw that people at many of the tables had nibbled their way through Russian rye, whole wheat, and sourdough rolls. What else were they supposed to do until the evening came off the pause button? Sylvia touched the back of one of the checkers from the grocery store.

"Glad you could make it, Jean."

Sylvia moved on quickly to another table, her churning stomach lodged in her throat but a smile pasted across her face.

"Henry, nice to see you."

Quinn, where are you?

And another.

"Bart Hendricks! I thought I saw your name on the RSVP list. Welcome back to Hidden Falls."

Please, God, let Quinn be okay. Wherever he

is, be there with him. I know You are, but please make sure he knows.

Sylvia worked her way past one table after another, smiling and calling people by name whenever she could but never slowing down enough for anyone to initiate conversation. When she picked up a shadow, she ignored it and moved between two tables especially close together.

The shadow pushed through as well. "Mayor Alexander, I wonder if I might have a word."

Sylvia exhaled slowly and turned around. "Why, of course. You're Quinn's friend from this morning, aren't you?" She extended a hand.

"Cabe Mueller."

She held her grip on his hand and gently guided him around so that she stood between Cabe and the nearest table. "I could see this morning how much it meant to Quinn that you came. We've long since lost track of addresses for most of his first year's students."

"Mayor, are you quite sure everything is all right?"

Sylvia smiled. "Unfortunately, our grand opening didn't go quite the way we rehearsed, but we'll be under way shortly."

"It's been quite some time —"

"As you can see, I'm making my way back to the front. Principal Devon will want me to give some further instructions."

Sylvia patted Cabe's arm and moved past him, stopping just often enough to appear congenial but not letting her eyes rest too long in one place. She could sound pleasant. She could appear reassuring. What she couldn't do was get bogged down in inquiries and speculation about how she could misplace Quinn on this night of all nights. Apart from her mother, Quinn was the dearest person to her in Hidden Falls, but she was the mayor and responsible to keep this event under control.

The evening bag that hung from Sylvia's shoulder was just large enough to hold her cell phone and a small wallet. With abrupt realization, she remembered she had silenced the phone hours ago. Now she fumbled in her bag, extracted the phone, and resisted the urge to rub her eyes while it came to life.

A text message.

From Quinn.

The assistant principal of the high school touched her elbow. Sylvia looked up, eyes unfocused.

"Miles said you wanted to show the PowerPoint now instead of over dessert," he said. "It's ready to go."

"Perfect." Sylvia gripped her phone, but her hand trembled. "Since it's mostly about Quinn's work at the school, maybe you'd like to introduce it."

He nodded and turned to ascend the stairs

to the stage. As the lights went down, Sylvia pulled up the text message again.

I KNOW I'VE WHINED, BUT I COULDN'T ASK FOR A BETTER NIGHT. THANK YOU.

Her heart knocked against her ribs. When the time stamp came into focus, she realized Quinn had thumbed this message even before she put him on his X.

Quinn, where are you?

On the fourth PowerPoint slide, a picture of the first debate team Quinn had coached — none of the pictures included Quinn — the image smeared and disappeared. The music cut off abruptly. Sylvia felt like her heart had been pounding for hours. The assistant principal looked at her, flustered. Sylvia marched down the side of the hall, past the remnants of the video booth, and to the audiovisual platform at the rear of the dining area.

The diagnosis was a bad projector bulb. The spare — if there was one — was in a closet at the high school.

Sylvia sucked in her breath, walked back to the stage, and stepped behind the microphone again. She was beginning to hate this.

The video booth.

The PowerPoint.

Both strategies were supposed to buy Sylvia some time while others searched the grounds for Quinn. What were the odds that both would fail in a matter of minutes? She had no more tricks up her sleeve for distracting people from the delay.

"I'm afraid technology has thrown us another curve," she said. "We beg your indulgence once again while we discover what the actual order of events will be."

She said nothing more before descending from the stage. Sylvia returned the smile of a frequent customer in her books and gifts shop and progressed toward the row of round tables closest to the stage, just short of the rectangular head table. Sylvia allowed her eyes to meet the gaze of her niece. Next to Lauren was Nicole Sandquist, and on the other side of Nicole sat Ethan Jordan.

Quinn would have liked that. He had said so just minutes ago. Nicole and Ethan together, and both of them with Lauren. Three of his favorite former students — perhaps the *most* favorite — at one table would have merited a whole-faced grin. Sylvia approached the table.

"Nicole. Ethan. I'm so glad to see you here," she said. "I'm sorry the evening has taken such an unexpected turn."

"Aunt Sylvia, what's going on?" Lauren's voice strained with query. "At first I thought it was nothing, just Quinn being funny. But it's been half an hour."

Thirty-three minutes, to be precise. Sylvia pointed at the empty seats on the other side of the table. The place settings appeared disturbed enough to think someone had been there. "Who else is at this table?"

"The Gardners," Lauren said. "And another couple I didn't recognize."

"Where are they now?"

"I don't know. When Quinn didn't come out and the applause died down, everybody got on their phones. The Gardners were calling all their kids."

Sylvia laughed nervously. "It appears I am not to be trusted with the guest of honor. I let him out of my sight for five minutes and I lost him."

"He seemed fine beforehand," Nicole said.

"He was," Sylvia said. "He absolutely was. Oh, he was protesting even up to the last minute that everything was over the top, but he gave me no reason not to expect his full cooperation."

"Well," Ethan said, "something changed."

"I sent Miles on an errand," Sylvia said, "and then we'll have to make a decision."

She scanned the room and almost didn't recognize Cooper Elliott coming toward her in a black suit. Around town he was either in his two-toned blue sheriff's department uniform or jeans and polos. The tailored black suit accentuated his height, even though Sylvia would not have described him as tall.

"Hello, Sylvia." Cooper smiled at the entire table. "We've certainly had some drama tonight."

"It's all right," Sylvia said. "You can speak freely."

"Cooper Elliott." He put out his hand toward Lauren, who took it.

"Lauren Nock," she said.

"I know."

Sylvia saw the blush in her niece's face. "Cooper Elliott, please meet Nicole Sandquist and Dr. Ethan Jordan."

"Welcome to Hidden Falls."

"Nicole and Ethan grew up in Quinn's neighborhood, in addition to being students of his."

"Then I'm sure you would like to find him safe."

"Of course," Nicole said. "This is all some kind of misunderstanding."

"Cooper is with the sheriff's department." Sylvia's feet suddenly ached.

"So you'll look for Quinn, then," Nicole said.

Cooper straightened his tie and buttoned his suit jacket. "While I am as curious as the next person about why Quinn didn't come off that stage, I'm not sure yet we have anything to be alarmed about from a law enforcement perspective."

"You don't suspect foul play?" Sylvia asked.

"*Suspect* is a strong word," Cooper said. "It's too soon to suspect anything. All we can say for sure is that we don't know what happened."

"Obviously," Nicole said. "Isn't the real question *why*?"

Cooper shrugged. "How can we ask *why* if we don't know what we're discussing?"

Sylvia was desperate to give in to the rubbery sensation in her knees. "Can we please not talk in code? Cooper, are you not concerned about what happened to Quinn?"

"That's my point," he said. "We don't know what happened to Quinn, so we shouldn't jump to the conclusion of foul play."

"How can you be so sure?" Sylvia said.

"We should be checking for his car," Nicole said. "Ethan and I looked around the lot, wondering what he drives these days."

"Same old green Olds," Sylvia muttered.

Nicole and Ethan looked at each other. "We didn't see that car. We would have recognized it."

"Are you sure?" Cooper asked.

"Positive," Ethan said. "We had quite the discussion about what Quinn would drive, actually. Seeing that old beater would not have slipped by us."

"Well then," Cooper said, "in my opinion the most likely scenario is that Quinn drove away. We'll double-check the lot, of course."

"That doesn't make sense," Sylvia said. "He was fine. I told him what to do. He knew to stay on the mark."

"Wait a minute," Ethan said. "Even if Quinn did drive off, where would he go?

Home? The lake?"

"We're a small county," Cooper said, "and he won't cross the county line. He'll turn up soon enough."

Sylvia jumped when she felt a touch in the middle of her back.

Quinn used to touch her like that.

She spun around. "Miles."

"I told Cooper he shouldn't talk to you out in the open," Miles said.

"It's all right." Sylvia waited for her heart rate to fall back into a normal range. "He thinks Quinn drove away of his own free will."

"The caterer is going a little crazy," Miles said. "She doesn't want her reputation ruined by a disastrous event of this scale."

"That's a good idea, actually," Cooper said. "Everybody's getting hungry, but nobody wants to leave the premises without knowing the end of the story. They paid for a meal, so feed them. In the meantime, we'll see if we can get Quinn back here."

"I agree," Miles said.

"I'll go out to his house," Sylvia said.

Cooper shook his head. "You are the public face of this event. You stay here. We'll all stay here, but I'll make sure a squad car goes."

"Fair enough." Sylvia took a deep breath. "Miles, get the sound system going again. Turn the houselights down."

Sylvia gave Miles a head start and then climbed the steps to the stage and crossed to the podium.

"Ladies and gentlemen," she said, "thank you once again for being with us tonight. We apologize for the delay in your dinner, but at this time we are going to ask the servers to begin with your Caesar salads. Your entrées will follow shortly. We all look forward to doing what we came to do, and that is to honor Ted Quinn for his unparalleled service to Hidden Falls."

9:13 p.m.

Jack Parker smashed his dessert fork into the last crumbs of the cheesecake crust and transferred the result to his mouth. The servers had rushed the entrée on the heels of the salad, essentially serving them at the same time, but they had also done a good job of keeping the bread baskets full. Then dessert carts rolled between tables, and diners had their choice of cherry cheesecake, double chocolate cake, or apple pie. All in all, Jack thought it was a passable meal.

Too bad it was such a ruinous evening.

"Does anybody here think there's really going to be a program?" Jack glanced around the table. He hadn't met any of his tablemates before tonight other than Gianna, whose foot he ignored when it landed on his in exactly the manner he anticipated.

"Surely they've sorted it out by now," said the woman across the table.

Raisa Gallagher. The color of her face hadn't been the same since being caught in the collapse of the video booth. Jack had tucked her name away an hour ago when the group made nervous introductions. A homemaker with two small children, she was not likely to need his legal services unless her marriage crumbled. But he never knew, so Jack nodded cordially. Her mind was probably on whether the sitter had gotten the baby to sleep. Her husband, on the other hand, was an animated conversationalist who claimed to be an amateur inventor. Jack made a mental note to bone up on patent law. If she knew what he was thinking, Gianna would accuse him of being sexist. Jack preferred to think of his assessment as shrewd.

"I don't see any sign of Quinn," Jack said. "If everything's all right, wouldn't he be eating?"

Faces turned toward the head table, which Jack had watched all through the meal. Quinn had not turned up even for a moment. The mayor sat beside Quinn's empty seat, but she didn't eat. Members of the town council, all facing the main audience, leaned forward to talk to one another up and down the line, but their plates were removed with most of the food untouched. Jack had worked with plenty of jittery clients. In his observation, the guilty ones never lost their appetite even when their cases seemed doomed. The innocent who were scared — those were the clients who couldn't make themselves take more than token bites.

Jack gestured that he wanted more coffee, and a server with a pot appeared to top off cups around the table. For both the sake of his business and peace in his household, Jack had not objected to coming to this banquet. He had even filled the time between Quinn's disappearance and the start of the meal by introducing himself to people at nearby tables and making pleasant conversation, including nodding in concern at Quinn's peculiar absence. But Quinn had been gone for an hour and a half now. The evening was a fiasco, and the sooner the dignitaries admitted the truth, the better it would be for everyone.

The server with the coffeepot wandered to an adjacent table, and in his place another balanced a large tray in one hand while deftly reaching with the other between diners to remove dessert plates and empty bread baskets and pile everything on the tray. The waitstaff were all on the clock. The caterer wouldn't be eager to pay them extra because the program planners didn't keep to a schedule. The mayor couldn't stall much longer.

"I'm going to stretch my legs." Jack pushed his chair back.

"You just asked for coffee," Gianna said.

"I changed my mind."

"Jack —"

"It's all right, Gianna. I won't be gone long."

He sauntered toward the front of the room, putting to use everything he ever learned in trial settings about appearing confident and unflustered no matter how thin his case was. Jack had not represented a client before a judge in more than a year, but he could still taste the craving as if it sat on his teeth like tonight's cheesecake.

Jack watched the waitstaff and timed his steps toward the mayor to follow the young woman who was removing dishes from the head table.

"Good evening, Mayor."

Sylvia Alexander looked up. Jack assessed what her eyes revealed. It wasn't the first time he saw irritation there, but the dominant sentiment was anxiety.

"I hope you enjoyed your meal, Jack," she said.

"I can never decide whether to get the steak or the fish at these events," Jack said. "Did you get a chance to eat in the middle of everything?"

"The servers were very attentive." Sylvia folded her white napkin and laid it calmly on the table.

She didn't answer his query, though.

"If there's something I can do to help, I am at your disposal." Jack crossed his wrists in front of him.

"Can you excuse me, Jack?" Sylvia stood up.

Jack followed her gaze to the end of the head table, where the high school principal assumed an expectant posture.

"Of course." Jack stepped back from the table and casually turned toward the exit into the corridor that ran alongside the banquet hall. He paced through the exit, put his phone to his ear though there was no call, and nodded at several other dinner guests coming and going. When Jack slipped back into the dining room, pleasure flushed down his neck at the confirmation that he had hedged his bets accurately.

Sylvia Alexander huddled with Miles Devon and the young man Jack recognized from the sheriff's office. Elliott something. No. Elliott was his last name. Officer Elliott, with a first name that sounded like a last name. Jack clucked his tongue in frustration that the man's first name did not come to him.

"Cooper, what did you find out?" Mayor Alexander asked.

Cooper. That was it. Officer Cooper Elliott.

Jack inched closer, his silent phone still to his ear, and angled his face away from the trio.

"A squad car went to Quinn's house," Cooper said. "The place is locked up tight."

"It always is," Sylvia said. "And his car?"

"No sign of it. The squad car went up to the lake, too. If he took his car up there, he didn't park in any of the usual places."

"Where else would he go?" Miles Devon said.

"I called the station in Birch Bend and asked them to keep a look out," Cooper said.

"Cooper," Sylvia said. "Tell me straight. What do you think happened?"

Jack closed his eyes to concentrate on the voices. The pause seemed elongated to him.

"I'm not going to speculate," Cooper said. "In the unlikely event of foul play — and I stress *unlikely* — we don't need a bunch of rumors flying around town that people will trace back to us."

"I think it's safe to say the evening is over," Miles said. "If we can't produce Quinn, we don't have anything left to do here."

Jack heard Sylvia's sigh.

"Yes, of course," she said. "We have to handle things. But this is very unlike Quinn. Very."

"Do you want me to make an announcement?" Miles offered.

"I'll do it."

"Keep it calm, Mayor," Cooper said. "These circumstances are unusual for Hidden Falls, but the town may take your cue. And whatever you do, don't answer any questions."

Jack turned around in time to see Sylvia

nodding. He dropped his phone in his pocket and picked up his pace, arriving back at his table just as the mayor took the stage.

"It's over," he murmured in Gianna's ear as he took his seat.

She turned quickly toward him. "What do you mean? Is Quinn — ?"

"They can't find him. That's what it comes down to." He lifted one finger toward the stage. "The mayor's going to send everyone home. We're done here."

"How do you know this?"

"I'm a good lawyer. I know things."

Sylvia stepped to the microphone for the fifth time that evening. This time the spotlight stayed off and the houselights up.

"Ladies and gentlemen, I hope you enjoyed your meal. Let's show our appreciation for the fabulous team of people who prepared the dinner and served us. Haven't they done an outstanding job?"

Mayor Alexander put her hands together to start a round of applause, and the audience complied.

"See what she's doing?" Jack whispered. "Acting like everything's fine."

"Perhaps everything *is* fine." Gianna clapped.

"I think we waved good-bye to 'fine' at least an hour ago." Politely, Jack contributed to the applause.

The mayor continued. "What an amazing

sight it is to look out from the stage and see so many of you here tonight. I know Hidden Falls is as dear to your hearts as it is to mine. Whether you came from across the county or across the country, you're here because of a remarkable citizen whose contribution to all of us calls you home."

She was smooth. Jack gave her that. This was probably the speech she had prepared, but she would have to go off script soon.

Sylvia paused for a breath.

"Here it comes," Jack muttered.

"Unfortunately," Sylvia said, "at this point we will bring our evening to a close. Drive carefully as you make your way to your homes or hotels."

Sylvia stepped away from the microphone.

The air went out of Gianna, and she put her hand on Jack's knee. "Is that really all she's going to tell us?"

"What else do you want her to say?" Jack said.

Sylvia walked across the stage and started down the steps at the side.

"Where's Quinn?" a voice demanded.

"That's the $64,000 question," Jack whispered.

Sylvia waved her hand and called out, "Thank you again for coming."

Jack stood up and picked up his wife's wrap from the back of her chair. As he dropped it around her shoulders, he kissed her cheek. "I knew there would be something interesting in this town if we dug deep enough."

9:29 p.m.

Dani folded her arms across her chest, resisting the tendency for them to slide across the unfamiliar satin. Frankly, the mayor's announcement didn't entirely surprise Dani. Yes, Quinn was the sort to persevere and finish what he started or to follow through on what he promised, but everybody had a breaking point. People had to stop thinking Quinn was next to God. Who could take that kind of pressure? Sylvia didn't say why Quinn didn't show up, so either she had no idea or thought it was nobody's business. Either explanation satisfied Dani.

Although Dani didn't expect to marry and was 108 percent sure she would make a terrible mother, she thought Sylvia should have married Quinn years ago. Everybody thought so — not that the topic was anybody's business, either. But if they had, their kids should have been bursting with pride at an event like this one.

Except for the part about their father disappearing. They might have found that slightly embarrassing. Or mortifying.

Dani had spent an awkward evening in an awkward dress lurking on the edges of awkward conversation. With enough people in her day to last her a week, she was exhausted.

And for what? If she had left for the lake ten minutes sooner or fifteen minutes later that afternoon, she wouldn't have seen Quinn and she wouldn't be wishing she had a dress that covered her knees. Or instead of letting Quinn talk her into coming, they might have made another choice together. Dani replayed the encounter in her mind with alternate endings.

She didn't take Quinn home. She took him to the lake, and they decided to do some night fishing.

Instead of dropping him off, she went in the house with him to look at his old laptop that might as well have been held together with chewing gum.

Quinn got in her Jeep, and Dani aimed it for the far side of Birch Bend, where the bridge spanned the river. Quinn liked to park at one end and walk along a narrow sidewalk to the crown of the bridge. There he would stop and stare into the distance. Always east, never west. And he didn't like to talk while he stared.

But they hadn't done any of those things. Quinn asked Dani to come to the banquet and she came. And then he left, confirming Dani's opinion that he hadn't wanted to be there in the first place.

Every clink of fork against china, each slosh of liquid poured from pitcher to goblet, the mindless inquiries from strangers about

"How do you know Quinn?" Dani's head was ready to burst from the pointlessness of it all. No one all evening had said a sentence to her that mattered, but she sat politely through every tortuous phase of the deteriorating event.

Dani pushed her arms into the sleeves of a brown sweater with a blue stripe, which she knew didn't match her gray satin dress. "I should have gone fishing like I wanted to do. I can still get to the lake tonight. So goodbye, everyone."

When Dani stood up, Liam looked up at her from his seat. "You're going to leave, just like that?"

"Yes, just like that. Putting on my sweater. Getting out my keys. That's the general pattern for leaving."

"I'm surprised you're not more worried about Quinn."

"That's because you don't know Quinn as well as I do." Dani plunged one hand into the bottom of the tattered leather bag that passed as a purse when she absolutely had to carry one and felt around for her keys. "Quinn changed his mind, and everyone should leave him alone."

Jessica spoke up. "I agree with Dani."

Dani's eyelids flicked up and she looked at Jessica directly for the first time in at least an hour. If she and Jessica found something to agree on, the universe must have rent in two.

Dani could almost hear the rip vibrating against her eardrums.

Jessica lifted the long strap of her own dainty gold bag from the back of her chair and slung it casually off one shoulder. "We should go, too, Liam."

Liam made no move to leave. "How can you two just go home like everything's fine?"

"I'm not going home. I'm going fishing," Dani said. "And everything *is* fine. The more everyone sits around dreaming up gloomy scenarios — well, what's the point?"

"Quinn is gone. That's the point."

Jessica stood up now, and still Liam didn't move. Dani was beginning to think she was going to have to dump the random contents of her handbag to find her keys.

"Are you all right, cuz?" Dani's pinkie finally grazed her key ring, and she hooked it through to bring the keys to the surface.

"I'm concerned about Quinn," Liam said. "You should be, too."

Jessica tapped Liam's shoulder. "Dani already told you what she thinks. Quinn changed his mind. Come on. Let's go. The night is young."

Liam finally pushed his chair back and stood up in slow motion. Dani saw the sweat beading at his hairline, evidence of the great effort it took to compose his face.

The "innocent look," Dani used to call it. When they were kids and somebody's mother came looking for the pack of cousins to ferret out who had split open the bag of flour at the back of the pantry or let the puppy loose in the flower beds, a chorus of "Not me!" inevitably rang up. Liam made the same claim as the rest of them, but his face took on the carved stone expression it bore now. He looked like he was about to be found out for doing something naughty and pushing the blame to another suspect.

Maybe it was Liam's guilty expressions that made Cooper decide to become a cop.

Cooper returned to the table now. "So that's it, folks," he said. "We can be on our way."

"What did you find out?" Liam asked.

Cooper had a stone face of his own. Liam tried too hard to appear innocent. Cooper never gave anything away.

"They'll find Quinn, or he'll come home on his own," Cooper said. "Everybody should just relax and go about their usual business."

Dani looked at the trickle of people drifting toward the doors. Like Liam, most of the crowd seemed hesitant to abandon their tables. "People aren't in a hurry to leave."

"If they think they're going to learn something by hanging around," Cooper said, "they'll be sorely disappointed. The cleanup crew will start any minute, and I promise you that will be the most exciting thing happening here."

"See, Liam? Your own brother says there's nothing to wait around for." Jessica laid a hand on Liam's chest. "What's this lump?"

When she started to open his jacket, Liam grasped her hand and kissed her knuckles. "Something from a client."

"You were working tonight?" she said.

"Just a chance encounter."

Dani wasn't going to get involved. Whatever was going on between Liam and Jessica was none of her business, but she wished they'd get their act together.

She would have to swing by her house in town and divest herself of the dress, but she could still drive out to the lake, sleep under the stars outside the cabin, and be ready to fish before dawn. Two days on the lake, or maybe three, and this would all blow over. She had not the least curiosity about the details. Dani wouldn't be surprised to find Quinn on the shores of Whisper Lake, too. If she did, she wouldn't interrogate him. His choice was his business, and Dani was the last person interested in demanding an explanation.

"The best thing any of you can do for Quinn," Cooper said, "is depart in a normal manner. Set an example by not freaking out."

Dani gripped her keys in her fist. "You don't have to ask me twice."

10:17 p.m.

"I'm going to change my shoes." Lauren reached under her chair for her bag.

After more than half an hour since the mayor's announcement, the hall was finally showing signs of emptying. Women gathered their wraps and bags. Men jangled keys.

"You carry spare shoes to a banquet?" Nicole bunched her features.

Lauren shrugged. "I always keep comfortable shoes handy. I don't drive, so I have to be ready to walk."

"You don't have to walk. I'll take you home."

Lauren shook her head. "I don't want to leave yet. I'm going to help clean up. Or something."

Or something. Anything to stay around and feed her hope that this evening might yet have a happy ending. Flat black shoes with thick, grooved soles sat side by side in the base of her bag. Lauren pulled them out, exchanged them with the three-inch strapped heels, and examined the resulting effect.

"Not much of a fashion statement," she said, "but efficient."

Lauren stowed her bag on an out-of-the-way ledge before snagging a rolling cart with plenty of space to load dishes.

"I'm sure the caterer has people lined up to do that," Nicole said. "They've already started with the tables in the back."

"You miss the point." Lauren transferred four coffee cups, six goblets, and three dessert plates to the cart. Then she bundled a white tablecloth and tossed it against the wall.

"You seem to know what you're doing." Nicole added two empty water pitchers to the cart.

"I used to work events like this in college."

"You're just waiting to talk to your aunt without the crowd around."

"Ah, your reporter's nose is in good working condition." Lauren glanced around. "Where did Ethan disappear to?"

"*Disappear* might not be the best choice of words under the circumstances." Nicole circled a table, picking up cloth napkins. "And the answer to your question is, I don't know."

"Are you guys going to figure out what this stuff is between you?"

"What do you mean?" Nicole tugged a tablecloth and tossed it into the laundry pile Lauren had begun.

"You invited him to sit at our table."

"We had an empty seat."

"I saw the way he was looking at you."

"I don't know what you're talking about."

"Yes you do." Lauren pushed the cart toward another table. "You should find him before he leaves."

"Maybe he already has."

Lauren didn't think so. Ethan ate his dinner, but he spent much of the evening watching Sylvia's movements. He was as puzzled and concerned as Lauren was. As Nicole was. As Sylvia was. As Miles was.

Cooper Elliott was oddly calm about the whole business. Was that his professional demeanor, or did he genuinely think the evening's surprise meant nothing?

"He could have left, you know," Lauren said.

"Ethan doesn't owe me any explanation for his departure," Nicole said.

"Quinn, I mean," Lauren said. "I know he's incredibly reliable, but it was no secret that he tried to avoid the attention of this banquet. When they first asked him, he said no. Three times."

"I didn't know that." Nicole grabbed two goblets in each hand. "But eventually he said yes. Isn't that what matters?"

"Even so, his hesitancy might mean something."

Sylvia still wore her heels, and Lauren recognized the sound of her aunt's determined steps as she crossed the stage one last time and picked up her notes from the podium.

"Did that sheriff's deputy leave?" Lauren paused with another tablecloth gathered against her chest.

"Cooper? Yes. A while ago." Sylvia folded her papers in half and pressed the crease.

"So he doesn't think there's . . . I don't know, evidence or anything?"

"He had a look around backstage." Sylvia descended the steps and approached Lauren and Nicole. "But there was no sign of disturbance other than that silly air cannon going off during my introduction. Everything was just the way it looked when I put Quinn's mark on the floor myself."

Lauren sat down. "So you think he left? Or should we be worried?"

Sylvia blew out her breath. "I have no idea. Cooper says they aren't calling it foul play because they have seen nothing to suggest Quinn didn't leave of his own accord."

"Other than being contrary to his character." Nicole moved glasses around on the cart to make room for three more.

"And he didn't go home." Sylvia dug her fingertips into her closed eyelids. "I have a splitting headache."

"You should go home and go to bed." The weight of her aunt's dismay shot pain through Lauren as well. "You don't need to stay, do you?"

"There's nothing left for me to do," Sylvia said. "The caterer's crew will finish up."

"That's what I said." Nicole flashed Lauren a look.

"I saw Ethan in the foyer a few minutes ago," Sylvia said to Nicole. "Maybe he's waiting for you."

"I don't know why he would be," Nicole said.

"Don't you?" Lauren taunted.

"Quinn was so glad the two of you came," Sylvia said. "I'm sorry he didn't get to see you sitting together."

The moment thickened. Lauren had a hard time breathing. Ethan and Nicole had known Quinn far better than Lauren had when they were teenagers — and they'd had each other. Jealousy washed through her.

Nicole rolled her eyes. "Fine. Just to suit the two of you, I will go say good night to Ethan." She took her purse and crossed the banquet room.

Lauren saw the slope of Sylvia's shoulders fall as, silent, the two of them watched Nicole's swift progress. Was it possible for a person to look a year older in just one evening?

"Go home, Aunt Sylvia." Lauren reached out and squeezed her aunt's hand. "Try to get some sleep."

"I'll take you home first," Sylvia said.

"No. I think I want to walk."

"It's late for walking, Lauren. Past ten thirty."

"I already changed my shoes." Lauren held up one foot. "I'll get the pepper spray out of my bag and make sure it's in my hand. Promise."

"Okay. But don't stay much longer. Let the

caterer do her job. She gets nervous about people who aren't on the payroll handling her dishes."

Lauren watched her aunt stop to thank the caterer and smile at the waitstaff. Sylvia could hold herself together in a crisis, but Lauren was sorry she had to showcase that particular character trait tonight.

Sylvia and Quinn. Quinn and Sylvia. People in Hidden Falls could hardly say one name without the other.

Lauren's turn to put on a good face would come tomorrow morning at Our Savior Community Church. Quinn didn't even like recognition for everything he did for the congregation — like organizing next week's health fair. News would spread overnight to anyone who wasn't present for the banquet. And if Quinn didn't appear in the morning to make the health fair announcement at church, Lauren would have to bluff her way through it. No one would be listening to the pastor's sermon that followed. Quinn's absence would have people whispering and wondering.

Walking briskly would burn through the energy amassing in Lauren's muscles for the last two and a half hours. No matter what the time, she knew she wasn't going to sleep anytime soon if she didn't discharge the concern creeping through her body. The humor she had first seen in the empty spotlight had dissipated hours ago. Anticipation for the antics Quinn might have planned morphed into apprehension. Even if he was physically safe, what must be his mental state to make him do the unthinkable?

Lauren didn't require words to pray. She needed movement. She would move hard and pray hard all the way home.

Tossing the tablecloth in her lap onto the heap against the wall, Lauren stood and paced to the ledge where she had left her bag. She looped it across her shoulders and took out the pepper spray, something she carried so she could honestly tell her anxious mother that she did. The waitstaff had dispatched their cleanup tasks with efficiency and now rolled one cart after another into the kitchen on the far side of the hall. Through the open door, Lauren heard water running and dishes rattling. She lifted a hand to wave at Zeke and wondered if she would see him in church the next morning.

Lauren didn't expect to find Nicole and Ethan still in the foyer. The lights, perhaps on a timer, had dimmed. With her hands behind her back, Nicole leaned on the push bar of one door, as if any second she planned to put her weight into the motion and make her exit.

"You're still here," Lauren said.

A look passed between Nicole and Ethan. Lauren stifled a smile. Something good might yet come out of this evening.

"We got to talking," Nicole said.

"Don't let me interrupt," Lauren said. One day Nicole and Ethan could joke with Quinn that if he hadn't made his secret escape they wouldn't have gotten together.

That is, if Quinn had made a secret escape, and if, given enough time, anyone could find the humor in it.

"I'd better get going." Lauren adjusted the strap that crossed her chest.

"Are you sure you should walk?" Nicole said.

"Positive." Lauren had never been one for praying on her knees. "I live on Main Street, above the barbershop. It's not that far."

"I guess it's all relative to how much you're used to walking," Ethan said.

Lauren could do it in thirty minutes, especially if she took a shortcut or two, but tonight she was more likely to lengthen the walk than concern herself with efficiency.

"Church tomorrow is at nine thirty," Lauren said, "in case you're interested."

Ethan smiled politely. "No thanks."

"Maybe." Nicole pushed on the bar behind her at last.

The trio stepped into the night, where the security light on the pole above threw radiance around them while its glare deepened the blackness beyond.

"Well, good night. It was nice to see you

both." Lauren maneuvered past Nicole and Ethan, since neither of them seemed inclined to move beyond the sidewalk.

11:14 p.m.

"How did we end up being the last ones here?" Glad for its warmth, Nicole pulled out her coat, draped it around her shoulders, and let the car door close softly behind her. She should have been on her way home — or in the old house getting ready for bed — by now. Instead, she leaned against her vehicle and raised her eyes to meet Ethan Jordan's.

Ten years.

Nicole had not seen Ethan or Quinn in that time, and in one evening her heart ached for them both. She couldn't see through Ethan's eyes the way she used to. He protected whatever was inside him now. And Quinn. A gasp slid past Nicole's lips.

"What is it?" Ethan said.

"I don't know what I was thinking," she said. "I always meant to come back to Hidden Falls for a real visit. Scooting in and out of town for Christmas with my dad or a Father's Day lunch doesn't count."

"You're way ahead of me." Ethan leaned against her car beside her.

Nicole inhaled deeply and pushed the air back out. She always told herself she would pop over and see Quinn the next time. And then her dad moved and there hadn't been a next time in the last four years.

Nicole looked away from Ethan. It seemed like another lifetime, those years of living next door to Ethan and the two of them slipping through the fence to traipse across Quinn's expansive backyard, leap the three steps to his patio, and knock on his back door. She thought of the time her editor asked where she would go if she could go back in time for a day. Nicole would choose one of those days, one of those exquisite moments perfectly cradling the weariness of two lonely children and calling to the wholeness deep within them.

"I don't even want to imagine the mess I would have grown up to be if I hadn't known Quinn," Nicole said softly. "I wish I had been more grateful."

"Don't use the past tense," Ethan said. "You heard what Cooper and Sylvia said. No sign of foul play."

"Then what happened?" Nicole slipped her arms into her coat sleeves.

"I don't know." Ethan's hands went into his pockets.

"It's hard for Quinn to be the center of attention, but I thought he looked genuinely happy to see people tonight."

Ethan nodded. "I'm certain he intended to go through with the evening."

"I heard him say he wanted to talk to you later."

"Eavesdropping?"

"Occupational hazard."

Ethan put a hand inside his suit jacket and pulled out an envelope. "It's too dark here for you to read this, but it's from Quinn. I think he knew I would conveniently lose the dinner invitation, so he made sure I knew he wanted to see me."

Nicole inspected the handwriting on the outside of the envelope. Even in the shadows where they stood, she could see that the slope and shape of the lettering were Quinn's. Envy pinged her chest, knowing that Ethan held something that had been in Quinn's hands so recently — and that he had received a personal plea to attend.

"He has something to tell me." Ethan took the envelope from her hand. "I don't have a clue what it is, but he was insistent that I come to the banquet."

Nicole buttoned her coat. "We know him better than just about anybody. And I think we know that Quinn wouldn't ditch an event like this."

Ethan shrugged. "We were kids. I don't fool myself into thinking I know everything about him. We don't know why he never drives beyond the county line, for instance."

"No one cares about that," Nicole said. "It's just Quinn."

"To kids, it's just the way things were. Now I wonder what it means."

"It doesn't have to mean anything more than he has a happy life in Hidden Falls," Nicole said. "We experienced his true character. He's warm, compassionate, solid, generous."

"People change."

Yes, they do, Nicole thought. Ethan had changed, after all. So much about him was familiar, recognizable. A habit rutted deep in her muscles made Nicole want to reach for his hand. Yet she stood beside a man she barely knew. She plunged her hands into her coat pockets.

Aloud she said, "You can't just turn off core traits."

Ethan didn't respond.

Nicole spoke. "You can't think Quinn would turn into a different kind of person — unless you think it's something in his brain."

"That's always possible."

"You're just saying that because you're a neurologist."

"Some illnesses will make people behave in uncharacteristic ways. It can be the first sign something is wrong."

"No. Quinn was fine. He *is* fine."

"I hope that's the case," Ethan said. "But the urgent note, his disappearance. If these things are out of character, then the question is why."

A chill shuddered through Nicole. "We have to find him, Ethan."

"If he left of his own free will and in his right mind, he may not want to be found."

"But if he's ill," Nicole said, "or if there's even the possibility that he's ill, it would be just like him not to tell anyone."

He gestured toward the sky. "The night is practically moonless. We could look all night and drive right past him in the dark."

Ethan was right.

"Well," Nicole said, "it can't be that hard for the sheriff's department to cover the county."

"The Quinn we grew up with didn't leave the county," Ethan said. "That's what we know. We don't know what he does now."

Nicole huffed. "You're nothing if not stubborn."

"I'm a scientist," he said. "Going beyond Birch Bend could be one more uncharacteristic behavior."

"So you do think he's ill." Nicole's stomach clenched.

Ethan shook his head. "I didn't say that."

"Ethan," Nicole said, "if something happened to Quinn or if he's ill . . ."

"One thing at a time. That's what I tell my patients. Let's not assume the worst."

Against her better judgment, Nicole linked an arm through Ethan's. "You were always the rock in our relationship. I could always depend on you."

Ethan was silent, but he covered her hand

with his.

"Until you couldn't," he finally whispered. "Somehow the hole inside me started to matter more than hanging on to you."

Nicole's throat thickened.

"Did you fall in love again?" Ethan asked.

"No." The answer came quickly. Nicole had tried. The bearded detective who fed her just enough leads to keep her working on a story without compromising his case. The rugged landscaper who worked on the grounds around her condo building. The restaurateur the Internet dating service had declared a perfect match.

None of them was Ethan.

"How about you?" Nicole asked.

"I didn't think you would wait for me," he said.

"What?"

"Med school. A long residency. The stress is enough to kill a relationship."

Trembling, Nicole withdrew her hand. He had found someone.

"When I started researching med schools," Ethan said, "I heard all sorts of horror stories about the toll it takes. I didn't want to take the chance of ruining the way we were."

Nicole absorbed his words. "You didn't trust me to be tough enough for our relationship to survive med school? Didn't you know I loved you?" *That maybe I still do?*

"I didn't trust myself. I'm capable of immense unhappiness, Nicole. I have chronic, huge dissatisfaction with my own efforts. I always have to do more."

"That sounds incredibly self-aware." And it was no surprise to Nicole.

"Seeing the problem and fixing it are two different things. I couldn't ask you to wait years and years for me to finish my training only to discover I wasn't good husband material anyway."

"It seems like that should have been up to me to sort out."

"Maybe. I was too young and dumb to see that."

"All these years, Ethan." Nicole blinked back tears. "All these years of wondering how I disappointed you. It took me a long time to get past blaming myself, even though I didn't know what I'd done."

"Nothing. You were perfect." His voice hushed. "You deserved a perfect life, not some poor jerk who doesn't even understand why he can't get along with his parents."

"But I didn't deserve an explanation?" Nicole's voice cracked.

"Yes," he said. "And no, I didn't fall in love again."

Nicole swallowed hard.

"My biggest regret is leaving you," he said, "and second is not talking to you about why."

"Now you can cross the second regret off your list." Nicole pulled the coat collar up against her face. "I would have tried to talk you out of it."

"I know."

It was too late now. Their lives had parted ways. They lived four states apart. And though she had never fallen in love again, Nicole had stopped waking up every day with her first thought wondering how Ethan was, or where Ethan was, or jumping when her phone rang because it might be Ethan. She had a job, friends, a life.

And maybe he was right. Maybe life together after the focus of college, beyond the safe haven of Hidden Falls, would have been more than they were prepared to face.

Now they would never know.

"I should get to my motel." His realism disturbed the spell that wrapped them in the moment.

"You're really not staying with your parents?" Nicole wasn't sure whether she was relieved or disappointed that Ethan wouldn't be sleeping — or lying awake — under the roof next door to hers.

He shook his head. "I just came for Quinn. If I see them, it will only complicate things. I have to head back in the morning anyway."

"Without knowing what happened to Quinn? How can you leave?"

"Two reasons: Brinkman and Gonzalez, both of whom would be glad to have my head if I don't get back."

Nicole didn't know Brinkman and Gonzalez, but how could they compare to Quinn?

"This is an emergency," she said. "Highly unusual circumstances. Can't you explain?"

He held her gaze until she was uncomfortable and broke away.

"I'm staying at the old house." She turned around and gripped the driver-side door handle.

"Nicole," he said softly. "I have to go."

Then or now? she wondered. Or was it all the same thing?

"It was good to see you." She opened the car door.

He reached out and grazed her cheek with two fingers.

Nicole kissed his knuckles. "Good-bye, Ethan."

Behind the steering wheel, she pulled forward through the empty parking spot in front of her car and didn't look back. She had a new final image in her mind: Ethan alone in the shadows in his dark suit looking as handsome as he ever had when he took her heart captive. At the parking lot exit, she took a moment to get her bearings and choose her route. She decided to go back through town rather than take the country road circumventing the collection of buildings that formed downtown. In a starlit canopy Nicole didn't often see above the lights St. Louis spread across the sky, the moon's absence left the night black. The roads were no longer familiar at every turn, and in the dark Nicole maintained a modest speed.

Coming around a bend, Nicole hit the brakes and skidded to the side of the road. Adrenaline stole her breath as she put the car in Park and opened her door to confirm her vision. A sedan lay on its roof, tires sprawled toward the branches of the tree the car had collided with.

A green sedan. An Oldsmobile Delta Eighty-Eight.

Quinn's car. Nicole snapped off her seatbelt and lurched toward the wreck. The passenger-side door hung open at an awkward angle, ripped from one hinge. Nicole scrambled around the car, peering into every window and seeing no sign of occupancy.

The trunk.

She banged on metal. "Quinn? Are you in there?" Why he would be in the trunk was a trail of thought she banished from the urgent moment.

Nicole stepped back to assess the balance of the overturned car. She had been in the vehicle dozens of times — maybe hundreds — and knew where the trunk release was. Ducking in through the open passenger side, she clamored across the ceiling that had become the floor and pulled the lever. Immediately she backed out again. The trunk hung open now, and Nicole squatted to peer inside.

The cracking branches behind her made her jump. Nicole spun around to face Lauren Nock.

3
A Town in Trouble

Sunday
9:23 a.m.

Lauren Nock pulled her apartment door closed behind her and made sure it locked. She was cutting it close. *Seven minutes to be on time.* She urged her sleep-deprived body to go faster than it preferred as she bounded down the flight of stairs to the street and set a lively pace down two blocks and around the corner to the church. By her own routine, she was at least an hour late. Lauren liked arriving early at Our Savior Community Church on Sundays, in time to listen to the musicians warming up and get a hint of what the morning's music would bring. In her office, she liked extra time to gather the handouts and sign-up sheets she intended to distribute to children, youth, and parents that day, giving people plenty of opportunities to participate, both to offer ministry and to receive it. And someone always popped in for a quick chat before the service.

Not today.

With only three minutes to spare now, she entered the church. The pre-service music was under way, and worshippers were curtailing their conversations over coffee in the foyer and drifting into the sanctuary.

"Good morning, Mrs. Berrill." Lauren's long habit had been to disregard the dour expression etched on Mrs. Berrill's face and greet her with cheer, no matter what. Ever since she retired and closed her hair salon, Mrs. Berrill seemed to require personal attention from every member of the church staff each Sunday or she mumbled to others in the congregation about how church leaders were too busy for her. Today Lauren dreaded mustering interest in which part of Mrs. Berrill's body hurt now. She suspected the root cause of the pain was in the woman's spirit, anyway. Thankfully, with the prelude beginning, even Mrs. Berrill wouldn't choose this time to start on her litany of ailments.

Lauren slipped into a random pew. This was the sort of day she wished she had a regular spot to sit and know what to expect from the others around her. Her intentional custom, though, was to choose a different part of the sanctuary each week so her greeting and chatting were not confined to the same predictable list of people every Sunday. How could she serve as director of family ministry if she didn't intersect with every family in the church?

On this morning, it didn't matter where she sat. She wasn't in any condition for socializing and doubted she would remember a thing anyone said to her.

She stood with the congregation for the opening songs, one hymn and one contemporary song to placate preferences for both styles of music. Even though her lips moved with the familiar words, Lauren's mind spun with the events of last night and the consequent lack of sleep.

Lauren spent enough of the night sitting across from Cooper Elliott to watch his face begin to advertise its need for a morning shave. He wasn't on duty, but someone — Lauren wasn't sure who — decided to wake him and bring him in to do the questioning because he had been present at the banquet when Quinn disappeared.

It was the sheriff's staff who asked Lauren to sit in a room by herself while Cooper further interviewed Nicole and then sent Nicole away during Lauren's interview. Lauren resented the implication of wrongdoing. To officers on the scene, Nicole reported finding Lauren standing near the accident, but not with rancor or suspicion. They had bonded in their worry about Quinn's welfare. Nicole didn't suggest Lauren had anything to do with the accident.

Cooper kept saying they needed to piece together separate testimonies and not have two witnesses confusing each other and potentially blocking independent memory of significant details. By two in the morning, the circular nature of Cooper's questions irritated Lauren. Cooper was making careful notes, but he didn't seem to grasp that Lauren didn't see the car's collision with the tree, and she didn't see Quinn get out of the car. She had no idea how long before her arrival the crash happened. She wasn't hiding information. No matter what angle Cooper's questions came from, the answers didn't change. Lauren knew *nothing.*

Around three in the morning, Lauren overheard confirmation that Quinn's house still showed no sign of his presence.

Now, Lauren spoke the words of a printed congregational prayer without taking in their substance. She sat when the congregation sat, hard-pressed to recall even a snatch of a phrase that might suggest the day's theme.

Next would come the announcements — and the moment Lauren dreaded. Quinn was supposed to briefly present the health fair and would have had something clever to say. His congenial manner alone would have stirred interest. Lauren hadn't stopped in her office for the sign-up sheets and hadn't even remembered to bring the clipboard she carried around town yesterday for some basic information.

Only yesterday.

It seemed such a long time ago that she ran into Quinn outside her apartment and heard his reassurance that all was in hand.

Today all was most definitely *not* in hand.

Lauren caught sight of Nicole sitting three rows forward on the other side of the center aisle. When her turn came during the night, Nicole had to remember everything she touched inside the overturned car, any place where investigators might discover her fingerprints. She had been at the station just as late as Lauren, and given Nicole's "maybe" answer to Lauren's invitation to attend church, Lauren hadn't expected to see Nicole in the service.

Someone nudged Lauren's shoulder and she stirred.

"The pastor is calling for you," Raisa Gallagher said behind Lauren. "Are you supposed to make an announcement?"

No, I'm not, Lauren wanted to say. *Quinn is going to do that.*

She stood up, arranged a smile on her face, and walked to the front of the sanctuary, where the pastor moved aside to give Lauren room to speak into the microphone.

Lauren saw in her mind the microphone and podium from the banquet hall. She saw her aunt's drawn face at the end of the evening when she retrieved a speech that for the most part had gone unspoken. She saw the forlorn stage.

Lauren closed her eyes for two seconds to push the image away and instead visualize the clipboard she ought to have had in front of her. She cleared her throat, chiding herself for not at least bringing a bulletin up with her.

"Good morning. You'll see in your bulletin that Saturday is the health fair we've been organizing for the last couple of months. I know that many of you are involved."

Lauren hadn't seen the final list of volunteers, but it seemed reasonable to give the congregation the benefit of the doubt. Quinn couldn't do everything himself, after all.

"This is an exciting outreach to our community and a chance for all of us to explore better health in body and spirit." Lauren could say this much with confidence because it had been her main argument for introducing the idea for a health fair in the first place. "If you haven't signed up to help, I'm sure we still have room for you. And no matter what, we hope you will come and enjoy the booths and demonstrations. It'll be a great chance to meet members of the community as well as learn something new about your own health."

This seemed like a good place to mention specific attractions, if she could just remember some of them. "We'll have . . . um, cooking demonstrations . . . um, immunizations and games for the children . . ." What else was there? "You won't want to miss the joke contest, because laughter is good medicine."

Chuckles broke out around the sanctuary.

"The list is too long to mention everything now. If you have questions during the week, you can call or e-mail me here at the church."

That was the best she could do. Lauren might not have answers for any questions, but she couldn't discourage people from asking. Quinn meant no harm yesterday by saying he had everything under control, but Lauren wished she had pushed harder, and sooner, for detailed information. The meeting they scheduled for Monday after school looked dubious.

Lauren needed Quinn to turn up soon. But after seeing the state of his car, she had to wonder what condition he was in for following through on the fair.

10:02 a.m.

Sylvia's eyes trailed Lauren's sluggish movement back to her pew. Next to Sylvia, her mother leaned against her shoulder and whispered, "Lauren looks tired."

Emma was right. Lauren usually had a crisp, perky appearance and demeanor. Today it seemed not to bother Lauren that her glasses slid down her nose, and she had done nothing more with her hair than pull it into a midweek afternoon ponytail. Even the dress she wore was faded. Sylvia was surprised her niece still had that old thing, much less that she would wear it on a Sunday morning. On the surface, her announcement about the health fair was fine. Not overly informative, but fine.

A trio of teenagers made their way to the front to sing for the offertory. Sylvia glanced at Lauren again, expecting she would look pleased. For months now she had lobbied for including a wider range of people in the music program as part of a ministry to families. But it looked to Sylvia as if Lauren barely registered that anyone was singing.

Just yesterday Sylvia assured Lauren that if Quinn was working on the health fair, she had nothing to worry about.

Everybody in town, whether or not they attended the banquet, would remember the night the mayor lost the favorite teacher. The evening was nothing it was supposed to be. Sylvia had tossed and turned through the lengthening hours of the night and supposed she didn't look much better than Lauren did.

Her mother phoned Sylvia at seven in the morning as she had for several years. Emma was awake to see the sun sneak out of its nocturnal cocoon most days and could tell anyone in town what the weather had been at dawn. If anything, aging had reinforced this habit, which now gave Sylvia peace of mind.

The jangle of her bedside phone at seven each new day meant her mother was fine. She was up eating Nutella on toast and reading the psalms she had loved all her life.

"It's warm in here," Emma whispered as she passed the offering plate to her daughter.

Warm or cold. In her mid-eighties, Emma seemed to have two temperatures these days, and neither one of them was particularly comfortable. Sylvia handed the offering plate to the waiting usher. The warbling teenagers arrived at their big finish and held the last note like professional choristers. A slight smile crossed Lauren's face, and Sylvia allowed herself a moment of relief.

Pastor Matt stood behind the pulpit and asked the congregation to pray with him.

"Why don't they adjust the thermostat?" Emma fanned herself with her bulletin.

"I'm sure it will feel cooler soon." Sylvia hoped her whisper would remind Emma to lower her voice.

The pastor began to read the New Testament passage he planned to preach on.

Emma shirked off her sweater. Sylvia ignored the rustling and focused on the voice coming through the sound system. Around them, most of the congregation settled in. Feet shuffled in search of a comfortable position, and Bible pages turned. A few rows behind Sylvia, a toddler whimpered.

"I have to go out for some air," Emma

whispered.

"Give it some time," Sylvia said.

"What?"

"Just wait a few minutes."

"I can't hear you." Emma picked up her purse. "I'll take a walk."

Emma stepped past Sylvia's knees and padded up the aisle. Sylvia pressed her lips together and made a rapid decision to follow her mother. Lately the confusion was unpredictable. Since the death of Sylvia's father seven years ago, Emma lived alone and managed fairly well — but when Sylvia visited several times a week, she noticed more and more items out of place. Her mother seemed to pour a lot of coffee she never drank and strewed shoes around the house after a lifelong rule of shoes belonging in closets.

Sylvia reached the foyer right behind her mother. "We can sit out here."

"I just needed some air. You didn't have to come."

"I wanted to stay with you." Sylvia pointed to a loudspeaker. "We can still hear the sermon out here."

"He's preaching on trust again." Emma sat in one of a pair of identical stuffed armless chairs with a round table between them.

"It's a series," Sylvia said. "Two more weeks, I think."

"Well, I trust he will bring it to a trustworthy end."

Sylvia tilted her head toward Emma as she took the other chair. "I don't think that's the lesson he wants us to learn."

"Let an old lady have her fun." Emma crossed her ankles.

"Would the old lady like a glass of water?"

"Don't call me old. No, thank you. I don't need water. I'm cooler already just being out here."

"Good."

"This business about Quinn is certainly mysterious," Emma said.

"Yes, it is."

Even though Sylvia purposely didn't discuss last night with her mother, there was no telling what Emma had heard. Any number of people might have phoned Emma with speculative information along with the sparse facts.

"It's not the first time somebody from this town has disappeared under mysterious circumstances," Emma said.

Sylvia angled her head to consider her mother, whose own face was poised on the precipice of recollection.

"It's a good story," Emma said.

"You'll have to tell it to me sometime." Sylvia glanced up at the loudspeaker in the ceiling and tried to tune in to Pastor Matt's voice.

"Now, I'm not sure I'll get all the details right." Emma tapped her fingers against the purse in her lap.

"There's no hurry. You can think about it

and tell me another time. Do you feel cool enough to go back in?"

"Let's see," Emma said, "actually there were two families."

"Mom," Sylvia said, "have you cooled off?"

Emma waved a hand. "Oh, trust God and pray. You know how the sermon is going to end."

Was it so much to ask that Sylvia have a chance to sit still and quiet in a place that represented God's presence to her?

"The two families didn't have much in common, as I recall." Emma pushed her lips to one side in thought. "Your grandmother used to tell the story. Actually, she didn't tell it so much as she talked about it as if she knew something."

Sylvia was trapped. If she walked away now, her mother would have every reason to take offense.

"And of course I haven't heard the story in decades," Emma said. "Not since I was a young woman. A girl, really."

"Mom, let's go back in to church."

"Just give me a minute. It will come."

An usher came out of the sanctuary. Sylvia recognized the Sunday morning attendance sheet he carried between thumb and forefinger.

"Hello, Henry." Sylvia hoped the interruption would distract her mother.

"I sure wasn't expecting to fill in for Quinn

on usher duty," Henry said. "I figured this was one weekend he'd be in church for sure."

"Yes, well, we're all a bit surprised."

"What a night it was for Lauren," Henry said.

"For Lauren?" Why should Henry Healy pick out Lauren, when Sylvia was the one the town would hold responsible for Quinn?

"I'm surprised she even came to church after being at the sheriff's office until the middle of the night."

Sylvia sat up straight.

"Oh, hadn't you heard?" When Henry raised his eyebrows, his whole face lifted. "I assumed someone would have called you."

"Perhaps you'd better start at the beginning." Sylvia pushed her internal professional button for outward calm.

"I'm trying," Emma said, "but I can't quite remember how the story begins."

Sylvia put a hand on her mother's knee. "I'm sorry, Mom. I meant Henry. I think he has something to tell me." She stood up and stepped several yards away from Emma. Henry followed.

"My son called me first thing this morning." Henry parked his pencil above one ear. "He works nights for the janitorial service and was cleaning at the sheriff's department last night. He said Lauren was there until all hours after the car wreck."

"I think I've got it now," Emma said.

"There were two families and it seemed like they had nothing in common and probably didn't even know each other."

"I'll be right there, Mom." Sylvia kept her eyes on Henry.

Emma scratched her chin. "Now, what was it? Maybe they knew each other after all. I'm trying to remember what Mama used to say. She was quite a gossip, you know."

Sylvia did know. "I'm sure it will come to you. Just give me a minute to talk to Henry."

"Is she all right?" Henry asked.

"Yes." Sylvia licked her lips. "What wreck, Henry?"

"Quinn's, of course. Didn't you hear they found his car?"

Sylvia determined her face would give away nothing.

"From what my son heard, Lauren was one of the people who found the car. That Sandquist girl was with her."

"Nicole?"

"Yes, she's the one."

Sylvia's heart thudded. "And Quinn?"

Henry shook his head. "No sign of him. They called in Cooper Elliott to take down the testimony."

Sylvia rapidly indexed the people she had noticed in the sanctuary. Cooper was not among them, but his attendance was erratic under normal circumstances. Why hadn't anyone called her?

Henry flapped the paper in his hand. "I'd better go count the kiddos in the children's wing."

"Do me a favor, Henry?"

"Sure."

"Don't mention this to anyone after church. Give me a chance to find out what's going on."

"You got it."

How many people had Henry already tried to impress with his advance information?

10:47 a.m.

Quinn was the one who got Nicole Sandquist started going to church in the months following her mother's death. Ethan Jordan came later, after Nicole knew every closet, coatrack, and drinking fountain in the building. She gloated in those days and doled out her stash of insider knowledge in measured weekly rations to the boy next door who was also the smartest kid in the class. They sat in worship on either side of Quinn. He didn't have to be a parent to know that if the two of them sat side by side they would spend the hour whispering. As it was, they folded notes and labeled them "very important" as an appeal to Quinn to allow them to keep passing messages back and forth.

Later, when they were teenagers, Nicole and Ethan sat together on their own, and often in the rear pews where most of the youth group seemed to congregate. On Sunday evenings the youth group met in their own space on the second floor of the educational wing. Ethan and Nicole rarely missed a meeting. But that was years ago, and while Nicole had a church in St. Louis that she called her own, in truth she was only there once every five or six weeks.

Now Nicole was sitting in the pew where Quinn ought to have been, on the left side of the congregation and about a third of the way back. She had no idea if he still gravitated to that spot, but it had been the pew of choice when she started coming to church. If she breathed deeply, she could nearly smell his aftershave in the pew upholstery, and it didn't require much imagination to sense Ethan sitting two spots over. Several times during the service, Nicole turned her head expecting to see them both and give herself over to the tug of those years. She would feel again the cushion that Quinn and Ethan, and all of Our Savior, had been for her during years of hard landings.

But they weren't there.

Nicole didn't know this pastor. The bulletin said his name was Matt Kendrick. Most likely he was doing a fine job of preaching, but Nicole was only hearing about every fourth sentence.

She would find Quinn. What was the point of training as a journalist and climbing out of the garden club and into investigative reporting if she couldn't put her skills to work when they mattered most? More than one case in St. Louis twisted on a peculiar fact Nicole uncovered and confirmed before feeding it to a detective with the authority to act on it. The fact that Cooper Elliott wasn't a detective became clear to Nicole in the middle of the night. He had some training, and he followed protocol in the way he questioned, but he wasn't going to smell a trail the way Nicole could.

Nicole flipped over the bulletin and found an open square where she could make notes.

Principal.
Other teachers.
Neighbors.
Newspaper archives.
Falls and lake.
Sheriff's report on accident.
Lauren.

She might have trouble getting the sheriff's report and photos, but she had her own memory of the scene. Nicole drew a line under Lauren's name. Sometimes people knew information without realizing it. The right questions could bring it to light.

The pastor closed his sermon with a prayer, and the congregation stood to sing one last time. Nicole folded the bulletin and stuffed it in her purse. As soon as the final syllable of the benediction faded, she turned toward the tap on her shoulder.

"It *is* you!"

Nicole looked into the bright blue eyes of the woman who had been her Sunday school teacher for most of high school. Benita Booker looked just the way Nicole remembered her — perhaps because her captivating eyes had always been the feature Nicole noticed most. Benita opened her arms, and Nicole happily leaned into the embrace.

"I was just sure that was you," Benita said. "I almost let my husband persuade me otherwise."

"It's me, all right. It's good to see you." Nicole meant what she said.

"Did you come home for the banquet last night?"

Nicole nodded. How many other people dear to her past had been in that confused crowd?

"What could have become of Quinn?" Benita said. "It must have shocked you even more than the rest of us."

Nicole resolved not to say anything about the accident. If she was going to find Quinn, the last thing she wanted to do was fuel the rumor mill with incomplete information.

"People are saying the most dreadful things." Benita shook her head with a sigh.

"Oh?"

"There was a couple at my table I didn't recognize, though I think they had to be at least ten years ahead of you in school. They went on and on about how Quinn and Sylvia never married and maybe it was because he already had a wife somewhere."

"I've never heard anything so ridiculous in my life."

"That's exactly what I said. What kind of person wants to sully the reputation of someone like Quinn at his own banquet? I nearly picked up my plate to look for a seat at another table."

"Don't pay any attention to idle gossip." Nicole seethed with indignation that such an explanation would be the first to spring to anyone's mind. The whole town would be in trouble if people resorted to thinking the worst. "What matters is finding Quinn and making sure he's all right."

"Do you think the police will find him?"

"I'm sure they intend to look." Nicole didn't add that she intended to search five times harder than anyone else. She wouldn't stop until she was sure Quinn hadn't come to harm — at least not more harm than slamming his car into a tree and perhaps wandering into the woods disoriented.

Ethan would have an opinion about whether disorientation could be a symptom of whatever was wrong with Quinn's brain. Nicole stopped herself. She might not have Ethan's scientific mind, but she was well trained not to jump ahead of facts she could prove. She didn't know that anything was wrong with Quinn's brain. Finding Quinn was all that mattered right now.

She spotted the mayor. "Excuse me, Mrs. Booker, but I want to catch Sylvia Alexander."

To Nicole's relief, she realized Sylvia was aiming toward her. Emma lagged behind Sylvia, stopping to chat with a couple of people. Unlike Benita Booker, Emma looked a great deal older than what Nicole remembered. Her hair had whitened considerably, and while her movements didn't look strained, exactly, they were slower.

Sylvia gripped Nicole's arm and pulled her toward a wall.

"I only found out a few minutes ago," Sylvia said, "that you and Lauren were at the sheriff's office well into the night. I haven't even talked to Lauren yet."

Nicole puffed her cheeks and blew out her exasperation as she mentally reviewed who had been present last night in a sparsely staffed sheriff's department. Any of the officers sworn to uphold the law would know better than to spread rumors.

"I was driving home," Nicole said. "Lauren was walking, but she had a healthy head start, so I was surprised to find her there when I saw the car."

"How bad was it?"

Fear flushed through Sylvia's face, but Nicole saw no point in holding back truth. Sylvia was sure to be on the phone to the sheriff before lunch. "The car flipped, probably when it went around a bend too fast. The front end hit one of the old maples at the side of the road."

Sylvia shook her head. "Quinn doesn't speed. He hardly goes the limit."

"We don't know what happened, Sylvia, but we're going to find out. I promise you that."

11:01 a.m.

Sylvia prodded her mother to recall that she had known Nicole as a child and left them to chat. She scanned the sanctuary, but Lauren had slipped out of sight. A couple of musicians were picking up sheet music, but otherwise the congregation had dispersed to the foyer or the fellowship hall. Sylvia didn't want to be drawn into conversation just then. She reached into her purse, woke up her phone, and found the nearly daily trail of text messages she exchanged with her niece. Sylvia wasn't as speedy on the miniature keyboard as younger people she observed, and she detested abbreviations, but she was accustomed to sending text messages like a citizen of the twenty-first century.

WHERE ARE YOU? she typed. CAN WE CHAT?

Sylvia held her phone in her hand and ventured into the corridor that led to the staff offices, hoping Lauren had not already bolted from the building. "Come on," she muttered. "Turn your phone on."

Just when she was about to concede that Lauren had switched off her phone before the worship service and had not yet reconnected to the world, Sylvia's phone vibrated.

IN MY OFFICE, was the reply.

ALONE?

AT THE MOMENT.

WAIT FOR ME.

Sylvia paced in a businesslike manner she hoped would communicate she didn't intend to stop for chitchat — a strategy that successfully carried her past two ushers bearing offering plates to the office to count and Raisa Gallagher cradling a baby while chasing a squealing toddler. If Sylvia offended anyone by not being sociable, she would make amends later. At Lauren's office door, Sylvia saw through the slim window that her niece was inside.

"Why didn't you call me?" Sylvia demanded as she closed the door behind her. "Why does Henry Healy know where you spent the night before your own aunt?"

Lauren sank into her desk chair. "It was late. You were exhausted. If you were asleep, I wanted you to stay asleep."

"I'm the mayor."

"Officer Elliott pointed out that a car accident is a legal matter, not a civic matter."

Sylvia swallowed the anxiety gathered in

her throat. Cooper was right. Technically. But Cooper had to know how she would feel about learning her niece had discovered Quinn's car under precarious circumstances — and Quinn nowhere in sight. She composed herself and sat in one of four chairs at a round table.

"Tell me what happened," Sylvia said. "I want every detail."

Her brow furrowed as Lauren recounted leaving the banquet hall, opting to stroll an indirect route home, coming upon Quinn's car, looking up to see Nicole scrambling around the car, and spending half the night telling the same details to Cooper Elliott. Dizziness took hold behind Sylvia's eyes as she tried to make sense of it all.

"Quinn had some kind of emergency." Lauren rubbed each temple with two fingers. "What was so important that he didn't think he could wait one more day — or even a couple of hours? And leaving his car makes no sense. He should have called 911 or the sheriff's office."

Sylvia sighed. "He probably didn't have his cell phone. He's always going off without it."

"He could have waved somebody down on the road," Lauren said. "If he was uninjured and could walk away, then he could just as easily have gotten someone's attention."

"He didn't want anyone's attention." Sylvia put a finger on the tabletop and drew idle circles on the waxy surface to help her think. Didn't Quinn know he could tell her anything? Disappointment mired her anxiety.

"How in the world did he get away from the banquet hall without anyone seeing him?" Lauren stood up and began to pace behind her desk.

"It's like a magician's trick," Sylvia said. "Everybody was looking somewhere else." It disturbed her that no one could say for certain whether Quinn was on his X when the prop cannon fired backstage while she was introducing him.

"He lost control of the car," Lauren pointed out. "Maybe we should be asking what happened to make him lose control even before we ask why he would leave the scene of an accident."

Sylvia snapped a tissue out of the box at the center of the table and blew her nose. She knew Quinn better than anyone, cared for Quinn more than anyone. She ought to be able to sift through the workings of his mind and come up with more than questions. They needed answers. The thought of Quinn being the object of gossip threatened to pound through her forehead. He would hate that.

A commotion burst out in the hallway. A child screamed and a woman shrieked.

"Raisa Gallagher." Sylvia jumped to her feet and opened Lauren's door. Henry Healy was awkwardly holding a fussing baby while Raisa grabbed a fistful of tissues from a box and dabbed at the flow of blood from her toddler's forehead. The child thrashed against her mother's efforts, and Sylvia stepped in to hold the little girl's hands out away from the wound.

"I'll find Bruce." Lauren ran down the hall, returning a moment later to report that Raisa's husband was pulling the car up so they could go straight to the hospital. She ran back into her office and produced a fleece blanket, and between the two of them, Sylvia and Lauren bundled the girl in a way that bound the girl's arms.

"It's a lot of blood," Sylvia said, "but I don't think it looks too bad." The little one would probably scream through the stitches she needed, but the cut was at the hairline and not on the eye as Sylvia had first thought.

"What happened?" Lauren asked.

"Kimmie wanted Quinn," Raisa said. "I kept telling her he wasn't here today, but she ran off and fell against a table."

Bruce Gallagher broke into the huddle and scooped up his daughter. Raisa took the baby from a startled Henry. In another moment, the Gallaghers were gone and the hallway was quiet again. Sylvia and her niece retreated into Lauren's office.

"An emergency," Lauren repeated. "It's the only thing that makes sense."

Sylvia wished it were that easy. If Quinn had a medical emergency, he shouldn't have been driving himself anywhere — and the road where his car was found was not on the way to the Hidden Falls hospital. What other kind of emergency could he have? He had no family, at least not any he had spoken of in years. Everyone came from some sort of family, Sylvia realized, but Quinn's ties were loose enough to be confined to memories he seldom felt a need to express. Something a teacher once said to him. A class he hated in college. The cousin who died from a rare brain tumor when she was three.

Quinn's life was in Hidden Falls. All of it. Sylvia was sure of this. Everything that mattered to him was in this town. *I'm here.*

So where was he racing to?

Lauren stopped pacing and looked out the windowpane in her office door. "Nana is out there."

Sylvia looked up to see Nicole standing behind Emma, shrugging. "I don't think she remembers Nicole very well." Sylvia stood up and opened the door, slightly irritated. She'd wanted more time to talk with Lauren.

"Your mom was anxious to know where you were," Nicole said. "It was her idea to look here."

"I'm not anxious," Emma said. "I'm just getting hungry. You know I eat breakfast at the crack of dawn."

"I'm overdue for some of your Saturday morning chocolate chip pancakes," Lauren said.

"Come next Saturday," Emma said. "But you might have to bring the chocolate chips."

"Next week is the health fair, Mom," Sylvia said. "Lauren will be busy all day."

"I thought Quinn was in charge of that," Emma said.

Sylvia and Lauren looked at each other.

"He was a big help," Lauren said, "but it's my job to make sure everything comes off according to plan. I'm responsible."

"Especially now that Quinn is gone, I suppose." Emma sat down at the table with Sylvia.

"Well," Lauren said, "we all hope Quinn will be back long before Saturday."

"That's rather hard to predict, isn't it?" Emma said.

Sylvia watched her mother's face. Though she still prepared her own meals and ate heartily, Emma had difficulty remembering what she had for lunch on any given day. She called Sylvia every morning on a precise schedule, but then she had trouble remembering what was on her calendar for the day. But in the moment, in a conversation, Emma still made accurate connections.

"We're going to be positive, Mom," Sylvia said.

"I think I'll head on home now." Nicole

still stood in the doorframe.

"When are you leaving town?" Lauren took a seat at the table across from Emma.

"Not until I find Quinn."

The determination in Nicole's voice puddled Sylvia's jumbled emotions.

"So we'll see you again," Lauren said.

"I'm sure." Nicole met Lauren's eyes, and then Sylvia's. "I wish our reunion was under better circumstances."

"We'll have a real celebration after Quinn's home safe." Sylvia had trouble recalling a time in the last fifteen hours that her thickened throat had not threatened to cut off her airway.

Nicole stepped out of the office.

"Quinn's disappearance is so curious." Emma set her purse on the table and smoothed her skirt. "I was getting ready to tell Sylvia a story earlier. You might find it interesting, too, Lauren."

"What's it about?" Lauren asked.

Sylvia had hoped to avoid another halting round of this story at least until after lunch.

"Some families who used to live in Hidden Falls a long time ago, when I was a girl." Emma tilted her head in thought. "I'm not sure when they disappeared."

"Disappeared?" Lauren said.

"Well, they left town suddenly and never came back," Emma said. "No one knew where they went, either. That sounds like disappearing to me."

"Me, too."

"During the Depression, I think." Emma leaned forward, elbows on the table. "Yes, not too long after the Crash."

Sylvia stood up. "Mom, you said you were hungry. Why don't we go back to my house? I'll make you some lunch."

"I feel like ham." Emma picked up her purse.

"I just bought some." Sylvia turned to Lauren. "How about you? Hungry?"

Lauren shook her head.

"We should all eat," Sylvia said.

"I need sleep. And I want to call Raisa and see how things went for Kimmie. But if you hear something —"

"I'll call."

12:07 p.m.

The old Adirondack chair was still on the Sandquist back porch, weathered but sturdy. Ethan angled the chair away from a view of the Jordan home next door and eased himself into it. Trees planted along the property line when he was a small boy towered now, with broadened branches and thickened trunks. Burnished leaves trembled against the threat of plummeting to the ground, obscuring the line of sight between the two houses, but Ethan didn't want to take any chances. The size of the chair would disguise his form lest one of his parents happen to step outside the Jordan house and glance toward the Sandquists' back porch. Sitting on the front steps would have left him exposed, and Nicole would pull her car around to the back even if she didn't bother with the garage. Ethan's Lexus was parked up the street.

He jiggled one foot while he waited. Church was at nine thirty. It was after twelve now. What was taking her so long?

His phone buzzed. "Hey, Hansen. What's the word?"

"I can help you out."

"That's good news."

"It's only one day," Hansen said. "And you'll still have to deal with Gonzalez."

"Rounds are covered tomorrow. That's all I wanted." *One day at a time,* Ethan told himself as he pocketed his phone.

Finally, he heard the engine of Nicole's white Hyundai purr into the driveway. He'd been right. She did pull the car to the back. Ethan sat still, listening to the sounds of her opening the car door and shuffling some bags. The door slammed and Nicole made her way along the path of narrow cement rectangles embedded in the ground. When she reached the edge of the porch, Ethan stood up.

She met his eyes and shifted a pair of paper sacks in her arms. "I stopped for food. There's nothing in the house, obviously."

"You knew I would be here, didn't you?" Ethan took one of the sacks from Nicole.

"You don't walk away from things, Ethan Jordan." Nicole fumbled with her keys and moved toward the back door.

He had walked away from her ten years ago, or more like slithered away.

Nicole unlocked the door. "The food is from Fall Shadows Café. I got the pot roast you used to like. You'll have to tell me if it's the same as it always was."

Ethan could think of no other person in his life with whom he could slip into old habits so comfortably. "It's good of you to feed me."

Nicole laughed. "Says the boy who is secretly relieved that the girl is not going to try to cook again."

"Have you given that up?" Ethan set the sack on the kitchen table, a flimsy maple set with four spindled chairs.

"Mostly."

"My recollection is you were starting to get good at it."

Nicole shrugged and lifted a Styrofoam container from one bag. "I live alone. It doesn't seem worth the bother."

He owned the zing she hadn't meant to shoot. Nicole stated a simple fact, but if Ethan hadn't slithered away, they could have been married, and she wouldn't be living alone.

"The other one is pork, if you'd rather have

that." Nicole opened both containers on the table and pulled two iced teas out of the second bag. "Extra sweet, no lemon."

She remembered everything. And she knew he couldn't leave town.

"I only finagled one more day." Ethan could stay until midnight on Monday and still be in Columbus in time for morning rounds on Tuesday and the surgery schedule that followed.

"Then we'll have to find Quinn in one day." Nicole opened a drawer, pulled out two dusty forks, and moved to the sink to rinse them. Old pipes rattled against the unexpected demand.

And if we don't? Ethan thought. He would still have to leave at midnight the next night or risk his residency.

"Do you keep the water on when the house is empty?" he asked.

"Quinn taught me to work a main valve when I was eleven." Nicole sat down and handed Ethan a fork. "There's something you should know."

While they ate, Nicole relayed details of discovering Quinn's car.

"Could he have an accident because he's sick?" Nicole asked.

"It's possible." Ethan forked the last of the pot roast. "But if he was that seriously impaired medically, I'm not sure he could walk away and out of sight so thoroughly."

"I want to start looking for him," Nicole said. "We can check things out at his house, for starters."

"I thought the police said he hasn't been there."

"A good reporter always double-checks her sources." Nicole stuffed the empty food containers back into the paper sacks. "If we don't find anything there, we can hike toward the falls."

"Seems like an obvious place to go for a man who is trying *not* to be found," Ethan said.

"First of all, we don't know he's trying not to be found, and second, I have to get inside his head. Try to think like he thinks. And the falls or the lake seem like the best place to do that."

She had a point.

"Just give me a minute to change into jeans." Nicole pushed the swinging door from the kitchen into the hallway.

Ethan heard the rhythm of her feet taking the stairs. He started to put the trash in the bin under the sink before remembering that an empty house wouldn't have any trash service. Though it had been unoccupied for years, everything in this house was exactly as Ethan remembered it, down to the collection of red and yellow wooden roosters on the shelf above the sink. Nicole's father must have decided to decorate from scratch in his new home. Perhaps there were too many memories in Hidden Falls, like the ones that pressed in on Ethan.

He wandered into the living room and found the major pieces of furniture covered in drop cloths, but their shapes and positions evoked the evenings he and Nicole sat on the couch to watch TV while they did homework. The dining room furniture was exposed and dense with dust. Ethan stood with both hands in his pockets, remembering Nicole's pile of cookbooks on one end of the table. What had become of them?

He took one hand out of a pocket, put a finger in the dust, and stacked two sets of initials. NS over EJ.

Ethan heard Nicole's steps on the stairs and moved to the foyer. "That was fast."

"No time to waste." Nicole squatted and tightened a shoelace on a running shoe. "I'm not sorry I went to church, but I'm ready to get moving."

"How was everything at Our Savior?"

"You should have come." Nicole hooked her keys around a belt loop.

Ethan shook his head. "I don't do that anymore."

"Maybe you should."

Ethan regretted asking about the church. "Let's take your car."

"You don't want to go through the fence?"

Ethan wasn't eager to be spotted in the

neighborhood, much less in his parents' backyard crawling between loose boards. "You're the same size, but I kept growing during college."

"Fine. We'll drive around the block. But then I want to hike so we can look carefully."

"Let's stop at my car," Ethan said. "My camera might come in handy."

Fetching the camera and driving around the wide block took less than five minutes.

Nicole parked as close to Quinn's house as she could get. "How do we get in?"

"Maybe we don't." Ethan winced at the blade Nicole's eyes threw at him.

"That'll make it hard to find any useful information." Nicole opened her door and got out. "The place looks the same on the outside."

Ethan circled the hood of the car to stand next to her. "Normalcy means something, doesn't it? He wasn't planning to leave."

Nicole cocked her head. "Why do you suppose he always locked up?"

"You locked your house when we left."

"I've been polluted by living in a city. Plenty of people in Hidden Falls wouldn't even be able to tell you where their house keys are, but even when Quinn is inside the house, he keeps the door locked."

Nicole paced toward the house, slipped between bushes, and pressed her face against the front window.

"Do you have X-ray vision to see through closed drapes?" Ethan stood behind her.

Nicole slapped his shoulder with the back of her fingers.

A teenage boy in running gear pounded the pavement down Quinn's street. "Now there's a man after my own heart," Nicole said.

At the sight of them, the boy stopped and, with his hands on his hips, let his chest heave while he eyed Nicole and Ethan.

"I suppose you're wondering what we're doing." Ethan had no plan for how he would answer that question.

"Looking for Quinn, I guess." The boy used the sleeve of his sweatshirt to wipe sweat from one side of his face. "He's not here, is he?"

"Nope." Nicole stepped away from the window.

"Too bad. He could have helped me smooth things over."

"You're in trouble?" Ethan asked.

"Seriously," the boy said. "I'll never live down knocking over the video booth at the banquet last night. My parents were mortified."

"Oh," Nicole said, a knowing grin coming over her face. "You're Zeke Plainfield."

"Does the whole town know it was me?" Zeke squatted and tightened a shoelace. "There are no secret identities in this town. If you'll point me to the nearest hole I can jump down, I'll be on my way." Zeke took off down the street.

Nicole turned to Ethan. "I think Quinn has a secret."

"And this secret explains his disappearance?"

"It's a workable theory," Nicole said. "Now we have to test it. Isn't that what you scientists do?"

"I agree."

Nicole narrowed her eyes at him. "You're full of surprises."

Ethan took three steps back and tilted his head to survey the upper level of Quinn's house. "Ever since I saw him last night, I've been thinking about something Quinn once said that I never understood."

"I need more than that to go on."

Ethan shrugged. "There isn't much more. He knew I didn't get along with my parents. One day when I was whining about it, he said that as estranged as I might feel, I had no idea what it felt like to truly be separated from people you love."

"I'll bet that was the end of that."

"Pretty much. I didn't dare ask what he meant." Ethan wished he had.

"He told me once how he used to play in the water sprinkler with his little brother," Nicole said. "But millions of kids do that every summer. All I ever knew about his family is that they were back East somewhere."

"So we grow up running to Quinn like he's

the parent we wish we had, and this is the best we can do?" Ethan spread his arms wide. "*Maybe* he had family somewhere between here and the Atlantic Ocean?"

They stood silent. A car swished past on the road behind them, and a crackling swirl of leaves blew up in its wake.

Finally, Nicole spoke. "Like you said last night, we were kids. We were so hungry for what he gave us that we didn't really see the world through Quinn's eyes."

"Do you think he was — *is* — happy?"

"Yes," Nicole answered without hesitation. "He helped — *helps* — people because he wants to, because he cares if they're happy. And he has his faith. It's real."

Ethan clamped his reply closed. He wasn't going down the faith trail.

2:19 p.m.

Jack Parker was starting to wonder what, precisely, his son did the night before. Colin was seventeen — closer to eighteen. Maybe Jack didn't want to know what Colin and his friends did. Next year at this time, Colin would be away at college, and Jack wouldn't see that his son looked slightly hung over at lunch on Sunday. The girls had gotten up and gone to church, but even Gianna gave Colin a wide berth these days and hadn't knocked on his door in the morning. Colin didn't say more than "I need the butter" for the entire meal when the family gathered in the formal dining room with its tall windows and wide crown molding. This was the room that sold Gianna on the house. She didn't seem to need much of an excuse to serve family meals in the dining room. Jack preferred the kitchen, figuring that since they spent a small fortune renovating it, they ought to use it.

Eva had come home for breakfast. The swim party last night turned into a sleepover, so she looked tired, but she made an effort to be pleasant. Thirteen-year-old Brooke chattered about the shopping spree her friend's mother took them on the night before and the chocolate-covered shortbread squares they baked. Perhaps Brooke's brightness was a sign that she didn't blame him for isolating the family in this small town. Gianna wouldn't tell Brooke directly that she didn't think the girl was ready to stay home alone in the evenings, even at thirteen. Somehow, Jack realized, Gianna made sure Brooke had something enticing to do whenever everyone else was out.

"I was going to tell Quinn I wanted to help at the health fair," Brooke said as Gianna began stacking dishes. "Now I guess I should tell Lauren."

"If that's what you want to do," Gianna said, "let her know. I'll make sure you can be there."

"Quinn will be back before Saturday, won't he?" Brooke said.

Jack and Gianna glanced at each other.

"What about school tomorrow?" Eva asked. "I can't give my family genealogy presentation to a sub."

"Quinn has many friends." Gianna laid the fifth dinner plate in her stack. "I'm sure he'll be fine. It's not something we have to fret about. Let's just enjoy our Sunday."

Colin unfolded out of his chair. "I have homework."

Jack watched his son slink from the room. No "excuse me" or "thanks for dinner." No taking dishes to the kitchen. It might as well have been Jack saying, "I have to work."

The guilt made Jack stand up and lift the stack of plates and silverware Gianna had assembled. "I'll do the dishes."

When Gianna caught his eye, she looked stunned. Other than her blinking eyes, nothing moved.

"I know I haven't cleaned up in about a hundred years," Jack said, "but I will today."

"Well, I *have* been looking for time to catch up on my scrapbooks." Gianna's face lit up.

"Then go on," he said. "I'll take care of this."

Gianna scooted her chair back. "If there's anything you don't know what to do with, just leave it on the breakfast bar."

Jack wasn't sure whether to be relieved at

this instruction or insulted. Gianna was already predicting he wouldn't know his way around the kitchen. Every time he emptied the dishwasher — usually under unexpressed duress — she later remarked about finding an item in an odd place. And by *odd* she meant *wrong.*

Eva picked up two empty serving bowls, and Brooke took the bread basket with the cross-stitched liner that draped an autumn leaf pattern over the rim of the basket. It was the perfect accent for the season and the room, Jack observed. That was Gianna. The perfect accent.

"Go," he said again. "Spend the afternoon doing exactly what you want to do."

Gianna smiled, and Jack bent to kiss her.

She stroked the side of his face. "Thank you."

He was making an effort. It didn't come naturally, but he was trying. Jack carried the plates into the kitchen. When he returned for the glasses, Gianna had left the dining room. In the kitchen, in addition to tableware, Jack faced the cookware required to produce a Sunday meal featuring meat, potatoes, salad, two hot vegetables, and rolls.

Folding up the sleeves of the dress shirt he had worn to church, Jack started in. Someone turned on the television in the other room and changed channels every eight seconds. Jack rinsed and scrubbed and loaded the dishwasher with Gianna's voice in his head at each task. He was pleased to leave nothing on the breakfast bar, and only twice did he put something in a cupboard without being certain the location was correct.

Having fulfilled his family duties and successfully lightened Gianna's mood toward him, Jack went upstairs to change clothes. The master bedroom stretched across one end of the house and included space Gianna used for whatever was her current project. Jack had never seen the need to keep up with what the scattered craft elements meant. Rather than working at her table, though, Gianna was asleep on the paisley chaise lounge with a quilt pulled up to her neck.

Good. She wouldn't miss him.

Outside, Brooke was playing with the puppy in the yard. The Airedale had a green chew toy between her teeth, and Brooke gripped its edges and shook it. Roxie's tail wagged.

"Hi, Dad." Brooke grinned.

She could be a calendar photo, Jack thought. A fresh-faced girl in a sweater playing with a puppy in a yard of fall leaves.

"Looks like you're having fun."

"I wish we'd gotten a puppy a long time ago." The dog released the toy, and Brooke tossed it several yards away. Roxie scampered after it and, panting, brought it back.

"Mom is napping," Jack said. "If she wakes

up and wonders where I am, will you tell her I went for a walk?"

"Yep." Brooke dropped to her knees and snuggled the puppy against her face.

Another calendar shot.

Jack was going to have to do something about the leaves in the yard, but not today.

He was aiming for his office. Jack would have preferred to live farther out of town in a newer subdivision. They could have avoided all the remodeling mess and expense of the last few months. But Gianna had wanted a house with character, so they bought a home built in 1906, knocked out a couple of walls to create the great room, and modernized the kitchen and bathrooms. From the outside, the old house maintained its stately charm and suggestion of gracious living.

Jack hated it. But Gianna was happy — with the house. She was less happy with Jack.

One advantage of living in town was that Jack could, in all honesty, say he was going for a walk and end up at his office in an old brick structure one block north of Main Street. He had inherited a number of loyal clients when he purchased the suite of offices and took over the law practice. He also handled the occasional real estate transaction. But Jack wanted something he could dig his teeth into.

A storeroom in the suite of rooms that housed his practice contained dozens of crates of old files. One by one Jack carried them to his desk, where he could sit in his high-backed leather chair and sort through folders looking for a random document or a handwritten note that might lead to a legal challenge that would make his heart race like the old days. Jack loved Gianna, and he loved his kids, but he was choking on the pressure to accept mediocrity and think it was a good life.

Now Jack wondered if his old files contained any records related to Quinn. One clue. That's all it would take to bring some excitement to practicing law in Hidden Falls.

2:58 p.m.

Liam Elliott hardly knew Jack Parker and surprised himself by lifting a hand in greeting, much less waving him over when he entered the Fall Shadows Café.

It was an impulse, and perhaps a desperate one.

Liam pushed away his plate with the remains of his roast beef sandwich and sweet potato fries. He came in for a late lunch after waiting as long as his stomach could take for Jessica to call. The baby shower for her coworker was supposed to start at ten thirty. Liam wasn't sure what a room full of women found to do for more than four hours. Last night Jessica had been eager to spend most of the day with Liam, so why hadn't she found some way to duck out sooner? He kept his phone on the table to be sure he wouldn't miss her call, but what was the harm in a little strategic conversation while he waited?

He was just exploring options, not making a commitment.

Liam had heard the rumors about Jack coming to town with his tail between his legs over some corporate scandal. Whether there was any truth to it or not, the suggestion had put Liam off getting to know Jack, even though Jack moved into the empty office suite in Liam's building months ago. Of course Jack had all the requisite qualifications for taking over a law practice, and the rumor mill also said some of the clients were satisfied that the previous attorneys wouldn't have turned over the business to a shyster. They intended to stay put unless Jack Parker gave them reason to look elsewhere for routine legal services.

Some of the clients, Liam had noted in conversations around town, not *most.* Liam couldn't afford to lose even some of his clients. It was hard enough to make a living as a financial consultant in a small town, traipsing all over the county every week — because if he waited for people to be willing to drive into town to meet at his office, he would never close a deal.

Now Liam felt some sympathy for Jack. News traveled fast in Hidden Falls because it didn't have far to go before falling on fresh ears. If a rumor started that Liam had been unethical in his business, it might as well be on a billboard over the WELCOME TO HIDDEN FALLS sign. Whether it was true or not, his business would never recover.

As much as Liam hated to admit it, Jack Parker, attorney at law, might be just the person he would need on his side if the question of the missing funds blew up in his face.

Maybe the operative word was *when,* rather than *if.*

Jack made his way across the café to the small table where Liam twiddled a fork.

"Heading to your office?" Liam asked.

"Thought I might. Just wanted a cup of coffee to take with me."

"Sit down if you have time." Liam gestured to an empty chair. "I'm about to order some myself."

Jack hesitated but took a seat and raised a hand for Gavin's attention. They ordered coffee. When Jack didn't ask for his "to go," Liam's mind churned over the challenge of managing this conversation. He managed conversations every day, but the stakes were steep in this one.

"I've got fresh blueberry pie." Gavin wagged his eyebrows and reached for Liam's empty lunch plate.

"Let me buy you some pie, Jack." Liam spoke quickly, before the opportunity faded.

"I was just lamenting that my lunch at home didn't include dessert," Jack said. "How about some ice cream on that pie, Gavin?"

"You got it. Two?" Gavin looked at Liam, who nodded.

"So as a lawyer," Liam said after Gavin left, "you must find last night's events curious. Have you dealt with missing person cases before?"

"In my experience," Jack said, "there are two kinds of missing persons. Those who don't want to be found, and those who have been strongly encouraged to go missing against their wills."

"And Quinn? Do you have a theory about him?"

"I never actually met him. How well do you know him?"

"Not as well as some," Liam admitted, "but we're working on a business deal." There seemed no harm in stretching that particular truth.

"Did he seem like someone who would up and walk out while five hundred people are applauding him?"

"I would have to say no." That was the truth.

Jack turned his palms up. "There you have it, then. Somebody got to him."

"Got to him?"

"A little chloroform, perhaps. A pistol in

the ribs. A chop to the neck. It could happen any number of ways. The closed curtain was a perfect cover — and that blast, whatever it was."

Liam grimaced. "That sounds a little dramatic." Just how much time did Jack spend working on criminal cases compared to how much time he spent watching reruns of *Law and Order*? He hated to think that something like what Jack suggested actually happened.

Jack shrugged. "I've tried enough criminal cases to face facts. It happens."

"I didn't realize you were that kind of lawyer."

"I spent a few years in criminal and a few years in corporate."

"I see." Either way, criminal or corporate, Jack could be of help to Liam — if it came to that. The combination could bode well.

Gavin returned with coffee and pie. Liam poured cream into his cup. Jack chunked off an ambitious bite of blueberries.

A commotion at the back of the café demanded their attention. A woman tripped over a chair and cried out, "My purse!"

Liam froze, but Jack bounded out of the booth and tackled a man with a lump under his sweatshirt. The thief sprang to his feet again and pulled his hood up to obscure his face. A woman's purse tumbled to the floor as he careened out of the café. Jack picked it up and handed it to the distressed woman.

"Thank you!" She hugged Jack and returned to her table. Someone started a rhythm of applause. Jack gave a dignified bow.

Gavin Owens dashed out the door after the thief but returned almost immediately shaking his head.

Liam was flabbergasted as Jack slid back into his seat. "That was some quick thinking."

"That's how fast crime happens." Jack picked his napkin up off the floor and sat back down. "Hidden Falls may be the kind of town where people think crime will never strike, but believe me, it happens everywhere. It just takes one person with one screw loose."

"So you think that petty thief has a screw loose?" Liam stirred his coffee. "Or are you saying somebody mentally unstable has Quinn?"

"I'm just saying that anything could have happened. That poor woman came in for a sandwich, and look what happened to her."

Liam picked at his pie. While he was as stunned as anyone by Quinn's disappearing act last night, until this moment Liam hadn't confronted probabilities. He swallowed a forkful of sweetened blueberries. If Quinn was taken against his will, his return was less predictable with every hour that passed. That meant Liam's options were narrowing as well.

"It sounds like you've seen some serious cases." Liam resumed his query for what he needed to know from this conversation.

"I've had my share."

"What about on the corporate law side? You must see some hanky-panky there, too."

Jack took a long sip of coffee. "Corporate law is all about money. Who has it. Who wants it. How they plan to get it. What price they are willing to pay. What they'll do to avoid responsibility."

Liam's gut tightened at the relevance of every one of Jack's points. He knew he didn't have the missing money. So who did? And how did they get it? Liam had only suspicions he couldn't prove — yet. If Liam didn't figure out something soon, he would be responsible whether he liked it or not. He cleared his throat.

"I suppose some of it has to do with creative bookkeeping," Liam said.

"More than a little. Corporate decisions often come down to technical interpretation and applied logic of the law." Jack had nearly cleared his plate already.

"Doesn't it ever come down to somebody covering up, say, embezzlement?"

"Only if they're not very good at it. You'd be surprised what people get away with."

"If they get away with it, how does anyone find out?"

"Eventually somebody slips. They get greedy, make one transaction too many, something outside the normal pattern of the accounts in question."

"And what do the attorneys do when that happens?"

Jack fastened his gaze on Liam. "Attorneys always act in the best interest of their clients. That's our job."

Liam looked down at his pie, wishing that the accounts he questioned didn't already meet Jack's description. Maybe it had been going on for longer than he realized, and only now had someone gotten greedy and made the first transaction that caught Liam's attention. Nobody would believe he didn't know, that he hadn't seen it sooner — that he hadn't done it himself. He had to protect himself. His vision of his future dangled precariously.

"Thanks for the pie." Jack laid his fork on his plate. "I think I'll get a second cup of coffee to take with me."

Liam picked up his briefcase, and they walked to the counter together, where Liam paid the bill before continuing down the street to his car. He drove south, toward the banquet hall. The parking lot was full once again. Liam guessed it was the sort of run-of-the-mill wedding reception that Jessica would have nothing to do with. Once he shut the engine off, he reached into his briefcase for the envelope. It was time to put it back — without raising questions about why he had it to begin with. Liam sat in his car and watched the front entrance for five torturous minutes. If he had worn a suit instead of jeans and a pullover, it would have been easier to go unnoticed. He concluded from the lack of foot traffic that events inside were in full swing. If he was lucky, they were doing toasts and giving speeches and cutting cake, traditions none of the guests would want to miss.

Liam tucked the envelope in his waistband and pulled his sweater down. He strolled toward the building, through the door, and down the hall with the certainty of belonging. Breaking in again wouldn't be necessary — as easy as it would be. Liam squatted to position the envelope under the door before giving it a swift two-fingered push. The angle was strategic, sure to leave the envelope in a place where it might easily have fallen off the corner of the desk.

The ring of his phone jolted Liam. With hastening steps, he answered it. "Hi, Jessica."

His brain didn't register her words. Liam powered past the doors from the banquet hall that opened into the hallway. When he heard steps behind him, he didn't turn. No one saw his face. Still on the phone, he sank into the driver's seat.

The envelope was out of his hands.

And he had what he needed from its contents.

5:12 p.m.

"I want to be kept in the loop at every step." Sylvia strode across her kitchen as she spoke into the phone, pivoted, and retraced her steps. "No matter how small the detail, tell me. It might mean something to someone who knows Quinn well." *Like me.*

"Mayor," Cooper Elliott said on the other end of the phone, "if there were something to tell you, I would. We've towed the car to a police holding lot. Tomorrow we'll see if we can get an investigator on it, someone with some forensics experience. We don't exactly have that specialty in Hidden Falls."

"I want to know the results."

"They won't be instantaneous. Even if they find prints or fibers, a lot of people have been in Quinn's car."

"Thank you, Cooper. I'll be in touch." Sylvia hung up the landline just as her cell phone sang the tune reserved for her niece. "Hello."

"Aunt Sylvia," Lauren said. "I wanted to see how you are."

"Bordering on frazzled." Sylvia sat down and put her elbows on the kitchen table. "Did you sleep?"

"Yes," Lauren said. "Some."

"Good." Sylvia's phones had been ringing in rapid succession all afternoon. Members of the town council. Quinn's neighbors. People from Our Savior. Everybody wanted to be the first to know when she heard from

Quinn. Opinion seemed uniform that if Quinn would contact anyone, it would be Sylvia.

She hoped so.

She was an intelligent, educated, thoughtful person, a leader in her town. And she couldn't think of one useful action she could take to help find Quinn.

"Aunt Sylvia?"

Lauren's voice pulled Sylvia back to the moment.

"Yes, I'm here."

"I've been going through my folder on the health fair," Lauren said. "Some of the information is old, I'm sure, but I see a note about items from your store. I'm not sure what it refers to."

"I told Quinn I would donate a few things for the silent auction," Sylvia said. "At least, Quinn was going to look at them and decide if he thought they would sell."

"Do you mind if I have a look instead?"

"Sure." Sylvia admired Lauren's practical approach. If Quinn were found well and safe before Saturday, he could still run the fair. But if not, Lauren had to be ready.

"Would tonight be too soon?"

Sylvia crossed the kitchen again and looked out into the living room, where Emma sat with a magazine in her lap. "Nana is still here. I want to give her another good meal, and then I'll take her home. I could meet you at the shop about a quarter to nine."

They said good-bye, and Sylvia set the cell phone down on the kitchen counter. She walked into the living room. "I'm sorry for all the phone calls, Mom. As you can imagine, everyone is worried."

Emma didn't answer.

Sylvia angled toward the chair where Emma sat with her eyes closed, her chin on her chest, and her hands slack over the magazine in her lap. Emma's chest lifted in a slow breath. Relieved, Sylvia put a hand against Emma's cheek. "Mom?"

Emma's eyes fluttered open. "I dozed off, didn't I?"

"How long have you been asleep?" With her spoken question, Sylvia also indicted herself for how long she had been on the phone and not paying attention to her mother.

Emma looked out the front windows. "It wasn't this dark when I sat down with a magazine. What am I reading, anyway?"

Sylvia flipped the magazine closed in Emma's lap.

"Goodness," Emma said. "This is some sort of mayors' magazine. No wonder it put me to sleep."

Sylvia hadn't noticed when Emma picked up the magazine. Who had she been on the phone with when her mother stopped puttering with Sylvia's houseplants and sat down?

"I haven't been very good company today,"

Sylvia said.

"I know," Emma said. "The whole town is in trouble because Quinn went missing."

"It seems that way."

"And you are the mayor, after all."

"That's right."

"I should go home."

"Let's have supper first, and then I'll take you."

"What do you have?"

Sylvia smiled. That was just like Emma, always one to find out what the options were before committing herself.

"Frozen spinach mozzarella ravioli," Sylvia said.

"I do like spinach. And mozzarella. And ravioli."

"I have fresh salad greens, too."

Emma scrunched her nose. "Salads are so much work to eat. An old lady should be able to take a pass on a bowl of weeds."

Sylvia chuckled. "Okay. No salad for you."

"Then I accept your invitation to dinner."

Sylvia's next words were pure impulse. "Why don't you stay the night in my guest room?"

Emma's jaw moved back and forth. "I'll think about it."

"Fair enough." Sylvia turned toward the kitchen, but not before she saw Emma pick up the magazine she had cast off only moments ago. Emma selected that magazine every time she came to Sylvia's house, and each time declared it unreadable to the common person.

Sylvia returned to the kitchen, filled a pot with water, and lit the gas burner underneath it. Leaning against the counter, she took five intentional deep breaths.

And then the phone rang. Sylvia snatched the cordless from the base and looked at the caller ID before pushing the button to answer.

"Good evening, Henry."

"Hello, Sylvia. Just wanted to know if everything got sorted out at the sheriff's office. You seemed surprised at the news this morning."

"Thanks for the heads-up. I'm up to speed now."

"So what are you going to do about it?"

"I'm letting the police do their jobs." Sylvia opened the freezer and dug for the bag of frozen pasta.

"What do you think they'll find?"

If she knew that, she wouldn't have to wait for them to find it. "I don't know, Henry. They have a plan, but these things take time." She moved a carton of ice cream and found the ravioli.

When Sylvia closed the freezer door again, her mother stood at the stove peering into the pot. "I've got to go, Henry. I'll talk to you later."

"You didn't have to hang up on my account," Emma said.

"I'm tired of being on the phone." Sylvia opened a drawer for a pair of scissors to cut open the bag.

"You should be. You've been doing it all day."

"I'm sorry."

"I picked up a magazine in there, but it's all about being a mayor. Normal people don't want to read that."

"I'm a mayor, Mom," Sylvia said.

"I suppose that's why you're on the phone all the time."

"Well, today it is."

"What's so important, anyway?"

Sylvia watched for the pot to bubble. "Quinn."

"Is something wrong with Quinn?"

Sylvia looked at Emma, and the familiar sadness over her mother's memory gaps swept through her afresh.

Emma had known about Quinn's disappearance. And now she didn't know. This was happening more and more. Sylvia was starting to wonder how much longer it would be safe for Emma to live alone.

"How's your appetite?" Sylvia decided to focus on dinner. The water was close enough to boiling that Sylvia dumped in the pasta.

"I'm famished. I've hardly eaten a thing today."

The ache rose through Sylvia's core. Emma

had eaten enough lunch for two growing teenagers.

"This only takes a few minutes," Sylvia said. "Why don't you get plates out?"

Emma glanced around the kitchen. Sylvia pointed to the correct cupboard. Emma opened it and took out one plate. Immediately she realized she needed another. Now that she was in the cupboard, she also removed two water glasses and filled them at the sink. Normal motions, Sylvia thought, but not quite automatic.

"I'd like it if you would spend the night," Sylvia said. "You like the guest room, don't you?"

"It'll do. Are we eating in here?"

"I thought we would." Sylvia took a colander from a shelf and set it in the sink before lifting the pot to dump the water through it.

"Quinn disappeared, didn't he?" Emma set the plates on the table.

Sylvia sucked in her breath. "Yes, he did."

"I remember." Emma sat down. "I remember a long time ago somebody disappeared. A whole family. Two whole families. No one ever heard from them again."

Sylvia's cell phone rang.

"That silly phone just doesn't stop," Emma said. "How do you stand it?"

Sylvia picked up the phone and, without looking at the number it displayed, turned it off. Even if it was Cooper Elliott, she would have to return the call later. Then she set the pot of pasta on the table and stuck a slotted spoon in it. "No more phone calls tonight. You can tell me the story that's been on your mind all day."

"I thought you were having salad greens," Emma said.

Sylvia smiled. There was no predicting what her mother would hang on to these days. "I changed my mind. We'll keep it simple. Tell me the story."

"Which story?"

"About the families who disappeared."

"I'm surprised you never heard your grandmother tell it."

"It doesn't sound familiar," Sylvia said. She spooned food onto her mother's plate and watched the ravioli slide into formation along the curves of the dish.

Emma picked up her fork. "It was during the Depression. So long ago. I was hardly old enough to be aware of what was happening. I suppose that's why I don't remember too much. People were so poor, and there were no jobs. Your grandfather lost his furniture store on Main Street."

Sylvia had heard that story. "Is that when he became a barber?"

"He'd been a barber before the store, I think. But that was before I was born. After the Crash, people did anything just to survive. Some of them moved away."

"They went to stay with extended family, I suppose." Sylvia stabbed a piece of ravioli.

"No doubt. But moving away is one thing. Dropping off the face of the earth is another."

"What do you mean?"

"Your grandmother used to talk about two families who left right around the same time. The odd thing was, one of them had money when no one else seemed to have any."

Sylvia chewed. The story didn't matter. She only wanted her mother to feel she was listening.

"I can't really remember much more." Emma took a bite.

"That's all right. If something comes to you, maybe we can write it down. The Hidden Falls Historical Society might be interested."

"It's so dark outside," Emma said. "As soon as it gets dark, I start thinking about going to bed."

"If you stay here tonight, you can go right to bed."

Emma nodded. "That has some appeal."

They finished eating. With a fresh nightgown over one arm, Sylvia went into the guest room and waited for Emma to emerge from the bathroom.

"I need something to read," Emma said. "I can't fall asleep without reading."

One of Sylvia's earliest memories was of her mother propped up in bed with a book when Sylvia woke thirsty one night. "Do you feel like a mystery?"

Emma was always a voracious reader. It was possible the story she was working so hard to reconstruct was an old plotline from decades ago, a book about the Depression.

It didn't matter.

6:19 p.m.

The water kindly lifted the rowboat and nudged it toward the shoreline, requiring very little from Dani Roose as she rowed. Nearly ten hours on the lake yielded six fish she had released back — and the seventh she kept for her dinner. Lapping lake water soothed her spirit. As the bow knocked against the pier, regret flashed for half a second that she had not stayed out another thirty minutes. Dani secured the oars, a task that announced the finality of coming off the lake.

Grabbing the rope from under the bench, Dani took a long step out of the boat and up onto the short pier. She tied the boat to a steel post her grandfather had sunk decades ago for this purpose. Dani wished she were still using his boat, but the wood had weathered and crumbled and Dani hadn't been able to keep it seaworthy. He would have been proud of the way she restored this one, though.

Dani rotated toward a brushing sound behind her but saw no one among the trees that marched in formation between the water and her cabin. She checked her knot before lifting her rod and reel in one hand and the trout in the other. It wasn't far to the cabin, and her grandparents had made sure a path through the trees would be lit by low-set solar-powered lights once the sun faded. On some days, like this one, Dani couldn't believe her good fortune that her two cousins still living in Hidden Falls had no interest in the cabin. She could have it to herself whenever she wanted.

Though slight, the noise she heard now was louder than the animals that made their habitat among the trees. Dani peered again but saw nothing but a leaf taking its autumnal journey toward the ground. She spent enough time alone in these woods to know the sound of another human wending through them. But she saw nothing.

She continued up the path and came to a log bench her grandfather had notched together to sit under a favorite tree and watch the lake.

A woman sat on the bench, and a few feet from her a man stood with a digital camera around his neck and an impressive zoom lens.

Nicole Sandquist and Ethan Jordan. Dani had been a couple of years ahead of them in school, but Quinn invited groups of students to his house often enough that everyone knew Ethan and Nicole lived in the next block.

Were they still together after all these years?

Ethan stood very still, capturing a view of the lake in fading light. Dani held her pose while he tinkered with the camera settings. Finally, he looked through the huge lens and snapped several pictures. Dani stepped toward the bench. Ethan was already setting up another shot.

"Looking for something?" Dani said.

Ethan lowered the camera away from his face and glanced at Nicole.

"Don't you recognize her?" Nicole popped up from the bench. "It's Danielle Roose."

"Just Dani." Dani shifted the grip on her rod. "You've come a long way in your taste in cameras since you worked on the yearbook."

"It's beautiful out here." Ethan raised the camera and pressed a button. The camera took a series of shots. "It always was."

Dani couldn't dispute that.

"I was always a little jealous your family had this place," he said.

"I'm the only one who comes out here now."

"Forgive us if we're trespassing." Nicole took several steps toward Dani. "We're looking for Quinn."

"He's not here."

"You've been out here all day?"

Dani nodded. "Since last night, actually. On the lake mostly."

"And you haven't seen or heard anything

unusual?"

"Besides the two of you turning up like a blast from the past? No." Until a few minutes ago, Dani hadn't spoken to a soul all day. Irritation stirred at the interruption to her peaceful retreat.

"We've been hiking all afternoon," Nicole said, "trying to remember the places Quinn liked to go."

"That makes sense, I guess," Dani conceded. "I thought he would come out here today, but he didn't."

Ethan was framing another shot, this time toward the woods.

"Aren't you wondering where he is?" Nicole burrowed both hands in her jeans pockets.

"Relax. He's fine."

"I thought you said you hadn't seen him." Ethan still peered through his camera.

"I haven't. But I know him pretty well these days." Dani reasoned she knew Quinn light-years better than these two did, acting as if they could swoop back into town and be his favorites again. "He needs some space. Being the center of attention at a banquet is not his thing."

Nicole ran one hand over an ear, taming her hair. "I don't think you've heard the latest."

"What's that?"

Ethan braced his camera with a hand under

the long lens. "He smashed his car into a tree."

Dani almost dropped her fish.

"It's true," Nicole said. "I saw it myself. But he wasn't there, so he must have wandered away on foot."

Dani carefully set her rod and reel on her grandfather's bench. "When you say 'smashed'. . ."

"The tree won the fight," Ethan said.

"Yes, that's true," Nicole said, "but he walked away. We just have to find him."

Dani picked up her gear. "What's with all the photos?"

"We may need to look at them more closely," Nicole said. "You know, something that might spark a memory of where else Quinn might go."

"I don't believe it," Dani said.

"I wish it weren't so."

"No, I mean I don't believe your theory."

Ethan took his camera off his neck. "Danielle —"

"Don't call me that." Dani waved her fish at him.

His phone played a few bars from *The Odd Couple* theme song, and he looked at the screen. "Sorry. I have to take this." Ethan put the phone to his ear and wandered away.

"Something tells me his phone rings a lot," Dani said.

Nicole nodded. "He's trying to get more

time off work so he won't have to leave before we find Quinn."

"What about you?"

"I brought a project with me. I can work from here for a few days."

"Quinn will turn up when he's ready." *And he wouldn't like you fussing over him.*

Nicole paced four steps and turned. "Maybe. But the accident raises a lot of questions."

"I haven't eaten all day," Dani said, "so you'll excuse me."

"Of course, but —"

"Stay as long as you like," Dani said, "but Ethan won't have much light left for his pictures."

She hadn't come to the lake to be chatty, and she wasn't going to get caught up in a web of false anxiety. The condition of Quinn's car didn't change anything.

Dani stepped from one stone in the path to the next without being tempted to turn her head and look back at Nicole and Ethan. They hadn't really been her friends in high school, and they didn't know Quinn now.

A *swoosh* made her freeze midstep and hold her breath. The sound was coming from the woods. Something was out there. Or someone.

9:28 p.m.

Lauren knocked on her aunt's front door.

Sylvia opened the door and a bath of yellow light spilled onto the porch. "Oh, Lauren. I'm sorry. I forgot."

"That's all right." Lauren followed Sylvia into the house. "If you're too tired, we don't have to do this tonight."

"No, I'm not tired. And you need to know where things stand with the fair." Sylvia swept her gray-speckled hair off her forehead.

"I'm still hoping for good news."

"We have to be prepared. You have a job to do."

"I'm mostly just trying to keep busy. If I sit around and think about things . . . well, you know."

"I'm sorry I kept you waiting. You walked all the way out here only to go back into town."

"I wanted to walk anyway." Lauren dropped her pepper spray into her bag. She had never needed it, but it was the only thing that gave her mother — and her aunt — peace of mind about her nocturnal wanderings.

"I got distracted," Sylvia said. "Nana and I decided she should stay here tonight."

"Nana is still here?"

"She's already been asleep for an hour and a half." Sylvia rescued a pair of shoes from under the ottoman.

"Is it all right to leave her?" Lauren wondered what Emma would do if she woke in a bedroom not her own.

"She won't rouse," Sylvia said, "and we won't be long. We'll take a quick look in the shop, and I'll run you home."

"Can I look in on her?"

"Of course. Just don't wake her."

"I won't." Lauren dropped her bag into an easy chair and padded down the hall to the guest room. She turned the knob with extra care and pushed gently on the door. As a girl, she had stayed in this room enough times herself to know precisely how long the door would stick before popping open and the degree of pressure needed to avoid a sudden sound.

Emma was turned on her left side, her face toward the dim light from the hall and one arm splayed across the quilt tucked over her torso. Thirty years earlier, Emma had hand-stitched the double wedding ring pattern. These days she was likely to say she had given up quilting because she ran out of scraps long ago. Lauren was grateful to have at her apartment both the quilt Emma made when Lauren was a baby and her grandmother's final creation, a tulip field in greens and yellows.

The day had been restless and wearing. Had Emma felt the tension Sylvia carried? If she had, she successfully released it when it was time to sleep. Her chest rose and fell in a gentle, unperturbed rhythm of a slumber Lauren envied. With slow steps, Lauren crossed from the door to the bed to give

Emma the butterfly kiss they had always shared, brushing her eyelashes across Emma's cheek three times.

When Lauren returned to the living room, she found Sylvia's feet clad and a light jacket over her shoulders.

"Ready?" Sylvia said.

Lauren picked up her bag, and they went out through the kitchen to Sylvia's red Ford Taurus.

"You know my offer to teach you to drive is open-ended." Sylvia closed the driver door and reached for her seat belt.

Lauren laughed. "If I learn to drive, people will think it even more odd that I prefer to walk or bike."

Sylvia smiled. They pulled out of the driveway in silence.

"Did Nana ever tell you the story she had on her mind this morning?" Lauren flipped up the visor, unnecessary in the nearly moonless night.

"She tried," Sylvia said. "It was disjointed, but it doesn't matter. I think focusing on the story was her way of trying to make sense of things. That's what we're all trying to do today, isn't it?"

"I suppose so."

"She just wanted someone to listen to her. And at least I did that much right today."

They were on the highway now. The turnoff to Main Street was only a mile away.

"So," Lauren said, "nothing new from Officer Elliott?"

Sylvia glanced over at her. "You do know that his thorough questioning was only because he wants to help Quinn as much as we do."

Lauren raised both hands under the lenses of her glasses and rubbed her eyes with her fingertips. "I can't believe this is happening."

"It's been a long day."

"This morning feels like another day. Last night feels like another year."

"With every ounce of mayoral authority I could muster, I firmly instructed Cooper to call me if he had the slightest movement on the case."

"The case," Lauren echoed. "I don't like talking about Quinn as a case."

"I know." Sylvia turned on her left signal and prepared for the maneuver.

"I've been wracking my brain all day trying to think what kind of emergency he could have had." Lauren's voice broke. "And then when I think how things went from bad to worse, I start to feel frantic."

Sylvia eased onto Main Street. Lauren tracked the rows of irregular lights and signs. This far out of downtown, the buildings were gas stations, repair shops, a lumberyard, a tackle shop — the kinds of businesses a community needed but not the sorts of structures with the charm of downtown.

"I have a set of devotional books you might want," Sylvia said, "and a set of candle stands. People always seem to be interested in nice picture frames, too. Maybe a clock."

"I appreciate your willingness to donate." Lauren lifted her heels in nervous tempo against the floor mat. "I don't want the silent auction to be ostentatious, but it might raise a little bit of money for the women's shelter in Birch Bend."

"We'll have a look around. I can always donate whatever you think will get a good contribution."

"I know you want to get home to Nana," Lauren said. "We'll make it quick."

Sylvia parked directly in front of the store on Main Street. On a Sunday evening, few businesses were open. Out of habit, Lauren glanced down the street toward the building where she lived.

In tandem they slammed their car doors. Sylvia put her key in the shop door and led the way in.

Lauren heard her aunt's gasp. "What is it?"

Sylvia grasped for the light switch, and the rank of fluorescent lights flickered on and began to buzz.

Lauren's stomach flipped. She liked to think she knew the store's arrangement nearly as well as Sylvia, but the disarray and breakage they faced now was so thorough it was impossible to discern what was missing. She fumbled for her phone and punched 911.

4
Unexpected Hero

Monday
8:30 a.m.

Side by side, Sylvia and Lauren stood on the sidewalk outside Waterfall Books and Gifts squinting into the sun's reflection against the display window. Yellow crime scene tape formed a giant X across the storefront.

"They won't even let you in?" Lauren said.

"My own store, and I'm denied entry." Sylvia rolled her shoulders, but the motion did nothing to release the tension that had built up overnight. "Did you get any sleep?"

"Not much." Lauren slid two fingers of each hand under her glasses to rub her eyes. "The police took two hundred pictures. What more do they need?"

Sylvia shrugged. "Fingerprints."

"It's a store," Lauren said. "Dozens of people are in and out all day, six days a week. Are they going to fingerprint everybody in Hidden Falls? What about all the tourists? Do they have a clue about how many items people pick up, even if they're just browsing?"

Sylvia turned her palms up at Lauren's tirade of frustration. "It's their show to run. I have to stay out of the way."

"They can't keep you closed beyond reason."

But who decides what's reasonable? Sylvia thought. Though images from last night still seared the backs of her eyes, she once again pressed her face against the glass to peer inside. The window display, featuring a rash of new novels, was undisturbed. Looking past it into the main gifts display, though, Sylvia saw the wreckage afresh. A heavy, solid five-shelf unit of clocks and figurines left no survivors when it tumbled. The book racks were bolted to the walls, but at least half of the volumes they held had been pulled from the shelves and tossed around in no pattern. Four paintings on the walls were slashed.

"Why didn't they just take whatever they were after?" Lauren said. "Why did they have to be so destructive?"

"We never know what's in somebody else's mind." Like Quinn's. What was going through his mind when he stepped off the backstage X where Sylvia emphatically told him to stand on Saturday night? And when he drove his car too fast around a bend in the road? Maybe amid the rage, the vandal had taken something from the store. Until Sylvia was allowed in to clean up and do a proper inventory, she couldn't be sure.

Behind them, footsteps on the sidewalk came to a halt. The image of Gavin Owens reflected in the store window.

"You're the headline of the breakfast rush," he said. "That yellow tape gets attention, considering how little we see of it around here. The sheriff must have pulled it out of a back closet."

Sylvia turned to face Gavin. "I hope you're telling people that if they saw anything suspicious last night they should call the sheriff."

"Either that or mind their own business. You want me to bring coffee or something to eat?"

"Thanks, but we're on our way to the sheriff's now." Sylvia hitched the strap of her purse over one shoulder.

"You're going to need a crew to help you clean up."

"Eventually."

"You let me know when. I'll make sure everybody gets lunch." Gavin gave a half salute and continued down the block to his café.

Sylvia looked at her watch. "We'd better get over there."

"After this," Lauren said, "I don't ever want to see the inside of the sheriff's department again."

Sylvia fell into the ambitious pace Lauren

set. "I had to call Lizzie Stanford and tell her not to come to work today." She'd had to explain, of course. Lizzie was a competent assistant at the shop, but she too easily jumped to conclusions. In this case, she would have worried she was losing her job if Sylvia didn't explain why the shop couldn't open. Everyone in town would know soon enough.

They had been spared spending half the night in the sheriff's office to complete the report on the break-in. As long as the store was secured, and because everything had been photographed, Cooper Elliott was satisfied they could leave the formal paperwork until the morning. The break-in had been through the back door, Cooper said. The lock on the door from the alley was intact, but scratches on the doorplate suggested someone who was not adept at picking locks had nevertheless succeeded.

It was an old lock. Everything on Main Street was ancient. Hidden Falls was one hundred and fifty years old, and Sylvia felt nearly that age herself. Even when she was young, she was never one to tolerate sleep-disturbed nights — and certainly not two in a row.

Quinn was her best friend, and he was missing.

The store was her livelihood, and it would take days to get up and running again.

And she was mayor of Hidden Falls. People wanted answers.

No one — so far — thought the burglary was related to Quinn's absence. Sylvia hoped they were right.

Lauren pulled open the oversized wooden door at the sheriff's office, and Sylvia stepped inside. For years she had been after the sheriff to come over from the Birch Bend station and figure out why the Hidden Falls building smelled distinctly musty, but he always countered that the task required a financial outlay his budget would not withstand. Maybe he was right and maybe he wasn't. Either way, Sylvia wrinkled her nose at the smell. She had no influence on the county budget.

A half wall divided the small waiting area, representing the public portion of the large room, from a quad of desks. Rarely were more than two desks occupied at the same time. Across the back were three small enclosed rooms with large windows looking inward and two jail cells that hadn't been used in years.

Lauren pointed to the room on the left end. "I was afraid that room right there was going to be my new home."

"Quite a downsize from your apartment." Sylvia flicked her gaze toward Lauren.

Beyond the half wall, Cooper sat at one of the desks, talking on the phone. Only one other person was on duty, and he seemed engrossed in waiting for the coffeepot to perk. Crime was small-time business in Hidden Falls.

Cooper waved them over while he finished his call.

"Let's get this over with," Lauren muttered.

They could get the report over with, at least. Then Sylvia was going to have to face the mess in the store and a fresh deluge of well-meaning phone calls. There was no telling what was waiting for her at her small office at Town Hall. Out of reflex, she felt in her jacket pocket for her phone, thinking to call Quinn and confide.

But of course she couldn't.

Cooper arranged two side chairs next to his desk. Sylvia was beginning to think the mustiness was baked into the fibers of the commercial upholstery.

"We just need to go over the basic facts for the report." Cooper clicked through several screens on his computer. "It's important that we're working with accurate information before we begin an investigation."

"Whatever you need to know." With reluctance, Sylvia sat in one of the chairs. Lauren took the other.

"So you weren't in the store at all after you closed up on Saturday?"

"That's right."

"And that was about six o'clock?"

"Yes."

Cooper tapped a few keys. "And you arrived at the shop around nine thirty Sunday night."

"That's correct."

"Were you on Main Street at all yesterday before that?"

Lauren broke in. "You asked us all this last night."

"I just want to be sure my report is right." Cooper was unflapped. "We're going to need to narrow the time down. What about after church yesterday?"

"I walked home," Lauren said, "but I didn't go past the shop."

"I drove straight to my house with my mother and didn't leave," Sylvia supplied. Cooper knew as well as anybody that next to nothing was open on Main Street on Sunday afternoon. Gavin opened the café for the diehards, and down the street Eat Right Here catered to the tourists looking for refreshment after coming in from the falls or the lake. But most people who ran small businesses six days a week valued a day off.

"But you went last night to look at possible donations to the silent auction at the health fair." Cooper's fingers were poised above the keyboard.

"That's right." Lauren's tone made clear her ongoing irritation.

"We're all tired," Sylvia said. "These last

couple of days have been stressful."

Cooper looked at Lauren. "This is the third time in a day and a half I've had the pleasure of meeting Lauren in the line of duty. I don't find that stressful in the least."

Sylvia froze her lips rather than let the corners turn up, because she suspected Lauren wasn't amused. Cooper Elliott wasn't doing a very good job flirting, Sylvia thought, but his intention cut through the heaviness of her mood.

The half door creaked on the short wall separating them from the waiting area. Sylvia looked up to see Jack Parker enter.

"Good morning, Jack," Cooper said. "If you're here on official business, I'll have to ask you to wait a few more minutes. And if not, well, I'm afraid I'm occupied."

"I'm here to offer my legal services." Jack buttoned his dark gray suit jacket. "I understand there have been several incidents in the last few hours."

"You can wait right over there." Cooper nodded at the bank of chairs by the door. "But seeing as how we don't have any suspects, I'm not sure who you're here to defend."

"No suspects?"

Sylvia followed Jack's eyes as they settled on Lauren. "This is not the place for your ambulance chasing, Jack."

"Yes, I can see it might be better to talk

with you in your office."

That was the last thing Sylvia wanted. "Lauren and I are just giving a report. I doubt we'll need your services, but we know where to reach you."

"Of course. And I'll see you tomorrow for our appointment." Jack laid a business card on the end of Cooper's desk before pivoting to depart.

Sylvia wished she didn't dislike Jack Parker so much. But she did.

Cooper clicked his mouse, and the printer on the end of his desk whirred. He pulled two sheets of paper off the tray and handed Sylvia a pen.

"Look it over and sign here," he said.

Sylvia signed.

"When can my aunt get back in her store?" If Lauren recognized Cooper's attention, she didn't let on.

"I have good news on that point," Cooper said. "We already had a forensics guy coming out to look at Quinn's car today. He can do the fingerprinting at the store as well. As soon as he gives the all clear, we can start cleaning up."

We.

Sylvia followed Cooper's gaze, which was still fixed on Lauren.

She stood up. "Good. I need to stop in at Town Hall. You can call me there or on my cell when he's through."

"I'll go with you." Lauren stood as well.

"I still need your signature, Lauren." Cooper slid the papers across the desk. "Can you look this over carefully, please?"

Sylvia patted her niece's arm. "Stay and see what else Cooper might need. I'll talk to you later."

Lauren's eyes widened into a glare. Sylvia allowed herself a close-lipped smile. Lauren had noticed after all.

10:46 a.m.

"I'll walk you out," he said.

Lauren looked from Officer Elliott to the door, a distance of about twenty feet. She hardly needed an escort. Before she could protest, though, Cooper was on his feet and cradled her elbow with one hand. The pressure was slight, and Lauren didn't resist. What was the point? They would be at the door within a few seconds.

"We have to stop meeting like this," Cooper said.

"Believe me, I plan to." She pushed her glasses up her nose. "I mean, well, the questions and reports. I could do without all that."

"That's what I mean, too." Cooper opened the door and stepped outside with her.

Lauren wondered just how red her face was at that moment. "So . . . you'll call if you find out anything."

"Your number's in the file."

"Right."

"Despite the circumstances," he said, "I'm glad we finally met officially. I've had my eye on you."

She looked at him in her peripheral vision. Lauren had been vaguely aware of Officer Cooper Elliott, but nothing more. She stayed on the right side of the law, and he came to church once every few weeks at best — and only to Sunday morning worship. Why should he have his eye on her?

"I hope you'll call soon." The blush rose through her neck immediately. "I mean — about my aunt's store. I hope the investigation turns up good news."

Lauren pivoted and put distance between herself and Cooper Elliott as rapidly as her feet would take her. Only when she was back on Main Street and turned the corner did she lean against a brick building to blow out her breath before inhaling again. She was twenty-eight and hadn't been on a real date in so long she was hard-pressed to say when it was. Obviously it hadn't led anywhere.

It didn't matter. Lauren wanted Cooper Elliott to find Quinn or find whoever wrecked Sylvia's store — preferably both. That's what mattered. In the meantime, Lauren wasn't going to sit around doing nothing. In trim khakis and a blue sweater, with stylish but sturdy walking shoes, her apparel was perfectly appropriate for the conversations she intended to have this morning. Sylvia was Quinn's best friend, but that didn't mean someone *else* didn't know a random bit of information that might explain what kind of emergency Quinn had.

Principal Miles Devon, for instance. Walking out to the high school wouldn't take more than twenty minutes.

Actual time in transit turned out to be seventeen minutes. Lauren headed straight for the administrative offices and presented herself to the secretary. It took another six minutes to talk her way into the principal's office.

"What do you hear from your parents?" Miles gestured to a chair where Lauren would be comfortable. "Fishing in Alaska! I can't imagine how beautiful that must be."

"I don't hear too much," Lauren said. "Phone reception is spotty up there." She hadn't come to discuss her parents' dream vacation. Lauren explained the purpose of her visit.

"I don't think I know anything relevant to your inquiry," Miles said when she finished.

"I asked a broad question." Lauren crossed her legs. The principal's office had been redecorated since her high school days — quite recently, Lauren thought. The table and chairs were still scratch-free. "What if I get more specific?"

"Such as?"

"You hired Quinn, right?"

"Yes. I don't see where you're going."

"How did you find him?"

"He applied. As I recall, we had an unexpected opening less than two weeks before the school year was due to start. His application came with an impeccable recommendation, and we did a couple of phone interviews. When everything checked out, I hired him."

"So you hadn't met him in person?"

"No, I hadn't." Miles cocked his head. "Lauren, where is this leading?"

"I just want to find Quinn." Lauren met his gaze. They weren't student and principal. Forty years apart in age, they both lived and worked in this town in high-profile positions that required some savvy in personal relationships.

"We all want to find him," Miles said.

"What he did was uncharacteristic. Aren't you curious what kind of emergency would make him behave like that? Something in his past?"

"Quinn was a very young man when he came to Hidden Falls, just a summer out of college. I don't suppose he had much personal history."

"You've known him a long time," Lauren said. "Surely over the years he must have said something about his past."

Miles leaned his chair back on two legs. "Quinn is one of the best teachers I've ever seen. Maybe even *the* best. And other than not taking students on field trips out of the county, he does everything I ask him to do. That's all I need from him."

"He's your friend, Mr. Devon."

"I like to think so. But he's always been reticent to talk about his background, and it isn't my business to push."

A knock on the door brought the principal's secretary into the office. "The Barkers are here for their appointment."

Lauren's stomach sank. "Can we talk more later?"

Miles lifted one shoulder. "I'm always glad to see you. But I don't know anything about Quinn before he came to Hidden Falls and very little about his personal life since then."

As she walked back toward downtown, Lauren made a series of phone calls that led her to the house where Sammie Dunavant was cleaning. Sammie met her out front with her hands still in yellow rubber gloves.

"I can't invite you into the house of one of my customers." Sammie pulled off the gloves.

"I understand." Lauren estimated the house was built in the 1950s, an era in between the early stages of downtown Hidden Falls and the upscale building patterns of the last several decades ringing the town's historic center. "I just want to ask some questions."

"Sure. Can't promise I'll know the answers." Sammie sat down on the front step.

"You clean house for Quinn, don't you?"

"I go in every other Tuesday and do the bathrooms, kitchen, and floors. He never asks for much more than that. It only takes a couple of hours."

"Were you there last Tuesday?"

"No. That was an off week."

"So you'll go tomorrow?"

"I always call to confirm." Sammie propped her elbows on her knees. "If he doesn't come home today, I won't go."

"I think," Lauren said slowly, "that something really serious must have happened to make Quinn leave."

"I heard they found his car," Sammie said.

"That only makes me more worried." Lauren adjusted her glasses. "I wondered if you ever saw something around Quinn's house that would be a clue to an emergency."

Sammie stood up quickly. "I'm running a business. I clean. I don't snoop."

"I'm sorry," Lauren said quickly. "I'm not implying anything. I'm just . . . you might have seen something and not known what it meant. A stack of papers, an envelope from out of town."

"I have to get back to work." Sammie pulled on one glove and put a hand on the doorknob. "I can't help you."

Sammie disappeared into the house. Lauren kicked a rock down the sidewalk. She was going to have to get better at this.

Lauren checked her phone three times as she scuffed her way back to town. No missed calls. No voice mails. No text messages. She might as well head to the church and try to get some work done. The details of the health fair loomed.

She walked past the Fall Shadows Café, and the wafting aroma exiting with a customer triggered Lauren's latent appetite. Dinner last night had seemed like too much bother, so she'd dismissed the thought. Neither had she eaten breakfast. Maybe a sandwich and coffee would help her think more clearly. Lauren retraced her last eight steps and entered the café.

When Gavin looked up, she said, "Can I get a tuna on wheat and a large coffee? To go, please."

"How'd it go at the sheriff's?" Gavin touched the buttons on his cash register screen to enter Lauren's order.

"Blessedly brief." She fished in her bag for her debit card.

"People are mighty curious."

"I can imagine." Lauren paused before continuing. "Gavin, Quinn comes in here a lot, doesn't he?"

"He's a regular." Gavin filled a "to go" cup with coffee and snapped on a lid.

"Maybe you know something about what kind of emergency he might have had." Lauren swiped her debit card. "Maybe he mentioned a friend in trouble? Some business he needed to take care of."

"Nope. Drinks his coffee black, eats eggs Benedict on Saturdays, says hello to everybody, thinks he knows how to spin a good pun."

"Well, he is pretty punny." Lauren cautiously sipped the coffee.

"Ha. He's an amateur. Just wait for the joke contest on Saturday."

12:59 p.m.

She was exiting the Fall Shadows Café with coffee in one hand and a small paper sack in the other when Jack spied Lauren. Based on the direction she headed, Our Savior Community Church was her likely destination. Her speed surprised him. Jack had to lengthen his stride to close the gap without looking like he was chasing her.

"I meant what I said." Beside her, Jack matched her pace on the sidewalk.

"What was that?" She didn't even turn her head to greet him.

"You might need legal help. You're bound to be a person of interest."

"What?" That got her attention. Her step faltered for half a second. "I'm not a suspect. I'm barely a witness."

"You never know."

"Jack," she said, "I'm sure you mean to be helpful, but I didn't see anything. I certainly didn't do anything to Quinn or my aunt's shop."

Jack put his hands in his pockets in a practiced casual mannerism and continued walking. "In my experience, it helps to be prepared even if you think it will never happen."

She stopped and turned to face him. "Officer Elliott gave me no reason to believe anything except that he needed my statement."

"Of course not. He's a competent officer. He knows he has to have a solid case before he moves forward." Jack smiled at Lauren's bewilderment. "But I can help you."

"I mean no offense, Jack," she said, "but Sylvia suggested you look elsewhere to build your practice, and I have to say I agree. I'm sure there are other people in Hidden Falls who need your services."

Jack pulled a card out of the inside breast pocket of his suit jacket and handed it to her. "In case you change your mind."

She stuck it in her bag. She didn't drop it into the cavernous abyss but tucked it neatly into a side pocket. He'd gotten to her. In another day, she'd be writing a retainer check. Jack couldn't bill at the hourly rate he'd charged in Atlanta or Memphis, but a high-profile client would be good for business.

Lauren glanced across the street. "There's

my aunt now. I want to catch her."

Jack didn't object. He simply followed.

"Any news?" Lauren asked.

Sylvia gripped her phone in one hand. "I just talked to Cooper. He says I can get back in the store in a couple of hours."

"That's good news," Lauren said. "The fingerprint guy came?"

Jack took one hand out of a pocket and buttoned his jacket again. "You'll want to be certain the police have been thorough. Once the scene is disturbed, you can't restore evidence."

Sylvia met his eyes. "I have confidence in Cooper Elliott."

"Well, I ran into Lauren and reiterated my offer to help, if there's anything I can do. If the criminal approach doesn't get you the results you need, we can always go the civil route."

"If we discover who did it, you mean."

"Right." Jack produced a cool smile.

"I don't think I need a lawyer," Sylvia said, "but I'm going to need help cleaning up the shop and getting it up and running."

"Sounds like a job for Dani Roose," Lauren said.

"I've been calling her." Sylvia waved her phone. "This could be several days' work. But —"

"Let me guess," Lauren said. "She's not answering her phones."

"I've left messages on both numbers. Multiple times."

"She's probably up at the lake." Lauren sipped her coffee.

"Ignoring your phone is an aggravating way to run a business." Sylvia reached for the sack in Lauren's hand. "I smell tuna."

"Take half." Lauren released the bag.

Jack watched the two of them move in synchronized familiarity. They were a lot alike. He could see the family resemblance in their features and gestures, even the timbre of their voices. Either one — preferably both — would make a great client. He would even be willing to handle mundane matters for them to build their confidence in him and be able to count them as clients.

"Why don't I drive out to the lake for you?" Jack turned his palms up and brightened his eyes. "Dani has a cabin, right?"

"Yes, but you don't have to go to that trouble," Sylvia said. "Dani will either call me back or I'll find someone else to do the work."

"It's no trouble," Jack said. "I would be happy to do it. I'll just go home and get my car."

He didn't wait for her to decline but reversed his direction and covered the blocks between downtown and his home. Getting on the mayor's good side would never be a lost effort. Smelling Lauren's tuna sandwich, though, made Jack hungry. At home he could grab a quick sandwich himself. As Jack let himself in the front door, the house felt empty.

"Gianna?"

No answer came. His wife's absence was not completely unexpected. She stayed on top of shopping and errands and every loose end while the kids were in school so she could be in the house when they came home. Gianna had been the same way when she worked as a paralegal, always anticipating the next step and finding order and logic where no one else did. Any attorney she was assigned to was lucky to have her. If Gianna were an employee, Jack could assign her to dig through the files in his office and be confident she would come up with something that would help build his business. As his wife, though, she would tell him he was wasting his time. So he flipped through the files on his own, pausing to read carefully if something out of the ordinary grabbed his attention. Quinn's disappearance two nights ago gave Jack a new trail to trace. When he figured out where Quinn had gone, Sylvia Alexander would be in his debt.

Jack was in the kitchen smearing mustard on two slices of dark rye bread when his wife and youngest daughter burst through the back door. Brooke was in tears, and Gianna's patience teetered. Her jaw was clamped shut in that way that meant one more wrong comment would break the dam.

Fresh sobs smashed over Brooke's face as she ran from the room.

Jack abandoned his sandwich in the making and looked at Gianna. "Did something happen at school?"

"She never made it to school." Gianna tugged off her jacket and tossed it over the back of a chair. "This morning I asked her to take Roxie out to do her business one last time, and she let her off the leash."

"So the puppy —"

"Is lost. And she ran in front of a car, which terrified Brooke. I heard the squeal of brakes myself. Apparently Roxie kept running and Brooke lost sight of her. We've been looking *all* morning. I'm glad you're home. It's your turn to do something now, Jack."

Jack wasn't sure what Gianna wanted him to do. Comfort Brooke? Promise another puppy? He resumed working on his sandwich, laying deli turkey on one slice of bread and positioning the other on top before picking it up.

"I'll talk to her," he said. "Then I have something on my schedule. I have to meet someone."

"Call whoever it is and reschedule." Gianna opened the fridge, stared for a few seconds, and closed the door without removing anything. "Your daughter needs you. Now is *not* the time to ignore her."

Jack bit into his sandwich. It was just a puppy. They'd only had her a few weeks, and he was sure they could get another one.

"I'm serious, Jack." Gianna fixed her eyes on his. "Brooke needs you, and I need you to take a shift looking for the dog. She'll be hysterical if you don't."

"Fine." Jack would take Brooke out looking for a few minutes, talk some sense into her, and get his day back on track. He carried his sandwich as he left the kitchen. Brooke was curled tightly on the couch, gripping the dog's leash and wiping tears.

"Come on," Jack said. "We'll go look a little longer."

"We have to look until we find Roxie." Brooke sat up. "Even if something really bad happened to her, I want to know."

Jack chewed. "Do you want something to eat first?"

"No. Every minute counts."

Jack swallowed. "Then let's go." He crammed the rest of the sandwich into his mouth.

"Where will we go?"

He had no thought. "Where do you think we should go? Which way did Roxie go?"

"She runs so fast." Brooke zipped her purple fleece-lined hoodie. "She must have thought it was a game."

"She probably saw a bird or a squirrel."

They stepped outside the front door.

"Maybe she'll come back." Brooke's voice trembled with hope. "Dogs do that sometimes, don't they?"

"Sometimes."

A gray-haired woman power walked toward them on the sidewalk. "Did you find your dog, Brooke?"

"No, Mrs. Winters. Not yet."

"I hope she turns up." Mrs. Winters charged on down her route.

"How do you know that lady?" Jack asked.

"She lives three doors over from us, Dad. She goes for a walk every day after breakfast and again after lunch."

Jack had hoped Brooke would not pick up that mannerism from Gianna, the tone that said, *You should know this.*

Brooke cupped her hands around her mouth. "Roxie! Roxie! Come here, girl!"

Jack scanned the view and saw no sign of the Airedale.

"We have to look in everybody's yards." Brooke started to march up a driveway.

"Whoa." Jack pulled her back with a hand on her shoulder. "That's trespassing."

"I just want to find my dog, Dad."

"I know. Let's knock on doors, and if someone is home, we'll ask permission to look around."

"And if no one's home?"

Jack hesitated. Brooke's eyes pleaded with

him to be a father, not an attorney. "Then we'll look really fast."

Thirty minutes, he thought. *Then she'll have to face facts.*

2:32 p.m.

"I just need a day or two." Speaking on the phone to her assistant, Nicole flipped a purple pen back and forth between her first two fingers. "I have my interview notes, and I can work on the rest of the research from here."

The knock at the door was the same rhythm Ethan had always used.

"Terry, I'll have to call you back," she said. Nicole set the phone down on the coffee table and crossed to open the front door. "Anything yet?"

"Nothing." Ethan stepped in and pulled his camera from around his neck. "I can't think where else to look."

"You want coffee?" Nicole picked up her empty mug and headed for the kitchen. "I broke down and bought some beans this morning."

Ethan followed her toward the coffeepot and reached into the cupboard where the mugs had always been. Earlier Nicole had discovered there weren't as many now. Her father had taken the favorites with him when he moved out of the house.

"How about you?" Ethan held his cup

under the stream of liquid Nicole poured. "What have you turned up?"

"Eerily little." Nicole filled her cup and leaned against the counter. "Oh, it didn't take long to find Quinn's name listed in property tax records and the school faculty. Those things are public records, but I didn't come up with anything else."

"No birth certificate? Military record?"

Nicole ran her finger around the rim of her mug. "Do you realize we don't even know his first name?"

"Ted. You know that."

"Is it Ted? Or is it Theodore? Theo? Or Edward? Or even Edwin?"

Ethan blew across his coffee. "I guess it could be any of those."

"And what about a middle initial? Or the city he was born in?"

Ethan shrugged.

"I need more to go on if I'm going to find someone who knows him outside of Hidden Falls." Nicole reached into a grocery sack, pulled out a bag of chips, and yanked it open. Along with the coffee beans, she'd also bought juice, milk, yogurt, apples, bananas, granola bars, and chocolate cupcakes. If she was going to stay in Hidden Falls for a couple of days, she would need something to eat.

"The mayor must know something," Ethan said.

"*We* should know something." Nicole put

four chips into her mouth. "Are you still leaving at midnight?"

"That's almost ten hours," Ethan said. "Anything could happen."

Or nothing could happen, and Ethan would still leave and Nicole would be on her own to track down Quinn.

"We can't waste time jabbering here." Nicole brushed crumbs from her hands. "I'm going to the newspaper office. What about you?"

"I don't know. I guess I'll find someplace else to look."

"Think fast," Nicole said. "Go back out to the lake. Ask around and see who might have seen him on Saturday — or even Friday night. Maybe he said something to somebody."

Ethan downed his coffee. "I'll try. Let's meet for dinner in town."

"Or sooner if you hear anything."

"Right."

They exited the house, got into their cars, and drove in separate directions. Nicole parked her Hyundai in front of the newspaper office where she had worked after school for her last two years of high school. She pulled open the door to the *Dispatch* and stepped inside, waiting for the old editor of the weekly to look up at her over his glasses.

"Why, it's my star beat reporter!" Marvin Stanford pushed his glasses all the way to the top of his now bald head and came out from around the desk to hug Nicole. "Is it true that you're working on a paper in St. Louis?"

"Your sources are impeccable, as always." Nicole kissed Marv's cheek. "Investigative reporting. Local political dirt, white-collar crime, that sort of thing. In between the juicy stories, I cover whatever they put me on."

"A good reporter digs up her own stories."

She waved a finger at him. "I learned that from you."

"What brings you into my humble establishment?"

"I'm returning to my roots. You were the first one to teach me about the trove of information a newspaper's archives can be."

"The paper is a hundred years old. Just how far back are you planning to go?"

"To the year Quinn came to town."

"Ah. So you're sleuthing for our mutual friend."

"It's been almost forty-eight hours." Nicole dropped her bag into a chair that hadn't moved from the spot she remembered. "We have to find him, Marv."

"My resources are your resources." He waved a hand around the room. "You know where everything is."

Nicole looked around. The arrangement looked the same — exactly the same. A wall of wide file cabinets divided the office area from the small printing press in the back.

While the view was nostalgic, it made Nicole's stomach sink. This was going to take a lot longer than she had allowed.

"I see the microfiche is still in the corner," she said.

Marv repositioned his glasses on his nose and looked over them. "You were hoping we had digitized, weren't you?"

"The thought had occurred to me."

"Sorry. Not that far back. Hidden Falls is still Hidden Falls, not the big city."

"It's no problem."

"No money. No time." Marv shuffled back to his desk chair. "Everybody wants us to live in the digital age, but they don't understand how expensive and time-consuming it is to get there."

"It's all right, Marv. It'll all come back to me."

"Anything in the last fifteen years is digital, but it's not on the web, so you'll have to use the computer here to search the database."

The dust on the machine told Nicole no one had hunted through microfiche files in quite some time. It wasn't even plugged in. She fished under the table for the cord and found the outlet before pushing the On button. While she waited for the *whirr* of the warming machine, Nicole tried to recall the last time she searched microfiche. It was at least five years ago, in a small Missouri town a lot like Hidden Falls.

In the meantime, Nicole started with the digital files. In high school she routinely tagged articles with key words or topics, never imagining that someday she might come back to use her own system. But she remembered it well enough to search quickly for articles mentioning Quinn. Once she found them, she would have to read every word of each one. A sentence or two used to fill out a column in the paper might now yield a clue she could chase down.

Announcements about school plays Quinn directed. A charity event to which he donated time. Quotes from students acknowledging the role Quinn played in their academic success. References to small speeches he gave at local events.

In other words, practically nothing.

Nicole turned to the microfiche and pulled the first reel from the year she knew Quinn moved to Hidden Falls. She had lost her touch and didn't control the speed of the reel at a consistent rate. Every time she spun past something without being able to read the headline, she backtracked. As the years moved forward toward the time Marv started keeping digital files and the ground Nicole had already covered, two things struck her.

Quinn was mentioned in small ways in plenty of articles, but the articles were never about Quinn himself. Considering how people in Hidden Falls felt about Quinn, this was a curious omission.

She raised her second question with Marv. "Why isn't there a single photo in the paper of Quinn?"

"If you look in the old files," Marv said, "you'll find some black-and-white prints. But Quinn would never let me use them."

"What do you mean, 'let' you?"

"Anytime I had a photographer at an event, I'd get a call from Quinn the next day asking me not to run the pictures. I used to argue with him about freedom of the press, but he was politely persistent. He didn't want his picture in the paper. Eventually I stopped shooting him."

Nicole leaned back in her chair. "That's odd."

"Did you ever notice he's not in the yearbook, either?"

"That can't be. They print photos of all the faculty."

Marv shook his head. "There are always a few who find themselves in a catchall category of 'not pictured.' Quinn is always in it."

"For more than thirty years? How can that be?"

"I'm just telling you the way it is." Marv's desk phone rang and he snatched it up. He spun his chair around.

Nicole could only hear Marv's side of the conversation, which consisted of a string of grunts and indefinite sounds, but the mention of Quinn's name urged her out of her chair to stand in front of Marv's desk.

He hung up the old phone and spun back around. "They found his glasses."

"Where?"

"In the glove compartment," Marv said. "They weren't even cracked."

Quinn had worn glasses for driving at night for as long as Nicole had known him. "But that means —"

"That's right. Quinn wasn't driving his car."

"But was he in it?"

"That's the question everybody's asking. If he was a passenger, then somebody out there knows something."

4:36 p.m.

Jack kept both hands on the steering wheel of his dated BMW, but he was watching his daughter more than he was looking for the puppy. They'd been at this for almost three hours, first on foot in their immediate neighborhood and then expanding the search radius in the car. His shoe barely touched the accelerator as they crawled down one side street after another. Brooke's window was down and she hung her head and arms outside its frame. Every few minutes she ducked her head inside to glance at the dashboard clock, and each time she looked a shade paler to Jack. Gianna spent the entire morning searching, and Jack the whole afternoon. He was beginning to wonder what the statistics were about finding lost puppies that had been missing for more than eight hours. Roxie could be trapped in a hole, spattered on the highway, or perfectly healthy and contentedly wandering the miles of woods along the river and around the lake. Or she might be safe in the arms of another child who thought God had overridden the will of parents and answered a prayer for a puppy.

"Roxie has her tags on, right?" Jack fished for some encouragement.

"Mom never lets me take the collar off." Brooke answered from outside the vehicle.

The BMW was moving so slowly that Jack figured Fred Flintstone could power it faster with his feet on the pavement. All afternoon Jack had tried to recall the conversations with Gianna about putting a chip in Roxie's shoulder that would identify her wherever she ended up. He hadn't been invested in the decision because he wasn't invested in the puppy.

"What about a chip?" he finally asked. "Did Mom get the chip?"

"Yes."

"That's good," he said. "You know that, right?"

Brooke nodded.

"If someone finds her, it will be easy to find us, too."

"Only if they want to find us." Brooke

rested her chin on her arms, filling the bottom rim of the open window. Jack could see only the back of her head.

He turned the corner into the next block. They were miles from their own neighborhood. Was it possible a three-month-old puppy could find her way home from this distance? He didn't know.

"Stop the car!" Brooke fumbled with the lock.

At the speed they were traveling, it didn't take much pressure on the brake to stop. Jack put the car in Park, and Brooke scrambled out. He didn't know what she'd seen, but he couldn't just sit in the car while his frantic thirteen-year-old hurtled down the street. Jack felt his age as he tried to keep up.

They came to a corner, and she stopped.

"What did you see?" Jack tried to catch his breath.

"It was Roxie. I'm sure of it. She ran this way, but now I've lost her." Brooke cupped her hands around her mouth to shout, "Roxie! Here, girl!"

Jack scanned the area but saw no movement to suggest the presence of a puppy. Maybe Brooke only saw what she hoped to see.

"There's an alley." Brooke began trotting down a narrow strip of road that led to garages behind several houses. When they emerged from the alley, a young man was getting out of a parked car.

"Did you see a puppy?" Brooke asked.

The man slammed his car door. "Brown?"

"Yes! And black. Was she brown and black?"

"I didn't notice the black." With his thumb he pushed a button on his clicker and his car doors locked. "That dog just about gave me a heart attack. Almost didn't see it in time."

"Thank you for not hitting my dog." Brooke rubbed her hands on her denim-clad thighs. "Did you see which way she went?"

He pointed, and Brooke began running down the street calling the dog's name.

Jack's stomach sickened at the thought of the puppy under the tire of a car or tossed to the roadside. There was no telling how many drivers that day had braked for a puppy oblivious to the danger. The imminent darkness would soon bring a stop to their search. Keeping an eye on Brooke, Jack pulled out his phone and hit Gianna's number on his contact list as he followed his daughter.

"Jack, where are you?"

"Some old neighborhood to the west. Brooke thinks she saw the dog."

"Then you're close."

"Maybe, maybe not. We don't know for sure it was Roxie, and she's nowhere in sight now." He moved his phone to the other ear. "It's going to get dark, Gianna. How realistic is it to keep looking?"

"She won't want to stop."

"I know. But we put a chip in the dog for a reason. Someone will call."

Gianna sighed into the phone. "I'll start dinner. You see if you can get Brooke to come home."

Gianna had the easier job, Jack thought as he dropped his phone back in his pocket and lengthened his stride to catch up with Brooke.

"Do you see her?" Jack scanned a block for the hundredth time that day.

"We have to knock on doors again." Brooke marched toward a house. If there was a system to her choice, Jack didn't discern it.

"We'll make posters," he said. "You can print them on the good photo printer, and I'll help you get them up first thing tomorrow."

Brooke halted. "Are you saying we should stop looking for Roxie?"

"Sweetheart, it's going to get dark. I think we have to call it a day."

"But we're so close! We can't stop now." Brooke punched her hands into the pockets of her hoodie and fixed her stare at her father's face.

Even if the dog Brooke spotted was the right puppy, she could be four blocks in any direction by now. It was like starting the search all over again.

"I just talked to Mom," Jack said. "She thinks we should come home, too."

"Fine. You go." Brooke turned away. "I'm

not leaving without Roxie."

"Brooke, come on. I promise we'll look again tomorrow."

Her face scrunched. "One more block. Please?"

Jack blew out his breath. "All right. But if no one has seen her in this block, we need to go home."

He stood on the sidewalk and watched her knock on one door, her shoulders raised in hope only to droop again as she turned around. At the second house, he saw the way she swallowed back her fear, but the woman in the door frame still shook her head. Jack held his tongue. He had promised her the whole block. She would be disappointed enough without being rushed.

In front of the third house, Jack took out his phone to look for an icon announcing a voice mail or text message.

"Dad!"

He glanced up. Brooke waved him up to the porch.

"They found a puppy. Just now!"

Jack raised his eyes to the middle-aged woman who stood on the step.

"That's right," the woman said. "I just put her in the garage. She wouldn't hold still long enough for me to get a look at her tags yet, but when I saw her in the yard, I knew a puppy that young and frisky had to be lost."

"Let's have a look," Jack said. It did sound

like Roxie.

The woman led the way to the detached garage, set slightly back from the house, and opened a side door. As soon as the light went on, the puppy pranced across the garage.

Brooke gathered the dog in her arms and buried her face in Roxie's fur. Jack had never seen such joy and relief on his daughter's face.

"Let's go home," Jack said to Brooke. He extended a hand to Roxie's rescuer. "Thank you. You've made my daughter very happy."

Brooke strapped herself into the backseat of the car where she could play with the puppy. Jack paused long enough to send Gianna a text.

FOUND ROXIE. COMING HOME.

As he drove, he glanced in the rearview mirror every few minutes. When he pulled into his own driveway, Gianna and Eva clambered down the front steps and out to the car, both eager to get their hands on the dog. Gianna looked over the heads of their girls and mouthed, "Thank you." Inside, Colin turned off the enormous flat screen and welcomed Roxie with her favorite green chew toy.

Jack closed the front door behind him and leaned against it. Not many things rallied his family. He was as guilty as any of his children of being antsy to be on his own, to be released from family togetherness and let his mind chase down what interested him. The moment before him now was the stuff of Christmas letters he rarely bothered to read, from people he barely knew anymore.

And he savored it in all its unfamiliarity.

He'd lost the entire afternoon. With a start, Jack remembered his promise to Sylvia Alexander to drive out to the lake and look for Dani Roose to see if she would help restore the mayor's bookshop. There seemed no point in driving out there now. Sylvia would have already tracked down Dani or made other arrangements. Whatever opportunity he'd seen that morning on the sidewalk with Sylvia and Lauren had evaporated.

A timer sounded in the kitchen, and Gianna left the puppy frolics to respond to whatever the noise meant. Jack followed her and went to the sink to wash his hands.

"Thank you." Gianna opened the oven and pulled out a casserole. "I don't know what we would have done with Brooke if you hadn't found the dog."

"Brooke found her." Jack snapped a paper towel off the roll and dried his hands. "I just did the driving."

"We have to stop talking about puppy training and actually find someone to help us." Gianna poked a fork into the hot dish and tasted the concoction. "I don't ever want to go through this again."

"I agree."

Gianna took a bagged salad out of the

refrigerator. "I'll make some calls first thing in the morning."

Jack opened a cupboard and removed five plates. He had watched deep dread roll through his youngest child that afternoon, but he'd also seen powerful resolve he'd never suspected she possessed.

5:03 p.m.

Sweat pooled at Liam Elliott's hairline all day, dripping onto the collar of his blue dress shirt and wicking through its fibers in a ring of perspiration that choked him every time he swallowed. He drank nine cups of coffee in a desperate effort to force his brain to see a way out. The piles on his desk, lugged from his apartment, were less haphazard now. He had sorted and re-sorted the papers and made his eyes bloodshot comparing printed numbers with the ones on the screen as he tried every display option available in the software.

An auditor would have to be an idiot not to conclude that Liam had embezzled seventy-three thousand dollars of his investors' money. Clearly the money was missing. Two thousand here. Four thousand there. Seven hundred from one of the smaller individual accounts, but seven thousand from a more robust company retirement fund. If he were going to embezzle, this would be the way to do it — amounts that would suggest an individual merely had an off quarter. The funds Liam managed were meant to yield well over the long term. An occasional dip didn't cause alarm.

But Liam hadn't done this.

And he couldn't take the chance that anyone would think he had — or reach the same suspicion that made more and more sense to him. Liam needed time. If he could get a couple of major investments, perhaps he could camouflage the records while he sorted out what really happened. The key was not to make things worse.

Liam clicked open his own account. For someone who made a living by impressing on people the necessity to plan for the future, he hadn't done a very good job for himself. It wasn't enough, and most of it was locked in at a disappointing rate for several more years anyway. If he invaded the joint wedding savings account he and Jessica held, he would have to come up with a credible explanation. He couldn't just tell her what he was doing.

Now *that* would make things worse. There wasn't nearly enough money in the account anyway.

He rummaged on his desk for the new-leads file he should have been working on all day. With his Bluetooth in place to free up his hands, he dialed a number.

"Hello, Mr. Plainfield. This is Liam Elliott, just following up on our conversation a couple of weeks ago."

"Oh, right. You're the investments guy."

Liam had learned long ago to push past the lukewarm reception he initially heard in people's voices. He wasn't trying to sell people something they didn't need, but a service to help them achieve an important financial goal.

"We only chatted for a few minutes," Liam said. "What evening would be convenient for me to meet with you and talk further?"

"I appreciate your interest, but we're not really in a position to consider investments right now."

"It doesn't take much each month to make a big difference down the line." Sweat trickled down the center of Liam's back.

"I know that's what they say," Dave Plainfield said, "but we're just not there."

"I'd be happy to look at your budget with you. Confidentially, of course. That's one of my free services. My clients are often surprised at how painless it is to find a few dollars."

"I have your card," Dave said. "When we're at a better place, I'll call you."

The call cut off. Liam would never hear from Dave Plainfield again. He dialed another number.

"Mrs. Gallagher? This is Liam Elliott at Midwest Answers. We met the other night at the banquet."

"Oh yes. That certainly was an evening none of us can forget. Have you heard anything about Quinn?"

"No, I'm afraid I haven't. I'm sure he'll turn up soon." *Not soon enough,* Liam thought. If Liam still believed he would be managing Quinn's money soon enough to camouflage the missing funds — at least temporarily — he wouldn't have called a long shot like the Gallaghers or toyed with a stolen bank account number. "Would it be more convenient for me to drop by on Wednesday or on Thursday to talk with you and your husband?"

A baby squalled in the background. Liam heard Raisa Gallagher shuffle across the room.

"I'll ask my husband to call you," she said. "He's the one who handles most of our financial matters."

"Of course. Can I leave my number?"

"Let me find a pencil."

Raisa shuffled around again. Liam heard the baby, probably on her hip now, cooing. He rattled off two phone numbers and hung up.

These two pitiful calls had been his best leads. He had meetings set up with three businesses to discuss retirement plans, but not for another two weeks. That could be too late.

Missing or not, Quinn was his best shot.

But if Jack Parker was right and Quinn was taken against his will, Quinn would be another dead end.

Liam rubbed his eyes, as if he could rub out the word that had crossed his mind. *Dead.* Even if Quinn didn't come on as a client, Liam certainly didn't want to imagine him dead.

There was still the mayor's office. Liam needed a way to jump over a lesser official who was the gatekeeper of town finances and have a direct conversation with Sylvia Alexander. He opened a new file on his computer to put together a fast proposal for what he could do for the town's investments if she gave him a chance.

He heard footsteps on the stairs leading to his second-floor office in one of the old downtown buildings and clicked open his calendar. Had he forgotten an appointment, someone coming by after work?

No.

That would have been too easy. Liam's entire day had been appointment-free, not a good sign in his line of work.

The footsteps stopped at the top of the stairs, outside Liam's office, rather than passing down the hall to one of the other businesses, perhaps to Jack Parker's office. His door opened.

Jessica entered and immediately leaned across the desk to offer a juicy kiss.

"Let's go to dinner." Her voice was velvet. "We can drive over to Birch Bend and get away from the doom and gloom around here."

"Doom and gloom?" Liam's head tilted back. What did Jessica know?

"About Quinn," she said. "Everywhere I go, it's all anyone is talking about. The world didn't spin off its axis."

Liam clicked the space bar on his keyboard, tempted to say he needed to spend the evening working. The truth was, he wasn't sure he could keep hiding from Jessica the reason for his recent intense burst of work. Just the day before yesterday he promised to spend more time with her.

Jessica came around the desk for a proper embrace and settled her lips on his again. She was still in the dress she wore to work, with no jacket. Liam could feel the heat of her skin under his hands at her waist.

She broke the kiss, cocked her head, and smiled. "You're not seriously going to tell me you have a better offer."

He swallowed and stepped back to turn off his computer.

6:34 p.m.

Nicole always preferred to run. Ethan wondered if she still did. As children, though he was stronger, Nicole was nimbler than Ethan. Inevitability this was her advantage.

Ethan had spent the afternoon hiking the sloped banks of the river, the shore circling the lake, the path cutting across the top of the falls. While he took advantage of the opportunity for photos, he also looked for people. Theoretically it was possible someone living closer to nature than to downtown would not have heard of Quinn's disappearance and perhaps had seen him and not thought it unusual. It was also conceivable that among the visitors who were a routine sight among the waterways was someone whose behavior made a Hidden Falls resident take pause.

It was a matter of asking the right questions, a diagnostic process that sifted symptoms until settling on the answer that made sense to pursue. Ethan did it every day. Now he had spent most of Monday doing the same thing around the lake.

He found a stump and sat down to read again the hours-long exchange of text messages with Nicole.

It had started when she wrote, THEY FOUND HIS GLASSES. QUINN WASN'T DRIVING.

FOUL PLAY NOW? he answered.

OFFICIALLY NO COMMENT.

WHAT'S UP WITH THIS COOPER DUDE?

NOT MUCH. TIGHT-LIPPED.

Ethan couldn't blame Cooper Elliott for withstanding the temptation to speculate. In itself, the fact that Quinn wasn't driving meant nothing about his volition at the moment of departure from the banquet hall. It did, however, increase the odds that someone out there had seen Quinn.

Unless . . .

Unless Quinn's disappearance and his car's disappearance were unrelated. Ethan turned the theory over in his mind, not quite persuaded. He scrolled to a later message.

I'M FINDING DIDDLY-SQUAT IN THE NEWSPAPER ARCHIVES.

NOTHING OUT HERE EITHER, he had answered. NO ONE I'VE RUN INTO HAS SEEN ANYTHING UNUSUAL.

I'LL GO TO BIRCH BEND TOMORROW.

WHAT'S THERE?

COUNTY CLERK'S OFFICE. YOU NEVER KNOW.

Ethan wasn't sure what Nicole could expect to find among mundane public records. And hadn't she said she already checked out property taxes and the like on the Internet? Since he would be rounding at the hospital in Columbus by the time Nicole woke up, he held his questions. Apparently her experience as a reporter told her public records could yield secrets — or at least bread crumbs on the trail — if she looked hard enough.

His phone sounded a text alert.

STILL UP FOR DINNER? Nicole's message said.

Ethan would need a few minutes to walk back to his car.

He thumbed, 7:30?

SEE YOU THERE.

Almost immediately the phone rang, and Ethan touched ANSWER on the screen. "Hansen, I don't want bad news."

"The chief is going out of town. It just came up a couple hours ago. Some convention where the hospital needs him to fill in at the last minute."

Ethan began striding along the path back to his car, aware that his pulse had just accelerated. "How long?"

"His admin says three days. They've culled the surgical schedule to emergencies only. You know how he is."

"Likes to see everything that goes on."

"Right."

"So he won't know if I'm not there," Ethan said.

"No guarantees. Right now you're not on the board for any procedures. Take your chances."

"I just might. Thanks, Hansen."

Ethan walked faster. He was still a good fifteen minutes from his Lexus. Leaves crunched under his feet as he hustled toward the orange span of the setting sun. His hand was on the driver's door handle when his phone rang again. Brinkman. Ethan answered.

"Just checking to see if you're on your way."

Ethan had no patience for the sneer he heard in Brinkman's tone. "Change of plans."

"No can do. We're busy."

"You're losing your edge, Brinkman." Ethan sat in the driver's seat and put the key in the ignition. "I know Gonzalez left town."

"Which makes us three surgeons short instead of two."

"We all know what happens to the surgical schedule when Gonzalez leaves town. You don't need me."

"People still get sick."

"I've got some stuff here to take care of. I'll let you know." Ethan ended the call before Brinkman could bluster further, sure that he had just bought himself an additional day in Hidden Falls.

Nicole had reached the restaurant first. Ethan saw her sitting at the table in the Main Street window of Eat Right Here. She always wanted to be where she could see what was going on, even in their tree house and comic book days. An amber light in a tightly woven wicker shade hung over her head, creating a dome of golden illumination that made Ethan sit in his parked car to savor the sight of Nicole studying the menu. The years shivered through him — a decade of lost years, and decades more ahead. As long as he didn't see Nicole, he'd persuaded himself the past was behind him. Now he wasn't so sure. Bound together again by Quinn even in his absence, Ethan and Nicole had sampled their old familiarity, the recognition of fleeting expression, the memories they alone would share if Quinn didn't come home.

And whether or not Quinn returned, when Ethan left Hidden Falls, this spell would break. How could it not? He pulled the key from the ignition, got out of his car, stowed his camera out of sight, and clicked the Lock button on his keychain. When he opened the door of the restaurant, Nicole looked up and smiled. Her dark hair hung loose around her face above a peach sweater.

Ethan slid into a chair across from her. "Good news. I'm not leaving tonight."

Her gasp delighted him.

"Can you go to Birch Bend with me tomorrow?" she said.

"I don't see why not."

Her face clouded over. "You know the trail is two days cold now."

Ethan accepted the menu the waiter handed him. "If it's any comfort, I don't think Quinn is sick. We've covered a lot of ground along the water and trails and talked to a lot of people who would've noticed him. Nothing."

"But you said he could have wandered off disoriented from the accident."

"That's when we assumed he was in the car in the first place."

"I know. Maybe he was, but maybe he

wasn't. But that makes even less sense." Nicole unwrapped the napkin around her flatware and put it in her lap. "I'm so frustrated — and worried."

Ethan laid down the menu that refused to come into focus. He would just ask for a hamburger and keep the decisions easy. He said, "I would lay odds that Quinn left town."

"But people in Birch Bend know to be looking for him. Somebody would have called Cooper Elliott."

"What if he went farther than Birch Bend?"

"You think that Quinn left on his own and that he left the *county*?"

"Stranger things have happened."

Nicole shook her head. "I've talked to Marv Stanford, Sylvia Alexander, Lauren Nock, and a dozen people I've run into in town. They all say Quinn still doesn't leave the county."

"No one can know *everything* another person does."

She pressed her lips together. Ethan could almost see the synapses firing in her brain as she tried to construct meaning from their conversation.

"His car is smashed," Nicole said, "and the bus stop is pretty far out on the highway. No trains run through Birch Bend after five o'clock on a Saturday night."

"I don't claim to have all the answers. We

have to be sure we're asking the right questions."

The waiter appeared. Ethan deferred to Nicole to order first and wasn't surprised when she made the same choice of a no-fuss burger and avoided protracted conversation about side dishes.

"What do you make of the break-in at the mayor's shop?" Ethan picked up his water glass, suddenly realizing how thirsty he was.

"Lauren seemed pretty rattled when I ran into her." Anticipating the arrival of a plate, Nicole arranged her fork on one side and knife and spoon on the other. "She's pretty close to Quinn these days, and now the news about her aunt's shop . . . It's a lot to take in, but she says she's trusting God. It turns out she walks as much as she does because that's how she prays."

Ethan flicked up his eyebrows. He'd left behind that way of looking at the world. Lauren's exercise would be good for her health, but praying wasn't going to find Quinn.

8:18 p.m.

Liam hardly ate any dinner, but he drank a lot of coffee.

Jessica, though, lingered over both *calamari alla piastra* and *insalata caprese* before the *ziti boscaliola* and *spinaci* arrived. Now she flipped the dessert card back and forth.

"I can't decide between the tiramisu or the

chocolate-filled cinnamon pumpkin roll."

"You can always get one to go," Liam said. Beneath the table, his left leg jiggled and he wasn't sure he could stop it even if he tried. When the server came by with a fresh pot of coffee, Liam nudged his cup to within her easy reach.

"Are you planning an all-nighter?" Jessica put a finger on the picture of the tiramisu.

If she had any idea how much coffee Liam had consumed before arriving at Vittorio's nearly two hours earlier, she didn't let on. But even what she had seen him drink was considerable this late in the evening.

"I had a rough day." Liam forced himself not to guzzle the steaming coffee.

"Then you should relax. If you weren't happy with what you ordered, you could still get something else. I'm in no hurry."

Clearly.

The evening was early still. Liam and Jessica never let their morning work schedules dictate how late they stayed out or what time either of them left the other's apartment. He couldn't simply suggest they cut off the meal without dessert.

"I haven't had much appetite the last couple of days," he said. "But you get whatever you want." In his mind, Liam was already adding up the expense of this meal. Perhaps if they had fewer extravagant dinners they would have saved enough for their wedding long before this.

He doubted it, though. The price tag on the wedding Jessica dreamed of seemed to increase with every conversation about it. She was up to seven bridesmaids, which meant he would have to find seven groomsmen. His brother, Cooper, could be best man, but that still left six vacancies. Hidden Falls had a dozen churches, and with the right decorator the banquet hall could be far more attractive than it had been for Quinn's dinner — but Jessica wouldn't hear of getting married in Hidden Falls. She had in mind the ballroom at a swanky Chicago hotel or a chartered boat with their vows coming at a precise moment on the middle of Lake Michigan, followed by an exquisite sit-down dinner. And considering the guest list she had in mind, the boat would have to be a high-end yacht.

Despite her expensive tastes, he loved her. No one made him feel the way she did.

Liam wanted to figure things out so he could live happily ever after and never speak the thoughts that overflowed his mind now. He watched her lips move and heard the silkiness of her tone against the controlled, dim hush of Vittorio's carefully appointed interior, but her words didn't register. The shirt collar he had perspired onto all day was uncomfortably dank, and he wished he had stopped by home to change before driving to Birch Bend.

Jessica rapped the table with the knuckles

of one hand. "Are you hearing a word I'm saying?"

"Sorry." Liam reached across the table and covered her hand with his. "I'm not very good company tonight."

"It's not Quinn, is it? Because you know it's not your responsibility to worry about him. He's a grown man."

A grown man whom no one could find. Liam could think of plenty to worry about. The jiggling rolled over to his other leg.

"That's only part of it," he said.

"Look, I don't want to be unsympathetic to your feelings for your old teacher or the pressure of your job, but you have to learn to take care of yourself, too. We never have fun anymore."

"Maybe I just need a good night's sleep." Liam picked up his coffee and moved it to the edge of the table, untouched. As it was, his heart was racing. Even an hour of sleep seemed a remote possibility.

"Maybe," she said. "Or maybe you just need some good news — and I'm not talking about Quinn."

"What, then?"

"I think we should set a date." She beamed.

Liam leaned across the table, studying her face. They'd been engaged for five years. His friends and business colleagues had stopped asking when they were getting married. Even Liam felt they were dragging things out beyond reason. Still, he knew what was in the wedding account, so he was surprised Jessica would bring up setting a date.

His stomach burned and acid traveled up his esophagus despite his lack of dinner. He could think of one possible explanation for why she would find this the right time.

The waiter returned with a polite inquiry about how they were enjoying their meal. Liam leaned back and unbuttoned his collar and loosened his tie while Jessica ordered both desserts with specific instructions that half of each one should be placed in a container that she would take with her.

"Are you surprised?" she said when the waiter left.

"A little, yes." More than a little.

"I've been saving money," she said. "I think we're within reach."

"The last time we talked about it, we seemed to be . . . quite a bit . . . short."

"Things change. For one thing, I got a raise I didn't tell you about. A promotion, really, with a lot more money."

He fumbled for words. "Why didn't you tell me?"

"I wanted to be sure it would work out. The position was on a trial basis. They promised if I wasn't happy I could have my old job back."

Jessica worked in accounting for a three-floor department store on Main Street. In the past, her chronic complaint was that she had no opportunity for advancement, though she was capable of far more complicated projects. Liam couldn't quite add this up to arrive at the explanation she offered.

"And are you happy?" he said.

"It's working out beautifully. I'm very happy and so are the owners."

"Well, then, I'm very happy for you."

"For *us*," she said. "There's nothing stopping us now. Let's get married on the second Saturday of April."

"A little chilly for a wedding on Lake Michigan."

She waved away his objection. "That was a passing fancy. Let's do the Chicago ballroom and all the trimmings."

"Maybe we should think about it a little more."

"That's an underwhelming response." Jessica tossed her napkin on the table. "Don't you want to get married?"

"Of course." Liam backpedaled as fast as he could. "I only meant we don't have to get attached to a date right this minute. Don't we need to call the venue to book a date? Check with the caterer's schedule? That sort of thing?"

Her face froze. "Maybe I'll get both those desserts to go."

When Liam dropped her off at her apartment a half hour later, he knew Jessica wouldn't suggest he come in. He leaned over in the car to kiss her before she got out, but she turned her cheek to him instead of her mouth.

During the silent drive from Birch Bend to Hidden Falls, Liam admitted to himself that he needed help. His cousin Dani was a whiz with computer software. He'd seen her make programs do things it never occurred to him to expect. If anyone could do what he needed — without being nosy — it was Dani. Could he trust her with the information that might emerge? That was the question.

Liam turned his car toward the end of town where Dani lived alone in a small house he would never choose. It wasn't late enough that she would have turned off the lights and gone to bed. He bypassed the broken doorbell and knocked on her front door. At the same time, he pulled out his phone and called her house number. After four rings, it rolled to voice mail. Liam dialed her cell phone number and took four steps to the right to peer through the slats of the old blinds. On the table in front of the window, he saw the glow of her ringing cell phone. It, too, rolled over to Dani's cryptic instructions about leaving a message. Liam didn't bother leaving messages because he knew Dani was never in a hurry to listen to them. No doubt she was out at that hut she called a cabin on the lake overlooking the falls.

9:07 p.m.

An evening that found all five Parkers at home was rare. The television was on, of course. Gianna's default station featured home-and-garden programs. She called it inspiration. Jack saw dollar signs in her eyes, like an old cartoon. Gianna was the one who wanted this house, and now she seemed intent on making it into something it was not. Colin had gone to his room, or he would have been flipping channels. The girls were content with HGTV in the background.

Eva was at the dining room table wrestling with geometry homework, and Gianna had just left the couch to help her. They learned with Colin to leave the math homework to Gianna — not that Jack had ever been around to help with Colin's homework. Jack sat in an easy chair with his feet on an ottoman and a legal thriller in his lap. He'd been reading the same novel for seven weeks and seriously considered either starting over or giving up. Brooke was on the couch ignoring the television and playing with the puppy. Roxie squirmed in Brooke's arms in a constant thrust toward freedom, but Brooke was equally determined not to release her.

"Brooke, it's time for your shower," Gianna called from the dining room.

"Not yet. I want to play with Roxie some more."

"Brooke."

Jack was glad not to be the object of the warning in Gianna's tone — this time.

"You'd better go," he said. "You've had a long day."

Gianna crossed the great room. "It's a school day tomorrow. And you're going to have makeup work."

"I know." Brooke snuggled the wriggling dog. "I'm just so glad Roxie is safe."

"Roxie is fine now." From behind the couch, Gianna nudged Brooke's shoulder. "But don't take her in the bathroom with you. She tears up the toilet paper."

Brooke stood up, still holding the dog. "Dad, will you hold Roxie while I'm in the shower?"

"Does she really need to be held?" Jack closed his book around one finger to mark his place.

"Please? I just want her to know how much we love her."

She's a dog, Jack thought. Trying to connect with his children confused him. Now he was supposed to be responsible for the emotional well-being of a three-month-old animal? The plea in his daughter's eyes was irresistible. Brooke loved the dog, and he loved Brooke.

"Okay." Jack set his book aside.

Brooke put the dog in his lap. To Jack's relief, Roxie sprawled across his thighs and put her head down on one knee.

"See, she likes you." Brooke stroked Roxie's permanently upright ear. "I'll be quick."

Her scampering approach to the stairs was convincing of her intention. Jack laid a hand on the puppy's back. Roxie blinked up at him and wagged her tail. Jack noticed the line of color change, from brown to black, across her forehead that he had never paid attention to before. He moved his hand to scratch under Roxie's neck. If they had to have a puppy, this one would do.

"She probably should go out," Gianna said. "You'd better take her now. Brooke will be nervous about going out with her after what happened this morning."

Jack hadn't taken a dog out in his life. Ever. "She has a leash, doesn't she?"

"Of course she has a leash. It's hanging in the mudroom."

Jack carried the dog through the kitchen to the mudroom, found the leash, and attached it to Roxie's collar. They stepped out into the backyard, and she immediately did her business. At the sound of a squirrel in the bushes, Roxie strained against the leash. Jack could see how easily she might have run off. He could already hear Gianna's voice in his head saying they were going to have to get a new gate in the back so the dog couldn't get out.

Inside again, Jack heard the shower shut off. Brooke had kept her word to be quick. A moment later, the old house creaked with her footsteps in the hall. Jack hung up the leash, and Roxie shook herself. Why dogs did that eluded Jack. He picked up the puppy, wondering how long it would take for Brooke to get some clothes on. Pajamas, probably.

Jack walked past Gianna and Eva still at work on the geometry. From the foot of the stairs, he heard movement in Brooke's room and began to climb the stairs, stroking Roxie's head all the way up.

He knocked. "Brooke?"

Brooke wore gray sweatpants and a faded pink T-shirt, an ensemble that passed for sleepwear. Her long hair, unbrushed, still dripped, but she immediately took the dog into her arms.

"Will you come in, Dad?" Brooke said. "I want to talk to you about something."

Jack looked in the room, wondering just where he was supposed to put his feet among the wall-to-wall clothing and towels. No wonder Gianna preferred to pull the kids' doors closed when she walked past them.

Brooke shoved a stack of DVDs away from the corner of the bed. "You can sit here."

"Okay." Jack sat tenuously and then scooted back for broader support. "What's on your mind?"

"Roxie."

He should have known that. "Mom and I have already talked about finding someone to help us train the dog."

"I want to be the one."

"The one what?"

"The one who trains Roxie." Brooke closed the door, let the dog loose, and picked up a hairbrush. That she knew where to find it astounded Jack. Roxie sniffed around in the bed before burrowing between the sheets and blankets.

"I suppose we'll all have to learn more about puppies," he said, though he hoped he would be at the bottom of the list of people expected to control the family pet.

Brooke tugged the brush through her tangled hair, spraying water on Jack with the motion.

"I was the one who lost Roxie," Brooke said. "I don't ever want it to be my fault again."

Jack watched Brooke with the brush and then moved his eyes toward the lump rooting around in her bed.

"I don't think it was anybody's fault," he said. "Dogs get lost every day."

"Not *my* dog," she said. "I should have known better than to let her be outside without a leash."

"I didn't hear anyone blaming you," Jack said. "Everyone was just glad to have Roxie back."

"I blame myself." Brooke dropped the brush back into the sea of clothing she had fished it from. "If something happens to

Roxie, I don't ever want it to be my fault again. So I want the job of training Roxie. I want to be sure she will obey me."

As his daughter sank onto her bed, Jack wondered why Brooke hadn't chosen to have this conversation with her mother. This was foreign territory for him. A few hours ago, Brooke was a little girl frightened she would never find her puppy. Now she was asking for considerable responsibility. Was being thirteen as confusing to her as it was for him to have his youngest child reach this stage? Jack was clueless about whether he should agree to the arrangement. Gianna would know what to say.

"Sometimes things happen," he said, "like puppies running after a bird, and it's not anyone's fault."

"That doesn't mean I shouldn't take responsibility to make sure it never happens again."

"Sometimes accidents can't be prevented."

"I know." Brooke pulled on the blankets to expose Roxie, whose tail wagged. "But I'm the one who begged for a puppy."

Jack hadn't known that. He just knew that one day they had a dog, and everyone except him seemed attached to her within the first twelve seconds.

"You've been through the wringer today," he said. "Tomorrow will be better."

"I'm serious." Brooke took the dog into her

lap and pulled the bedding up over her bare feet. "I want to find a trainer who doesn't believe in hurting dogs to make them obey, and I want to go to all the training classes."

"We'll have to see who we can find."

"Talk to Mom, okay?" Brooke's eyes pleaded again. "Make her understand that I want to do this. I don't want her to sign up for something while I'm at school."

Jack nodded. "I'll talk to her." He wasn't sure how much weight his opinion would have, but he could broach the topic with Gianna.

"The other thing I want to say," Brooke said, "is thank you for helping me find Roxie. I know you wanted to come home and you probably have cases to work on or something. You're my hero. So thanks."

Jack squeezed her toes through the bedding to buy himself time to swallow the lump in his throat and breathe. "You're welcome. I learned some things about you today."

"You did?"

"I did. You're determined when something is important to you. You don't give up."

"Mom says I'm stubborn."

Jack chuckled. "She says that about me, too."

"I'd be proud to be like you."

Jack's chest warmed. It had never occurred to him that one of his children would ever speak that sentence. "Maybe one of these days we can find something else to do together that doesn't involve a puppy crisis."

"Really? Can we?"

Brooke might be his first step, Jack thought. He had missed so much of her childhood with his self-absorption. He disappointed Gianna, and Colin and Eva had already moved into the stage of adolescence when they wouldn't admit to needing a father. But Brooke was still on the brink.

"Absolutely," he said.

"I want to help with the health fair on Saturday. They need face painters, and I'm pretty sure I can do that. Maybe you can come with me."

"Face painting it is, then."

"I'll call Lauren tomorrow."

The broad grin on his baby's face redeemed every moment of the frustrating afternoon. Jack stood up to kiss her on the forehead, something he hadn't done for years.

9:42 p.m.

Dani pulled on the oars with an urgency she had felt only a handful of times on the waters of Whisper Lake. Being on the lake after dark didn't frighten her. Night fishing was a lifelong habit, and Dani knew the pattern of lights along the shore that would guide her safely to the dock when she was ready. Sometimes on the weekend, when he didn't have to be at school early the next morning,

Quinn came with her and they stayed out as long as they felt like it. They would talk or not talk. It didn't matter. The water would lap against the swaying boat, and every now and then one of them would cast a fresh line under the stars.

But on this night, Dani's feet were getting wet. The boat was taking on water.

She latched the oars in place, reached behind her for a pail, and bailed for a few minutes. Water was not accumulating rapidly enough to fill the pail quickly, but neither was the level subsiding. It seemed to invade the boat at the same rate Dani could dump it out. She pulled out the oars again and rowed faster. Land was her only goal at this point. Though she could still see the shadows of her own short dock and the solar lights that had come on outside the cabin, it wasn't her best bet.

At intervals of decreasing length, Dani alternated between bailing and rowing. Despite her efforts, the boat was drifting and deepening.

Whisper Lake was a gentle body of water, but it was fed by a small river and dumped over the Hidden Falls rock formation for which the town was named.

Dani's focus shifted from the familiar lights on her side of the lake to the nearest point she might find land. She couldn't afford to lose her sense of direction in the dark. The sky of the nearly moonless night would be no help.

She bailed.

She rowed.

And she was coming out on the losing side of the equation.

Dani was a stickler about water safety. Her grandfather had refused to let her step foot in a boat the first time without hands-on safety lessons. Every time they went out together — *every* time — he insisted they visually inspect the boat and all its gear. Dani had done this yesterday and again this morning, and she'd seen nothing that alarmed her, nothing to suggest the boat wasn't watertight.

The water climbed above her ankles. Dani could see the widening hole now, as if it had been drilled and a plug was easing out. Dani released the oars to bail furiously. The pail filled as quickly as she dipped it into the bottom of the boat. Water was coming in faster.

As the rate of drift increased, Dani stared into the darkness once again to hang on to her bearings. Under the lapping sounds of the lake, Dani also heard the rush of moving water. The boat was headed toward the falls. Dani dropped the pail, ignoring the splash it created inside the boat, and reached into the storage space under the bench for a life jacket. She'd had to prove she could swim a quarter of a mile before her grandfather would even let her get in a boat without wearing a life jacket. Dani hadn't used one in years, at least a decade, but this wasn't the time to debate the necessity. She slipped her arms through the openings, pulled the straps together, and double-checked to be sure they latched completely.

Then she gripped the sides of the rowboat and sat as still as she could to judge the shifting sounds and sensations. Dani could neither bail nor row fast enough to avoid the impending catastrophe. Either the boat would sink or it would go over the falls.

The falls were not huge, but they were craggy. The boat would never withstand being lifted into the air for a terrifying moment before slamming against the rocks and dropping into the spot where the river that fed the lake continued its course. It wouldn't matter that the river didn't amount to much in that place. The fall, rather than the landing, would destroy the boat.

Dani didn't intend to be in the boat when that happened, but if she didn't get out soon the current would carry her toward the falls, boat or no boat. She fumbled for her water bottle and guzzled its contents.

Then she stood in the boat and, with water halfway up to her knees, kicked off her shoes before diving over the side.

She swam hard toward the only spot on the lake's shore where she could still see lights, not daring to stop and tread water lest she forfeit even a foot of the progress she made.

Breathe. Stroke. Breathe. Stroke. Breathe. Stroke.

Only when the tug of the water subsided did Dani pause to assess her bearings, and only for two or three seconds at a time.

Breathe. Stroke. Breathe. Stroke. Breathe. Stroke.

The light on the shore brightened and enlarged steadily until Dani believed she was close enough to feel for the bottom of the lake with her feet. She stood and turned toward the place where she had left her boat, not knowing whether it had yet tumbled over the falls but certain of its destiny. Rapidly exchanging air in her lungs, Dani half walked and half swam to the edge of the water. She was a long way from her cabin, but at least she was on solid ground and no longer feared becoming disoriented about which direction to go.

Somebody had tampered with her boat. The hole that grew into this disastrous hazard was deliberate — and recent.

Sopping wet, Dani pulled herself upright and began the rugged walk back to her cabin. Her chest still heaved as she twisted her shirttail to wring it out. The night was bottomless by the time Dani, shivering, rounded the final curve and saw the cabin.

Something moved in the woods beyond her.

"Who's there?"

Silence.

"Answer me!"

The ripple through the trees betrayed movement.

Dani filled her lungs. "I will find you!"

5
THE MAYOR'S QUANDARY

Tuesday
7:06 a.m.

Dani Roose turned over in bed, shoving against the weight of four quilts. The fire in the cabin had gone cold during the night, sometime after Dani's teeth stopped clacking and she let go of her exhausted fury long enough to sleep a few hours. Behind her closed eyes now, she saw the rising water in the bottom of her boat and the shape of the hole that permitted its entry.

Her boat.

It was only a rowboat, but Dani had spent months of her spare time restoring it, and she couldn't afford to replace it.

Not to mention her rage that someone had endangered her life.

Dani gripped all four quilts in her left fist and threw them off in one harsh gesture. The lake-drenched clothes she had peeled off last night still hung damp over a rack in front of the fireplace, but she had other jeans and sweaters in the battered armoire her grandmother had stored at the cabin four decades ago. She flung the fleece pants and sweatshirt she slept in onto the rumpled bed and yanked on fresh clothes. Not bothering with a brush, she moved through the movements of daily habit and rapidly braided her waist-length, silky black hair.

In less than nine minutes, Dani was in her Jeep and gunning the motor. Ethan Jordan never liked his parents much even in high school, so Dani's hunch told her he'd checked into the old motel across the lake. He and Nicole Sandquist were poking around the lake Sunday afternoon, and Ethan was back on Monday afternoon, just yesterday. Chances were he hadn't left town yet. Dani should have thought of it last night. The motel was no farther than her cabin was from the spot where she swam ashore, just in the opposite direction. She accelerated along the low bridge at the top of the falls and whizzed past the parking lot where tourists left their cars while they explored that end of the lake.

Dani leaned into the lobby door at the motel, rousing the overnight clerk from the chair where he had nodded off to the drone of a television behind the desk.

"Which room is Ethan Jordan registered in?"

The clerk, a gangly young man, unfolded himself from his chair. "The owner doesn't like me to give out that kind of information."

"So he is registered here."

"Didn't say that."

"Fine. Then call his room, please."

The clerk clicked a few keys on the computer. "No can do."

"You don't know how to use a phone?"

"Dr. Jordan has a DO NOT DISTURB until nine o'clock." He laughed. "Must have had some night."

"Whatever. Go back to sleep."

Dani didn't need his help. It wasn't rocket science to look for a car with Ohio plates that seemed like a surgeon would drive. It was a one-story motel. Paying guests parked right outside their rooms. She strolled the parking lot across the front of the building, down one side, and around a back corner.

There it was. A black Lexus with Ohio plates.

Dani pounded on the door. She didn't hear a voice calling out within a few seconds, so she pounded again. This time shuffling answered her call. Someone — Ethan, presumably — knocked against a piece of furniture, and after about half a minute, he opened the door.

"I need to see your pictures," Dani said, "the ones you've been taking the last couple of days."

Shirtless and wearing plaid flannel lounge pants, Ethan rubbed his eyes and ran a hand through unkempt hair. He really had still been asleep.

"What are you doing here?" He stood with one arm on each side of the door frame, oozing irritation. "I told the front desk I didn't want to be disturbed."

Dani ducked under one arm and pushed past him. "Where's the camera?"

Ethan grabbed her arm. "You can't just barge in here and go through my stuff."

She shook him off. "Fine. Whatever. But I need to see those pictures. Somebody vandalized my boat. I nearly went over the falls, and you might have a picture of the perp."

"The 'perp'?"

"What, you think I don't watch crime shows?"

"I'll tell you what," Ethan said. "There's a diner just down the road. Wait for me there."

"How do I know you're not blowing me off so you can go back to bed?"

"You don't. I recommend the skillet omelets."

"I know all about their skillet omelets." Dani pivoted toward the door. "Bring a laptop, too."

She didn't believe anybody traveled without at least a decent tablet, but Ethan Jordan thought himself a photographer. He'd have a laptop, and it wouldn't be a dinky thirteen-inch screen, either.

Once she was back in her Jeep parked

outside the lobby entrance, Dani drove around the building to be sure she saw light through the drapes of Ethan's room. She'd drag him out of bed a hundred times if that's what it took to make him understand she meant business.

The diner was nearly deserted, which didn't surprise Dani at seven thirty on a Tuesday morning. She preferred to make her own omelets over a fire at the cabin, but occasionally she went down the road when she wanted to fill a thermos with coffee to take out in the boat or down a trail.

Quinn hated the diner's coffee, but Dani's standard response to his objection was for him to bring his own. He scowled at her every time, but it stopped his protesting.

Dani judged Ethan to be a meat eater and ordered him a skillet omelet with extra ham, onions, and green peppers with hash browns on the side. Waiting for him to read the menu would only waste time. She was halfway through the first pot of coffee when Ethan showed up, showered and shaved.

Dani turned his mug open side up and poured. "Took your sweet time."

"Look," Ethan said, "I'm sorry about your boat, but I didn't mess with it, so back off."

"Let's just look at the pictures."

"I've taken close to three hundred," he said. "Mostly landscapes. It's absurd to think you'll see anything."

"Is that what you tell your patients when you scan their brains? That it's not worth looking?"

Ethan set his camera on the table. "I haven't even imported them yet."

Dani rolled her eyes. "That's why I told you to bring the laptop."

"Can I order breakfast first?"

"Done. You took so long you're lucky it's not already cold."

"Look, Danielle —"

"Dani."

"Look, Dani, I'm here. I brought my camera and computer. Clearly I'm going to cooperate, so put on your party face."

"Just hook things up." She crossed her arms across her chest. "I want to see every single frame."

Their skillets arrived. Impatient with Ethan's pace and detailed interest in his breakfast, Dani swiveled the computer toward her and picked up his camera. She'd accurately assessed the age and models of the devices and correctly concluded that connecting them would require a cord — and now wasted no time finding the ports and spurring communication.

"Hey," Ethan said as he took a bite, "don't snoop around on my hard drive."

"Don't flatter yourself."

"Are you sure you know what you're doing?"

Dani deadpanned. She already had the photos importing from camera to computer and took advantage of the slow processing speed of his laptop to stab her omelet and tear off a piece of a biscuit. Did he have any idea how behind the times his technology was? For the sake of his patients, she hoped he didn't practice medicine this far back into the dark ages.

"If you want to update your computer, I can give you some tips," she said.

"I thought you did odd jobs." Ethan slurped his coffee.

"Nothing odder than thinking like a computer."

"Computers are supposed to think like people."

"If you only had a Mac," Dani said. "At least you have decent photo software."

Ethan glared at her. "What exactly are you looking for?"

"I'll know it when I see it." Dani clicked through several dozen photos before pausing to capture a small section of an image and enlarge it. She leaned toward the screen to study the result.

"What?" Ethan said. "Why are you stopping?"

"There's a person. A man." Dani turned the laptop toward Ethan. "Do you recognize this guy?"

Ethan looked carefully enough to persuade

Dani he was at least trying to be helpful. Somebody trained to read X-rays and scans ought to be able to see what she saw.

"No," he said. "Should I? You can hardly tell it's a person. It's just a shape in the trees."

He probably said that about tumors. "It's a person, all right."

"You think it might be the person who wrecked your boat?" Ethan scooped hash browns into his mouth. "What if it's somebody who had something to do with Quinn's disappearance?"

"You all need to relax and give Quinn some space." She was getting tired of stating the obvious. These people were like a brick wall. Dani clicked the next photo, another shot of the same scene. "He does sort of look like the guy who visits Quinn."

Ethan dropped his fork. "A guy visits Quinn?"

Dani shrugged. "About once a year, usually in the late fall. They meet out on the lake and pretend to fish, but they never come back with anything."

"How long has this been going on?"

"Don't know. It's been the same dude for about fifteen years. Before that I was too young to notice."

"What does Quinn say when you ask him about it?"

"Why would I ask him? It's not my business. If he wants to borrow my boat, I trust him."

"Dani," Ethan said, "this could mean something. Who is this guy?"

"I told you, I don't know." She enlarged another segment of a photo. "Besides, I don't think this is Quinn's friend after all. He's not old enough."

Dani opened up her own Dropbox account and moved copies of twenty photos to it. She would enhance them later. This might not be Quinn's friend, but it could be her vandal. She needed a better look at his face.

9:16 a.m.

Sylvia Alexander wished she had dropped a charging cord for her cell phone into her purse that morning. She had a feeling she was going to need it. The phone, sitting squarely in its holder affixed to the dash in her car, rang and she reached to push ANSWER and SPEAKER.

"Good morning, Marianne," she said.

"I wish it were a good morning, Mayor," her assistant at Town Hall responded. "I'm just calling to give you a heads-up that things are already crazy around here."

Sylvia thought she'd done a reasonable job calming everyone the day before. Yes, Quinn was still missing, and yes, her shop had been vandalized, but the sheriff's department was on top of both situations.

"We need to continue to communicate our confidence that the proper authorities will lead the search for Quinn and my store will be open again soon."

"No, Mayor, it's not that. Something else happened."

Sylvia pulled out of her subdivision and onto the highway. "I didn't get a call about anything else."

"Someone just called Cooper Elliott a few minutes ago. It's about Dani's boat."

Sylvia clenched the knuckles of both hands around the steering wheel. "What about Dani's boat?"

"George Kopp found it at the bottom of the falls this morning. Or at least he found pieces of it. He's sure it was Dani's because of the green stripe. She painted it that way herself."

"Back up," Sylvia said. The boat didn't matter. "Is Dani all right?"

"George didn't see her. He went to her cabin, but she wasn't there, and she's not at her house in town, either. That's why he called the sheriff."

Sylvia refused to panic. When she wasn't fishing, Dani often hiked, or someone could have called her to fix a broken pipe. Not being able to reach Dani immediately meant precisely nothing.

"Keep trying to call her, will you?" Sylvia said.

"I'll try, but what should I do about all the people here to see you?"

"I only have one appointment this morning." Jack Parker was due in at about ten. After that meeting — which Sylvia hoped would be blessedly short — she planned to spend the day cleaning up the shop, whether or not she got hold of Dani to help. Dressed in jeans and a cabled sweater Quinn had given her for her birthday years ago, she wanted to feel close to him today.

"I keep telling everybody that," Marianne said. "They all say they *have* to talk to you."

Sylvia blew out her breath. "I'm almost there. I need to call Lizzie before I come in."

She ended the call and at the next stop sign pushed Lizzie Stanford's number on her speed dial.

"I'm going to be a little later than I thought." Sylvia spoke with practiced calm to Lizzie's voice mail. "You can either go in by yourself and get started on cleanup or wait for me later. I'll call when I'm on my way."

Lizzie would prefer to wait, but Sylvia always liked to give her the option to take initiative.

At the edge of town, Sylvia turned off of Main Street and steered toward the street two blocks south where Town Hall was situated. The two-story limestone building was compact but pillared in a manner no doubt meant to make an authoritative statement seventy-five years ago. It housed the chamber of commerce, the mayor's office, the town council chambers, and the Hidden Falls Historical Society. Because it was two blocks off of Main Street and not an immediate neighbor to any business more exciting than the mortuary, normally Town Hall was a quiet place. Governing a town of ten thousand people wasn't time-consuming. The mayor didn't even receive a stipend worth accepting, and the administrative assistant only worked three hours each morning.

Today, though, people loitered on the sidewalk. They ought to have been tending their own businesses or getting on with their errands. Sylvia parked her car, knowing she had approximately twelve seconds before someone would realize she had arrived.

It was Betty Pullman who spotted her first. She lurched from her huddle outside Town Hall and toward Sylvia.

"I always thought Hidden Falls was a safe place to live," Betty said. "I'm starting to wonder if we ought to move to Birch Bend."

Sylvia sidestepped this trap. She wasn't going to advise anyone on where they should live or why. If she pointed out that Birch Bend was a good deal larger than Hidden Falls and closer to the interstate, both factors that likely increased exposure to crime, she would only further frighten Betty.

"Good morning, Betty." Sylvia adjusted her

grasp on the small brown briefcase she carried back and forth to Town Hall. For the most part, she kept important active documents in her possession.

"Have you heard from Dani Roose?" Betty stood between Sylvia and the group lurking on the steps of Town Hall.

"No, I haven't." Sylvia touched Betty's shoulder and smiled at the others on the sidewalk, trying to read their faces.

Shock. That's what she saw. Betty's sentiment about the safety of Hidden Falls was widely held. Three peculiar episodes in as many days were disconcerting. Certainly they were disconcerting to Sylvia. She had been on the town council for many years and mayor for a good deal more, and never had Hidden Falls experienced anything that remotely resembled a crime wave.

Sylvia reminded herself that this wasn't a crime wave. It was still possible Quinn left under his own steam, and anyone could have untied Dani's boat with benevolent, if misguided, intentions.

"Tell us you're going to get to the bottom of this." Patricia Healy, Henry's wife, fixed her enormous brown eyes on Sylvia. Behind Patricia stood three people Sylvia recognized as employed in Main Street shops.

Sylvia pointed toward the door of Town Hall. "I'm going to go in that door and do the job you all elected me to do. When the time is right, we'll let you know what we find out."

The huddle parted, and Sylvia climbed three cement steps. She always suspected the architect of the building meant them to be marble and went to his grave shrouded in disappointment with a town council that voted down the expense. Inside the building, Sylvia paused halfway up the stairs to her office and took out her cell phone to dial Dani's numbers. She still had the phone to her ear, listening to the vacant ringing, when she pushed open the door to the small anteroom outside her office.

Marianne sprang to her feet, which signaled three women and two men to do the same as all heads turned toward Sylvia's entry.

"Who are you calling in to find Dani's body?" one of them asked.

Body? All anyone had seen so far was a broken boat and they had Dani halfway into her grave.

"Let's take one step at a time." Sylvia dropped her phone into her purse. "I'll need some time before I can say anything definitive."

"Have you spoken to anyone in the sheriff's office?" Marv Stanford, Lizzie's father, had a pen poised over a miniature yellow legal pad, ready to craft an account for the *Dispatch*.

Sylvia didn't blame him. The last few days were the busiest news days Hidden Falls had seen in years, maybe even decades.

"When I have something worth your ink to print, you'll be the first to know." Sylvia lifted her eyes to the group as a whole as she moved toward her office door. "In the meantime, we should all keep calm."

Marv cleared his throat. "George Kopp says he found a piece of the hull that looked like it had been drilled through."

"You know I can't comment. We'll have to wait to hear from Cooper."

Why hadn't Cooper Elliott or someone else from the sheriff's office called her before letting her walk into this bundle of anxiety? Cooper wasn't in the habit of revealing information prematurely — or at all — but he had to realize people would expect Sylvia not to be the last person to hear the news. Getting hold of Cooper went to the top of her mental list.

The faces in the room, including Marianne's — and even Marv's — weren't merely curious. Events of the last three days, whether crimes or not, were unsettling. Sylvia was the mayor. It was her job to do what she thought was in the best interest of the residents of Hidden Falls.

Quinn would have offered some wise advice. The damage in Sylvia's shop would have pained him, and he would have been out looking for Dani. Sylvia missed him. She wanted him to walk through the door. Now would be an ideal moment.

"As I said, we'll take things a step at a time," Sylvia said. "I encourage all of you to go about your normal day. If you see or hear something you think may be significant, call me or speak directly to Cooper Elliott." When they had something definite to say, word would get around. It always did in Hidden Falls.

She strode across the room, past Marianne's desk, and into her private office.

Dumping her briefcase in a side chair, Sylvia again pulled her cell phone from her purse.

Nothing from Quinn.

Nothing from Dani.

Nothing from Cooper.

She'd said the right things to the people on the sidewalk and in the anteroom. She would say them again, she was sure. Calm, professional, official. Sylvia wanted to do nothing that might interfere with any of the investigations.

Investigations. What an odd word to use about anything that happened in Hidden Falls.

Sylvia set her cell phone on her desk in plain sight and went through the motions of powering up her desktop computer and flipping through the file of correspondence Marianne had laid beside it. Even mayors got junk mail — leadership conferences a small town couldn't afford to send anyone to, offers of business services she didn't need, newsletters she hadn't subscribed to.

And a hand-addressed, square gray card envelope with no stamp. *Quinn.*

Sylvia scooted around her desk and pulled open her office door. A new set of faces stared back at her.

"Marianne," she said, "can I see you, please?"

Once the door was closed again, Sylvia held out the envelope. "Where did this come from?"

"Quinn gave it to me with strict orders to give it to you with today's mail."

"Quinn said that? When?"

"He came by with it last Thursday, I think it was."

Sylvia focused on breathing normally as she tore the flap open. She carried this card in her shop, a simple "thinking of you" greeting. A drawer in her study at home held every card Quinn gave her over the years.

But why today?

Congratulations, he had written inside. *Twenty years in business is an accomplishment worth celebrating.*

It was the anniversary of opening Waterfall Books and Gifts. Sylvia doubted anyone else in town would have realized that. She'd forgotten herself. Of course no one else was there every night after work for two months arranging stock and preparing for the opening. Quinn had done that for her. Even now the thought warmed her.

"Is everything all right?" Marianne asked.

Sylvia slid the card back into the envelope. "Very. Now tell me about the people out there."

"As soon as the others left, more came in. They all want to see you."

"I suppose I should speak to them."

Marianne opened the door. Sylvia looked across the waiting room to see Jack Parker enter.

"There's your appointment," Marianne said.

"Good morning, Jack." Listening to Jack's pitch for handling the town's legal affairs was the last thing on Sylvia's mind, but she had promised to hear him out. "Come right in."

"Hey!" A man scrambled out of his chair. "Why does he get to go right in when we've been waiting our turn?"

Sylvia smiled. "Because Mr. Parker has an appointment, which he made two weeks ago. I know you all have questions and concerns. Please feel free to leave detailed messages with Marianne, and I promise to read them all carefully."

She closed the door on the protests and shook Jack's hand properly. "The latest news is causing quite a stir."

"I don't know Dani Roose personally," Jack

said, "but she seems to be all anyone is talking about this morning."

"Dani grew up in this town." Sylvia gestured to a chair where Jack would be comfortable. She chose to sit behind her desk in case she had to remind Jack whose territory they were in.

"I've heard she's a bit of an odd bird," he said.

Sylvia shifted in her chair. "She has her own approach to life, but people have known her a long time. Hidden Falls is a tight community. These last few days have been unnerving."

"I could make some calls," Jack said.

"What kind of calls?" Sylvia was dubious.

"I have connections with people who might help track down Quinn. I can call in some favors. It won't cost anything." Jack turned a palm up. "Wouldn't it help settle things down around here if people knew what really happened?"

"I'm sure it would." Quinn had been gone three nights and two days. No one wanted to know what happened to him more than Sylvia did.

"Then I'll get on it as soon as I get back to my office."

The smugness of his tone grated against Sylvia's polite smile, but what could it hurt to let him try?

10:22 a.m.

"I just want to get my run in." With a foot up on a kitchen chair, Nicole Sandquist leaned forward to tie her laces and spoke toward the cell phone set on speaker and laid on the table.

"So maybe noonish?" Ethan said.

"That sounds about right, but you'd better wait for me to call you." Nicole liked to run at least five miles and often ran seven or eight. She could run toward town, loop around downtown, catch some of the river trail on the way back, and still have time to shower.

"I thought you'd be in more of a hurry to get to Birch Bend."

Nicole stretched her hamstrings. "I think better if I run."

By dinnertime, Quinn would have been missing for seventy-two hours. Nicole didn't have time for muddled thinking. Hours on the Internet and at the local newspaper archives the day before had turned up nothing about Quinn's past before he moved to Hidden Falls. Everybody had a past and people who knew them before. The vacant column under Quinn's name niggled at Nicole more persistently with each hour that ticked by.

After jogging for a few minutes to warm up, Nicole ran hard. As soon as she was out of the stately subdivision where she grew up in the block behind Quinn's house, she was off the harsh sidewalks and lengthening her stride on the softer shoulder of the road into town. A gap of three-quarters of a mile had somehow escaped the developers in the history of Hidden Falls's gradual expansion like concentric rings around the shops on Main Street. Nicole had first started running along here when she was about twelve. She ran with a backpack in those days, getting off the school bus long before her assigned stop to discharge the anxiety that built up over seven hours in the classroom. Nicole hated being the only girl without a mother, agonizing over how to become a grown-up woman with no mother to show her or being jealous of all the girls who complained about their unreasonable mothers. At least they had mothers.

Nicole got over being anxious and jealous, but she never let go of running.

Quinn found her one day right along this stretch of road when she had run herself breathless and stood with her hands on her knees, trying to fill her lungs. He said he was on his way to get an ice cream cone and figured she would want one. Many years passed before she realized he was driving the wrong direction for an ice cream cone. More likely he was headed toward the lake to walk or fish on his own. He'd given up his afternoon to make a lonely child smile.

Nicole's feet thudded against the ground in

unvarying rhythm. Her running shoes were worth every penny of the exorbitant price she paid for them at regular intervals. She catered to few indulgences, but new running shoes in the budget every three months was not negotiable.

Her eyes soaked up the view. Reds and golds and browns rustled against one another in autumn breezes that swirled them, one by one, to the ground. In another couple of weeks, nearly bare tree branches would herald the unstoppable turn of the seasons. The sun would provide more light than warmth in the middle of the day, and one morning not long after that, snow would startle the county — and like all good Midwesterners, the residents of Hidden Falls would hunker down.

Quinn would be assessing whether his firewood supply would see him through a winter of the roaring blazes he relished. He never had them growing up, he'd said once. His family never had a fireplace.

Nicole stumbled with the memory and uncharacteristically halted her run. She stood with hands on hips, breathing hard.

The lack of a fireplace hardly narrowed the possibilities of where Quinn might have lived, but the fact that she knew this bit of his past bolstered Nicole's conviction that a clue would emerge if she only dug for it hard enough and deep enough. And if she could find where Quinn came from, she might also find where he had gone to.

She could almost feel him there on the side of the road. Quinn had seen this same view three days ago, the same riotous swaths of competing color, the same midmorning brilliance of the sun. Perhaps he had stood in this spot.

Had he known then whatever it was that made him leave?

Nicole resumed running, suddenly feeling the urge to see if that old ice cream parlor was still in business. Instead of skirting around downtown, she would run right through it. She could go by Our Savior Community Church. If she remembered right, the frozen treats of her childhood were four blocks west of the church. Her path sloped gently now, and Nicole saw the steeples of several churches amid the patchwork of rooflines ranging from forty to one hundred years in age. Hidden Falls was a picture-postcard small town. Nicole had grown up here, but Quinn chose this town and liked it so well he never wandered more than fifteen miles to the west or south. On the other side, the county line ran just north of the river and just east of the falls. Still, the county covered over three hundred square miles.

Nicole's mental calculations had carried her into downtown. Rounding the corner at the church, she saw the woman with the baby and toddler a fraction of a second too late.

She stumbled for the second time that morning, this time stepping off the curb before she judged its depth.

Her ankle crumpled beneath her. Pain shot through her lower leg. Lying between two parked cars, Nicole tried not to shriek.

"I'm so sorry, I'm so sorry." The woman scrambled off the sidewalk. "I didn't see you. I was looking at the baby."

The infant bawled now.

Rolling to one shoulder, Nicole breathed rapidly in and out. Her foot screamed. "I didn't see you either. Accidents happen."

"Are you all right?"

Nicole maneuvered to all fours, holding the injured ankle off the ground, and concentrated on not biting her tongue.

"I'll find help." The woman took the toddler's hand. "Come on, Kimmie. We'll go in the church."

Nicole gripped the grill of the nearest car and pulled herself upright, amazed at the way pain superseded the instinct to breathe. She leaned on the hood of the car and tentatively tested her weight on the ankle — and immediately shifted to the other foot. As a runner, Nicole had her share of sprains. This was no sprain.

The side door of Our Savior swung open and Lauren hustled toward Nicole.

"Raisa Gallagher told me what happened." Lauren ducked under Nicole's arm to brace her weight. "What are you doing trying to stand up?"

"It seemed like a better idea than lying in the street." Nicole grimaced. "I think it's broken."

"Lean on me."

With her foot off the ground, Nicole's ankle dangled at a precarious angle. "Didn't there used to be a little urgent care place around here?"

"It's part of the hospital now. We have to get you up there."

"This would be a really good time to tell me you have a car nearby."

"I don't drive, remember?" Lauren tightened her grip around Nicole's waist. "I think you're leaning on Jack Parker's car. Oh, there he is now. Jack!"

Across the street, Jack's head turned.

Nicole didn't know Jack Parker, but if he had a car and knew where the urgent care center was, then he was about to be her new best friend.

1:42 p.m.

"How am I going to find Quinn when I'm doped up on painkillers, with my leg in a boot cast?"

In the urgent care exam room, Lauren offered a sympathetic shrug in response to Nicole's question. "You have to take care of yourself. Other people are looking for Quinn."

"Are they? What has that Cooper Elliott of yours turned up?"

"He's not *my* Cooper Elliott." Refusing to blush, Lauren settled into a side chair to await the physician's assistant who would return with final discharge instructions. "I hardly know him."

While Lauren was sorry to hear about Dani's boat being smashed, she was also relieved that the latest incident had not taken her once again to the sheriff's office for another round of questions with Cooper Elliott. At least — as far as Lauren knew — there had been no gruesome discovery of what became of Dani herself.

"I *cannot* do this," Nicole said. "I *cannot* be laid up like this. Not right now. There's too much to do."

"One thing at a time." Lauren examined the boot cast carefully wrapped around Nicole's swollen ankle. The ankle was indeed broken. For now, the boot would immobilize it. Whether Nicole would need surgery was undetermined.

"I know, I know. It's just so frustrating. I don't even care about my foot. We have to find out what happened to Quinn."

Maybe, Lauren thought, she would suggest that her aunt Sylvia call a special town meeting. Cooper could run it. The other officers could help with interviews. There had to be a faster way to find out who was the last person to see Quinn — and when and where.

Lauren quickly dismissed the idea. Sylvia's shop was in shambles. Asking her to take on a town meeting was out of the question.

Nicole's phone buzzed for the fifth time from its secure place in the sport band wrapped around her bicep.

"Maybe you should answer that," Lauren said.

"It will either be my editor — and I don't know what to tell him — or it's Ethan wondering why I haven't called. We were supposed to go to Birch Bend."

"Either way," Lauren said, "somebody's probably worried."

And they were going to need a ride. Jack Parker had safely transported Nicole and Lauren to the hospital, but he hadn't even come inside. He muttered something about an important phone call and left them as soon as Lauren scrounged up a transit wheelchair for Nicole from inside the clinic. Lauren didn't want to call her aunt, who had a pile of her own problems right now.

"Ethan would come and get us, wouldn't he?" Lauren said.

"Probably." Nicole rubbed her forehead. "I would have thought they'd offer me something stronger than ibuprofen by now."

"Your stomach is too empty for narcotics."

Lauren stood up and took Nicole's phone from the strap on her arm, surprised Nicole didn't protest. "Call Ethan."

The exam room door opened just then, and the physician's assistant entered with papers in his hands.

"Okay, we'll have you out of here in a jiffy," he said. "We just need a few John Hancocks. First, I need to know where you plan to go from here."

"To my house, I suppose."

"Alone?"

"I'll be fine."

"Do you have a ground floor bedroom and bath?"

Nicole sighed. "No."

"Then I don't recommend you go home. No stairs."

Lauren shifted her bag to the other shoulder. "She can come home with me. There's an elevator in my building."

"I'm not imposing myself on you," Nicole said. "Thank you, but I'll manage."

"Perhaps I wasn't clear," the PA said. "No weight on your foot. None at all. You have to be extremely careful until you see the orthopedist and get a determination about surgery. I want you in a comfortable chair with your foot elevated, icing every three or four hours for the next three days."

"She's coming home with me." Lauren had a chair in her spare room that would fold out to a twin bed. The apartment was small enough that Nicole wouldn't have to hobble too far for anything, and since it was right downtown on Main Street, checking in and making sure Nicole had everything she needed would be easy.

"Good." The PA checked some boxes on a form. "She shouldn't be on her own until after she sees the surgeon."

"What about medication?"

"I'll give you the prescription. She shouldn't take more painkiller than she needs, but she shouldn't skimp either."

"*She* is right here," Nicole said, "and not nearly as unconscious as you might think."

"Sorry," Lauren muttered.

The PA flipped over a page. "I see you live in St. Louis."

"That's right." Nicole tried to readjust her position and winced.

"I'd like you to stay in Hidden Falls for at least a week. I can understand that you may prefer to have surgery in St. Louis, but you'll need someone to help you get there. And you'll have to hang up your car keys for a couple of months."

A protest formed on Nicole's lips, but Lauren was relieved she had the good sense not to voice it. "You can stay with me as long as you need to," she said.

"I'm not being given much choice, am I?" Nicole reached for the pen the PA held.

"What do you want me to sign?"

"Right here." He handed her the form. "And here's your prescription for pain meds. They should hold you till you can see the surgeon."

Nicole scribbled her signature.

"I'll send someone in to help you get outside and make sure you have your X-rays on a CD." He looked at Lauren. "You can pull your car around anytime."

The door closed behind him. Lauren looked at Nicole. "You have to call Ethan."

"I guess." Nicole looked at her phone. "Four calls and five texts from him."

"He's worried."

"Or at least curious." Nicole scrolled to find Ethan's number in her list of recent calls and tapped it.

Lauren looked around the exam room to make sure they wouldn't leave anything behind. The shoe and sock taken from Nicole's injured foot were in a plastic bag with the sweatshirt she'd worn tied around her waist. Lauren picked up the bag and her own purse, trying not to eavesdrop on Nicole's conversation with Ethan.

Something was going on with the two of them. Lauren slapped down a twinge of envy and decided to look in the hall to see if anyone was coming to help them out. She and Nicole would have to wait for Ethan in the waiting room or on a bench outside the urgent care doors. The clinic would want to free up the exam room.

She nearly didn't hear her own cell phone ring. Lauren dug in her bag and extracted the phone between the third and fourth rings. The number was unfamiliar, and Lauren couldn't immediately place the area code her screen displayed. She didn't get a lot of phone calls from other cities. She tapped the ANSWER button and raised the phone to her ear.

"Hello?"

No response.

"Hello?"

She heard only the notes of a faint tune — a music box? A whistle? A flute? Lauren couldn't be sure. When the sound stopped, she looked again at the screen. The call had disconnected.

The tightness in her chest was both distant and familiar. She was back in high school, a pleasant student with a few close friends but not remarkable in any way that would launch her into popularity beyond her cafeteria crowd. For most of a school year, she received calls from at least a dozen different numbers but always with the same low, mocking chuckle. When Lauren stopped answering calls, the caller began letting her voice mail catch a few seconds of his amusement. When she began ignoring any number she didn't immediately recognize, he called repeatedly until she shut off her phone. Then she started leaving her phone at home on purpose and deleting voice mails without looking to see who left them.

Why she was a target, Lauren never knew.

Just before graduation she heard the laugh for the last time — at the back of a classroom. She turned and caught his eye. Nevin Morgan. He never called again.

When Lauren returned to Hidden Falls after college, he'd moved away. She didn't care where. She was just glad he was gone.

Until three days ago when she saw him on Main Street and he turned up at Quinn's banquet.

2:56 p.m.

The clinic doors slid open with a squeaky *whoosh* and Ethan stepped through. "There you are."

Nicole looked up at him from six feet over, seated in the same kind of curved vinyl seats he saw in the ER of his own hospital. A monthly twenty-four-hour shift sprinting through emergencies gave Ethan extra income that made paying down his student loans look like an achievable goal. A long-term goal, but a goal at the top of his list — right under being the best neurosurgeon in the country.

Nicole sat in one chair with her injured foot propped up on another and cushioned with a wadded sweatshirt. She looked tired and frazzled, but her face carried the same determination it always did.

"Thanks for coming," she said.

"Of course." Ethan looked around. "Where's Lauren?"

"At the hospital pharmacy getting my drugs."

"I hope they gave you something strong." Ethan dropped into the chair beside Nicole.

"If it makes me woozy, I'm not going to take it."

Stubborn as ever. "It's going to hurt for a while, Nicole. Controlling the pain will also keep you comfortable enough to be still and let the break heal."

"I don't need drugs for that."

"Maybe I should go talk to the guy who treated you."

Nicole put a hand on his arm. "Thanks, but I don't see the point. It's broken. I have to wait for the orthopedist's office to call about scheduling. I'm going to push for tomorrow."

"They'll want to wait a few days," Ethan said, "for the swelling to go down."

"Great." She snatched her hand back from his arm, and instantly he felt cold rush into the place she had warmed.

"Every day will be better." Ethan said what he told most of his patients in recovery.

"Not as long as Quinn is missing," Nicole

said. "What are we going to do about that?"

He had no answer.

"Are you leaving tonight?" Nicole asked.

Ethan gave a slow shrug and blew out his breath. Nicole's injury changed his agenda — again. He would have to call Hansen, but Ethan wasn't sure how many more favors he had in the bank with Hansen. He avoided Nicole's question.

Instead, he said, "Do you know how to use these crutches?"

"I'll manage."

Ethan swallowed and picked up Nicole's hand. "It's okay to accept help while you're injured." This was something else he often told patients. "Let people who care for you look after you."

Her emerald eyes, fixed wide open, stared into his. He smoothed back the disheveled hair hanging over the side of her face. In the old days, this would have been a moment when he'd lean in and kiss her. The old impulse was still there, but he'd forfeited the right long ago.

Nicole's eyes shifted to look over his shoulder. "There's Lauren."

Ethan released Nicole's hand and stood up. He took the white paper bag from Lauren's hands. "Let's see what they gave you."

"Thank you for coming," Lauren said. "They said it's a narcotic."

Ethan read the label on the bottle. "They

told you the truth."

Lauren handed a package of crackers and a bottle of water to Nicole. "You're not supposed to take it on an empty stomach."

Ethan recognized conflict flickering in Nicole's eyes as she gritted her teeth against the pain in her ankle and calculated its relief versus the prospect of losing her mental edge.

"Take it." Ethan twisted the cap off the bottle, dumped a pill into his palm, and offered it to Nicole. "At least today."

Nicole closed a fist over the pill and then tore open the crackers. She chomped down two of them before she swallowed the pill.

"Eat a couple more," he urged.

To his surprise, Nicole complied. "Let's get out of here." She reached for the crutches leaning against her chair.

Ethan grabbed the crutches and held them steady. "Push up through the heel of your good foot."

"I know, I know." Nicole grasped the handles of the crutches and slowly brought herself upright.

Ethan assessed how well the crutches fit her height. "We should take these down a notch at the bottom."

"You can fuss with them later," Nicole said. "I just want to get out of here."

Ethan wanted to put an arm around her waist, but an extra pair of feet at the base of the crutches would only increase her risk of stumbling. He glanced at Lauren. "My car is right outside the door. I'll go get it ready."

He stepped toward the doors and turned his head to watch Nicole's slow progress. She knew how to handle the crutches — something must have happened during the last ten years to teach her this skill — but she winced at the pain of holding her booted foot off the ground. If Lauren didn't have a comfortable chair for Nicole, he would go to Birch Bend and buy one.

Ethan had all four doors of his Lexus open by the time Nicole and Lauren conquered the few yards separating the clinic entrance from the vehicle. Nicole carefully maneuvered herself to sit on the edge of the backseat and handed her crutches to Lauren.

"I feel like I have to think about every stinkin' move I make," Nicole said.

"You do," Ethan said. "Successful rehab begins now by not making things worse."

Ethan was full of good advice for patients. Some of it he even believed.

Gently, an inch at a time, Nicole scooted back on the seat until she rested her injured foot on the padding. She twisted, looking for a seat belt. Ethan leaned into the car, found both ends of one, and fastened them across her lap. His face was inches from hers.

She put a hand on his shoulder. "Thank you, Ethan. It means a lot that you would come for me. But you never answered my question. Do you have to leave tonight?"

"Let me make some calls before I answer." He gave the seat belt an extra tug to be sure it was latched.

Lauren settled in the front passenger seat, and Ethan started the engine. He glanced in the rearview mirror at Nicole.

"I had an interesting conversation with Dani Roose this morning," he said.

Lauren twisted under the constraint of her seat belt so fast Ethan thought she might fly over the center console at him.

"You saw Dani *this morning*?"

"Yes." He glanced at Lauren as he backed out of the parking spot. "What's the big deal?"

"Have you been under a rock all day? Dani's boat went over the falls."

He nodded. "That's what she said. Good thing she wasn't in it at the time."

Air swished out of both Lauren and Nicole.

"What's going on?" he said.

"George Kopp found pieces of her boat, but no one has heard from Dani all day." Lauren leaned against the headrest. "Have you told anyone you saw her?"

"She roused me out of a sound sleep, demanding to see the photos on my camera. We had breakfast at that old diner on the other side of the falls. I wasn't the only person to see her."

"There must have been a shift change at

the diner," Lauren said. "People have been looking for her all day. When we get Nicole settled, you have to tell Cooper Elliott what happened — or my aunt."

"I don't know what happened." Ethan pulled out of the parking lot and turned south toward downtown. "She took a few images off my computer, and there wasn't much more to it. Except she said Quinn has a friend who comes to fish with him once a year."

"That's something to work with." Nicole slapped the seat. "If we can find Dani to tell us more."

Ethan glanced in the rearview mirror again. Nicole's head lolled slightly. The medication was kicking in. The best thing at this point would be to make sure she got a good night's sleep.

"I live above the barbershop," Lauren said.

Ethan tried to imagine Lauren's life — an apartment in town, blocks from where she worked, walking as a primary form of transportation. Ethan hoped she at least had a bicycle. It seemed like a small life. She had been away to college, and so had her aunt. What would bring them both back to this small town with its limited prospects? Didn't they have any ambition?

He parked and shut off the ignition.

Upstairs, Lauren cleared a stack of magazines out of a recliner, and Ethan helped Lauren ease into it and put the padded footrest up.

"I'll get the bed made up in the guest room," Lauren said.

"We should ice her ankle," Ethan said.

"Plenty of ice in the freezer."

Ethan put a throw pillow under Nicole's ankle before leaving her alone in the living room. In the kitchen, he found ice, gallon-size ziplock bags, and a dish towel. By the time he returned to Nicole to begin unstrapping the boot cast to expose her swollen ankle, she was on the phone with her office.

"What are you talking about, Terry?" she said. "Nobody said anything to me."

Ethan couldn't hear the response, but he didn't like the way it made Nicole tense up. He folded the makeshift ice pack into the towel. As gently as he could, he lifted the ankle to secure the ice pack at the point of swelling. Nicole's foot was well into a typical black-and-blue inflammatory response.

"I'll have to call you again tomorrow," Nicole said into the phone. "My meds are kicking in and I can't think straight."

She tossed her phone on the end table.

"Everything okay?"

"They killed my story."

"You need to get some rest."

"I wish everyone would quit saying that." Nicole winced under Ethan's touch as he arranged the ice. "Tomorrow we're going to get back to looking for Quinn. We'll start by figuring out who this guy is that Dani has seen."

Nicole wasn't likely to cooperate with her need for rest as long as Quinn was missing. Ethan would have to stay around to insist she behave sensibly.

4:04 p.m.

Marianne had left Town Hall two hours ago, which was two hours past her usual nine-to-twelve work hours. On a normal day, Sylvia spent a couple of hours in the morning efficiently attending to her duties as mayor from her office in Town Hall. Her home phone number was in the book, everyone knew she owned Waterfall Books and Gifts, and half the town seemed to have her cell phone number or know someone who did. Sylvia was hardly inaccessible because she limited her office hours.

Today, though, had been one relentless interruption after another. The waiting room filled and refilled with people demanding to know what the mayor was going to do about the spate of alarming events over the last three days. Sylvia's office phone rang so persistently that she and her assistant agreed Marianne would answer line one and Sylvia would pick up line two. With her cell phone she played a day-long round of telephone tag with Cooper Elliott. They left each other cryptic messages in the hope they would have a full conversation before the day was out. Now it was after four in the afternoon, and Sylvia hadn't yet stepped foot in her shop despite being dressed in jeans and tennis shoes for a cleanup operation.

She powered down the computer on her desk, held her breath, and cocked her head to listen to sounds from the waiting room. To her relief, Sylvia heard no shuffling, no coughing, no outdated magazine pages flipping, no cell phones playing silly tunes. Was it possible she was alone? Sylvia slid a few essential folders into her slim briefcase and picked up her cell phone and purse. Cracking her office door, she made sure the anteroom was indeed empty before snapping off the light switch and exiting. Her car was on the street in front of Town Hall and about five blocks from her store. Sylvia opted to move the old Ford now. After getting such a late start, the chances were good she would be at the store past dark.

Sylvia met no one on the stairs on her way out of the building and kept her head ducked to avoid eye contact until she reached her car with her key in hand ready for a swift entry into the vehicle. She was still tugging on her seat belt as she backed out of her parking spot. Transit time to the shop was only a couple of minutes, and Sylvia chose to park in the alley behind the store.

Her heart sank when she saw two figures approaching her car. As mayor, Sylvia believed in being approachable. She always told people to call her anytime with their questions or suggestions. Her philosophy was that the citizens of Hidden Falls had to work together to keep their town charming and inviting. Customers dropping into her shop often concluded their purchases with a comment about something happening around town that they thought she, as mayor, would want to know. For the most part, she listened carefully and politely, even to remarks that bordered on gossip. But this day had overflowed with questions for which she had no answers.

No, she didn't know where Quinn was.

No, she didn't know who broke into her shop.

No, she didn't know what happened to Dani's boat.

No, she didn't know when Quinn would come back.

No, she didn't know when her shop would open.

No, she hadn't spoken to Dani.

No. No. No. All day long, Sylvia felt as if she knew next to nothing about anything, and it had worn her out. The best she'd done was to remain calm and even-tempered enough to listen to the nineteenth iteration of the same question as carefully as she had to the first.

The two figures ready to greet her as soon as she opened her car door worked in adjacent shops. There was no telling what gossip they had heard all day from people coming in and out of their stores.

Sylvia opened the driver's door, stepped out, and smiled. "Good afternoon."

"We're hearing a lot of rumors, Mayor," one of the women said.

"I know." Sylvia had probably heard most of them herself in one form or another. "I assure you we're not hiding information. Careful, proper investigations take time. We want to be sure any information we give out is factual and reliable."

"We trust you." The second woman nodded in satisfaction. "We just want to help."

Too quickly, Sylvia had concluded these women wanted answers like everyone else in town. She softened. "Thank you."

"What can we do?"

"Just tell folks I'm working closely with the sheriff's office. Tell them to go about their usual routines." The last three days had been eventful, but Sylvia saw no reason anyone should think the townspeople were at more risk for a mishap than they had been on Saturday afternoon.

Sylvia turned her key in the alley door lock, the one that had been violated but not destroyed on Sunday night. First thing tomorrow morning she would go to the hardware store and see what they had in stock. She'd meant to go today. Now she didn't want to risk another distracting conversation by going down the block.

Lizzie was already inside, standing in the office doorway surveying the main store with a broom in her hand and her dark eyes wide with the impossibility of the task. She looked up at Sylvia. "I just got here. I had no idea."

"Thank you for coming." Sylvia was glad now she had not asked Lizzie to face the mess on her own earlier in the day.

"I thought . . . well, I don't know what I thought, but not this."

"I just wanted us to make a plan for how to go about this." Sylvia pushed her sleeves up over her elbows. "I'll hire some help, but they'll need supervision from someone who knows the store."

"Of course. I'll do whatever I can."

Sylvia had no doubt Lizzie meant what she said. She also had no doubt Lizzie would become overwhelmed easily and need frequent breaks. Lizzie thrived on order and predictability, and the view before them couldn't be further from those conditions.

Dani Roose was the sort of person who could come in, intuitively break down the task into steps, and methodically make her way through each one without getting emotional about how many more still lay ahead.

Sylvia had stopped trying to leave messages for Dani. She would have to hire someone else. Frustration over Dani's lack of response had slid into concern for her welfare, but Sylvia still needed to get her shop up and running.

"Let's clear a path," Sylvia said, "from back here to the front of the store." Fallen shelving in the center of the display floor would prevent a direct path, but they needed to be able to move safely through the store.

"I don't know where to start." Lizzie gripped her broom with both hands.

"Go along the book wall." Sylvia pointed. "Sweep aside whatever might hurt you if you stepped on it. Pick up books and stack them along the wall. Don't worry about sorting them." They could decide later which volumes might still be sold, even if deeply discounted, and which were a complete loss. Sylvia would follow behind Lizzie with another broom and dustpan.

Lizzie got started. Sylvia set her purse on the desk in the back room and went into the alley for one of the large trash bins on wheels. She was pushing it through the office when her cell phone rang. Sylvia abandoned the bin and fished the phone out of her purse.

"It's me," Lauren said into her ear. "Got a minute?"

Sylvia watched Lizzie's tenuous efforts. "Of course."

"I have Nicole at my apartment," Lauren said. "Ethan's here, too."

"Sounds like a party."

"Hardly. Nicole broke her ankle this morning."

Sylvia sank into her desk chair. "My goodness. She's not going to like being held down."

"That's clear. At this point, medically it seems straightforward. She'll have to see a specialist to be sure. Ethan is trying to arrange to stay in town and help."

"That's good."

"What I'm really calling about is Dani."

"I've heard nothing." Sylvia sighed. How many more times today would she have to say that? "Cooper has been to all her usual haunts and come up with nothing." As well as being a sheriff's deputy, Cooper was Dani's cousin. If anyone was motivated to find her, Cooper was.

"Well, she's just giving him the slip," Lauren said. "Ethan had breakfast with her and she was in one piece."

Sylvia exhaled with deliberation. "Doesn't she know the whole town is looking for her?"

"Apparently not," Lauren said. "Ethan says Dani told him someone vandalized her boat."

"That's George Kopp's story." Sylvia picked up a pencil and wrote George's name on a scrap of paper. "He claims he found the piece that proves it."

"I hope Cooper took it into evidence."

"He did. But Cooper said he had no proof George didn't drill that hole himself."

"That's an awful thing to say!"

"That's off the record." Sylvia didn't want her remark turning up on the rumor mill. "Cooper only means he has to have a strong case before any charges can be filed."

"He also needs a suspect," Lauren pointed out. "And it's not George."

"I'd like to bring dinner to your place." Sylvia had no time to cook or even to go by her house, but she could phone an order over to Gavin at the Fall Shadows Café and tell him what time to have it ready.

"Aunt Sylvia, you must have a million things to do."

She did. But her day already was so far off track that probably it was not worth rescuing. It would be better to start fresh tomorrow on that million-item list.

If Quinn were here, he'd be taking dinner to Nicole and Ethan. Sylvia was certain of that. When Sammie Dunavant had her appendix out, Quinn arranged an army of caregivers to make sure she had everything she needed and then some. Anytime Sylvia so much as sniffled, Quinn showed up with home remedies. And he'd want to hear about Ethan's conversation with Dani.

"I'll get some ice cream, too," Sylvia said.

"I'm sure we can manage," Lauren said,

but Sylvia heard no real protest in her voice.

"I'll send you a text when I'm on my way." Sylvia was now jotting down a list of dishes to order from Gavin. "In the meantime, fix Nicole a cup of tea. I seem to recall Quinn used to give it to her with honey."

Sylvia set her phone on the desk and concentrated on the order. A moment later, she had Gavin on the phone, ordering enough food for Nicole and Lauren to last three days. Then she added one more dish, hoping Ethan would also be around for meals during the next few days. A final serving would feed Cooper Elliott. Whatever Ethan knew about Dani, Cooper needed to hear it firsthand.

A good meal soothed a multitude of nerves, in Sylvia's opinion.

This whole business had started over a meal, the banquet to honor Quinn's steadfast contribution to Hidden Falls students and their families — only Quinn went from being the honored guest to the absent guest, and matters rolled downhill from there.

Even if Sylvia were not the mayor of Hidden Falls, she'd want to do something to make things better. People needed things to be normal — at least for one day. Meals, shopping, errands, friends. Until that moment, Sylvia's concern to get her store open again was to minimize the financial price she would pay for being closed. She had separated the task from her duties as mayor. Now she saw that opening her Main Street shop was one of the best things the mayor of Hidden Falls could do for the town's morale. Cleaning it up would remove the eyesore reminding everyone to fret. Opening for business would show people it was okay to go about their normal lives. Ringing up sales would tell residents they still could depend on her.

Sylvia sent Cooper yet another text before jamming her phone into the back pocket of her jeans and grabbing the trash bin again. She had given Gavin one hour to get the food ready.

5:58 p.m.

"Yes." Jack tapped the eraser end of a pencil against his desk. Talking to Gianna on the phone was the main reason he kept pencils around. Most of the time he didn't sharpen them. His own wife's name on his caller ID made him jumpy, never sure whether she was calling about something ordinary or because he had disappointed her in a new way. Or an old way. Tapping an eraser she wouldn't hear helped even his mood.

"So you'll be home by seven?" Gianna said.

"Yes." *Tap. Tap. Tap.* "Absolutely. I just have a few loose ends to tidy up while things are fresh in my mind."

"Good. We can have a family dinner."

Moving to Hidden Falls eight months ago had made Gianna Parker hunker down into domestic aspirations. Jack hadn't thought it possible. No longer was it enough for the five Parkers to eat together a couple of times a week. Now Gianna aimed for five nights out of seven. And picking up take-out wasn't good enough anymore, either. She had untethered a vast range of recipes and let them loose on her unsuspecting husband and children. Jack tried to be grateful. He knew plenty of lawyers who would have grabbed at a chance for a home-cooked meal at a table at seven rather than food they unwrapped to eat at their desks at nine o'clock at night.

But would they feel the same way if it meant practicing law in a small town like Hidden Falls?

Yesterday had been a throwaway day as far as his practice. He couldn't point to one thing he'd accomplished to further his career. But it wasn't a throwaway day for his family. Jack spent the afternoon with his youngest daughter looking for her lost puppy, and it turned into a day he wouldn't trade for anything short of being exonerated from the career gaffe in Memphis that had exiled him to Hidden Falls. He'd taken Brooke to school this morning and wondered what it might be like to take her every day.

Jack had told Gianna the truth about having a few things to tidy up before he could leave. He reached for the yellow legal pad where he had made his list after he left the mayor's office that morning. He'd written four names.

One of the private investigators Jack's Memphis firm frequently hired.

A friend in the sheriff's office in Memphis who primarily pursued missing persons cases.

A paralegal still employed by the Atlanta firm where Jack worked before Memphis, with a nose that could have made him an investigator if he wanted to be one.

A law school classmate who'd recently joined the staff of the Cook County State's Attorney's Office. Jack figured it could help to talk to someone in the State of Illinois, a conversation that might lead to someone closer to Hidden Falls who might have some inkling of how to get things done more efficiently.

So far Jack was underwhelmed at the efforts of the local sheriff's office, and if the sheriff in Birch Bend didn't stop farming out the work to low-levels like Cooper Elliott, Jack didn't see how the case of Quinn's disappearance would ever be solved.

He'd spent the entire afternoon strewing messages from Atlanta to Chicago. In the late afternoon the cryptic responses began.

The Memphis investigator asked a part-time clerical support person to call Jack and tell him she didn't have time for any uncompensated cases right now.

"Who said anything about

'uncompensated'?" Jack had snapped at the young woman.

"I'm sorry, Mr. Parker."

Jack hadn't pushed back. He knew what kind of fees private investigators commanded if they knew what they were doing, and he didn't have that kind of money to spend on a case without a paying client to bill.

The friend in the Memphis sheriff's office sent an e-mail saying that without more proof that the individual in question was actually missing or had fallen victim to a crime, it was probably too soon to worry about looking for an adult. His caseload, he said, was full of children who didn't come home from the playground — and besides, he couldn't offer much assistance from another state. He claimed he didn't have the necessary connections in Illinois.

The paralegal in Atlanta rattled off a series of starting points for a search — public records, eyewitnesses, coworkers. He said nothing imaginative — leaving Jack wondering if he had overestimated the man's abilities all these years — and his tone made clear he wasn't supposed to be talking to Jack. What exactly had the Atlanta partners said to the staff after Jack's departure?

Jack picked up his desk phone. He could make one last call to his buddy in Chicago. Certainly the fact that they both had joined the Illinois bar would provide a starting point of conversation if Jack could just catch him. It was only a little after six — early for someone in the state's attorney's office to quit for the day but late enough that the person who answered his phone during business hours might be gone.

His hunch paid off when he heard "Doug Davies" in his ear.

"Doug! Jack Parker here."

"Oh. Hi, Jack. Sorry I haven't had time to get back to you today."

"No problem. I'm just glad I caught you now." Jack gave the bare facts of the case as he knew them, beginning with Quinn's disappearance and on through his smashed car, Sylvia's vandalized shop, and Dani's sabotaged rowboat.

"I'd like to help, Jack," Doug said, "but it's not a state's attorney's kind of case. Coincidence is not the same as causation, as you know."

"You have to admit it's peculiar," Jack said. "Why should a little town like Hidden Falls suddenly have so much excitement?"

"I don't really do small towns."

Jack heard Doug shuffling papers in the background. "Come on, buddy. I'm sure if you put your thinking cap on, you can give me a name I can call."

" 'Fraid not. It sounds like petty crime to me, if that, and you should just let the system play out. I can't get involved in overriding a local sheriff's investigation."

"It's not much of an investigation."

"Sorry, Jack. Call me if you ever come to Chicago. We'll have lunch."

The call disconnected, and Jack dropped the receiver into its cradle. He had expected more from Doug Davies.

Jack checked the time displayed on the base of the desk phone. He had his car in town today, so he could wait until the last minute and still be home by seven. He never should have promised the mayor he could make some calls. He should have just made them. If they'd turned up someone actually interested in helping solve small-town mysteries, Jack would have gotten what he wanted from the effort without the egg on his face. He kicked the side of his desk, and it was no accident.

Jack went through the motions of packing a briefcase, an old habit more than necessity. He had a commercial real estate contract to review at the request of a farmer who didn't want to be swindled by the developer buying his land. And a woman from a town beyond the county line outside Birch Bend had sought Jack out to ask questions about a legal separation — without being seen doing so by anyone who knew her. He had taken notes on their conversation about marital assets. People around Hidden Falls expected a lawyer to be a generalist. While Jack was sure he could handle filing for a separation, he had done very little family law in Atlanta or Memphis. Even if he had, he would have to read up on the Illinois statutes.

Small potatoes. How was this ever going to be enough?

In the hall outside his office, Jack ran into Liam Elliott. "Heading out with that fiancée of yours?"

"I wish." Liam ran his hands through his hair. "I still have a lot to do tonight. I'm just going over to Main Street to get some dinner and bring it back."

"I'll walk over with you," Jack said.

Seven o'clock was far enough off that he could come back for his car. Jack had known a lot of nervous people in his law career. Either Liam was one of them, or Jack was no judge of character at all.

"Business is good?" Jack asked as they fell into stride.

"Business is . . . complicated." Liam scratched the back of his head.

Yep. Nervous. But why?

Jack didn't care why. Innocence, guilt, motivation. None of it mattered. Nervous people needed bulldog attorneys.

"I don't think we've ever exchanged cards." Jack casually reached into his breast pocket. "Obviously you know where to find me, just down the hall, but it can't hurt to have me in your contacts."

Jack waited for the hesitation that often came when he offered his card. Either people couldn't imagine needing an attorney or they didn't want him in particular. Jack was used to seeing people take his card and drop it in a purse or briefcase without even pretending to be interested in his services.

But Liam read the business card and carefully tucked it into his shirt pocket. "Thanks."

They turned onto Main Street beside the barbershop.

"I think I'll stop for a paper," Jack said. He would play this cool and reel Liam in at the right moment. "Get food you like for dinner. If you have to work late, you should at least enjoy something about your evening. Listen to the voice of experience."

Jack ducked into the barbershop, where he'd risked having his hair cut a few times, and waved at Henry Healy getting a trim in one of the three barber chairs.

Trace Hulett, the barber, made a couple of snips. "I'm getting ready to close up."

"No problem. I just came in for a newspaper." Jack picked up a copy of the *Dispatch* from the stack on the counter and left fifty cents.

Outside, he opened the paper, which he read more for amusement than information. The paper came out on Tuesdays but was printed on Monday nights. This edition had headlines about the failed banquet on Saturday night, the unknown driver of Quinn's crashed car, and the vandalism and theft at the mayor's bookshop. Marv Stanford was probably kicking rocks at the missed opportunity to cover the damage to Dani's boat while it was fresh. It would be old news by next Tuesday.

It all would.

Jack leaned against the building, scanning the newspaper's columns and finding nothing he hadn't already heard by roaming the sidewalks. Voices approached, and Jack looked up to see Sylvia Alexander and Cooper Elliott, their arms full of food bags.

"Evening," he said.

"Hello, Jack," they said in unison. Both seemed equally surprised to see him there.

"Did Lauren tell you about Nicole's ankle?" Jack said. "I took them to the hospital."

"Yes," Sylvia said. "We're just heading up to Lauren's with some food."

"I haven't forgotten about making those calls," Jack said. "I'm still following up on a few things."

"What calls?" Cooper held open the door to the hall leading to apartments above the barber and newspaper shops.

"Jack thought he might know some people who could help us." Sylvia shifted the load in her arms.

"I see." Cooper looked at Jack. "Our investigation is progressing satisfactorily, if not as rapidly as some might hope."

Sylvia elbowed Cooper. "Jack's only trying to help."

"That's right." Jack folded the newspaper in half.

"Dani's fine," Sylvia said, "at least we think she is. We found someone who spoke to her this morning. She wasn't in the boat when it went over the falls."

"That's good news." Jack returned Cooper's glare. "Do you have a suspect for that crime, or has it fallen into the same category as the others?"

Cooper cleared his throat. "As you know, the legal system runs on evidence. We're not in the habit of making accusations prematurely."

Jack stuck his tongue into a cheek.

"I'm sure you have matters in your own practice to attend to," Cooper said. "You don't have to feel any obligation to meddle in the sheriff's affairs."

Sylvia went through the door Cooper held open. Cooper followed without looking over his shoulder at Jack.

Meddle.

Jack wadded up the worthless newsprint people in Hidden Falls thought passed as a newspaper and stuffed it in a trash can.

7:32 p.m.

Sylvia lifted Nicole's plate from the awkward

lap that results from eating in an extended recliner.

"You didn't eat much," Sylvia said.

"Too much work." Nicole put her head back. "I feel rubbery."

"It's the medication."

"I know. But I still hate it."

Sylvia handed Nicole a covered cup with a straw. "You should stay hydrated."

"For a broken ankle?"

"In general. Water helps most everything." Sylvia had the same conversation with her mother on a regular basis and wondered how much hydration accounted for the hours, or even days, when Emma seemed in good shape cognitively compared to the times when she seemed more confused.

Nicole took a long sip through the straw. "I can't believe how one step changed everything."

"Tomorrow will be better." Sylvia stacked her own plate on top of Nicole's. "Years ago I had surgery on one knee. I bet you didn't know that."

"No, I didn't."

"It hurt a lot, so I took the painkillers. Quinn was pushing water on me like he owned the utility company. Even in the hospital, he kept coming around with my favorite foods to make sure I ate."

Nicole drew the back of her hand across her forehead. "I miss Quinn."

"So do I." Sylvia picked up two more plates from the coffee table. "My point is that it's all right for you to let people look after you."

"I know. But how am I going to help look for Quinn laid up like this?"

Sylvia had no answer.

"I know Quinn would want to help you," Sylvia said.

Lauren emerged from the kitchen carrying a tray of bowls filled with generous portions of butter pecan ice cream and set it on the coffee table.

"Quinn's favorite," Nicole muttered.

Nicole was right. When Gavin asked what flavor of ice cream Sylvia wanted him to pack in with the food, she said the first flavor — the only one — that came to her mind. Quinn was there in her thoughts at every turn.

Ethan and Cooper came out of the kitchen with a coffeepot and mugs. When Ethan offered a cup to Sylvia, she accepted it. Normally she didn't drink coffee past mid-afternoon, not even to be sociable. It kept her awake. But she suspected she would be awake tonight anyway, so she might as well feel alert enough to think rather than thrash in the bed to no avail.

Nicole dozed off. Sylvia couldn't be sure Nicole was actually sleeping, but with her head back and eyes closed, she made no further effort to engage in conversation. While the others grasped ice cream bowls and murmured about the day's event, Sylvia tapped her mother's number in the favorites list of her cell phone. The busy signal, which she heard again now, had been steadfast for close to an hour. Emma was never one to stay on a call very long. Her phone must be off the hook.

"I should go," Sylvia said. "I still want to run by my mother's tonight. Tomorrow is sure to be busy."

Cooper set down his bowl. "All right. I'll walk you back to your car."

Sylvia waved him off as she stood up. "It's only three blocks. Stay and enjoy your dessert and some good company."

He glanced at Lauren and settled into one end of the sofa.

Cooper deserved to avail himself of a few relaxing moments, Sylvia thought. If the last three days were any measure, there was no telling what the night or the next day would bring for the sheriff's deputy. Sylvia made herself hope for good news. Besides, she saw the way Cooper followed Lauren's movements all through dinner. When these compounding conundrums cleared up, maybe something would come of the two of them.

Lauren followed Sylvia to the door. "Aunt Sylvia," she said half under her breath.

Sylvia turned and raised her eyebrows.

"You're leaving Cooper Elliott here?" Lauren whispered.

"He might as well finish his dessert," Sylvia said. "He's a perfectly nice man, Lauren. We all want to find Quinn. Cooper is doing everything he can to help."

"I know what his job is." Lauren glanced toward the sofa.

Sylvia squelched a smile. "Relax, Lauren. It's just ice cream and coffee with friends."

She slipped out the door before Lauren could protest further. Lauren was a lovely young woman. She deserved to have someone look at her the way Cooper had in the last few days. Quinn looked at Sylvia that way in their early days. Sometimes he still did. And she always wanted him to. Sylvia would have married Quinn, and he knew it. On the brink of proposing, he backed away without explanation. Sylvia had tried to be angry, to be hurt, to be disappointed. Her friends said there were bigger fish in the sea.

The problem was that Sylvia couldn't imagine her life without Quinn. Not then, and not now.

She walked down Main Street with the lump in her throat threatening to cut off her air. These last three days were the first time since meeting Quinn more than thirty years ago that Sylvia had gone so long without speaking to him at least on the telephone. Three days might have been thirty years for the ache they sent throbbing through her muscles.

Sylvia reached her car and slid into the driver's seat. Before turning the ignition, she hunched over the steering wheel, eyes closed.

Quinn. Where are you? Come home.

God, keep him in Your care.

She sucked in a deep breath and drove the mile and a half to her mother's house. From the driveway, Sylvia saw that nearly every light in the first story burned bright. She rapped on the front door and then turned the knob and went in.

Emma Alexander dozed in her favorite armchair with her feet on an ottoman while the television blared. Sylvia scanned the room. Emma ate her meals in the living room in front of the television, and Sylvia didn't blame her mother for seeking a semblance of company. Not all the dishes found their way back to the kitchen, though. Sylvia picked up a plate of bread crusts piled on the remains of egg salad along with two bowls bearing evidence of chocolate pudding. Three cups of coffee were half drunk, and two glasses of water looked untouched.

Emma roused. "Oh, it's you."

Sylvia bent and kissed her mother's dry cheek. "How was your day, Mom?"

"Dullsville. I haven't been out of the house in two days."

For now, Sylvia was content that Emma didn't know the latest events rattling Hidden Falls. Soon enough someone would tell

Emma the extent of the damage to Sylvia's shop and Dani's boat, if she hadn't already heard.

"I tried to call," Sylvia said. "I think your phone is off the hook."

"I don't know where I left it."

Sylvia looked under a couple of throw pillows. It wouldn't be the first time her mother's phone, base and all, explored the depths of the couch, but it wasn't there. She picked up a pile of newspapers from an end table and found the receiver with the Talk button still lit. Sylvia turned off the phone and returned the receiver to the base.

She picked up a soiled dish towel. "Maybe I'll start a load of laundry for you while I'm here."

"I'm perfectly capable of doing my laundry," Emma snapped.

"I know. But you look so comfortable sitting there."

"I am."

"I'll go get your hamper."

Sylvia wasn't surprised to find the hamper in Emma's bedroom held only a few items, but that didn't mean there were insufficient clothes for a load to wash. As she did every couple of weeks, Sylvia quickly pushed through the hangers in Emma's closet to spot soiled clothing her mother had hung up. More and more of her shirts had food stains just below the second button as she ate more meals from her lap in front of the television. Sylvia grabbed four shirts, two pairs of pants, and a nightgown. In the bathroom across the hall, she took three towels. She carried the hamper, now full, to the laundry room at the back of the kitchen and started the load.

The front door opened. From the kitchen, Sylvia looked through the house and saw Sammie Dunavant enter.

"How's my favorite neighbor?" Sammie said.

Emma's face brightened. "That chili you brought over last night made a delicious lunch."

"Great! I have a lot more if you want some."

"I'd eat it if someone put it in front of me."

Sammie laughed and swooped around the room, swiftly picking up newspapers, dishes, and two sweaters. She stacked the clutter on a long table behind the couch, folded two afghans, and tossed a pillow into the chair it matched. Within a couple of minutes, the room transformed. Sammie cleaned houses for a living, so it was no surprise to Sylvia that she could be efficient, but Sammie moved around the room with familiarity and intimacy, as if she knew what to expect. Abruptly, Sylvia realized Sammie did this often. She'd brought food just last night.

Sylvia stepped out of the kitchen. "Hello, Sammie."

"Hey, Sylvia. Just checking on our Emma."

Our Emma. It was the sort of phrase Sylvia expected to see in a British novel. The affection in Sammie's face as she spoke it warmed Sylvia.

"Did Celia from across the street come over with the groceries?" Sammie asked Emma.

"I'll get fat on all that food," Emma said.

"It's just a few extra things we thought you might enjoy. No point having that stuff kicking around our pantries if you can use it."

Guilt and gratitude mingled in Sylvia's chest. Did her mother need more attention than Sylvia realized? Perhaps. But if she did, she was getting it from people who cared about her and knew her well.

Sammie folded the sweaters she'd left on the long table and then picked up the dishes and newspapers and carried them into the kitchen.

"Thank you," Sylvia said. "Mom hasn't mentioned that you come over like this."

"It's nothing." Sammie set dishes in the sink and dropped the newspapers in the recycling bin. "Just being neighborly."

"I'm touched."

"I'm very fond of Emma," Sammie said. "And you must have enough on your mind to make your head explode."

"I see you're keeping up with local news."

"We all just want to help." Sammie opened the refrigerator, sniffed the milk, and returned it to the shelf. "I'm sure you know Emma does pretty well with a routine."

"She's always been that way," Sylvia said.

"I'll just say good night and be on my way." Sammie ran some water on the dishes in the sink. "She's probably had her evening snooze, and now she'll be ready to go to bed."

Sammie touched Emma's shoulder, leaned over, and said something that made the older woman laugh. Watching, Sylvia smiled. It was almost eight thirty, which had long been Emma's cue to take a book and go to bed. Sammie wiggled the fingers of one hand as she went out the front door. She had been in and out of the house in less than ten minutes, but her presence lingered in Emma's grin and Sylvia's gratitude.

"Well, it's time for me to go to bed." Emma stood and picked up a book from the end table.

"I'll stay long enough to get the laundry in the dryer," Sylvia said.

"Don't do that," Emma said. "That old machine takes forever to wash a load. I'll do it in the morning. But leave me a note on the kitchen table or I'm liable to forget."

Emma spoke truth. The washer was old and inefficient. And — at the moment — Emma seemed aware of her limitations and had a strategy to compensate.

Anyone could forget to move a load of laundry. Sylvia did it all the time.

"You might as well go," Emma said. "I'm

headed for bed, anyway."

"If you're sure you don't need anything." Sylvia followed her mother down the hall.

"I've been going to bed all my life," Emma said. "I'm pretty sure I know how to do it."

Sylvia laughed. "Good night, Mom."

"Lock up, please. I'll call you in the morning."

Emma shuffled into her bedroom, the room that had been Sylvia's father's den until he died and Emma decided she'd rather live entirely on the main floor. Sylvia leaned against a wall in the hallway and considered the array of photos documenting her family's life — her grandparents, her parents' wedding photo, childhood portraits of Sylvia and her sister and brother, favorite family vacation photos, Lauren and her cousins on Whisper Lake and in Christmas jammies. Sylvia was so used to the arrangement that she rarely saw individual images anymore.

It was a beautiful life. Emma Alexander loved well and was well loved.

We all just want to help, Sammie had said, and so had the shop clerk in the alley.

Hidden Falls was that kind of town. The frustrations of the day — the constant queue of people hovering for Sylvia's attention, the undercurrent of concern about the unusual events since Saturday, the determination of citizens to do something. They all just wanted to help. The town came together to look after their own, whether Ted Quinn or Emma Alexander or Dani Roose.

Life was exquisite. Sylvia relished every moment just as it was. People sometimes pitied her for never marrying, but love was wondrous in any form.

Now if they could just get Quinn home.

9:04 p.m.

Liam Elliott went out of his way to the gas station on the highway east of downtown. The price per gallon was not less than anywhere else. The pumps were not more modern, and access was not easier. It was the opposite direction out of town from where he lived.

But from this station, Liam could see the square brick building of eight apartments where Jessica lived on the third floor in the front unit.

They hadn't spoken in twenty-four hours, not since he dropped Jessica off at her building the previous evening. She hadn't called him, and Liam hadn't reached out to her. He didn't know what to say.

I'm sorry I disappointed you. Again.

If you think we should get married in April, we'll get married in April.

I think there's something you're not telling me.

I know there's something I'm not telling you.

I don't want to believe it, but I think I have to.

Give me a little more time, and we'll have a great life together.

All day long, Liam had turned the options over in his mind. Some of them rang truer than others, but all of them asked for compromise. Or downright deceit.

Liam wasn't opposed to compromise. One slippery millimeter at a time, compromise was what got him in this predicament in the first place. The world ran on compromise, it seemed to him. How would people, much less nations, ever get along without give-and-take? But in his current circumstances, Liam would have liked his options to be a little more clear-cut. His brother, Cooper, worked in law enforcement and believed in rules and boundaries. Their cousin, Dani, was a free spirit who didn't care what people thought about how she lived. Liam was squished somewhere in between, like the third child sitting in the middle of the backseat in a car. No one ever chose to be in the middle. They just got stuck there.

Liam swung around the gas station lot so he could park with the nose of his blue sedan aimed at Jessica's building. A light went on in the corner of the third floor. Jessica's bedroom. She never went to bed this early. Liam could still call her, still drive across the street and take the elevator up to her floor. He could still be abject, still tell her what she wanted to hear. They could still set a date and move toward their wedding.

If only the stakes were not so high this time.

He got out of the car and pulled a credit card from his wallet. Forcing himself to look away from Jessica's building, Liam slid the card into the pay-at-the-pump slot and picked up the nozzle for regular unleaded gasoline.

"Hello, Liam."

His head snapped up and he stared into the eyes of Mayor Sylvia Alexander as she filled her tank next to his. "Good evening."

"It's not often I see both Elliott brothers in one evening," Sylvia said.

"I hope Cooper's behaving himself." Liam opened his tank and inserted the nozzle. He smiled. Liam knew the mayor preferred Cooper, but he would play along with her friendliness if for no other reason than the meeting he had scheduled with her in a couple of weeks.

Of course, he could be on his way to prison by then. Cooper would probably be the one to come and arrest him. Liam squeezed the nozzle with one hand while he felt for Jack Parker's business card with the other.

"Any word on Quinn?" Liam asked. Two days ago, Quinn seemed like Liam's last hope, but that was before Liam found the missing pieces of his puzzle.

"No, but I remain optimistic," Sylvia said. "We'll find him and he'll have an explanation."

If Quinn had an explanation for what he'd

done, he'd be ten steps ahead of Liam, whose only way out — possibly — was to point a finger in a direction that made his gut twist just thinking about it.

The mayor's nozzle shut off, and she replaced it in its cradle on the pump. "I guess I'll call it a night."

Liam nodded. "Let's hope for good news tomorrow." He certainly needed some.

While his tank filled, rather than look at Jessica's building, Liam watched the numbers on the digital display flip. Maybe tomorrow he would know what to say to her. He drove back through downtown and west to the complex of apartments where he lived. With the strap of his briefcase hanging off one shoulder, Liam turned the key in the lock. He had everything from his desk at the office in that bulging, soft-sided leather computer bag. He wasn't letting the incriminating papers out of his sight. Someone in the corporate office might still trace the electronic trail, but Liam saw no point in making the job easier.

As Liam flipped on the light switch next to the door, his foot scuffed against something on the floor. He squatted to pick up a nine-by-twelve-inch manila envelope and turned it in every direction.

He found no mark. The flap was sealed. Supposing it to be a communication from the building owner to the tenants, Liam tore off the top edge and slid out the single page of contents.

Centered neatly on the sheet of ordinary white copy paper, the message was simple.

I know. For a price, I'll help you.
Breakfast in Birch Bend at seven.
You know the place. Don't be late.

6
No Time for Answers

Wednesday
7:42 a.m.

Liam Elliott was first aware that his right elbow hurt. Then his neck abruptly announced its discomfort. He swam up toward consciousness as his back demanded repositioning. The yawn that followed, huge and devouring, reminded Liam of the chronic lack of sleep over the last few days and the persistent sensation of waking up without feeling refreshed. He rubbed his eyes, stunned that he had fallen asleep at all.

He hadn't dared go to bed.

Liam had laid the note on the breakfast bar and stared at it for two hours. Before its arrival, in the last few days Liam had imagined the shame of being confronted by a corporate executive about seventy-three thousand dollars missing from the client accounts Liam managed. He had imagined the embarrassment of being arrested, of having his hands locked together behind his back. He had sickened over the possibility of losing Jessica. He had known the dismay of a suspicion he could not yet prove.

But he had not imagined a blackmail note.

By midnight Liam was playing snippets of old movies in his head. A clever detective noticed a swirl in the handwriting or the texture of paper that gave away the blackmailer. For Liam, there were no handwriting clues.

By 2:00 a.m. Liam was thinking about the old typewriters, where no *e* was like any other, so finding the blackmailer was a matter of locating the typewriter and following the trail from there. The note Liam found under his door was printed in a common default font on ordinary printer paper that anyone could buy in an office supply store or a big-box store. How many computers were there in Hidden Falls? How many printers?

At 3:00 a.m. his brain was empty of possibilities for who might have slipped that note under his door.

I know, the note said.

Who could know? Liam had only discovered the missing funds a few days ago, and he had spoken to no one about it. He carried his papers and his laptop everywhere he went. The screen on his office desk was only a monitor. Without the hard drive of Liam's laptop, the screen could give away nothing.

Who could possibly know?

At 3:30 a.m. Liam jammed his swollen briefcase in a backpack in the rear of his closet and buried it among the camping gear he never intended to use again, hoping it would be safe there for a few hours.

At 4:00 a.m. Liam made coffee and resolved to shower and put on a business suit before driving to Birch Bend. He wouldn't go to this meeting looking disheveled and frightened and vulnerable.

At 5:00 a.m., dressed, he sat at the breakfast bar staring at the note again and wondering about fingerprints.

At 5:30 a.m. he folded his arms on the breakfast bar and laid his head in their nest just for a minute.

Now Liam shot off the stool, the red lights of the digital wall clock in his kitchen finally registering in his weary brain. 7:43! His heart pounded and his eyes refused to stop blinking. He gasped at irregular intervals.

Breakfast in Birch Bend at seven, the note said.

Liam had no idea who left the note, so he had no idea whether the person would wait. He slid the note into its envelope, snatched his keys off the breakfast bar, and ran out of the apartment.

You know the place, the note said.

Liam wasn't certain. Birch Bend was larger than Hidden Falls, and Liam had a couple of favorite places to go for breakfast. Was the note writer someone who knew his haunts? In the twenty minutes it took to drive to Birch Bend, he would have to decide which was the right place.

Liam imagined it was sacrilegious for a supposed embezzler to pray about a meeting with a probable blackmailer, but he didn't know what else to call the sensation of trying to conjure hope. He had no hope within him. It had to come from somewhere else.

One restaurant edged out the other in his head, and he drove there, arriving at 8:10 — more than an hour after the appointed time. A waitress in a green apron put a menu in front of Liam and offered coffee. He raised the menu to read it, but the words blurred. Blood pulsed through his temples as he looked around the restaurant for anyone he recognized. He had clients in Birch Bend. He had clients all over the county, but his files were confidential. Midwest Answers had one security system layered on another. Hacking in would have taken serious expertise, and a second person discovering the missing money — if it was a second person — screamed against the odds.

Yet Liam sat in a restaurant, suspicious of every face that looked vaguely familiar. He ordered a tall glass of orange juice and a muffin. Food in front of him, whether or not he consumed it, gave him a reason to remain in his booth and watch people. Liam didn't know who he was looking for, but if the author of the note was still in the main dining area, he or she would see Liam.

When it arrived, Liam sipped the orange juice.

His eyes met the gaze of a fiftyish man six tables away, his stomach burning at the realization that he knew this man. Burt. Bart. Something like that. Henderson or Hendricks. They stared at each other. Liam sipped his juice again without moving his eyes.

Finally Burt — or Bart — dropped his napkin on the table and zig-zagged between diners. Liam stood up, wondering if a handshake was appropriate under the circumstances.

"It *is* you," the man said, extending his hand.

Liam accepted the handshake, which felt anything but sinister. Wouldn't someone who wrote a blackmail note be certain whom he was meeting?

"I know it's been a few years since you set me up," Bart — Liam was sure now — said. "I just wanted to tell you how well that fund you suggested for me has worked out. I didn't believe you when you said it would yield as well as it has, but I'm glad to admit I was wrong."

Liam eased out the air lodged in his throat. "I'm glad to help. Call me anytime you have questions."

"I live out of the area now and I'm going home tomorrow, but I just might do that."

Bart turned to go. Liam's knees barely held his weight, finding security in the booth bench behind his legs just in time. His throat parched, and he dumped the juice in his mouth and downed it in one long gulp. It was past eight thirty now. Liam scanned the room one more time. No one stared back. Leaving his muffin untouched, he tossed a ten-dollar bill on the table and walked out into the sunlight.

Liam wasn't ready to get in his car and drive back to Hidden Falls — not while his heart beat so fast. There were always errands to do in Birch Bend. He could check his UPS box, for starters. He had several around the county so clients and vendors in each area would feel they were dealing with a local consultant. The county was too thinly populated for Liam not to cover as much territory as he could, and he and Jessica were in Birch Bend often enough that checking the box was never an inconvenience. Liam walked the four blocks to the UPS store, flipped through the keys on his ring to find the right one, and withdrew a stack of envelopes.

What he needed were the responses to corporate mass mailings or paperwork from clients. Liam riffled through the contents of the box, prepared to toss junk mail before he even left the store. As he pulled one pale yellow envelope from the stack, Liam's fingers trembled.

Mr. Ted Quinn, it said.

Quinn had a UPS box, an alternate address. The three digits in the box number were an inverted arrangement of the same three in Liam's number. Liam understood his own business reasons for the box he kept in Birch Bend, but why would a schoolteacher pay for a box? He flipped the envelope over and inspected the seal, which was firm and flat. Liam glanced up at the clerk busy behind the counter with a customer and three stacked boxes to ship.

He ought to give her the envelope. Liam knew that. He didn't need to add another form of theft to the list of crimes he might be accused of.

But what if the contents of the yellow envelope contained a clue to Quinn's whereabouts? Liam knew enough about direct mail to recognize this was not an impersonal advertisement. Neither was there a glassine pane to show an address on an invoice or a statement. This had the feel of a true letter. The name of the business, however, gave nothing away about its nature.

With one fingernail, Liam again tested for a loose edge at the end of the seal, but nothing gave. Short of taking it home to steam it open and reseal — a procedure Liam had no experience with — he couldn't open the letter without ripping the envelope.

Liam propped the envelope up against a sample shipping carton and took his phone out of his pocket. With a swift click, he photographed the envelope, and with a second he zoomed in on the return address. Then he put on his congenial face, approached the clerk, and returned the mysterious envelope.

10:04 a.m.

"I know the health fair was my idea," Lauren said, "and I still believe in it. I'm just not sure we can do it well without Quinn, and I would hate for it to be a sloppy catastrophe. So I wonder what you think is the best way to let people know it's canceled."

She raised her water bottle to her mouth and waited for what the pastor of Our Savior Community Church had to say. They sat at the round table in Lauren's office at the church.

"I don't think we should cancel."

Lauren had expected Matt Kendrick to say that. Still, its reality stung.

"I made a little progress on Monday," Lauren said. "But I lost all of yesterday looking after Nicole Sandquist and her broken ankle."

This was Wednesday. The health fair was scheduled for Saturday. Lauren didn't see how she could pull it off. Quinn had been the primary organizer, and Lauren didn't even have his notes. Nicole needed help whether or not she admitted it, and Ethan could be leaving town at any minute. Lauren hadn't had a decent night's sleep since Quinn disappeared on Saturday evening.

"I thought there was a committee," Matt said.

Lauren shifted her weight to one hip. "There is, officially." But Quinn was running the show, and Lauren had been glad for his enthusiasm.

"Then we can start there."

By *we* he meant *you.* Lauren knew Matt well enough to understand that.

"I'm not usually a quitter," she said, "but the circumstances this week have been especially stressful."

"I know." Matt leaned on the table. "Quinn gone, finding his car wrecked, the burglary at your aunt's shop. And now your friend Nicole."

"Right. It adds up."

"And I don't want to be unsympathetic. But we made a promise to the community. Families are counting on us. Kids need their immunizations, and we've collected a pile of winter coats to give away. Any day now the temperatures will start dropping at night. A lot of our church members are looking forward to the event, as well. Why don't we do what we can?"

Church attenders had been bringing in coats for two months, and backpacks and school supplies lined one wall of a classroom in the education wing of the church. Lauren might not be able to organize all the booths Quinn had in mind, but the fair could still cover some basics.

"All right." Lauren took a deep breath and reached for her clipboard. "I'll get started."

Lauren took three battered yellow sheets of random notes off her clipboard and laid them on the table. What she needed was an organized list of action steps. She gripped a favorite purple gel pen and wrote in tidy straight letters. The list filled every line on the page. Lauren went back through and starred essential entries.

Taking her clipboard, with the random notes behind the numbered list, Lauren went down the hall to the classroom where coats and backpacks awaited. She would find someone to sort them. Zeke Plainfield and a couple of other kids from the youth group could handle the job. Maybe Eva Parker would like to help. Lauren separated a few of the tangled sleeves and decided she would have to give guidelines for which coats were suitable to give out and which ones the donors should have thrown away. She pushed aside a few more and pulled out a brown-and-green child's coat that looked brand-new. The zipper worked smoothly and the hood was securely attached. If most of the coats were in this condition, the church volunteers could make a lot of children happy and warm.

Lauren suspected Quinn would have talked with merchants in the downtown businesses about the health fair. Taking her clipboard, she set out to make the rounds. All she had to do was ask business owners if Quinn had spoken to them about participating in the health fair. If they said no, she would move on. If they said yes, she would get the details of donations or volunteer time. Once she knew where everything stood, she would call the health fair committee members and distribute the tasks of following up and having everything ready by Friday night for the fair to begin on Saturday morning.

Later she would call the rental store out on the highway to see what Quinn had arranged for equipment. He would have extracted a steep discount if not outright donation. Then she would bike to the community center. When she saw Quinn last Saturday, he'd said something about exercise classes and recipe exchanges. A nurse in the congregation of Our Savior would probably know who was going to provide the immunizations and blood pressure screenings.

Who would run the book fair, the joke contest, and the cooking demonstrations were mysteries to Lauren at the moment, but Brooke Parker had called her, eager to do face painting. She even said her father was going to help. Lauren had a hard time imagining Jack Parker painting the faces of little children. She made a note on her clipboard to find someone to organize games for the children and another entry to find a couple of compassionate church members to be available to pray with people on Saturday. They could use the church prayer room for that.

The plan was coming together, but Friday was the day after tomorrow. On paper the fair looked good, but Lauren was going to need information, volunteers, and equipment. If only she had a month instead of three days. Lauren popped a piece of gum in her mouth, picked up her water bottle, and left the church building.

This would all be so much more fun with Quinn.

While she walked up toward Main Street, Lauren called Nicole's cell phone and promised to swing by and fix her some lunch. Ninety minutes later, Lauren had worked her way back and forth through the downtown blocks. Finding people who had agreed to help turned out to be surprisingly easy, and Lauren regretted doubting Quinn's preparation. The time-consuming part of the task was having the same conversation over and over.

Is it true you found Quinn's car?

You're the mayor's niece. What's she telling you about where Quinn is?

What's your theory about what really happened?

When is your aunt going to open her store again?

Lauren pitied the poor souls at the end of her circuit. Though she was fairly certain she hadn't said anything unquestionably rude, she'd come close a few times. She understood their concern — and shared it. But Lauren didn't have Quinn's gift of patiently listening as if the person in front of her was saying something new when, in fact, everyone up and down the block scratched their heads and said the same thing. She had a long task list, and she hadn't factored in how much everyone wanted to talk.

When she came to Sylvia's shop and saw the lights on and activity inside, she couldn't resist. The Closed sign hung in the window, but Lauren knew the rear door off the alley would be open.

Dani's Jeep was parked in back next to Sylvia's Ford, a vision of relief to Lauren that at least her aunt was getting the help she needed. As she passed through the office at the back of the store, Lauren looked around for a broom or a rag or something she could use to be helpful. The closet was empty of cleaning supplies, though, and Lauren walked on into the store.

"Hey, Dani."

Dani attacked a pile of rubble with a broad push broom. "Hi, Lauren."

"I'm glad to see you." Lauren was heartened both by the physical evidence that Dani was all right after having her boat sabotaged and the progress made in the store since Lauren was there two days earlier.

"Can you pull that trash can closer for me, please?" Dani pointed.

"Of course." Lauren set her clipboard down and dragged the can toward the heap of splintered wood and glass that Dani had contained against one wall. "I can't tell you how relieved I was yesterday when Ethan said he'd seen you in the morning. I'm sorry about your boat."

"I'll find the guy who did it."

As full as she was of questions, Lauren reasoned Dani would tell her story if and when she was ready. Frankly, at the moment, Lauren didn't have space in her brain to store the details anyway.

Lauren looked up to see Sylvia and Lizzie Stanford dragging a large cardboard box from the front of the store. It clattered with broken contents, and the sound made Lauren shiver. Deep in the recesses of the box, a small bell tinkled with the constant shifting of porcelain shards scraping against each other. Lauren's eyes automatically went to the spot in the store where the display rack that had been the bell's home should have stood.

Fresh discouragement surged through her. Whoever had done this either had a warped sense of amusement or no conscience.

"We're making progress," Sylvia said. "I want to open by the weekend."

Lauren wondered what Sylvia would have left to sell.

"It's not so bad," her aunt said.

"Not so bad?"

"It's a lot to clean up, but we're finding a surprising number of items in good shape. In fact, I've had a creative idea for the auction."

"Oh, Aunt Sylvia, you shouldn't be thinking about that under the circumstances."

"I need some distraction." Sylvia bent to pick up a book and inspected it front and back before flipping through the pages and setting it deliberately in a pile. "Lizzie, I think these we'll keep. We can sell them 20 percent off."

"I can do a table in the front window." Lizzie picked up a stack of books and carried them forward. "I'm putting the keepers up by the counter for now."

Sylvia trailed after Lizzie, picking up odds and ends and rapidly sorting them into various piles. Lauren followed. As she got farther from the trash bins at the back and into the shop, she saw that Sylvia, Lizzie, and Dani had established a system that looked more hopeful than she first thought.

"So what was your idea?" Lauren asked.

"With the books that are slightly damaged, we'll make up mystery packs for the silent auction." Sylvia thumped a stack of books and glanced at Lauren. "We have a lot of perfectly fine books that will bless the people who read them, but one little ding in the cover will make people pass them over in the store."

Lauren blinked while she thought about it. "We could start the bidding low enough that people can't resist the idea of getting a stack of books for that price, even if they can't see them first."

"Precisely. The money will go to a good cause, so people will be less particular than they'd be in the shop."

"This could work. Let me write it down." Lauren's eyes flashed around the room. Panic welled. Where had she left her clipboard?

Dani walked past her and pointed a thumb over her shoulder. "In the back."

"What?" Lauren spun around.

"Your clipboard. That's what you're looking for, isn't it?"

Lauren let out her breath. "I'm so scatterbrained." Somehow Dani remained calm and methodical after what she'd been through with her boat, and Lauren couldn't even keep track of a clipboard.

"And while you're at it," Dani said, "I promised Quinn I'd do a cooking demonstration grilling lake fish."

Lauren sucked in surprise. "He mentioned cooking, but I had no idea who."

Dani chuckled. "And you sure didn't think it would be me."

"No, I suppose I didn't." Lauren blushed.

"Well, it is. Also, Margie Bayly plans to make little sample cups of her favorite salads and share the recipes. They're all low-fat."

Relief warmed Lauren's chest.

Dani tied an extra-strength garbage bag closed. "And Mrs. Healy will answer questions about vegetable gardens."

"I really have to write this down." Lauren scrambled for her clipboard.

12:27 p.m.

Ethan Jordan ducked into the nearest store on Main Street. Immediately his sinuses told him the shop was full of scented candles, but he wasn't in a position to be picky. He moved away from the door and apologized for nearly stepping on a child's foot in his distraction. Then he positioned himself where he could see out the store's display window. Beyond the artful arrangement of candles and baskets, Ethan found the object of his search.

Yes. It was her. Kay Jordan, Ethan's mother, stood on the sidewalk across the street, casually gazing through the glass of a narrow electronics store and fussing with the collar of the blue jacket she'd worn forever. Though she carried a white sack, she seemed in no hurry. The hardware store was only a few doors down, Ethan realized. His mother probably was waiting for his father to emerge with supplies for a fix-it project. She turned and scanned the street before settling her eyes on the candle store. Reflexively, Ethan stepped back against the shadowed side wall of the shop. Though she seemed not to see him — which was his intention — Ethan saw his mother's features clearly for the first time in ten years.

She hadn't changed all that much. Perhaps Ethan had always thought of her as older than she was, and now she had finally attained the age he had assigned to her in his mind.

Did she think of him? Did she remember that day? Ethan had put on a white shirt and blue tie and waited for his parents to get ready for his eighth-grade awards program, where he would receive five different academic recognitions. His father, Richard, sat in his easy chair with the newspaper after dinner, and Kay was at her sewing machine.

She looked up at him and smiled. "You look nice."

"It's time to go," Ethan said.

Richard turned the page in his paper.

Ethan hated being late. He caught his mother's eye.

She took a pincushion out of a basket. "Your father is tired. We decided to stay home, but you go on and have a good time."

Even now, standing in the candle store, Ethan felt the weight of disappointment that should not have surprised him. His parents had chronically disappointed him for all of his fourteen years, his father with his passivity and his mother with her reluctance to stir things up. But that day, at the end of eighth grade, was the day Ethan decided not to care. His older brother was already out of the house and out of town. Ethan was on his own.

He'd turned, wordless, and left the house. Next door, Nicole Sandquist was getting into the car with her father. She waved him over, and he rode to the junior high with them. Nicole never asked about his parents. She knew.

Now Kay Jordan stepped down the sidewalk toward the hardware store. Ethan barreled up the short aisle of the candle store, grateful that Lauren Nock's apartment over the barbershop was in the opposite direction of his mother's path. He shoved open the shop door without looking.

"Hey! Watch out!"

The warning came too late. Ethan collided into the form of a person whose face he hadn't seen, a tangle of blue and khaki as she tumbled to the sidewalk. Sheets of yellow paper fluttered in three directions when a standard brown clipboard slammed the pavement.

"My notes!"

Ethan grabbed at a sheet wafting past him with one hand and offered the other to his victim. "Lauren," he said. "I'm so sorry!"

"Just get my notes!" Lauren gripped his hand long enough to get to her feet then gently removed her glasses from her face.

After swooping in every direction, Ethan returned with five yellow sheets, two of them torn. "Are you all right?"

"Did you find all my notes?" Lauren picked up the clipboard.

Ethan handed her the pages. "Are your glasses broken?"

"They'll at least need some major adjusting." Lauren put the glasses on, but the frame was so cockeyed that she immediately removed them and folded them closed. "Why were you in such a hurry to get out of that store?"

Ethan looked down the block. Kay Jordan walked past the hardware store and disappeared into a card shop. He blew out a long breath.

Lauren stood in front of him with her glasses in one hand and the clipboard braced against one hip as she wrestled with getting the papers back in place.

"Can you see without your glasses?" Ethan asked.

"Not very well. I hope everything is here."

"I have my car," he said. "I'll take you somewhere to get your glasses fixed."

"I have another pair in my apartment. You didn't say what your big hurry was."

Ethan glanced down the street again. "Um . . . Nicole. I was on my way to see how she is. She seemed agitated when I spoke to her on the phone awhile ago."

"She's frustrated." Lauren brushed off her knees. "I'm on my way to fix her some lunch."

"I'll help you. I owe you."

Lauren cocked a smile. "I'll tell you what you can do. Help me at the health fair on Saturday."

"That's three days away."

"I know! I'm frantic to pull things together without Quinn."

"What I mean is, I don't think I can stay in town that long."

Even without Brinkman and Gonzalez to contend with, the longer Ethan stayed in Hidden Falls, the more likely he was to run into one of his parents. Today's close call unnerved him. Despite Nicole's determination, he wasn't sure he would be much practical help looking for Quinn. When Quinn got home, Ethan would try to arrange another weekend off and come back.

"You're a doctor." Lauren began walking. "There must be something a doctor can do at a *health* fair."

"I'm a neurologist." Ethan worked on brains. Health fairs were about blood pressure and sugar screenings and heart rates and body mass index.

"Think about it."

"I'm lucky to be here this long," Ethan said. Saturday seemed an impossible objective.

"Everything's a blur," Lauren said.

"We'll get your glasses fixed."

"I don't mean that — though I can't see my hand in front of my face without my glasses. I mean, it's hard to make sense of this whole week. Four days without Quinn is a ridiculous thought, but it's happened."

They reached the barbershop and entered the door beside it. Ethan pushed the button in the elevator, and they rode to the apartments above. Lauren turned the knob of her door.

Inside, Nicole sat in a small rolling office chair rather than the recliner Ethan had expected to find her in. With her good foot, she propelled herself across the living room's wood floor.

"Nicole," Ethan said, "you're supposed to keep your foot elevated. The orthopedist, remember?"

Nicole scoffed. "I've been on the phone to every orthopedist in the county, and nobody will see me until Friday."

"That sounds about right. I told you they'd want the swelling to go down first."

"Excuse me," Lauren said. "I'm going to find my other glasses."

She went down the hall.

Nicole gave the armless rolling chair another shove.

"Maybe we should get you a wheelchair," Ethan said.

"This works fine." Nicole progressed toward the kitchen. "I get wherever I want to go. I don't intend to be sidelined for two more days while Quinn is missing."

"I don't see that you have much choice."

"There's always a choice." With another push, Nicole swiveled the chair to change directions and misjudged the stopping point. She grasped at something to steady herself, but instead, she knocked over a small accent table.

Ethan lurched toward her and intercepted Nicole's trajectory before she went the way of the table. He held the chair, and she leaned against him to straighten herself. Her hair slid loose from the clip she had used to pile it on her head, and she snatched the clip and hurled it at the recliner.

"I hate this," she said. "I hate that Quinn is gone, that I hurt my foot, that I'm cooped up here."

"I know." Ethan stroked her hair, running his fingers through it as he pushed it away from her face, away from the mole she always tried to hide in the way she let it hang. The first time he did that fifteen years ago, she had almost stopped him. But she hadn't.

And she didn't this time.

He wanted to kiss her.

12:47 p.m.

Lauren halted without crossing the threshold into the living room. Ethan was on one knee, leaning in toward Nicole, who had one hand on his shoulder. It didn't seem like the kind of moment she should interrupt, but neither did it seem like the kind she should spectate.

Lauren cleared her throat.

The pair looked up.

"Grilled cheese and fruit all right for lunch?" Lauren said.

Ethan stood up. "I'll cook."

Nicole laughed. She sounded nervous to Lauren.

"Nicole, how about some ice?" Lauren said.

"And a pain pill," Ethan added.

"Yes to ice, no to pain pill." Nicole started to push the chair toward the recliner.

Ethan put a hand on her leg. "I'll drive."

Nicole picked up her good foot, and Ethan rolled her back to where she belonged and helped her move between the chairs. Lauren went into the kitchen and started a gas burner under a frying pan.

An hour later, Nicole dozed off in the recliner with her foot elevated. It had taken all the time Lauren spent eating her sandwich, but Ethan convinced Nicole to take a pill and rest. When Lauren left in the morning, she had planned to meet with Pastor

Matt, cancel the health fair, and come home to look after Nicole. Instead, she had walked miles around town already and now had a clipboard full of details to check on before the day was over.

"She needs you." Lauren said.

"I'll stay with her this afternoon," Ethan said. "I know you have things to do."

"I appreciate it, but that's not what I meant." Lauren saw the way the two of them looked at each other over cheese sandwiches and apple slices.

Ethan leaned against the refrigerator and looked across the apartment at Nicole in the chair. "How much time do you need this afternoon?"

"I just need to see a couple of people. Then I'll do what I can by phone from here."

"Take your time. I'll keep the rebel forces under control."

Nicole shifted in her chair. "I heard that."

Lauren went down the stairs and out the back way, where she kept her bicycle tied to a pipe at the rear of the building. She pedaled down the alley, onto Main Street, and on out to the highway. If she hadn't felt pressed for time, Lauren gladly would have walked, but today the bike would save her time reaching the community center. Hopefully someone there would know what they had arranged with Quinn, but in Lauren's experience the phone went unanswered much of the time, instead giving callers automated options. This wasn't a day when Lauren wanted to leave messages. She needed solid information. Lauren leaned her bike against the side of the building, straightened the cross-body bag that held her clipboard along with the usual items, and entered the building.

No one was at the reception desk. The phone rang as Lauren walked past. The exercise room had an aerobics class going, but Lauren recognized the instructor and knew she only came in a couple of hours a week. In search of the full-time director, Lauren strode down the hall. Outside the director's office, five plastic chairs strewed the corridor. On one of them, a small boy sat swinging his feet and banging the legs intermittently.

Lauren slowed. The child didn't look older than five, and Lauren had never seen such a somber face on a little one. When he saw her, he stilled his feet. The director's door was closed. Lauren raised her hand to knock.

"My mom is in there."

His voice barely rose to an audible pitch. He needed a haircut, and his T-shirt was the thinnest Lauren had ever seen.

"Has your mom been in there a long time?" Lauren asked.

His eyes lifted to a large clock on the wall. "I don't know how to tell time."

Lauren sat next to the boy. "Does it seem

like you've been waiting a long time?"

He shrugged.

Lauren watched the second hand sweep around several times. She removed the clipboard from her bag and pulled out a pen. There must be something she could do now that would be more productive than waiting. Lauren took out her phone. She could at least call the rental company about the tables and chairs. Beside her, the little boy folded his hands in his lap and hung his head.

The owner of the rental store answered the phone himself. Within a few minutes, Lauren had notes on the tables and chairs, as well as the helium tank for the balloons. She hadn't thought about that. On a fresh page on her clipboard, she started a list of items to purchase before Saturday: helium balloons, face-paint kits, sidewalk chalk, paper goods. No doubt she would think of fifty other things before Saturday. Lauren glanced up at the director's door, still closed.

The child next to her was statue still.

"I'm Lauren," she said. "What's your name?"

He didn't answer — didn't even turn his head.

She tapped his knee. Finally, he looked up at her with eyes of dark wavy pools.

"If we're going to wait together, we might as well get to know each other." If he was five years old, he was a small five. Lauren was surprised his mother would have left him in the hall alone. "Maybe I can guess your name. Shall I try?"

He twisted his lips and looked away.

"Let me see. Maybe your name is Aladdin?"

He shook his head.

"How about Methuselah?"

Confusion ran through his eyes. "That's not a real name."

"Well, it is, but I can see why a little boy wouldn't want that name," Lauren said. "Something simpler, then. John. Is your name John?"

He rubbed one eye.

The director's office door opened.

"Christopher, have you been good?" A young woman knelt in front of the boy and looked at Lauren. "I hope he wasn't bothering you."

"I would say it was the other way around," Lauren said. Christopher was a quiet child. He didn't smile much, either. Lauren met the weary eyes of his mother.

"I'm sorry if I took a long time in there. I just . . . had a lot of questions." The young woman, who Lauren was sure was a good four years younger than she was, took Christopher's hand. "Come on, sweetie. Mommy needs to see someone else."

He stood up and tolerated his mother's motions to straighten his shirt. Lauren winked at him and then looked at the clock and at the clipboard in her lap, making sure she had the correct page of notes before knocking on the director's door. She approached the door and raised her hand.

The sound of the young mother's shuffle tugged on Lauren's gaze, but the clipboard weighed heavy in her grip and the health fair heavy in her mind. She blinked and turned back to the director's office, but her knuckles refused to make contact with the door. Lauren looked again at the mother whose shoulders drooped as she stroked the back of her son's head.

"I'm Lauren." She stepped down the hall.

"Excuse me?" The woman stopped walking and turned.

"I'm Lauren, and I have a feeling you could use a friend right now." The sensation had started the moment Lauren saw Christopher, and Lauren was glad to speak it aloud.

The woman's face blanched and her eyes reddened. "I'm Molly. And you're right."

Lauren jammed the clipboard into her cross-body bag. "Do you mind if I ask what you need to go see someone else about?"

"Gas. For starters."

Lauren paced toward Molly, who picked up her son. "And what else?"

Molly moistened her lips. "Groceries. Someone told me there was a food pantry here, but I guess they were confused."

"I can help you." Lauren couldn't believe

she'd almost ignored her instincts about this mother and child because details of the health fair overwhelmed her. She reached into her bag for an item she always carried on behalf of the church. "Could you use a gift card for the gas station down the road?"

Molly's eyes widened.

"Please," Lauren said. "Take it. I don't have a car, but if you don't mind an extra passenger, I can open the food pantry at the church where I work."

"You work at a church?"

"I do." Lauren tilted her head back toward the director's office. "If you'd like, we can go back and talk to Mrs. Hubbard. She'll vouch for me."

Molly kissed Christopher's face. "You know what? I trust you."

Christopher raised his head off his mother's shoulder. "My daddy went away. He doesn't love us anymore."

Lauren's stomach churned. No child should ever have to say those words.

"It's complicated," Molly said quickly. "We married young and had Christopher. Then we had a baby girl, but she was sick."

"My sister died."

Lauren was stunned at the flat tone in Christopher's voice. Did he understand death? The permanence of it?

Molly put a finger over Christopher's lips. "We couldn't keep up with the medical bills . . . or the funeral. My husband said he needed a break. But it's been over a year. He's not coming back, and I don't believe in lying to my son."

Lauren doubted she would be as brave under similar circumstances.

"You don't have to explain," she said. "Let's just get you the help you need."

"Thank you."

"Could Christopher use a new winter coat? I have one I think would fit him perfectly." Lauren saw no reason why the boy should wait until Saturday for the jacket he was meant to have.

2:46 p.m.

"I hate ice." Nicole winced as Ethan secured the ice pack around her ankle.

"Ice is your friend." Ethan gently repositioned her ankle. "It's the best anti-inflammatory there is."

Nicole knew she was grumbling too much. Despite her best resolve, though, the complaints came out of her mouth. Her ankle throbbed. Pain pills helped, but they made her groggy. If it weren't for Quinn's absence, maybe she'd be a better patient, but she wasn't going to get a chance to find out.

"We should have gone to Birch Bend," she said. "We would at least be doing something useful while you're still here."

"Nicole, we already talked about this."

She put her head back against the chair and sighed. "I hate ice. I hate pain. I hate the stupid pills. I hate not knowing where Quinn is. I hate that I let ten years go by. I hate it all."

"I know." Ethan adjusted the pillow under her foot.

"Has Hansen called you back?"

"Not yet. Do you want something to drink?"

"Juice, please." The sugar might jolt her brain into action.

She could ride in the backseat of Ethan's car with her foot elevated on as many pillows as he wanted to prescribe. Except when she was icing her ankle, it was immobilized in a boot cast — and considering how much it hurt, Nicole was certain she would remember not to put any weight on it while using crutches. Birch Bend had the county clerk's office and a larger regional newspaper than the few pages Marv Stanford produced every Tuesday.

Ethan handed her a glass of cranberry juice. "Friday is only the day after tomorrow. You can see the orthopedist and, if you feel up to it, make some inquiries in Birch Bend."

Nicole drank half the juice in one long gulp. "Maybe you should call Hansen again."

"He'll call when he has something to say."

"If you leave, who will take me to the orthopedist?"

Ethan sat on the end of the coffee table and rearranged the ice pack on Nicole's foot. "We'll figure it out. I'm sure Lauren can suggest someone who might help — someone from the church, perhaps."

Nicole sipped the juice, this time with less vigor. Ethan was right. Lauren had a lot on her mind, but she wouldn't leave Nicole stranded on Friday.

Nicole wanted Ethan to take her, though, and not just because he would indulge her investigative urges.

Nicole handed the empty glass to Ethan. "I should call my office again."

She was going to have to rearrange her life for a couple of weeks even if she managed to get home to St. Louis and even if she didn't need surgery. Nicole had been trying to reach Terry, the administrative assistant who provided support to a cadre of reporters. It was unlike Terry to go all day without responding to a phone message. Nicole called Terry's direct line once again and got her voice mail for the fourth time that day.

Ethan took the juice glass to the kitchen. Nicole heard running water and clinking plates as Ethan cleaned up the lunch dishes. She looked at the time displayed on her cell phone, anxious to get the ice off her ankle and the boot back on. Ethan was a stickler, not willing to shave even two minutes off the twenty-minute icing cycle. Lauren had made

Nicole comfortable in a set of sweats, but if Nicole was going to be confined to Lauren's apartment for at least the next two days, she was going to need her own things. Ethan would have to go to the Sandquist house and gather up the contents of the suitcase Nicole had traveled with. Already she'd exceeded the number of days she planned to stay in Hidden Falls.

At least the recliner was next to the big window overlooking Main Street. Nicole rolled her head toward the outside view of a sunny fall day identical to yesterday. An Indian summer might still erupt, but for now, most people moving around town wore a sweater or light jacket. Without leaning against the window more precariously than Ethan would permit, Nicole couldn't see the sidewalk below the apartment, but she had a clear view of the other side of the street. A small park interrupted the row of specialty shops, and Nicole's eyes settled there. The trees at the center of the park had dropped another layer of leaves since Nicole looked on the same scene the day before. Ragged points of maple leaves curled in as the breeze clustered fallen colors against the trunks of the trees.

A man walked through the park, and a flare of recognition made Nicole's head leave the back of the chair as she leaned toward the glass. A second man followed, his manner a little too precise to suit Nicole.

"Ethan."

His steps brought him out of the kitchen. "Need something?"

"Come here. Isn't that your dad down in the park?"

Ethan made no move to cross the room.

Nicole looked up at him. "I have a bad feeling. Maybe you should go down there."

Now Ethan stood beside the chair and looked out.

"That *is* your dad, isn't it?"

"Yes, but you know I wasn't planning to see them."

"This is different. That other guy —" Nicole lurched as much as the sprawling recliner would allow.

In the park, the second man came up behind Richard Jordan and reached for his back pocket. Richard responded to the man's touch with a swift pulse of his elbow, and the two of them tussled. Richard fell to the ground and the other man — younger and someone Nicole didn't recognize — ran back in the direction he'd come from.

"Did he get your dad's wallet?" Nicole asked.

"I couldn't tell."

"You should go down there and make sure your dad's all right."

Ethan didn't move. "He's already getting up. He's not hurt."

Richard Jordan resumed his walk, crossed Main Street, and went out of view.

"It's been ten years, Ethan." Nicole caught his eyes and held them.

"I know."

"You're not a kid now. You know how the world works."

Ethan stepped away. "I'm aware of my age. Some things don't change."

"They might. Besides, sooner or later, someone is going to mention to your parents that they saw you."

Ethan picked up Nicole's phone and tapped an application. "Here. See if you can beat yourself at Scrabble. No Internet browsing allowed."

Nicole took the phone, but her eyes returned to the empty park.

4:13 p.m.

When Jack Parker heard a door close down the hall and recognized the anxious gait that followed, he got up and left his own desk, walked past the as yet unoccupied secretary's desk in the outer office of his suite, and stepped into the hall just in time to intersect Liam Elliott.

If possible, Liam looked even worse than the last time Jack saw him less than twenty-four hours earlier. He had an all-nighter look about him. At least Liam wasn't wearing the same suit.

"You doing okay, buddy?" Jack fell into step with Liam as they reached the top of the stairs.

"It's a hectic time." Liam didn't meet Jack's eye.

"I sure hate seeing you look so worn out these days."

"It won't last forever. You know how work can be. Feast or famine."

Jack kept pace with Liam descending the stairs. "I do know."

Jack thrived on feasting. He got by the last few months with routine work from established clients who stayed with the practice after Jack took it over, but it was no feast. His practice needed an injection of interesting work, something that would justify the expense of finding someone to replace the legal secretary who retired when her employers turned the practice over to Jack.

The overstuffed leather computer bag Liam carried around would suggest his business was doing well, but Jack was unpersuaded. Liam didn't look harried by work. Jack had seen enough frightened clients to recognize the face of fear.

"Do you have time for a cup of coffee?" Jack asked as they reached the sidewalk.

Liam shook his head. "I'm hoping to catch the mayor."

"I thought she kept morning office hours."

"I heard she was in her store today."

They rounded the corner and walked over one block to Main Street.

"Something's going on in the park," Jack said.

Liam hesitated long enough to turn his head.

"Isn't that your brother?" Jack nodded toward the uniformed sheriff's deputy taking notes while an older man pointed and waved his arms.

"With Richard Jordan." Liam looked toward the park and then down the street.

"You know him?"

"He's a client."

"Maybe he needs help." Jack stepped off the curb to cross the street.

"I'll catch you later, Jack." Liam continued down the sidewalk.

Jack knew where to find Liam. This skirmish in the park would be a brief diversion, but if it had legal overtones, Jack didn't want to miss it.

"Did you see what he looked like?" Cooper Elliott said as Jack reached him.

"Young. Dark. Strong." Richard thrust an index finger toward the back of the park. "He came from that direction. He was trying to get my wallet."

"Did you see his face?" Cooper asked, his pen poised over the form he was filling out.

Richard shrugged. "He never looked at me full on."

Jack cleared his throat. "What I think the good officer is getting at, Mr. Jordan, is whether you would be able to identify your assailant if you saw him again."

"Hello, Jack." Cooper gave Jack a cool look.

"How do you know my name?" Richard asked.

Jack extended a hand. "Jack Parker, attorney. I only want to help."

"Jack." Cooper cocked his head. "Let me get the man's report."

"Of course." Jack stepped back to where he could casually look over Cooper's shoulder at the makeshift map of the park drawn with stick figures and arrows.

"I think he was following me ever since I left the hardware store," Richard Jordan said. "He was dressed all in black and gray, but I remember noticing he was wearing green tennis shoes. Seemed odd to me."

Cooper made notes. "But you didn't see his face?"

"It was just a face. Who notices the face of everyone you see when you're out running errands?"

"And no suspicious behavior?"

"Not until he tried to steal my wallet."

"We're right off Main Street," Jack said. "Someone else must have seen something."

"I already told Officer Elliott I didn't notice who else was around. Not anybody I know, I guess."

"That's right." Cooper clicked his ballpoint pen. "We've already been over that ground. I think I have everything I need for now. I'll see if there have been any other reports of pickpockets lately. Maybe we'll find a pattern."

"Be sure you talk to Gavin Owens about the attempted purse snatching in his restaurant." Jack reached into his breast pocket, withdrew a business card, and handed it to Richard. "I'm experienced with criminal cases. I might be able to help you remember something you don't realize is significant."

Richard put the card in the pocket of his brown flannel-lined jacket. "I have to go meet my wife."

"Call me anytime if you want some help."

Jack looked down the street. Liam was out of view. Jack found it hard to believe Liam and Cooper were brothers. Beyond a vague family resemblance, they seemed nothing alike, even when Liam was not the ball of nerves he'd become in the last few days. By now Liam was probably at Waterfall Books and Gifts. Jack crossed the street and strode down the sidewalk.

At the mayor's shop, Jack tried the front door and found it locked. He could see into the store, though, and watched Liam set his lumpy bag on the counter. Jack jiggled the doorknob again, and Sylvia looked up and pointed at the sign. CLOSED. Unperturbed,

Jack waved through the glass but made no movement away from the door. When he had Sylvia's eye, he pointed at the door. A moment later she turned the latch.

"We're not open, Jack. It's still a mess in here."

"I just thought I'd see if I could be helpful." Jack pushed into the store.

"We have it in hand," Sylvia said.

Jack spotted Dani Roose toward the back of the store. She was definitely someone he should speak to soon. He could represent her interests in making sure any suspects in the vandalism to her boat were prosecuted as thoroughly as possible. Probably there were grounds for a civil case on top of criminal charges.

"I haven't heard back on the calls I made yesterday," Jack said. "It takes time, though. I'll be sure to let you know as soon as I hear anything."

Silent, Liam shifted his weight from one foot to the other.

The poor guy can hardly stand up, Jack thought.

Sylvia turned to Liam. "As I was saying, the best thing is to call Marianne and make an appointment to see me. Then we can talk without interruption."

Liam glanced at Jack and ran his tongue over his lips. "I appreciate your willingness to see me in your office, but I believe this is an urgent matter."

Jack knew when to keep his mouth closed. He stepped back two paces to listen.

"You can see I'm in the middle of my own muddle. I could give you my full attention at Town Hall."

Liam glared at Jack. "I was hoping to speak privately."

Jack gave a smug smile. He wasn't going anywhere.

"I've told you before," Sylvia said, "the town council can't look at your proposal until the comptroller has vetted it."

"This is about Quinn."

Sylvia froze. "What about Quinn?"

Jack leaned with one palm on the counter.

Liam took his phone out and tapped a few buttons before turning the screen toward Sylvia. "This was mixed in with my mail. I couldn't keep the letter, obviously. I hope it's not a crime to take a picture, but I thought it might mean something. Look at the next one, too."

Sylvia held the phone in both hands, studied the image, and scrolled to the second one. "What kind of business is that?"

"I tried to find it on the Internet," Liam said. "They don't seem to have a website."

"Everybody has a website," Jack said. "Mind if I have a look?"

He ignored the reticence in Liam's face and

reached for the phone. Sylvia handed it to him.

"Santorelli," Jack read aloud the single name of the business. The address was in Pennsylvania, but it was only a PO box. "In my experience, this sort of letter comes from an organization whose greatest value is being discreet, like a private detective or an adoption search."

"Adoption search," Sylvia said. "Why would Quinn . . . ?"

"Some sort of search," Jack said. "It might not be an adoption, but Quinn is probably looking for somebody."

4:44 p.m.

Sylvia could tell nothing from the photo.

It could be a private letter from an old friend. Liam had held it, though, and insisted the paper inside felt like business weight, the kind companies used to print letterhead on before the world defaulted to economical photocopy paper for ubiquitous use.

Sylvia took the phone from Jack and handed it back to Liam. "Will you send that image to my e-mail address, please?"

Liam tapped a few prompts, and Sylvia heard the alert sound on his phone that meant the message was en route. She would look at it later, at home, where she could hold it before her eyes for as long as she liked. Maybe a full-size image on her computer screen would reveal more than what she could see on a cell phone.

Not that Sylvia would know what to look for. The return address was just one name, the PO box, and a city Sylvia recognized as a suburb of Philadelphia. Quinn's name and address had come off a laser printer. Whatever kind of company Santorelli was, their standards for being discreet didn't preclude contemporary office technology.

Liam and Jack still huddled uncomfortably close.

"Thank you, Liam. You did the right thing by insisting I look at the photos." What she would do with the information, Sylvia didn't know. Philadelphia was a long way from Hidden Falls, and she didn't even have a street address.

"I'll call your office about the other matter." Liam tucked his phone away.

"I'm sure Marianne can set you up."

"I'll ask for the next available appointment."

"There's no rush. As I said, I can't do much until the comptroller finishes his work."

"I understand. I just want to be sure I have the opportunity to address questions you might have."

Sylvia was ready to be done with both Liam and Jack badgering her for town business. She wasn't sure she could trust either one of them, but even if she did, the town council had several members savvy about financial contracts. The decision to give Liam investment accounts to manage or Jack legal contracts to review wouldn't be up to Sylvia. People tended to think the office of mayor held far more power than it did. Even a small town had ordinances and bylaws to abide by.

Still, she was grateful Liam had brought her the photo, even if he did have ulterior motives.

Liam picked up his black bag. "I'd like to say hi to Dani before I go."

He moved toward the rear of the store, leaving Sylvia with Jack's overeager expression.

"Let me check out that address," Jack said. "If this is a clue about what happened to Quinn, we'd all like to know."

Sylvia's mind was unclear what Jack had invested in finding Quinn. It certainly wasn't personal. Quinn welcomed the Parker family to town with the same cordiality he extended to anyone, and one of Jack's daughters was a student of Quinn's, but as far as Sylvia knew, the two men barely knew each other. Jack's chronic zeal to be the winner — when there was no contest — grated on Sylvia.

But Sylvia would never forgive herself if she didn't do everything she could for Quinn. All day, every day, between responsibilities — Town Hall, her mother, the shop — Sylvia tempered the anxiety for Quinn that broke over her spirit in fresh waves.

What could it hurt to let Jack try to find out who or what Santorelli was? She couldn't stop him, anyway. He'd seen the address. If he came up with something, she wanted him to bring it straight to her. Brushing him off at this point would be counterproductive.

"It's kind of you to offer your time and experience," Sylvia said.

"I'll get back to you."

Sylvia wondered what kind of lawyer Jack had been in Memphis and Atlanta. Perhaps despite his overconfident yet needy demeanor, he was a competent professional. When it came to finding Quinn, Sylvia would like nothing more than to be proven wrong in her instincts about Jack Parker.

Jack went out the shop door, and Sylvia locked it behind him. Out of deference to Dani, she quashed the urge to rush Liam out.

Sylvia went down the shelf-lined wall to check on Lizzie's progress with sorting books according to degree of damage. Each hour brought more encouragement about the store's inventory. The insurance policy would compensate Sylvia for most of the losses, but it was still nice to see they wouldn't have to reopen with empty shelves. Already the UPS truck had brought two orders Sylvia placed before the burglary, and Lizzie had entered orders with two other distributors with expedited delivery. Between new items and salvageable items, the store would look fairly normal in another day or so.

In the back of the store, Dani was replacing bent brackets on a shelving unit that had otherwise survived the assault. Dani typically didn't stop what she was doing to talk to people, and the conversation with Liam was no exception. She ducked her head at an odd angle to position a screwdriver while Liam spoke to her.

Liam looked alarmingly pale to Sylvia. Distraction seeped through his every gesture today, and his grooming seemed a shade off of his usual personal presentation.

Sylvia stopped to chat with Lizzie and then moved through the store toward the office in the back.

"Fine, come," Dani muttered.

"Your house at seven?"

"Yes." Dani withdrew the screwdriver. "But you'd better bring something I feel like eating."

"Pretty sure I can manage that." Liam adjusted the strap of his bag as he turned toward Sylvia. "I'll get out of your way now."

"I'll walk you out," Sylvia said.

Once he was out of the store, Sylvia bolted the door again. This time she pulled down the shade that covered the glass in the door and then reached for the cord to release a shade over the front window, something she hardly ever did.

She wanted no more interruptions. CLOSED

meant CLOSED.

7:02 p.m.

Dani was tempted to sit Patricia Healy down for a lesson on rewiring a lamp. If Patricia was going to persist in blowing out lamps at the rate Dani had seen during the last two years, she ought to learn to repair them. This one had been on Dani's garage workbench for four weeks already. If she didn't fix it soon, Patricia would start leaving daily messages on Dani's old answering machine in the kitchen. Further delay wasn't worth that aggravation. Dani popped the old socket out of the lamp and tossed it aside before cutting the wires and pulling out the cord. She had just starting pushing the new cord through the bottom of the table lamp when she heard Liam's car.

Dani didn't interrupt her project. Liam would know where to find her. His car door slammed, and his steps crunched on the gravel driveway. Dani counted seventeen steps and looked up to see her cousin standing in the door with a sack of food from Eat Right Here.

"I got cake, too," he said.

"What are we celebrating?" Dani pulled the cord through to the top of the lamp and reached for the wire strippers.

"How about the fact that you're alive and

not in the hospital after being tossed over the falls?"

"You must have heard some wild stories." Dani stripped a half inch off the wires. "Hand me that new socket, will you?"

Liam set down the food bag and found the socket.

"Now the screwdriver," Dani said. "That little one."

He gave her the tool. "I was relieved to find you in Sylvia's store today and see for myself that you're all right."

"I think in my case you can assume that if you don't hear from me, I'm not dead." Dani wrapped wire around a screw. "You're my local next of kin."

"I'm honored. But seriously, I was glad to see you weren't more banged up."

Dani tightened down both screws and reached for electrical tape to wrap the terminals. "I just need a few minutes to finish this."

"I'm in no hurry."

"Isn't Jessica waiting for you or something?"

"Jessica doesn't run my life."

Dani flashed him a look but managed to refrain from laughter. "What did you do now?"

Liam reached into the food sack and pulled out a french fry. "I'm not going to dignify that crack."

"Whatever." Dani tore a paper towel from the roll over her workbench and wiped her hands. When Liam opened the sack and unleashed the smell of food — Reuben sandwiches along with the fries, if Dani's nose was any judge — hunger overtook her. "Let's go eat. I'll finish this later."

Before she had swallowed her first bite, Liam put his phone on the table in front of her. Dani looked at the photo of an address.

"I'm not sure I trust Jack Parker," he said. "Do you?"

Dani took another bite and chewed slowly. "Who's Santorelli?"

Liam swiped to another photo. "And why is he writing to Quinn at a UPS box?"

"You're full of surprises." Dani set down her sandwich. "How did we get from Jack Parker to Quinn's *private* mail?"

"Jack says he can find out who Santorelli is, but I would put my bet on your sleuthing abilities."

"That's Quinn's business," Dani said.

"And maybe it had something to do with what happened to him."

"That's a pretty big leap."

"It's possible, isn't it?"

"Anything is possible. That's not the point."

Liam rearranged his sandwich. "Yes it is. Even long shots are possibilities when no one's heard from Quinn in four days."

"So now you've talked to every resident of Hidden Falls."

"I'm pretty sure Cooper's on top of that."

"Then let him do his job." Dani filled her mouth again. No matter what anyone said, she wasn't inclined to worry about Quinn. "I've got my own mystery to solve if I want justice about my boat."

"Isn't that Cooper's job, too?"

"This is different."

Half of Hidden Falls were sticking their noses into Quinn's business and thinking they knew his mind. Dani was minding her own business. She had every right to try to assemble the puzzle pieces when it came to the destruction of her boat. Dani wanted to get back to her work enlarging and enhancing Ethan's photos. She wasn't going to waste time debating the merits of her strategy with Liam.

Liam chewed and stared. Dani did not relent.

"Follow me." Dani led Liam into the other room, where her computer displayed a photo from the edge of the lake.

Liam leaned in for a closer look. "That's the woods outside the cabin. So?"

Dani zoomed in and put a finger on the screen. "Here, where it's darker. See that shape?"

Liam peered but shook his head. "What am I supposed to see?"

"A person. A man, I think."

He shrugged. "It could be, I guess. You

think this is the person who put a hole in the boat?"

"I think it's somebody who doesn't want to be seen. If you were going to commit a crime, would you want to be seen?"

Liam paled.

Dani clicked the photo closed. "Why are you so bent on finding out who Santorelli is?"

"Because of Quinn, of course."

"You're not even that close to him."

"But you are. After four days, aren't you starting to wonder?"

Wonder, yes. Worry, no. "He'll turn up when he's ready."

"I'm impressed with what you're doing with those photos," Liam said. "I wouldn't know where to begin."

Dani shrugged. "People learn what they're interested in learning. It's easier than a lot of people think."

Liam chuckled. "That sounds like the kind of thing a gloating hacker would say."

Dani saw no humor in the remark. "I'm not one of those people who steals information or creates viruses."

Liam backpedaled. "I didn't say you were."

Then what exactly was he saying?

"But you understand how to hack into a system, don't you?" Liam asked.

Of course she did. "It's not usually that hard. People are careless about passwords."

"If someone's computer was hacked, would you be able to trace how it happened?"

"Depends." Whatever Liam was trying to say, Dani wished he would get to the point.

"I've been having some trouble with my computer," he said. "Maybe I'll have you take a look."

"It's not my favorite thing to do." If he'd been hacked, Dani hoped Liam hadn't been stupid.

"Nothing competes with fishing."

Liam had that right.

"Back to Quinn," Liam said. "I know you can track anything. I really want you to try to dig up something on this Santorelli business."

"I told you —"

"I know. But if there's even a remote possibility something happened to Quinn, don't you want to help?"

7:31 p.m.

"I love macaroni and cheese." Christopher stood on a chair pulled up next to Lauren at the stove and stirred the pasta and powdered cheese together.

Molly was at the cupboard putting away peanut butter, tuna fish, spaghetti sauce, pastas, bread, breakfast cereal, and assorted canned vegetables. Bananas and apples sat in a basket on the counter. The refrigerator was stocked with milk, juice, eggs, and yogurt. A generous gift card to the nearest grocery store would ensure Molly could get more fresh food.

Lauren patted Christopher's back and smiled over his head at his mother.

"He doesn't remember that we didn't always eat out of boxes," Molly said softly. "I pureed his baby food out of organic ingredients."

"Don't be embarrassed," Lauren said. "You're taking care of your son the very best way you can right now."

"This is the fourth place we've lived in a year," Molly said. "Each one is crummier than the one before."

"Christopher knows you love him. That's what matters." Lauren put her hand over his and stirred the mixture with slightly more force.

The house was dismal. Lauren wouldn't deny that reality. Standing next to the back door, she felt the draft that came in through the cracks around it. The curtains looked like they hadn't been replaced in twenty years, and the linoleum floor had a crack that ran the length of the room. None of the chairs matched the table or each other. In the living room, the unpolished wood floors were gouged and lacked the rugs that would have warmed up the room.

Christopher hadn't taken off the brown-and-green winter jacket since Lauren first helped him zip it up. It fit him well, with plenty of room for the growth spurt he might have over the winter. When they got home, Molly had coaxed him to take off his hat and gloves with the compromise that he could sleep in his new jacket that night even though the house was comfortably warm.

"This looks just about done." Lauren glanced at the green beans heating on the rear burner. She had already promised Christopher she would eat with them and confided that mac and cheese had been her favorite food when she was his age.

Molly lifted Christopher off the stool, and they moved to the table. Lauren sat between mother and son and offered her open hands.

"I'd like to ask the blessing," she said.

Christopher sobered, shook his head, and put his hands in his lap.

Lauren raised her eyebrows toward Molly.

"We haven't asked a blessing in a long time," Molly said. "He's not used to it."

"Do you mind?" Lauren asked.

"I wish you would. I'm so grateful tonight."

Lauren kept her prayer simple and childlike, using words she hoped Christopher would understand. They ate macaroni, beans, and salad greens. Christopher asked for two refills of milk, making Lauren wonder about the last time the child had unlimited access to filling food.

"Time for your jammies." Molly prodded Christopher when he had scraped his plate clean. "You can put your coat back on after you change."

Once her son left the room, Molly turned tear-filled eyes to Lauren. "I was so desperate this afternoon when I found out the community center couldn't help us. And then there you were."

"We were both where we needed to be." Lauren had come so close to simply phoning the community center and taking her chances with leaving a message for the director. Even after she was there, she'd almost let Molly and her son walk out of the center. The clipboard was still in her bag, untouched for the last few hours. Tomorrow was Thursday. She had only two days to pull the fair together. When she got home tonight, she would call the other members of the committee and begin trying to share the load — if it wasn't too late to make phone calls.

"We've taken up so much of your time," Molly said.

"I was glad to give it." Lauren stacked the plates. "I hope you'll come to the fair on Saturday. We're planning fun for the kids, and I think you'll meet people you'll really like."

"The only thing that will keep us away is if I find a job."

Lauren wondered who would look after Christopher when Molly found work. He had just missed the cut-off for being old enough to go to school. *One challenge at a time,* she reminded herself.

Christopher returned to the kitchen in Thomas the Tank Engine pajamas that were too short and his new coat. "I can't zip it myself."

"We'll have to work on that," Molly said.

Rather than standing before his mother, Christopher presented himself for Lauren's assistance. "Can you tell me a story while I fall asleep?"

"Oh, honey," Molly said, "Lauren has done a lot for us today."

His face fell.

"I would be happy to do it," Lauren said. She didn't care if she didn't make her calls that night no matter what the consequence would be tomorrow.

"At least let me help you brush your teeth." Molly steered the boy toward the bathroom.

Lauren ran water in the kitchen sink and started on the dishes while she waited for Molly's return.

"He's ready," Molly said. "But make it a short story. He needs his sleep, and you have things to do. We've imposed enough."

Lauren found Christopher's bedroom. There were only two rooms at the other side of the house. He was in his jacket and under a quilt. In the background, Lauren heard his mother cleaning up after the meal.

She sat on the bed. "This story is about a

little boy who *loves* macaroni and cheese."

Lauren filled the story with bits and pieces of Christopher's own day — at least the good parts she had witnessed for herself. After only a few minutes, his eyes closed and his shoulders drooped. She lowered her voice and spoke more slowly, matching her cadence to his even breathing until she was sure his slumber had passed the fragility of waking. Lauren managed to stand up without disturbing him and, on impulse, leaned over his face to give him the butterfly kisses she had learned from her Nana, her eyelashes barely brushing his cheek. Christopher shifted his head on the pillow but didn't wake. At his door, ready to pull it closed behind her, Lauren turned to watch him. A prayer welled in her for this little boy to know blessing more than fear.

Molly was in the hall and embraced Lauren. "I can't remember the last time someone was so kind to me. You've given us both a beautiful day. It gives me hope in my spirit. I had just about given up on hope."

Just about.

Lauren patted Molly's back. When Molly woke in the morning, she would still have no job and crushing debt. She would still be raising a child alone. She would still be living in a dismally furnished rental house. She would still grieve the little girl she had laid in the ground last year and the dismantling of a life where she had been loved and happy. Lauren knew nothing she had done that day would solve the disappointments of Molly's existence. But for now, her son had a warm jacket, new shoes, and food. It was a start.

Outside Molly's house, Lauren remembered she had ridden her bicycle out to the community center. Molly drove them around town to the various businesses that allowed Lauren to find a chink in the desperation of Molly's day and ignite hope. Lauren could walk to her apartment easily enough from the edge of town. The movement would give her time to pray for Molly and Christopher.

Nothing about the last four days had been what Lauren expected. In her small corner of the world, Lauren had just about given up hope herself — hope for the health fair, hope for being able to do it well, hope for caring enough to carry through when she was exhausted.

She had lost another precious day.

And she would do it again in a heartbeat.

8:36 p.m.

"Tell me you're not on the Internet." Ethan snatched the phone out of Nicole's hands and closed the search window.

She looked up at him. "I'm not on the Internet."

"Funny." He set her phone out of reach. "If it rings, I'll let you answer."

"I remember your being a lot more entertaining to be around."

"Yeah, well, you weren't so grumpy in those days."

"I thought Lauren would be home by now," Nicole said. "I was going to ask you to go over to my house and get my stuff. Lauren can go along if you feel weird about doing it."

"I'm sure you think it will be easier to scour the Internet for clues about Quinn on your laptop instead of your phone."

"Don't forget my iPad." Nicole raked her fingers across her scalp.

They'd tried the TV, but Lauren didn't have cable and Nicole wasn't satisfied with broadcast options. Ethan snooped in the hall closet and uncovered a Scattergories box, but Nicole found him such a pitiful opponent that she refused to play more than two rounds. Ethan called in an order to the Fall Shadows Café and left Nicole alone long enough to run down the street and pick it up. When he got back, she was rolling around the apartment in the swiveling desk chair again. He wasn't an orthopedist, but he'd seen enough broken bones to know she was in pain, and she refused to take another painkiller before bedtime. The lack of response by her assistant to her phone messages increasingly bothered Nicole. Her uninjured foot jiggled almost nonstop.

She was anxious, in pain, tired, and bored — though Ethan doubted Nicole would admit any of it. Her general state of agitation underscored for Ethan why he became a physician and not a nurse. He was used to being in and out of a patient's room within a few minutes. He counted on nurses to let him know when his skills were needed or when a change of meds might be helpful, and he'd never developed the ability to patiently respond to shifting moods and chronic discomfort.

"I hear footsteps." Nicole straightened as much as she could in the recliner.

Ethan breathed relief at the sound of the knob turning. Lauren came through the door.

"Nicole was about ready to send out a search party."

"Sorry." Lauren dropped her bag on a chair next to the door. "I kept meaning to call."

"I hope you were able to get some work done on the health fair," Nicole said.

"Not really," Lauren said. "Something else came up."

Despite Lauren's words, Ethan thought, she looked less stressed than she had when she left after lunch. She went into the kitchen for a glass of water and then stretched out on the sofa.

"I hope you ate," Lauren said.

"We did." Nicole rubbed her eyes. "How about you?"

"Yes. Has Ethan been taking good care of you?"

"No comment."

They laughed.

"Actually," Nicole said, "I was hoping you and Ethan could run out to my house to get my things."

"Sure. I'm willing." Lauren sipped water. "I wish that as long as we're in the neighborhood there was some way to get Quinn's notes on the fair. I still think it would make my job easier."

"The place is locked up," Ethan said. "We'd have to climb a tree to see if Quinn ever fixed that window into the attic."

Silence slid into place as the women froze.

"Ethan," Nicole said, "are you saying that all this time you knew a way to get into Quinn's house?"

"Well . . . no," he said. "That was years ago."

"What are you talking about?" Lauren asked.

"Quinn's house has a full attic with windows at the back," Ethan said. "I used to climb the maple that shades his deck and get into the house that way."

"Why did I never know this?" Nicole asked.

"I only did it a few times when I just had to get out of my house," Ethan said. "It was a scary climb and it's a small window, which was probably why Quinn never got around to fixing it."

Nicole reached for the lever and lowered the footrest on the recliner. "My crutches, please."

Lauren rose from the couch and handed Nicole the crutches. "I'll find your shoe."

Ethan stared at them. "You're not seriously thinking about breaking into Quinn's house."

"What's to break?" Nicole said. "We just need to find out if the window still opens."

"I'm not twelve years old," Ethan said. "I'm not climbing three stories up to an attic window."

"Lauren needs Quinn's notes," Nicole said, "and we might find a clue about where Quinn went."

"I am *not* going to climb that tree."

Lauren was on hands and knees looking for Nicole's single shoe under the sofa. "Well, I'm not going to do it, and Nicole is in no condition. That leaves you."

"I don't recall putting this to a vote." Had they lost their capacity for rational thought? When he was a neglected preadolescent, Ethan lacked the sense of danger he felt now. And while he kept himself in good shape, he wasn't as nimble as he was at twelve — and weighed eighty pounds more than the last time he climbed the tree. He wasn't even sure if the branches that high up would support his weight. Testing the notion had no appeal.

"Come on, Ethan," Nicole said. "*Four days.*

If you're going to leave in the morning, then let this be your parting contribution to the cause."

"Getting arrested will not be a great career move." Neither would falling out of a tree and breaking his back. He wasn't going to listen to this nonsense. Ethan put both hands up. "Lauren, I'll take you to get Nicole's stuff, but that's it."

"I vote we take Nicole with us. Once you get in and get the door open, it won't be that hard for her to hobble in the back door."

Ethan squeezed his head between his hands. "You've lost your minds. Why don't you just call Cooper and tell him there's a way in?"

Nicole waved off the suggestion. "He'll make a fuss about needing a search warrant or something. An officer of the law can't just go into somebody's house. He's a by-the-book guy."

"Well, maybe there's a good reason for the book."

"Nicole, do you need a jacket?" Lauren asked. "I've got a spare."

"Good thinking." Nicole was upright now, leaning on crutches and holding her booted foot off the floor. "What did you do with my house key when we got here yesterday?"

"In my bag." Lauren opened the front closet and pulled a dark jacket from a hanger. "Where are you parked, Ethan?"

"Look, I'm taking you to Nicole's house,"

he said, "but Nicole does *not* need to come." She might get a crazy idea like trying to climb the stairs.

Nicole laughed. "I'm not missing this for the world."

Twenty minutes later, Ethan stood at the base of the mature maple tree in Quinn's backyard. He judged the attic window to be at least twenty-five feet off the ground, maybe closer to thirty. Nicole sat on the deck with a flashlight. Lauren stood directly below the window in question with another light. The tree was closer to the house than Ethan remembered. He was surprised the roots hadn't caused issues with the home's foundation, but the proximity meant it wasn't as far from the tree's trunk to the window as he'd pictured. This wouldn't be the first time he'd climbed in the dark — only the first time he did so knowing the ludicrous danger of climbing at all.

They should have left this to Cooper and his team. If Ethan got any whiff of a four-day-old decaying body in the house — he banished the thought. Cooper had sent a squad car to the house within minutes of Quinn's disappearance at the banquet. The premises had been undisturbed.

Ethan checked to make sure the flashlight app on his phone was working. Though he knew its rays would be a pitiful weapon against the darkness inside the tree, Ethan didn't want to carry anything heavier. He intended to stop every few branches to shine the light and get his bearings and make sure he was on a path toward the window and not above it or behind it.

Sweat plastered his shirt to his skin before Ethan was ten feet off the ground. Where had his twelve-year-old self gotten such bravado? The higher he got, the more slowly Ethan climbed. He didn't look down at Nicole's flashlight beam and then Lauren's without first grasping a branch with both arms. If this had been the middle of summer when the tree was in full leaf, he would never have seen the house from the interior branches. When he was fairly certain he had reached the right height for the window, he began scooting slowly out on the thickest branches he could find, making sure he also had a good grip at all times on a branch other than the one he sat on.

Inch by inch, Ethan by turn held his breath and deliberately exhaled. The branch he slid out on thinned. Finally, he saw the glass in the window reflecting the beams angled from the ground.

Ethan couldn't get it open with one hand. He counted to three under his breath before releasing his security grip and leaning his weight into pushing the window up with both hands.

Its resistance felt like it hadn't been open

since the last time Ethan made this climb.

But it gave.

He slid off the end of the branch and was in.

Ethan closed the window behind him and leaned against the wall to wait for his heart to stop pounding. He turned on his phone light and gave his eyes time to adjust before finding his way across the attic, down the stairs, and into the upstairs hall. There he paused long enough to send a text message.

I'M IN.

Without turning on more lights, Ethan descended the carpeted stairs, paced to the back of the house, and unlocked the patio door.

"No lights," he said to Nicole and Lauren. The last thing they needed was someone in the neighborhood calling the sheriff's office because of suspicious activity in a house everyone in town knew was locked and empty. After what he'd just been through, Ethan wasn't interested in answering Cooper Elliott's questions.

"Let's check his den first," Nicole said. "He used to spend a lot of time there."

Lauren pointed her beam at the floor, keeping it one step ahead of Nicole's crutches. Ethan followed, ready to catch Nicole at the first sign that she had put a crutch down on the edge of a rug or another spot that wasn't clear and level. Cutting into someone's brain was less nerve-racking than this.

In the den, Lauren rifled through the papers on top of the desk while Nicole started on a file cabinet.

Ethan just wanted them to finish whatever they were going to do so they could all get out of there.

Lauren gasped.

"What is it?" Nicole closed a file drawer.

"I think I found his notes." Lauren held her light steady. "Yes! Booths, supplies, volunteers. It's not very organized, but it's all here."

"Good," Ethan said. "Let's go."

"I'm not finished." Nicole pulled open another drawer. "Lauren, bring your light over here."

Lauren folded the papers she took from the desk and stuffed them in her bag. Then she held her light, the brightest one, over the drawer Nicole had open.

Nicole flipped through files with a rapidity and efficiency that astonished Ethan. Obviously she'd done this sort of thing before.

"Bingo," Nicole said.

"What?" Lauren asked.

Even Ethan couldn't deny his curiosity. He was in too deep now to claim not to be party to the search.

"It's a photograph." Nicole laid the picture flat on top of the contents of the drawer.

Lauren looked at the photo, at Ethan, and

then back to the photo with disbelief in her eyes. "Do you see what I see?"

7
Yesterday's Promise

Thursday
6:54 a.m.

Three more days.

The good news was that Dr. Gonzalez, surgical chief overseeing Ethan's neurosurgical residency, decided to follow a conference with a long weekend. Ethan had bartered his shifts to gain three more days in Hidden Falls.

The bad news was he would be in serious debt to his colleagues when he returned to Columbus in time for Monday morning rounds, exactly one week after his scheduled return.

And there would be Gonzalez to deal with. Ethan reasoned he had three days to produce an explanation that the chief might accept. Somebody who survived four years of medical school and five years of a six-year residency should be smart enough to come up with something, even if he would probably be on probation for the entire final year of his residency.

What mattered at the moment was Quinn. And Nicole. And what Ethan had let her drag him into last night. He was going to need some help getting out of this mess.

Walking away wasn't an option. Not this time.

Ethan glanced at the clock in the motel room. Instead of guzzling bad coffee and hitting the interstate, Ethan now planned to drive across the bridge above the falls, go into town, and find the house Dani Roose lived in when she wasn't incognito up at the lake. Ethan left his half-packed suitcase on the bed and went out to his car.

The night had been late. Ethan could have used some coffee, but he didn't dare delay or he could spend all day guessing at Dani's movements. He wanted to catch her before she left.

And he would do it without remorse in repayment for the morning she banged on his motel room door not much later than it was now. She'd needed something he had. Now he needed something she had.

Ethan pulled up to Dani's house on the north edge of downtown, wagering that her fishing habit was temporarily curtailed by the loss of her boat and that seven in the morning was too early for Dani to be working on a project in someone else's home. At her front door, he knocked sharply twice before stepping back to await her response.

When she opened the door, she was dressed and her long hair was braided. One hand gripped the handle of a large mug. She stared at him and sipped coffee.

Ethan's envy magnified his sense of morning caffeine withdrawal.

"I need your help," he said.

Dani turned around and walked back into the house. Since she left the door open, Ethan followed her through the sparsely appointed living room and into the kitchen, where she took another mug from the cabinet and filled it. She set it on the table and sat down to finish her half-eaten breakfast.

When he picked up the coffee, Ethan knew he had lost the edge he'd felt a few minutes ago. With the first sip, he was in her debt.

"My day is scheduled." Dani used a corner of toast to scoop eggs.

"Then I need you to reschedule it."

She scoffed. "You're a piece of work."

He plunged in. "I'm guessing you've worked on Quinn's laptop."

She raised one shoulder about an inch and let it fall. "That's not exactly a secret."

"Recently Quinn's computer has been . . . transferred to a new location, and it doesn't seem entirely happy with the change in locale."

"I can't help you if you're going to talk in code." Dani took a long draft of coffee.

"We took Quinn's computer to Lauren's apartment."

"We?"

It hadn't been Ethan's idea. He'd argued against it — vehemently — to Nicole and Lauren. No doubt by taking it they'd added some technical degree of theft to a particular form of illegal entry. Cooper Elliott would know the specifics, but Ethan hoped the whole business would be cleared up long before Cooper needed to know anything about it. Ethan decided not to mention the spare house key that Nicole knew where to find inside Quinn's kitchen and had dropped in her pocket.

"The computer won't power up," he said.

"Doesn't surprise me." Dani put the last of the eggs in her mouth.

Good. If she recognized the computer's behavior, then she probably knew how to resolve it.

"Perhaps I was chewing too loudly to hear you," Dani said, "but I think you skipped over the part about why you stole Quinn's laptop."

Ethan didn't know Dani well, and he was tiring of parrying every time they conversed. But he needed her on Team Find Quinn.

"So the computer is not dead?" he said.

"Quinn refuses to let it die with dignity. There may still be some extraordinary measures worth trying."

"I want you to come to Lauren's and try

them." Ethan took a deep breath. "And then I want you to help us find some information that may be on the computer."

Dani laughed. "No. I think I have a Styrofoam cup around here if you want to take your coffee with you."

Ethan didn't move. "I'm serious."

Dani stood and set her breakfast plate in the sink. "Let me see if I have this straight. You broke into Quinn's house. You stole his computer — and who knows what else. Now you want me to join your ring of thieves to gain access to private information to which you are not legally entitled."

"We didn't break anything." Ethan swirled the coffee in his mug. "And I prefer to think of the computer as borrowed." Since they had a key now, they could put it back.

"And the private information?"

"It might help us find Quinn."

"I have somewhere to be by seven thirty. And it sounds like you have a busy day of criminal activity ahead of you."

Had Dani been this harshly unsympathetic when she was in high school? Ethan couldn't remember. At the time, he hadn't known her well enough to care.

"Think about it, Dani," Ethan said. "It's been five days now. Even you have to admit that's extremely unusual for Quinn. If he's not up at the lake, where else would he be?"

She hesitated, a brief interruption to her

motion of reaching for her orange North Face vest.

"No," she said. "I have to go, and so do you. No offense, but considering what you just revealed, I'm not comfortable leaving you alone in my house."

Ethan followed her out. She started up her Jeep and backed out of the driveway.

Ethan banged a hand against his steering wheel. He was never going to persuade Gonzalez to forgive his transgressions if he couldn't even persuade someone who cared about Quinn to help with a simple skill. His car lurched as Ethan backed out of the driveway and turned the wheels to follow Dani before he lost sight of her Jeep.

She headed southwest of town. Ethan tried to remember the geography and what might be out that direction or how far she might drive. He made no effort to disguise his efforts to follow Dani because he knew he wasn't any good at stealth, and he didn't want to risk losing sight of her vehicle among the rural back roads. When she pulled up in front of a house in a subdivision that had not existed when Ethan lived in Hidden Falls, he was right behind her.

"Is this some kind of a joke?" Dani took her toolbox from behind the driver's seat and slammed the door.

"I'm not letting go of this." Ethan braced one arm against the Jeep to block her path.

Dani pivoted and walked the other direction around the car. Ethan met her at the walkway leading to the front of the house.

"I have a job to do here," Dani said. "You're not invited."

"I'm not leaving." He matched her stride. "You can show your tough exterior all you want, and I respect it, but I know you care about Quinn."

At the front step, she glared at him. When she reached for the doorbell, Ethan covered it with his hand.

"Don't do this for me or Nicole or Lauren. We're nothing to you. I get that. Do it for Quinn."

"Fine." She rolled her eyes. "I'll come this afternoon. But I'm not making any promises beyond that."

7:46 a.m.

Lauren pulled open three drawers in the kitchen and came up empty-handed. In the bedroom, she went through her dresser drawers, and in the second bedroom, she rummaged through the desk drawers. She couldn't remember the last time she had used a magnifying glass.

It turned up in the hall closet.

Lauren carried it out to the living room, where Nicole sat in the recliner with her foot propped up and a photo in her lap, and snapped on the lamp above Nicole before handing her the magnifying glass. Lauren sat on the arm of the chair, and together they hunched over the image.

"It's freaky how much this guy looks like Ethan," Nicole muttered as she adjusted the distance between the glass and the picture.

Lauren had to agree. The man in the photo had a beard, but it wasn't thick enough to obscure the lines of his jaw or cheeks. In a black-and-white photo, it wasn't possible to judge the mixed shades of his hair color or the pigment in his eyes, but the angle and width of the man's nose could have been Photoshopped in from Ethan's face. The same was true of the distance between his eyes and the precise point at which the hairline began to slope back. The age of the photo made it impossible for the image to be Ethan, or even his father. Based on the cut of the suit the man wore, the picture had to have been taken before 1940.

But why would Quinn have this photo tucked away in a folder in his filing cabinet? The folder had otherwise been empty, and the ones around it contained a variety of documents with no bearing on the photo — expired car insurance policies, receipts for tools long past their warranty periods, paint color samples.

"Who files paint swatches?" Lauren had said aloud when Nicole pulled the samples from the file drawer she was rifling through the night before. Apparently Quinn did.

Lauren couldn't see very well. Nicole had the magnifying glass adjusted for her own vision and angle. "What can you see?" Lauren asked.

"Other than Ethan's twin? It's hard to say. The photo is pretty grainy." Nicole handed the glass and picture to Lauren.

The picture was taken outside. That much was indisputable. Grass filled in much of the lower part of the photo. Dense summer grass, Lauren thought. The man stared at the camera almost as though he didn't see it or was looking beyond it at whatever demanded his focus. He wasn't a happy man, at least not on the day the shutter captured this moment. If there was any difference between his eyes and Ethan's, it was that they were sunken, strained.

"It looks like a full lawn," Nicole said, "but there are tiles or stones of some sort. Maybe they made some kind of design if you stood back from them."

And that's when Lauren knew.

"Graves," she said. "The kind of markers that lie flat on the ground."

Nicole grabbed Lauren's wrist. "You're a genius."

"Ethan should ask his parents about this picture," Lauren said.

"He won't. He doesn't want to see them."

"But this changes things, doesn't it?"

Nicole sighed. "I doubt it.

"He's got to be curious."

"We need more to go on," Nicole said. "We're already on thin ice after we made Ethan climb that tree. I thought he was going to have a stroke when I said we should take the computer."

They looked at Quinn's computer set up, but silent and lifeless, on Lauren's small dining table. They'd been up half the night trying to get it to turn on, but it kept shutting off before all the applications cycled into action.

"One thing at a time," Lauren said. "If this is a graveyard in the photo, where is it?"

"Here," Nicole said. "Hidden Falls Memorial Garden goes back a long way — much further than this photo."

Lauren squinted at the picture. "How can you be sure?"

"It's a hunch, I admit," Nicole said. "We need a name. Can you make out any of the lettering on the graves?"

"It would be easier if they were tombstones." Lauren adjusted the magnifying glass. "The ones around his feet are too flat to read."

"Look behind him." Nicole took the photograph back. "That thing shaped like a tower could be a tombstone."

Lauren leaned over Nicole's shoulder. "Maybe." It seemed too far away from the man to be the grave he was there to see. He had the sorrowful look of a mourner.

"K . . . maybe *K-R."*

"K-R-A-V or *W."* Lauren nudged Nicole's arms toward the lamp.

"You live here," Nicole said. "Can you think of any family names that start with those letters?"

Lauren shook her head. "Besides, what does this have to do with finding Quinn?"

"Yes, that's the main thing."

Nicole set the photo aside, but Lauren could tell her mind had not let go of the mystery. Lauren was curious, too. Her day, however, already overflowed. Last night's escapade had yielded Quinn's notes about the health fair, and the event was the day after tomorrow. Lauren's first thought that morning was a prayer for efficiency and insight to recognize each next task that needed to be done.

Nicole lowered the footrest and took both crutches in one fist. "I have to try the computer again."

The old PC laptop had been unused for the last five days during Quinn's absence. They didn't know when it had last been turned on successfully. Lauren doubted one more night of inactivity on her dining table would have made a difference. But while Nicole stabilized her balance and crutched her way over, Lauren turned on the computer.

The right lights went on and the machine made noises. But the flash of encouragement was misleading. The screen went dark nearly as soon as it lit up, and the cycle of noises stalled in a high-pitched *whirr.*

"Nuts," Nicole said. "I'm good at a lot of things, but resurrecting computers is not one of them."

Someone with the right skills could probably tell them within ten minutes whether the computer would ever function, but under the circumstances they couldn't simply carry it into a shop.

"Why hasn't Ethan called?" Nicole lowered herself into the forbidden desk chair parked at the table.

"Careful," Lauren said.

"I *am* careful. Rolling in a chair is not rocket science."

Nicole glanced at the door and then pulled her phone from the pocket of her pajama bottoms.

"Would you like a shower before I go?" Lauren said.

"Are you saying sitting around for two days has ripened me?"

Lauren chuckled. "You have your own things now. Maybe you'd feel better if you freshened up. I have a plastic lawn chair downstairs that I sometimes take to the park across the street. You can sit in that."

Nicole sniffed her own hair. "I admit it's time."

"I'll be right back with the chair."

"Thanks. But when I get out, I'm going to figure out what to do about the computer. And Ethan had better get here soon."

Lauren ran downstairs to a small storage area tenants shared, brushed off the chair, and carried it upstairs. She started the shower, and in a couple of minutes she heard Nicole hopping around the bathroom. Lauren was eager for Ethan to arrive, too. He would reinforce efforts to keep Nicole's ambitions for the day within reason.

Lauren picked up the clipboard, which now held her own notes on yellow sheets and Quinn's half sheets of white paper. She adjusted her glasses. This pair didn't fit her as well as the pair bent out of shape the previous day, but they would have to do until after the fair. With a pencil, Lauren underlined on Quinn's pages details that she hadn't thought of. Next to each entry, she wrote initials of committee members she would ask to follow up on the task.

When her cell phone rang, Lauren answered.

"Lauren, this is Benita Booker."

"How are you?"

"I'm fine. I'm calling because most of my day is free, and I have a feeling yours is not. What can I do to help?"

Lauren's feet jumped a little as giddiness ran up her legs. This was a great start to the day. Benita Booker wasn't on the health fair committee, but she was one of the most dependable people at Our Savior Community Church. Lauren picked up the clipboard and assigned five tasks to Benita with certainty of her ability to accomplish them. Lauren wouldn't wait for Ethan. As soon as Nicole was out of the shower and settled again, Lauren would make sure everything her nonambulatory houseguest needed was within reach, and then she would attack the list with a furious squall of organization and productivity.

The shower shut off. Lauren studied the list again, marking it up with a code of check marks, stars, and brackets.

Her phone rang again, and Lauren answered. Her cheerful greeting brought no response.

"Hello?" she said again.

She heard enough noise to know the call had not dropped, but no voices. Had someone's phone accidentally dialed her from a pocket or the bottom of a purse? Lauren looked now to see what the number was. She recognized it — the same one she'd seen two days earlier, while she was at the urgent care center with Nicole.

Lauren was no closer to knowing the identity of the person this number belonged to.

Her stomach roiled with the familiarity of a sensation she thought she'd left behind ten years ago.

She was *not* going to call the number back.

8:16 a.m.

Lauren was gone. Nicole didn't know where Ethan was. He could be on the way to Columbus, for all she knew. They were years beyond his owing her an explanation for his decisions, but disappointment mingled with irritation that he hadn't at least sent a text by now. On Saturday night, she didn't see how he could go home without knowing what happened to Quinn. But five days changed that. No one could put life on hold indefinitely. If she hadn't broken her ankle, Nicole would be wrestling with the same decision. Was it time to go back to work and wait for news from the authorities?

Nicole adjusted the pillow under her foot and picked up her phone from the side table. She wasn't used to how quiet her phone had been without the frenzy of an active story to work on for the St. Louis newspaper that employed her. No sources to confirm, no facts to check, no quotes to capture, no long text message threads with the detective who was her first contact on any crime story. The only project she brought with her when she left St. Louis was a tame background story on St. Louis history that wasn't due for another two weeks. She'd already done the interviews and research she needed in order to write it, and the latest information from Terry, the administrative assistant, was that the editor no longer wanted it. The lack of an investigative assignment didn't explain the silence from Nicole's editor — especially since Nicole had left multiple messages about her injury. She could believe no one had time to be chatty on the phone, but she at least expected a sympathetic e-mail. Nicole lifted a finger to call again but changed her mind. What good would one more message do? They knew where she was.

Mentally Nicole reviewed the facts surrounding Quinn's absence, as if organizing them for a story and searching for the overlooked detail that would unlock the mystery. She looked across the room at Quinn's unyielding computer, and frustration welled. Computers were like brains, she mused. They held memories and evidence of fleeting thoughts and the language that distinguished one person from another. She'd never had a story where she got access to a computer and didn't find something — a new fact, confirmation of a suspicion, a downloaded photo, a revealing Internet search history, a deleted e-mail thread that still existed in the ghostly interior of the computer's memory and came to life in the hands of a computer specialist. Usually, though, she had help discovering what a computer held.

She'd never stolen a computer before. She told herself that in Quinn's neighborly spirit he'd never denied her the loan of any of his belongings. Ethan had guessed that Quinn's computer was at least seven years old — ancient by technology standards. No wonder it didn't have the energy to cooperate with her inquiry.

Before she left, Lauren had pushed the recliner closer to the window with the remark that Nicole might enjoy a better view that didn't require twisting her spine. Now Nicole turned her head to the window and the brightness of the day. The whole week had been stunning, stirring in her a craving to be outside. Each day, though, rattled Hidden Falls. Nicole was used to finding answers. People called her persistent — or downright stubborn — but no one would describe her as patient.

Main Street was full of memories, some of them welcome and some less so. Nicole could see the bench across the street, where in his grief her father had once left her and forgotten to come back. She'd waited and waited, clinging to his promise that he'd be right back. In the end, it was Quinn who found Nicole shivering in fear and warmed her with the jacket that swallowed her as she plunged her face into the inner panels that smelled most like Quinn.

Nicole took a deep breath, wishing she could find the place in her own brain where that smell was stored so she could inhale it again and peek up at Quinn's reassuring face with his amber eyes and ruddy cheeks. Her father loved her, but it was Quinn who made her feel safe.

Was he safe now?

A store now heralded by a sign about natural organic foods had once been a sweets shop, an irony that made Nicole smile. The sweets shop had been there for decades and featured old-style display cases and dispensers that Nicole hadn't seen anywhere since she left Hidden Falls. St. Louis had its share of business history, but perhaps she was no longer in the habit of seeking out quaint little shops. As a child, if she had a dollar of her own, Nicole went into that store and calculated carefully what she could get. As a teenager, when she had money from babysitting or working for Marvin Stanford at the *Dispatch,* Nicole enjoyed surprising her friends with small gifts of fancy handmade candies. Quinn had always been partial to cherries covered in dark chocolate. Nicole gave him a box of twelve every Christmas, and every year he offered the first piece to her and then took one himself. They grinned at each other as they synchronized the first bites.

Did any place in town sell handmade

chocolates now? Or did Quinn have to go to Birch Bend to search out his favorites?

She watched the park across the street. It looked the same as it always had, with a clump of towering maples at the center and evergreen bushes around the edges. The bricked path circled the park with an outlet on Main Street and another on the next street south. The cast-iron benches required minimal maintenance and contributed to the sensation that the little park was a vestige of another era. Perhaps once it had been larger before businesses built up around its edges. Nicole's mother used to let her run on the brick path as long as no one else was in the park. In the weeks after Nicole's mother's funeral, Quinn twice took eight-year-old Nicole to the park to run the small circle as many times as she needed to, sitting patiently on one of the benches where she could wave at him as she came around the curves.

Had she ever said thank you for any of it?

A pit of regret deepened in Nicole's stomach. She took Quinn for granted as a child, and in the last ten years, she took him for granted as an adult. She'd never imagined Quinn wouldn't be there if she reached out for him.

Five days.

Now it might be too late. She'd written enough missing persons stories to know the odds of a good outcome — the outcome loved ones yearned for — dropped with each day. Someone gone five days might never come home.

Nicole banished the thought. He could be sitting in an airport in San Francisco, for all she knew, or in New York waiting for a flight to France. He could be anywhere.

In the park, a little boy in a brown-and-green jacket ran the circles Nicole used to run. She doubted the day's temperature required a winter jacket, but its bulk didn't hold him back any more than it would have restrained Nicole when she needed to run. A young woman Nicole presumed to be his mother met him on each lap with a hand outstretched for him to slap as he passed.

Nicole sat up and put a hand on the windowsill. Cooper Elliott was walking through the park. Probably he was simply using the park as a shortcut from the sheriff's station up to Main Street. He seemed in no particular hurry. Considering that Quinn was missing and his car smashed, Sylvia's store had been burgled, and Dani's boat was sabotaged, it seemed to Nicole that anyone on the sheriff's staff should look busier. Whatever their usual routine was, they should all have plenty to do this week. As the most senior of the handful of deputies working from a base in Hidden Falls, Cooper in particular should be swamped. So why did he look so unflustered?

Nicole made a mental note to track down Cooper's cell phone number. Lauren's aunt would have it. Cooper had seemed like a nice man when he was at Lauren's with Ethan and Sylvia for dinner on the day Nicole broke her ankle, but if his work ethic would benefit from a little pressure, Nicole would be happy to supply it. She wondered if he'd looked over his shoulder to see that his brother was not far behind him with a white bakery bag and hesitant steps. Cooper turned one direction on Main Street, and a few minutes later, Liam turned the opposite way.

Nicole watched the little boy take three laps before the mother grabbed her son's wrist and guided him off the path. She immediately saw why. An old man shuffled on the bricks. His gait didn't look particularly unsteady, but given his age and frail appearance, any mother would have been sensible to make sure her child was not the cause of harm.

The old man raised his hat in the kind of greeting he must have learned as a young man. No one did that anymore. But the gesture revealed his face just long enough for Nicole to recognize him — the man from the cemetery on the western edge of Hidden Falls.

Even when Nicole was a child and her mother died, he had seemed old to Nicole. He had guided the mourners to the gravesite, where the minister had said, "Ashes to ashes, dust to dust." Now he was unquestionably at least eighty, maybe older.

Tom. Was that his name? It didn't sound quite right. Nicole fished deeper into her memory.

Not Tom. Dom. "Old Dom," people had called him.

Short for Dominick. Nicole wasn't sure if that was his first name or his last name, but it didn't matter.

She picked up the photo of Ethan's look-alike and set it on the arm of the recliner. In her lap, she positioned her iPad and opened an Internet search.

9:14 a.m.

Liam could smell the drizzled blueberry scone, still warm in the bag and nestled next to the steaming cup of rich Ecuadorian coffee, both Jessica's favorites.

Yesterday had been the longest day of his life. In the middle of the night, Liam looked at his image in the bathroom mirror and thought he had aged five years in five days. How long could he endure by substituting coffee for sleep? The swelling dread of knowing someone else knew his secret tormented him. Even without near intravenous caffeine levels, his heart would be racing alongside his imagination.

He had to talk to Jessica. He would grovel an apology to get her to listen, and then he would speak the words that seemed to be his only way out. His options were to give himself a heart attack waiting for the blackmailer's next move or to risk a broken heart with this conversation with Jessica. He couldn't stand the waiting, so he approached Jessica's office with gifts to soften his unplanned appearance.

Jessica worked in accounting for a small department store, Hidden Falls's answer to Sears or JCPenney. Liam suspected that what kept them in business was old-fashioned credit based on relationship rather than credit scores, along with a population dominated by an aging generation less and less inclined to drive to Birch Bend for their first-choice item if they could find their second choice on Main Street between stops at the pharmacy and the bookstore. Jessica's office was on the third floor with all the business workings of the store. Liam paced through the first-floor clothing and housewares sections to the stairwell tucked away at the rear of the store. The employees knew him. No one would question his presence passing the second floor on his way up. He turned left at the top of the stairs and entered the maze of offices. The building was historic, a hundred years old, and the offices hadn't been converted to the impersonal cubicles of more modern buildings.

At her open door, Liam knocked twice and

held up the bakery bag. "Truce?"

She looked up from her computer, but Liam couldn't read her expression. Either her mind had not yet shifted from the preoccupation of her work or his visit was unwelcome even with a scone and coffee.

"I'm sorry about the other night," he said. "I should have been thrilled that you were ready to set a wedding date."

"But you aren't," she said.

"Of course I am." He would have married her years ago if she hadn't wanted a lavish wedding they couldn't afford. "I stuck my foot in my mouth at Vittorio's. I was just stunned that we went from scraping for wedding money to having it. I love you and want to marry you."

Liam's words were true on both counts, but he doubted that the first truth would lead to the second.

She waved him in. He closed the door behind him, wondering if the old walls between offices were as soundproof as they looked.

"Will you forgive me?" he said.

Her lips pouted. He kept going.

"No matter how much I had on my mind, I should have taken you in my arms and kissed you and then announced to the whole restaurant that I was going to marry the love of my life."

"Now that's more like it." Jessica swiveled

in her chair to face him.

"You looked fantastic that night. You always do. I'm so lucky to have you in my life." *And letting go of you will be the hardest thing I've ever done.*

The door opened and a buyer for the women's department stuck her head in. "My distributor says we didn't pay them."

"Of course we did," Jessica said. "I'll send you the info on the electronic transfer."

"ASAP, please. They're holding up my next order."

The buyer ducked out.

"Just give me a minute." Jessica swiveled back to her computer and clicked around before hitting Send with a flourish.

Liam opened the bakery bag and laid the scone before her, followed by the coffee.

"None for you?" Jessica took a bite.

"I just wanted to see you smile." *One last time.*

She tilted her head and obliged him. Her phone rang, and she reached for it.

"It should be here later this afternoon. . . . Yes, I'll bring it right to you. . . . Let me know if you have more questions."

Liam got up and closed the door again.

Jessica hung up the phone. "Good move, bringing a scone to apologize." She stood up, came around the desk, and leaned into him, pressing him up against the wall behind the door to kiss him hard.

His hands circled her waist. Jessica had a habit of wearing slinky clothes, not immodest but silky enough to slide over her skin with the slightest touch or movement. As her mouth made a fresh attack on his lips, his hands slid up. He could feel the heat of her skin under his fingers and deepened the kiss. A moan escaped her lips just as a knock on the door startled them both. They jumped apart.

"Come in." Jessica moved away from the door.

Liam recognized a clerk from the men's department.

"Here's the envelope for the group gift for Mr. Swift. Just pass it on when you're finished."

Jessica took the envelope and tossed it on her desk. "Now where were we?"

Liam took hold of her hands and held them. "Maybe this isn't the best place for a private conversation. Is there somewhere we can go?"

"Sounds serious."

"It is."

"I can meet you tonight."

Liam's resolve might shatter if he waited that long. "If you can get away, I'd like to talk now."

She pressed her lips together in thought. "There's an empty office near the receiving dock. No one would bother us there."

He took her hand, and they rode a freight elevator down to the dock. Two small trucks were backed up against the receiving platform. Jessica led Liam past the unloaders and into a windowless room.

She flipped on the lights. "What's on your mind?"

Liam's heart crashed against his ribs. "I didn't listen to everything you wanted to say the other night about your promotion and the extra money."

She shrugged. "I told you. I have more responsibility, and they gave me a pay raise. I've been putting all the extra money aside for the wedding."

"It must have been quite a raise."

Her jaw stiffened. "Don't you trust me?"

If he did, he wouldn't be sweating through this conversation. "If we're going to be married, I think we should be transparent with our finances, don't you?"

"I'm used to my independence. I've always supported myself."

"I know. But we've talked so much about what the wedding would cost and how we would pay for it."

"I would think you'd be happy I came up with a solution."

"Of course I am. My business hasn't been great lately. I'm sorry I haven't been contributing more to the joint account."

"It'll get better. We still have a few months before the wedding."

Liam leaned one shoulder against a wall. "I should tell you what's really happening."

Her eyes met his.

"I'm pretty sure I've been hacked," he said. "Someone has been messing with my accounts."

"Are you missing money?"

She asked the question without missing a beat. Shouldn't she have been surprised? Sympathetic? Liam hadn't thought his gut could burn any hotter than the last five days, but now it did. Truth was a searing sword.

He and Jessica had been a couple for six years. Though he changed his passwords frequently because the corporate system would lock him out if he didn't, Liam had his own backup system for remembering them. Jessica wouldn't have had to hack his passwords but only into the site where he stored them. Decoding one password would get her into his entire list. Bank accounts, social media, online retailers. He supposed a husband and wife ought to know each other well enough to think as the other would in a crisis, but he had thought this ability would be based on trust, not used for distrust.

"What do you think I should do?" he asked tentatively. "Go to the police? Find a way to borrow the money and replace it?"

Jessica stepped back from him. "If you're

hinting at borrowing from me after I've sacrificed for our wedding —"

"I didn't say that."

"You don't have to. I know how you think."

And I know how you think.

"Maybe I could find the money," Liam said. "You could help me trace back the financial transfers. You understand these systems. We could get it back."

"I can't get involved, Liam."

"If we're going to be married, we'll be in this together."

"I love you, Liam, but I'm not going to tamper with bank accounts for you."

No. Only for yourself. "And I love you. We could fix this and never have to talk about it again."

"Talk about what, Liam?"

He saw no question in her eyes as he moved toward her. "We don't have to have a fancy wedding."

"We don't have to have any wedding at all."

"Jess, come on. Let's figure this out together." He stroked her shoulder.

"I don't like your tone." She pulled the ring off her left hand and pushed it into his palm. "I've been thinking since the other night, too. I don't believe in you anymore, Liam, and you don't know me at all."

More hurtful than her words was the truth that he did know her. He closed his fist around the ring.

"Good-bye, Liam." Jessica yanked open the door and left.

Liam opened his hand and studied the ring. The fluorescent lights were starkly bright in the empty room. He stared at the setting Jessica had been so particular about.

Something was not right. What had she done with the money? And the diamond?

9:56 a.m.

Nicole rolled across the living room to answer the knock on the door. Ethan stood there in jeans and a sweatshirt.

"I thought you were never going to get here." Nicole shoved herself away from the door.

"Good morning." Ethan closed the door.

Nicole braced for a scolding about being out of the recliner and skipped mentioning that the door hadn't been locked. "Don't get comfortable. We have to go out."

"Didn't last night's adventure satisfy your wanderlust?" Ethan dropped his keys in a pocket.

"Don't put your keys away," she said. "I want to go see that new attorney, Jack Parker."

"Never heard of him."

"He's just over in the next block. He bought out Morris and Morris." One phone call to Benita Booker had caught Nicole up on what the town knew about its newest attorney. "Just give me a minute to find what Lauren did with my running shoe."

Ethan stepped into her path and caught the chair. "Can we slow down a little bit?"

"I've already lost two days." Nicole tried to roll back, but Ethan gripped both sides of the chair's seat, stooping to put his face level with hers. For a few seconds, she stared into his wide brown eyes and felt his exhaling breath on her neck. Neither of them spoke.

"I'm sure you have a good reason to see Mr. Parker," Ethan said, "but let's get on the same page."

"Sorry." She sucked in a filling breath and let it out with considerable control. "First of all, I'm really glad you're here — in Hidden Falls, I mean. I thought maybe you'd left for Columbus."

"I would have told you." He released his hold on her chair and sat on the sofa, stumbling over her shoe in the process.

Nicole caught the shoe when he tossed it and bent over to put it on, avoiding Ethan's eyes. "Second, I've been staring out that window feeling afraid I've missed my chance to tell Quinn how grateful I am and apologize for taking him for granted all these years."

"He knows how you feel about him — how we both do."

"I suppose," Nicole said, "but that doesn't excuse me from saying thank you. My parents brought me up better than that." *And so did yours,* she wanted to add but didn't.

"I want him to know," Nicole said. "He gave so much love. I want him to know it wasn't wasted."

"Love is never wasted," Ethan said.

Nicole looked at Ethan now, straining against the lump in her throat. Even after he walked away from her ten years ago, she never felt her love had been wasted.

She broke the gaze. "I still can't get Quinn's computer to power up properly."

"I have good news on that."

Ethan leaned back and laid an ankle on the opposite knee, as if he were planning to settle in. Nicole bit back on prodding him to get out the door and instead gave him the most expectant look she could muster.

"Dani's coming this afternoon."

Nicole's stomach flipped. "You told someone we have the computer?"

"I didn't think you'd want to take it back to Quinn's after what we went through to get it."

He was right about that. Other than laying hands on the computer and wondering if God answered technology prayers, Nicole didn't know what she was going to do, but returning the computer without getting into it hadn't entered her mind. It held too much potential — both for Quinn's whereabouts and the mysterious photo — to abandon the effort.

"I thought maybe you would look at it again," she said.

He turned both palms up and spread his fingers. "These are the hands of a brain surgeon, not a technology expert. I used up my last trick at two in the morning."

So had Nicole. She'd hoped Ethan was just tired and would put his analytical skills to good use in the light of day. Nicole double-knotted her shoe. She couldn't afford to trip over a loose lace right now. "What makes you think we can trust Dani?"

Ethan laughed. "Even in high school she would never rat anybody out. I don't think much has changed. If she turned us in, she'd have to get involved — and that would cut into her fishing time."

He was right again.

"Not turning us in is one thing," Nicole said. "Actually helping is another."

"Getting her here is the first step."

Nicole nodded. She'd persuaded plenty of people to do what they said they wouldn't. She would handle Dani Roose when the time came.

"In the meantime, let's go see Jack Parker," she said.

"I have a feeling this is against my better judgment." Ethan stood up.

"You can torture me with ice all afternoon."

"Is he expecting you?"

Nicole looked away. "Bring the photo,

please. And my iPad." Jack Parker would have no reason to know Ethan Jordan. She wanted the full effect of laying the photo on Jack's desk while Ethan was sitting right in front of him.

"Do I at least get to know what your hunch is?"

Ethan never had been one for blind obedience.

"It's the cemetery," she said. "Your twin is standing in Hidden Falls Memorial Garden."

"And Mr. Parker?"

"Has old things in his office. Very old." She didn't make an appointment because experience told her that catching people off guard gave her the advantage in establishing the path of the conversation. Surprising people was a well-cultivated investigative habit.

"I had to park down the street." Ethan stood up.

"I'll wait on the bench outside the barbershop."

They spent far more time getting Nicole in and out of Ethan's car than they did driving around a couple of street corners to find the brick building of stately office suites. Nicole had never been in this building. An elevator followed by wide halls with gray marble floors guided them to the second-floor suite that bore the sign JOHN H. PARKER, ATTORNEY AT LAW. Ethan held the door, and Nicole took careful steps with her crutches.

In the outer office, the sleek modern desk looked out of place with the high ceilings and crown molding. It had a phone, a stapler, and a tape dispenser but no computer. The credenza behind it supported only a vase with silk flowers. In one corner were a gray leather loveseat on one wall and two chairs upholstered in a blue-and-gray plaid on the adjoining wall, with a square coffee table pulling the pieces together. The furniture was in near pristine condition. Certainly Jack Parker had redone the decor. And certainly he worked alone.

Ethan gestured that Nicole should sit down, and she didn't object. Resisting the habit of putting weight on her injured foot made for tedious progress, and she was tired. The door to the inner office stood open.

"Hello?" Nicole called out.

After a brief shuffle, Jack Parker appeared, wearing a starched blue dress shirt and a tie with a sophisticated classic stripe over navy trousers. Nicole was sure a matching suit jacket was arranged on a hanger on the back of his office door. His hairline was impeccably trimmed and not a wave was out of place.

"Miss Sandquist," Jack said. "I didn't expect to see you up and around."

"Thanks for taking me to the urgent care the other day." The smile with which he greeted them, however, seemed a tad too wide to Nicole. She felt like fresh meat.

Jack offered a hand to Ethan. "I'm Jack Parker."

Ethan shook the attorney's hand. "I'm Ethan Jordan."

Jack tilted his head. "I met a Richard Jordan yesterday. Any relation?"

Nicole knew Ethan wouldn't answer that question, and he didn't.

"Is this a good time?" Ethan asked without sitting down. "We can make an appointment to come back later."

If Ethan were in reach, Nicole would have kicked him. They would *not* come back with an appointment.

"I realize we may be interrupting your day." Nicole gestured to her crutches. "But as you can see, I've gone to considerable effort to come see you, so I would appreciate your time."

"Of course." Jack waved an arm toward his private office.

Nicole glared at Ethan as she hobbled past him. Jack hadn't spared expense in his furnishings. Even the side chairs for his guests were plush and soft.

Once she was seated, Nicole put out a hand for the folder Ethan held. "I understand your practice inherited some files that go back quite a ways."

Jack nodded. "Morris and Morris were in business for fifty years, I believe, but I suspect there was another practice here before them."

That's what Nicole wanted to hear. The further back the files went, the better.

"My inquiry is straightforward," Nicole said. "If I provide you with a few names, would you be able to tell me if the old files contain any documents reflecting legal transactions involving the names?"

Nicole felt Ethan's eyes on her but didn't turn her head.

"I might," Jack said, "though many legal matters are confidential, if not technically then certainly out of deference to clients."

"I'm quite certain the individuals I have in mind are deceased." Nicole changed her strategy on impulse. She wouldn't show Jack the photo of the man who looked like Ethan. Her instinct was not to stir up more curiosity in Jack than necessary for what she needed to know. Right now, she only needed to know if Jack had documents related to the graves around the towering tombstone.

"Well, if the individuals are deceased and there are no heirs, then in some instances the files may be available."

There could be heirs, Nicole conceded. She could be sitting right next to an heir.

Rather than pulling out the photo, she flipped open her iPad. "I made a list of names of people buried in a particular section of the local cemetery. These are the individuals concerned."

Ethan turned toward her in his chair. "How did you —"

Nicole cut him off with one shake of her head and kept her eyes on Jack. There was time later to explain to Ethan that Hidden Falls Memorial Garden was an old enough cemetery to be of interest to some historians and genealogists, and she'd found an online map of numbered graves and a corresponding list of names of people buried. Once she'd found the name that started with *K-R-A* — Kravicz, it turned out — it was easy enough to match grave numbers with names within a thirty-yard radius. Based on the perspective in the photo, Nicole was fairly certain the distance was closer to twenty yards, but she couldn't discern directions from the photograph.

Jack looked at her list. "This could take some time."

Possibly. Without seeing the condition of the old filing system for herself, Nicole couldn't dispute Jack's observation. Glancing at the names on file folders wasn't exactly strenuous work, even without an alphabetized system. He would know fairly quickly whether he had anything related to the names. Going through individual files looking for relevant documents — a will, for instance — would be more intensive.

"I'm happy to leave a retainer for your time," she said.

He named a modest figure that would cover a few hours of work and gave her a standard agreement to sign about payment beyond the retainer. Nicole pulled a credit card out of her back pocket.

2:44 p.m.

Dani didn't bother taking her Jeep to Lauren's apartment. It was easier to park at home and walk the few blocks. The park across the street tempted her to find a sunny patch of grass and sit with a book.

Quinn had told her five days ago that his computer was on the fritz again, so the news hadn't surprised her. The main reason she agreed to Ethan's request to look at the computer was because sooner or later she would end up doing it. She might as well do it while Quinn wasn't hovering over her shoulder trying to understand everything she did. It wasn't that he didn't have the smarts to learn. Dani just didn't have the patience to teach him — or anyone. There were classes at the community college in Birch Bend, but the most motivated people would figure it out the way she did. Just start doing it. If you're good at it and manage to solve a practical problem, keep doing it. If you're not good at it, then find something else to do. Dani had learned to fix most anything around a house by the same reasoned approach of testing a theory and learning from the experience, whether in failure or triumph.

Dani had never been up to the apartments above the shops on Main Street. On the street level, shops with varying signage and entry styles broke up the monotony of red brick. On the second story in this block, four sets of windows were evenly spaced across the front. Quinn once told Dani that almost certainly the original shop owners had lived above their enterprises because they rarely had time off, and of course the Main Street structures were built before the advent of automobiles. Only the wealthiest Hidden Falls families operated businesses in town but lived on outlying acreage. Where Quinn came up with that tidbit, Dani didn't know, but it was the sort of thing a history teacher would tuck away in his brain. Maybe he read it in the files of the Hidden Falls Historical Society.

Or maybe he made it up to see how many legs he could pull.

Dani ignored the elevator and took the stairs up to the apartments and found the one marked *D.* She only knocked once and the door opened. Dani looked down at Nicole sitting in a chair with a boot cast on one foot.

"Thank you for coming." Nicole rolled away from the door.

"What happened to you?" Dani stepped into the apartment.

"Clumsy."

Dani scanned the apartment, which was a cozy mixture of historical ambiance and modern convenience, from the original fireplace to the mismatched built-in cabinets to the unskillfully cut baseboards. The house Dani rented was a 1950s prefab down the block from the one her parents had occupied before they finally admitted that, though they had grown up in Hidden Falls, they detested small-town life. Her landlord gave her a steep break on the rent in exchange for handling all the upkeep for the three houses he owned and rented out.

"The computer is over here," Nicole said.

Dani could see it just fine. She didn't need a guided tour.

"Ethan said he explained to you what we're trying to do." Nicole used her good foot to steer from the door to the table. "The first question is whether or not you can get it running. I sure hope so."

"Sometimes I think Quinn holds it together with chewing gum." Dani pulled out a chair, sat in front of the computer, and pressed the power button. Ethan and Nicole flanked her. "Um, can I have some room to work, please?"

Ethan rolled Nicole around to the other side of the table, where he sat down directly across from Dani. She would have preferred they go wait in the other room but supposed it would be rude to say so. Necessity had developed in her some tolerance of hovering customers desperate either not to lose data or not to have to shell out for a new computer — or both. Quinn's laptop whirred and then shut off, just as she had expected it would. In response, Dani simultaneously pressed an arrangement of several keys, a strategy that worked often enough that she defaulted to it when she was troubleshooting PCs. If the computer stayed on, she could run diagnostics and narrow down where the glitch was happening.

Across the table, Nicole responded to the encouraging sounds by wiggling and leaning forward.

Dani clicked for a list of Wi-Fi networks. She could guess from the name, Faithworks, which one was Lauren's. She allowed herself a half-inch shake of the head when she saw the network was unsecure. Why did people leave themselves so vulnerable and then complain about being hacked?

It took another twenty minutes before Dani was reasonably certain that the computer was not in danger of imminent death. Quinn was going to need a new one soon. Dani would steer him toward a Mac if for no other reason than she preferred fiddling with them, and Quinn was sure to keep coming to her with his questions.

"Okay, I think my work here is finished," Dani said.

"Wait!" Nicole's urgent tone made Dani look up. "Didn't Ethan tell you we're looking for some information?"

"He mentioned it."

"I can snoop around for half the night," Nicole said, "but I have a feeling you know Quinn's computer pretty well. You know how he stores information. Just think how much faster it would be if you helped us."

Dani looked from Ethan's brown eyes to Nicole's green eyes. She was in this far. She might as well find out what they had in mind. "What are you looking for?"

"Try to reconstruct where he has spent his time online in the last thirty days." Nicole licked her lips. "Credit card activity, bank accounts, deleted e-mails."

She's done this before, Dani thought.

"That's a lot of personal information."

"In my experience as an investigative reporter, that's where the clues are."

"Does Cooper know you're doing this?"

Nicole huffed her breath out. "Do you really think he'd turn his head if he did?"

Never.

Dani knew the password to Quinn's Internet browser, and unless he had heeded her recent warnings, his e-mail password wasn't much different. People would be surprised at how many passwords Dani had in her head — or could figure out — because they'd made no effort to keep them secret when

Dani needed access to an account to troubleshoot. Most people seemed to think of a password as a necessary nuisance for getting onto sites they used frequently, rather than considering what would raise a barrier to someone else trying to get on those same sites. If Ethan and Nicole thought long enough, they would come up with Quinn's password. Dani saved them a couple of days — during which time Quinn probably would come home anyway — and scanned the list of sites Quinn had visited in the last few weeks.

"Nothing here," she said. "Just the usual stuff."

"What does that mean?" Nicole said. "What's his usual stuff?"

"Book orders, the place he likes to buy his shirts from, teacher resources, history sites."

"Can't you be more specific? Broad categories won't give me anything to chase down. And you didn't mention anything financial."

"Hacking into his bank account is over the line."

"You don't have to look," Nicole said. "Just get me in. I'll look."

Dani wasn't going to let two people who hadn't seen Quinn in ten years look at his bank records. "*If* I get in," she said, knowing that she would, "I am getting right back out if I don't see anything suspicious."

"Who's to say what's suspicious?" Nicole

started to roll herself around the table.

Dani closed the browser window. "Either you trust me or the deal is off."

"Why can't you trust me enough to believe I want to help Quinn?" Nicole parked herself next to Dani and stared at the background on Quinn's screen.

"Why can't you keep your nose out of Quinn's private business?" Dani turned her head and glared at Nicole, who apparently didn't understand the concept of asking nicely for favors.

"I want to find Quinn." Nicole spoke through a clenched jaw and gritted teeth. "After five days, during which no one has seen him or heard from him, you can't possibly be a hundred percent sure that he's all right."

"And you can't be sure anything is wrong." Dani leaned in near Nicole's face, daring her not to pull back.

"Ladies!" Ethan was on his feet now. "Let's all keep our cool."

"Shut up." Nicole and Dani spoke in unexpected unison, though neither turned to look at Ethan.

He came around the table and pulled Nicole's chair back about two feet. "Nobody is going to help Quinn this way."

Dani leaned back in her chair and eyed Nicole. "Here's my final offer. I will look at his bank account, which is way out of my comfort zone. In exchange, you have to admit that I know him better than you do right now and trust my judgment about whether anything looks unusual. And I'm not looking back any more than thirty days."

Nicole pressed her lips together. "Fine. Thank you."

The arrangement wasn't anywhere close to what Nicole wanted, but Dani was more interested in protecting Quinn's privacy than satisfying Nicole's curiosity.

Dani logged onto the bank's website and tried slight variations of core password elements she knew Quinn had used in the past on various accounts. She watched the clock at the top of the computer screen, knowing she had limited time before the site would lock her out.

"I'm in," she said finally.

Nicole started to roll forward.

"You come any closer, I'll shut this down." Dani held a finger over the computer's power button.

"Sorry," Nicole muttered. "Reflex."

Dani's eyes widened at what she saw.

"What?" Nicole said.

Dani turned slowly toward Nicole. "If we can believe these transactions, he's in St. Louis."

4:27 p.m.

After Ethan and Nicole left, Jack turned off

the ringer on his desk phone. Voice mail could pick up for the afternoon.

Jack recognized some of the names on Nicole's list. He'd been passing time crawling around in the old files for months now. Though he didn't recall anything noteworthy in the folders he'd flipped through so far, Jack printed the list Nicole had e-mailed from her iPad and labeled three columns so he could track which files he found, which names were missing, and whether there were any documents that matched Nicole's specification: wills, birth and death certificates, transfers of property. He was sure that at some point in the history of the law practice, the files were in alphabetical order. But the files Nicole asked about were old and, through the decades, were moved further and further out of the way of active work. Jack had discerned little order to the way they were stored other than where they seemed to fit the available space in a box or drawer.

Nicole's list included nearly forty names. So far Jack had uncovered twenty-three folders. One held the incorporation documents for a business that no longer existed, and a handful of others were straightforward real estate purchases of homes that most likely had changed owners several times since. These Jack set aside.

The rest were thicker folders reflecting clients who must have used the services of

Morris and Morris, and their predecessor, on a regular basis. Two of these Jack recognized as ancestors of clients he had inherited with the practice. He read both files carefully, along with several more. Jack expected to find wills, and he did, but nothing more complicated than spouses leaving their worldly goods to each other, and no worldly goods out of the ordinary.

The piles on his desk grew as Jack sorted files and made check marks on the printed list. Before he was finished he would double-check the names for whom he found no files.

Jack reached for another tattered file, this collection of documents in an expanding file with a narrow cord wrapped around a clasp to fasten it closed. When Jack touched the cord, it crumbled in his hands. Lacking sufficient clear space on the surface of the desk to lay out the elements of the file, Jack carried the brittle case to the space he called the *conference room* even though so far he hadn't held a conference within its walls. The table and six musty chairs were relics of Morris and Morris. When it came to the least public space of the suite, Jack had lost the budget war for remodeling dollars to his wife's agenda for the new powder room. He slid the papers out of the expanding jacket. Even as dated as they were, he could quickly recognize the types of documents and sorted them swiftly.

And then one seemed to stick to his fingers. Jack scanned the first page then flipped to the next one. And the next.

This could be it.

Jack pried off the old blue legal backing paper and carried the pages to his desk, where the printer on his credenza also functioned as a scanner. He certainly wasn't going to give Nicole Sandquist the original. The scanner rattled into service, and Jack began placing the fragile pages on the glass one at a time until he had an electronic version of the entire document.

Next he picked up the phone and dialed his home number.

"Gianna," Jack said when his wife answered, "I think it's better if you don't wait dinner for me."

"Jack, you might as well come home at least long enough to eat."

He steeled himself against her protests. "I had a walk-in client this afternoon with a time-sensitive matter. I'll make a sandwich later."

"How late will you be?"

Jack fingered the thick document. "I'm not sure."

"All right. Brooke is right here. She wants to talk to you."

Jack glanced at the photograph of his three children that sat on his desk. The faces of Colin and Eva were obscured by the corner of a stack of folders, but Brooke's face smiled out at him from under the clutter.

"Hi, Dad."

Brooke's lilting voice cheered him even on the phone.

"Hi, sweetheart. Sorry I'll miss dinner."

"Just don't forget about tomorrow."

Jack mentally rustled through recent domestic conversations to find the one that related to tomorrow and his youngest child.

"The puppy trainer," he said.

"Right. I have to go right after school, and you promised to take me."

"I remember."

"And I need to practice face painting before Saturday. Can I practice on you?"

Jack was glad Brooke wasn't there to see his face grimace at the thought of little balloons or ponies adorning his cheeks.

"It's washable, right?"

"Don't be silly, Dad. Of course it's washable. It's not a tattoo."

"Well, then, maybe one little practice spot."

They said good-bye, and Jack reached behind him and extracted a fresh yellow legal pad from the credenza and took a new pen from a drawer. He printed the scanned document — he wouldn't mark up the original — and leaned back in his leather chair.

Before Jack finished the first paragraph, he was making notes.

By the end of the first page, he saw through

the legalese to the relevant details.

By the top of the third page, Jack knew this wasn't a routine old will that had been executed long ago and lost its relevance. Otherwise Nicole Sandquist wouldn't be looking for it.

6:31 p.m.

Ethan rubbed the back of Nicole's neck. "You've been hunched over that laptop for two hours."

"There must be something here." Nicole rubbed one eye and continued clicking keys. "Dani had a lot of gall telling us Quinn's in St. Louis and choosing that moment to decide she wasn't going to snoop anymore."

"We're lucky she did that much."

Nicole closed her eyes for a moment, giving herself over to the sensation of Ethan's hands digging into her shoulders. He used to do this when they studied together. Nicole always offered to reciprocate, but she doubted her small hands could approach the results Ethan's widespread fingers accomplished. His thumbs pressed into the muscles running out of the sides of her neck and down into her back. Increasing pressure told her that he'd discovered the resistance points in her tensed back.

Ethan was right about Dani's general attitude toward gleaning information from Quinn's computer, but Nicole remained aggravated. One bank transaction had him paying for gas at a St. Louis station, so he must have rented a car. If Dani had been willing to find his credit card account, they might have tracked down where the car came from. In a second debit transaction, Quinn paid for a meal at a St. Louis location of a national chain restaurant. Judging from the amount, he hadn't eaten alone.

"His wallet could have been stolen," Ethan said.

"I'd be more likely to think that if Quinn weren't missing." Nicole's gut told her Quinn and his cards were together — even if it was against his will. A stolen card would have been used more recklessly and widely than two transactions in five days.

Nicole had already telephoned all the major St. Louis hotels and ascertained he hadn't registered at any of them — at least not under the name Ted Quinn. She'd even tried giving a physical description to the desk clerks, but it was too generic. Quinn had no visible distinguishing marks, no limp, no twitch, nothing that would set him apart from hundreds of people who walked through a hotel lobby in the course of a day.

But why only two transactions in five days? The rest must be on Quinn's credit card.

"We have to go to St. Louis." Nicole wriggled out from under Ethan's mesmerizing touch. It was only two hours away. She knew the city. She'd be able to track Quinn — or his cards — starting with the gas station and restaurant.

"Or," Ethan said, "it might be more logical to go to Cooper Elliott."

"Don't you think he would already be looking at Quinn's accounts?"

"He'd have to have a warrant or something, wouldn't he?" Ethan asked.

Probably. Nicole wasn't an attorney, but since Quinn had gone missing the same night his car was found wrecked — and he hadn't been driving — there might be enough suspicion of foul play to persuade a judge in Birch Bend. Maybe Cooper had held back information from Nicole — even from Sylvia. If the mayor knew Quinn was in St. Louis, would she have withheld that information even from Lauren?

"How can we find out if Cooper knows about this?" Nicole reached for her crutches. She had to stand up and stretch her spine.

"Tell him what you know," Ethan said. "Basic exchange of information."

"You're adorable," she said, "but it's too late for that." They'd have to start with explaining how they got into Quinn's house, the decision to take the computer, Lauren's knowledge, Dani's reluctant complicity. But if they went to St. Louis themselves and found Quinn, no one would care how they accomplished it.

"You see the orthopedist tomorrow," Ethan pointed out.

Nicole rolled her eyes. "That can be rescheduled. And we have orthopedists in St. Louis, you know. Find some paper. I'll leave Lauren a note."

Ethan cleared his throat. "Nicole, I'm not going to drive you to St. Louis."

Her heart jolted from its rhythm. "I can't drive myself. It's my right ankle that's broken."

"Let's sit down." He gestured toward the sofa.

"Don't waste my time, Ethan."

"Please, Nicole. You make me nervous trying to pace with crutches."

She brandished one crutch at him. "Fine. But keep this short."

They settled next to each other on the sofa. Ethan took one of Nicole's hands.

"I think Quinn wants to be in St. Louis," he said.

She stared into his wide, earnest brown eyes. "Quinn has never been to St. Louis in his life. Why would he suddenly decide to pick up and take the trip?"

"That's a legitimate question, and I don't know the answer." Ethan lifted her fingers and kissed Nicole's knuckles. "But he used his debit card for normal kinds of activities that people do, whether at home or on vacation."

"What's your point?" Nicole's brain said she should pull her hand out of Ethan's grasp, but she didn't. His touch, his nearness, his chocolate eyes inches from her face — Nicole was lucky her tongue could still form sounds against her teeth.

"If he didn't want anyone to know he was in St. Louis, would he use a debit card?"

"Everybody needs to use money. He didn't plan this escape, after all. He didn't have a roll of cash in his tux the night he disappeared."

"Or," Ethan said, squeezing her fingers, "if someone took him against his will, wouldn't they make sure he *didn't* use his card?"

"That's it!" Nicole did snatch her hand back from Ethan now. "It's a signal, a call for help, a way of telling us where he is."

"I don't think so." Ethan gripped both of Nicole's crutches and moved them out of her reach. "Besides, those charges were three days ago now. He could be anywhere."

"All the more reason to see his credit card account." Nicole eyed her crutches, dismayed that Ethan had maneuvered her away from both the rolling desk chair and the crutches and trapped her, immobile, on the sofa.

"Then you're going to have to take your chances with Cooper," Ethan said.

She wasn't ready to do that.

He slipped a hand under her hair at the side of her face and stroked her earlobe with one thumb. "I can't take you to St. Louis."

Nicole didn't expect the sting of tears in her eyes. "We have to find him."

"I think we have reason to feel encouraged. He's not lying in a ditch. He just decided he had somewhere to go."

"But what if he doesn't come back? What if I never get to tell him how much he means to me?"

Ethan leaned his forehead against hers. "I understand how you feel. I've been gone from Hidden Falls for the same ten years you have, and I never so much as sent him a Christmas card."

Nicole swallowed hard but didn't move. If anyone could know what she was feeling right now, it was Ethan.

"Let's not create any more regret," Ethan said. "Not about Quinn, not about each other."

"If I stop looking for him," Nicole said, "I'll regret that."

"If you don't let yourself be grateful for him, even if you can't tell him, you'll regret that."

Her chest rose in a sharp spasm. "But I am grateful."

"We both let a lot of opportunities pass us by." Ethan moved his hand to the back of her neck. "These last few days have reminded me of that."

His breath blew warm against her cheek,

and Nicole's breathing grew shallow.

"What if we don't get another chance with Quinn?" Her hushed voice cracked.

"His disappearance may have given us another chance with each other," Ethan said, "and I think Quinn would want us to take it."

All day long, Ethan was right with one observation after another. And he was right about this. If Quinn hadn't disappeared on Saturday night, she would have gone back to St. Louis and Ethan would have gone back to Columbus. They would have had no reason to see each other except across the banquet hall, and she would have spent her visit to Hidden Falls reminding herself that she got over Ethan Jordan a long time ago.

But Quinn had disappeared.

And Nicole hadn't gotten over Ethan Jordan, it turned out.

He closed the remaining inches between their faces, pulling her mouth against the eagerness of his. He tasted as he always had, and Nicole savored the familiarity and all that it stirred in her. She had never been sure what a second chance might feel like — or if she would take it. No matter what happened with Quinn, Nicole was grateful for this moment.

Nicole broke the kiss and gasped for a breath that would fill her lungs. She was letting emotion overwhelm her. One kiss didn't change what had happened between them ten years ago or the reasons for it.

"The photo," she said.

Ethan said nothing while he continued looking into her eyes.

Nicole leaned away, and his hand slid down her neck and off her shoulder. "The photo is the reason Quinn wanted you to come to Hidden Falls. He has something to tell you about it. He would want you to know what that is."

Ethan picked up the picture from the coffee table in front of them.

"You do see the resemblance, don't you?" Nicole asked.

Ethan nodded.

"If you won't take me to St. Louis, then I have a request for another destination — a local one. It won't take very long."

"We should ice your ankle."

"Forget about my ankle. It'll still be broken when we get back."

7:03 p.m.

Lauren followed her aunt up the narrow stairs to the attic.

"I should have thought about these clothes when you were here on Sunday night," Sylvia said. "I'm glad you brought it up. Quinn and I talked about it, but that was ages ago."

It hadn't occurred to Lauren to include vintage clothing in the silent auction until she found Quinn's brief note about some clothing Sylvia had — a note Lauren avoided mentioning directly. Considering how she came into possession of Quinn's notes, she watched her words carefully, even with her aunt. Lauren vaguely remembered the fancy gowns and dresses her Nana had worn when Lauren was little, though she suspected at least some of her memory came from photographs from long before Lauren was born showing Emma in satin skirts shaped by underlying crinoline layers, and velvet bodices and matching gloves.

At the top of the dim stairs, to Lauren's relief, her aunt found a light switch.

"I don't know what condition the dresses are in," Sylvia said. "I haven't looked at them in years. I don't even remember why they ended up in my possession."

"Are you sure you don't want them now?" Sylvia asked. "Vintage seems popular these days."

"They would never fit me. Besides, I don't have the kind of class that Nana has." The extended family still repeated Emma's favorite advice. *A classic dress never goes out of style. Don't skimp on a good investment.*

Sylvia opened a tissue-lined box, and they took turns lifting garments and releasing into the air the scent of the cardboard storage.

"Don't feel obliged to take all of them — or any of them." Sylvia smoothed a hand across blue satin. "It was only an idle thought at the time."

Lauren found the dresses stunning. She wouldn't take them all, though. They would fetch a better price if there weren't too many. Three, or perhaps only two, would drive up bidding. If they did another auction the following year, Lauren would gladly revisit her aunt's attic.

"We should have brought a bag up." Lauren hesitated to set the dresses down among the rough edges of the attic flooring.

"I think there are some empty boxes over there."

Sylvia pointed, and Lauren scooted about ten feet to the right where an old shelving unit held boxes, some full and some empty. On the top shelf was a wooden box, about ten inches by ten inches, and perhaps four inches deep.

"What's this?" Lauren picked up the box.

"I haven't seen that in years, either."

"It's beautiful." Lauren picked up the box and trailed her fingers along its carved lines. She started to lift the lid.

"Don't open that!"

The edge in Sylvia's tone startled Lauren. "I'm sorry."

"No, I'm sorry," Sylvia said. "It's just that the box doesn't belong to me."

"But it's in your attic."

"Quinn gave it to me nearly twenty years ago," Sylvia said. "He said it was for safekeeping and asked me not to look in it."

"So you never have?" The box's lid was hinged on one side, but Lauren saw no latch. Anyone could open it.

"No, I never have. Quinn and I trust each other."

"You've never been curious?" Lauren put the wooden box back on the shelf and checked several cardboard cubes until she found one that was empty. She shoved it along the floor to the dress pile.

"It doesn't matter if I was curious," Sylvia said. "Quinn asked me not to look in it . . . unless . . ."

"Unless what?"

"Never mind." Sylvia held up a red silk dress. "I would think this one would do well in your sale."

Lauren knelt beside her aunt and let the silk of the shirred skirt slide between her fingers. "Aunt Sylvia, why didn't you ever marry Quinn?"

"He never asked me." Sylvia folded a straight black skirt and balanced it on the edge of the open box.

Quinn was at Sylvia's side during holidays and family events all through Lauren's childhood and youth, in the days when the extended family gathered. She saw the glances that passed between them and the thoughtfulness of the gifts they exchanged. In many ways their intimacy was more profound than the interactions Lauren observed in most married couples.

"If he had asked, you would have said yes?"

Sylvia didn't meet her niece's eye. "Yes, I would have."

Maybe you still would, Lauren thought. Surely in all the passing years Sylvia had other opportunities. She must have known other young men who would have jumped at the chance to live out their days with a generous, compassionate, capable woman like Sylvia. How many of them had she turned away after the first date because they were not Quinn?

Lauren reached for Sylvia's hand, stilling its wrestling with a crinoline-lined skirt. "I can't imagine what you must be going through these last few days."

"Quinn's absence is hard on all of us."

"But especially you."

Sylvia leaned back on her heels. "When Quinn gets back, he will be so glad to know you went ahead with the health fair."

Lauren hoped so.

Mostly she hoped Quinn would come back soon, or at least let someone know where he was. Lauren decided to take the red silk and vacillated between the sheer lace over blue satin and a pearl gray she suspected was cashmere.

"What about you?" Sylvia asked. "Do you hope to meet someone? Cooper Elliott cuts a dashing figure in his dress uniform."

Lauren tried very hard not to blush.

"I have a good life, Aunt Sylvia. I'm not unhappy on my own." Lauren had her moments of envy when she saw couples — like Ethan and Nicole, who had returned to their inseparable status in the last few days. Did they have any idea of how rare the bond they had was? But Lauren meant what she said to Sylvia. She enjoyed her life in Hidden Falls and working at the church and meeting people like Molly and Christopher.

"I feel the same," Sylvia said. "I wouldn't trade a moment of the happiness I've known."

Lauren leaned over and kissed her aunt's cheek. "I think I'll take these three." She put her final selections in the empty box.

"I'll get them dry-cleaned tomorrow and have them ready first thing Saturday morning," Sylvia said. "Now, can I give you a ride into town?"

"I need to go to the community center." Lauren folded the flaps of the box down. "My bike is there."

In the car, Lauren described her encounter with Molly and Christopher and the reason she'd left her bike at the community center. When Lauren got out of the car, Sylvia stayed long enough to make sure the headlamp on the bike worked and that Lauren's helmet still hung from the handlebars.

Lauren never minded riding in the evening

any more than she minded walking after dark. She strapped her cross-body bag to the back of the bike and pushed off. Her apartment was her eventual destination, but right now she wanted to pedal as hard as she could and feel the rush of air against her face. She rode north through the stately neighborhood west of downtown, where she knew she would encounter little traffic, and toward the edge of the cemetery. From there she could follow a well-lit road back toward Main Street.

When her phone rang, Lauren braked. Trying to grab the call before it went into voice mail, she didn't look at the number on the screen. She expected it would be Benita Booker with a report on her accomplishments of the day.

Lauren heard city noises — the *hiss* of bus brakes, a car horn, a street musician. This definitely didn't sound like Hidden Falls.

The call cut out. It was the same number as that morning and two days ago.

Had he left town that day? Was he going to torment her all over again, just like in high school? Lauren jammed her phone back in her pocket. She didn't have a landline. Everyone called her on this number. Changing numbers would be a major hassle that would have to wait until after the health fair. For now, it was enough to know that he had left Hidden Falls.

Lauren put her bicycle in motion again and

rode up to the cemetery. She didn't intend to ride in, but only to pick up the road that would take her home. But she saw a car turn slowly into the entry to the cemetery.

A black Lexus.

Nicole was up to something, and she had dragged Ethan into it.

8:09 p.m.

"One stop," Jack said into the telephone. "After that, I promise I'll be home. I'll come in and say good night."

He dropped the phone into its cradle, satisfied that his wife and youngest daughter were placated for the evening. If he went home now, they would see the distraction in the creases of his face, the glaze in his eyes when he didn't quite focus on whatever it was they would want to show him. It was better if he went now, even in the dark, to get the curiosity out of his system.

Jack stacked the four pages of notes he had written, stapled them to the marked-up copy of the will, and slid the whole packet into his briefcase. Then he spun the combination wheels to ensure it would not be an easy task for anyone to get into it.

This was the most interesting project he'd undertaken in more than a year. He was going to get it right.

It could unfold in one of several different ways, and Jack didn't want to be surprised.

Nicole Sandquist had paid for his time to search old records, and he'd done that. Almost certainly she hoped he would hand over a copy of whatever he discovered. Like other journalists Jack knew, Nicole likely thought she had entitlements. He didn't agree. She needed his legal expertise, whether she admitted it yet or not. When the moment came, he wanted to be prepared with a foolproof interpretation of the facts, a rock-solid strategy for exposing the truth and all its ramifications.

If what Jack suspected was right, Hidden Falls would be stunned.

The downtown area was settling in for the night. Lights illuminated the occasional office window still occupied. Most of the shops had closed at six, and those that remained open through the dinner hour now prepared for the end of the business day. Signs flipped from OPEN to CLOSED. Ranks of overhead lights went off in favor of interior security lights. Window shades came down. Latches turned. Cars rumbled out of the alleys that ran behind the main streets. Jack backed his car out of his designated parking spot behind his building.

He had a general idea of where the cemetery was. Brown signs alerting drivers of the vicinity were everywhere.

Jack found the main entry easily. Before leaving his office, he'd studied the online map enough to know which turns to take even though he wouldn't recognize the landmarks families might use to find graves of loved ones. The darkness would complicate the task. As soon as he was certain he was in the correct section, Jack pulled his car to the side of the road and grabbed a flashlight from under the driver's seat. Gianna insisted that he keep one there in case of an emergency. Jack doubted she would call this an emergency, but it seemed like a fine time for a flashlight to him. He pushed the ON button, and an intense beam rewarded his efforts. This would do nicely.

Sometimes old graves were marked only with words like *wife* or *beloved son,* and observers could only be certain of *whose* wife or beloved son by scoping out inscriptions on surrounding graves. The names Nicole had given him were only surnames. The family he'd found had been prominent and prolific going back almost to the earliest days of Hidden Falls. Jack needed confirmation of names, along with birth and death dates, before he announced that any of the graves matched up with what he'd been looking at for the last three hours.

He traipsed through the aisles of graves, flashing his light to read the lettering carved into limestone or marble and muttering to remind himself of his location. As Jack started his third aisle, he heard voices.

He turned off his flashlight.

"Nicole, you *have* to be careful. It's only been two days since you broke your ankle."

So Lauren Nock was in on this conspiracy.

Jack watched her drop her bicycle and stomp toward the two figures who had visited his office that afternoon.

She jabbed Ethan Jordan in the chest. "And you! You're supposed to help take care of her, not lose yourself to her persuasive charms — much less bringing her here in the dark."

Sitting in an open car door, Nicole laughed brightly. "It's hardly the middle of the night."

"I made her promise to stay in the car," Ethan said.

"Good, because if she steps in a hole and breaks the other ankle, it'll be up to you to explain to that orthopedist tomorrow."

Ethan stood at attention and saluted. Nicole laughed again.

Jack turned his light back on.

"Who's there?" Ethan called out.

Jack stepped forward. "It's Jack Parker." His light flashed across Lauren's astonished expression and the flash of surprise in Ethan's eyes.

Nicole pulled herself upright against the car's door. "I knew it! If you're here, that means I was onto something this afternoon."

Jack had hoped to contain what he suspected at least until morning.

8
All You Need to Know

Friday
8:03 a.m.
Another late night.

The whole week was full of surprises, and Lauren Nock didn't think she could handle another one. Nor could she keep pushing her tasks off until the next day. She'd run out of days. This was it. Friday. Tomorrow at nine in the morning, the health fair had to be ready.

Nicole was awake, dressed, and fed. Ethan had promised to come early. Nothing was keeping Lauren in her apartment except for the first destination on her list for the day.

Quinn's notes said he wanted Cooper Elliott to do a safety demonstration. Lauren had called Cooper yesterday, but he preferred to talk in person. At the moment, Lauren regretted not moving this particular task to Benita Booker's list. But she hadn't, so now she had to go see Cooper face-to-face at the sheriff's department.

Being there would remind Lauren she found Quinn's car smashed into a maple tree last Saturday night — and was detained at the sheriff's office into the wee hours convincing Cooper she didn't know how it got there.

It sure felt like he'd needed a lot of convincing. Sylvia said Cooper was just doing his job with his careful questions.

And, of course, there was Cooper himself. He made Lauren nervous. Nothing came out of her mouth right whenever he was around, and that was a horrible feeling.

Lauren double-checked the contents of her cross-body bag and put her head through the strap.

"You look nice," Nicole said from the recliner, where she sat with her broken ankle elevated.

"Thank you." Lauren didn't want to look nice. She just wanted to get the job done. She'd pulled on khakis and a lightweight sweater, as she did most days this time of the year, and corralled her overgrown bangs on the top of her head and held them there with a large brown clip. The rest of her dark blond hair tumbled around her face, and she would probably end up hooking it behind her ears at moments when she concentrated hardest.

"So you're off?" Nicole tapped the screen of her iPad.

"Yep. Call me after you see the orthopedist."

Lauren chose to walk through the park across the street and down two blocks before cutting over toward the sheriff's department. When she passed Town Hall, she wondered if her aunt was in her office yet. The box she'd seen in Sylvia's attic last night had floated through Lauren's dreams. It wasn't locked. Quinn must have expected Sylvia would need to be able to open it at some point.

Safekeeping, Sylvia said. Sylvia would keep the box safe, but what was Quinn trying to keep safe?

Outside the old sheriff's building, Lauren took a deep breath. She had a standard list of questions she was asking everyone about the health fair now. All she needed was a little information and she would make sure Cooper had everything he needed tomorrow. She tugged the door open and entered.

Cooper sat in his chair at the quad of desks clumped in the center of the main room. As far as Lauren could see, he was the only officer on the premises. No one hovered at the coffee machine or fiddled with buttons on the old photocopier.

Cooper looked up. "Good morning, Lauren."

"Good morning." Lauren opened the door in the half wall separating the waiting area from the officers' desks.

Cooper arranged a chair for her beside his desk. Lauren set her bag on the floor and extracted her clipboard.

"So," she said, "I understand you and Quinn had an initial conversation."

"We did." Cooper held a pen between thumb and forefinger and tapped against a pad of paper on his desk. "Quinn's logic was that you first need to feel safe to have good health in body and spirit."

Lauren could follow the reasoning. Sort of.

"I thought I would do something about bicycle safety," Cooper said, "and maybe fire safety. Then I can talk to the kids about what to do if an adult, even someone they know, makes them feel uncomfortable in any way."

So far we could have done this on the phone. Lauren flipped a few pages on her clipboard until she came to her standard questions. She asked them systematically. How much space did he require? Did he need electricity? How many times did he plan to present? Would he like chairs or was open space better?

Cooper gave answers, and Lauren made notes. This wasn't so bad, she decided, as long as they stuck to the details of the fair. When she prepared to put away her notes and pen, Cooper leaned forward and touched her knee.

"I can see you're doing a terrific job," he said, "but I'd like to know how you are."

Air refused to flow through her throat.

"You've had a lot to deal with," Cooper said. "I know you were counting on Quinn for the fair, and you've really stepped up for Nicole by taking her in."

"Ethan is the one taking care of her most of the time," Lauren muttered into her bag. She'd hardly been home the last two days. All she'd done was give Nicole a place that was easier to navigate than Nicole's empty two-story family home.

"I'll be there all day tomorrow," Cooper said. "Could you use some help early to set up?"

So far the setup crew was Lauren, Benita, Pastor Matt, and maybe Ethan. He still hadn't promised he'd be around to help. If he came to set up, then who would look after Nicole?

Yes, Lauren could use all the help she could find. But did it have to be Cooper?

"Of course," she heard herself say, with a frightening flash of insight that she was probably underestimating the task. "Can you be on the lawn behind the church at six thirty tomorrow morning?"

"I'll do your bidding every moment of the day."

Lauren couldn't decide if the offer was kind, romantic, or creepy. "I'm sure there will be plenty to do."

"And when it's all over and things start to settle back down, I hope you'll agree to go out with me."

"Out?" Lauren's stomach fluttered in a way

it hadn't in years.

He smiled. "A date."

"Um . . . it's hard for me to think about anything but the fair right now."

"I understand. I'll ask again, if that's all right."

Lauren's ringing phone saved her from having to give an immediate answer. She pulled it from her pocket and looked at the number she had begun to dread.

"Do you have to take that?" Cooper asked.

"Nope." Lauren hit Ignore, and the phone silenced. For two days she hadn't had a spare moment to look up the area code. "Do you know where a 918 number comes from?"

Lauren shocked herself by asking, but Cooper calmly pulled a binder from a row on his desk, flipped a few pages, and put his finger on a map.

"Oklahoma."

"I don't know anybody in Oklahoma."

"People mix up numbers all the time," he said.

"I suppose so." But usually the person who answered the mistaken call heard a voice on the other end. And usually the same wrong number didn't show up on a phone four times in three days.

Lauren fastened her bag closed and stood up. Cooper rose as well.

"I'll see you bright and early, then," he said. "Thank you again for your help."

Outside, alone on the sidewalk, Lauren let out her breath and tried to remember where her next stop was supposed to be. The church was just down the street. She could go there and get herself organized.

And then there he was, across the street. After hearing city noises on the last call she answered, Lauren thought Nevin Morgan had left Hidden Falls. Had he gone and come back? For what? Lauren's stomach clenched with dread, which in that instant became an unacceptable way to live. Turning in the opposite direction from Our Savior Community Church, Lauren began to follow Nevin's path. He turned toward Main Street, walking past the dry cleaner and a vacuum repair shop. Lauren followed his turn with one of her own but remained behind him and across the street. When he made another turn and approached a parked car, Lauren had just about decided to call out to him. She could get this over with right now.

He unlocked his car, a midsize beige Chevy. Lauren increased her speed.

"Oh good, there you are!" An arm reached out to grab Lauren's elbow.

She turned to see Benita tugging on her.

"I know you have a million things to do," Benita said, "but I've been working on the sketch for how to set things up. Do you have time to look at it?"

His car was running now, and he backed

out of his parking space. Lauren released him from her sight and tried to focus on the graph paper Benita handed her.

9:43 a.m.

The will and the graves last night gave Jack Parker a jolt. He'd gone home in time to say good night to his family, as he promised, and then he unlocked his briefcase and took out the file. Jack added to his notes the cemetery information he'd typed on the tiny keys on his cell phone as he stood in the dark with Lauren, Nicole, and Ethan. He'd stayed up late, sitting in the high-back leather recliner in his home office, jotting the questions that prevented any consideration of sleep until one in the morning.

Jack couldn't bill Nicole for this time, of course. He had already done what she asked him to do, and when they met in the graveyard last night, she seemed satisfied with what he turned up. But he couldn't let go of this until he made sense of his suspicions.

The disadvantage was now Nicole Sandquist was on the trail of the same information.

The advantage was if there were legalities involved, Jack would have the upper hand. He had the files.

What Jack didn't know was *why* Nicole was so interested in an old will executed long before she was born by someone she had no connection to — at least not that Jack had found.

Yet.

Maybe impending surgery on her broken ankle would slow her down. He could only hope.

Names multiplied. Marriages introduced new names and new trails. Jack now had his own list of surnames of interest that took him back into the old files. And this was what brought him to the point of canceling two appointments, rolling up the sleeves of his bold yellow dress shirt, and sitting on the floor of his office. He'd entered the suite at seven in the morning and started all over again with a new system for sorting files that quickly overtook the surface space of his conference room table. He set the business lines to go directly to voice mail if someone called and turned off the sound on the cell phone and put it out of sight in his briefcase. Jack wanted full concentration.

There was something here, and he was going to find it if he had to create a cross-referenced inventory of every single yellowed document in every single brittle file.

Using a permanent marker and sheets from a yellow legal pad, Jack labeled stacks, making sure he knew which file every document he removed came from. All those clandestine sessions looking through these old folders were starting to pay off. He felt a jump-start familiarity with their contents now that he had a specific task to pursue.

With two doors closed between his piles and the hall outside his office, Jack blocked out the usual sounds of the building — approaching footsteps or the turn of the doorknob on the heavy door or a voice in his outer office. A rap on his inner door made him close a folder over his hand before he looked up.

"Jack?"

Gianna.

"Come in." Jack braced himself for the onslaught.

The door opened. Gianna scowled. "What in the world are you doing?"

"Working." He ought to get up and kiss her cheek, he thought, but his piles left him little space to maneuver.

"Is this the same client from last night?"

Jack couldn't say yes because he was off the clock. To say no would trigger an interrogation.

"Jack?" Gianna rarely had patience when Jack hesitated to reply.

"It's complicated," he said.

"Try me."

He didn't find the right words quickly enough.

"Jack, this looks . . . entirely unprofessional. What are you doing?"

"I wasn't expecting you," he said.

"Clearly."

"Did you need something?"

"I've been trying to call you for an hour. What happened to answering the phone?"

"I wanted to concentrate."

Gianna made a wide gesture. "On cleaning dusty old files?"

"I'm sorry I didn't answer." It wasn't the truth, but it seemed the right thing to say — what she would like him to say. "What did you want to tell me?"

"Never mind. Since I came into town to see if you're all right, I'll do the errand myself."

He was going to have to tell her something or she wouldn't stop. Next would come a speech about how he was losing perspective about what really mattered, or how he was letting his obsessions control him, or how he couldn't just cut himself off from real life. He had responsibilities and relationships, after all.

Jack retrieved the pad of sticky notes he'd lost under one thigh and peeled one off the stack to affix to the document he'd been reading. He let it hang off the edge of the page so he could find his place easily again.

"Jack?" Gianna still stood in the doorway.

"Let's go sit in the reception area," he said. "We can talk there."

Jack carefully stood up and took a long step over one pile to get to the clear space where he could put down a foot. He followed Gianna to the corner seating arrangement and sat next to her on the love seat.

He didn't tell her everything. He didn't know everything yet. He didn't say who his client was. But Jack told his wife more than he had in a long time.

"So you think this all has to do with a prominent family in Hidden Falls," she said when he finished, "and there's some secret from seventy-five or eighty years ago."

"I do." He refused to feel apologetic.

"Why is this so interesting to you?"

Because I'm bored in this little town. Because I want you to be happy, but I'm not sure if I can stand it.

"Because it's not straightforward," he said aloud. "Because it's something to figure out, something that has ramifications. This could change somebody's life." *Maybe it could change mine. Ours.*

"I don't understand." Gianna crossed her legs. "I don't think all the puzzle pieces are in the box. You could be wasting your time and never get the whole picture."

Had she always been so utterly practical?

"Gianna, please don't stomp all over this."

"But, Jack —"

"Please."

She sighed. "Okay."

"Do you remember," he said, "in the beginning? When you were a paralegal in Atlanta, and then Memphis? I was always glad to have you assigned to work with me because I knew you could dig like no one else."

"That was another life, Jack."

"I know. You don't want to be a paralegal anymore. You want to be there for the kids. But I remember how good you were at your job, and I learned from you."

"What did you learn from me?"

"How the odd fact is the one that matters. How hunches are worth chasing down. How finding the string that connects two random facts can break a case wide open."

"You make me sound like an investigator, not a paralegal."

"You investigated documents in the files like no one else."

"But those were the days of billable hours." Gianna uncrossed and recrossed her legs.

"It was billable hours that brought us together," Jack said, "but you had such a thirst for the truth."

"I guess maybe I'm chasing a different truth these days."

Home. Family. A legacy. Remembrance.

Jack knew what Gianna wanted now. Couldn't she see it wasn't incompatible with what he wanted?

"I miss the days we were in sync with each other," he said.

She waited a beat and said, "And I'm afraid

we'll miss the days of being in sync in the future."

Jack leaned over and kissed his wife full on the mouth, something he hadn't done in a long time. He lingered and heard her breath catch.

"I don't want to miss those days either," he said, his voice hushed. "But I'll be a happier husband and father if I know I can jump on opportunities that get me excited."

"Wow, Jack, that's quite a speech from you."

"I mean it. I want to be a good husband, but I have to be me in the process." Jack hovered over her, one hand on her waist, wondering if the gesture meant anything to her.

Gianna's phone rang. Jack leaned away from her, uncertain whether anything he'd said would sink in.

"It's Eva," she said.

Jack listened to Gianna's side of the conversation.

"Again? . . . Are you sure? . . . I'll be right there, then." Gianna hung up.

"Did she forget something?"

"Another stomachache," Gianna said.

Jack did his best to disguise his lack of awareness that there had been a previous stomachache.

"I think she should stay at school this time," Gianna said, "but I'll go talk to her."

11:13 a.m.

"So no surgery?" Nicole swung her cast-clad leg over the side of the examination table. She had insisted she could handle a simple doctor's appointment on her own and left Ethan sitting in the waiting room.

"We don't gain a lot from operating on this kind of break," the orthopedist said. "But you should plan on being in the boot for eight weeks, followed by physical therapy. Do you have an orthopedist in St. Louis?"

"I'm sure I can find one."

"Just let us know where to send the records."

"I will."

"And be careful. Take it easy as much as you can."

Nicole wasn't going to promise that aloud, not when there was so much to do.

He tapped a few times on the iPad that held her electronic record, shook Nicole's hand, and left the room.

Nicole crutched her way out the door and to the main desk. She could see Ethan sitting in the waiting room looking at an old magazine. How did doctors feel when they were on the waiting end of the health care system? She folded the papers the clerk gave her and held them between her middle and ring fingers as she hobbled out to Ethan.

"No surgery," she said. "Next stop, county records."

He held the door open for her and offered to fetch the car. Nicole declined. If she gave him reason to think she couldn't handle being up and about, he would get some silly notion in his head about going straight back to Lauren's apartment and a bucket of ice. On a good stretch of sidewalk, she could move fairly well.

In the car, Ethan asked, "Do you know where this place is?"

She'd already noted the address in her phone and now rattled off driving instructions.

A few minutes later, Ethan again held open a door while Nicole hobbled through. "What exactly are we looking for?"

"I'll know it when I see it."

"That's a pretty wide field."

Nicole had two agendas. First, public records related to Quinn that might not have been online when she searched. Second — and she likely would have to make a special research request for these because of their age — records related to the Tabor, Fenton, and Pease families in the 1930s and 1940s. It was still a broad search with a wide margin for error.

"Ted," she said. "His name is just Ted."

When Quinn first disappeared, Nicole and Ethan realized neither of them knew if Ted was short for another name. She'd started with his address and backtracked through property records until she found the deed to his house showing his name as simply Ted Quinn. No nicknames, no middle initial.

Ethan kissed her cheek. "We'll see him again."

Ethan should know better than to make promises that were not within his power to keep. Even if Quinn was safe in St. Louis right now, which was far from certain, maybe he was never coming back to Hidden Falls. Maybe whatever made him leave was so huge that anything could happen now.

Nicole read instructions posted in large letters, sat down at a carrel with a computer terminal, and began the process of making requests for copies of documents. First she tried several searches to determine whether she could narrow down what might be in the system.

Ethan stood behind her, watching her click through various screens. "You look like you know what you're doing."

"Every county's system is different," she murmured, "but the same information should be available in some form."

Deeds, liens, mortgages, marriage certificates, tax bills, bankruptcies, birth and death certificates, divorce decrees, probate records.

Probate.

"Did you ever hear Quinn say anything about an inheritance?" Nicole asked.

"Who would he inherit from?" Ethan

rubbed her shoulders.

The kiss yesterday started with a neck rub. Nicole hadn't made up her mind whether she wanted to repeat that experience.

Well, she knew she did *want* to repeat it, but it might not be the smart thing to do.

"I don't know," Nicole said. "Nobody, I guess." Probate was a much more logical lead for the Tabors, Fentons, and Peases, though. Nicole filled in the form with the broadest request possible for these three families. As she suspected, the fine print at the end of the form explained that documents dating that far back might not be digitized and would take a few days for staff to locate. Nevertheless, Nicole supplied her e-mail address for notification, asked for electronic versions, and submitted the form with a credit card for the fees.

Nicole moved her feet and knocked her broken ankle against a chair leg. Gritting her teeth, she waited for the pain to pass. She wasn't going to let Ethan see her wince.

"Is that your phone buzzing?" he asked.

When the wave of pain subsided, she felt the vibration in her pocket and answered the phone.

"Hey, Terry." Finally, someone from the newspaper was responding to all the messages Nicole had left.

"Sorry not to call you sooner," Terry said. "It's been crazy here."

"Big story?"

"More like big shake-up, so I'm out of here."

Nicole reached up to still Ethan's hand on her neck. "You're quitting?"

"The department has been reorganized. They offered me an insulting reduction in responsibility and pay, so I told them where they could put it."

Terry had been at the St. Louis newspaper for twelve years. Nicole tried to picture the city desk without her, but the image wouldn't form.

"What does Reggie have to say?" Nicole would call her editor as soon as she got off the phone.

"I suspect they've instructed our fearless leader not to talk to me. And maybe not you."

"What?"

Nicole tried to think whether she had Reggie's home phone number in her contact list — or whether he even had a landline anymore.

"Heads are rolling, Nicole. I wouldn't take anything for granted."

"You can't think Reggie has anything to do with this," Nicole said.

"I don't even know what *this* is," Terry said. "I only know I'm not sticking around. I just wanted to give you a heads-up that you might want to keep your options open, too."

"I don't have any options open."

"Then you might want to create some."

12:34 p.m.
Dani Roose wiped polish into the bottom shelf of the repaired rack in Waterfall Books and Gifts. It looked good to her — probably better than it had before the break-in. It was overdue for the sanding and staining she'd given it.

The whole shop looked to be in good shape, even if the shelves had slightly fewer items for sale than usual. It wouldn't take Sylvia long to fill up the space, and after the store's five-day closure, the whole town would be curious and make a point to stop in. For Sylvia's sake, Dani hoped at least a few of the looky-loos would spend some money. Lizzie Stanford had lobbied for a special name for the sale that would herald the shop's reopening: Break-in Bash, Steal of a Sale, Pitch It Pickings. Something like that. Dani figured Lizzie was working too hard if she thought Sylvia would spend advertising money on such silliness. Curiosity would do the job of getting people back into the store.

The tables in front offered attractive price reductions on slightly damaged items. It seemed to Dani most people wouldn't even be able to discern the damage, so they'd think they were getting an even better deal. Sylvia had been particular about not trying to pass anything off as being in new condition if she could see it wasn't, no matter whether anyone else could.

Sylvia pushed her reading glasses to the top of her head and set down the sheets of orange price stickers in her hands.

"Thanks for coming back today." Sylvia rubbed the bridge of her nose. "The extra pair of hands really helped. We should be ready to go in the morning."

"I thought you'd want to be at the fair tomorrow." Dani tossed the staining rag into her toolbox.

"I'll pop back and forth. Lizzie will be here."

"Let me just check that new lock again." Dani didn't like the way it was sticking. A new lock shouldn't do that. If she had to take it back to the hardware store, she would, but she hoped it would smooth out because she wanted to get a good hike in that afternoon.

Sylvia handed Dani the shiny keys. Dani had replaced both locks, front and rear. She saw no point in replacing only the compromised back lock when the front one was just as pitiful as the one the thief violated. While she was at it, she drilled into the antique doors and added deadbolts. It was the back deadbolt that refused to turn without a minor wrestling match.

Dani put the key in the questionable lock and met with resistance. The same key worked effortlessly in the front lock. She went back into the store for her toolbox. She'd have to take the lock out of the door to get a good look. When she had it out, she laid the pieces on Sylvia's desk and examined them. The mold on the bolt was off just slightly along an almost invisible seam, she decided. But it wasn't worth the bother of taking the assembly back down the street when Dani could file off the offending protrusion and be on her way.

The lights went out.

"Hey, I'm still back here," Dani called.

"I know," Sylvia answered. "I didn't touch anything."

"Flashlight?"

"In the bottom left desk drawer."

Dani felt her way around the desk and rummaged for the grooved cylinder of the light. It went on with one touch of the button, and she went to the breaker box. All the switches were properly aligned, which is what she expected. If every light in the store went out at the same time, the problem was likely the utility company's. She stepped out the rear door of the shop and saw heads poking out doors into the alley.

"It's the whole block," she called to Sylvia.

Dani picked up the pieces of the lock, along with her toolbox, and carried everything to the front of the store.

Sylvia had kept the front shades down ever since Jack Parker and Liam Elliott descended on her two days ago, but now she pulled the cord to raise them and allow daylight through the display window.

"They'll probably have the power back on in a couple of minutes," Sylvia said.

"As soon as I get this lock back in, we'll be finished, anyway." Dani took a metal file from her toolbox, discerned the protrusion with one finger, and began filing it off.

Sylvia locked the shade into the up position and released the cord. On its arc down, her hand caught the edge of a display shelf in the window, part of Lizzie's arrangement, and a mirror with only a slight scratch in the frame now tumbled to the wood floor.

Dani and Sylvia both jumped back from the shards.

"Wouldn't you know it," Sylvia said, "just when we thought everything was under control."

"It'll be fine." Dani reached under the counter where she knew she would find a small broom and dustpan because she had put them there only two hours ago. She began to sweep up the glass.

"Thank you," Sylvia said.

Dani glanced up. Sylvia sounded exhausted — and why shouldn't she? Quinn gone. Her shop wrecked. One person after another asking something of her all week. Constant phone calls. Even a temporary power loss would aggravate most people with a lot less on their plates than Sylvia.

"You'll be glad when things are back to normal," Dani said. Getting the shop open was the first step.

"What's normal?" Sylvia asked.

"Good question."

"Having Quinn back would help a lot." Sylvia's voice wavered for a fraction of a second. "Everyone's nerves would settle down if we just had a few answers about him."

Even for Sylvia, Dani wasn't going to be the one to reveal that she had tracked Quinn to St. Louis. Dani wanted a peaceful hike this afternoon, not an interrogation from her cousin the deputy about how she came to have the information that Quinn was spending money in St. Louis.

"Quinn will come back," Dani said. "When he's ready, he'll tell you all you need to know."

"*Need* being the key word," Sylvia said.

"He's okay." Dani dumped the broken glass into the trash can Sylvia held in place for her.

"I know you think that," Sylvia said. "At this point, it's hard to know what to believe."

Dani turned back to the lock and ran a finger over the smooth edge she'd created.

The lights came back on.

"See, I told you." Dani blinked at the sudden brightness. "I'll just pop this back in."

"Thanks again for all your help."

Dani walked to the back of the store while Sylvia rearranged the items in the window.

The lock worked now. Dani had one more stop before she could find a trail. She loaded her tools behind the seat in her Jeep and drove over to Liam's office. As she went around the corner at the top of the stairs, she wondered if Jack Parker had come up with anything on the address he'd shown Sylvia. In the end, it wouldn't matter if he found anything, because Dani's efforts had been fruitful — at least partially. As soon as she told Liam what she knew, he would tell Sylvia, and Dani wouldn't have to be in the middle of any of it.

She was surprised to find the door to Liam's office locked and the lights obviously off. He was notorious for leaving the lights on even when he went home for the night. She silently congratulated him for turning them off just for an errand or an appointment.

Dani pulled out her cell phone and selected Liam's number. After four rings, his voice came on with a cheery encouragement to leave a message.

As a matter of principle, Dani didn't leave voice messages. It was enough aggravation to have to listen to them in order to earn a living.

She found somebody's business card in her vest pocket and jotted a note.

Have news. Will come by tonight. — D

Dani slid the card under the door.

2:07 p.m.

She knew his name, and she knew his parents' names. Lauren made steady progress down her list. Three phone updates assured her Benita was doing well with hers, too. But simmering below every check mark, every note, every star was determination that this time she wasn't going to withdraw into a shell for someone else's amusement. When the simmering crossed into boiling, Lauren couldn't leave the task on the back burner for another hour.

The outdated phone book in her office at the church yielded an address. Lauren estimated a twenty-seven minute walk, less if she burst into powerwalk mode as soon as she hit the curve where Main Street bent into Tabor Avenue and the shops gave way to wide, stately homes west of town. She didn't care if she arrived a sweaty mess. Marching out there, telling Nevin Morgan to leave her alone unless he wanted to hear from the sheriff, and marching back to her apartment could be accomplished in an hour. Lauren wasn't interested in conversation. She only wanted closure. If her legs went rubbery when it was all over, so be it. One way or another she was going to be through with this.

Lauren didn't intend to be rude. Just firm, unwavering.

As she paced down the sidewalk, she formed her sentences.

I'm not seventeen anymore. I know it's okay to stand up for myself, and I'll do it.

I have every right to expect to live my life without harassment, and I'm here to ask you to respect that right.

If you choose to persist, I will take action. Maybe Jack Parker's professional services would come in handy after all.

Consider this a cease and desist order. If I have to ask again, it will be in writing from my attorney.

Yes. Jack would love an excuse to bury somebody in legalese. How much could it cost to get an attorney to write a couple of threatening letters?

Lauren's speed slowed a bit when she took the final turn onto the street where the Morgans lived.

"Let your gentleness be evident to all." Lauren exhaled. Those weren't her words. They belonged to the apostle Paul, who clearly had never met Nevin Morgan.

But he'd met a lot of other people who wished him ill.

Okay, gentle. Gentle could still be firm. Gentle didn't mean being a wimp. Gentle didn't mean getting walked all over.

She wouldn't make legal threats — yet. If he would listen, she would tell him how his calls made her feel. And if he wouldn't, she would excuse herself — gently — and then decide what to do.

But living under a curtain of dread wasn't an option.

Lauren could see the house now, just two doors down and across the street. A woman pushing a stroller came toward Lauren and smiled.

"What a beautiful day to be out walking." The woman stopped and leaned over the stroller to straighten the green hat on her child's head.

Lauren returned the smile, unsure what expression her face must have carried before the choice to be friendly. Anger? Tension? Fear?

The toddler in the stroller grinned up at her and swatted a spinning toy hanging in front of him Lauren squatted and jiggled the toy herself, sending the little boy into giggles.

"I won't hold you up." The woman gripped the stroller handle. "He's going to be ready for a nap soon."

"Have a lovely afternoon," Lauren said, some of the tension out of her back. She was always surprised at the power of a simple beautiful moment.

"You, too." The young mother looked both ways before crossing the street and angling toward a white house with blue trim.

The Morgan house? She couldn't possibly be headed there. Lauren followed a few yards behind, until she was certain the woman was going up the walk to the Morgan front door.

"Wait," Lauren called out.

The woman rotated.

"I'm looking for the Morgan house. Do you know where they live?"

"Right here. I'm Becky Morgan."

Lauren didn't remember that Nevin had a sister. A cousin, then?

"It's Nevin I'm looking for," Lauren said.

"My husband?"

She was his *wife*? This adorable three-toothed baby was his?

Lauren licked her lips. "I'm Lauren. We were in high school together. I haven't seen Nevin in a long time, but I thought I spotted him in town this morning."

"You probably did. He met someone for breakfast, but the baby was fussing so I stayed home."

"Is Nevin home now?"

Becky gestured toward the empty driveway. "No, but I just asked him to go for diapers. He should be back soon."

"I'll come back in a few minutes then." Lauren stepped back. Maybe she wouldn't return. It hadn't occurred to her that he might not be home, or that there might be an audience for her outpouring, whatever its tone turned out to be.

"Don't be silly," Becky said. "Come in. I'll put the baby down for his nap, and we'll have some tea."

"I don't want to intrude." *What about his parents?* Lauren thought. "Did you come to town for the banquet last weekend?"

"For the high school teacher? Not exactly. Nevin's mother had some minor surgery scheduled, and he thought we might be some help. His father's at the hospital now. But since we were here, Nevin went to the dinner."

Becky Morgan unbalanced Lauren. Talk about gentleness. How in the world did she end up with someone like Nevin Morgan? Then again, Lauren would never have pegged Nevin as someone who wanted to help out because his mother had surgery.

Becky lifted the baby out of the stroller. "Here's Nevin now."

The beige Chevy turned into the driveway, and Nevin got out, a package of thirty diapers in his hands.

"Your friend Lauren dropped by." When her husband drew close, Becky raised her face for his kiss.

"Lauren?" He inspected her expression.

"Lauren Nock," she said. "We had a few classes together."

"Oh yes, I remember. I was there the other night when Quinn went missing."

Nevin sounded sincere. Likable. He took his son from Becky's arms and let her unlock the house unencumbered.

"I invited Lauren in for tea," Becky said.

"I'll get the baby settled while you two catch up."

If Lauren had any thought to back out of the confrontation, Nevin's wife was making it hard. Lauren was relieved when Becky took the baby down the hall so she could focus.

"How are you, Lauren?" His hand, the palm upturned, invited her to sit down.

"Thank you, but I'm not going to stay long. I have no desire to be rude or to upset your wife, but I'd like you to stop making those calls."

"Calls?"

"You know what I'm talking about."

"I'm afraid I don't."

"Let me back up, then. I know it was you who made those calls to me all during our senior year."

He winced. "I was pretty obnoxious in those days. I'm sorry for the way I behaved."

If he was so sorry, then why was he doing it again? If this was some kind of show because his wife would walk back into the room at any moment, Lauren would push back — gently, of course.

"I'm getting calls again. They're just like before. I saw you at the banquet with all your old buddies."

"So you tracked me down because you think it's me?"

Lauren wasn't sure of anything at the moment.

"Please stop," she said.
"It's not me," he said.
"You can't blow in here from Oklahoma and pretend everything's different."
"Oklahoma? We live in Minneapolis."
"Do you have a cell phone?"
"Of course."
"May I see it, please?" She trembled, but she put out her hand.
Nevin laid his phone in her palm. Lauren dialed her own phone number, and when her phone rang, she looked at the number it displayed.
It wasn't the 918 number.
"It's not you." She met his eyes. "I apologize."
"I'm really sorry about high school," he said. "I didn't do a great job of picking friends in those days. With a few beers in me, I would do whatever they asked and think it was hilarious. Mostly I didn't remember what I did."
Lauren scratched the back of her neck, unsure what to think.
"I don't even know why I agreed to sit with them the other night." Nevin returned his phone to the holster on his hip. "I guess I should have put you on my list of people to make amends with."
"Amends?"
"It's one of the Twelve Steps. Make amends. I'm seven years sober, but I hurt so many

people, I've been making amends all this time. Maybe I always will be. I'd like your forgiveness for the way I used you for my own amusement. If someone did that to my son . . ."

Never in a million years would Lauren have expected this.

"I take responsibility," Nevin said. "Will you please try to forgive me, even if you can't do it right now?"

Lauren straightened her glasses. "Please thank Becky for the offer of tea."

"You can still have tea," he said.

"Thank you, but I'm really very busy today. I'd better go."

Lauren raced out of the house, down the street, and around the corner before leaning against a stop sign. She was glad she'd faced Nevin Morgan, surprises and all. Maybe now she'd finally be able to throw off the shame she felt when she was seventeen.

But if Nevin wasn't making the calls, who was?

3:44 p.m.

They didn't say much driving back from Birch Bend to Hidden Falls.

While Ethan drove, Nicole sat with the folder in her lap. Along with her list of names and the photo from the cemetery, it now contained copies of a few public records pertaining to Quinn, but nothing especially revealing — his property tax bills for the last five years and the deed to his house showing that he'd paid off his mortgage three years ago. She felt no closer to finding Quinn than she had three days ago.

She'd also dug up several property sales for the family names Jack had narrowed her list to, but she'd have to wait for the details to come in the official documents. Some discrepancies in lot numbers made it difficult to be certain which properties were in question, but Nicole figured they could at least drive through the neighborhoods. Her hunch was that some of the lots were either combined in a sale or split up in a sale — or both, at two different points in history. She could always go back to Jack and see what else was in his files — if she got that desperate.

Nicole felt the pressure of a Friday afternoon. The county records office would be closed for two days. Jack struck her as a workaholic, but he also had a family, so it was hard to guess what his weekends were like. Tomorrow marked a week since she arrived in Hidden Falls. If she had known that five minutes talking to Quinn before the banquet began was all she was going to get, she would have chosen her topics more carefully. She'd blathered on about some man with a birthmark when she should have been thanking Quinn for his presence in her life.

She opened the folder and pulled the

photograph to the front.

"Has no one ever told you that you look like your grandfather or something?" she said.

"That man is not my grandfather." Ethan kept his eyes on the road. "I knew my Grandpa Jordan, and my mother's father was a fair-haired Swede. I've seen pictures."

"Then somebody else. An uncle? Cousin?"

"I've never seen that photo before. I'm sure the resemblance is just coincidence."

"Ethan, look at this!"

"I'm driving."

"This is no coincidence." Nicole closed the folder. "Lauren thinks you should just ask your parents. I told her you wouldn't do that."

"You were right."

"I know. But I agree with Lauren. If we want to find out who this is, then your parents are the best bet."

Ethan gave her a fast glance. "I think I'll take my chances on Quinn coming home. If that picture has anything to do with what he wanted to tell me, I'll find out soon enough."

Six days was already too late for "soon enough" in Nicole's opinion.

Her foot throbbed, but if she asked Ethan for some ibuprofen he would insist on taking her home for ice and a pain pill. It was hard to think straight. Nicole reached for her water bottle and dumped the last of its twenty ounces into her mouth.

"I'm usually better at my job than this,"

she said. "I can't remember the last time I came up so empty-handed." And now perhaps she didn't have a job to go back to. She checked her phone again, looking for an e-mail, a text message, a voice mail icon — anything from Reggie telling her what was happening at the paper.

"Quinn was in St. Louis, and he was fine," Ethan said. "He's going to come home."

"You could drive me to St. Louis now," she said. "I don't need surgery. I just have to be careful."

Ethan didn't speak. Nicole watched the way he worked his lips in and out.

"Just say it, Ethan."

"I have to go home to Columbus. I'm probably in serious hot water as it is."

"How bad is it?" Nicole had gotten so used to having him at her side she'd forgotten Ethan had his own dilemma.

"I don't think I've let any surgeries fall through the cracks, but my chief is not going to be happy with me."

"Are you going to get kicked out of your residency?"

He didn't answer.

"Ethan?"

"I don't know. It's possible. Are you losing your job?"

"It's possible." She looked out the passenger window at the fall countryside. "I should never have questioned how you could leave that first night without knowing what happened to Quinn. Just because I couldn't go didn't mean you shouldn't have."

"I made my own choice, Nicole, and for my own reasons."

He reached across the console for her hand, and she gave it to him.

"I can't say I'm sorry you're here," she said, "but I'm sorry you took such a risk and it turned out like this."

"I'm not."

Nicole held on to his hand but didn't look at him. She had nothing to do with the changes at her paper, but if Ethan lost his job — his career — it could be because of her, no matter what he said.

"Are we still going to the cemetery now?" he asked.

"Old Dom," she murmured. "He may be our best hope now."

Ethan turned into the cemetery from the back side and circled around the curved roads to the main building that housed the offices. Nicole waited for him to come around and hold the door open while she got her crutches situated.

At the desk inside, Ethan asked for Dominick. They still didn't know if the name was his first or last.

"Mmm," said the pleasant looking young woman at a computer. "Not too many people come looking for Dom. He keeps his own hours."

"So he still works here?" Given his age, Nicole wasn't sure whether to be shocked or relieved.

"Not officially." The nameplate said the young woman's name was Jasmine. "But he likes to putter around, and he knows a lot of things no one else does, so they don't mind if he comes and goes."

"If he's on the grounds, where would he likely be?" Nicole asked.

Jasmine pointed out the door. "Just go around the back of the building. There's a room he calls his office."

Nicole hopped on one foot to turn around and set her crutches in a new direction. Ethan went ahead of her to open the door. Outside, a sidewalk ran alongside the building, easing her effort.

At the back of the building, Ethan tried the only door they saw. It opened.

"It looks more like a storeroom than an office," he said.

"He was a groundskeeper," Nicole said. "It wouldn't be the kind of office you expect."

Ethan felt around for a light switch. An overhead lamp went on, revealing an old wooden desk and the most uncomfortable looking chair Nicole had ever seen. But she needed a chair just then, so when Ethan pulled it out for her, she sat in it.

"He may not even be here today," Ethan said. "Do you want to wait? I could go ask some other people."

She wanted to put her foot up. Instead, she stretched it out in front of her and tried to find an angle that didn't shoot pain up her leg.

"You're not feeling well," Ethan said.

"No, Dr. Jordan, I'm not."

"Let's go," he said. "We're going to get you home."

Nicole took a deep breath and let it out slowly. "Unfortunately, I have to admit you're right."

Ethan held her crutches and Nicole pulled herself upright. She looked up to see an old man shuffle through the doorway.

"Goodness," he said, "if I'd known I was having company, I'd have brought hot chocolate for you." He sipped from a steaming cup.

"Excuse us," Ethan said, "we're actually just on our way out."

"No," Nicole said. "He's here now. We might as well ask our questions."

"What questions are those?" Old Dom set down his hot chocolate and pulled a handkerchief out of his pocket to blow his nose. "Are you looking for your mother's grave?"

She blanched. Nicole hadn't been to her mother's grave in fifteen years. "You remember me?"

"I remember a lot of folks."

"Do you know Ted Quinn?" she asked.

"Of course. He hasn't been out to visit me for a couple of weeks, though."

Nicole's eyes widened. "Quinn comes to visit you?"

"He likes to look at my books."

"Your books?" Nicole saw nothing around the office but sparse furniture and a space heater.

Old Dom shuffled across the room, taking keys off a chain hanging from his belt. He unlocked a door Nicole hadn't even noticed and turned on a light.

"I started keeping these books with my daddy when I was just a boy."

The room was only about nine by twelve, but three walls had counters and shelves. Several oversized record ledgers lay open. Nicole could see they were filled with handwritten entries.

"Quinn always said genealogy was a hobby," Old Dom said. "I let him think I believed him."

"But you didn't?"

"He was looking for something. Lately I got the idea that he might have found it."

4:02 p.m.

The trail wasn't one that recreational visitors to Hidden Falls used, which was why Dani chose it. The only sounds she wanted to hear were her own feet hitting the ground, breaking the occasional twig underfoot, and the orchestra of nature. Birds calling to each other, squirrels chasing each other up one tree and down another, wind scratching leaves, insects buzzing, water hitting rock in the distance — those were the sounds that would soothe Dani. At this time of year, she could count on a thick layer of fallen oak and maple and river birch leaves swirling, dry and shriveling, as Dani shuffled through them.

Quinn always liked the crunching sound. He said stepping on leaves and watching them crumble was his way of making sure the organic matter got back into the soil. Some future generation would thank him.

Dani and Quinn had hiked this trail together about three weeks earlier. If she followed the path in a strict way, Dani would end up at a high point overlooking the river. By then she would be ready to sit for a few minutes in the dirt on the bluff, with her feet dangling over the river.

At the sound of a crunching step that wasn't hers, Dani paused. Slowly, she put her foot down and turned to look behind her. A white tennis shoe disappeared into the brush on one side of the trail.

Dani peered into the trees. "There's poison oak in there."

The warning caused a brief flurry of movement, but the owner of the tennis shoe did not emerge onto the trail.

Dani knew she couldn't prevent others from using the trails, but that didn't stop her from wishing for solitude each time she set out to hike. She turned back to the trail and pulled a bag of dates from her vest pocket. Sliding one into her mouth, Dani chewed into its sweetness with deliberation but hiked at a normal pace. A couple of glances over her shoulder revealed no one behind her on the path.

Yet she knew she wasn't alone.

The woods were thick in this stretch, with low-lying growths filling in places where sunlight wormed its way through branches. But Dani knew well the sounds of the forest, and what she heard now didn't belong there — any more than the shadows she'd seen outside her cabin on the lake belonged there.

This white tennis shoe could belong to some kid avoiding homework, or it could belong to someone who knew how to drill a hole in a boat and camouflage a plug that was sure to work loose. Either way, Dani wasn't going to put up with someone following her now. She knew these woods better than she knew the quirks of Quinn's ancient laptop. In another twenty yards, she could ignore the sign to remain on the trail and the yellow arrow pointing to the approved path. Dani would know where she was going, but a less experienced hiker would get lost. In the woods, every turn looked the same as a half dozen others.

Dani veered off the path. She didn't have to listen hard or long to know that her shadow now flailed against sticky bushes and tripped on tree roots. Following someone in the woods wasn't as simple as lurking at the edge of a well trampled trail. Dani kept going, choosing a route that grew even denser. It was only a matter of time now.

The thud she'd been waiting for was followed by a sharp cry of pain.

Now Dani turned, retraced her steps, and saw the girl sitting in the dirt with a fresh rip in one knee of her jeans.

Some kid, Dani thought. *She won't know poison oak from a four-leaf clover.*

Dani stomped toward the girl, put her hands on her knees, and leaned into the frightened face.

"Why are you following me?"

The girl tried to scoot back in the dirt, but Dani moved with her.

"I come here to be alone." The only exception Dani made was hiking with Quinn, because he knew how to keep his mouth shut and enjoy the view.

The girl said nothing, her chest heaving. Whether it was from the exertion Dani had induced or fear, the movement made her look frail.

Dani knew this girl — or at least she'd seen her somewhere.

"You're Jack Parker's kid."

The girl nodded. "I'm Eva."

Dani had never known her name and didn't particularly have a use for it now. "Stand up."

Eva complied.

Dani assessed the girl's size. She was tall enough to match the shadow Dani saw moving through the trees at the lake, but she seemed more slender. Then again, a shadow was never an exact match to the shape that cast it. Angles and levels of light could distort anything.

Eva gasped when Dani grabbed her arm and felt the muscles under her long-sleeved T-shirt. Dani only wanted to know if this kid could have the strength required to get a boat out of the water and apply sufficient force with a drill to tamper with Dani's boat.

"It's not you." Dani pushed the girl's arm away.

"What's not me?"

"Never mind. But leave me alone."

Eva started to cry.

Dani rolled her eyes. "Look, I'm sorry if I scared you, but you were following me, and I don't like that."

"I hear what people say about you." Eva choked back a sob.

Dani knew she was going to regret this. "What are you talking about?"

"I just want to know how you do it."

"Do what?"

"You don't fit in, and it doesn't bother you."

At least the girl had her facts straight. "What does that have to do with you?"

"I don't fit in either," Eva said. "But it bothers me, and I *hate* that it does. I don't want to care that I don't fit in. Like you."

Dani sighed. "We're not very far from the river. Let's go there."

She turned and resumed hiking. Behind her, Eva shuffled but kept pace. Dani followed an arc of bushes back to the main trail and eventually emerged at the bluff she'd been aiming for all along. With the swift motion of experience, she sat on the ground and hung her feet against the rock.

"Is this safe?" Eva asked.

"Is that what matters?" Dani tuned into the sound of water flowing beneath her and watched a couple of kids fishing on the opposite shore.

With some care, Eva lowered herself to the ground beside Dani. Her fingers probed the tear in her pants.

"Okay," Dani said, "if you insist on talking, this is where you do it."

Below the bluff was the promise that the river would widen into the lake. From experience, Dani knew the kids would find better fishing if they went downstream about half a mile.

Eva's voice was tiny. "Have you always been so . . . independent?"

Independent was a kinder word than many people would choose.

"I suppose so."

"Everyone says you don't like to be around people much."

Dani puffed out her cheeks. "Certain people in small doses are all right." Liam called her socially inappropriate. If he weren't her cousin, he might not make the list of people she tolerated.

"That's how I feel!" Eva picked up a rock and dropped it down into the river. "I had friends in Memphis who understood me. But here everybody wants me to be like them."

"And you're not?" Eva looked like a pretty normal teenager to Dani.

"I went to a party last Saturday, and all I could think about was how I wished I could call my parents to come get me. But they were at that banquet for Mr. Quinn."

"Well, I know how the banquet came out, but what was wrong with the party?"

"Nothing, I guess," Eva said. "Except that it feels like so much *work* to go to a party."

Dani knew the feeling. "So don't go."

"My mom thinks I need friends."

"Do you think you need friends?"

"I feel like I'm supposed to say yes."

"You're not supposed to say anything."

Eva was silent for a minute and then said, "It was Melissa's birthday. She's nice to me and I like her, but I *hated* being at that party."

"So next time don't go." What was unclear about this dilemma?

"Is that what you do?"

"Look," Dani said, "I'm no role model, and I don't want you thinking I am."

Eva's head turned toward the lake, and she maneuvered to her feet and shaded her eyes for a better look. "I can see his truck from here. I have to go!"

Dani saw no reason to protest the girl's departure. She wanted peace and quiet, and now she had it.

5:02 p.m.

Old Dom lifted a volume off the second shelf up. The ledgers were so tall that the only way to store them was to lay them flat. Ethan had been scanning the room, trying to discern a system to the way the books were organized.

"This was the one where Quinn left off," Old Dom said.

"Left off?"

"He studied quite a few." Dom laid the volume on a clear space on the counter and opened the cover. "But he kept coming back to this one."

Ethan kept a hand at the small of Nicole's back in case she lost her balance leaning on her crutches. The first page — and all the others, Ethan supposed — was marked off like an oversized sheet of notebook paper, with a red line down the left margin and rows of faint blue lines.

"Are these the official cemetery records?" Ethan asked.

"Might as well be." Dom shuffled out of the way so Ethan and Nicole could get closer. "My father copied over all the entries in the official records."

"But why?"

Dom pointed to a notation. "So he could write what the records left out."

Ethan peered at the florid handwriting. After a few seconds, he began to see the system to the flourishes and cramped spacing between words. This particular note said, *Infant. Bad breather.*

"What does that mean?" Nicole asked.

"Cause of death," Ethan murmured. He looked at Dom. "Your father made notes about what he thought caused the deaths of people buried in this cemetery?"

Dom nodded. "Sometimes he took it from the death certificate. Sometimes he took it from what folks said. And sometimes he had his own ideas."

"Was he a doctor?"

"No sir. He was a groundskeeper, same as me. Started tending graves in 1918 after his own father died. Folks were afraid of anything to do with dead bodies because of the Spanish influenza, but Daddy figured he'd already been exposed. He started digging graves and stayed on."

Nicole gingerly lifted one of the thick pages to turn it. It made the sound of creasing cardboard. "And Quinn was looking at this book?"

"Last I saw."

Ethan scanned the dates copiously entered in the left margin next to the names on the first page. "This is from the early 1930s."

"Well, he's a history teacher. I figure liking old records comes with the occupation." Dom scrunched up his wrinkled features to inspect Ethan. "What did you say your name was?"

He hadn't. "I'm Ethan Jordan."

"Richard's boy?"

Ethan winced but nodded.

"You don't look like him."

Ethan had heard that all his life. His older brother was the spitting image of their father. Ethan had his mother's eyes but little other family resemblance.

"Jordan was one of the names on Quinn's list," Dom said.

Nicole looked up. "Quinn had a list?"

"Just a scrap of paper he kept in his shirt pocket." Dom patted his own pocket. "He borrows my pencil a lot. He'll scratch something out and write something else in and make his thinking noises. But I saw it once. He wrote *Jordan* in big letters."

It made no sense. Ethan's parents didn't move to Hidden Falls until his father started working at the screw factory in Birch Bend after they were married. Ethan had no relatives buried in town, and Quinn knew that.

"My hot chocolate is getting cold," Old Dom said. "You folks stay as long as you like. I'll just be in the other room."

"Wait," Nicole said. "Can you tell us what else Quinn was looking at?"

Dom pointed. "Those right there. That was his stack."

Ethan glanced at Nicole, balancing on her crutches, trying not to put weight on her bad foot while using her hands to turn pages in the records book.

"I don't suppose there's a stool Nicole could use."

"Maybe in the front office. Tell them I said it was okay."

Dom left the room. Ethan heard the creak of Dom's chair as he sat and the slurp of hot chocolate that followed.

"Are we staying?" Ethan said to Nicole.

She looked up. "How can we not?"

"Then I'm going to find you a stool. And there's a pain pill in your future."

She nodded. "I know. I need one. But we might not get another chance with these books."

Ethan was persuasive in the front office and returned with a wooden three-legged stool. It wouldn't be comfortable, but at least Nicole would be off her feet.

Dom whistled softly at his desk and turned on a radio.

"Old Dom doesn't know about the photo," Nicole said softly as she adjusted herself on the stool with the oversized volume on the counter in front of her.

Ethan agreed. "So what are we looking for here?"

"We go back to our own list of names, especially Tabor, Fenton, and Pease." Nicole looked at the stack Old Dom had pointed them to. "Can you pull those books down and see when they're from?"

Ethan laid two more volumes on the counter and opened one to a random page toward the back. "June 3, 1934."

"And the other? Earlier or later?"

He opened to another random page. "September 8, 1956."

"So we have three volumes covering roughly twenty years."

Ethan put fingers to his temples. The cemetery wasn't large, and the population of Hidden Falls had always been small and was probably smaller in the decades represented in these books than the present ten thousand residents. Old Dom's father wouldn't have needed so many pages to record basic information about deaths. There had to be more to it. He flipped to the back of one book and found rubbings of tombstones pasted in.

"What are these marks?" Nicole's question

broke into Ethan's thoughts.

"What marks?"

"Look." She placed a finger above a line. "Little pencil dots and dashes. You don't think it could be Morse code, do you?"

Morse code? In cemetery records? Ethan took the book into his hands and carried it to better light. He turned a few pages. The pencil markings, faint and smudged, didn't appear on every page, and slanted ascenders and descenders of inked handwriting nearly obscured the marks.

"Quinn borrows Dom's pencil," Nicole said.

Ethan looked up. The markings, whatever they were, came from Quinn's hand. Ethan took his phone from his pocket and opened an Internet search bar to tap in Morse code.

"We're going to need some paper," Nicole said.

Ethan selected one of the search results. Just as he turned to ask Old Dom if he had any paper they could use, a website for decoding Morse code popped open.

6:07 p.m

The first question that niggled at Dani all afternoon was how Eva Parker got out to the trail in the first place.

The second question was whose truck Eva saw and why it spurred her into running back down the trail.

Dani didn't want to be the last person to see Eva Parker.

When she got back to town, Dani drove straight to the Parker house and climbed the front steps to ring the bell.

As soon as Gianna Parker opened the front door, Dani could see Gianna wasn't pleased to see her. Since the two of them had never spoken five words to each other, Dani wasn't clear just what objection Gianna had already formed. Dani wasn't completely incapable of appropriate manners. She'd put on a dress for Quinn's dinner, after all, and she pleased people enough that they called her back for small home repairs and computer work. This was one of those moments where Dani had to reach inside herself and pull out the manners she knew were there.

"Hello, Mrs. Parker. I'm Dani Roose."

"What can I do for you?"

"I'm looking for Eva."

"For what purpose, may I ask?"

Purpose? Dani smiled. "Friendship."

"Aren't you a bit old to be friends with a fifteen-year-old?"

Dani was now counting the remaining life of her smile in single-digit seconds. This was the mother who thought her daughter needed more friends. Apparently Gianna meant friends she could personally approve of.

"Is Eva here?" Dani's primary objective was to be sure the girl had gotten home safely.

"My husband will be home any minute, and we'll be sitting down to dinner."

How was that an answer to a simple question?

"I only need a minute," Dani said.

"Eva hasn't been feeling well," Gianna said. "I'd rather not disturb her."

The answer was still indirect, but it seemed to indicate Eva was home. Dani looked past Gianna and saw the movement behind her.

"Hello, Eva," Dani said over Gianna's shoulder.

"It's okay, Mom." Eva came to the door.

Gianna scowled, an expression Dani suspected was well practiced and which Dani disregarded.

Eva slipped past her mother. "We'll just wait for Dad and Brooke in the yard."

With a sigh, Gianna surrendered and withdrew into the house. Eva pulled the door closed and led the way across the yard to a two-seater glider under a spreading oak tree. Dani followed.

Eva started a swinging motion. "What are you doing here?"

"You were a long way from home," Dani said, "for someone who looks too young to drive."

"I have my permit."

"But you weren't driving today."

Eva swung a little harder. "No."

"That trailhead is a good three miles from here."

"I know."

"Whose truck did you see?"

"You have a lot of questions."

Two cars drove past the house. Dani waited for answers.

"I know this boy, Zeke. His uncle works at a bait shop at the lake," Eva said. "Sometimes his uncle asks Zeke to bring him things he needs from town."

"And sometimes you ride along with Zeke."

"He doesn't mind giving me a ride. I can walk for a few minutes while he makes his delivery. But he borrows his dad's truck, so he can't be late getting back. Please don't tell my mother."

They swayed with the glider. Dani had the information she'd come for. Eva was doing something behind her parents' backs, but it wasn't nearly as creepy as some of the alternatives that had passed through Dani's mind after Eva ran off. She didn't like to be in between people who ought to be talking to each other. Eva and Gianna would have to work this out.

"Why does your mother think you're not feeling well?" Eva looked fine to Dani. No one could be certain what was going through another person's mind, but Eva didn't act sick.

"I get a lot of stomachaches. I had one

today, but she made me stay at school."

Going to school used to give Dani a stomachache, too. If she hadn't been able to sign up for a class with Quinn every semester, she would have gone bonkers. At least for fifty-two minutes every day, she was in a room with someone who made an effort to understand her.

Dani buzzed her lips.

"What's wrong?" Eva said.

"Look, kid . . . Eva . . . I don't know why you chased after me today, but there are no easy answers to what you're going through. You just have to be who you are, that's all."

"I don't think I've figured out who that is yet."

"You're fifteen. You have time." Dani gave the swing a fresh push. "This Zeke, does he give you a stomachache?"

"Not exactly."

Dani waited.

"He tried to kiss me last week."

"Tried?"

"I . . . ducked. I didn't know what to do."

"Then you're not ready."

"Melissa has a boyfriend. All the girls at our lunch table wish they did."

At least Eva had a lunch table crowd. Dani was glad for that much on her behalf.

"So do they know about Zeke?"

Eva shook her head. "I hear how they talk. They would tell me stuff I should be doing with a boy, and I don't want to do it."

"Then don't."

"Why is everybody in such a hurry?" Eva's voice cracked. "I want to go to college. I want to live on my own. I want to find a job I love. I want to do lots of things before I worry about having a boyfriend."

Dani was starting to wish she'd left after she was sure Eva was safe.

"I just thought you would understand that," Eva said.

"Well, I wasn't cut out for college, and some people would say I don't pay enough attention to my work." Dani reached out and caught a leaf on its way down from the oak tree.

"But they still call you when they need something," Eva said. "I bet you didn't know that you fixed Melissa's laptop after her dad was sure it was toast."

Dani fixed a lot of laptops. Every time she did it, she promised herself she would never be so attached to something outside herself that she panicked if it stopped working. But Eva wasn't really talking about deficient technology.

"You don't have to be like everybody else to find your place," Dani said. "You make the place where you want to live your life. Then if you're happy there, you protect it."

"What about love?" Eva whispered.

"Love comes in all shapes and sizes," Dani

said. Quinn. Liam and Cooper. Sylvia. Dani's married sister and her new baby. Her parents. "Don't pass it up thinking it has to look like Zeke and drive a red truck."

Eva giggled, breaking the tension of the moment.

"Could we go hiking together sometime?" Eva asked. "I promise not to talk."

Dani nodded. "Okay, kid, I'll think about it."

A BMW that could no longer be called new turned into the driveway

"There's my dad and my sister, Brooke." Eva hopped off the glider. "They've been to their first puppy training class."

The back door of the vehicle opened, and a girl younger than Eva got out with her fist firmly wrapped around one end of a leash. A puppy romped out of the car and tugged on the leash.

Eva knelt in the grass, and the puppy strained toward her. Brooke gradually let the dog move toward the goal until Eva put her face straight down into the dog's neck.

"Thank you," Eva said when she looked up.

Dani shrugged and got off the glider.

Gianna appeared in the yard, and Jack walked over to kiss her cheek.

"How did it go?" Gianna asked.

Jack tilted his head toward the puppy. "The trainer said it wasn't bad for a first session."

"I have to have treats in my pocket all the

time now," Brooke said. "I have to reward her when she does the right thing."

"Hello, Dani." Jack looked puzzled and for good reason. A few hours ago, Dani would have been just as bewildered at the thought of finding herself in Jack Parker's front yard.

"Dani's going to take me hiking," Eva said. "I hope that's okay."

Jack glanced at Gianna. "Sure. I guess."

"Dinner's ready." Gianna turned toward the house. "I want to hear how you came out on your search through the old files."

Dani paced to her Jeep, parked on the street. Jack wouldn't find in his old files what she had already dug up.

7:02 p.m.

Sunset lowered darkness like a blind around Liam's apartment building.

He hardly noticed the difference between the shadows and the brilliance of midday, though. Liam kept his drapes closed and his door bolted now. For the last twenty-four hours, he'd alternated between not sleeping in the bedroom and not sleeping in the living room. The more he thought about it, the more he was persuaded he might as well have shot himself in the foot yesterday when he went to see Jessica. Now she could report his words to anyone she chose.

His brother.

His boss.

The mayor.

The sheriff.

Free of context and body language between the two of them, his words would sound like an effort to cover up a crime. Technically, he supposed, they were. If Jessica had miraculously agreed to produce the needed funds, he would have figured out some way to put them back, to trace the trail backward and turn back time to before any of this started. Going forward he would have been vigilant about every transaction made on his accounts and hoped — prayed — that once they were married and Jessica didn't have the wedding to obsess about, she would be happy with the life they shared.

There was no going forward now.

For the last week, Liam slept only when exhaustion overwhelmed fear and his body gave out. Then he would start to dream and wake with a jolt to realize it was all still true, and the cycle would begin again. The master of being cool, reassuring, and confident to close the deal was defeated. Belief that every circumstance contained an answer fled. Liam was past staring at his computer screen or printouts of the various reports. Inhaling the fragrance of Jessica's blueberry scone yesterday was the closest he'd come to eating in two days. Now he sat on the couch chewing his thumbnails, uncertain how many hours he'd been in that same position. What did it matter? Without Jessica, his future was a formless void.

The only question now was how long it would take for someone to knock on his door with a search warrant.

And whether he would be there.

Liam put his head back and closed his eyes. The digits of the account numbers he'd stolen on the night of Quinn's banquet burned against his eyelids, memorized. He doubted he would ever forget them. If he had used them, perhaps he wouldn't have derailed his future with Jessica. Maybe he could have fixed this mess. But he hadn't used them, and now there was no point in even trying.

The rap on the apartment door that woke him could have been a dream. His eyes popped open, but he didn't move, instead listening for whether the sound would recur.

"Liam, are you in there? Don't mess with me."

Liam let his breath out. He got up, stumbled to the door, and took off both locks before falling back onto the couch.

The knob turned, and Dani entered. "What's up with you? I had to knock three times."

Liam glanced at the clock and saw that he had been asleep for twenty minutes.

"Sorry. I dozed off." Liam got up and moved away from her stare. "I was just about to make coffee. Want some?"

"No offense, but I think you should back off the caffeine," she said. "You look even worse than you did two days ago."

"I just need to shower and shave."

"I'll say." Dani waved a hand in front of her face.

Simultaneously, Liam was relieved to see his cousin and wished she would go away.

"I have some information for you." Dani dumped herself into the recliner. The way she moved reminded Liam of Cooper, who did the same thing every time he came over.

Liam rubbed one eye. "I'm sorry. Information?"

"Dude, you need to wake up. Or sleep. Or something."

Or something, he thought. He bypassed the coffeepot and instead went to the sink to splash cold water on his face.

"That address you gave me," Dani said. "It's a private investigator's off-the-record address."

"I don't understand." Liam guzzled cold water straight from the faucet.

"And you say I'm socially inappropriate." Dani swung her legs around and they hit the floor with a carpeted thud. "It's a Doing Business As of a Doing Business As of a private detective outfit with three investigators."

"Speak English, please."

"It's a subgroup of a subgroup of the real

company. Somebody is trying to separate what people see from what the company really is."

"Sounds clandestine." And it sounded like someone Liam could really use. Too bad the firm was three states away.

"Quinn's looking for something. Or somebody."

"I'm glad to hear you use the present tense." Liam took a glass from the cupboard and stuck it under the ice dispenser before filling it with water.

"Why wouldn't I? He's away, that's all."

"Okay, let's not go there." Liam willed his eyes to stay open. "So what's he looking for?"

"You didn't ask me to find that out."

"Danielle Elaine." Why did she have to be that way?

"Liam Maurice."

"You must have a theory."

She shrugged. "An adoption? Maybe he has a child he just found out about, or maybe he was adopted himself and just discovered it."

Equally unlikely possibilities, Liam thought. But maybe with some sleep, they would make sense.

"You can't think of anything else people look for?"

"Relatives of some sort. Money they left in an old bank account. Some kind of inheritance."

"Quinn doesn't have any relatives, and he

has plenty of money." Liam didn't know exactly how much, but Quinn had at least two accounts he wanted to roll over into a new investment. "And why use a UPS box in Birch Bend?"

"There's this modern concept known as right to privacy. Lately people in this town act like there's a ban on the idea."

Sometimes Liam felt the childhood urge to punch Dani for being so aggravating. But she was younger and a girl, so when he tried that strategy as a boy he was always the one to get into trouble — no matter how much of a smart aleck Dani was.

"So you'll tell Sylvia, then?" Dani stood up with her hands in the pockets of her orange North Face vest.

"I guess so." Sylvia was the one Liam first went to with the information. She was entitled to the results of Dani's search.

"And Cooper."

"Not Cooper. He'd come up with a statute that says my photographs were illegal." Besides, learning that Quinn might be looking for somebody didn't point to where he was right now.

"Nicole Sandquist, then," Dani said. "She'll know what to do with it. She's staying with Lauren Nock in town."

"Maybe. I'll think about it and decide in the morning."

Dani wandered across the apartment and

sat on a stool at the breakfast bar. Too late, Liam saw what she reached for.

"Jessica's engagement ring?" Dani held the ring up to the light between thumb and forefinger.

Liam set his glass down slightly too hard and scratched his head vigorously with both hands.

"She broke up with you, didn't she?"

"Yes." That much was certainly true. The reasons were another matter. "Do you know a jeweler in Birch Bend I can trust?"

"More intrigue."

Liam took the moment for a long drink of cold water. He didn't dare go to the only jeweler in Hidden Falls and suffer the embarrassment of everyone in town knowing this piece of truth.

Dani peered at the ring.

Liam lurched across the breakfast bar and snatched the ring from her hand. "Fine. She scammed me. I think she took out the diamond before she returned the ring. That's how much a sucker she thinks I am. Is that what you want to hear?" It wasn't the stone that gave it away, because honestly he couldn't tell the difference between a diamond and cubic zirconia, but the setting now had a slight scratch that Jessica wouldn't have tolerated if she'd planned to wear the ring. She hadn't gone to the Hidden Falls jeweler, either. He wouldn't have made that scratch.

Dani swiveled the stool back and forth. "Liam, as annoying as you are, you're the closest thing I have to a brother. No, I don't want to hear that Jessica scammed you. But only a jeweler can tell you for sure."

"I'm sorry I snapped at you. It's been a rough few days." He finished his water. "Are you willing to do me another favor?"

"I am not taking that ring to a jeweler."

"No. Bigger than that." He watched her impassive face while he told her about the accounts.

"You need Cooper," she said.

"I need to be sure my suspicions are right."

"It seems pretty clear Jessica threw you over for the money."

"Maybe I can still fix everything somehow."

"Why would you want to?"

Liam turned to the sink for more water. He was being stupid. But the thought of releasing Jessica once and for all cut into his heart too painfully to accept.

"It gets worse," he said.

For once Dani didn't shoot off a smart remark. Liam unfolded the blackmail note, which he now carried in his back pocket, and slid it across the table.

Dani read it without picking it up. "Okay, now you really need Cooper."

"It's too risky. I don't have proof of anything."

"You're going to look guilty if someone

finds all this."

"I know. But before I draw fire, I want a defense strategy. You can hack into the accounts and find where the money went. You know how to do that, right?"

9:18 p.m.

Sylvia deserved a piece of pie.

A busy stint at Town Hall in the morning, a long afternoon putting final touches on the shop, and a session of straightening up and folding laundry at her mother's house all added up to pie. Sylvia hoped Gavin Owens had baked blackberry today. She drove past the shop one last time, admiring the display Lizzie had created for the reopening, and pulled into a parking spot in front of the Fall Shadows Café.

Inside, she was surprised to see her niece at the counter, leaning over her clipboard with Gavin.

"I want to have all the details in my notes," Lauren said, "in case somebody asks me a question I can't remember the answer to."

"Relax." Gavin patted Lauren's hand. "It will be what it will be."

"But I'm responsible for whatever it will be." Lauren smoothed out the ragged corner of a page.

"Food, fun, friends. I'm supplying the food. How can you go wrong?" Gavin looked up. "Here's your aunt."

Lauren turned.

"Gavin's right," Sylvia said. "It's time to take your list home and get some rest before tomorrow."

Lauren stuck the clipboard in her bag. "I guess so. Six thirty in the morning will come way too early."

"The food won't be far behind," Gavin said.

"I'll be there as soon as I can," Sylvia said. She'd have to wait until after her mother's daily call at seven before she could leave the house.

"I'm craving a piece of pie." Sylvia looked hopefully at Gavin. "Am I too late?"

"Blackberry?"

"Of course."

"You're in luck." Gavin pushed through the swinging door into the kitchen. "I'll make it to go."

"I'm glad I ran into you," Lauren said. "I've been thinking about that box."

"Quinn's box?"

"Yes." Lauren pushed up her glasses. "Are you sure you shouldn't open it?"

Quinn gave the carved box to Sylvia when she first moved into her house. They'd carried empty cartons up the stairs, and Quinn lifted the box out of one of them. He asked if he could leave it there undisturbed, and Sylvia agreed without thinking twice. When he was ready, he would tell her what was in it and why he wanted to leave it at her house.

He never had, and Sylvia only saw the box one or two times a year when she had a reason to go up into the attic. It had been absorbed into the clutter.

"I really think you should consider it, Aunt Sylvia." Lauren put her head through the strap of her bag and arranged it over one hip. "Didn't Quinn give any instructions about . . . well, what to do with the box if . . . you know."

"That hasn't happened," Sylvia said immediately. Without a body, there was no proof of death or foul play. She was a long way from concluding Quinn would never come home.

"I just meant . . . well, there might be extraordinary circumstances, and Quinn would understand."

Twenty years that box sat in Sylvia's attic. Now Lauren suggested Sylvia set aside two decades of trust because of one mysterious week.

"Jack Parker is onto something," Lauren said. "I've run into him a couple of times this week, and he's determined to be a hero."

"I'm aware of his efforts." Sylvia doubted Lauren knew about the address Jack was supposed to be tracking down.

"Ethan and Nicole are hard at it, too. I haven't talked to them today, but I'm sure Nicole isn't going to let go of this."

"No, she won't."

Lauren laid a hand on Sylvia's arm. "If

there's something to discover about Quinn's past, I would rather Nicole be the one to find it. Or you. And maybe the truth is in that box."

Lauren left, and Gavin returned with Sylvia's pie. She drove home and sat at the kitchen table to eat it.

"Quinn," she said aloud. "Quinn."

Sylvia lost interest in the pie halfway through the piece. It was almost ten o'clock. She knew she should take the advice she'd given Lauren and go to bed and try to sleep.

Instead, she climbed the attic stairs and carried the carved box down.

She set it on the coffee table in the living room, unopened, while she got ready for bed.

At ten thirty, she went through the house turning off lights. She was down to just the bedside light and the table lamp in the living room when she sat on the sofa and stared at the box.

At eleven, she picked it up and sat with it in her lap and ran her fingers along the edges and in the crevices of the intricate leaf carving. It was the sort of box that had a story of its own, no matter what it contained.

It was past midnight when Sylvia raised the lid and looked inside.

9
A Fair Refuge

Saturday
7:34 a.m.
The lawn behind Our Savior Community Church had its share of the town's fallen leaves. In this case, most descended from the two towering oak trees in the middle of the lawn. Those old oaks created a wide circle of shade for church picnics and were the traditional location for photographs of Sunday school children every autumn. A medley of river birch and maples provided irregular adornment of the outer portions of the grass.

It will do well for the fair, Sylvia thought as she took a distant parking spot in order to leave the best slots for fair visitors. Only ten minutes behind the arrival time she'd aimed for, Sylvia was eager for the day. She still had more than two hours before Waterfall Books and Gifts would reopen. Everything was ready at the store, and Lizzie would be there soon, so Sylvia could relax and be helpful setting up at the church.

In navy slacks, a white blouse with a gray cardigan, and comfortable shoes, Sylvia progressed across the parking lot. From fifty feet away, she could see blue and white stripes of four canopy tents forming a row along one edge of the lawn. Quinn had acquired them for the church several years ago at a clearance sale at the hardware store on Main Street. Instant pop-up canopies had swept into vogue all over Hidden Falls, and the hardware store's owner had gotten desperate to get the older style out of his storeroom. Sylvia was pretty sure there were two more. The six tents were a mainstay of outdoor events of Our Savior.

Everything reminded Sylvia of Quinn. She could hear his voice in her head using humor to put people at ease on a day like this one.

Lauren was more than capable of running the fair — it had been her idea, after all. But all week Sylvia hoped Quinn would return in time to see the fruit of his organizing labor. When he did come back — even after all this time she refused to say *if* — the whole town would want to hear his story.

And there would be a story, because nothing else would explain why a man who hadn't left the county in more than thirty years suddenly was nowhere to be found.

Sylvia reached the church's sidewalk and started to cross the lawn. At tent number five, a sea of blue and white tumbled down.

"Hey!"

Sylvia recognized Lauren's voice — from beneath the canopy.

"I thought we had a system." Lauren fought her way out from under the canvas.

"Sorry. My bad." Cooper grappled for an edge to hold up while Lauren crawled out.

Sylvia couldn't help laughing. And it felt good.

Lauren emerged. "I thought we were trying to avoid a repeat of what happened with the video booth at the banquet."

"Today we scheduled the equipment collapse for before the main event." With Lauren clear of the canopy, Cooper straightened out the canvas and positioned it in line with the tents they'd already erected.

"And we'll give Zeke Plainfield something to do that doesn't involve tent poles."

Lauren smiled, something Sylvia hadn't seen her do much lately. Her niece was in close proximity to Cooper Elliott and not scowling or trying to escape. This was progress — and it would make Quinn smile.

"Hello, you two." Sylvia grabbed hold of one corner of the canvas and freed up Cooper to wrestle with the poles and connective framing that would hold the slight structure together.

"I'm glad you're here." Lauren gripped a pole in one hand and a canvas edge in the other. "The clock is ticking, but I think we'll be ready."

Lauren's glance at Cooper didn't escape Sylvia's notice.

Sylvia surveyed the lawn, discovering more help than she'd realized they would have. Benita Booker was busy directing a crew of four or five.

"Where did I leave my tools?" Cooper looked around before finally releasing the piece of framing in his hand and wandering off to search.

"I feel silly standing here holding parts of a tent." Lauren's eyes trailed along Cooper's path.

Sylvia glanced around. "I'm glad to catch you in a quiet moment. I thought a lot last night about what you said about opening Quinn's box."

"And?" Lauren gave Sylvia her full gaze now.

"Your argument started to make sense to me."

A honking horn made both of them shift attention to the street, where Gavin Owens's gray van pulled up. He jumped out of the driver's seat and went around to open the rear doors.

"Have we got electricity?" Gavin hefted a tub of supplies as he started across the grass.

Lauren tilted her head toward the building. "Benita put everyone who needs power over there."

"Great. The breakfast burritos are hot, and I'd like to keep it that way."

"I'll help you." The angle and size of the tub made Sylvia nervous, and she grabbed one end of the tub from Gavin. They carried it between them to an arrangement of tables and chairs.

Once it was out of the tub and on the table, Gavin found the cord and plugged in the food warmer. "No eggs Benedict for you today, but the burritos are low fat in whole-wheat tortillas. We've got regular, black bean, and spinach."

Sylvia made several trips with Gavin back and forth between the van and his assigned station, carrying paper goods, another warmer of individually wrapped burritos, bottled juices, and two fifty-five-cup coffee brewers.

"It's a lot of food," Sylvia said.

"I'm hoping for a lot of people. At lunch-time we'll change up the menu. When that's over, I'll mosey over and win the joke contest. I've been saving up a doozy."

Sylvia laughed and wondered what Quinn's entry would have been.

It was after eight now, less than an hour before all the booths and activities were scheduled to welcome visitors. Lauren and Cooper got the final tent up. Every time Sylvia looked at the street or the parking lot, she saw more cars lining up and volunteers taking up their positions on the lawn. This was the first time the church had done something like this. It was impossible to predict what the turnout would be or how foot traffic would rise and fall with the hours.

When Sylvia saw Lauren standing alone, leaning against the brick wall of the church, flipping sheets on her clipboard with a pen between her lips, she headed toward her. Lauren looked up, and Sylvia waved.

"I did open the box," Sylvia said when she got closer.

Lauren's eyebrows went up in expectation.

Benita Booker angled in at a speed Sylvia hadn't known she was capable of.

"I need Lauren for a few minutes." Benita took Lauren's hand and drew her away from the wall.

"Stay right there," Lauren called over her shoulder. "I'll come back."

Sylvia hadn't known what to expect when she opened the box. Before last night she'd never considered looking inside, so it hadn't seemed like a profitable use of mental energy to speculate. But she had expected that the contents, if she ever saw them, would be more self-evident.

Contrary to Lauren's instructions, Sylvia wandered down the side of the building to the area where silent auction items were displayed between two large posters on easels assuring bidders that proceeds from the auction would go to the support of a women's shelter in Birch Bend. Four mystery packages from Waterfall Books and Gifts, meticulously wrapped by Lizzie, sat on a draped table. Farther down, the vintage dresses from Sylvia's attic hung on a makeshift clothesline. Sylvia found a small box of bidding sheets and tape and began securing sheets next to the items they described — a weekend in a Chicago hotel, a fishing rod, pairs of concert tickets, meals at restaurants, children's toys. Bidders with a variety of interests could find something to consider.

"There you are."

Sylvia looked up to see her niece. "I thought I would make myself useful."

"Please do! I hope the auction will be self-explanatory and low maintenance."

"I'll check in on it when I can during the day."

"Perfect." Lauren set down her clipboard. "Now, you were going to tell me something about the box?"

Movement in her peripheral vision made Sylvia step back. A bell dinged, and Cooper rode by on a bicycle far too small for him. His knees pumped up close to his chin as he pedaled around with a grin on his face.

"At least I'm wearing a helmet!" He whizzed past them.

Lauren laughed. "I'm tempted to go get my bike and race him."

Sylvia's cell phone rang, and she lifted it to her ear as she watched Cooper circle around and come toward them again.

"This is Sammie Dunavant."

"Sammie, is everything all right?"

"I think so. Your mother called me because she was concerned she couldn't reach you this morning."

Sylvia was grateful her mother had a caring neighbor to call — but she had spoken to her mother barely an hour ago.

"I guess she's forgotten that we spoke." Sylvia shifted the phone to the other ear as she turned away from Cooper's shenanigans.

"She seems agitated. Do you mind talking to her again?"

"Of course not. I'll call her right now."

She hung up and dialed Emma's number. "Hi, Mom."

"I wondered if you were coming by today," Emma said.

Sylvia had just been to her mother's home the evening before. Barely ten hours had passed between the time Sylvia left last night and when her mother phoned her in the morning. Emma had seemed fine, but Sylvia heard anxiety in her voice now.

"I'm forgetting something," Emma said. "I'm sitting here working the muscles of my face, but it's just not coming to me."

"If it's important, you'll remember." Sylvia said this to calm her mother, knowing that it was less and less true for Emma.

"It's the babies, I think."

"The babies?"

"They were sick. Or one of them was, anyway."

The babies.

"Mom, I'm going to come over. Can you put the teakettle on?"

"Of course I can. Don't be silly."

Sylvia hated to leave. Between the fair and her shop — which would open in an hour — her day was full. But after seeing the contents of Quinn's box, Sylvia realized Emma might know more than she thought she knew.

But would Emma remember the babies by the time Sylvia got to her house?

9:31 a.m.

The only reason Liam showed up at all was because Benita Booker roused him with a reminder call at eight o'clock on Saturday morning, waking him from three consecutive hours of sleep, a duration that was beginning to feel satisfying compared to most stretches. Her husband had been a steady client for seven years. Liam couldn't afford to offend Benita by backing out.

Besides, he'd promised Quinn. If Quinn ever found whatever, or whoever, he was looking for and returned to Hidden Falls, Liam hoped they would pick up their conversations where they left off. That scenario seemed unlikely given Liam's current circumstances, but Liam had always been one to keep his options open and hope for the best.

"Oh good, you're here." Lauren waved Liam over. "I'll show you your table."

Liam sipped coffee from a covered mug and followed her.

"Hey, bro!" Cooper grinned from behind a poster featuring diagrams of the proper way to wear a bicycle helmet.

Liam waved at his brother, wishing the most popular Hidden Falls deputy was somewhere else tracking bad guys.

Ahead of him, Lauren paused and turned to look at him. Liam realized he was dragging too slowly. Or Lauren was moving too swiftly because she was the peppy, busy type. He picked up his pace and managed to stay beside her as they crossed the lawn. People wandered with burritos or muffins in their hands while others clumped around displays or began to form lines.

It finally came to Liam what he had said he would do — help people fill out forms. Essentially he did that whenever he enrolled a client in a new investment. He was glad to discover that Lauren led him to a table under a canopy.

"Hi, Christopher!" Lauren squatted to look a small boy in the face. "I'm really glad you're here today. I've been wondering how you are."

The boy leaned against his mother's thigh.

"Are we in the right place for his immunizations?" the young mother asked.

"Yes, Molly, this is it." Lauren stood and brushed the boy's hair out of his eyes. "This is Liam Elliott. I'm going to get him set up to help with the paperwork, and the nurse from the public health office will be here in just a few minutes to give the shots."

The boy stiffened. "I don't want a shot!"

"Christopher," Molly said, "we talked about this."

He pushed away and started to run. Molly followed.

Lauren grimaced at Liam. "Hopefully they won't all be like that."

Liam offered a smile he didn't feel. He didn't have much experience with small children, but in his opinion, they lacked appeal.

Lauren reached into a tub and took out a set of two pages stapled together. "Don't worry. Your job is just the paperwork. It's not complicated, and the nurse can answer a lot of questions."

Liam nodded at appropriate intervals as Lauren explained the essential information he should check for on the forms that parents filled out. She pointed to a few places on the sample form and then showed him the tub where the papers were, along with clipboards and pens for parents to use. Vaguely, he heard her caution against trying to leave too many forms on the table at a time. One ill-timed gust of wind could make a mess. Liam had an odd awareness that most of what Lauren said wasn't sinking in but comforted himself with the thought that it couldn't be too difficult to hand parents a form and then take it back.

"Oh, here's the nurse now." Lauren turned to help the nurse with supplies and setup.

Liam sat in the lawn chair behind a plastic folding table and tried to make his eyes focus on the questions the form asked. How long had he said he would do this? Had he promised all day? Liam wasn't sure, but he hoped not. At least under the canopy he was out of the sun.

A large hand thudded against the plastic table. Liam grabbed the jiggling edge. "Cooper, knock it off."

"I didn't know you were coming." Cooper rubbed his hands together in anticipation. "It's a beautiful morning."

"If you say so." Liam laid three pens across the front of the table. "How's the crime spree coming?"

"We've managed to put a stop to all that. No new crimes in three days." Cooper cocked a smile. "Today we're all about community service."

"I heard the mayor's shop is opening today."

"Good news, eh?"

Liam scanned the fair. "Is Sylvia here?" He would need a private moment to talk to Sylvia about what Dani found — though the fair might not be the right setting.

"I saw Sylvia earlier," Cooper said. "Not sure what happened to her."

Cooper rotated to the left, and Liam followed his line of sight. His brother was looking with great interest at Lauren Nock.

"Cooper, is there something you want to tell me?"

"About what?" Cooper didn't turn his head.

"I don't know. Something new in your life?"

"You know I can't tell you anything about any cases I'm working on." Cooper took four steps and grabbed a tub Lauren had bent to pick up.

Throbbing pain shot through Liam's gut — followed instantly by guilt. He ought to be glad for his brother, even if his own relationship had crumbled.

"Oh, hello, Liam."

The voice was familiar, but it wasn't until Liam turned to see the face that he made the connection. Miranda lived in his apartment building. He ran into her sometimes in the laundry room or at the mailboxes.

She stood in the booth behind him, flipping through a box of brochures. "They have me handing out flyers about warning signs of heart disease and stroke."

Liam waved a form. "Checking immunization paperwork."

"I'm supposed to be walking around. Do you mind if I leave my box behind your chair?"

"No problem. I'm not going anywhere."

Miranda pointed beyond Liam. "Looks like you've got a line."

Liam straightened in his chair and stared into the faces of four parents and seven preschool children. He clapped his hands. "Okay, then, let's get this going."

He assembled clipboards, passed them out, and then glanced at the nurse with her vials and needles and labels and little yellow immunization cards. The first clipboard came back to him, and Liam read the lines, making himself see each question and each answer. He handed it to the nurse, who invited a mother with a tiny girl to sit in a chair. While the nurse asked more questions and reviewed the form, the line in front of Liam lengthened. Two parents returned their forms at the same time. Liam decided to stand up to move more easily and keep things sorted. His chair pushed against Miranda's box and dumped the contents. When he lurched to correct his clumsiness, he only made things worse.

Liam scooped brochures back into the box. They would never be the neat piles Miranda would expect to find.

The envelope slid out from between *Heart*

Disease and *Stroke* and landed at Liam's feet. It was just like the other — unmarked, sealed, and thin. Had it been there a moment ago, when Miranda was choosing flyers to carry around the fair?

"Looks like you could use some help."

Jessica.

He dropped the envelope back into the jumbled box.

A parent set a completed form on the table. Jessica picked it up and ran a finger down the center of it.

"We're missing a phone number." She handed the paper back to the parent. "Who's next, please?"

The line was growing now, but Liam watched Jessica seamlessly organize the traffic flow of paperwork into piles and small children toward the nurse.

"What are you doing here?" Liam spoke when all the parents in line were occupied with their forms.

"Two hours of community service. Everybody who works at the store has to do it."

Liam offered her the only chair. "But why here?"

"They don't know I dumped you."

Her tone stung even more than the words.

He glanced at the bare ring finger on her left hand and then at the envelope sticking out from a pile of brochures. Volunteers moved back and forth between the tents. The lawn was full of visitors roaming the displays. Dozens of people might have had the opportunity to drop an envelope into that particular box. But Miranda was the one who left the box in a spot where Liam was likely to knock it over at some point.

The boy who had run from the prospect of an injection when Liam first arrived was approaching the tent again. This time his mother had a firm hold on his hand. Liam tried out a smile on the boy — Christopher, wasn't it? — and handed the paperwork to his mother. Jessica arranged the small tub of supplies where they could reach it more easily and tidied a stack of forms on the corner of the table. A few feet away, the nurse put a cartoon bandage on a tiny arm.

Liam felt trapped in slow motion. Around him everything moved normally, but he couldn't make his fingers close around the pen he intended to pick up. It rolled off the table. Liam watched it knock into his shoe and then bounce into the grass. His knees wouldn't bend. He couldn't pick it up. When another parent came to the table and Liam didn't move quickly enough, Jessica stood up and gave the young father what he needed to begin the immunization process. Her arm brushed against Liam's, but still he didn't move.

Jessica's sigh of exasperation as she picked up the fallen pen finally pierced Liam's inertia, and he stepped out of her way.

In that moment, Liam made a decision.

10:17 a.m.

Behind a trifold screen with red paisley fabric stretched between its supports, Ethan pointed to the solid wooden table he was fairly certain once had been in a small conference room inside Our Savior. Maybe it still was the conference room table, but someone had wisely decided a surface for children's health screenings ought to be sturdy enough to sustain the erratic movements that could result from poking and prodding small bodies. A strategically placed step stool helped independent climbers scale the height.

Permission to climb on a table was an attraction among the preschool set. A little girl attacked the task with exuberance, but in the end her mother had to help her get turned around and dangle her feet off the edge.

"I hope you're keeping that stethoscope warm." Nicole sat on the other side of the screen. "I'd hate to think you would torture innocent little children."

"Shh." Ethan made eye contact with the child to see how well she would respond. "Her mother is standing right here. You're blowing my cover."

The mother chuckled.

"Can I look in your mouth?" Ethan said to the child.

"Open your mouth, Kimmie," the mother said.

Ethan took a fresh depressor and gently kept the girl's tongue in its place while he looked down her throat and found everything right where it belonged.

"Any particular concerns?" he said to the mother as he inspected the child's ears and nose before using his stethoscope to listen to her heart and breathing.

He moved quickly through the fundamentals of a well child physical. He wasn't a pediatrician, but he treated enough kids when he was on call in the ER that he liked to think he'd spot a sick kid sitting right in front of him.

When Ethan was finished, he lifted the girl off the table and pointed the mother toward a vision screening station. No one else was waiting at the moment, so he stepped around the screen to see what Nicole was up to. She sat in one chair with her foot propped up on another and her crutches on the ground beside her. In her lap were several sheets of paper and her iPad opened to the most helpful Morse code site they'd found yesterday. They'd stayed at the cemetery as long as Old Dom's patience lasted, copying sequences of dashes and dots. In the dim light, Ethan took the best photos he could of the ledger pages that seemed to have interested Quinn the most — if the markings were indeed Quinn's.

Ethan was inclined to think they were.

"These phrases just don't make sense." Nicole chewed the top of her pen. "Maybe we mixed up some dots and dashes."

Ethan's photos captured the handwriting squiggles and flourishes of Old Dom's father well enough that he and Nicole could read the information recorded in cryptic phrases, but most of the images didn't capture the faint points of contact between Quinn's pencil and the thickly textured paper that swallowed up ill-placed markings. For that, they had to depend on their best guesses.

"What have you got that you're sure of?" Ethan asked.

"Not much."

Nicole reached for her foot as if she wished she could scratch it. It was probably swelling under the boot cast.

"Boy ill," Nicole said. "But that could be any number of boys who died as children. It's a cemetery record, after all. Then there's *right age,* but that was pages and pages later."

"Nothing else?" Ethan glanced up at a mother and son he suspected were coming in search of his services.

"Both. Here before. Sure. Not sure."

"Can't make up your mind?"

"No, I mean that's what it says. *Sure. Not sure.* About six pages apart."

The boy approaching the booth had a yellow balloon tied to one wrist. His feet halted, and he seemed to stare at Ethan. After a few seconds, his mother picked up his hand and tugged. The boy looked up at her and then at his balloon as she led him forward again.

"I'm Molly," the young woman said. "This is my son, Christopher."

Ethan took the paperwork she offered. "How old is Christopher?"

"He just turned five."

Ethan left Nicole to her puzzling and escorted Molly and Christopher behind the screen. Christopher hesitated once again.

"Come on, Christopher." Molly ran her hand down the side of her son's face. "Let's not daydream right now."

At the stimulation of her touch, Christopher blinked his eyes.

"Does that happen often?" Ethan helped Christopher up onto the table.

"The daydreaming? Some days I notice it more than others."

He's the right age, Ethan thought. The boy's mother couldn't be expected to know that the condition could emerge at this age.

"I just have to remind him to listen," Molly said. "He gets so caught up in what he's thinking about."

Ethan found nothing else wrong with the boy in the cursory examination he was able to do behind a screen on the church lawn.

"I'd like your son to see a doctor," Ethan said.

"I thought you were a doctor." Her face paled.

"I am. But I'm only visiting in Hidden Falls, and I'm leaving later today. Christopher needs to see a neurologist."

Her eyes flicked wide open. "Something's wrong with his brain?"

"I can't be sure just by looking at him." Ethan remembered Lauren had said there would be a public health nurse at the fair. Maybe she would know the name of a pediatric neurologist. "Why don't you bring Christopher, and we'll see if we can connect you to the right help."

Molly lifted Christopher, and the child wrapped his legs around his mother's waist.

Ethan scanned the activity and spotted the sign announcing immunizations hanging from one of the blue-and-white tents. The couple at the table seemed to have a system going, though the dark-haired man appeared the more frazzled of the two.

Christopher thrashed against his mother's hold, and Ethan turned rapidly, thinking the child's condition was worse than he'd realized.

"I don't want another shot!" Christopher shouted.

Molly tightened her grip. "Sorry. We were here a few minutes ago."

Ethan put up both hands in a stop gesture. "Then let's not torment him. I just want to talk to the nurse. You can wait here if you'd like."

Molly nodded.

Ethan waited for the nurse to finish an injection before interrupting the flow of the line. He introduced himself and explained what he needed.

The nurse shook her head. "There's Dr. Glass, but he's mostly retired. We don't have as many neurologists around here as we could use, and none of them are pediatricians."

"I need to give her a name." Ethan was almost certain Christopher was having seizures that lasted a few seconds at a time and needed an EEG.

The nurse reached for a scrap of paper and wrote on it. "She could try this place in Birch Bend. If nothing else, they'll give her a good referral."

"Thank you." Ethan turned around and found the spot where he'd left Molly empty.

"Did you see where they went?" The man behind the table looked vaguely familiar.

"Who?"

"The young woman who was standing right here."

"Oh, the one with the kid who screams."

"I don't know if he screams or not, but I need to find them."

"He saw Lauren Nock and took off like she was his long-lost friend."

Ethan glanced back at his own station. Nicole was upright on her crutches talking to a couple of families and handing them forms. That would give him some time.

"Which direction?" he asked.

"Toward the church. I think they went inside."

Ethan pivoted and faced the brick structure of Our Savior. He hadn't been inside the church — or any church — for ten years.

But that little boy needed to have a workup.

And it was just a building.

Ethan crossed the lawn, smiling vaguely at a couple of people who seemed to recognize him and trying to recall how well they knew his parents. He entered the side door of the church.

"Would you like to use the prayer room?" a woman said. "We have someone available to pray with you, if you like."

"No thank you." Ethan looked past the woman into a dimly lit room with a makeshift altar and candles. "I'm just looking for a woman with a little boy. Five years old, blond hair, skinny. Have you seen them?"

"Molly and Christopher?"

"Yes, that's right." Ethan scanned the hall.

"They're right inside." She gestured.

"In the prayer room?"

"You're welcome to quietly step inside and have a seat."

Ethan pressed his lips together and looked away. He didn't see another place to sit, and he didn't want to risk losing track of Molly altogether. He sucked in his breath and slipped into the prayer room, where he found a lone chair against a back wall. Other chairs were arranged in pairs or trios around small tables with Bibles opened.

Molly was there, with Christopher on her lap and both their heads huddled with Lauren's. Wondering how many more parents were at his booth, Ethan waited for Lauren to finish praying aloud.

When she looked up, Molly saw Ethan. "I'm sorry. Christopher wanted to see Lauren, and then we stayed to pray."

"It's all right." Ethan stood up.

"I admit I got scared when you said something was wrong."

"I have the name of a practice for you." Ethan handed her the scrap of paper the nurse had written on. "You can tell them I said Christopher *may* have a seizure disorder. If I'm right, it's very treatable."

Lauren stood with an arm around Christopher's shoulders. "Thank you, Ethan. There's no telling how long it would have been before another doctor noticed something. I'll make sure Christopher gets an appointment."

"Good." Ethan turned to leave. "Nice to meet you, Molly."

He walked across the grass, which now had the beginnings of trodden paths as the size of the crowd increased. Back at his paisley screen, three families waited.

Nicole waved a sheet of paper at him.

"Did you find something more?" he asked.

"It says, *this matters.* It was next to a notation about a death in the Tabor family in the 1930s."

Her green eyes captured sunlight and spun it back out of her face. Ethan was going to have a hard time getting in his Lexus and driving away in a few hours.

11:02 a.m.

Jack saw the little fist on a trajectory that would take it not only to the table but straight into a small square pod of purple face paint.

If his kids had moved that fast when they were this little, he didn't remember it.

Brooke lunged too late.

The little girl pulled her fist out of the pod, spread her fingers, and wiped them with glee across her own cheek. If she had stopped there, it might have been cute, but the next landing place for her fingertips was the wobbly card table where Brooke had meticulously laid out her supplies. In one swoop of a toddler arm, purple streaked the table and four other open tubs tumbled to the ground. Two of them landed upside down. When Brooke squatted to pick them up, the contents slithered out into the grass. The little girl giggled and slapped her hands against Jack's knees. He pushed her hands away, but not before she transferred paint to his palms.

"Kimmie!" Bruce Gallagher removed his daughter — now squalling — from the scene of the crime, leaving Jack's daughter with her mouth hanging open and random paint splotches along the fleshy sides of her hands.

"What just happened?" Brooke stared at the tubs in her hands and the two at her feet.

Jack pulled several wipes out of a plastic dispenser and used them to salvage the pods on the ground before another child stepped in them. He set them on the table and squatted to scoop up paint from the grass, a nearly impossible task. With two fresh wipes, he took his daughter's hands and wrapped them, pulling streaks of purple off her skin. A set of four siblings were next in line to have their faces painted. None of them looked to be older than seven. All of them creased the skin over their noses. Jack had never seen such identical consternation. When he looked at their mother, he saw where they'd learned it.

"Just give us a moment." Jack dabbed at his jeans, uncertain whether trying to wipe the paint out of the denim would just make things worse.

"What am I going to do now, Dad?" Brooke tossed a wipe in the small trash can under the table and pulled another from the container.

"We'll just clean things up and keep going." Jack's strategy was not so different from practicing law. When he worked in Memphis, messes happened every day. It was his job to clean them up — until the mess got so big that the only way to please the client was for someone to be fired.

That someone was Jack.

He recognized the dismay in his daughter's face because he felt it every day. Careful planning and systematic arranging were not supposed to end up splattered on the ground waiting for someone to step in the mess and make it worse.

Jack picked up one of the towels Brooke had been using to protect children's clothing from the paints and reached for her hands to dry them.

"It'll be all right," he said into her ear. "We still have a few good colors. Take some deep breaths."

Brooke squeezed her eyes shut but nodded.

Jack picked up the stool children had been sitting on and repositioned it out of the path of the spilled paint before pulling the table over as well. Then he took a clean towel from the stack and picked up a large clip. With a smile, he turned toward the four children with pinched faces. "Who's next?"

The littlest one raced forward and came to an abrupt halt in front of Brooke.

"Dad, maybe you should hold him," she said.

"You got it." Jack sat on the stool and lifted the squirmy boy to his lap. He held the child's hands out of the way while Brooke fastened a towel around his shoulders.

He wished he could remember what it felt like to hold Brooke like this, or Eva or Colin. When was the last time Brooke sat in his lap? If Jack had known it wouldn't happen again, maybe he would have paid more attention to the moment. Instead, he inhaled the shampoo scent of somebody else's youngest child.

"A puppy!" One of the other siblings fell to her knees.

The boy in Jack's lap tried to turn his head. Brooke had a firm grip on his chin, though. Jack looked into her focused eyes and admired her ability to resist the urge she must have felt to look at her own dog.

Gianna stood beside him with Roxie's leash wrapped several times around her hand to keep the dog near.

"Unless you came for paw painting," Jack said, "don't let the dog under the table."

Gianna leaned to one side to inspect the ground. "Looks like you've had some excitement."

Brooke finished a simple red balloon on the little boy's cheek and set her brush down long enough to snuggle Roxie.

"Is that *your* dog?" one of the kids asked.

Brooke nodded. "Would you like to pet her?"

The face painting line dismantled in favor of puppy adoration. Brooke took the leash from her mother.

Gianna turned to Jack. "How's she doing?"

"Very well, actually. She's pretty good drawing the animals."

"Considering how much she doodles, I'm glad to see the skill put to good use."

"We should get her some lessons."

"I'm sure she'd like that." Gianna ran her hands through her loose hair. "Thank you, Jack."

He raised his eyebrows.

"Brooke really wanted you to do this, and here you are. I just want you to know I appreciate the effort you're making. And not just with Brooke. Thank you."

"You're welcome." Other than the flash with the two-year-old in the paint, it had been a nice morning. And Jack hadn't seen that look in Gianna's eyes in a long time.

"Would you be willing to keep the dog for a few minutes?"

Jack glanced at the puppy in the middle of the cluster of children. Brooke would probably like to have the dog around, and Jack would enjoy the way Roxie lit up his daughter's face.

"Sure," he said.

"I won't be long," Gianna said. "I'm only going over to the silent auction."

How much would this cost him? he wondered.

"I'll keep the bidding reasonable." Gianna seemed to read his mind. "There's a gorgeous red silk dress that has to be thirty or forty years old, but I couldn't get a good look while I was watching the dog."

Jack supposed Gianna wanted to buy an old dress to go with her old house. When he caught himself wondering if she planned to remodel the dress beyond recognition as she had the house, he put his hands in his pockets and did his best to banish the thought before it fully formed. It would only spoil the moment between them.

"The money is for a good cause," he said. "I promise not to get into a bidding war."

Gianna sauntered away, and he watched her turn her head a few times at the displays she passed, looking but not deviating from her mission. Sunlight tugged at the natural reddish highlights in her brown hair.

Jack turned to the growing huddle of children. "Brooke, let me take Roxie. You can paint a few faces."

Brooke released the leash and her puppy into his care, and for a while Jack stood near her stool watching her interactions with the kids, some of them not much younger than she was. She had prepared a chart of the choices she could paint — a puppy, a kitty, a giraffe, a bird, one balloon, three balloons, a rainbow, a caboose. Jack listened to her negotiate with a boy who came with his own idea and decided she was managing the endeavor well. The puppy, on the other hand, was straining at the leash amid the activity of the fair.

Jack caught Brooke's eye as she fastened a towel around another child. "I'm going to walk with Roxie."

She nodded.

He took the dog through a small aisle between booths and out to the sidewalk that ran along one side of the lawn. People were coming and going at a steady pace. Jack was glad for a few minutes to think. He'd found something in those old files still spread around his office floor, and unquestionably Nicole and Ethan would be interested. Did Jack want them to know? That was a separate question.

The sidewalk ended, and Jack let the dog choose a route back into the main fair area, though he shortened the leash. From here Jack could see Ethan with his own line of children, and Nicole with her foot propped up and her head bent over something in her lap. Jack was too far away to know what she might be looking at. At one point, Ethan put a hand on Nicole's shoulder and leaned in to talk to her. She raised her face and nodded. Ethan put his hands in his pocket and began to zigzag between fairgoers toward the side of the building.

Jack tugged the leash, redirecting Roxie toward a path that would intercept Ethan's. Jack stepped ahead of the puppy to set a brisker, more focused pace. When he caught Ethan's eye, he waved and made known his intention to catch up with him.

"We should talk," Jack said. "I found something more in the files."

Ethan looked over his shoulder at Nicole. "I was just getting us something cold to drink. Can you walk back with me? I'm sure Nicole will be interested."

Roxie sniffed Ethan's feet. They moved together toward a refreshment stand. Roxie got distracted by fallen bits of food, and Jack stooped to pick her up in order to keep pace with Ethan.

Ethan handed a couple of dollars to Gavin Owens. "Two lemonades, please."

"It will be up to you what you want to tell Nicole, of course." Roxie settled in Jack's arms. "But this really concerns you."

"You found something in your files about me?"

"Possibly." Jack didn't have it all worked out yet.

Brooke swooped in and took the dog from Jack's arms. He hadn't seen her coming from behind.

"Come on, Dad," she said. "A lady asked if it was true that my father was a lawyer. She's waiting to talk to you."

Ethan snapped lids on the two paper cups Gavin set in front of him. "You're busy, I'm busy. Let's talk about this after the fair."

11:48 a.m.

Though she felt slightly mean, Dani got ready to laugh when Eva put her hand on the ice chest lid. "Are you sure you want to do that?"

"I told you, I want to help."

"Okay, then."

Eva lifted the lid and recoiled. "Eww. You didn't tell me . . . yuck."

"Haven't you ever seen a fish before?" Dani slid both hands into the ice and lifted out a trout.

"Not with the . . . well, you know, this is the whole fish. I didn't expect it to stare at me. It doesn't look like that when my mom buys it."

"I take it your dad never takes you fishing."

"*My* dad?" Eva laughed. "He doesn't even eat fish unless my mom makes him."

Dani laid the fish on the small table at the side of the charcoal grill she had been heating for the last half hour and peeked at the coals. "The next one has no head."

"Yeah, I think maybe you should get that yourself." Eva grimaced and took another step away from the cooler. "Is this going to be some kind of step-by-step fish show?"

"Something like that." Dani pulled the next

fish out, minus the head and tail. The next one was filleted open, ready for the grill. Eva's reaction confirmed Dani's suspicion that some of the people stopping by for her demonstration of grilling fresh fish could use a reminder of where fish came from. Dani had caught these three specimens about four hours earlier in Whisper Lake, fishing from a borrowed rowboat. When she said *fresh fish,* she meant *fresh fish.*

"I want to help," Eva said, "but touching fish skin?"

Dani rolled her eyes. Did Eva think fish came from cosmic packaging plants that removed all potentially bothersome parts before making overnight delivery to supermarkets?

"Forget the hiking," she said. "Next weekend you and I are going fishing."

"Isn't there something else I could do right now to be useful?" Eva scrunched up her face.

Dani pointed to two sacks. "Set out paper plates. Forks and napkins, too."

"I can do that."

Dani opened the grill and redistributed the graying coals. She was well aware that most of her observers today would go home to gas grills on their decks in the firm conviction that gas was no different than charcoal when it came to outdoor cooking. Dani didn't buy it. A little patience and well-timed attention made an enormous difference.

Her presentation was scheduled to begin in a few minutes. She wouldn't wait until she had a crowd. Whoever made the effort to arrive at the posted time, or to wander in during the middle, deserved to take the samples that would come off the grill.

A moment later, her cousin's eyes smiled at her across the grill.

"Hey, Cooper."

"What time shall I be back for lunch?"

"I'd say about eighteen and a half minutes."

"Perfect. I expect to be hungry in nineteen."

"You could eat in seven and be hungry again in nineteen." Dani arranged her sprigs of rosemary and thyme.

"Enough with the banter." Cooper folded his arms across his chest. "I'm worried about Liam."

"Am I my cousin's keeper?" Dani avoided Cooper's eyes. "He's *your* brother."

"Has he talked to you?"

"Have we exchanged conversation?" Dani sliced two lemons. "Sure. We do that from time to time. You should try it."

"Dani, I'm serious." Cooper pointed across the lawn with a tilt of his head. "Liam looks awful."

Dani didn't have to look up to know that statement was true. "Jessica dumped him."

"But she's at the tent with him. She seems to be doing all the work."

That didn't surprise Dani. She cut a slit

lengthwise through the belly of the whole fish and prepared to stuff it with herbs.

"I saw Liam a couple of times this week," Dani said, "and things aren't going well for him in general. But that's as much as I'm going to say."

If Cooper wanted to know what was going on in his brother's life, he would have to ask. Dani didn't like being in the middle of things, and Cooper knew that.

Eva brought back an empty sack. "What else should I do?"

"Come here," Dani said. "You're going to season a fish."

"Ick."

"Get over that. It's just a little oil with sea salt and pepper." Dani set out the fillet.

With Eva's presence, Cooper stopped asking questions.

"I'll be back in ten minutes and twenty-three seconds," he said.

"I'm serving samples, not lunch," Dani said.

Cooper should go talk to Liam. As fragile as he was, Dani suspected Liam would crack. He'd tell his brother everything, and Dani wouldn't have to be in the middle of anything.

Eva held a bottle of olive oil. "I don't know what I'm doing."

Dani handed Eva a small brush. "Just put oil on the fish, skin side, too."

The cooler contained several other fish that Dani caught the last time she was on the lake with Quinn. More accurately, Quinn had caught them, but he insisted Dani take them home to her freezer. That was when the idea of this grilling demonstration arose. If anyone was interested in stuffing a fish, rather than only watching Dani do it, she could accommodate them.

Eva gingerly brushed oil on the fleshy side of the fillet. Dani waited for the moment when Eva would need to turn it over. She could have prodded Eva to stuff the whole trout with a fish eye staring up at her, but Dani was not completely without pity.

"Use the spatula," Dani said.

Eva rummaged in the bag of supplies and came up with the utensil. Dani checked the coals again. They were very close to ready. Four people had found seats around two rectangular folding tables.

Sylvia approached.

"How's the shop?" Dani asked.

"I just came from there. Business is brisk."

"That's good."

"Lizzie has everything in hand for the moment." Sylvia examined the rosemary sprigs spilling out of the trout Dani was preparing.

Dani glanced over at Cooper helping a small child sit on a bicycle.

"Has Liam talked to you?" Dani asked.

"Not since that day he came into the store with the photo."

Dani moved away from where Eva was still

oiling the fish. The girl didn't need to hear this. "I know Jack wanted to help. Has he come up with anything on that address?"

"Not that he's told me." Sylvia shielded her eyes to look around the lawn.

Dani puffed her cheeks to keep from sighing. Sylvia didn't know Liam had asked Dani to track down the Santorelli address. Neither did Jack. But with Eva Parker standing five feet away, Dani held her tongue. Why had Liam bothered her about the address if he was going to keep the results of her search to himself? Surely Sylvia wasn't really depending on Jack Parker to solve that particular mystery.

Hidden Falls pulsed with mystery these days. Where did Quinn go? Even Dani, who at first figured he just needed some space, wondered where he was now. What was in St. Louis? Who was Santorelli?

Dani wished she had resisted Liam's urging to find out what kind of business the Santorelli name represented. She also wished she had resisted Nicole's urging to look at Quinn's bank account.

She was going to cook some fish and perhaps persuade a few people to try it at home. Then Dani could say she'd kept her promise to Quinn to work at the fair. After that, she would focus on replacing her destroyed boat and finding the guy who wrecked it. Maybe she could scrape up enough money to buy one that didn't need a lot of work. It would be nice to have a boat to take Quinn out in once he got back.

"I'm going to check on things at the auction," Sylvia said. "Then I think I need to talk to some people."

Yep, you do, Dani thought as Sylvia turned and walked toward the auction tables.

"I really do want to learn to do this. How do you know when the coals are ready?" Eva lifted the grill's lid, the brush in her hand still drenched in oil.

"Be careful —" Dani's words were too late.

Oil dripped onto the hot coals and flame blasted up. In her fright, Eva's fingers opened. Simultaneously she let go of the lid and the brush. One tumbled to the ground and the other fell straight into the grill. People gathered for the demonstration now jumped from their seats and backed away. Dani yanked Eva away from the rising fire.

"I'm so stupid!" Eva wailed.

Dani had no time to comfort Eva — and she wouldn't have known how. Flare-ups happened during grilling when fat naturally dripped, but Dani wondered just how much oil Eva had been putting on that fillet. She scrambled to grab the bouncing grill lid and circled to the back of the grill to replace the lid and smother the flames. In the commotion, the fillet had been dumped in the dirt.

"It's all right," Dani said to onlookers. "We

just may be a couple of minutes late getting started."

Eva had fled the scene of her failure. Dani watched her run across the lawn, dodging and weaving through the crowd. Where was she likely to go?

It didn't matter. Dani couldn't chase her now. She'd have to find her later.

Dani had amassed extra spectators because of the burst of flames. She might as well take advantage of the attention. The cooler contained several more trout. Now the demonstration would include the added feature of how to fillet a fish. Then it would pick up with Dani's plan to grill both a whole fish and a fillet. Samples would be slightly delayed but still delicious. Fifteen minutes from now no one would remember the unplanned diversion. They would be too busy salivating over bites of perfectly grilled fish.

The look of the sky suggested Dani might not have the opportunity for a second demonstration. If she were out on a hiking trail under a darkening sky like this one, she would be planning how to take cover.

12:39 p.m.

Nicole lost her grip on two pages of notes and they fluttered away in the wake of two children, with painted faces and balloons, running perilously close to her propped-up boot cast.

"Hey!"

They didn't hear her above their own squeals.

Ethan was busy looking in another set of facial openings. Nicole leaned over for the crutches tucked against the side of her chair. She had enjoyed the morning's sunshine but now wondered if she would have been better off spending the day in Lauren's apartment. The cast and crutches made mobility difficult, so she had only been up and about a few times, and no matter how many times she set down her pile of notes, determined to enjoy the day, she picked them up again. The mystery filled the crevices of her mind, leaving room only for frustration that she was missing something obvious. She hadn't been much help at the fair. Maybe she'd even been in the way.

The breeze gusted, threatening to take Nicole's pages farther from her reach. She swung toward the nearest sheet and stabbed it with a crutch to hold it still while she went through the laborious steps of balancing to keep weight off her injured foot as she bent to pick it up. In the meantime, the second page skidded across the grass.

"I got it." Lauren swooped down to rescue the second page.

"Thank you." Nicole straightened up, relieved to lean on two crutches again.

"What's all this?" Lauren scanned the paper

she held.

"I wish I knew." Nicole took the page from Lauren and nested it against the other, arranging her armpits on the crutches while she examined her own scribbles and arrows and question marks. In the last hour she'd made little progress in deciphering the relationships between the bits of information she'd collected.

"Mind if I pull up a chair?" Lauren filched a rented chair from a nearby assortment and set it beside Nicole's. "I've been on my feet all morning, running every which way."

Lauren's efforts had paid off, Nicole thought. The fair had come together even without Quinn. Once they'd found Quinn's planning notes, Lauren went into high gear with the details. If any of the planned activities were absent, no one would know. For nearly four hours now, the lawn was host to a steady stream of visitors.

"We're almost there," Lauren said. "In another couple of hours, we can declare the first community health fair a rousing success."

"Quinn will be proud when he hears how you stepped in and pulled it off." *St. Louis,* Nicole reminded herself. Quinn had been in St. Louis. He bought gas and dinner. He was all right. Or at least he had been a few days ago.

"Benita Booker is a lifesaver." Lauren's eyes

scanned the grounds constantly, sweeping one direction and then arcing back again. "And Ethan saved the day after the pediatrician on Quinn's list left us hanging."

"I didn't think Ethan liked kids, but he's doing all right." Nicole had checked the time on her phone only a few minutes ago. It wouldn't be long now before Ethan left. Already he'd checked out of the motel on the other side of the lake and stowed the few personal belongings he traveled with in his Lexus for the drive back to Columbus.

"I'm sure he'll stay in touch," Lauren said softly. "It won't be like before."

"We haven't made any promises." Nicole fiddled to reunite the rescued pages with the rest of her collection of notes.

"Without you he would have found a reason to leave before now."

"He took pity after I broke my ankle. That's all."

"Well, that's not what I think."

What did it matter? In a few hours, Ethan would be on his way to Columbus, and Nicole would have to figure out how to get home to St. Louis. She could take all her notes and photos with her. Maybe she'd get somebody to take her back out to the cemetery to look at Old Dom's ledgers one more time first, but St. Louis might still be the best place to track Quinn's recent movements. Nicole knew people there, and with the right provocation they would help her.

And then there was the matter of her job. It would be a lot easier to get to the bottom of whatever happened at the newspaper if she went home.

Nicole would miss Ethan. She was fooling herself if she thought otherwise. It had been easy to slip into the understanding they shared of each other's lives. It had even been easy to slip into his embrace, into his kiss.

But it was all because of Quinn. They came to Hidden Falls to see Quinn. They stayed because Quinn disappeared. But they couldn't remain in romantic nostalgia indefinitely. Ethan had to save his job, and Nicole had to find out whether she had one to save.

Lauren's phone rang, and beside Nicole she dug into her pants pocket to pull it out.

"Not again," Lauren muttered.

"Not again what?"

Lauren waved a hand across her face. "Just a wrong number. They keep calling."

"Then why don't you answer it and tell them they've got the wrong number?"

"It's not that simple."

"Lauren Nock, you tell me what's going on." Nicole rotated in her chair as best she could to look more directly at Lauren. A minute ago Lauren's face flushed with pleasure in the fair. The color that rolled through it now was anything but pleasure.

"I've gotten these calls," Lauren said.

"Actually, I don't think they're wrong numbers. It's somebody's sick idea of fun. I've been through it before, and I'll get through it again."

"Have you told Cooper? If you're being harassed, he might be able to help."

"No, I haven't told Cooper. I hardly know him."

That might have been true a week ago, but Nicole wasn't blind. Although Cooper was supposed to be running his own booth, all day long he still managed to show up wherever Lauren was with impressive frequency. Nicole could see it all from where she sat — and it seemed to Nicole that Lauren was glad to see him. Lauren had come a long way from the reticence of the evening Cooper showed up with Sylvia at Lauren's apartment bearing dinner.

"If you're not going to tell Cooper, then tell me," Nicole said.

Lauren crossed her legs. "There's not a lot to tell. Somebody with an Oklahoma number keeps calling me, but they never say anything. Sometimes there's noise but nothing I can identify."

"So you stopped answering."

Lauren nodded. "Voice mail kicks in. They still don't say anything. I just get a message of strange sounds."

"The same number every time?"

Lauren tilted her phone's screen toward Nicole. "See? I didn't answer, and now there's a notice I have a voice mail. I'm just going to delete it again."

Nicole reached for the phone. "Put in your password and let me listen to the message."

"I'm telling you, it's nothing. Street noises, whistling. Maybe I'm wrong and it's not on purpose. It's like someone is pocket dialing me. Maybe they don't even know it."

"Just let me listen." What could it hurt for Nicole to hear the message? At worst, she'd be as puzzled as Lauren. At best, she'd have an idea for how to stop the bothersome calls.

Lauren tapped a few buttons on the screen, and Nicole lifted the phone to her ear to listen to the automated voice announce one unheard voice mail.

The message began — and Nicole's heart crashed into her throat. She screamed.

Lauren snatched the phone out of Nicole's hand.

"No!" Nicole nearly tipped over her chair lunging for the phone. "Don't delete that!"

"Why not? What did you hear?"

"Have you deleted all the messages from this number?"

"Yes, of course." Lauren's finger was poised over the phone.

Nicole groaned. "I want you to listen to this one and tell me if you've heard that sound before."

Lauren moistened her lips and then complied.

"Yes," she said. "Not exactly the same. This was somebody whistling. Last time it sounded more like a tinny out-of-tune piano. But it's the same tune."

Sylvia Alexander rushed toward them. "I heard a scream. Is everybody all right?"

Ethan came out from behind the screen and hurriedly handed a form to a parent. "What happened? Your foot?"

Nicole shook her head. "Give me the phone, Lauren. I'm going to call that number back." Trembling, she found the number in the phone's log and tapped it. A few seconds later it rang four times. No one answered, and no one's voice invited a message. In an unsteady hand, Nicole scrawled the number across the top of one of her note pages and checked it three times.

Nicole handed the phone to its owner. "Lauren, have you ever heard the tune before these calls started?"

"No."

Nicole looked at the trio of expressions locked on her face. "Well, I have. It's Quinn's tune."

"Quinn's tune?" Sylvia echoed. "What are you talking about?"

Nicole could hardly breathe. Her pulse hadn't raced this hard in a long time.

"After my mother died," she said, "my

father was so bereft he didn't know what to do with me. But Quinn was there. He knew I was scared and lonely, and one day he said I needed a song."

"What kind of song?" Ethan asked.

"A song that was just mine," Nicole said. "It didn't even have to have words. We sat at his piano and I picked some random notes. Quinn turned them into a few bars of music. After that he whistled them to me when he knew I was feeling low. Even in high school, when he saw me in the hall, he whistled those notes."

Six eyes around her widened into stunned discs.

"That voice mail is someone whistling Quinn's tune. It's not Quinn — I would know his whistle — but no one could know that tune if they don't know Quinn." And it would have to be someone Quinn trusted. Why else would he share something that was just between him and Nicole?

Fifteen seconds passed before anyone spoke. Finally, Sylvia took control.

"We need to have a meeting, and we need to do it soon. We're all circling each other with pieces of information that might be relevant, and it's time to get everything on the table." Sylvia checked her watch. "I want all of you to find a way to get away from your stations and meet me over behind the auction tables in thirty minutes."

Nicole nodded.

"Lauren," Sylvia continued, "get Dani, Jack, and Liam. And Cooper. Everybody we need is here today. Don't take no for an answer."

Ethan left to see another child waiting to have his tonsils examined, and Sylvia pivoted to march across the lawn to the silent auction.

"What just happened?" Lauren's face blanched.

"You've been walking around with a clue for days." Nicole stilled the shaking in her limbs.

"I didn't know! I thought it was the guy who bullied me in high school."

"No one's blaming you," Nicole said. "But Sylvia's right. It's time to find out what everyone knows."

Lauren jaunted across the lawn and halted in front of Liam's table.

Nicole hadn't trusted anyone else to find Quinn, but she hadn't found him, either. All of her digging through information hadn't revealed why Quinn would leave Hidden Falls. It was Dani's skills that turned up the lead that Quinn had been in St. Louis. Could he be in Oklahoma now?

Ethan dismissed his patient and came back around to kneel in front of Nicole. "Are you all right?"

"I don't know what to think, what to feel."

Breath was still elusive. "This could be big."

"I hope it is. I hope it breaks Quinn's disappearance wide open."

Nicole's stomach hardened. She didn't want to hear what was coming next.

Ethan put a hand on her knee. "I have to leave as soon as the fair wraps up."

"I know."

"I hope you also know I don't want to." Ethan leaned toward Nicole. "Especially now."

Nicole swallowed. "We'll find Quinn. I'll make sure he calls you."

"Nicole." Ethan's voice thickened. "No regrets, right?"

She welcomed his kiss but felt the goodbye in it.

1:16 p.m.

Not everyone seemed eager to be there, but that didn't deter Sylvia. She needed only enough cooperation to glean information.

"We don't have much time." Sylvia made no suggestion that anyone should sit down, not even Nicole. They stood a few yards away from the end of the silent auction table because it seemed like the best option for staying out of major traffic flow around the lawn while still observing the fair. Already Lauren had positioned herself to look out on the activities she felt responsible for.

"What are we doing here?" Liam looked

like he could barely stand up.

"I'll get right to the point." Sylvia met each gaze around the circle. "You may not all know each other, but we all want to see Quinn come home. I've had enough conversations with each of you in the last few days to suspect that if we all threw our thoughts against a canvas, we might be surprised at the picture that resulted."

Jack looked lost and defensive.

Liam clearly was exhausted by something other than Quinn's disappearance.

Nicole's face was white with intensity.

Ethan's was full of remorse. Or dread.

Dani, as usual, wore a deadpan expression that meant she didn't intend to invest herself in this conversation.

Lauren paled with confusion.

Cooper's stance next to Lauren appeared protective.

"No offense, Cooper," Sylvia said, "but we need to speed up the process of sorting things out. You and your team might not even be aware of some of the information floating around, so you can't possibly evaluate whether it's worth investigating. As mayor, I believe this conversation will be in the best interest of the whole town."

"Please proceed, Your Honor." Cooper crossed his wrists in front. "I respect both your authority and your wisdom."

"Here's what we're going to do," Sylvia

said. "One at a time, I'm going to ask you to share with the others what you've shared with me — or anything else you know that may be relevant. Think of this like a brainstorming session. There are no wrong answers. Every idea matters. We get everything out there, and then we decide what to do with it."

Sylvia wasn't sure whether the squinting in some faces was because of the sun — which wasn't as bright as it had been earlier — or doubt about the usefulness of the analogy. As mayor, Sylvia had led enough meetings to understand that people don't always know what they know and that how the pieces fit together mattered more than individual agendas.

"I'm depending on you to be straightforward," Sylvia said. "Even if you think I already know something, the point is to tell everyone else. Understand?"

Heads nodded.

"Liam." She pointed at him. "You first."

He shifted his weight from one foot to the other. "I think what the mayor has in mind is my accidental discovery that Quinn uses a UPS box in Birch Bend. The number is similar to mine, and I mistakenly got a piece of his mail."

"Why does he have a UPS box?" Cooper asked.

"That's what we don't know," Sylvia said. "Keep going, Liam."

He wrapped his arms across his belly and grasped his own elbows. "You mean the pictures?"

Sylvia nodded.

"I took pictures of the envelope before I turned it in, and I gave them to the mayor. I thought she might know something about it."

"But I didn't." Sylvia turned her attention. "Jack? You were going to investigate the return address."

Jack shrugged. "Sorry, I didn't come up with anything. Whatever it is, it's buried pretty deep."

Sylvia saw Liam's eyes flick toward Dani. "Liam, do you know something?"

"Only what Dani told me."

All heads turned toward Dani, whose eyes had taken on a glare.

"It's not buried so deep," Dani said. "The envelope is a small holding of a detective agency. My guess is Quinn's looking for someone and got the box in Birch Bend because he didn't figure it was anybody's business. Which it isn't."

"That fits." Nicole adjusted the stance of her crutches. "He's been doing genealogy research at the cemetery. You wouldn't believe the books Old Dom has out there."

Interest flickered through Dani's eyes. "But at the cemetery he'd be looking for someone who is dead, someone who died in Hidden Falls. I don't see how that fits with a detective agency in Pennsylvania."

"I wonder if he went to Pennsylvania," Sylvia said. "He came from back East somewhere."

"Doubtful," Jack said.

He was posturing because his own efforts had turned up nothing, and it irritated Sylvia. But she had said every idea mattered, and she held herself to her own instructions and didn't comment.

"Jack is right," Ethan said. "Quinn didn't go east. He went west, to St. Louis."

Sylvia felt her own eyes widen. This was the first she'd heard about St. Louis.

"He was there a few days ago," Ethan said. "Right, Dani?"

Dani held up both hands, palms out. "It wasn't my idea to snoop."

"Snoop where?" Cooper asked.

"Just a quick peek at Quinn's bank account," Nicole said. "It was my idea. If it matters to anyone, Dani didn't want to do it and she stopped almost immediately."

"How exactly did you gain access to this information?" Cooper asked.

"Nicole stole Quinn's computer." Dani's statement assigned no blame, simply provided facts.

"And I twisted Dani's arm into hacking in," Ethan said.

Cooper rolled his eyes. "I see the Hidden Falls crime spree has been more widespread than I realized."

"I agree," Jack said. "If Quinn's privacy has been invaded, he will have solid grounds for legal action."

If Jack thought Quinn would take legal action against his worried friends, he didn't know Quinn at all. In fact, Jack didn't seem to know anything. Maybe it had been a mistake for Sylvia to invite him to this gathering. There was no telling what he might do with what he learned.

"Back to St. Louis," Sylvia said.

"Quinn bought gas and a meal," Nicole said. "Or at least someone with his debit card did. The transactions are right there on his bank account."

"When?"

"A few days ago."

"Where has he been since then?" Sylvia asked.

Nicole shrugged. "Dani shut down the computer. As far as I know, she hasn't looked again."

Sylvia turned to Dani. "Have you?"

"Of course not. Quinn was fine and safe in St. Louis, probably having dinner with a friend."

"But what friend?" Ethan shifted over a few steps to stand closer to Nicole. "The friend who visits him every year?"

Adrenaline rolled through Sylvia's stomach. "What friend who visits him every year?"

Liam asked.

"Dani knows him."

Dani seemed to know a great deal today, Sylvia thought.

"I do *not* know Quinn's friend. All I ever said was that a guy comes to see him in the late fall, and they go fishing. Sometimes they used my boat."

Sylvia fought the blanch draining her cheeks. How could she be so close to Quinn for more than thirty years and not know who visited him in Hidden Falls every single autumn? Quinn rarely mentioned any old friends, and never with any suggestion that an old friend was still active in his life. Sylvia was his oldest friend. His closest friend.

So why did she feel so far from him right now?

"What else?" She needed to keep the conversation rolling before anyone interpreted the lag as completion.

"Maybe," Lauren said, "it's the friend who helped him get his teaching job here. Miles Devon said Quinn came highly recommended. He never even had a personal interview before he got hired. Isn't that odd?"

"The cemetery business is curious," Jack said. "Nicole is the one who got me into that."

"Yes," Sylvia said, "let's go back to those old records for a moment. Did you figure out what he was looking for?"

"Not exactly," Nicole said. "Does Quinn

know Morse code?"

Sylvia had never heard him mention it. "Why would he need Morse code at the cemetery?"

"Dots and dashes make letters and words," Nicole said. "Somebody has been making pencil marks in Old Dom's records, and I think it was Quinn."

"What kind of letters and words?"

"Clues. But they're cryptic. I haven't quite figured out what they mean, but I will."

Sylvia believed her. Nicole was not the sort to give up.

"Do they have to do with the names you had me research?" Jack asked.

Sylvia had suspected she wasn't getting a full picture from the bits and pieces of information that had come her way during the week, but the level of what she had missed astonished her.

"You and Jack are researching cemetery names?" Sylvia said.

"I have it narrowed down to three surnames," Nicole said.

"Me, too," Jack said.

"Maybe you'd better share the names." Sylvia was tempted to shift her posture, but she didn't want to appear nervous.

"I guess so," Nicole said. "Tabor, Pease, and Fenton."

"Yep, those are the ones," Jack said, "though I'm pretty sure one of them is a red herring."

Sylvia knew the names, all well revered in Hidden Falls history. "But why would Quinn be looking at those names?"

"Probably because of the picture," Lauren said.

"What picture?"

"A photo, actually." Between one fist and a crutch, Nicole still grasped the folder Sylvia had seen her with earlier. She opened it now and handed a photograph to Sylvia.

Sylvia's eyes went back and forth between the photo and Ethan several times.

"I know, right?" Nicole said. "There has to be a connection."

"Let me see that." Jack reached for the photo, and Sylvia didn't resist for fear of causing it harm. Immediately Jack saw what she'd seen. He looked at Nicole. "You didn't tell me you had this when you came to my office on Thursday."

"I wasn't sure it was relevant. I still don't know."

"A photo in the cemetery. This is how you came up with your original list of names. You only wanted me to narrow them down."

"It hasn't gotten me anywhere," Nicole said. "A few cryptic notes about babies are not much to go on."

Sylvia's heart rate jumped about twenty beats per minute. "What babies? When?"

"As far as I can tell, sometime during the 1930s," Nicole said.

Jack scratched his chin. "Yes, that would be about right."

"Lauren," Sylvia said, "remember that story my mother wanted to tell us last Sunday?"

"Yes."

"It was about babies in the Depression."

Cooper cleared his throat. "Haven't we wandered a long way from what took Quinn out of town? If this photo and the graves and Emma's story have any connection to each other, that's all right here in Hidden Falls. It doesn't explain Quinn's disappearance."

"Keep in mind he reappeared in St. Louis, giving us every reason to believe he's fine," Dani said. "Are we about finished here? I left Eva Parker in charge of my grill, and considering she already set one fire today, that makes me a little nervous. No offense, Jack."

"I talked to her about that. She's sorry."

"I know. But still."

Sylvia met one last gaze, and Nicole took the cue.

"The reason the mayor called us together," Nicole said, "was because of what I heard. Actually, Lauren has heard it, too."

"But I had no clue what it was," Lauren said.

Nicole explained the tune and whistled the opening notes.

"Somebody out there knows Quinn," Nicole said. "But why would Quinn use *my* tune?"

Blank expression answered her inquiry.

Sylvia blew out her breath. "Okay. I realize we all have responsibilities this afternoon, but we haven't put the pieces together yet. I'd like to meet again when the fair closes. How about at three thirty after the stragglers are gone and before we start breaking down the booths?"

"I won't be able to stay long." Ethan glanced at Nicole.

"I hope the weather holds up that long," Dani said.

Sylvia raised her eyes to approaching darkness far too early in the afternoon. The greenish hue was disconcerting.

2:07 p.m.

Lauren watched Ethan's attentiveness to Nicole. He reached for her hand, but it was occupied with the grip of a crutch. Instead, he carried the folder with her notes and the photo and matched the pace she could manage across the lawn. A couple of kids and their parents stood outside the area screened off for his examinations. Ethan had taken few breaks of any length. Somewhere in the back of Lauren's brain, a note formed that next time the church organized a health fair, they should make sure they had several doctors.

Cooper had found so many excuses to be at her elbow all day that Lauren expected to find him there now, but he had left when the group dispersed. It was her aunt whose proximity she discerned.

"You didn't say anything about Quinn's box," Lauren said. Hours of curiosity about what her aunt found last night had battered the day, but there was always something else Lauren needed to attend to.

"There will be time to tell the others later." Sylvia put a hand in the middle of Lauren's back. "I thought I would start with you and see what you think."

"Okay." Lauren looked around. The fair had just started its final hour, and everything seemed to be going well. No one would miss Lauren if she ducked out of sight for ten minutes. In fact, the crowd was the thinnest it had been all day, which brought some relief. A drastic weather shift seemed imminent. Lauren dreaded the thought of the canopies getting wet before the crew could get them down and stowed. The gusting wind of half an hour ago had died down, but Lauren had been a Midwesterner all her life. The sky did not promise a fine evening.

"Let's just go into the back hall of the church," Sylvia suggested.

But the thought was tardy. Cooper was on his way toward them.

"We have to shut down," he said.

"It's only a few more minutes," Lauren countered.

"One of the other deputies called me."

Cooper waved his phone as if Lauren required proof. "The National Weather Service has declared a tornado warning. It's coming up from Springfield and will be here soon."

Lauren scanned the lawn. Even with a thin crowd, the visitors still strolling the grass and the volunteers at the booths were easily seventy people.

"They haven't sounded the siren," Sylvia said.

"It's coming, believe me." Cooper wiped a hand across his chin. "We have to get people out of here. Even if it just turns into a thunderstorm, we can't have everyone out here under the trees."

"The church basement, then," Lauren said. "I've got keys."

"People will want to go home," Sylvia said. "They'll want to know their families are all right."

"I don't advise it," Cooper said, "but we can't stop them."

"We can try to persuade them," Lauren said. Tornado sirens were nothing new in central Illinois. Most likely the tornado wouldn't touch ground, or at least not in the tiny dot Hidden Falls made on a map. The same logic, though, would make people feel there was no urgency to take shelter.

Sylvia examined the sky. "If you have to, tell them the mayor is closing the fair, but get people off the lawn."

"I'll get the basement doors open." Lauren fished in her pocket for her church keys. "Cooper, will you —"

"I'm on it. I'll use the authority of the sheriff's office, too."

"I'm right behind you," Sylvia said.

Lauren opened two sets of doors leading directly into the basement of Our Savior Community Church. When she returned to the lawn, she saw Sylvia and Cooper hustling between booths and clusters of people.

The siren still had not sounded. Lauren prayed that meant they had some time, but the sky was greener every time she glanced up. Lauren stopped at the balloon booth. Henry Healy was on duty.

"We're closing up, Henry. Take shelter."

Immediately he shut off the helium tank that had been filling balloons all day and began rolling it toward the church building. Lauren handed the final six balloons to the next child who walked by and encouraged the family to leave immediately.

Sylvia was at the auction tables now, where someone produced boxes and tubs from their hiding places and began tossing items inside them. Gavin Owens and a couple of other men were folding tables and chairs. Zeke Plainfield and a couple of his buddies were pulling tent poles out of the ground.

Lauren wished people would worry less about the booths. As much as her stomach turned at the thought of the dampness and damage that might result if items were left outside when the weather blew through, it wasn't worth jeopardizing anyone's safety. As she and Cooper and Sylvia made the rounds with news of the tornado, people tended to look up at the sky as if to evaluate the merit of the meteorologists' prediction for themselves. Again and again, she encouraged people to take shelter in the church basement. Some did. Others meandered toward their parked cars or down the streets that would take them to nearby homes.

Lauren glanced toward the space Ethan had been using just in time to see him scoop Nicole out of her chair. Crutches dangled from Nicole's grasp, but Ethan made steady progress across the lawn. Lauren allowed herself a breath of relief that at least Nicole could not be stubborn about this one thing.

Someone grabbed her elbow, and Lauren spun around.

"Are you going to open again after the storm blows through?" Mrs. Berrill, the weekly hypochondriac of the congregation, asked her ludicrous question with all sincerity.

"No, I don't think so," Lauren said. "Please take shelter."

"You're still out here."

"I'm trying to get everyone to safety as quickly as possible."

"But I just got here," Mrs. Berrill said. "I wanted to pick up some brochures and recipes. Will they be available later?"

"Mrs. Berrill, why don't you go in the church basement, and I'll try to answer your questions once we know we're safe."

Mrs. Berrill huffed. "I think I'll just go home if you're going to be that way."

"Please go inside."

Lauren hoped Mrs. Berrill wouldn't put herself in peril just to spite Lauren, but the outcome of the conversation was beyond Lauren's control. A slender figure ran toward her.

"Molly, where's Christopher?"

Sudden tears streaked Molly's face. "I can't find him. I turned my back for a few seconds, and he was gone. He's probably playing hide-and-seek, but I can't find him!"

"We'll look together."

The eerie sky swirled around them, the stillness of a few minutes ago lost in a howling wind.

The siren sounded, drowning out Molly's screams for her son. The boy would never hear his name over the deafening screech of the warning. Lauren spun around trying to think where a five-year-old could hide. Beside her, Molly's frantic gestures accelerated. Lauren grabbed Molly to keep her from running. She couldn't look for them both.

Under the ear-splitting siren, people

dropped whatever equipment they were trying to salvage and ran for the basement doors. Cooper rounded the lawn one last time, physically turning people around and pushing them toward the building. When the lawn was almost cleared, he raced toward Lauren and Molly.

"Come on!" he yelled. "It's time."

Lauren cupped her hands around her mouth. "We can't find Christopher!"

"He'll be so frightened by the noise," Molly screamed. "I won't leave him out here."

The big oaks. Lauren dashed toward the twin trees at the center of the church lawn. She climbed them when she was younger, and now nearly every Sunday in nice weather she shooed children out of their branches. The lowest branches were higher than Christopher's height, but what if he'd had a boost from an older boy when he was hiding from his mother? Or what if he was skilled at shimmying up the trunk of a tree?

The roar really did sound like a freight train, just like everything Lauren ever read about tornados said. The storm was close. Too close. Lauren spotted Christopher gripping a tree trunk, his eyes frantic. With the camouflage of his brown pants and green-and-brown jacket, it was no wonder he was so hard to find.

Lauren stood below the boy and opened her arms, praying she could catch him.

"Christopher! Let go!"

He shivered and shook his head.

"You have to!" Lauren shouted.

Christopher didn't move.

Cooper shoved Lauren out of the way and braced one foot against a knot low on the tree's trunk. With two swift swings, his wide arm span easily reached the branch where Christopher sat, but the boy still refused to unclench his grip. Cooper stabilized himself enough to pry the child's fingers from the bark and handed Christopher down to Lauren. Molly immediately grabbed him. Christopher began to wail, whether in fear or relief, Lauren did not know.

"Go!" Lauren pushed Molly behind both shoulders. "Run!"

Cooper dropped out of the tree and landed with a thud behind Lauren. He snatched her hand and they began to run. Ahead of them, Molly raced with astonishing speed with her child molded against her form. When Molly reached the basement, a half-dozen arms pulled her in — and then the door slammed.

All the church doors automatically locked. Lauren had propped the doors open without taking time to reset the latches to open from the outside.

Cooper's hand tightened on Lauren's as she pointed. She groped her pocket as they ran, feeling for the lump that would be her keys, but the pocket didn't have even the bulge of a wadded up tissue. The keys were lost. Lauren had unlocked two sets of doors into the basement, and now she tugged Cooper in the direction that would take them to the other doors — with no guarantee they would be open.

Lauren stumbled.

Cooper's pace was too rapid to resist the interruption to their grip on each other. Lauren's hand slid out of his as her knees and then her face slammed into the ground.

The last thing Lauren saw was Cooper's startled grasping at the empty air where she had been.

The last thing she heard was a break in the siren and the groaning split of an oak.

10
ONE FAMILIAR TUNE

Sunday
6:03 a.m.

Where was the nurse?

It was time for someone to wake Lauren, to check her pupils, to see if her speech was slurred, to ask what she remembered.

Someone was supposed to make sure the stillness of her sleep didn't mean she had slipped away into a coma.

Sylvia stared at the clock on the hospital wall, as she had all through the night in dim light while the hours crawled. Outside the window now, the sky began to pink up and coax another day to life. In an hour, Sylvia's mother would dial her home phone number, and Sylvia wouldn't be there to answer. Instead, she would have to call Emma and calm anxiety before it stirred. They had spoken last night when everything was over.

After the storm.

After the sirens.

After the oak tree shuddered and split.

After the ambulance.

Emma was fine. She went to her basement when the tornado warning siren sounded and stayed there until the wind subsided. Sammie Dunavant was already at the house checking on her when Sylvia phoned. Emma seemed to understand Sylvia's explanation of what happened to Lauren, though whether she would remember this morning was uncertain. Emma might look out the window at the sunrise, predict a beautiful day, and not remember yesterday's storm.

The funnel hadn't actually touched down in Hidden Falls, but the wind had scattered aimless debris. Sylvia had seen enough television news at the hospital to know that the storm cut a swath across central Illinois that left every town in its path in cleanup mode. Downed power lines, tree limbs — like the one that nearly landed on Lauren — strewn trash bins, twisted street signs, dangling traffic lights, broken storefront windows.

At some point, Mayor Sylvia Alexander would have to emerge from the hospital and get a full assessment of what the whirlwind storm had done to Hidden Falls. Right now she only wanted to be aunt to the young woman lying in the hospital bed.

Where was the nurse?

Sylvia had emerged from the basement of Our Savior Community Church to find Cooper Elliott shielding Lauren with his body and making sure she didn't try to untangle herself from the web of small branches that camouflaged them. The tree limb itself had just missed them. A gash on the side of Lauren's head marked her impact with the sidewalk. Though she regained consciousness after only a few minutes, Lauren was confused about what happened.

Ethan was there, and the ambulance responded in record time. The ER doctor quickly concurred with Ethan's opinion that Lauren was severely concussed but otherwise unharmed. Lauren was well cared for. Still, she looked frail asleep in the bed. Sylvia had helped to keep her niece awake through the elongated afternoon and evening. Finally, Lauren had been allowed to sleep for two hours at a time.

It was time for a nurse to come in and wake her.

Sylvia's cell phone jangled, and the noise made her jump. As she reached to answer it, she glanced at Lauren, who gave no indication that she'd heard the sound. Sylvia decided to take the call in the hall where she could also track down the nurse.

"Hi, Larry," she said to her brother-in-law, Lauren's father.

"Janet just listened to your message," Larry said. "There aren't a lot of cell phone towers in this part of Alaska. Is Lauren all right?"

"They say she's doing well." Sylvia relayed

as much medical information as she knew. "I know you're in the middle of the vacation of a lifetime, but I thought you would want to know."

"Of course we do. The fishing here is great, but there's only one little plane out every two days, and then it's another whole day to get home."

"Stay. They're only keeping her for observation. She'll be home before you get here, anyway. I'll look after her." Sylvia took comfort in her own composed tone. Millions of people suffered concussions every year, she told herself. If she set aside the dramatic circumstances of Lauren's injury and believed Ethan, Lauren could be released later that day. She would just need rest.

Sylvia finished the call and caught the eye of a nurse.

"Go ahead and wake her," the nurse said. "I'll be in soon. If her stomach has settled, we'll see about breakfast."

Sylvia returned to Lauren's room and gently nudged her shoulder. When Lauren didn't wake, Sylvia stroked her face and called her name. After Sylvia raised her voice a couple of notches, Lauren's head turned and her eyes opened. Sylvia wished Ethan were there to determine whether Lauren's eyes looked right. Ethan had left two hours ago, headed for Columbus to see if he could salvage his residency.

"Hi." Lauren's voice was breathy and soft, but she seemed to focus on Sylvia's face.

"How do you feel?" Sylvia asked.

"My head hurts." Lauren's eyes moved from side to side. "I don't remember. . . ."

"Would you like to sit up?" Sylvia found the remote control and pushed the appropriate button. The head of the bed rose slowly.

"Did someone find Christopher?" Lauren rubbed her eyes.

"You did," Sylvia said. They'd had this conversation several times already.

"He was in the tree. I was running."

"I know. You got there. Cooper got Christopher out of the tree."

"Cooper did?" Lauren leaned forward a few inches.

"You both did."

"So Christopher is safe?"

"Yes."

"And Molly?"

"Also safe."

"That's a relief." Lauren sank back against the bed. "Was that today?"

"Yesterday."

"So today is Sunday?"

"That's right."

"I should go to church."

Sylvia picked up Lauren's hand and squeezed it. "I'm sure everyone understands that you can't be there."

She wasn't sure what was happening at Our

Savior or any of the other churches in Hidden Falls. What happened in this room is what mattered.

"I can't see without my glasses," Lauren said.

"They broke when you fell." During the night, Sylvia had offered to fetch Lauren's spare glasses from her apartment, but Lauren said they were broken as well.

"Did someone find Christopher? Is he all right?" Lauren's face filled with anxiety.

"Yes, he's fine." Sylvia would reassure Lauren as many times as it took. Eventually Lauren would remember the answer to the question, even if she never remembered racing against a tornado to find a little boy who climbed a tree and couldn't get down.

"I'm thirsty," Lauren said.

Sylvia picked up the water pitcher and took it to the sink to freshen it before filling Lauren's cup.

Lauren sipped through the straw and swallowed. "What time is it?"

Sylvia pointed to the clock. "The sun's just up."

"It's Sunday morning, right?"

"Right."

"You should go home," Lauren said. "I bet you've been here all night."

She had been.

"There's a whole hospital to take care of

me," Lauren said. "Make sure Nana's all right."

"She is." Sylvia kissed Lauren's forehead. She wasn't going anywhere.

6:24 a.m.

The ER had treated and released Cooper ten hours ago. His arms and face were a patchwork of bandages and minor scrapes, but the injuries weren't serious.

So why, Liam wondered, had they sat together in a hospital waiting room all night, periodically changing places with their cousin Dani or Nicole Sandquist? At first, others from the church had come to the hospital, anxious to know the latest about Lauren's condition. By suppertime, though, the crowd thinned, and by bedtime, only Liam, Cooper, Nicole, Ethan, and Dani remained. Every now and then, one of them left for the restroom or the coffee machine outside the cafeteria. At two in the morning, Dani scrounged up some doughnuts, probably abandoned at the nurses' station. Around three, Ethan got a phone call, and by four he said good-bye.

For a week, Liam had avoided looking his brother in the eye. Now he'd spent an entire night within six feet of Cooper. If the oak limb had crashed eighteen inches to the left of where it landed, it could have smashed Cooper's skull or broken his back. Picturing a very different scenario, Liam was unable to simply say good-bye to his brother and walk out of the hospital.

He wouldn't have slept anyway.

Liam didn't have the second envelope. He didn't know what became of the box of brochures he'd found it in and into which he dropped it without reading it. Had someone carried it to safety? Where? Had the contents scattered in the gale-force wind? Had the sudden afternoon rain drenched the envelope in a ditch?

He would never know what the note said. And it didn't matter, because Liam had made a decision while sitting under a blue-and-white-striped canopy at the health fair, watching Jessica behave in a cool, telling manner devoid of distress — while his own heart shattered like Dani's boat smashing against the rocks of the falls. If Liam had needed any confirmation of his disturbing suspicions, he found it in Jessica's unflapped demeanor.

Nicole was stretched out on a sofa, her fingers winding under the latches of her boot cast to scratch her leg. She had refused to let Ethan take her somewhere more comfortable before he left town. Liam understood why she remained. Nicole was enough younger than he was that she would have known Lauren Nock in high school. Liam had seen them sitting together at Quinn's banquet last weekend, and they seemed friendly. Dani's presence was more puzzling. Liam had expected her to leave hours ago, with the pronouncement that none of them could do anything for Lauren, so they might as well go home and sleep. But perhaps she stayed for the same reason Liam did.

Because they could have lost Cooper in one unpredictable moment.

And because Cooper wouldn't leave, not while Lauren was lying in a room down the hall and he wasn't permitted to visit. Liam hadn't realized until the yawning hours of the night how attached his brother had become in the last few days. If only one of them could be happy in love, Cooper deserved it.

A nurse stepped into the waiting room, and all four vigil keepers braced for news. Cooper immediately stood up. Nicole gripped the back of the sofa.

"She's awake and talking." The nurse tipped her head forward and looked at them over the tops of the half-size frames of her reading glasses. "I can't give you any more information than that, and Dr. Glass doesn't want a room full of visitors. I'm sure Lauren would want you all to go home and get some rest and a decent meal."

She turned on one heel and departed. Postures around the room went slack.

"Maybe she's right," Liam said. "In a few hours, they might let Lauren have visitors."

"I'm not going anywhere just yet." Cooper sat down and leaned forward with his elbows on his knees.

"The mayor's with her," Liam said. "She won't be alone."

"Don't feel you have to stay."

Liam leaned back in his chair. He couldn't leave if Cooper wouldn't.

"The cafeteria will be open by now." Dani stood up and dug in her pants pocket for money. "I'll get us some breakfast."

Nicole reached for her crutches. "If you don't mind my pace, I'd like to come along."

Dani nodded and waited for Nicole to get herself organized for ambulation. Liam watched the unlikely duo move slowly into the hall.

"I don't want to hurt Dani's feelings," Cooper said, "but I don't feel much like eating."

Liam didn't either. "I have to talk to you about something. It's important."

Cooper glanced up at Liam. "More important than what Lauren's going through?"

"A different kind of important."

"It can't wait?"

After avoiding this conversation for so long, now that they were alone in the waiting room, Liam didn't think he could stifle himself.

"I'm in trouble, Cooper," Liam said. "I need your help."

"What kind of trouble?"

"Big trouble. Legal trouble."

Cooper took in a slow breath. "I'm a sheriff's deputy. You can't tell me you're in that kind of trouble and not expect me to think like a cop. Maybe you should talk to Jack Parker before you say anything else."

"You're my brother," Liam said. "You're the one I need."

"Be careful, Liam. There won't be any way to back out. If you put me in a compromising position, I will be obligated to do the right thing."

"That's what I'm counting on." Liam chose a path and began to pace back and forth.

He started with the day he realized something was amiss with one account, and then another, and another. He moved on to how he arrived at the total of seventy-three thousand dollars and the panic that surged through him by the night of the banquet. Liam skipped over breaking into the marketing coordinator's office at the banquet hall and taking an envelope from a bank. If he had to, he would confess later. Right now he didn't want Cooper to trip over that technicality. He had put the envelope back, and he'd done nothing with the information it contained. Cooper — so far — had overlooked a litany of infractions by Ethan, Nicole, Dani, and even Lauren in the search for Quinn, but Liam knew that when it came to his own brother, Cooper wouldn't risk being thought complicit in a crime. It could destroy his career.

Liam watched the clock, unsure how long it would take Nicole to gimp to the cafeteria and back. He moved on to the first note, the missed breakfast meeting, his suspicions about Jessica's newfound money, the breakup, the scratched setting of her ring.

Stone by stone, weight lifted off Liam's chest.

"You have to help me," he said. "I did *not* take that money, but I don't know how to prove it."

"And you think Jessica has it," Cooper said.

"I don't know how to prove that, either." Liam peered into his brother's face, aching for a glimmer of belief. Liam was always the gullible Elliott brother and Cooper the one whose face gave away nothing. It had always been that way. "Cooper, I'm telling the truth."

Cooper moistened his bottom lip. "I know."

Liam let out his breath. "So you'll help?"

"Within the constraints of the law, yes."

"Do I need to talk to Jack Parker?"

"I promise to let you know if you should."

"Thank you."

"It's Sunday," Cooper said. "I'm not sure how fast I can turn the wheels of bureaucracy on the weekend, but I'll try."

"Anything you can do, I'll appreciate it."

"Here's my deal," Cooper said. "I was going to go over to the church later. People will want to know how Lauren is, and there's a lot of cleanup to do."

Liam nodded. He'd seen the soggy detritus that had overtaken the church lawn in the wake of the storm.

"My guess is the trustees aren't going to leave that mess alone any longer than they have to," Cooper said. "There's too much risk of someone getting hurt."

Liam scrunched his forehead. What exactly was Cooper getting at?

"I want you to go over to the church," Cooper said. "Go to the service, find out what the plan is, and do what you can to help."

Liam swallowed hard. Yesterday's reluctant community service was the closest he had been to attending church in years, but he would do whatever it took to keep Cooper on his side.

"I'm going to go make some calls," Cooper said, "and then I'm going to the church. So if you want to know what I came up with, then that's where you'd better be."

7:07 a.m.

Nicole wrinkled her nose at the scrambled eggs. Few things were more disgusting than cold scrambled eggs, and even if they were hot when spooned onto a plate, they'd be cold long before she sat down to eat them. A bagel with cream cheese was a much safer choice, and she could never go wrong with a banana.

Dani pushed a tray along the rails of the cafeteria line and loaded it with an assortment of rolls, fresh fruit, and juices. Nicole admired the decisiveness Dani displayed without frittering away time speculating about what her cousins might want to eat. She made straightforward choices in efficient succession. If Cooper and Liam couldn't find something appealing on the tray, it would not be for lack of options.

"You were awesome yesterday." Nicole moved her crutches along behind Dani.

"What do you mean?" Dani picked up three pats of butter.

"You kept the looky-loos out of the way." While Ethan's medical training kicked in and he examined Lauren and Cooper, Dani had taken control of the crowd, impressing on everyone that they had to stand clear while a select few dragged the tree limb out of the way and the EMTs came in with a stretcher.

"Lauren will be fine." Dani stopped in front of the cashier and waited for the total before handing over several bills.

"I'm sure she'll be grateful to hear what you did."

"Nothing to hear. Sometimes a situation just calls for someone to be sensible."

They started back down the hall toward the elevators, Nicole's crutches clunking rhythmically against the tile floor as she swung her good foot between them. The heels of her hands were sore, but she progressed confidently alongside Dani, who carried the laden tray.

Nicole pressed the button that would bring the elevator to them and eyed her bagel on the tray. Hunger had kicked in, and she salivated for the cinnamon raisin meld of flavors. If she weren't on crutches, she might have reached for the bagel and bitten into it while they waited. The numbered light above the door changed with a *ping,* and the elevator doors opened. Nicole readjusted the grip on her crutches. Behind her, footsteps thumped rapidly toward the elevator. She started to turn to assure the person they'd hold the doors, but instead of a polite, grateful face, Nicole saw only the blur of a form pushing her aside and kicking one crutch out from under her. Hopping, she caught herself against the wall as the doors closed in her face. Dani's carefully balanced breakfast tray clattered to the floor as she pounded on the doors.

"Green shoes!" Dani shouted.

"Dani, what — ?"

But Dani was already yanking open the door to the stairwell.

Nicole surveyed the damage. Breakfast for four spilled across the floor — including a hefty slosh across her fallen crutch. She looked in both directions down the hall.

"Of course, nobody's around when you need help," she muttered as she balanced carefully and leaned forward to pick the crutch out of the mess. Nicole's admiration only moments ago for Dani's organization and calm evaporated in the reality that Dani had abandoned her. And the tray hadn't been knocked from Dani's hands. She'd dropped it in favor of hotheaded pursuit.

They could have pushed the button again and still had their breakfast.

Nicole had seen enough of the elevator thief to recognize the blue scrubs of a nonmedical employee. It was a man with dark, close-cropped hair. Beyond that, Nicole wasn't sure.

The handle of her crutch was sticky with jelly, but Nicole gripped it enough to safely report to the cafeteria cashier that there was a mess in the hall. Then she went into the restroom to clean up. By the time she returned to the elevators, an employee from housekeeping was dropping the breakfast remains into a rolling trash can.

The hospital wasn't large. There were only three floors. Nicole went up one story to tell the Elliott brothers that the breakfast plans had gone awry — but the waiting room was occupied only by a young couple Nicole had never seen before.

"There were two guys in here," she said.

"Did you see which way they went?"

The couple blinked at her and shook their heads.

Cooper and Liam should have been expecting breakfast. Why would they both leave?

Nicole huffed back into the hall. There weren't many places they could go. In one direction was a set of swinging doors leading to two squares of patient rooms around central nurses' stations. In the other was an EMPLOYEES ONLY sign. Nicole did due diligence and hopped a short distance in both directions to satisfy herself that Cooper and Liam were not simply loitering just out of sight.

Ethan had left for Columbus.

Dani got a bee in her bonnet about chasing somebody just for being rude.

Liam and Cooper had disappeared without explanation.

She didn't even have a cell phone number for Dani or her cousins — or Sylvia Alexander, who was probably still down the hall in her niece's room.

Nicole pressed her lips together and hopped back into the waiting room. Her stomach still rumbled for breakfast, but at the moment, she needed to sit down and give her sore hands a break. The young couple were both absorbed in magazines. Nicole moved past them and settled in a chair against the opposite wall.

Ethan would be more than halfway to Columbus by now. Nicole had been dozing with her head on his shoulder when his phone rang at three in the morning and he eased away to take the call in the hall. When he returned, he didn't say anything more than that he would have to leave.

Nicole had wanted to protest.

What about Lauren?

What about me?

What about Quinn?

But she'd held her tongue. She knew no more about the reality of Ethan's life in Columbus than he knew about hers in St. Louis. With the upheaval of the newspaper she worked for, the future of her job likely was beyond Nicole's control, but Ethan might still have a choice. He deserved the chance to choose.

They'd had no privacy or time for the conversation Nicole wished for.

The one where she'd look in his eyes to discern what he felt for her.

The one where she'd say that the storm had frightened her with the thought she might lose Ethan as well as Quinn.

The one where she'd agree he was right when he said they should have no more regrets about each other.

The one where she'd wish he would kiss her.

Instead, they'd stared at each other over

the cup of vending machine coffee Ethan would depend on to keep himself awake for a hundred miles or so when he pulled out of the hospital parking lot long before dawn.

Ethan promised to call, that it wouldn't be like last time.

Nicole wanted to believe him.

She took her phone from her pocket. Nicole's only charger was at Lauren's apartment. During the night, Ethan had brought in the charger he kept in his car, so Nicole had some juice, but the battery was not full. She opened her contact list just to stare at the entry under Ethan's name. Nicole knew the name of the hospital where he worked, and she had his cell phone number. This was more information than she'd had for most of the last ten years. Nicole shut off the phone to save the battery and instantly felt disconnected from Ethan. With the top of the phone pressed against her forehead and her eyes closed, she pictured him in his Lexus driving on Interstate 70 into the rising sun.

He would call. He would.

In the meantime, Nicole kept watch for Lauren, not even knowing if her friend was conscious. Nicole supposed she could call Benita Booker for a ride, once the morning progressed further toward a reasonable hour, but if Sylvia came down the hall with news of Lauren, Nicole didn't want her to find the room empty of her niece's friends.

Where had they all gone?

Her eyes still closed, Nicole leaned her head back against the wall. Every time she closed her eyes, she felt Lauren's phone against her ear and Quinn's tune playing from somewhere in Oklahoma.

Or anywhere. If the 918 number belonged to a cell phone, its owner — and Quinn — could be anywhere. Nicole wondered if anyone at the newspaper would still talk to her. She needed investigative help, but maybe none of the people she trusted still had jobs. Later Nicole would turn on her phone and try to reach somebody.

While the tune played in her head, the sequence of pitches formed in Nicole's throat, and she softly released them to the empty corner where she sat. She longed to hear Quinn's soothing whistle. Ethan's scent wafted around her, and for a moment Nicole marveled at how real it seemed even in his absence. When someone dropped into the seat beside her, Nicole's eyes fluttered open.

The scent was not a memory.

Ethan's dark eyes were inches from her.

"What are you doing here?" Nicole's heart raced. He should have been closing in on Columbus by now.

"Aren't you glad to see me?"

A grin split her face. She drew in breath. "What about your job?"

He shrugged one shoulder. "Whatever damage I've done to my career is not going to get worse at this point."

Nicole swallowed the thickness in her throat. "I'm glad you're here." She was — though she hoped he hadn't thrown away his residency in his decision to turn around.

"As long as I'm here, I might as well act like a neurologist," he said. "I want to see Lauren's chart and check her CT scan."

"Will they let you?"

"I might be able to prevail on professional courtesy, especially if Lauren says she'd like my opinion."

"I'm sure she would."

"It's almost the start of visiting hours, anyway," Ethan said. "Let me go see what I can do."

He stood up, and she tilted her face up at him. When he bent to kiss her cheek, Nicole said, "Bring me breakfast."

8:06 a.m.

Ethan figured twenty-four minutes before the official start of visiting hours was close enough to push through the swinging doors. He hoped one of the nurses on duty would remember his presence yesterday afternoon, when he followed Lauren's transfer from the ER to a regular room. A gray-haired woman in the corner, probably the charge nurse, looked up from her stack of paperwork.

"Dr. Jordan, isn't it?"

"Good memory, Nurse Wacker."

"What can I do for you?"

"I'm looking for Dr. Glass."

"Right. About your friend with the head trauma."

"I was hoping for sort of a professional courtesy conversation."

The nurse picked up her phone. "I'll page him."

"Thanks."

Ethan wandered a few yards away from the nurses' station but stayed within sight. When his phone rang, he glanced at the ID.

BRINKMAN.

He ignored the call. Ethan had nothing to say to Phil Brinkman, and he doubted his friend Hansen would call. Good news from Columbus, scarce to begin with, was out of the question now. If Dr. Gonzalez had not already returned to the hospital, he would within hours. Brinkman would alternate between a martyr who never left his duties in the chief's absence and a tattletale about Ethan's negligence. Ethan hoped Hansen had covered his own tracks enough not to be caught in the fallout. The next conversation Ethan expected to have would be with Gonzalez himself.

And it was not going to be pleasant.

"Dr. Jordan." Nurse Wacker signaled from the nurses' station. "Dr. Glass just got here. He's in the lounge down the hall and would like you to join him. Just push the buzzer by the employee doors and he'll let you in."

Ethan hadn't met Dr. Glass yesterday. A generalist in the ER had treated Lauren and admitted her for observation. But Ethan remembered the public health nurse mentioning Dr. Glass yesterday at the health fair.

That was less than twenty-four hours ago, and once again, everything had changed in Hidden Falls.

Ethan buzzed the doors, and a man more than twice his age peered through a narrow pane of plexiglass before opening the door.

"Dr. Jordan, I presume."

"Thank you for seeing me."

"I understand you're a friend of one of my patients." Dr. Glass led the way down the hall to a staff lounge.

Ethan took the chair Dr. Glass offered. "I haven't seen Lauren in the last twelve hours. I wondered about her status."

"I haven't seen her yet this morning, either, but my understanding is she had a good night, considering. My orders were for the nurses to wake her every two hours."

Ethan nodded. "Do you think I could see her chart?"

"Don't worry. We did all the scans. She has a significant concussion, but we're following protocol."

"I'm sure you are. I'm a neurosurgical

resident. If you could indulge me, I'd appreciate it."

"Neurosurgical, eh?"

"Nine months to go."

"Where?"

Ethan named the hospital in Columbus.

"Ah. Gonzalez still running that program?" Dr. Glass asked.

Ethan blinked.

Dr. Glass laughed. "Did you think a small-town doctor like me wouldn't know his reputation?"

"I meant no disrespect, sir."

"He was full of himself even in med school."

Ethan allowed himself a half smile. "You know Dr. Gonzalez?"

"I'm not sure he'd admit to knowing me. We had rather differing perspectives on the human side of practicing medicine when we started out, but I have no doubt he runs a fine residency."

"I'm there because of him."

"Despite his quirks."

Ethan relaxed. He liked Dr. Glass.

"Where are you going when you finish?" Dr. Glass asked.

Ethan shrugged. First he had to figure out if he still had a residency to finish. If he survived this crisis, maybe the hospital in Columbus would keep him on. "I haven't thought that far ahead."

"I've been trying to retire for years. I send

as many surgical cases as I can somewhere else, but they keep calling me in for emergencies. We could use someone like you around here."

Ethan smiled blandly. "I'm not sure Hidden Falls is for me." He was sure it wasn't.

"You're here now."

"I came for Quinn's banquet last weekend."

"Well, we all know how that went, don't we?" Dr. Glass stood up. "Let's go see our patient."

They stopped at the nurses' station, and Nurse Wacker handed Dr. Glass a chart. He read the overnight notes and then handed it to Ethan.

"See?" Dr. Glass said. "Nothing out of the ordinary."

Relieved, Ethan agreed. The radiologist's notes on the CT scan mentioned nothing remarkable, and other than a mild headache and residual memory issues, Lauren had no significant symptoms.

When they entered her room, Lauren gave them a drowsy grin. "They're not going to charge me extra for two doctors, are they?"

"Maybe you're just seeing double." Ethan held a finger up to see if she would follow it with her eyes and then automatically lifted the bedding off her feet to check her response to his touch.

"I feel everything I'm supposed to feel," she said.

As he checked Lauren's grip, Ethan glanced at Sylvia, settled in the chair beside the bed. "Is she behaving herself?"

"I'm here to be sure she does," Sylvia said.

"Do you remember what happened?" Ethan asked.

"Not exactly. But I remember that Aunt Sylvia told me what happened. Does that count?"

He nodded. "It counts for something."

Ethan listened while Dr. Glass asked some questions about headache and nausea and made some notes in Lauren's chart.

"I'd like to keep you until we're clear of the twenty-four-hour mark," Dr. Glass said. "But right now I don't see any reason why you should spend another night in the hospital."

"You can come home with me," Sylvia said, "at least for a night."

"What about Nicole?" Lauren asked. "I'm supposed to be looking after her."

"She can come, too, if she'd like," Sylvia said.

"Nicole's in the waiting room," Ethan said. "She'll be glad to hear you're doing better."

"Your friends can visit now." Dr. Glass clicked his pen closed and slipped it into the pocket of his white coat. "But they shouldn't stay long."

With a wave, Dr. Glass left the room, taking Lauren's chart with him.

"Would you like to see Nicole?" Ethan asked.

"Has she been here all night?" Lauren asked.

"We all were. Dani, Cooper, Liam, Nicole, and me."

"Goofballs. You should have gotten some sleep."

Ethan watched as Lauren rolled her head to one side and sighed. Clearly she was concussed, but her condition could have been much worse. She seemed in good shape to him for sixteen hours after a head trauma.

"Nicole's the only one still in the waiting room," Ethan said.

"Cooper's gone?" Disappointment tinged Lauren's voice.

"Maybe he went for breakfast or a shower," Ethan said.

Sylvia patted Lauren's hand. "He'll be back. He was anxious to see you."

"Is he all right?" Lauren asked.

"Scraped up," Ethan said, "but all the parts are working properly."

"Good." Her eyes closed.

"Looks like you could use a nap," Ethan said. "I'll let Nicole know how you're doing, and we'll figure it out from there."

"Thank you." Lauren was already drifting off.

She conversed coherently. Ethan was satisfied she was progressing well.

"I promised Nicole some breakfast," he said. "I'll see you later."

He went down to the cafeteria and picked up orange juice, coffee, bagels, and bananas before returning to the waiting room.

Nicole moved magazines aside, and Ethan set the tray on a coffee table.

"She's doing well," he said.

Nicole exhaled. "Good."

"I think you're both going home with Sylvia tonight."

"I could be on my own."

Ethan laughed softly. "I think it's already been decided."

Nicole rolled her eyes. "I'd be fine."

Ethan opened the juice bottles and handed one to Nicole, but she seemed more interested in lathering a bagel with cream cheese. She'd always liked three times as much cream cheese as he did. Closing her eyes, she moaned as she bit into her breakfast.

Ethan turned toward steps slowing on the tile in the hall and saw Jack Parker pause in the doorway.

"Here you are." Jack came in and sat across from them. "My daughters made me promise to come and see how Lauren is doing."

"She's doing well." Ethan gave a brief report.

"The girls will be glad to know that," Jack said. "They both like her a lot."

Ethan took a long swig of juice, suddenly

realizing how thirsty he was. “You wanted to talk to me about something yesterday, before all this happened.”

Jack tapped his knees with his fingertips. “It was about that will I found earlier in the week.”

Nicole leaned forward. “The Tabor will?”

“Right.”

“What about it?” Ethan asked. “I thought you said you wanted to study it some more.”

“I did. Harold Tabor stood to inherit a great deal of money.”

“But he had to have a male heir,” Nicole said. “That’s what you told us the other night. Otherwise the money went to his brother.”

“Correct,” Jack said.

It seemed to Ethan an odd provision in a will, but in a time of higher infant mortality, perhaps a child who survived to five had better odds of reaching adulthood.

“And he did have a son,” Nicole said. “A boy named Merrill.”

“Correct again.”

Ethan looked from Jack to Nicole. What had she figured out and not told him?

Nicole put her bagel down and wiped her sticky fingers with a napkin. “But the Tabors left town when Merrill was two.”

“Was that in Old Dom’s ledgers?” Ethan asked.

“Those notes I was puzzling over yesterday," Nicole said. "They had something to do with Merrill Tabor. But there was another family involved."

Jack nodded.

"The Peases," Nicole said.

Jack nodded again. Ethan felt lost.

"There's some connection between the Tabors and the Peases," Nicole said.

"I think I know what it is." Jack raised his eyebrows. "And I think you'll find it very interesting."

8:55 a.m.

Jack had their attention now. "The man in the photo who looks like Ethan is standing in front of a Pease grave."

Nicole nodded tentatively. "I want to go back to the cemetery to double-check that with Old Dom, but I think you're right."

"I haven't quite got it sorted out," Jack said, "but there's a red herring involved — something that looks like it should matter, but it doesn't."

"You're losing me," Ethan said.

"I found a contract between Harold Tabor and Stephen Pease."

Ethan turned his palms up. "So they had a business deal."

"The Tabors were a wealthy family," Jack said. "Back in the day, they owned half of Hidden Falls and had business ventures all over the Midwest. They had losses during the

Depression, like everyone, but they came out all right in the end. Harold was a fourth-generation business tycoon. Stephen Pease was an uneducated man who drove a fruit truck when he could get the work."

This contract could be nothing, some technicality an attorney advised. Or it could be much more. That's what Jack didn't know yet.

"Buying and selling fruit?" Nicole said. "Did the Tabors have orchards?"

Jack was impressed. "As a matter of fact, they did. Apples mostly. I have a stack of contracts six inches deep profiling the business operations of the orchards until they were sold." Jack knew the fruit truck drivers were day laborers — and they had to have their own trucks.

"I still don't understand what we're talking about," Ethan said.

Jack leaned forward and made sure he had eye contact with both Ethan and Nicole. "Why would a man like Harold Tabor draw up a contract with a transient worker like Stephen Pease for a vague transaction that on the face of it has no value?"

Jack let the question sink in. Ethan's brow furrowed in confusion and impatience, but Nicole sucked on one corner of her mouth, thinking. Jack didn't have all the answers to his own questions, but he felt fairly certain he was still a few steps ahead of Nicole.

"What exactly was this transaction?" Nicole tore off a piece of her bagel and tucked it into her mouth. "And what kind of money was involved?"

"Depends on your perspective," Jack said. "To Harold Tabor it would have been pocket change, even in the Depression. To Stephen Pease? It would have meant a fresh start. Options. A chance to get out of debt."

"And what did Pease have to do?"

"Deliver a package."

Nicole leaned back in her chair. "Must have been some package."

"The contents were never specified in the contract," Jack said. "It was Harold Tabor's prerogative to consider the package satisfactory, and Pease would get his money."

"Sounds like Tabor had all the power," Ethan said.

Nicole chewed. "Not necessarily."

"He has the money, and he has the prerogative to call the deal null and void," Ethan said. "What does Pease have?"

She smiled. "The package. Whatever it was, it mattered enough to Tabor to tempt Pease with the money."

Jack waited. If Nicole solved this, he would know immediately. And he had the evidence she would need to prove any theory.

"So," Ethan said, "what could the package have been?"

The three of them stared at one another.

"The babies," Nicole said. "Quinn's notes in Old Dom's ledgers were about babies."

Jack held his breath, his mind rapidly indexing the pages of notes he'd taken as he sorted files. Harold Tabor's younger brother had three children — all sons. But Harold had married after his brother, and his only child had not come easily. If he did not have a living son on his fortieth birthday, his brother would inherit the lion's share of the family business.

Yes, babies were an important link. But Harold had a son who would be five, two years before Harold turned forty. All had been well.

Jack looked up to see Sylvia Alexander enter the waiting room. "Good morning, Mayor. How is your niece?"

"Doing well, thank you." Sylvia paced toward the group. "She's sleeping at the moment. It seemed like a good time to get up and stretch my legs."

"I could go sit with her," Nicole said.

"Not just yet." Sylvia pulled a chair up to the huddle. "Nicole, what babies were you talking about when I came in?"

"I'm not sure," Nicole said. "Those Morse code notes Quinn was making in the cemetery records seemed to be about the age of some babies during the thirties. But what stumped me is that I don't think it was necessarily about the *death* of the babies. Old

Dom's father had all sorts of notes in those books about the families."

Jack cleared his throat. "It could be useful to compare those notes against my files." He was not entirely comfortable with Nicole's access to information that he hadn't seen. She might get ahead of him.

"Babies during the Depression?" Sylvia tilted her head.

Ethan grunted. "Somebody has to catch me up. We were talking about a contract between Tabor and Pease about some package, and now we're talking about babies? And what does any of this have to do with Quinn? Why was he making those notes?"

"Oh my goodness," Sylvia said. "My mother's story."

"What story is that?" Jack asked.

Sylvia blinked three times. Something was coming together behind her eyes, Jack realized.

"Sylvia?" Nicole said.

"My mother was young during the Depression," Sylvia said. "Her mother was the town gossip, so it's hard to know if the stories she told were true. But just a week ago, my mother was remembering a story about two families with little boys about the same age. Both families left town and no one heard from them again. But there was money involved, and at least one of the boys was sickly."

"That fits," Jack said, nodding.
"What fits?" Ethan asked.
Nicole's eyes widened. "That grave. It's the marker for Stephen Pease's little boy."
The pieces snapped into place for Jack. "A little boy would be a valuable package to a man who needs a healthy male offspring in order to inherit a fortune."
Nicole's face simultaneously filled with horror and certainty. "*One* of the boys got sick. It just wasn't the one everybody thought. Old Dom's father figured it out."
"Wait a minute," Ethan said. "You think Tabor bought Pease's kid?"
The outrageous truth swirled around them.
"My word," Sylvia muttered. "Why didn't I see this before now?"
Jack scratched his nose. What did the mayor know? He folded his hands in his lap and waited.
"I found some things of Quinn's on Friday night." Sylvia stared at a spot on the floor, concentrating. She covered her mouth with three fingers.
Nicole scooted forward in her seat. "What did you find, Sylvia?"
"A Matchbox collection."
Now Jack felt as lost as Ethan had been looking for most of this conversation. "Matchbox? Like the little toy cars?"
Sylvia nodded. "I guess they're Quinn's, but I never knew he had them. Sports cars, I

don't know. I didn't pay much attention."

"They must have been his when he was little," Nicole said. "Why would he hide them in your attic?"

"I don't know."

"What else?" Jack asked. A few small metal cars didn't connect to anything except perhaps Quinn's mysterious past.

Sylvia shrugged. "A hood ornament. At least that's what I think it was."

Ethan spilled half a bottle of juice over his knees. Nicole fumbled with a pile of napkins to help with the mess.

Ethan soaked up the liquid haphazardly. "Kind of a rocket-looking thing?"

Sylvia looked up. "Yes! How did you know?"

"It's from a 1955 Oldsmobile. I gave it to him when I was in college."

"Why didn't I know about this?" Nicole asked.

"It was just something I found online," Ethan said. "It was a lot older than Quinn's Oldsmobile, but I thought he would like it."

Sylvia stood up and began to pace. "You gave that to him when you were in college? Like when you were nineteen or twenty?"

"Something like that."

"So only ten years ago?"

"Yes, I think it was the last time I saw him."

"The box has been in my attic for twenty years."

"What box?"

"The box with the Matchbox cars. But the hood ornament couldn't have been in it twenty years ago." Sylvia paced faster. "And that means the documents might not have been there all that time, either."

"Documents?" Jack said. He thought he was the only one in possession of relevant documents.

"A few weeks ago," Sylvia said, "Quinn volunteered to take some boxes from my garage up into the attic. I didn't think it was urgent, but he insisted."

Nicole reached for her crutches and pulled herself to her feet. "So you think —"

"He put something new in the box."

"My hood ornament?" Ethan asked.

Sylvia turned to look at him. "And the papers. The hood ornament means he meant them for you."

Jack thumped one hand on the arm of his chair. He didn't want to admit he was losing the line of logic.

"Nicole," Sylvia said, "are you still willing to go sit with Lauren?"

"Of course."

"Then, Ethan, I think you should come with me to my house."

Jack took comfort in the fact that Ethan looked as disoriented as Jack felt.

"Quinn must have meant for you to have the documents," Sylvia said. "That's why he put them in the box. They were safe there. No one else even knew the box was in my attic, and he knew I wouldn't look in it."

"But you *did* look," Jack pointed out.

"Well," she said, "circumstances changed when Quinn disappeared."

"What do these documents say?" Ethan asked.

"Come with me and I'll show you," Sylvia said.

Ethan looked around the room. "I think we're all in this together at this point. What did you see?"

"Are you sure you wouldn't rather wait to see for yourself?"

"Please, just tell me."

"Well, first of all, there was a marriage certificate for Kay Petersen and Richard Jordan."

Nicole's jaw dropped open. "Why would Quinn have a copy of the marriage certificate for Ethan's parents?"

"It's like your dots and dashes," Sylvia said. "One thing leads to another. There's also an adoption certificate."

Jack's stomach fell away.

"I'm adopted?" Ethan looked dumbfounded.

"No," Sylvia said. "Your mother was. The document shows Kathleen Pease will henceforth be known as Kay Petersen."

Jack heard the breath of every person in the room.

"Her original birth certificate shows her parents as Dennis and Linda Pease."

Jack's chest heaved. When he'd opened this can of worms, he hadn't expected to hear any of this.

"Maybe we should have a look at those documents together," Jack said.

"Pease," Nicole said. "Your mother is a Pease. But . . ."

"I really wish you'd let me look at the documents," Jack said. He was an attorney. He would know what they meant better than anyone else present.

"Just hold on." Nicole put her fingers to her temples. "The man in the picture — he's a Pease? Is he Stephen or Dennis?"

"I only had a cursory glance at the picture yesterday," Jack said. "We'd have to pin down the date." And he would have to sort out the relationship between Stephen and Dennis. Getting at the truth was going to require a few more birth certificates.

"But the babies," Nicole said. "The package changes everything."

11:07 a.m.

"You have to go see your parents."

This wasn't the first time Nicole made this statement, but it was the first time Ethan thought she might be right. They stood murmuring outside the waiting room while Sylvia checked on Lauren before leaving the hospital.

"What in the world will I say to them?" Ethan opened his hands in a wide gesture. "Hi, Mom. Did you know you were adopted?"

Nicole rested a hand on his arm. "First go with Sylvia to see the documents. I hate to say it, but I think Jack's right. He should have a look. And I don't think he's telling us everything he knows."

Ethan eyed her. "I don't think you're telling him everything you know, either."

"*Know* is a strong word. It's more like *suspect.*"

"Okay, *suspect.* You found something in the cemetery notes, didn't you?"

Nicole looked over her shoulder and shuffled her crutches a little farther down the hall. "This is going to sound gruesome."

"More gruesome than the possibility of a rich man buying a poor man's baby?"

Nicole sucked in a deep breath. "When we were at the cemetery that night looking at grave markers, I noticed that sometimes when a baby died, the marker might only say *infant* or *baby* with a year. Not even a last name."

"So?" Ethan knew sickly babies did not always receive a name, and grieving families might find it costly to purchase and inscribe a tombstone.

"So . . . the grave the man in the photo is standing in front of is near two markers with the name Pease. But Old Dom's father didn't think it was a Pease baby buried there."

"Who did he think it was?"

Nicole shrugged. "The notes just say a Tabor child took ill."

Ethan stiffened. "A Tabor?" Harold's younger brother, Truman, also had several children. It could have been any one of them.

"Quinn's code says things like *right age* or *this one.*"

"So you think —"

"Don't you see, Ethan? If the 'package' in the contract Jack found was a baby, we're in a new game."

Jack lurked, leaning against the wall a few yards away with his hands in his pockets. Sylvia's steps slapped the tile floor as she approached. "Lauren's waiting."

Nicole gripped her crutches. "Then I'll go."

Ethan caught the gaze of her emerald eyes and wished he didn't have to leave her behind. "I'll call you."

Thirty minutes later, Sylvia lifted Quinn's box from her mantel, and Ethan's trembling hands unfolded the documents.

The marriage license.

The adoption papers.

A birth certificate listing Dennis Pease as the father of Kathleen Pease, born in a town in Kansas that Ethan had never heard of.

Ethan laid the papers in a neat row on the coffee table while he rubbed his eyes. He'd been up more than twenty-four hours now. Small letters typed into tiny boxes were running together, but Ethan had the feeling he was missing something obvious. He felt the same way on a regular basis when he was running through diagnostic protocol but not coming up with an answer that made sense for a patient's symptoms or treatment didn't relieve the symptoms. It had to be here. If Nicole were there, she'd have a hunch, a theory to turn and look at from every direction.

Sylvia sat quietly across from him.

Ethan looked at the morphing forms of his mother's names. Kathleen Pease. Kay Petersen. Kay Jordan. He looked again at the names of the men identified as her father. Dennis Pease. Carl Petersen. He blinked at the names of the women identified as her mother. Linda Pease. Linda Petersen.

"My grandmother," he murmured.

"What about your grandmother?" Sylvia asked.

Ethan pointed to the names on the birth and adoption papers. "Linda. It's Linda on both forms. I think she was married twice. The adoption was so my mother would have her stepfather's name — Petersen."

The doorbell rang. Sylvia stood up. "That

must be Jack with the papers from his office."

Ethan was reluctant to change position or even turn his head for fear of losing the thread that was beginning to make sense. Jack shuffled across the carpet and dropped onto the sofa next to Ethan to examine the pages Ethan had laid out.

"What did you find?" Ethan asked without looking up.

Jack reached into his briefcase, riffled through notes, and tapped the information he sought. "Dennis Pease was the only son of Stephen Pease. He was born here in Hidden Falls — a home birth, which was typical at the time. According to official records, he died eight months later, and his parents ran out on their lease and left town the day they buried him."

Ethan ran his tongue over his lips. "Then how is it he grew up to be listed on my mother's birth certificate?"

"How indeed?"

"Identity theft?" Sylvia speculated. "Someone found a record of an infant no one would miss and used the name. People still try to do that."

Jack nodded. "With enough basic information, much of which would be available in public records, it's possible to get a birth certificate."

That struck Ethan as random. He was a

man of science — of patterns and predictability. Even in treating disease, he depended on understanding causation and consistency.

This was no disease. This was his mother. And there was causation and consistency. No one had to obtain a birth certificate by fraudulent means when already in possession of one that would never be questioned.

"Jack," he said, "what was the date on that contract you found between Harold Tabor and Stephen Pease?"

"Why does it matter?" Jack gripped his notepad.

"I suppose the date doesn't matter," Ethan said. "What matters is the time between when the contract was drafted and when it was considered fulfilled."

Jack flipped a couple of pages. "Two days."

"And the money was paid?"

"In full. In cash."

Ethan stacked the documents. "May I take these with me?"

Jack jerked slightly. "I think we need to make sure those documents remain in safekeeping."

Ethan wasn't asking Jack's opinion. He raised his eyes to Sylvia.

"Of course," she said. "I believe Quinn meant you to have them. That's why he asked you to come to town."

Jack protested. "We should at least make photocopies."

"These are not original documents." Ethan folded the papers. "Wherever Quinn got them from, we could get them again."

"Santorelli is my guess," Sylvia said.

Ethan nodded.

"I have to advise against this recklessness." Jack stood when Ethan did.

Ethan wasn't interested in Jack's advice. He thanked Sylvia with his eyes and went out her front door, leaving Jack with his jaw hanging open.

He drove straight to Quinn's house and parked in front. When he spoke to Nicole, Ethan wanted to give his full attention to the conversation.

"That package," he said when she answered her cell phone. "I think it was a two-way exchange. And I'm not talking about the money."

"It's the only thing that makes sense," Nicole said.

Ethan hadn't expected her to be surprised. He was confident she knew what he was talking about. A substitution. A trade. A sickly baby boy for a healthy one of the same age.

"My mother doesn't have to know," he said. She had lived her whole life without the truth. Ethan was certain of that. What would it change now?

"She deserves to know," Nicole said.

"It's not what's between us," he said.

"No," she said. "Your father is what's

between you and your mother. Don't add this. Everything can change in a day. Remember — no regrets."

They hung up and Ethan sat in his car in the full light of day, staring at the features of Quinn's house.

The shutters Ethan had once helped to paint.

The hail-struck dent in the gutter above one window that Quinn never replaced because it didn't leak.

The strip of siding that he had replaced because squirrels nibbled through it.

The polished door knocker Quinn shined with his handkerchief nearly every day when he left the house.

It all looked so ordinary, as if the house itself was waiting for Quinn to pull into the driveway, turn his key in the front lock, and resume his life. Tomorrow he would go to the high school and relieve the substitute teacher who had taken his classes. The next day he would decide that his lawn needed mowing one last time before winter. He would be the same reliable Quinn so many people in Hidden Falls depended on, with that understanding gleam in his eyes that made people want to tell him their troubles.

Ethan was sure Sylvia was right when she said Quinn wanted him to have the documents. He was equally sure Quinn had wanted him to stay in town for a few days because he knew this moment would come and Ethan would resist it. Quinn had been patient with Ethan's sullen nursing of familial wounds but never accepted that Ethan's sense of rejection was final.

Ethan removed his keys from the ignition and opted to walk around the block to the Jordan household, where he stood on the sidewalk and took three deep breaths before knocking on the front door. His father, Ethan knew, would leave it to his mother to see who stood outside the house. He would have the TV on, and he wouldn't turn it off if the president of the United States came through the door. It had always been that way. Richard Jordan put in his hours at work and figured he'd fulfilled his obligation to support his family. Beyond that, his time was his own. It didn't matter how tired his wife got keeping up with everything else or what was going on in the lives of his sons. His father's passivity had fed Ethan's ambition for as long as he could remember.

"Hello, Mom." Kay Jordan paid the price for the difference between Ethan and his father. Ethan fished around in his mind for a memory of his mother standing up to her husband. He had none.

He had startled his mother. Maybe she never expected to see him again. Maybe her life had been more peaceful that way. Ethan hadn't even spoken to his mother on the phone in over a year.

"Can I come in?"

"Of course." Kay Jordan leaned her head over one shoulder. "Richard! Ethan is here."

Ethan stepped into the entryway and closed the door behind him while he waited for his father to appear. The paint on the walls looked reasonably fresh, and a vase on an accent table held a vivid array of flowers, probably from the grocery store. The accent rug was plush and bright with color. Hanging from a decorative ribbon was a framed photograph of Ethan's older brother with his wife and son — neither of whom Ethan had ever met. He wasn't sure what he'd expected — that life would have frozen the day he left? Obviously his parents had gone about their lives.

Richard Jordan came into the hall in a faded cardigan with a newspaper folded under one arm.

"Hello, Ethan."

"Dad."

"I'm surprised to see you here."

Ethan didn't know what to say. He heard the TV.

"I'll make some coffee." Kay smoothed her gray hair, still cropped at shoulder length as it always had been when its hue was darker.

Coffee would only make him more jittery, but Ethan didn't stop her. He could nearly feel both Nicole and Quinn nudging him into his parents' living room to accept their hospitality. Ethan sat in a chair at a right angle from the one his father had always preferred. This would be easier if he didn't have to look Richard in the eye.

"Dad," Ethan said, "would you mind if we muted the sound? I'd like to talk to you and Mom."

Richard huffed slightly, but he picked up the remote, and the droning from the television dropped out of the room.

"I didn't know you were in town," Richard said.

Ethan said nothing. Would anything be different if Ethan had let his parents know he was coming? If he had stayed with them?

To Ethan's relief, just then Kay returned with a tray of sandwiches and cookies to go with the coffee. Ethan forced himself to answer the perfunctory questions about his career before clearing his throat and unfolding the papers and explaining each one in chronological sequence.

His mother blinked in disbelief as she looked at the dates on the documents and discovered that she was a year old when her parents married and nearly two when her name changed from Kathleen Pease to Kay Petersen.

Richard scrunched his face toward his wife. "You're adopted and you never knew it?"

Kay picked up the adoption decree. "I used

to ask my mother to show me pictures of when I was a baby. I'm not so old that people didn't routinely have portraits made of their babies. The answer was always that she didn't know where they were. And then when she died and I went through her things, I never found a single one. But both of my younger brothers had baby pictures."

"So you have no recollection of the man who claimed to be Dennis Pease?" Ethan asked.

"Claimed?" Richard pointed at the birth certificate. "His name is right there."

Ethan nodded. "He might not have known himself."

"Known what?" his mother asked.

"I think he was Merrill Tabor."

"Tabor?" Richard sat up straight in his chair. "Like Tabor Avenue? Tabor Orchards? Tabor Mills?"

Ethan nodded.

Merrill Tabor was not supposed to survive. That's why his father needed a healthy infant of the same age. Ethan suspected the two children also must have had some resemblance.

What Ethan had not yet figured out was what had become of little Dennis Pease once he was taken into the Tabor household.

And if the infirm child had not been buried — regardless of what name was used at the cemetery — then whose child was in that grave?

And who was the man standing in front of it who looked so much like Ethan?

12:13 p.m.

Liam couldn't make himself go inside Our Savior Community Church. His justification was that after going home to clean up, he'd arrived too late for the start of the service, though he had dawdled intentionally to create this excuse. Then he told himself the parking lot would be full, left his car a few blocks away, and ambled to the church in no particular hurry. Eventually Liam reasoned there was no point in going in, and he sat on the cement steps outside the front entrance until an usher pushed open the doors and worshippers spilled out of the building.

Liam was only there because it was part of his deal with Cooper. That was hours ago. What was taking so long?

The day's weather carried no vestige of yesterday's wreckage. Midday sun illumined branches stripped of leaves the previous afternoon and spread its pervasive glare as if the occasion were only another mild September afternoon. Puddles formed in worn depressions of earth and asphalt bore witness to the brief drenching rain that followed the howling wind, but most of the water had run off as quickly as it came down. Debris, however, was widespread. Television meteorologists named the places where the tornado had touched down, and Hidden Falls escaped all the lists. No structures had splintered or collapsed. Nevertheless, a force beyond anyone's control left its evidence in papers scattered in the wind, downed branches, trash cans rolling through the streets blocks from where they belonged, tumbled signs, broken glass, shingles in all the wrong places.

The church had not been spared. Liam noticed now that the second-story window above the main entrance had cracked, and the church's sign on the corner was missing most of its letters. A tent pole was lodged in the bushes across the front of the building, carried all the way from the back lawn. Most of the booths at yesterday's health fair had been abandoned before they were fully disassembled. Liam hadn't made much of an effort to deconstruct the tent he'd occupied, choosing instead to heed the warning to take cover.

Liam wasn't sure what to do. He had to stay. This is where Cooper would come — and he'd be expecting to find Liam hard at work. Liam moved out of the way of Bruce and Raisa Gallagher, who carried their two little girls down the front steps. He looked up and spotted Henry Healy from the sporting goods store.

"You here to help?" Henry raised his bushy

eyebrows.

Liam nodded. “Figured there would be plenty to do.”

“You figured right. Somebody’s gone for pizzas to feed the crew, but Pastor Matt wants everyone out on the back lawn as soon as possible.”

“Then that’s where I’ll go.”

“First come with me to the shed for a couple of the big trash bins,” Henry said.

Liam followed. Henry unlocked the shed, and they rolled two massive waste receptacles out to the lawn. Matthew Kendrick righted a collapsed table, and a couple of women folded back the tops of pizza boxes and set out a stack of paper plates. Liam wondered if anyone had more recent information about Lauren than he did. If anyone asked, he would tell what he knew. She’d come through the night well and shouldn’t be in the hospital too much longer.

The group of workers gathered around the pizza table. Liam hung back. Pastor Matt whistled for attention.

“We’re going to give thanks,” Matt said, “for willing workers, for the fact that more people weren’t hurt in yesterday’s storm, and for the ministry of Lauren Nock, who helps so many people. I want to offer the opportunity for any who wish to pray aloud for Lauren’s healing and recovery, and then we will bless the food.”

Liam bowed his head but looked out of the sides of his eyes at the people circling the table. He hadn't done this in years, but something about it comforted him. People cared about Lauren, and their heartfelt words were persuasive that God cared. A soft angst oozed through Liam. He couldn't think of anyone who would want to pray for him. Besides, his mess was more complicated than praying for healing.

He wished Cooper would show up. Instead of taking a slice of pizza, Liam picked up a large, thick plastic trash bag and moved to the outskirts of the lawn. Soggy papers littered the grass — blank forms and food wrappers and blurred recipes. Liam picked up one piece or sometimes a fistful at a time and stuffed it all in his bag. Others joined him. A chain saw started up, and a group of men attacked the fallen tree limb that easily could have killed Liam's brother. Someone backed a pickup truck onto the lawn; volunteers tossed bent poles and ripped canvas and broken folding chairs into the truck's bed to be hauled to the dump. When Liam filled his bag, he tied it closed, tossed it into one of the huge receptacles, and pulled another bag off the roll. He murmured greetings to people who were no doubt surprised to see him there but offered no explanation. After filling another bag, Liam switched to helping stack the pieces of oak that the chain saw trimmed to size. A couple of trustees inspected all the trees on the lot and designated a few more branches to be cut down before they fell.

Liam wiped an arm across his forehead, drawing sweat away from his eyes. When he looked up again, Cooper fell into step beside him. They crossed to a quieter corner of the lawn.

"I only have a preliminary opinion," Cooper said.

Liam welcomed any encouragement he could get.

"It would have helped," Cooper said, "to have the second note for comparison."

"The storm," Liam said. He'd never meant to leave yesterday without picking up the envelope from where he'd dropped it in the box of health brochures.

"I know." Cooper stooped and picked up a two-foot piece of tree limb. "The note you did have uses a mixture of complete sentences and fragments, but everything is spelled correctly and punctuated. That seems to indicate a level of sophistication."

Liam had never thought of blackmailers as sophisticated. *Sinister* was the word he would have chosen.

"There's a certain cadence to it," Cooper said, "a certain structure in the three lines."

"And what does that mean? Is it a clue?"

Cooper cocked his head. "It might indicate a person with a mathematical bent. Or a highly organized person."

"Like Jessica, you mean."

Cooper put up one hand. "I'm not pointing fingers. I'm just giving you the preliminary profile I got from my buddy."

Liam swallowed. "What else did your friend say?"

"It's a person who likes to be in control, to call the shots."

In other words, just like Jessica. "I've been an idiot, Cooper."

"Yeah, well, I've been saying that for thirty years, but in this case, let's not jump to conclusions." Cooper adjusted the Cubs hat on his head. "I kept my inquiries general. If you want to take this further, the sheriff is going to want to know more."

"They'll suspect me."

"Maybe. But do you have a choice?"

"Do I need a lawyer?"

"You haven't been accused of anything yet."

Liam looked away. The men with the chain saw dropped a tree limb.

"I didn't do anything wrong," Liam said, "except be stupid in love."

"Innocent until proven guilty."

"Why doesn't that comfort me? I've been over those accounts enough times that I could practically prove myself guilty. It won't take much to make a case against me."

"If there's a crime," Cooper said, "I can't be complicit in concealing it."

"I know." Liam had set his own course when he confided in his brother. "When can you get more information for me?"

"Probably tomorrow."

"You'll have someone look at the accounts?" Liam asked.

Cooper nodded. "If that's what you want. We'll need your cooperation. But there won't be any turning back from what we find."

"So maybe I should put Jack Parker on retainer after all."

Cooper let out a controlled breath. "I'm not going to advise you on that."

"You don't like Jack."

Cooper pressed his lips together. "Not too much, no. But that's no indication of his legal abilities."

"I'm innocent, Cooper. Embarrassed, and probably naive, but innocent."

1:22 p.m.

Dani wasn't leaving. It had taken her all morning to get this far. Apparently Sunday mornings at the Hidden Falls hospital were not highly administrative, but she had eventually wormed her way into the human resources offices at one end of the third floor.

Green shoes.

Why hadn't she realized it sooner?

The assistant to the human resources director blinked and squinted and gingerly rubbed a spot in one eyelid.

He should just take out those stupid contact lenses, Dani thought. People did the oddest things in the name of vanity. Dani had no pity for someone who continued to cause their own discomfort.

"I just want you to help me find this man." Dani crossed her legs and her arms. If her body language made her appear hostile, all the better in this situation.

The assistant looked at her and tilted his head. "You do realize that we don't track employees according to the style of their footwear."

What an idiot.

"I don't care how you track employees as long as we find this one. Male. Thirties. Dark hair." And green shoes.

He pulled open a desk drawer. "We have a form appropriate to situations like this one. If you fill it out in detail, we will call the incident to the attention of the shift managers, and they will remind their staff of our policy."

"What policy is that?"

"Defer to hospital guests in the use of elevators, stairwells, and common areas, except in the case of medical emergency."

This guy could probably quote every policy in the five binders on the shelf behind him — if Dani didn't choke him first.

"I mean no disrespect," she said carefully, "but I am not here to fill out a form. I want to know who this man is."

"And no disrespect to you, Miss Roose, but I can't point fingers at employees. This is a hospital. We are a significant employer in this community. We have policies in place for the sake of everyone's safety and confidentiality."

Dani uncrossed her limbs and then folded them in the other direction. "Dark blue scrubs. What is that code for around here?"

"Code?"

"You know what I'm talking about." He couldn't stand behind patient safety on this question. A system of colors was supposed to help patients identify types of caregivers and employees.

One eye twitched when he met her gaze. "Dark blue is the uniform of our well-trained patient support staff."

Dani didn't need this guy. If she had to, she would ask every employee on duty in the hospital. Someone would have noticed a patient support employee who wore green tennis shoes.

It was a daring touch, those green shoes. *Catch me if you can,* they said.

Well, she would.

In a hospital, green shoes would pass for a statement of quirky personality. In the woods outside Dani's lake cabin, they would pass for camouflage — especially in the dark.

She stood up. "I commend you. You've done your job well and have been only the most minimal help to me. Perhaps you would like me to write that on a form."

Dani gave the door an extra tug on her way out to make sure it slammed.

When Green Shoes nearly knocked Nicole over and stole the elevator, Dani had raced up the stairwell. But she was too late. Both elevators were idle and the hall around them empty. Ignoring signs about where she was and was not permitted to enter, Dani strode through the corridors glancing into rooms and under desks. She loitered in the cafeteria watching people come and go and made another round of the hallways. Eventually she made inquiries that sent her to the fruitless session in the hospital's administrative offices.

Dani hadn't gotten a good look at Green Shoes's face, but she had an idea what it looked like. She paused in the hall to take out her phone and scroll through a set of photos she had transferred to it two days ago. They came originally from Ethan's camera, but Dani had cropped and enhanced small pieces of the images. Clothing, height, body shape, face — she had tried to capture it all. But she hadn't thought about the feet. Now nothing on her phone looked like it would hint at footwear.

But she had the side of a face, with one eye peering out from leaves hanging over the forehead. Olive skin. Dark hair. High cheek bones. Brown eyes.

It wasn't a photo Dani could show anyone and ask, "Do you know him?"

She practiced putting a smile on her face and sauntered away from the administrative offices and into a patient area.

"I'm looking for a guy who works in patient support services." Dani smiled at the nurses at their station. "Dark hair, wears green shoes?"

The nurses shrugged. Dani thanked them anyway and moved on down the hall to a nurse standing at a computer and filling little paper cups with various assortments of medications.

"Maybe you can help me?" Dani gave her description again, but the meds nurse just shook her head.

Dani made another stop at the end of the hall that yielded nothing. She turned around and headed back toward the elevators. A young woman in maroon scrubs emerged from a patient room and tossed a wad of sheets into a hamper stretched open on a cart.

"You looking for Bobby?" the woman said.

Dani smiled. She'd been asking the nurses. How many people on the housekeeping staff had she walked past?

Bobby.

"Yes," Dani said. "Have you seen him?"

"They keep him pretty busy on Two. He doesn't get up here to Three much."

"Oh. Okay, thanks. I'll look for him there."

"If he's not on Two, try the basement. He transports patients down for X-rays and scans."

"Thank you. You've been very helpful." Dani wondered if this young housekeeper was aware of hospital policies safeguarding employees from wild, aggravated strangers.

Dani strode to the elevators and punched the button. When she emerged on the floor below, she looked both directions. She had abandoned Nicole six hours ago. Pretty soon she was going to feel guilty about that.

When she ducked her head into the second floor waiting room and saw no one she knew, Dani decided to check on how Lauren was doing. Maybe Cooper was there holding her hand or something.

He wasn't. Instead, Dani found Nicole at Lauren's bedside. Lauren was sitting up in bed, picking at a turkey sandwich on wheat, red grapes, and cottage cheese. She looked good. Maybe Cooper had satisfied himself that Lauren was fine and dared to leave the premises.

"Sorry about this morning," Dani mumbled.

"As you can see, I survived."

Nicole looked none the worse for wear to Dani. "I thought Cooper might be here."

Lauren shrugged. "Haven't seen him all morning."

Lauren didn't fool Dani with her nonchalance. She was disappointed Cooper wasn't there. As soon as Dani found Bobby Green Shoes, she would track down Cooper and tell him to get himself back to the hospital. She was going to need him to arrest Bobby, anyway.

"How's the head?" Dani asked.

"Hurts. But they say I'm better."

"They're probably right." Dani looked at the clock, wondering what time Bobby had come on duty and when his shift would end. If she didn't find him in the hospital, he could be anywhere.

There was no place to sit, which suited Dani. She was glad to know Lauren was in good shape, all things considered, but she didn't want to feel obliged to sit and chitchat.

She heard the wheels of a gurney in the hall and reflexively looked toward the rapid rhythmic rattle of emptiness.

It *was* empty.

And it was being pushed by a man wearing green tennis shoes.

Dani bolted into the hall. "Hey!"

Bobby glanced over his shoulder, showing half his face. He couldn't know that he'd given Dani the exact pose she needed to be sure the face matched the image on her phone.

Dani ran with her phone in her hand, taking one photo after another. *Click. Click.*

Bobby put the gurney between himself and Dani and gave it a shove. She leaped out of the way. *Click. Click. Click.* Dani ran hard. Staff and visitors in the corridor pressed up against the walls. Bobby was headed for the stairwell, and Dani intended not to let him reach it. She dove for his ankles, and he tumbled. Dani scrambled to sit astride his chest.

The elevator doors opened, and Cooper stepped out.

7:17 p.m.

Ethan opened a deep lower kitchen drawer and found the dish towels neatly folded, just as he'd expected. They weren't the same dish towels as ten years ago, of course, but floral patterns in blues and greens still dominated the collection. Beside him, his mother rinsed the platter she'd served baked chicken on.

"You don't use the dishwasher?" he asked. She used to.

She turned the platter over and rinsed the other side. "It's only the two of us, and I cook fairly simply these days. It seems easier to wash up the old-fashioned way."

Ethan took the platter, dried it, and put it away. So far he hadn't yet opened a cupboard and not found essentially the same contents they'd contained since the Jordan family first moved into the house when he was a little boy.

His father, of course, sat in the living room watching the TV. His mother was making an effort, Ethan realized. Perhaps she always had. Perhaps she had never shared her husband's passivity and disinterest in their children. Because she had never put her foot down and made her husband do the right thing for their boys, Ethan had lumped her in with him. Now he realized the dynamic of their relationship was more complex.

This day had proven anything could be more complex than it seemed on the surface.

Kay was eager to please her younger son, pointing out that she still kept his favorite chewy chocolate chip cookies in the cookie jar and showing him that a houseplant he'd once given her for her birthday was thriving and enormous. Ethan hadn't expected to spend the whole afternoon or sit at his mother's dining room table after all these years. When he arrived, he hadn't thought beyond her right to know the truth of her own heritage. The way she paled surprised him. His medical training made him want to check the pulse in her wrist, but he refrained. He settled for restoring color to her face simply by not leaving an hour after he got there.

The antique clock in the dining room sounded.

"I suppose you'll need to go." Kay wrung out the dishrag and used it to wipe down the counter.

"Soon." Ethan neatly hung the damp dish towel through the round wooden hoop above the sink. He wanted to see Nicole one more time. Then he would have to make a decision about driving straight through to Columbus or sleeping a few hours first.

"I'm glad you came."

"Me, too." Ethan put his hands behind him and leaned against the counter. "Mom, how are you feeling about what I told you today?"

Kay scrubbed at a stubborn spot on the stove. "Your grandmother used to call me Katie-bug."

"I never knew that."

"I'd forgotten until today. My father didn't like it. He scolded her once about it. Do you know that's probably my earliest memory of him?"

"I'm sorry it wasn't happier."

"I've been thinking about that all afternoon. My mother still called me Katie-bug when we were alone, but she made a big game of how it was our secret. But do you know what I think?"

"What's that?"

"I think my birth father gave me that nickname. Dennis Pease or Merrill Tabor or whoever he was. I think my dad was trying to erase the fact that my mother had been married before, that I'd had another father."

Ethan scratched the back of his neck. "Well,

I suppose he loved you. He adopted you, after all."

"I never doubted he loved me." Kay rinsed out the rag and draped it over the faucet. "But why should he be jealous of a man who was dead and someone I was too young to remember anyway?"

"Because your mother remembered him, I suppose. She'd loved him first."

Kay took in the thought. "I hadn't got that far in figuring it out."

Ethan said nothing but only watched the muscles of his mother's face move as her next words formed in her mind. Outside the window above the kitchen sink, the day had sunk into darkness.

"I'm the same person I always was," Kay said. "Blood doesn't make you who you are."

Ethan had never thought of his mother as pensive. As she looked into the darkness, wistfulness crept through her expression.

"I'm curious," she said. "I'll admit that."

"About your birth father?"

"No. Maybe someday I'd like to know what happened to him, but I was thinking of the Tabors."

As far as Ethan knew, there hadn't been any Tabors in Hidden Falls in decades. Their businesses had been sold or merged through the decades.

"Somewhere out there," his mother said, "is a man who thinks he's Merrill Tabor — if he's even still alive. I guess he'd be close to eighty. Maybe he has children and grandchildren and great-grandchildren. And none of them knows what you and I know now."

"Maybe," Ethan said. "It's ironic that you and Dad ended up in Hidden Falls so long after all this happened."

"I suppose so, though I lived here when I was very small."

"What?" That didn't make sense. Ethan's parents had moved to Hidden Falls together.

"I told you I went through my mother's things when she died."

"Right. You were looking for baby pictures."

"I was looking for all sorts of things, anything I might find that would make me feel close to her. I found an old letter addressed to her, with a return address from Hidden Falls."

Words refused to form on Ethan's tongue.

"It was just a note," Kay said. "Somebody forwarded an electric bill with a few cheery words about how lovely it had been to know my parents for their few months in Hidden Falls."

Few months. "When was this?"

"Judging by the postmark, before I was old enough to go to school. Now I wonder if my mother knew something — if my birth father knew something and might have told her. Maybe that's why they came here."

It hadn't occurred to Ethan that either of

the boys who had been exchanged — a premise that remained an unproved theory — would have learned the truth.

"I guess there's no way to know that," he said.

"And I guess it doesn't matter anyway." She touched his cheek. "I know you need to go."

Ethan took his mother in his arms. Very little mattered in that moment except that they were together. Why had he thought all these years that his mother understood so little of the world? That she hadn't crafted a life for herself? He inhaled the fruity scent of her shampoo.

"I'll come back," he whispered.

"I'll be waiting." She kissed his face.

Ethan moved into the living room.

Richard looked up. "Are you leaving?"

Ethan nodded.

"Don't forget your documents," his mother said.

Ethan picked them up. "Would you like to keep them?"

Kay shook her head. "You'll do the right thing with them."

Ethan picked up the papers from the end table. His father stood up to shake his hand, but his eyes didn't leave ESPN. Ten or fifteen years ago, Ethan would have found only insult in his father's habit. Today it didn't matter.

His phone rang as he stepped out the front

door and began the walk around the block to where he'd left his car parked in front of Quinn's house.

"Hi, Nicole."

"Where are you?"

"Just leaving my parents' house. Where are you?"

"At the hospital."

"Still? I thought they would have discharged Lauren by now."

"Something happened, Ethan. She was doing fine, and then all of a sudden — I don't even know. They made everybody get out of the room. Cooper's going crazy, the nurse is trying to find Dr. Glass, people are going in and out of Lauren's room. Some doctor from the ER came up."

Ethan's phone beeped in his ear to alert to him to a call waiting. He pulled the phone away from his ear long enough to look at the caller's name.

GONZALEZ.

He let it go to voice mail and began to jog.

"You have to get over here, Ethan," Nicole said.

"I'm coming."

They ended the call, and while he ran toward his car, Ethan listened to the voice mail Dr. Gonzalez left.

"If I find out you are still in that Podunk town, I will throw the book at you. I want to hear from you in the next three minutes.

Whatever shenanigans you've been up to are over, Dr. Jordan. I seriously doubt you can offer any persuasive justification for your professional negligence, but if you are not in my office at six o'clock tomorrow morning, you can consider your career ended."

11
When Memory Came

Monday
4:03 a.m.

"So I'm good to go?" Ethan rubbed his eyes as he sat up on the sofa in the staff lounge at the Hidden Falls hospital. He looked up at Dr. Glass.

"How long have you been sleeping?" Dr. Glass asked.

"On and off about six hours." It wasn't much for almost forty-eight hours since Ethan's last full night of slumber, but exhaustion had made the sofa more restful than he'd expected, and only twice had anyone else come into the room in the middle of the night.

"The hospital board has cleared you for emergency privileges." Dr. Glass removed his spectacles and rubbed the sides of his nose between thumb and forefinger. "I'm getting too old for this middle-of-the night stuff. I'm grateful you're here, but I'll be responsible if you operate when you haven't slept."

"I slept." Ethan threw off the blanket one of the nurses had scrounged up for him. "I know we only met a couple of days ago. I appreciate your willingness to go to bat for me, and I don't intend to let you down." He wasn't going to let Lauren down, either.

"I'll be in the OR," Dr. Glass said. "That was one of the conditions of emergency privileges. But the scalpel will be in your hand."

"Thank you." Ethan would need someone there who knew his way around the unfamiliar facility. There was no time for tours and orientation.

"Your association with Dr. Gonzalez's program went a long way to commend you," Dr. Glass said.

They must not have called Gonzalez, Ethan thought. They would have gotten an earful. Nobody wanted that in the middle of the night. The hospital board members probably wanted to go back to sleep.

"How soon do we cut?" Ethan stood up.

"They're getting the OR ready now. The nurses tell me some of your friends are still down the hall."

"I'll go talk to them."

"Fine. I'll make sure the paperwork is above reproach and meet you in the OR."

Dr. Glass left, his long white coat flapping over his green scrubs. Ethan crossed to the kitchenette, found a clean tall tumbler, and downed two full portions of cold water from the faucet over the sink. The hydration made him feel more alert almost immediately.

Ethan went down the corridor to the waiting room and stepped from hallway brightness into the dim shadows. The only light came from a low table lamp in one corner. Nicole and Cooper were the two who had refused to go home when even Ethan said he was going to find a place to sleep. Nicole was stretched out on a couch with a throw pillow, and Cooper sat in a chair with his legs extended in front of him and his head tilted against the wall. Ethan paused in the doorway long enough to hear the even breath of sleep. Nicole had been ignoring her own need for rest and healing all week. Ethan was glad to see her conked out, her jaw slack and her mouth open slightly. For a moment, he considered not waking them. In a little while, he could come back with news that the surgery was over. But Cooper stirred and his eyes opened.

When he saw Ethan, Cooper reached over to nudge Nicole's leg. "How is she?"

Nicole pushed up on one elbow.

"They're going to let me do the procedure," Ethan said. "I don't expect it will take very long. I have every expectation Lauren will be fine."

"I want to see her." Cooper got to his feet.

"I doubt she'll know you're there," Ethan said.

"That isn't the point." Nicole reached for her crutches. "We'll know. Sylvia will know."

"All right."

They moved quietly through the hall down to Lauren's room, Nicole's crutches thumping against the tile and Cooper barely able to keep himself from running ahead of her measured pace. At the head of the bed, Sylvia was alert and lit by the bank of lights that stayed on all the time with patients who needed extra attention from the nursing staff.

It had been Sylvia who realized Lauren was not simply sleeping. Though Sylvia had been able to rouse Lauren and alerted the nurse, Lauren was extremely lethargic and barely responsive to questions. The possibility of being discharged evaporated into the reality that pressure was building on Lauren's brain. Dr. Glass had returned to the hospital about the same time Ethan did and ordered another scan.

"She hasn't woken up," Sylvia said softly. "I call her name every now and then, but she doesn't answer."

"We're going to fix that," Ethan said.

"We should pray for her." Cooper moved to the bedside and lifted Lauren's limp hand.

"The OR should be ready any minute," Ethan said. Prayer was not going to heal Lauren. She had a bleed in her brain and treatment protocol was proven and clear.

"Please," Sylvia said. "Just until they come for her."

Other than his own unbelief, Ethan could think of no reason to deny them the comfort of their faith. It would do no good in a medical situation, but neither would it cause harm.

"All right," he said, "but it won't be long."

Nicole shuffled over to the far side of the bed. Sylvia moved to the foot and put her hands on Lauren's blanketed ankles. Surrounding her on three sides, Lauren's friends bowed their heads.

Ethan stepped back and turned his head toward the door to watch for the transit staff. He didn't listen to the words Cooper murmured. In fact, he was surprised Cooper had been the one to suggest prayer. Cooper didn't strike Ethan as the faithful sort. Then again, Ethan would be hard-pressed to describe the faithful sort, and crisis tended to make people hedge their bets in favor of religion. He'd seen it before.

A young man in blue scrubs and soft-soled shoes entered. "I'm here from transit."

Ethan cleared his throat, and the others raised their heads. The transit employee looked at the name on the papers in his hands and checked the hospital bracelet around Lauren's wrist.

"I'm Dr. Jordan," Ethan said. "I'll be doing the surgery."

The young man looked doubtful, and Ethan didn't blame him. Ethan wore street clothes and had no hospital ID badge.

"My job is just to take her down to pre-op." The man began exchanging the stationary machine that monitored Lauren's vitals for the portable model that traveled with the bed. "After that you can take it up with them."

"I'll come find you as soon as it's over." Ethan herded Cooper and the others toward the door.

"I hope you don't mind if we pray for you, too," the mayor said.

Ethan shrugged. If it made them feel better, what was the point of protesting? What mattered to him was the confidence that he was well trained — and that this was not a particularly difficult procedure for a neurosurgeon. Based on Lauren's symptoms and information available from routine tests, Ethan was hopeful he would only need to bore two holes and suction the excess fluid away. Ethan did procedures like this every week.

Cooper had his phone out. "I'm going to call Liam and Dani."

"I'm sure they're asleep," Ethan said.

"I need them here. They'll come."

Ethan shrugged again. Liam and Dani couldn't do anything, but he wasn't going to argue with Cooper. His focus was his patient.

The young man from transit released the brakes on Lauren's bed and swung it toward the door.

5:16 a.m.

"Sylvia, trade places with me." Nicole leaned on the end of the waiting room couch and stood up on her good foot.

Sylvia was satisfied with the chair she occupied, but since Nicole was already up, she complied with trading seats.

"It's not a bad sofa for a doze," Nicole said. "You should at least try to catnap."

"I feel surprisingly good." Before Lauren's downturn ten hours ago, Sylvia left Lauren in the company of Nicole and Cooper and went home for a few hours. She changed clothes, ate a good meal, checked on her mother, and straightened up two guest rooms — one for Lauren and one for Nicole. Sylvia even managed to work in a short nap before returning to the hospital to await Lauren's discharge and bring her home.

Beside the bed, Nicole believed Lauren to be sleeping. Cooper had stepped out of the room. The peaceful scene erupted when Sylvia called Lauren's name and got no answer.

Sylvia, Cooper, and Nicole hadn't spoken much since resuming their vigil in the second-floor waiting room. They were all equally exhausted from the last two days, but for Sylvia, at least, the spike of worry fractured soon enough. Even Dr. Glass agreed his patient was fortunate Dr. Ethan Jordan was available for the procedure, and the bleed was slow. Lauren was in capable hands, and ultimately she was in God's hands.

Sylvia had a harder time letting go of her worry about Quinn. In the eight days since his disappearance, Sylvia's hours filled with her duties as mayor, reopening her shop, checking on her mother, and now being on hand as Lauren's closest family. Undulating beneath the rise and fall of sunrise and sunset was swirling disappointment that she couldn't call and confide in Quinn. She didn't know what happened to him, so she didn't know whose hands he was in.

Quinn was still in God's hands, Sylvia reminded herself. Somehow that assurance was less comforting without the visible form of a trained physician like Ethan Jordan. She closed her eyes to pray.

Squeaking steps in the hall carried in Liam and Dani. Cooper perked up. Dani dropped into a chair next to him.

Liam was neatly dressed in pressed khakis and a dark green polo shirt. And he looked rested — more rested than Sylvia had seen him appear in the last week. His eyes, though sad, had lost the frantic expression Sylvia saw the day he came into her shop and on Saturday at the health fair before the storm hit. The tension had vacated his shoulders, and he offered his brother an embrace.

Now they were five. Still silent, for the most part. Still waiting. Still captive to their own thoughts.

Nurse Wacker entered the room, and as if on a conductor's cue, all five of them sat erect.

"I see the gang's all back." The nurse looked at Dani and smiled. "I hear I missed quite a tackle yesterday afternoon."

Liam furrowed his forehead into four rows. "Excuse me? I don't understand."

"Dani knows," the nurse said. "Nicole and Cooper, too."

Sylvia sighed. Why was it that lately she was the last to hear about anything?

"Dani took down one of our transit employees," the nurse said.

"I had a good reason," Dani muttered.

"Is Lauren out of surgery?" Cooper asked.

"Not quite," Nurse Wacker said. "But Dr. Jordan wanted me to tell you —"

A shriek pierced the early morning tranquility, jolting everyone but the nurse.

"That will be Room 231, right on schedule," she said.

After a few seconds of silence, a fresh scream filled the hall.

"I'm sorry," the nurse said. "I'll have to go help settle her down or she'll keep doing that and have everyone on the wing awake."

She turned and left before any of them

could protest.

Liam turned to Dani. "What was she talking about? Who did you tackle?"

"Bobby somebody." Dani leaned back in her chair with her hands on her hips. "And I'd do it again."

Sylvia folded her hands in her lap. "Maybe this would be a good time to hear the story." She was the mayor, after all.

"I tracked down the guy who put that hole in my boat," Dani said. "He works here. Somebody had to catch him."

Sylvia's eyes moved to Cooper. "Oh? I didn't hear about this." Even while she was sitting with Lauren, Sylvia's cell phone had been within reach. If even one of the recent crimes in Hidden Falls was solved, the mayor would like to know about it.

"There wasn't much to hear about," Cooper said. "Witnesses say Dani assaulted Robert Doerr."

Dani shuffled her feet. "Think of it as a citizen's arrest."

"We don't do that around here." Cooper's voice remained as calm as it always did. "I wish you'd clued me in to what you suspected."

"Was I supposed to let him walk out of the hospital?" Dani glared. "You could give me credit for nabbing him."

Sylvia tilted her head at Cooper. "Is he the guy?"

Cooper shrugged. "Innocent until proven guilty."

"Did you arrest him?"

"We took him in, but it was because he took a swing at me when he was trying to get away."

"Sounds like suspicious behavior to me," Sylvia said.

"I wasn't in uniform," Cooper said. "The man had just been knocked down by a stranger."

"I can see your point." Sylvia glanced at Dani.

"Whose side are you on?" Dani rolled her eyes. "This could be the guy who smashed up your store, too."

Sylvia knew better than to try to persuade Dani when she was in this kind of mood. "Cooper, if you took him in, what happened?"

"The sheriff ordered his release a few hours later. We don't have anything to tie him to Dani's boat."

"I'll show you the pictures," Dani muttered.

"You didn't even take the pictures you think incriminate him," Cooper said, "and happening on somebody out in the woods is hardly the same as catching him at the scene of the crime."

"Did you even question him?"

"We didn't get much out of him before he played the 'I want a lawyer' card." Cooper gave a sly smile. "But we got his fingerprints."

Dani elbowed him. "Don't give me false hope."

"We can at least see if he has a record, or if he matches any of the prints we've taken."

Sylvia inhaled slowly. "You mean in my shop?"

Cooper nodded.

"And Quinn's car?"

He nodded again.

Sylvia wasn't sure if she hoped the prints would match any in Quinn's car or not. Fingerprints belonging to somebody with a record might point to foul play. While Sylvia couldn't imagine why Quinn would decide to pick up and go to St. Louis after not leaving the county for more than thirty years, she preferred that mystery to the possibility that someone meant him harm.

"You know you can't get prints from my boat," Dani said. "What are you going to do about that?"

"One step at a time," Cooper answered.

"What motive would tie everything together?" Sylvia asked. She could understand the thefts, but putting Dani's life in danger was a different sort of crime, a fiercer vandalism even than the unbridled destruction in Sylvia's store.

"We're working on that," Cooper said, "but sometimes people like to see what they can get away with. I doubt Dani was supposed to figure out it wasn't an ordinary leak in an old rowboat."

Quinn's disappearance.

The vandalism in Sylvia's store.

Dani's boat wrecked.

Lauren in surgery.

Sylvia rubbed one eye. "Cooper, I'm confident you'll do what you think is right. But if you get any matches on the prints, I hope you'll keep me in the loop."

"Yes, Mayor."

Liam was quiet but peaceful. Dani, usually unflapped, was visibly irritated. Cooper would have to go to work in a couple of hours, but his mind was on Lauren. Nicole hadn't left the confines of the hospital since she and Ethan followed the ambulance from the church the day before yesterday.

If Quinn would only come home. Or contact somebody.

"What happened to Lauren's phone?" Sylvia asked. "Do we still have that voice mail recording?"

Cooper shook his head. "It took one whack too many — from a tree. I don't think we'll get anything off of it."

"I know what I heard," Nicole said. "It was Quinn's tune, but I don't know who was whistling."

Nurse Wacker returned and stood in the doorway. The hall was quiet again.

Nicole leaned forward. "What's the word?"

"Lauren should be going into recovery soon. Mayor, you'll be welcome to see her then. The rest of you will have to wait until Dr. Jordan gives the okay."

"How is Dr. Jordan?" Nicole asked. "I mean, operating here for the first time."

"I think we can presume the surgeon is fine." The nurse left.

Sylvia smiled, watching Nicole settle back into her chair. If Quinn didn't come home soon, he was going to miss the unfolding reunion between two of his favorite people.

7:46 a.m.

Lauren recognized the sensation as what came just before she would wake. Light from somewhere saturated the backs of her eyelids with a thick orange haze, and she could tell she was lying flat.

The hospital.

Surgery.

Aunt Sylvia.

Sylvia had spoken to her, leaning over the bed and looking down at Lauren's face. How long ago had all this happened?

Lauren felt the mattress beneath her, the blanket over her legs, and the itch at the side of her head.

No, not an itch. Something was there. She raised an arm — and felt the hindering grasp of fingers around her wrist. Her eyes fluttered open.

The word formed in Lauren's mind. *Cooper.* Not Sylvia. Where was Sylvia?

More words formed in her mind. "My aunt?"

"I talked her into going to the cafeteria for breakfast."

Lauren realized she'd spoken aloud. She swallowed and ran a dry tongue over chapped lips.

Cooper guided her hand back to the mattress. "I don't think Ethan would be happy if you pulled out the drain he went to so much trouble to put in."

"I didn't know." What else didn't she know? Her eyes searched Cooper's. "What did Ethan do?"

"The simplest procedure possible. Two very small holes and a drain that he wants to leave in place for a while."

That didn't sound so bad. Considering. Her headache was better, and she didn't feel like she was going to empty her stomach involuntarily.

"Your aunt said you were awake earlier," Cooper said.

Lauren was uncertain whether she was actually nodding, but she meant to. She had been awake. She remembered now. It was in another room. Recovery. Lauren stared at Cooper, trying to make out his features. Perhaps the fuzziness was due to lingering anesthesia, but it might just as well be because she was so nearsighted.

"My glasses," she said.

Cooper winced. "Broken when you fell."

Lauren remembered now. All day yesterday she'd instinctively looked around for her glasses. But both pair had been broken in the last few days. She wished she could see Cooper more clearly. When she thanked him properly for getting Christopher out of one tree and then throwing himself between her and another as it splintered, she would like to be able to look into his eyes. Instead, she turned her palm up to squeeze his hand. They had run together on Saturday afternoon, holding hands, but it had not been a time to notice the softness of his touch or the gentleness of his grasp. Now she did.

She hadn't held hands with a man for a long time. Saturday didn't count. Lauren wasn't sure this counted, either. Only three days ago she had tried her best to avoid spending a moment longer than necessary with Cooper Elliott. Now she resisted the creeping disappointment that he would likely have to leave.

What day was this? Not Sunday. That was yesterday. Monday. Her impulse was to shake off the fog wrapped around her brain, but she remembered the fall, the concussion, the headache, the promise of surgery. Fading away when it became too hard to remain alert.

"I remember you prayed," she said. "When was that?"

"A few hours ago. We thought you were . . ."

"Unconscious."

"Yes."

"I just know that I heard you. Thank you."

"You're welcome."

Lauren heard the waver in his voice. "And I keep hearing Quinn's tune. Will it help you find him?" She tried to hum the notes, but no sound came out of her throat.

"I think," Cooper said, "that you should be a lot more well before we talk about that."

He was probably right. "Are you going to work today?"

Cooper squeezed her hand and said, "I don't want to."

"At least the storm was not another crime. And no one else was hurt, right?"

"Not that I've heard of."

She knew he should go. And she knew he would be back.

The door creaked open and several shadowy forms entered. Lauren turned her head carefully toward them.

Cooper let go of her hand and stood up. "You guys are not supposed to be here."

"Neither are you."

The voice belonged to Nicole, who now stepped farther into the room, where Lauren could recognize her posture leaning on crutches.

"Ethan will have all our heads if he finds out four of us were in here at one time."

"We'll make a pact of silence," Liam said.

Dani scoffed. "I could describe at least four people who saw us come in here together."

"Ethan doesn't scare me." Nicole nudged her crutches closer to the bed. "I wanted to see for myself how you are."

Lauren attempted a smile. "They tell me things went well."

"I'm glad it was Ethan taking care of you," Nicole said.

"Me, too." Lauren wished she could catch Cooper's eye. He had stepped away from the bed when the others came in.

Cooper slapped his brother on the back. "I guess I'd better go put on my superhero cape and fight some bad guys."

"You'll call me?" Liam said.

"If I hear anything."

Lauren rooted around her brain for the meaning of the brief exchange between Cooper and Liam but came up with nothing. Why would Cooper promise to call Liam about any of the recent crimes? She had to let the thought go. Hanging on to it entailed too much effort. Lauren was fairly sure Cooper was looking at her now, but he was too far away for her myopic eyes to be certain where his gaze fell.

"Nicole can stay until Sylvia gets back,"

Cooper said. "Liam and Dani, you need to leave."

"You're not the boss of me," Dani said.

Lauren looked down at her hand and pulled up the sensation of Cooper's fingers wrapped around hers. This was a thought she wanted to hang on to.

"At least let Nicole sit down," Cooper said.

Somewhere amid the shuffling that ensued, Cooper left. Lauren felt his absence the instant he crossed the threshold. Outside the door, the hallway was coming to life with the steps and voices of the day shift nurses and rolling carts of breakfast trays. Cooper had stepped out into a normal day. Lauren closed her eyes, trying to picture a normal day.

She prayed that this would be the day that Quinn came home. That would be the beginning of normal.

8:23 a.m.

Ethan heard laughter before he reached Lauren's room. He stood in the door and waited for them to observe his scowl.

"Uh-oh." Nicole giggled. "Busted."

"Last I checked," Ethan said, "none of you qualified as next of kin." Liam and Dani didn't even know Lauren all that well, other than growing up in the same town.

"You can't pick us up and throw us out," Liam said.

"Wanna see me try?" Ethan spread his feet

in a solid stance and crossed his arms, Lauren's chart enveloped in his stance and held flat against his green surgical scrubs. "I only got privileges a few hours ago. I don't want to start out my relationship with the hospital by being a rebel."

"Someone should be with Lauren," Nicole said.

Ethan waved Lauren's chart. "*I'm* here." And the nurses' station was only a few doors down the hall.

Liam, leaning against a wall, shifted his feet. He wasn't as tough as he liked to sound. Dani rolled her eyes, a gesture Ethan had come to expect from her. They were waiting on Nicole, Ethan realized. She was the ringleader. He set the chart on the bed and picked up Nicole's crutches to hand to her.

"I mean it, guys," he said. "Lauren doesn't need a bunch of people in her room."

Lauren hadn't said anything yet. Ethan glanced at her to make sure her eyes were open. They were, and he saw gratitude in them.

Nicole pulled herself upright. "When can we come back?"

"I'll let you know," Ethan said, "but one at a time, please. Right now I want Lauren to rest."

The trio shuffled out of the room. Ethan closed the door behind them.

"How are you feeling?" Ethan flipped the

blanket back from Lauren's ankles and ran fingers up the soles of her feet. She flinched, just as she should.

"What's this thing in my head?"

Ethan explained the drain. The tubing would come out soon enough if there was no further evidence of blood accumulating.

He picked up a hand. "Squeeze my fingers." Lauren's grip was satisfactory. Ethan moved quickly through a standard neurological assessment. Her responses were just what he expected they would be. Lauren's eyes tracked well, her tongue stuck out straight, and she pushed her hand well against his resistance.

"When can I go home?" Lauren asked.

"I just drilled into your head," Ethan said. "Give us a couple of days to be sure everything is all right. You can sleep if you'd like. The nurses will keep an eye on you, and I'll be back."

"Dr. Jordan, I presume."

Ethan pivoted and smiled at Sylvia, who entered with a tall, disposable cup of coffee. "I went for breakfast."

"Smart idea."

Sylvia raised her eyebrows in an unspoken question.

"She's doing fine," Ethan said.

"Do I need to have somebody here?" Lauren asked.

He shook his head. "You're in a hospital.

Nobody is going to leave you alone for long."
"Aunt Sylvia," Lauren said, "I think you should go home."
"You're kicking me out?" Sylvia said.
"I still don't remember what happened, exactly." Lauren readjusted her blanket. "But I'm pretty sure you were here all night."
"I was," Sylvia said.
"And the night before."
"Guilty as charged."
"Then go home." When Quinn got back, Lauren didn't want to have to explain to him that Sylvia collapsed from exhaustion because she was looking after her.
"She's right." Ethan made notes in Lauren's chart. Sylvia needed to take care of herself and rely on the nurses to follow the orders he would leave.
"I'm going to sleep." Lauren closed her eyes.
Sylvia sat in the chair next to the bed. "I'll just stay long enough to be sure that you do."
"Of course you will," Lauren said without opening her eyes.
Ethan allowed himself a smile at the two of them, wondering if he and his mother would have the same comfortable familiarity if one of them were a patient in a hospital. He supposed not, unless their relationship underwent its own surgery. Perhaps yesterday's long afternoon visit was the beginning of a new season, a small hole to relieve the ac-

cumulating pressure of the last decade. After all, he and his mother shared a new understanding of their own family history.

"My work here is finished." Ethan flipped the chart closed and tucked it under one arm.

In the corridor, he turned toward the nurses' station. Lauren was his only patient. He could go back to the locker room where he'd left his clothes in the wee hours of the morning and figure out his next step after that.

"Ethan."

He recognized the thumping behind him and turned to see Nicole. "Were you waiting outside the door all this time?"

"You didn't really think you were going to chase me off that easily, did you?" Nicole halted and leaned against the wall.

He chuckled. "No. I was just going to find my own clothes before I came looking for you."

She met his gaze. "I've never seen you in scrubs before. You look like a real doctor."

"I'm practicing for when I play one on TV."

"How was the surgery?"

"You saw for yourself how well she's doing."

"No." Nicole's emerald eyes held his. "I meant for you."

"I do this procedure all the time."

"Not in Hidden Falls. Not after everything you found out yesterday."

Ethan had returned to the hospital last night because Nicole called him when Lauren's deterioration began — or at least when someone noticed it. Through the crisis hours, they hadn't had a chance for a private conversation. He'd left her in the waiting room while he prevailed on his fledgling acquaintance with Dr. Glass to discern the particulars of Lauren's condition and express his opinion about appropriate treatment. Then he set aside the tangle of personal conundrums and focused on being the best doctor he knew how to be for someone he'd come to care about in the last seven days.

"I have so many questions," Nicole said. "How it went with your parents. What's happening in Columbus. What you meant when you said you were starting a relationship with the hospital here."

"I know." Ethan moved the hair off the side of her face. He didn't have answers to all her questions. "We have a lot to catch up on since yesterday at this time."

"How about breakfast?"

The flash of a white coat caught the corner of Ethan's eye. He stood up straight. "Dr. Glass."

"I've been looking for you." Dr. Glass looked from Ethan to Nicole. "I hope I'm not interrupting something."

"This is my friend, Nicole Sandquist," Ethan said. "She's a friend of Lauren Nock, as well."

Dr. Glass extended a hand and Nicole shook it.

"Lauren is in good hands," he said. "But if you know Dr. Jordan, then you already know that."

Nicole nodded. "Thank you for all your help, as well."

"Just doing my job. Can I steal Dr. Jordan for an hour or two? We have some business to take care of, and I want to introduce him to a couple of people who were kind enough to agree to give him emergency privileges when I woke them in the middle of the night."

"Of course," Nicole said.

Only someone who knew her as well as Ethan did would see the slight droop of disappointment that overtook her eyes. She wanted to talk, and so did he. He would have to go with Dr. Glass, though. He couldn't — wouldn't — snub the man who had welcomed him into Lauren's care.

"It was nice to meet you." Nicole adjusted the crutches under her armpits. "Thank you again for everything."

Ethan felt Dr. Glass's hand on the back of his shoulder as she thumped away.

"Are you hungry?" the older doctor said.

Ethan had only this moment realized the inadequacy of the snack he'd had at five in the morning on his way to the OR. "I could eat."

"Good. Why don't I buy you some breakfast? We can eat in the conference room off the cafeteria where we'll have some privacy."

"That sounds great."

"I've been making a series of inquiries." Dr. Glass set a determined stride toward the elevator. "I had a most enlightening conversation with Dr. Gonzalez."

Ethan's stomach dropped. His hunger vanished. "I can explain."

Dr. Glass punched the elevator button. "I just want to have a friendly conversation to set a few things straight."

8:47 a.m.

Nicole turned around only long enough to watch Ethan and Dr. Glass disappear into the elevator. Questions thickened in her throat, but answers would not come by standing and gawking in the hospital hallway.

What she needed was a ride, and not back to Lauren's apartment.

The folder of notes and photos Nicole had dragged around for the last three days was getting ragged stuffed in the only bag she could carry and still manage crutches, but Nicole was certain it contained more clues. Additional information could tie up some loose ends. Ethan had been her chauffeur the last few days, but Nicole didn't want to wait two hours for Dr. Glass to finish whatever he had in mind. If no one was in the waiting room, Nicole would call a cab. Hidden Falls had taxi service, didn't it? She wasn't entirely sure, a reminder Nicole wasn't in the city she'd called home since right after college.

But Quinn was in St. Louis, or had been.

Maybe now he was in Oklahoma, where the tune whistled into Lauren's cell phone had originated.

What could possibly be in Oklahoma of interest to Quinn?

Thump. Swing. *Thump.* Swing. Nicole made her way to the waiting room, where Dani was the only face she recognized. Three other people, guarding their personal space by strewing personal belongings in the chairs on either side of them, flipped magazine pages or leaned over their phones. Only Dani sat with nothing in her hands and her gaze out the window.

Dani's eyes turned toward Nicole, and Nicole swung herself over to Dani.

"I wasn't sure anyone would be here," Nicole said.

"Cooper went to work," Dani said. "I don't know what happened to Liam. I figured Ethan might need to hang around the hospital and you might want a ride back into town."

Nicole's assessment of Dani warmed. She'd been surprised when Dani turned up early that morning to sit with Cooper during Lauren's surgery. Now she was surprised that Dani was the one who patiently waited for her. Nicole reluctantly admitted to herself that she'd been prepared to go off to breakfast with Ethan without wondering if anyone was waiting for her.

"I could use a ride," Nicole said. "But I don't want to go home. I want to go to the historical society. Will you go with me?"

Nicole braced herself. If she had to, she would get Dani to drop her off at the historical society and worry about getting back to Lauren's apartment later. One thing at a time.

Dani took several slow breaths. "What are you expecting to find there?"

"I don't know. It just seems like a logical place to go. It's the kind of place Quinn would go, don't you think?"

Dani pushed her lips out and nodded.

"If you have to go to work, you can just leave me there."

"I haven't checked my messages," Dani said. "Work can wait."

Nicole smiled. "So you'll go with me?"

"Yes, I'll go." Dani stood and they moved toward the hall.

"Cooper seems pretty attached to Lauren," Nicole said. "And I think she might be coming around."

"Yeah."

Thump. Swing. *Thump.* Swing. Nicole made no further attempt at chitchat. She was tempted to ask Dani about taking another look at Quinn's bank account to see if they could track him to Oklahoma, but she was afraid if she did that, Dani might abandon her. Nicole wanted to avoid that complication.

Nicole resolved to call her detective friend before day's end and persuade him to make some inquiries. They could at least explore Quinn's movements in St. Louis, and maybe the detective knew someone in Oklahoma. All they had to go on was an area code, though, and Oklahoma had plenty of rural areas. If only they had a way to narrow the search.

She was also going to try to get hold of somebody at the newspaper or her editor at his home. On a Monday, administrative operations would be in full swing. Did she or did she not still have a job?

A few minutes later, Dani parked her Jeep in front of the Town Hall. As Nicole eased herself out of her seat — a little high for someone with a bum foot — another car pulled up.

"That's Marianne," Dani said. "Sylvia's assistant." She made the introductions.

"I'm dreading this morning," Marianne said. "The phones were ringing off the hook all last week as it was, and now Lauren. Is it true she had brain surgery?"

Nicole blinked, surprised that the rumor could have spread so efficiently by nine in the morning. "Not exactly. Fortunately something less drastic seemed to work."

She gripped her crutches and faced the task of mounting the steps to get into the building.

"If you've come to see the mayor," Marianne said, putting a key in the door, "she's not here. I don't think she'll be in today."

"Actually," Nicole said, "we're here to visit the historical society. Will they be open?"

"Should be. It's all volunteers, you know," Marianne said. "For the most part, they keep the posted hours, but Patricia Healy seems to have her own time zone."

Nicole glanced at the hours posted on the door. It was already a few minutes past nine. It looked like she and Dani were in for a wait of indeterminate duration. Nicole hoped there was a place to sit down.

She hadn't been in this building in years, even before she finished college and moved away permanently. It was a popular field trip destination for school children in younger grades learning about local government, and Quinn brought his tenth graders to the historical society every year to inspire the genealogy projects that were a rite of passage at the high school. Nicole was fairly certain she'd come in one other time during high school on an errand for Marvin Stanford while she worked for the *Dispatch.* But that was a long time ago.

Marianne paused at the bottom of the

stairs. "The historical society is still straight back on the first floor. I'll give Patricia a call and make sure she's on her way."

Nicole moved as nimbly as she could on crutches, and Dani patiently restrained herself to Nicole's pace as they progressed alongside the staircase to the rear of the building. Dani tried the door to the historical society, but it was locked just as Nicole suspected it would be.

A portrait secured to the wall beside the door made Nicole gasp. She moved closer, reading the label affixed to the wall below the painting.

MATTHIAS TABOR WITH WIFE MATILDA AND SONS HAROLD AND TRUMAN, 1915.

"Wow." Dani stared at the painting.

"Yeah, wow," Nicole said. "How long has this been hanging here?"

Dani shrugged. "Museums are not really my thing."

"Months? Years?"

Dani bent her head to one shoulder. "I installed a new projector in the town council chambers seven or eight months ago. I don't think it was here then."

"But you're not sure."

"No, I'm not sure."

"Look at that," Nicole said. "It could be Ethan in high school. Regardless of when it went up, this is where it all started. Quinn saw this."

"Now you're making stuff up," Dani said.

"Just filling in the gaps," Nicole retorted. "Why would Quinn have that photo of the graveyard? He was probably here helping to organize his students' essays and saw the painting. He saw what we see, and it made him ask questions."

"If it's been hanging all this time, how come Sylvia never saw it?" Dani asked.

"Her office is on the second floor. She comes in the front and goes up the stairs." To Nicole, it didn't seem out of the realm of possibility that Sylvia simply hadn't walked to the rear of the first floor recently. Even if she did, Ethan had been away a long time, and Sylvia hadn't been his teacher or neighbor.

It was Quinn who would have seen the resemblance. It was Quinn who would have dug up the photo she'd found in his den. It was Quinn who researched the birth and adoption records he left in Sylvia's attic. It was Quinn who sent Ethan a personal note urging him to come to the banquet.

And it all started here.

For the first time, Nicole felt as if she were at the beginning of the trail instead of somewhere in the middle.

She heard footsteps on the old tile floor and pivoted on her good foot. Patricia Healy approached.

"Oh my goodness," Patricia said. "I will have to make a note of this historic occasion

— visitors eager and waiting to get into the historical society. I don't think that's ever happened before." She turned a key in the door.

"This portrait has me curious." Nicole hobbled through the open door. "I suppose you have a lot of information about the Tabors from the era of the painting."

Patricia stepped behind a desk and dropped her purse into a lower drawer. "The first part of the last century was the heyday of the Tabor influence on Hidden Falls."

Patricia's reply sounded like it came straight out of an essay. Nicole suppressed a smile.

"Are there photos from those years?" Nicole surveyed the space, trying to recall what it looked like when she was fifteen. If she'd seen photos of the Tabor sons at that time, she would have seen the resemblance to Ethan.

"We're all in a dither these days," Patricia said. "An old storage building on orchard lands formerly owned by the Tabors was scheduled to be torn down, and the current owner found several crates of items we believe belonged to Matthias Tabor or one of his sons."

Nicole's heart skipped ahead of itself. "And the portrait hanging on the wall in the hall? That was in a crate?"

"That's right," Patricia said. "We had some restoration work done, based on some of the other photos of the family in the collection."

Nicole wouldn't leave without seeing those photos, but for now she wanted to know who else had seen them. She calmed herself and said, "That sounds like just the sort of thing Quinn would be interested in. He's always been curious about family trees."

"As a matter of fact, Quinn surprised us one morning not long after we got the crates. It was early in the summer, I think. He sometimes helps out. As soon as he saw the portrait, he volunteered to index all the items. He was a great help."

Nicole glanced at Dani and then back at Patricia. "Would you mind showing us what Quinn looked at?"

"You'll have to be very careful," Patricia said. "We haven't finished archiving everything."

"I promise," Nicole said. "We'll be careful not to disturb your organization of the photos."

"Why don't you have a seat at that table?"

Patricia gestured to a wooden table with six chairs that Nicole guessed was a hundred years old. Dani followed her, and they waited for the past to unfold before their eyes.

10:26 a.m.

Jack walked his new client to the door. They'd had a brief conversation at the health fair before the storm rolled in, and she had been eager to come to the office for a consultation about the status of her aging mother's estate. A retainer check sat on Jack's desk. The facts seemed straightforward, but he'd verify a few points of Illinois law before writing a letter that would serve as his opinion. He shook his client's hand a final time and returned to his office to review his notes. While she was talking, he'd thought briefly about whether he should bone up on elder law and promote that part of his generalist portfolio. He saw plenty of gray heads around Hidden Falls. With the right wording added to his business card, it could be a steady income stream.

But it wouldn't be as interesting as proving that Ethan Jordan was a Tabor descendant. If Jack did that, the entire town would take notice.

Jack heard movement in the outer office. "Did you forget something?" he called out.

Even on carpet the footsteps sounded heavier than the slight woman who just left.

"Jack?" The voice was male.

Jack got up and went out into the reception area, his mood lifting immediately at the sight of Ethan Jordan.

"Come in, Ethan." Jack offered a vigorous handshake. "It was quite a weekend, wasn't it?"

"Certainly not anything I expected," Ethan said.

Jack led the way back into his office. Instead

of sitting behind his desk, he angled two visitor chairs toward each other and sat in one of them. Ethan took the other.

"How's your patient?" Jack said. "My wife forwarded an e-mail from the church prayer chain that said you did brain surgery this morning."

"It was a simple procedure," Ethan said, "and Lauren is doing well."

"Good. Glad to hear that."

"I thought maybe we should talk about what happens after this," Ethan said.

Jack reached for a folder on the corner of his desk and handed Ethan a printed document. "I'm one step ahead of you. Here are some avenues I recommend we explore."

While Ethan scanned the document, Jack launched into his explanation. First, he would take steps to legally establish Ethan's genetics. Proving a connection by using DNA might depend on finding the current generation of Tabors, but the documents they had looked at the previous day would be extremely helpful. Jack was not convinced the Santorelli firm had been involved in Quinn's investigation — why would he use a private detective so far away on this matter? Nevertheless, Jack would contact them to be sure. Perhaps Quinn had traced Tabors to Pennsylvania.

Next Jack intended to investigate what was left of the Tabor fortune, if anything. No doubt their business interests had been folded into larger concerns or taken on new legal identities, but all indications in the files Jack possessed pointed to the fact that the family's finances had survived the Depression and thrived in following decades.

Then Jack wanted to locate the man known as Merrill Tabor. He would be about eighty, so he could very well still be alive, but if he wasn't, he might have several generations of descendants to whom Ethan was related.

Jack tapped his file folder. "I have Merrill Tabor's date of birth. I suspect it will only take a day or two to find that Dennis Pease was born on or around the same day. That will beef up evidence that Harold Tabor was willing to trade his sickly child for Stephen Pease's healthy boy. He had a fortune at stake. He had motivation."

Ethan flipped to the second page of the document. "I didn't realize you were going at this with such . . . enthusiasm."

"I think we have a strong case," Jack said. "Of course the transaction was completely unethical and illegal. No doubt all the individuals who were party to the agreement — which I suspect was just the two fathers — are deceased, but if we discover that any succeeding generations had any knowledge of the contract and made personal gain by suppressing the information, this could be fascinating for both of us."

Ethan looked up from the document. "I keep thinking about the man in the photo who looks like me."

"Harold Tabor. Your great-grandfather."

"He's standing in front of a Pease grave, an infant grave."

"That's what we believe, yes."

"I don't suppose we'll ever know who took his picture," Ethan said, "but Harold Tabor must have been there because he believed it was his son's grave."

Jack nodded and tented his fingers in front of his chest. "Based on what we know, that's a reasonable conclusion."

"He looks sad," Ethan said simply.

For a second, Jack let the sensation float through him of what it might feel like to stand at the grave of one of his children. Even a man heartless enough to reduce his son to a business deal that would protect his fortune would feel something. After all, his son had been sick. Harold Tabor expected him to die. Yet he could not mourn publicly, because everyone believed he had a healthy heir at home. Ethan raised a good question — who had taken the photo? A cemetery was not a typical backdrop for casual photos. Did someone else know? Maybe Harold Tabor had paid off the photographer — purchased the image in exchange for the silence of the person who took it. Jack would have to go through the old files again, looking for another suspicious transaction. If Harold Tabor would put in writing his agreement with Stephen Pease, he would also want assurance that he could not be blackmailed again. Jack reached for a pen to make a note of what to look for.

"I wonder what his wife thought," Ethan said. "What about his brother? Or his parents? Wouldn't they see the change in the baby?"

Jack smiled. He liked the questions Ethan was asking. "I doubt Harold chose a random child of a poor truck driver. He must have seen the child and knew there was a resemblance. And a sickly child who seems to improve dramatically could take on a new appearance that people would attribute to better health."

"I suppose so," Ethan murmured. "But a mother knows her own child."

Jack turned his palms up and stated the obvious. "She was in on it. She wouldn't be left childless. It wouldn't be the first time a woman lavished love on a substitute child to cover her own loss."

"I hope she did love him. I hope they both loved him and that Merrill Tabor, whoever he was, grew up happy."

Jack sucked in a controlled breath. The conversation was taking a turn he had not prepared for. Ethan Jordan didn't sound ready to strike out on the path to the justice he deserved. Jack decided to follow the lead of Ethan's mood with a point already on his list.

"Since we know that the child Stephen Pease took in grew up to be your mother's father," Jack said, "and we know Harold Tabor raised a son named Merrill, we have to wonder who *is* buried in that grave. Perhaps there's another suffering family out there, and we could bring peace somehow."

Ethan took too long to reply, and Jack's thumb began to twitch.

"I appreciate everything you've done," Ethan said. "You put a lot of thought into this, but I didn't come here because I was planning to take any legal action."

"If you're concerned about the fee, we can come to a contingency agreement," Jack said.

"Well, it's true that legal fees could be difficult. I already have a mountain of debt from medical school." Ethan handed back to Jack the pages outlining legal options. "I'm not trying to upset anyone's life. I just thought I might like to have photocopies of the documents from your files. There might be a time in my future when I need to put the pieces together."

"That's what I'm offering to help you do," Jack said.

"I'm not being clear," Ethan said. "I mean just for my own understanding. Maybe for my mother, if she decides she wants to know more. I'm not going to track down the Tabors and disrupt two or three generations of family."

"But they're your family."

Ethan shrugged. "Genetically, perhaps, but that's all. I just want to be able to answer my mother's questions. After all, she's my mother no matter who her father was."

Jack was starting to panic. "You only found out all this information in the last few days. You don't have to decide anything right now. I was surprised you came in today at all."

"Jack," Ethan said. "I know you'd love to chomp your teeth into this just the way I love a good medical case. But I don't want to do it."

Jack stared into unbudging brown eyes.

"Will you make me photocopies?" Ethan asked. "I'm happy to pay some sort of document fee, if that's the way lawyers do things."

Jack's stomach sank.

"I'd like the will and the contract, and anything else you might think is relevant — birth certificates? Marriage certificates?"

If Ethan intended to take this information to another attorney, Jack hoped he would have the good sense not to do it in legal circles Jack would hear about.

"After that," Ethan said, "I would really like you to just lose the file again. It's been buried all these decades already. You can burn it or shred it or do whatever lawyers do with files they are not required to maintain."

If Ethan had any smarts, he would ask for the originals, not photocopies. As long as Jack kept the originals, Ethan might still come back.

"I won't destroy them," Jack said. "A few months from now, a few years — you might change your mind."

"I won't." Ethan's tone sounded final, even to Jack.

Jack's mind raced. Perhaps he didn't need Ethan at all. Harold Tabor's brother had three sons who would have inherited if Harold had not bought another man's son. There could be three or four generations by now who were cheated out of a substantial inheritance.

And what about the family whose child was buried? Was Jack just supposed to let go of another action that almost certainly involved a crime?

"I'll make those copies right now." Jack got up, found the papers, and turned on the small photocopier behind his desk. He put the copies in a fresh manila envelope and handed it to Ethan.

"Thank you," Ethan said. "I'm asking you, please, to let this go. Will you?"

Now it was Jack's turn to be slow to answer. "I'll need to think about that. I'll want to be certain of my own obligations under the law with the information I know."

"Jack."

"I'll have to let you know. Why don't I walk

you out?"

11:05 a.m.

For the first time in more than a week, Liam was productive at his office. He still lacked the number of leads and appointments needed to sustain a healthy business, but that wasn't on his mind. He spent the time cleaning client files, making sure all information was current and records above reproach. The risk was still great that his career would be halted with a phone call or a knock on his office door. He chose not to hide or to behave as if he'd done something illegal with any of his accounts. Instead, if he was plucked out of his routine, anyone who came in after him would find everything in order.

It was a good feeling.

The morning had started early with Cooper's request to have Liam at his side during Lauren's procedure. After days of not eating, and with the upheaval of the weekend, Liam's appetite was unpredictable. When it surged, though, he paid attention, and this brought him to the Eat Right Here diner on Main Street for a very early lunch. In fact, he ordered a hearty breakfast platter minutes before the kitchen shifted to its lunch offerings and now inhaled its mixed fragrances. Liam had his eyes closed with a deep breath of anticipation when someone slid into the bench on the other side of the booth. His respiration caught briefly as he imagined who might be there to confront him and bolstered his determination to remain calm, whatever happened.

Liam opened his eyes. "Dani." Beside his cousin was Nicole, still arranging herself and her crutches before maneuvering into the seat.

"Hey." Dani reached for a menu propped up in a shiny holder. "So nice of you to buy us lunch."

"My pleasure." Liam turned on the charm. "Have you been at the hospital all this time?"

"Nope. Historical society."

Liam laughed. "No, really."

"It's the truth," Nicole said. "I haven't heard from Ethan all morning, so I assume Lauren is still doing well."

Liam picked up a slice of bacon. "Wait. Go back to the part about the historical society."

"You think I don't have any culture?" Dani stole a slice of bacon off Liam's plate.

"Not the historical society kind of culture. We're both deficient in that regard."

"Well, there's some pretty interesting stuff happening there these days."

"I'm listening."

Liam's chewing slowed down as Nicole explained the painting in the Town Hall building and the assortment of Tabor photos that had come into the historical society. A waitress came, and Nicole and Dani ordered.

"I haven't figured out how Quinn talked them into giving him that picture," Nicole said. "And I didn't ask in case he didn't ask, if you know what I mean."

"Quinn wouldn't steal a marshmallow at the county fair," Liam said.

"I know. But just in case." Nicole arranged her silverware. "We didn't find any other copies of that particular photo, but we found enough to remove any doubt that the man who looks like Ethan is Harold Tabor. He's holding a baby in one of them."

Dani slapped her palms on the table. "I don't believe it."

"You were there," Nicole said. "You saw for yourself."

"No. Not that." Dani looked over Liam's shoulder. "Robert what's-his-name is here."

Liam turned his head. "The guy with the dark hair and the hoodie eating pancakes at the table by himself?"

"That's him."

Liam reasoned it was a good thing somebody with a broken ankle was between his cousin and her suspect or Dani would have leaped out of the booth to tackle Robert Doerr again.

"I can't believe they let him go." Dani slumped and stared.

"That guy is *your* guy? The guy you think vandalized your boat?"

"In what way am I not being clear?" Dani

said. "Yes, doofus, that's what I mean."

"Then Cooper should have held him while he had him," Liam said. "It's pretty gutsy for Doerr to show his face, but he has to eat, and I guess he wouldn't go back to the Falls Shadow Café."

"Why not?" Nicole asked.

"Because last Sunday he tried to steal a purse at the café. Jack Parker is the one who ran him off, but I don't think anyone knew who he was."

"Jack Parker?" Dani said. "Annoying, superior attitude Jack Parker?"

"He's not so bad." Liam kept Jack's card in his wallet now. He had made up his mind that if he needed an attorney on short notice, he would call Jack.

Dani waved off Liam's remark. "Now we know this guy's name, and you and Jack could identify him. I hope Gavin knows the woman whose purse he took. We're going to need her to press charges."

Liam lifted his chin to point toward the door. "Take it up with Cooper right now. Here he comes."

Nicole lowered one shoulder to look over it. "Uh, I think this is not the moment. I don't think Cooper is here for lunch."

In his uniform, Cooper had another sheriff's deputy at his side. The two of them marched through the restaurant. Robert Doerr pushed his chair back and knocked it over as he scanned for a way out. When Cooper moved closer, Doerr gripped the edge of the table and turned it on its side. Gasps rose up around the restaurant as people scrambled out of the way. A third deputy emerged from the kitchen and blocked the only rear exit, trapping Doerr.

"Robert Doerr," Cooper said, "you're under arrest for grand theft auto and burglary."

Cooper's companion moved in with handcuffs while Cooper identified specific charges and read Doerr his rights. The two junior deputies marched the suspect out the front door. Liam saw now that a squad car was parked directly in front of the diner.

Cooper stopped at his brother's booth.

"Bro!" Liam said. "I've never seen you do that before."

"Car theft and burglary?" Nicole said. "Do you mean Quinn's car? Sylvia's shop?"

"I'm not at liberty to discuss active investigations."

That was all Liam needed to hear. He was pretty sure there were no other active investigations into auto theft or burglary in Hidden Falls. If there were, the rumor mill would be buzzing.

"Wow," Liam said. "You caught him."

"It was the prints," Dani said. "You caught him because of the prints you got because he took a swing at you — which only happened because I caught him first."

"I am not at liberty to discuss active investigations," Cooper repeated.

Liam saw the gleam in his brother's eye.

"So now you believe me?" Dani said.

"All I ever said was that we didn't have evidence," Cooper said. "We still don't."

"What about the purse snatching?" Liam asked.

"In Gavin's café?" Cooper said. "Already have a report on that."

"What do you know about Robert Doerr?" Nicole asked. "Arrest records are public information. Save me some time."

"True," Cooper said, "but you're not going to find anything under this name. Running the prints tells us he has a record, but the details are vague. Robert Doerr is probably an alias. We're still looking for a real name."

"I could ask around and find out in under thirty minutes how long he's been in town." Nicole looked up at Cooper hopefully.

"Less than a year." Cooper looked out the front door. "I gotta go and make sure these junior deputies do things by the book."

Liam watched his brother nod his head at a couple of people on his way out. The squad car was still waiting for him.

"Mmm." Nicole picked up her spoon and tapped it against an open palm.

"Nicole," Dani said, "spill."

Nicole shrugged. "It's nothing. I was just

thinking about something my detective friend once told me. He was trying to prove charges against a man he discovered was in the witness protection program. It turns out that most witnesses have criminal pasts and often get into trouble again in their new communities."

Liam leaned back in disbelief. "You think Robert Doerr is in the witness protection program just because he uses a false name?"

"I know," Nicole said. "It's silly. It was just the way Cooper said he had a record, but I wouldn't find it. I'm pretty good at finding these things."

The waitress arrived with the food Dani and Nicole had ordered. They settled in to eat.

Liam chewed slowly, thinking. Quinn wasn't driving when he disappeared. He used his debit card in St. Louis while Robert Doerr was working at a hospital in Hidden Falls. Dani's theory that Quinn left town because he wanted to was beginning to make the most sense. Liam would be relieved to learn — officially — that his brother had caught the person who stole Quinn's car and smashed Sylvia's shop. And it would be reasonable to at least look into the possibility that Robert Doerr had something to do with Dani's boat going over the falls.

What Liam wanted most of all, though, was for his brother to solve Liam's case before someone from the corporate offices of Midwest Answers swooped in to have him arrested.

2:13 p.m.

"Are you here for more blood?" Lauren didn't open her eyes to see which category of hospital employee had just shuffled into her room.

"Are you having vampire dreams?"

Lauren's eyelids flipped open. It was Cooper, in the blue-and-gray uniform that was his daily garb.

"I thought it was someone from the lab." Lauren wished she had something more clever to say, but even on her best days, her wit was never what she wished it was.

"You look good!"

Lauren turned her face away from Cooper for a few seconds. She couldn't possibly look good. He was either very sweet or a very good liar.

"How do you feel?" Cooper asked.

"A whole lot better than last night."

"That's what I want to hear."

Cooper rearranged the chair at the side of the bed so he could face Lauren. *So this is not a pop-your-head-in visit,* Lauren thought.

"You gave me a fright last night," Cooper said.

Gave me a fright? Lauren wasn't used to hearing such an antiquated phrase from anyone except her Nana. Or maybe Quinn, but that was probably because he was a history teacher and read a lot of old books.

A week ago, Lauren barely knew Cooper. Even three days ago she dreaded having to sit down and talk to him. She still barely knew him, but she had trusted him and put her hand in his while they raced against a storm. Oddly, that counted for something at the moment.

Cooper scooted the chair closer. "I wanted to make a few things clear."

Uh-oh. Cooper was using his cop voice. Considering that Lauren had been in the hospital for the last two days, what could she have done to deserve that?

"Yes?" she said.

"First, I want to be clear that when I said I wanted to spend some time with you, this is not the venue I had in mind."

Lauren's chest released.

Cooper leaned one arm on the bed. "It wouldn't be fair for you to hold these last two days against me when I ask you out for a proper date."

Lauren sucked in both lips to control the smile trying to break across her face. "I'll try not to."

"Because even I know that almost getting crushed by a cracked tree is a really bad first date."

The smile escaped. Lauren was glad he had

come, even if she was uncertain about whether she should let him know. She had never been confident around men of the attentive and available variety.

Lauren recognized the knocking pattern on her open room door. The nurse was right on time for asking questions about headaches and nausea and what day it was. It seemed to Lauren that Ethan had gone overboard in his instructions for people checking on her, but she had no experience with which to compare this one.

"Well, if it isn't the hero of Hidden Falls," Nurse Wacker said.

"Just doing my job," Cooper said.

"It seems you have done it particularly well today."

Lauren looked at the blurred faces of Cooper and the nurse. If she had a headache, it was because she'd been straining to see.

"Cooper, what is she talking about?" Lauren said.

"I made an arrest this morning. I've done it before, and I'll do it again, I'm sure."

Nurse Wacker looked at the monitor tracking Lauren's pulse, respiration, and blood pressure and made a few notes. "Sheriff's Deputy Cooper Elliott is being humble. It's all over town that he arrested someone for stealing Quinn's car and breaking into the mayor's store."

Lauren felt her eyes widen, even if their

focus did not improve. "When were you going to tell me this?"

"All in a day's work."

"Someone will be in to draw blood," the nurse said on her way out.

"Cooper Elliott," Lauren said.

"That's my name."

"You caught the guy? It was the same guy in both crimes?"

"Fingerprints don't lie. If you're going to hot-wire a car or break into a cash register, you should be careful what you touch. Theoretically speaking, of course."

"Does my aunt know?"

"Certainly. I promised to keep her in the loop, didn't I?"

If Lauren weren't nervous about the drain in the side of her head, she would have swung out of bed to hug Cooper. This arrest was going to make a lot of people feel better about life in Hidden Falls.

"I had a couple of good breaks," Cooper said. "The pieces came together just like they should, and we have a strong case in both charges. The legal system works if people give it half a chance."

He'd been so calm and patient in the face of rising panic around town. Even Lauren had been annoyed by Cooper's understated thoroughness when he seemed like he ought to *do* something, go out and *catch* somebody.

And now that he had, he didn't gloat or

boast. Was "congratulations" the right thing to say?

"On behalf of my aunt, Quinn, and all of Hidden Falls, I thank you," Lauren said. "Marv Stanford will think it's awesome it happened today. It'll make the headline for tomorrow's *Dispatch.*"

"Okay, I'm done with that topic." Cooper reached into a shirt pocket. "I brought you something."

Cooper's humility was endearing. Lauren took the solid oblong case he offered and opened it. Inside, against a blue felt lining, lay a pair of glasses identical to the two pair that had been wrecked in the last few days. She unfolded them and slid them onto her face. The room came into focus. The clock. The whiteboard telling her the name of her nurse and CNA. The sign reminding patients to be careful about falls. The menu sheet for the next day. It was all utterly ordinary and in that moment stunningly beautiful.

"Cooper! Thank you! How did you do this?" The prescription in the lenses was perfect.

"One of the advantages of wearing a badge and living in a small town is that it doesn't take much to discover where you might have gotten your glasses. The optometrist at the one-hour place in Birch Bend was eager to cooperate."

Lauren laughed. "I'm so relieved to be able to see."

Now that Cooper was in focus, self-consciousness tangled itself around Lauren. She couldn't remember the last time anyone had tried to comb her hair — certainly she hadn't — and the hospital gown with its blue and beige stripes and the opening in the back was the most hideous, shapeless thing she'd ever worn. She didn't even know what disgusting substance might be dripping through the tube coming out of the space under her skull, or what was going into the tube from the pole into her hand. Her aunt had remarked earlier about the colorful phases of the bruises on Lauren's face. She was only sitting up with the assistance of a button that raised the head of the bed.

"It's a good thing this is not a date." Lauren raised a hand to tame her hair. "I promise I can do better at putting myself together."

Now that she could see Cooper's face, Lauren found herself dodging his eyes.

Cooper wanted nothing to do with her evasion and leaned his head toward her. "I'm going to be here, you know."

She swallowed the thickness in her throat.

"You don't know me well, and I don't know you well," Cooper said, "but I would like to."

What did he see in her that he should be so eager? No doubt his patience in following procedure and gathering facts had laid the foundation for the strong case he felt he had now against the person he'd arrested today. Lauren had expressed only annoyance at the thoroughness of his questions when Quinn disappeared and Sylvia's shop was burgled. For the most part, she'd brushed him off when he turned up at her apartment with Sylvia on the night Nicole broke her ankle. Lauren had resisted having to meet with him in person to plan for the health fair.

And Cooper persevered. He was here. He was the one who was willing to throw himself between her and a falling tree. He had prayed for her and sat through her surgery. He thought to have her glasses made and to bring them to her. Lauren didn't know what she'd done to deserve his attention.

"I mean it," Cooper said. "We'll have a proper first date, and I'll try not to bungle it. If I do, I hope you'll give me a second chance, anyway."

A peculiar happiness streamed through Lauren, warming her from the inside out. Perhaps it was the drugs the nurse administered according to Ethan's specific schedule, but Lauren hoped not. She wanted to remember this moment when she was on her feet again or sitting across from Cooper at a restaurant. A nice restaurant with candles and soft music.

Lauren closed her eyes, not entirely voluntarily. Sleep overtook her, and when she opened her eyes again, Cooper was gone.

4:42 p.m.

Dani held the door open for Nicole as they left the hospital after checking on Lauren. If anyone had suggested to Dani that she'd spend as much time with Nicole as she had the last few days, Dani would have scoffed. They had almost nothing in common.

Except Quinn. Dani knew him well, and Nicole liked to think she did just because she used to. They had one thing in common.

"Can you take me back to Lauren's apartment?" Nicole asked. "You can just drop me off."

"Sylvia said you're supposed to go to her house."

"I'm not going to do that. I have everything I need at Lauren's."

Except someone to look after you. Dani wasn't going to argue with Nicole, though. Instead, she conceded that the second thing she had in common with Nicole was a stubborn streak. They were outside the hospital now. Nicole had already made clear that she could get to the car on two crutches and one good leg. There was no need for Dani to provide curbside service. Dani wouldn't have wanted the fuss, either.

Nicole's phone rang, and she leaned against a car to stop and answer it. "My detective friend. I've been playing phone tag with him all day. I need to take this."

"No problem." Dani put her hands into the pockets of her vest. She'd left her own phone turned off all day. Being at anyone's beck and call never interested Dani. As much as she tried not to hear Nicole's side of the conversation, it was hard not to.

"Do you know anything about what's happening at the paper? . . . If you hear anything, please let me know. . . . I have some questions about the witness protection program. . . . That's right, witness protection. . . . I thought you worked on a case once. . . . Hello? . . . Are you there?"

Dani could see that the screen of Nicole's phone had gone dark.

"Nuts." Nicole exhaled heavily. "I've been nursing the battery along all day."

"Let me guess. Your charger is not in your purse."

"I didn't think I was going to need it when I left for the health fair on Saturday. I haven't juiced up since yesterday when Ethan loaned me the charger he keeps in his car."

Nicole stared at the screen. Did she think the phone would magically turn back on?

Dani pointed toward her vehicle. "Get in the Jeep. You'll be at Lauren's in ten minutes."

It took seventeen minutes to get to the Jeep, drive down to Main Street, find a place to park in reasonable proximity to the barbershop under Lauren's apartment, and push the elevator button.

"Tell me you have a key," Dani said as they stepped off onto the second floor of the building.

Nicole's face paled.

"Stay here," Dani said. "The landlord leaves emergency keys with Trace Hulett in the barbershop."

"And you know this because . . . ?"

"I just do."

Simply because technically Trace had the keys didn't mean he knew where they were. Another sixteen minutes passed before Dani returned to the hall outside Lauren's apartment with a key that successfully admitted them.

Nicole hobbled to the recliner that had become her second home, dropped into it, and leaned over one side to the outlet. Her phone beeped when she plugged it in.

"Thank you, Dani." Nicole looked up, cradling her phone in one hand. "You don't have to hang around. You've given me enough of your day."

Dani had one more stop in mind before heading home herself, but she was fairly certain Nicole would try to call her detective back, and Dani was curious.

Nicole pushed a button and raised her phone to an ear. After about twenty seconds, she left a brief message and dropped the phone into her lap. "Back to playing phone tag."

"He really knows about the witness protection program?" Dani threw her long braid over her shoulder.

"A little, I'm pretty sure. He could find out more."

This was nonsense. Nicole couldn't think Quinn had anything to do with the witness protection program.

"I know what you're thinking," Nicole said, "but it could be true."

"What?" Dani bristled at the notion anyone could know what she was thinking.

"Virtually no one in the program has met foul play unless they broke the rules and made contact with someone from their old life."

"Are you talking about Bobby Doerr?"

"Maybe." Nicole pushed back the recliner and propped up her feet. "But you're thinking about Quinn."

"That's ridiculous." Dani wasn't going to confirm that Nicole had wormed her way into her thoughts.

"Is it? Is it so far-fetched to think Quinn's life has been as self-contained as it has been for over thirty years because he had a reason to leave a former life behind?"

"You said yourself that most of the people in witness protection have some criminal past." That couldn't be Quinn.

"That's right."

They stared at each other. Dani refused to follow this trail.

"You said you didn't need me." Dani would leave it to Nicole and Sylvia to duke out where Nicole should spend the night. "I'm out of here."

Dani pulled the apartment door closed behind her, took the stairs quickly, and drove her Jeep the few blocks to the Hidden Falls sheriff's office. She wanted to see for herself that Bobby Doerr was in custody. Inside, Dani walked right up to the gate in the half wall separating the waiting area from where the deputies sat and pushed in.

Cooper looked up from his desk. "Dani, this isn't a good idea. We have him, and we have enough to charge him."

"Not with my boat, you don't."

"Give me a chance to get there."

Dani strode past Cooper to the small holding cells at the rear of the building. She supposed they were occupied from time to time, but this was the first time she saw a prisoner stretched out on a narrow bed.

"Why?"

"Dani," Cooper said, warning in his tone.

She ignored him and stood three feet outside the cell that held Robert Doerr. In no hurry, he swung his feet over the side of the bed and righted himself to meet her unflinching gaze. His dark eyes didn't even blink.

Cooper pulled on her elbow. "Danielle, you cannot do this."

"Don't call me that." Dani pushed off his touch. "Are you going to keep him here?"

Cooper stepped between Dani and Bobby and put his hands on her shoulders. "Mr. Doerr will remain in custody until the opportunity comes for him to exercise his rights before a judge. If you're really interested in justice, you won't jeopardize the process."

They both turned their heads when they heard the door from the street slam shut.

Jack Parker entered. "Deputy, I'm here to see my client. We will require a confidential room to consult."

"You're kidding me," Dani said.

Cooper nudged Dani away from the cell. "Mr. Doerr has the right to an attorney. You know that."

"But *this* attorney?" Dani doubted Bobby Doerr had the resources for any attorney other than a public defender.

"This is the one he asked for."

Dani gritted her teeth and lowered her voice. "Don't you know a conflict of interest when you see one?" Liam had identified Jack as the one who tackled Bobby Doerr when he tried to steal a purse in Gavin's café. Jack was a potential witness. He couldn't be the defense attorney.

"The district attorney's office has not agreed to press the purse-snatching charges — yet." Cooper's murmur was barely above a whisper. "For the moment, the law says we have to let this play out."

"Is he going to get bail?"

Cooper didn't answer.

"Cooper Elliott, if you lose him again, you have me to answer to."

Dani marched past Jack Parker out to the street.

6:14 p.m.

At the four-way stop sign outside the hospital, Ethan sat with his foot on the brake even though no other cars approached the intersection. If he turned right, he could go into town, where he knew Nicole would welcome his company.

And pepper him with questions and speculation.

If he proceeded straight ahead, he could get a short hike in before darkness arrived to close out the day and catch the departing light for a few photos. And he could return to the motel on the other side of the falls and see if they'd give him back the room he had vacated very early yesterday morning. He wasn't sure there was any point in going back to Columbus, except to move out of his apartment, and there was no hurry about that.

Ethan accelerated through the intersection. He'd be better company for Nicole if he sorted the decisions that spread themselves before him like so many patient charts, each one needing his attention. Ethan wanted to return to the hospital later for one last check on Lauren. First, though, he needed to breathe some outdoor air and clear his head. Following the old road that curved with the turns of the river gave Ethan panoramic views he had not yet seen during his unplanned week in Hidden Falls and took him past the irregular placements of riverside homes and cabins, past the turnoff to Quinn's house and the neighborhood where Ethan grew up.

After delivering the jarring news the day before of their connection to the revered Tabor family, Ethan hadn't intended to see his parents again before leaving Hidden Falls, but his mother would be glad to have him back. Ethan had no doubt. His boyhood room might be untouched except to keep it clean. Maybe his brother's family slept in there when they visited. Kay Jordan would find some way to make her son comfortable.

Ethan wondered what his mother would think about Jack's determination to construct some kind of case out of events that happened eighty years ago.

I'll have to let you know, Jack had said. What was there to think about? Several issues in Ethan's life were muddled at the moment, but he didn't want to disturb the lives of people who had no more to do with those long-ago decisions than he did. And he doubted his mother would be party to Jack's efforts. If Ethan returned to Jack's office to reiterate his position — and warn him off of approaching his mother — the action might backfire and egg Jack on. But if Ethan left Jack alone, he couldn't be sure what he would do.

He pulled into the small parking lot at the top of the falls and retrieved his camera from where he'd stowed it out of sight in the back of his car. Ethan wasn't even sure he wanted this Lexus anymore. The purchase had been a moment of triumph — pride, really. He'd just performed an intricate surgery for the first time, a procedure that was sure to put him in an exclusive bracket of neurosurgeons one day when he'd done a few more and was in charge of his own OR instead of having Gonzalez looking over his shoulder.

Gonzalez.

The shock that Dr. Glass in a small hospital in Hidden Falls had spoken with Dr. Gonzalez in Columbus left Ethan rattled all day. Their conversation never would have happened if Ethan hadn't turned around when he was halfway to Columbus on Sunday morning. It never would have happened if he hadn't done a procedure on Lauren that he could do by touch in the dark if he had to.

But it changed everything.

He was going to have to tell Nicole what happened. Ethan had dodged her calls all day before promising he would see her in the evening. Guessing at her reaction was beyond him right then. Putting words on his own reaction was difficult enough.

Ethan hung his camera around his neck with the long lens on it and walked slowly to the highest point of the bridge above the falls, a place where he knew he could safely lean over the railing and frame river water tumbling over boulders. The rapid shutter speed would capture droplets of spray reflecting the evening light. Certain he'd get some shots worth printing, Ethan took about forty photos. The image of Dani's rowboat riding the water's crest before dropping over these rocks invaded his mind, and he shook it off. Ethan had always loved this place, this spot. He didn't want it spoiled by picturing what had happened to the boat — or what might have happened to Dani if she were not such a strong swimmer.

When had she come to know Quinn as well as she did?

Ethan walked along the bridge, taking idle shots — trees, ground vegetation creeping along the edge of the footpath, leaves fallen in abandonment, evidence of the presence of birds and squirrels and insects. Without an intentional plan, Ethan snapped whatever caught his eye. When he reached the end of the bridge, he turned around and took some wide shots of the river. Occasionally the distant timbre of a voice rising in the split-second vacancy between bursts of rushing water fell on his ears.

Back at his car, Ethan held the camera at an angle to look at the screen and scroll through the images, looking for shots he would never use — badly framed, blurred, unsatisfactory light. He moved swiftly from one picture to another, deleting some and granting reprieve to others that he might later decide were not worthwhile. His finger paused over the DELETE button as he examined a photo he had taken at the far end of the bridge. Though he was vaguely aware that a few other people were around, Ethan hadn't been interested in capturing the images of strangers.

A breath away from deleting an unwanted picture of two men, Ethan jerked his finger back. His breath caught, and his heart pounded in sudden velocity.

He knew one of these two men. The slope of those shoulders belonged to Quinn! The hairline — though thinner and grayer than ten years ago — was Quinn's. Even from the back, Ethan was sure. This wasn't a hidden shadow like the image Dani had been so sure was the man who destroyed her boat. Despite the distance, this was a clear shot, with the two men walking out of the frame on one side, their backs to the lens.

And one of them was Quinn.

Ethan gripped his camera and raced full speed across the bridge, past the place where he had stood with the camera and toward the spot where the men must have been standing — all the while trying to calculate how many minutes might have passed since his eye failed to notice them in the shot.

Too many.

His chest heaved as he spun in three widening circles and then let his feet slide down a gentle slope toward a narrow trail they might have taken out.

"Quinn!" he yelled.

Silence.

12
The Groundskeeper Remembered

Tuesday
7:17 a.m.

Ethan's level of sleep deprivation was starting to remind him of the early years of his long residency — which quite likely had come to an abrupt halt.

He was exhausted.

He was overwhelmed.

He was bewildered.

And he hadn't slept. How could he sleep after capturing Quinn with his camera yet being unable to track him on a hiking trail? Ethan was twenty-five years younger than Quinn and in good condition. Nevertheless, despite running down the trail as far as he could follow it, backtracking to try another offshoot, and racing back to his car to drive around to the road where several trails merged on the other side of the lake, Ethan found no sign of Quinn or his companion.

Ethan hoped the other man *was* a companion and not an assailant. In the photo, the two men seemed to be strolling in an agreeable manner, but an image wouldn't frame an unspoken threat.

Weary, he gripped one shoe and tugged it onto his foot, and then the second one. Other than the suit he wore to Quinn's banquet, Ethan had been dressing from an overnight bag for ten days. One trip to a Laundromat and one to the men's section of the department store on Main Street kept Ethan limping along, and every day he thought he would be making the simple drive back to Columbus and his full wardrobe. After yesterday, though, a return to Columbus was less imminent. Ethan stood in the motel room in jeans that were beginning to feel like second skin and one of three shirts he rotated through.

After pulling a comb through his damp hair, Ethan was as ready as he could be to confront the questions the day held. Last night, after seeing Nicole and checking on Lauren, Ethan drove past Quinn's house. It was just as he, Nicole, and Lauren left it six days ago after they removed the mysterious photo of the man who looked like Ethan — dark and unoccupied. Ethan had even rung the doorbell and knocked heavily on the front door. Then he sat in his car in front of the house waiting for the swing of headlights that would come with a vehicle turning into Quinn's driveway. Finally, Ethan gave up.

If Quinn was in Hidden Falls — and he was — why hadn't he come home to his house?

Ethan pulled out of the motel lot, drove across the bridge over the falls, followed the edge of the lake, and headed into his old neighborhood. Quinn might have come home a few minutes or a few hours after Ethan abandoned his vigil. He could be there now.

Taking his black vehicle through the brightening morning light, Ethan didn't care who saw him. He pulled into Quinn's driveway and as close to the house as he could get before taking out his phone and dialing the landline number Ethan had memorized twenty years ago. It didn't surprise him at all to realize he still knew it. The longer he stayed in Hidden Falls, the more details of his years there came to the front of his mind.

Quinn didn't answer, though. An automated voice came on and informed Ethan that the voice mailbox he was trying to reach was full. Ethan smiled at the thought that Quinn must have finally given up his antiquated answering machine and learned to use the message feature that came with his phone service. Pacing briskly to the front door, Ethan raised the brass knocker and pushed it heavily against the door. He rang the doorbell. He knocked again. Then he circled the house, examining every window, every curtain, for any sign of occupancy or disturbance.

Nothing was different. No one was home. No one had been there.

Ethan hated to admit it, but he needed Dani.

Back in his car, he drove to her house. At least this time, he wasn't asking for anything but a single piece of information.

Was the man in the photo the same man who came to see Quinn every year out on the lake?

Ethan's stomach sank when he didn't see Dani's Jeep in her driveway, but he didn't want to make a wrong assumption. He got out and rapped on her door. Hearing no sounds from inside the house, he knocked again, this time less vigorously.

He'd missed her already. Ethan leaned against the hood of his car and ran his hands through his hair, frustrated. Nicole would be waiting for him, and he needed to go see Lauren. It would be up to him to decide whether to discharge her or not, and he wanted to be certain. But Dani was the only person who could answer the question on his mind right now.

An engine cut off, and Ethan realized someone had parked a car in front of Dani's house. Cooper got out of a sheriff's department squad car.

"Morning," Ethan said.

"Morning. Let me guess. She's not here."

Ethan shrugged. "I guess we're both too slow today."

Cooper scratched his chin. "I was really hoping to make sure she got hold of herself last night. She was pretty upset the last time I saw her."

"I heard you arrested the guy she thinks wrecked her boat."

"Yes, but not for that. She's steamed we don't have enough to charge him, when she practically delivered him to our door."

"I can see her point."

"The law is the law." Cooper glanced toward the house.

Ethan slid one hand into a pocket and jingled his keys in the other. He could tell Cooper about the image he caught last night. They'd been through enough the last few days that he trusted Cooper to do the right thing. So far his by-the-book personality had paid off. He had in custody the man who stole Quinn's car, smashed Sylvia's shop, and probably drilled a hole in Dani's boat.

"I guess I'll be dropping by to see your father today," Cooper said.

"Oh?" Ethan hadn't expected that.

"Maybe you know your father was attacked in the park a few days ago."

Ethan did know. He saw the incident from the window in Lauren's apartment. So did Nicole.

"The green shoes," Cooper said. "That's

what Dani said tipped her off. And that's the one thing your dad remembers about the guy who tried to grab his wallet. I just wish I could find a witness."

Ethan's gut heated. But he hadn't seen the man clearly either. He hadn't even noticed the green shoes.

Cooper tossed his keys up a few inches and caught them again. "Guess I'd better get to work and make sure Bobby Doerr didn't break out overnight. Maybe I'll see you later at the hospital."

Cooper walked to his car without looking back. The impulse to call him back strangled in Ethan's throat as he got in his own car. He wouldn't hold out on Cooper — or the mayor — all day. Just a little longer. Just until he found out what he wanted to know from Dani.

Which meant he had to find Dani. Ethan didn't have any idea who she might be working for today, but maybe it didn't matter. She preferred to be up at the lake whenever she could. If Cooper was right about how upset Dani was last night, Ethan suspected he knew where to find her.

Ethan started his car.

When he pulled up to the cabin, he saw Dani on the pier. She wasn't fishing, to his surprise, just standing at the end of the short platform jutting into the lake and cradling a large mug between both hands. If she heard the approach of his car, she didn't let on. Ethan lifted his laptop off the passenger seat and closed his door as unobtrusively as he could before walking slowly toward the pier. He stood, wordless, beside Dani.

Dani sipped her coffee. "We have to quit having these early-morning meetings."

"This shouldn't take long," Ethan said.

"I'm having a pretty good morning so far. Please don't ruin it."

"I think I took Quinn's picture last night," Ethan said.

Dani turned her head, expectantly.

"No," Ethan said, "I *did* take Quinn's picture — by accident. But there's someone else in the frame, and I want to know if he's the person who comes to see Quinn every year. You're the only one who can tell me."

She flicked her eyes down at the laptop he held in one hand like it was a book. "Show me."

Ethan opened the computer, tapped the space bar to wake it up, and watched as the photo filled the screen before turning it toward Dani.

"I know right where that is," she said. "And yes, it's Quinn."

"By the time I realized what I'd caught, he was gone," Ethan said. "What about the other man?"

"Too short," Dani said. "It's hard to tell someone's age from the back, but the guy

I've seen is taller than Quinn."

"You're sure?"

"You asked a question, and I answered it." Dani turned her eyes back to the view of the lake. "I kept telling you that when Quinn was ready, he would come home."

Ethan closed the laptop. "Thanks for taking a look."

"Talk to Cooper," Dani said.

"Enjoy your morning." Ethan didn't commit himself.

He returned to his car and decided his next stop would be the hospital. Once he satisfied himself that Lauren was progressing well, he would go to her apartment and see Nicole. Last night she'd been eager to hear about his visit with his parents. It was a long and complicated conversation, and Ethan didn't want to incite wild ideas by telling Nicole about his photo of Quinn. But she would be the next person he told.

He went in through the main entrance and passed the gift shop on his way to the elevators. On the second floor, he stopped at the nurses' station to pick up Lauren's chart, which showed nothing noteworthy. Her vitals were within normal ranges, she was eating well, she'd slept well, her pain was well managed and decreasing. Most important, the amount of fluid collecting in the drain was notably less.

Nurse Wacker swiveled in her chair to face

him and removed her reading glasses. She seemed to work long shifts, and Ethan had come to expect to see her there at any time of day.

"Good morning, Dr. Jordan."

"Good morning."

"Dr. Glass was looking for you a few minutes ago."

Ethan looked up from the chart. "Do you know where he is now?"

"He has office hours this morning, but he asked me to tell you he'd like to see you in the staff lounge at about five this afternoon."

"Thank you." Ethan closed the chart and suppressed his urge to exhale heavily. "I guess I'll go make my rounds now."

"Funny." She turned back to her paperwork.

Ethan knew what Dr. Glass wanted to ask him. He just didn't know what his answer would be.

9:40 a.m.

Nicole slept late. Two nights in the hospital waiting room and a late evening with Ethan had caught up with her, and even pulsing pain in her ankle didn't keep her awake. She woke grateful for a solid night's sleep in a real bed.

A week earlier Nicole was charged up to find Quinn — as soon as she took a run that turned her week inside out. She hadn't found

Quinn, and now she hobbled around in a cast on crutches and was staying in Lauren's apartment instead of her childhood home. Waking up without Lauren in the apartment felt odd. Even though she knew Lauren was in the hospital, subconsciously Nicole expected to hear the shower start or the clink of dishes in the kitchen or one of the network morning TV shows. Instead, only an occasional street sound permeated the closed second-floor windows while Nicole got herself dressed and managed to pour herself a bowl of cereal and brew some coffee.

No matter how many times Nicole told herself to stop looking at the clock, she glanced at it again. A string of messages to people in St. Louis were still unanswered, which only aggravated her restlessness. Nicole liked excitement. She liked puzzles. Without those two traits, she wouldn't be as good as she was in her work as an investigative reporter. But the upheaval of the last ten days had punched the air out of her, and impatience flooded the crevices of her mind. Was there a neatly typed letter awaiting her return to St. Louis — the sort of communication an employer would not trust to e-mail? Where was Quinn? Was Ethan going to repair his relationship with his parents, or was his visit with them on Sunday all there was to it?

Nicole wanted answers.

Ethan hadn't said what time he would come

by, but Nicole hoped that when he got there he would be ready to tell her whatever it was he had avoided last night. He probably thought he'd done well at controlling the conversation, of keeping her on the topic of what he'd learned about his own heritage in the space of twenty-four hours. But Nicole knew he was holding back — something about his parents or his job or she didn't know what. But something. While she rolled in Lauren's small desk chair, carrying a second cup of coffee, Nicole reminded herself that Ethan didn't owe her an explanation of every detail of his life. Circumstances had thrown them together, and Nicole believed Ethan did feel something for her, but they hadn't had a conversation that entitled her to more.

Still, Nicole's antennae were up.

Finally, his knock came on the door, and Nicole rolled over to turn the locks. When he bent to greet her with a kiss, Nicole offered her lips without reluctance.

"How's Lauren?" Nicole asked.

"Downright perky, I'd have to say." Ethan set his laptop on the dining table.

"Can she come home?"

"I think we'll wait another day before we consider that question. And I want to get one last scan."

"Was Sylvia there? Or Cooper?"

"No." Ethan opened his computer. "And

I'm glad. They don't need to hover over her at this point. They'll do themselves good to do something normal."

Nicole chuckled. "That arrest yesterday wasn't exactly a normal day in the life of a Hidden Falls deputy."

Ethan didn't respond, instead absorbed in arranging his computer.

Nicole rolled up to the table. "What's going on?"

"Something happened last night that I didn't tell you about."

No kidding. Nicole waited.

"Take a look at this picture and tell me what you see." Ethan nudged the laptop toward her.

Nicole leaned in to study the screen. Less than two seconds passed before she gasped. "When did you take this?"

"Yesterday, just before sunset."

"That's Quinn."

"I know."

"Why didn't you tell me?"

"We covered a lot of ground last night."

"Not about this, we didn't." Nicole pushed back from the table so she could give Ethan a full-on glare.

"It was an accident," Ethan said. "I didn't see them in the frame when I snapped it, and I had the telephoto lens on. They weren't even in shouting distance. By the time I realized I had it and went looking for him, they were long gone."

Nicole's brain sorted possibilities.

"I scoured the trails before I came here." Ethan pulled out a chair and sat. "And when I left, I went to Quinn's house and sat in my car for half the night. He didn't come home."

"Maybe you dozed off."

"No. He didn't come home."

"But —"

"I went back this morning in the daylight. Nothing has changed since the night we were there."

With her good foot, Nicole rolled the desk chair forward and backward, forward and backward. "And your theory about the other guy?"

Ethan shook his head. "I saw Dani this morning. She says it's not the man who comes to visit Quinn every year."

"Did she recognize who it was?"

Ethan didn't answer. He only ran his tongue over his lips.

"Ethan?"

"I don't think I asked that specific question."

"Dani isn't going to volunteer information."

"I know."

Nicole bit back her frustration. Ethan's face told her he felt bad enough as it was. Obviously Quinn had a secret.

"What if Quinn broke the rules?" Nicole asked.

"Rules?" Ethan echoed.

"Of the witness protection program. They keep people safe as long as they follow the rules. But what if he broke the rules, and you caught the consequence on camera?"

"You think Quinn is in the witness protection program?"

"He could be. Maybe this other guy is keeping him from going home."

Ethan looked doubtful but had the kindness to keep his thoughts to himself.

"Quinn came home to Hidden Falls," Nicole said. "I don't know why he didn't go to his own house, but if he was out walking in a place where someone could take his picture — even accidentally — that means someone else could have seen him, too."

"I'm going to get a few prints made and start asking some questions," Ethan said.

"I'm coming with you." Nicole started to roll into the hall. Her shoe was in the bedroom.

"No, you're not." Ethan caught the seat of her chair and impeded progress.

"Ethan." Nicole pushed against his grasp, but he held firm.

"You have a broken ankle, Nicole. Even in a wheelchair, the trails wouldn't be accessible. I'd be crazy to take you out there on crutches."

"I'll sit in the car."

"You'll sit here."

"You're not the boss of me." She protested, but with reduced vigor.

"I promise I'll stay in touch at every move." Ethan squatted in front of her chair and held her gaze.

"Cooper," Nicole said. "And Sylvia. We have to tell them."

"I know. And I will."

"But you're not going to depend on them."

"Would you?"

Ethan had her there. As an investigative reporter working on criminal stories, Nicole had been told on several occasions to step back and let professional law enforcement do what they knew how to do, but she always found a way to steer clear of official channels while also digging up her own information. The important thing was to find Quinn. They'd lost a whole night already since Ethan's photo, and Cooper's plate was full. What could it hurt for Ethan to show the photo around?

"Then that's what we'll do," Nicole said. "You see what you can dig up, but be careful. And call me — often."

As much as Nicole hated to admit it, it would be easier for Ethan to move quickly through his inquiries and to be smart about any oddball responses he received if he didn't also have to worry about Nicole's inability to run if necessary. Quinn wouldn't have been on the trails if he was trying to hide. Nothing about his posture in the photo alarmed Nicole. His head was up, his shoulders relaxed, his distance from the other man comfortable. All four of their hands were visible. Nothing looked sinister in the least.

"Do you need anything before I go?" Ethan stood and closed his laptop.

"Thanks, no." Nicole didn't want to hold up Ethan a minute longer than necessary. "My phone will be within reach every minute."

"I'll call."

"Do you want me to talk to Sylvia and Cooper?"

"Give me a head start," Ethan said. "I don't want them to tell me not to do this."

Nicole grinned. That was exactly the right answer.

He took his laptop and left. Nicole transferred herself into the recliner in the living room and used the remote control to turn on the television for some diversion, though she didn't understand how anyone lived with the limitation of broadcast channels only. With a game show in the background, Nicole looked out the front window. Other than the annual Founders' Day or the peak of summer weekend river tourism, Main Street was never crowded, especially at midmorning. Nicole saw a young woman with two small children come out of the park across the street, and she realized it was Raisa Gallagher. A week ago Nicole had avoided falling over the toddler only by stepping off a curb and breaking her ankle. Raisa was running after Kimmie now.

"That child must be a handful," Nicole muttered to herself.

She looked down the street and saw a squad car parked. Two deputies got out and sauntered up the block as if they were on a casual morning patrol. One of them stopped in front of the department store, though, while the other continued farther down before pausing, lifting his chin, and nodding. A second squad car turned into view and pulled across three open parking spaces outside the department store. A third officer emerged.

Nicole shut off the game show. Events on the street below were far more interesting.

Three officers — but not Cooper. Where was he? At the hospital?

Nicole sighed, reached for her crutches, and pulled herself to her feet. She would just go downstairs and see what it was all about.

11:11 a.m.

If nothing else, Liam would be well organized when he resumed working regular hours. He wadded up the paper towel he'd used to wipe dust from his shelves, dropped it in the trash can, and took a fresh pad of lined paper from a drawer. Would it seem more or less incriminating if someone from the corporate office of Midwest Answers entered the office and found supplies and files looking as if Liam was expecting not to work again?

He'd done nothing wrong. He would work again. He still had appointments on the books for next week, and since he wouldn't be spending so many evenings with Jessica, he would have plenty of time to go through leads, as thin as they might be. For now, Liam wanted the productive sensation that would come from a list of action steps that implied he expected his life and career to move forward. He had several mailboxes around the county. This was as good a day as any to make the rounds and collect the response cards that might have accumulated since last week's roundup, and he had a folder of unread materials from the corporate headquarters about new products consultants could offer to their clients. Out of habit, Liam turned to where his computer normally sat to check for new e-mails, but the space was empty. Cooper had taken Liam's computer for the technology team at the sheriff's office in Birch Bend to inspect and see if they could turn up any trails to explain the missing seventy-three thousand dollars. Liam had exposed himself, he knew. His eagerness to cooperate might be mistaken as a cover-up effort, but he hoped not. It had taken him so long to see that something was amiss with the accounts that he didn't feel smart enough to have masterminded the thievery.

Liam made a list of tasks in small straight script, and to the left of each entry he drew a neat square that he would X out when the task was complete.

The office door was propped wide open. Liam wasn't hiding anymore. When he heard footsteps in the hall, he cocked his head and held his pen still.

That was Cooper's walk. Liam blew out a controlled long breath and waited for his brother to appear in the doorframe.

"Hey, Coop."

"Hey, Liam."

Liam waited. Whatever it was Cooper came to say would take form soon enough. Liam briefly glanced over Cooper's shoulder to make sure there were no other officers, as there had been yesterday when Cooper arrested Bobby Doerr in the restaurant. Still, Liam couldn't seem to fill his lungs.

Cooper repositioned a chair opposite Liam, sat down, and laid one ankle on the opposite knee.

Liam cleared his throat. "How's Lauren today?" His brother's face sported fewer Band-Aids than it had the last couple of days. Gratitude for Cooper's safety flushed through Liam in a fresh wave, as it did several times a day since Saturday's storm.

"I spoke to her," Cooper said. "She sounded well. I hope to see her later this afternoon."

"Good." Liam had never noticed before how intimidating his brother's uniform made him look. Cooper even had a gun hanging from his hip.

"Something is happening this morning," Cooper said.

"That's what we wanted, right?"

"I just want to make sure you're ready."

Liam's breath caught again, but he gestured around the office. "It won't be hard for anyone to find what they need."

"No one's coming here, Liam." Cooper put both feet on the floor and leaned forward on his knees.

"What's going on, Cooper?"

"I'm glad you're here and not grabbing an early lunch."

Liam wished Cooper would just say whatever it was.

"There are three officers on Main Street," Cooper said. "In a few minutes, two of them will go into the department store."

Liam's stomach lurched. "Jessica."

Cooper nodded. "I suppose she thought she was pretty clever."

"She fooled me on my own computer, after all," Liam said.

"I didn't mean that."

"I know." Liam laid his pen down on the pad on the desk. "What did you mean?"

"It only took the white-collar crime guys

one day."

"And they're sure?"

"They think they are. There are some irregularities about the way she navigated your company's system that apparently are quite distinct from the way you normally do things."

"But they're sure it was Jessica?"

"Yes. The money is all in an account in Springfield."

"She went to a training conference there a few months ago." At least that's what Jessica had told Liam.

"And the note?"

"We haven't tied that to her. It might not be what you thought it was."

"You saw it." Liam pushed his chair back from the desk. What else could it be if it wasn't a blackmail note?

"I can't manufacture evidence, Liam."

Liam spun his chair around and looked out the window at a day like any other. People on the sidewalks. Cars parked in the street. A canopy of blue sky. Did no one else feel the seismic shift under his feet?

"Liam?" Cooper said.

"If you're ready to arrest her, what are you doing here?"

"I've been assigned to a different detail."

"But you're the senior deputy in Hidden Falls."

"And I'm your brother."

Liam twirled the chair to face Cooper again. "They can't think you have a conflict — that you would compromise the case."

"No," Cooper said. "They're worried about you."

"Me?"

"The problem with living in the small town where you grew up," Cooper said, "is that people remember what you were like when you were little."

"What's that supposed to mean?"

"It's just a precaution."

Liam understood now. Cooper was there to make sure Liam didn't do something impulsive to interfere with the arrest. And maybe it had been smart to send Cooper. Despite everything, Liam's impulse was still to protect the woman to whom he had given a diamond ring. They were supposed to have a future.

"What about the ring?" Liam asked softly.

"You were right. It's been tampered with. The stone that's in the setting now is worth a fraction of what you paid for the original diamond."

Of all the times in Liam's life to be right.

Cooper rubbed a knuckle against his chin. "I hate to ask, but have you checked the balance on the account you shared with Jessica recently?"

"The wedding account?"

Cooper didn't speak.

"No," Liam said. It hadn't occurred to him.

He'd been so frenzied at the thought of facing criminal charges himself, and then with the agony of his own suspicions about Jessica, that he hadn't done the one simple thing that was most obvious.

"We'll need you to look," Cooper said.

It was a joint account. Either one of them could have emptied it at any time. "I don't want that money anyway."

"It goes to her motivation."

Liam stood up, put his hands in his pockets, and jiggled a knee. "If I promise to behave, will you let me go see what's going on?"

"That's a bad idea, Liam."

"Maybe from your view. Not from mine."

Cooper moved his head back and forth slowly several times. "See, now this is why they thought it was a good idea to send me over here."

"I want to see for myself." Everybody in town would assume Liam knew more than he did about the events that were about to transpire. How many of them would see the officers going into the store and up to the third floor? Probably they already had. Cell phones would come out of pockets and purses to spread the news. Store employees, shoppers, curious gawkers — it didn't seem fair to Liam that they would witness a scene he was barred from. He was the wounded party, in more ways than one. Liam stared at his brother, unblinking.

"You need to let go," Cooper said.

"You don't know what I need," Liam snapped around the desk. "I need to see what's happening to Jessica."

Cooper stood quickly. "All right, but if you interfere in any way with the actions of the officers making the arrest, I cannot be responsible for what it might mean for charges you'll face."

"I'm not going to do anything. I just want to see."

They left the office. Liam flipped the lights off and pulled the door closed behind him. Their feet found a simultaneous rhythm on the stairs, around the corner, and down one block to Main Street.

"Stop here." Cooper grabbed Liam's arm.

Liam complied. He was just in time. Two officers flanked Jessica. Her wrists were cuffed behind her back, but she held her head high. Even now she had no shame.

Why had he never realized that about her before?

11:40 a.m.

Lizzie Stanford hustled into the store after her usual morning break and whispered to Sylvia behind the checkout counter, "You won't *believe* what's happening down the street."

Sylvia handed a customer his two dollars and forty-six cents change and waited for him to leave the store.

"What are you talking about, Lizzie?"

Lizzie straightened her sweater over her hips. "*Three* deputies."

The adrenaline that surged through Sylvia was becoming all too familiar lately.

"They arrested the accountant at the department store," Lizzie said.

"Jessica McCarthy?"

"Yes! How did you know it was her and not one of the others?"

"Just a guess." It didn't take much for Sylvia to put two and two together. Liam had been a wreck for most of the last ten days. He must have seen this coming.

"Apparently two deputies walked through the store acting perfectly normal and then went up to the offices. When they came back down, they had her — handcuffed and everything."

"Did you see this for yourself?"

"I didn't see them in the store, but word gets around fast. Half the town is standing out there gawking right now."

Sylvia widened her eyes. "They're still out there?"

"Yep. Squad cars and everything."

It was time for Sylvia to put on her mayor hat. "I'd better see what's going on. You can handle things here, can't you?"

"Of course."

The only people in the store were Raisa

Gallagher and her two little girls in the children's book section, and she was likely to spend a long time looking and then purchase only a couple of coloring books. Sylvia pushed briskly out the door and hurried up the street, abandoning decorum along the way.

Lizzie was right. The front of the department store was mobbed with bystanders. Most likely everyone in the store at the time of the arrest now stood on the sidewalk, along with dozens more who had been in adjoining businesses when news of the excitement burst. One of the deputies was fully occupied insisting that onlookers remain a reasonable distance from where another officer hemmed in Jessica against a squad car. A third officer was in the vehicle using the radio.

Sylvia had assumed Cooper would be leading the arrest effort, but instead he was farther up the block, well away from the commotion. He stood with his body positioned slightly in front of his brother's. Cooper didn't block Liam's view, but Sylvia suspected he didn't trust Liam to stay out of official sheriff's business.

Sylvia jostled through the crowd.

"Did you know about this, Mayor?" someone asked.

Sylvia gave a diplomatic answer. "It's a matter for the sheriff's department."

"Yes, but did you know?"

She didn't answer. "Stand back, please. There's no need to loiter." Sylvia pushed on through, keeping an eye on Liam. She'd known Liam for a long time — nearly all of his life. She hadn't always liked him, but she tried to be cordial. He could be pushy and self-centered and just a little too suave for her liking, but Sylvia was not without sympathy. He and Jessica had been an item for years. Whatever had led to the morning's dramatic events, Jessica's arrest was sure to affect Liam in some way. He was as pale as Sylvia had ever seen him.

Only when Sylvia reached Cooper and Liam did she turn around to see the view from their perspective. Jessica was dressed with as much chic as ever in a gray skirt hitting above the knees and a fitted rose-colored silk blouse. She wore three-inch heels, and her hair and makeup were flawless. Her head tilted slightly to one side, unimpressed with the events swirling around her.

"Good morning, Mayor," Cooper said.

"Good morning, Deputy Elliott." Sylvia took a position beside Cooper. As hesitant as she was about Liam at times, she liked his brother a great deal.

Cooper's eyes were fixed on Jessica, with a glance every few seconds at his brother in his peripheral vision.

"One arrest on Main Street this week was not enough excitement for you?" Sylvia said quietly to Cooper.

"Just doing our job."

Sylvia looked at Liam, trying to think of words to offer. "I don't know what's happened, Liam, but I'm sure this must be hard for you."

"It's my fault," Liam muttered.

Sylvia glanced at Cooper, who shook his head about half an inch. She didn't envy Cooper, caught between his brother and his job, but if anyone could walk that fine line, Cooper could. The crowd showed no sign of dispersing. In fact, it thickened.

Marvin Stanford turned away from the deputy doing crowd control and strode toward Liam. Sylvia slipped around Cooper and stood on the other side of Liam. While she might not know what to say to comfort him, her presence could spare him some derision or harassment.

"Did Lizzie call you?" Sylvia asked when Marv approached. He was rarely in town on a Tuesday morning, after working late on Mondays to print the *Dispatch* and bundle it up for the three boys who rode their bicycles around town throwing papers onto porches and sidewalks.

"This is a pretty obvious news story," Marv said. He took a pen from above his ear. "Liam, I'd like to ask you a few questions."

"Marvin," Sylvia said, "you can't print this story for a week. What's the rush for your questions?" The arrest of Robert Doerr amid dozens of onlookers had already given Marvin a better story than he had most weeks.

"I've been known to run a special edition," Marv said.

Sylvia didn't recall a single time in the last ten years that Marv had run a special edition. "Don't bother Liam now."

Marv angled himself toward Cooper. "Can I get a statement, on the record?"

"As you can see," Cooper said, "we are arresting Jessica McCarthy. When she has been duly processed, the details will be a matter of public record."

"Then why make me wait?"

"Marvin," Sylvia said. "I will personally guarantee that you get the information you need for a front-page story, but this isn't the time."

Marvin shuffled a few yards away, but he was already jotting notes.

Sylvia touched Liam's shoulder. "Is there something I can do? I'd like to help."

"Thank you." Liam hadn't budged since Sylvia first spotted him from down the street. "I got myself into this, and now I'll have to see it through."

Sylvia wanted to know what had happened as much as Marvin did. For the good of Hidden Falls, she needed enough information to help manage the fallout of this public scene. But she couldn't ask now. Cooper would fill her in during a more private conversation.

She looked up to see Nicole thumping toward her.

"What's going on?" Nicole asked.

Sylvia couldn't — wouldn't — answer that question with Liam standing right there, but how was Nicole to know? She gestured for Nicole to follow her and moved well down the sidewalk, behind Cooper and Liam. Neither one of them would take their eyes off the scene outside the department store.

"I saw the deputies arranging themselves awhile ago," Nicole said. "It took me longer than I'd like to get down here."

Sylvia told Nicole what little she knew, certain that Nicole had never met Jessica McCarthy and would not have recognized her as Liam's fiancée.

"This doesn't have anything to do with Quinn, does it?" Nicole asked.

Sylvia didn't honestly know. "I don't think so." She was going to have to quash that rumor, she realized. If Liam had been anyone but Cooper's brother, Sylvia would have pulled Cooper away to get at least the bare facts of the case.

"Did Ethan call you?" Nicole leaned against the brick of a building.

"No. Is Lauren all right?" Sylvia realized she'd left her cell phone at the store.

"Yes. It's not that," Nicole answered quickly and glanced toward Cooper. "Cooper is go-

ing to need to hear this, too."
"Cooper is occupied."
"I know," Nicole said, "but it's about Quinn. I'm not sure it should wait."
"I'm the mayor of Hidden Falls." Sylvia straightened her spine. And when it came to Quinn, she was far more than a local official. "Perhaps you should tell me what's on your mind and let me decide what to make of it."
Nicole tucked her hair behind her ear on the right side of her face. "I think he's back."
Sylvia's knees went soft, and she balanced herself against the brick beside Nicole. As she heard the account of Ethan's accidental photo, her breath quickened.
If Quinn was back, why hadn't he called her? Why hadn't he rung her doorbell or shown up in Waterfall Books and Gifts?
"Thank you," Sylvia said. "I'll take it from here."
"What about Cooper?"
"I'm sure we'll be in touch. You've done your part."
Sylvia left Nicole and took a few steps toward Cooper. She tapped his elbow and he turned his head slightly, keeping his eyes on the arrest scene.
"We need to talk," she said softly.
"This will only take a few more minutes," Cooper said. "I'll find you when it's over."
Sylvia wouldn't lose another minute waiting for Cooper's availability or fretting about

the welfare of the town. She could get back to the shop, grab her car keys, and start looking for Quinn within seven minutes.

11:57 a.m.

Liam had kept his promise. He'd stayed put while deputies escorted Jessica out of her workplace. He did nothing to interfere with any of the activities or movements of the deputies. She was arrested and handcuffed, and even from his position down the street, Liam could see it was only a matter of minutes before Jessica would be in the back of the waiting squad car and on her way — where? Would they keep her in Hidden Falls or take her to Birch Bend?

"I have to see her." Liam dodged around his brother's form.

Cooper took one long step to block Liam. "We had a deal."

"And I've kept my part. Nothing I do now will change what's done."

Liam avoided Cooper's eyes and pushed past him, throwing off Cooper's grip on his elbow. He paced up the sidewalk and wormed through the gawking crowd until he was within five feet of the woman he had thought he would marry.

Jessica looked up at Liam, but it felt as if she were looking through him or beyond him. Had she ever truly looked *at* him? She must have seen something in him six years ago when they began dating, and five years ago when she accepted his proposal and wore the ring he gave her.

Now the ring was only one more way she'd tossed him aside after she took what she wanted.

Hair fell across one side of Jessica's face and she blinked a few times at the irritation, but with her hands cuffed behind her, she could do nothing. Liam moved closer.

"It's all right," Cooper said from behind Liam. Nevertheless, a deputy established his position two feet to one side of Liam, while another kept a hand on Jessica's elbow.

Liam took the three steps that closed the gap between him and Jessica. Her focus changed now, and she looked into his eyes but offered no intimacy. He put his hands on her shoulders but felt no sense of recognition in his touch. Liam leaned in. With the squad car right behind her, Jessica had no place to go. Her scent, so familiar after so many years together, was both delicious and cold. Liam kissed her full on the mouth, lingering in inquiry.

Jessica offered nothing in return. The same softness of her lips and shape of her mouth that she had given so freely over the years now carried nothing. No surprise at his action. No regret at her own. No saucy temptation.

Liam broke the kiss. "If only we could have

trusted our love."

She ran a tongue over the lips he'd abandoned.

"If we had married years ago," he said, "we could have been happy. This would never have happened."

Jessica shook her head and let out a slow breath onto his face. "I gave you every chance to make something of yourself."

The words stung, and Liam stepped back.

"If you'd done your job and gotten Quinn's accounts when I first suggested going after them," Jessica said, "maybe we could have avoided this."

"Quinn has nothing to do with your choices," Liam said.

"You've never had enough ambition. I had to have ambition for you, and now you've ruined even that."

"I have plenty of ambition."

She scoffed in laughter. "I'm the one with all the guts. You had opportunity, but I was the one who knew what to do with it. We could have been partners."

"I was going to marry you. We were going to be life partners."

"And I could have made sure we had a good life, but you weren't even smart enough to see that."

"I only wanted you, Jessica. You would have been enough."

"You're so naive."

"You could have just broken up with me. Why did you do this?"

"Do what?" She looked at him with clear, untroubled eyes.

"Jessica." His voice hushed with hurt.

"Liam, don't pretend like you're going to stand by me now," Jessica said.

He could hardly say he would. Undoubtedly he would have to testify against her and give voice to the suspicions that ultimately led to enough evidence for her arrest.

"Go away." Jessica turned her face away from him.

Cooper tugged on his shoulder. "That's enough for now, Liam."

"It's enough, period," Jessica said. "I don't want to talk to either of you."

One of the deputies opened the rear door of the squad car while the other put his hand on Jessica's head with enough pressure that she folded herself into the backseat. In a few seconds, the engine was running and the vehicle carried Jessica away. If the trip — for now — was just to the small Hidden Falls sheriff's station, it might as well be to the moon. Jessica was lost to him.

Liam turned to Cooper. "Did you hear what she said?"

Cooper nodded.

"She's acting like she's innocent — like this is *my* fault."

"It's not," Cooper said.

"She was prepared to ruin me to get what she wanted." Liam shoved down the knot in his throat.

Cooper said nothing, which was just what Liam wanted him to do. He didn't want anyone to say he was lucky this happened before he married Jessica, or that she never deserved him, or that clearly she'd never loved him, or that he was better off without her. Behind his back, someone would say they never understood what Liam saw in her in the first place. People would say all sorts of things because they thought it was helpful to take his side, and none of it would be. In the face of the truth, no one would understand Liam's pain.

"Do you want a ride home?" Cooper asked.

Liam shook his head. "I'll go get my car."

"I'll make sure she's treated well."

"Thank you." Liam turned to walk back to his office.

Cooper's voice rose over the murmurs of the crowd, encouraging people to disperse and go on about the day.

When a woman's voice called Liam's name, he didn't turn around. Behind him, her footsteps quickened.

"Liam! It's Miranda. I just need a minute."

He stopped and let the woman who lived in the apartment directly above his catch up, steeling himself to politely tell her he wasn't in the mood to talk about what she had seen outside the department store.

"I just have a question," Miranda said. "I knocked on your door a couple of times."

"I haven't been home much the last few days." Liam couldn't force a smile, but he provided an appropriate pause into which she could speak.

"I left my box of heart disease brochures with you at the fair on Saturday," she said.

Liam nodded. "I'm afraid the storm got them."

"I don't care about the brochures," Miranda said. "But there was a manila envelope in the box. Did you see it?"

His heart crashed against his breastbone.

"Any chance you picked it up and took it to safety?"

Cautiously, he shook his head. Was she asking whether he'd read the note the envelope contained? Was she the one who left it there for him — the one who'd sent the first blackmailing note as well?

"I think that's all moot now," he said, guarding his tone.

"What's moot?" Miranda looked genuinely puzzled. "Did you read the note?"

"No."

"Well, neither did I. Now I'll never know what it said."

Hadn't she written the note?

"You've lost me," Liam said.

"My friend is organizing a murder mystery

dinner as a fund-raiser for the high school drama department," Miranda said. "She thinks she's having great fun writing cryptic notes about meetings and the like."

"Notes?"

"In unmarked manila envelopes. I already missed one envelope she claims she slid under my door, but I never got it. Apparently I missed a breakfast meeting in Birch Bend, and she was not in the mood for excuses."

Liam could hardly breathe.

"Oh well," Miranda said. "I knew it was a long shot that the envelope might have made it to safety, but I thought I'd ask."

"Sorry I couldn't help."

"I know it's silly to worry about the note. It just struck me that in the wrong hands someone might read something sinister into it. I guess I'm not very good at this mystery business."

Neither am I. "Your friend can't hold the storm against you," Liam said.

"I suppose not. Sorry about . . ." Miranda waved a hand toward the space the squad car had occupied.

"I have to go." Liam turned and lengthened his stride as fast as he could.

The note was not for him. All those sleepless nights. All those jittery cups of coffee. All those hours of fear and dread.

It was all a mistake. The note was not for

him. No one had known about the missing money.

At the corner, Liam leaned against the wall of the sporting goods store and let his shoulders heave with the effort of regaining breath.

"Liam?" Cooper was beside him. "You okay?"

"It was all a mistake," Liam muttered. He told his brother about the conversation with Miranda. "I put all of this in motion because I thought somebody else knew. Nobody knew. I was paranoid."

"That's a strong word," Cooper said. "You still did the right thing."

"I thought it was too late to undo everything."

"It *was* too late. You would have only implicated yourself in the crime."

Liam didn't speak aloud how close he'd been to covering up Jessica's actions if it had been within his abilities to do so.

Cooper glanced back down the sidewalk. "The mayor wanted to talk to me, but she's gone now. Are you sure you don't want a ride home?"

3:33 p.m.

"Can we stop for pie?"

As Jack pulled out of the junior high school pickup line, he glanced at the hopeful face of his youngest child.

"Please?" Brooke used her big eyes to their

fullest effect.

"Don't you want to get home to the dog?" At his wife's request, Jack was fetching Brooke from school, but he wasn't planning to call it a day quite this early.

"Roxie can wait a half hour. Please? I really want pie."

Half an hour. Jack's eyes flicked to the clock in the dash as he headed for Main Street. He was ready for his afternoon coffee anyway. "The café or the diner?"

"Café. The cream pies are creamier."

Jack hadn't been in the café in more than a week, not since the Sunday afternoon he and Liam had speculated on the harm that might have befallen Quinn the night before. Now Liam was in his own mess — indirectly, at least. Jack didn't know any details other than that Liam's fiancée was arrested a few hours ago. Observing Liam coming and going from their shared office floor in a deteriorating state every day, Jack suspected the arrest had not been a surprise to Liam.

He parked and followed Brooke into the café, letting her choose a booth and sliding in across from her.

She pulled the dessert menu from its holder and studied it. "Should I have chocolate cream, peanut butter cream, or banana cream?"

Jack didn't answer. Brooke wasn't asking his opinion as much as she was thinking aloud. He preferred berry pies, and Gavin knew that. While Brooke pondered her choices, Jack caught Gavin's eye and raised the coffee mug at his place setting. It struck him that the café was unusually busy for this time on a weekday afternoon. Gradually the chatter around them sorted into words and sentences and implying tones.

"I don't see how Liam Elliott could *not* have known she was doing something illegal. What kind of relationship could they have if he didn't know what she was up to?"

"That Jessica McCarthy has been a snob since the day she came to town."

"Did you see the way he kissed her? Right out there on the street."

"Cooper should recuse himself, even if he is the senior deputy. That woman was practically his sister."

Brooke stuck the menu back in the holder. "Why is everybody being so mean?"

Jack had hoped she wasn't listening. "I don't know. People like to talk."

"What happened, anyway?"

"I'm not sure, other than that a woman who works at the department store was arrested for some financial transgression."

"Is she going to need a lawyer?"

"I suppose so."

Gavin arrived with coffee. "Are you going to take the case? Could be an interesting one."

Brooke's eyes moved from Jack to Gavin and back again.

"That question may be premature," Jack said.

"Looks to me like she's in big trouble," Gavin said as he poured. "You should make sure she knows who you are."

"Did you decide what kind of pie you want?" Jack asked Brooke.

"Banana cream, please."

"I'll have whatever fruit pie you have," Jack said. "Thanks."

Gavin moved on to the next table.

"Will you be her lawyer?" Brooke asked.

"She hasn't said she wants me to be her lawyer." When Bobby Doerr called and requested his services, Jack figured he had come across one of the many business cards Jack spread around town. He would walk Doerr through the arraignment process at least. As soon as Jack arrived at the sheriff's office, he recognized Doerr as the man who'd stolen a purse in the same restaurant where Jack sat with his daughter now — and he saw the flicker in Doerr's eyes indicating he also remembered their encounter. That would be a separate matter in the legal system, though, and in light of the weightier charges Doerr faced, perhaps Jack would persuade his client to confess to the smallest of his violations. Ironically Doerr had been successful in more serious crimes while failing to complete a simple purse snatching or pick Richard Jordan's wallet out of his pocket.

"What if she does say she wants you to be her lawyer?" Brooke's inquiry brought Jack back to the present question.

"Then I would meet with her, and we would decide if I'm the right lawyer for her," Jack said. "Everybody accused of a crime is entitled to a strong defense, and no one should think they know the truth because they heard gossip somewhere."

Jack didn't think Jessica McCarthy would call him, though. She never regarded him with anything other than arrogant distaste. In the past, he wouldn't have cared. He would have done anything to bring in a fee or to bring a new client to the firm — which was precisely the attitude that got him in trouble in his corporate work in Memphis. Sitting in a small café with his thirteen-year-old daughter, Jack was certain that was not the image he wanted her to see of him. As tempting as it was to try to insert himself into the case, he wouldn't.

"Tell me about your day," Jack said, and Brooke launched into her usual vivid accounts.

Thirty minutes later, Jack dropped Brooke at home and turned his attention back to the question niggling his brain all day. Stephen Pease had exchanged his healthy child for the sickly son of Harold Tabor and a significant amount of money. Shortly thereafter, the Peases went through the motions of burying an infant, yet they had raised a boy who lived long enough to father a daughter — Ethan's mother.

So who was in that grave?

Rather than returning to his office, Jack drove to the cemetery. He didn't know Old Dom, the groundskeeper who had provided Nicole with the records that led her into the mystery of several babies, but it wouldn't be difficult to spot a man in his late eighties who seemed to feel at home on cemetery grounds. Jack's BMW crawled around the widest loop first as he looked in both directions for any sign of grounds-keeping activity. As he drove nearer to the heart of the cemetery, Jack spotted two young men clearing away fallen tree branches, likely remnants from Saturday's sudden storm. He eased alongside their pickup truck to inquire whether they knew Old Dom. Following their instructions, he found the caretaker with his knees on a pad while he pulled weeds from among a bed of flowers in their last gasp of bloom. Jack introduced himself, and Old Dom tilted his face up in greeting but did not stop plucking weeds and tossing them into a bag.

"I need to get this done," Old Dom said.

Jack squatted beside the old man. "I understand you know a great deal about the history of this cemetery."

"A fair bit." Dom pinched another weed. "You can pull weeds, can't you?"

Jack hadn't pulled weeds since he was a boy when he was sentenced for some infraction with a summer of tending his mother's vegetable garden. He didn't remember what his crime had been, but he remembered that he hated pulling weeds. Nevertheless, he reached among the flowers and pulled a greenish-yellow stem he was certain didn't belong.

"Lots of people asking questions these days," Dom said. "What's yours?"

"It's about the Pease graves," Jack said.

"We only have a couple of those."

"Two adults and an infant."

"That's what the records say."

Jack reached for another slender but stubborn stem, making sure to get his fingers close to the root. "Do you suppose I could see the records?"

"For that, you want to talk to Jasmine at the front desk in the office." Dom picked up the nearly full bag and shook its contents down.

"I understand you have some records that might be more informative," Jack said.

Old Dom smiled with one side of his face. "I do indeed."

"Then if you would allow me to give you a ride, maybe I could have a look while I'm here."

Dom folded the weed bag closed. "First I have to put this bag where it belongs."

"We can do that." At this point, Jack would do whatever it took to see those records, including haul a bag of weeds in the back of his spotless BMW. He picked up the bag, surprised at its heft and wondering how long it would have taken the old man to carry it. Jack opened the back of his car and set the bag inside, then held open the passenger door for Old Dom.

They drove to an enclosed trash and recycling area, and Jack gladly set the bag of weeds among others like it. Then Dominick pointed toward the main building and directed Jack around to the back.

"It's curious how many people are interested in my father's records," Dom said. "First Quinn, then Richard Jordan's boy and the Sandquist girl, and now you. I ought to get some chairs. I've only got the one."

Dom led the way through a door at the rear of the building. Jack followed through the underfurnished room Old Dom referred to as his office. Dominick took a key from his pocket and opened another door and flipped a light switch.

"What you're looking for is in here," Dom said.

Jack saw the books lying open on a counter. "Thank you for indulging me."

"What are you all looking for?"

"I'm sure you know Quinn disappeared," Jack said. "We're looking for whatever he saw when he looked at these books." The answer was overly simplistic, but Jack hoped it was enough to keep Dom talking. Jack didn't think the cemetery records had anything to do with Quinn's disappearance, but he had discovered months ago that merely dropping Quinn's name into conversation seemed to improve people's moods and cooperation.

"Like I told the Sandquist girl, those are the books Quinn was looking at. But since you mentioned the Pease graves, I'll save you some time. My daddy never believed that infant was the Pease baby."

Jack's head snapped up and he raised his eyebrows. "What makes you say that?"

"Daddy knew things. That was the way of him."

"The official records say the Peases lost an infant son."

"There's official records, and then there's what really happened," Dom said.

Jack gently laid his fingers on an open page of an oversized volume. "What do you think happened?"

Dom shook his head. "Can't say. I was just a boy myself. But I remember a lot of children took sick that winter. Whooping cough and measles are hard on the little ones. My own baby brother had the croup all winter. My mama was scared something awful that we'd lose him."

"But you didn't?"

"No sir. He pulled through."

"That's good to hear."

"But many families were not so blessed."

"Like the Peases?"

Dom removed his hat and scratched the top of his bald head. "That's hard to say."

Jack waited.

"So many babies were sick, and of course it was the Depression. If a grieving family turned up at the funeral home with a baby wrapped in a blanket and no money for more than a pauper's burial, nobody asked many questions. My daddy and I just dug the graves. Daddy had nothing to do with who went in them."

"But he had his ideas," Jack said.

"Yes sir, he had his ideas."

"Do you mind if I look at these books for a while?"

"That's what you're here for, isn't it? You seem like a smart man. You'll see soon enough what I'm talking about. But I'll tell you something else Daddy didn't write in those books."

"What's that?"

"Stephen Pease had a bicycle. He dropped by the next morning in his rattletrap of a car and asked me if I'd like to have it. Of course I said yes."

"Of course. What boy doesn't want a bicycle?" What did a bicycle have to do with the grave? Jack hoped Dom would get to the point.

"It was a heap of rust," Dom said, "and I had never ridden one before. Mr. Pease got back in his car and I waved. And that's when I heard a baby cry."

"A baby? In the car?"

"That's right."

"Did you tell your father?"

"Yes sir. He said he already knew and I shouldn't worry about it."

Jack's heart lurched ahead of itself. There was a crime. Multiple crimes.

Who — or what — was in that grave?

4:48 p.m.

Lauren smiled at the face she'd been hoping all day would turn up. "Hey, Cooper."

"Hey you. You're looking good."

Lauren hoped he would pull the chair close. She was ready for him this time, with her hair brushed, her bathrobe cinched, the head of her bed up, and her glasses on straight — more than presentable by hospital standards.

While Cooper, still in uniform, adjusted the chair to his liking — and Lauren's — a CNA stuck her head in.

"Do you need anything? Fresh water? A snack?"

"No thanks," Lauren said. "Someone said my dinner would be here soon."

The CNA let her glance settle on Cooper as she half-backed out of the room.

"Funny," Lauren said, "when my mouth is parched, I can't get anyone to come in and freshen my water pitcher for the life of me."

Lauren heard indistinct voices in the hall, which she ignored in favor of giving Cooper her attention. "I hope you've had a good day."

"Some highs, some lows," he said.

"Oh, what happened?"

Someone from food services came into the room. "I just wanted to confirm your dinner order. Pork chop or baked chicken?"

"Pork chop."

"Brown rice or potatoes?"

"Brown rice."

"Vegetable?"

"Whatever you have."

"Perfect."

Once the hospital employee left, Lauren looked at Cooper, puzzled. "That was weird. I don't always get what I mark on the menu, but they never come in to double-check."

"So you like pork chops better than baked chicken," he said.

Lauren laughed. "Let's just say I've had their chicken. What happened to give you a low day?"

Before Cooper could answer, the nurse came in with Lauren's chart and looked at the readouts on the monitor. She left without writing anything down but threw a smile at Cooper.

The hum in the hallway rose to a buzz.

"What's going on out there?" From the bed, Lauren didn't have a clear view of the door.

The food services person returned. "I forgot to ask if you wanted lemon cake or butterscotch pudding for dessert."

"It doesn't matter," Lauren said.

Cooper stood. "I notice there's a an unusual amount of activity right outside the door."

"Mealtimes are busy," said the food services employee.

"I have an idea what's going on out there," Cooper said. "On your way out, maybe you can let everyone know I'm off duty and there will be no further drama today."

The young woman blushed. "Sure." She turned and left.

"Cooper, what is going on?"

"You really haven't heard?"

"Heard what?"

"I'm guessing Ethan laid down the law about hospital staff coming in here bothering you with news."

Lauren put her hands flat on the mattress to push herself more upright. "And what news would that be? You said drama."

"Well, yes."

Lauren sucked in air. "Have you found Quinn?"

"No, I haven't heard anything on that front." Cooper resumed his seat.

"Then what?"

"We made an arrest today."

Lauren closed her eyes for a few seconds. She'd thought she was over being confused about the passing of time. "Oh. I thought that was yesterday."

"It was. There was another one this morning."

"Whoa."

Lauren listened to Cooper's brief account of his brother's suspicions, now almost certainly proven true except for presenting the case to a jury.

"I never got to know Jessica," she said. "Did you get along?"

"Well enough," Cooper said. "If they'd married, there wouldn't have been any fireworks in the family as long as Jessica stayed out of Dani's way. Obviously that's all down the tubes."

Lauren's head spun. Liam had always grated on her nerves for reasons she couldn't specify, but now she saw him through Cooper's eyes.

"Liam must be a mess," she said.

"He is."

"I'll call Pastor Matt. He has a way of making people comfortable even if he doesn't know them very well."

"You'll do no such thing."

"But I —"
"I just meant I could do it," Cooper said. "Your job is to get well. I'm pretty sure you're on official leave from your duties as director of family ministries."
"You promise you'll call Matt?"
Cooper nodded. "I'm not sure Liam will agree to talk to him, but I'll at least make sure Matt has the right facts about what happened."
That would have to do. Someone rapped on the door.
"What now?" Lauren said.
"I see you have your cheerful disposition back." Ethan came in and stood at the foot of the bed.
"Sorry," Lauren said. "It's been a parade in here the last few minutes."
"And if you're well enough to feel grumpy about that, I'd say it's progress." Ethan flipped a couple of sheets in the chart.
Lauren readied herself for the paces he would put her through checking various responses.
"Everything is looking good," Ethan said. "I can't find much to complain about."
"You're not going to chase Cooper out again, are you?"
Ethan glanced at Cooper. "I think he can stay as long as you'd like him to, if you promise to let him know when you're tired."
"I will."

Lauren's eyes focused on a smudge of dirt on Ethan's forearm. Then she noticed the layer of dirt across the tops of his shoes.

"What have you been up to today?" she said. "You look woodsy."

"I was out and about for a while today."

"More photos?"

"Not today." Ethan closed the chart and glanced at the wall clock. "I'm already late for a meeting with Dr. Glass, but, Cooper, I'd like to check in with you later about something. Will you be available?"

"Call me," Cooper said.

"When are you going to spring me?" Lauren asked.

"We'll talk about that tomorrow. I think we'll take the drain out in the morning and see where we go from there."

"You're throwing me a bone, aren't you?"

Ethan tucked the chart under his arm. "I'll make sure all this gets into your electronic medical record so it can haunt you for the rest of your life."

"Aren't you sweet?" Lauren grinned.

"Later." Ethan left.

"Is it my imagination," Lauren said, "or is everyone acting weird today? I asked an innocent question about what he did today, and he didn't want to answer it."

Cooper shrugged. "He's entitled to privacy."

"After everything we've all been through? I

thought we were past that."

"He's your doctor now. Professionalism and all that."

"Maybe." Lauren wasn't convinced. "What do you suppose he wants to talk to you about?"

"I don't know." Cooper leaned back in his chair. "But it reminds me your aunt wanted to talk to me earlier, and I never got the chance to find out what was on her mind."

"Off duty or not, it looks like your day is far from over."

"It does seem that way."

"You'll call my aunt, won't you?"

"I'll do my best to track her down. Maybe I'll buy her dinner and find out what's going on."

Cooper would be waiting for Ethan's call now, as well, and there was no telling what his evening held when it came to Liam. Frustration washed over Lauren. It wasn't like her to stay in bed. She wanted to be up and doing something. Problem solving was in her nature.

"Are you sure you haven't heard anything about Quinn? Did you question Bobby Doerr?"

"He's adamant that he didn't see Quinn — that he doesn't even know who Quinn is."

"Don't you find it odd anyone would want to steal a car as old as Quinn's?"

"Doerr says his uncle used to have one just

like it. He was feeling sentimental." Cooper caught himself. "You can't tell anyone I said that. It's an active investigation."

Lauren sighed. "I only wish he'd seen Quinn at some point."

"No one's giving up," Cooper said.

"I'm going to nag Ethan to discharge me tomorrow."

"You're going to do what he tells you to do."

"I don't think Ethan can imagine living in a small town again," Lauren said, "but I really want my quiet small-town life back."

"I know what you mean." Cooper stood up. "I should go check on things, but I have one question before I go."

"What's that?"

"Can I take you to dinner on Saturday night?"

Lauren flushed. "I would love that."

5:41 p.m.

The problem was that half the town knew who Dani's cousins were.

She had dodged the morning's events as much as she could, but when one cousin was a popular sheriff's deputy and another was engaged to marry a woman who exuded enough chic to make a hundred women jealous, suddenly everyone wanted to pick Dani's brain.

What did Dani really think about Jessica

McCarthy? Did she think Jessica was guilty? What about Liam? Had he embezzled as well? Was Cooper going to arrest his own brother next?

It would have been a great day for Dani to ignore her phones and go hiking, but before the arrest, she had committed herself to a minor plumbing repair, giving a quote on some painting work, and looking at a desktop computer on which the warranty had expired three weeks before the machine started freezing. That meant at least three lengthy conversations during which Dani said little while she concentrated on working but her clients speculated at length, plus a string of efforts to trap her by store clerks or people who happened to cross the street at the same time Dani did.

When were people going to learn?

The cumulative effect, though, was to make Dani wonder. She didn't devote much mental energy to Cooper. He'd done what everyone depended on him to do and upheld the law. It was Liam who was on Dani's mind. Despite overlapping hours at the hospital over the weekend and being together when Cooper arrested Robert Doerr, she hadn't had a private conversation with Liam since the day she discovered Jessica had put him at risk and broken his heart. While Dani wouldn't satisfy the misplaced inquisitiveness of people who didn't know Liam well and would jump to their own conclusions anyway, she did wonder how Liam was doing.

So at the end of her day, Dani swung by Liam's apartment hoping he was there alone.

He was.

Liam answered her knock within only a few seconds and admitted her without resistance. Dani surprised both of them by kissing his cheek.

"What was that?" Liam asked.

Now she slapped his shoulder. "It'll never happen again."

"Thanks for coming over."

The television wasn't on. No reading material lay open.

"Were you sleeping?" Dani asked.

"No."

Dani couldn't see that Liam had been doing anything else. "Just sitting?"

Liam nodded.

He looked relatively calm to Dani, considering that his world had disintegrated in the last few days. His briefcase was missing from its usual spot on the corner of his desk. Dani saw no sign of food or even an open can of pop.

"So I guess you heard." Liam put his hands in his pockets and pressed his lips together.

"Cooper has got to stop arresting people on Main Street," Dani said. "It gets people riled up."

"Right. Not at all like taking a guy out at

the knees in a hospital hallway."

"That was different."

"I don't really want to talk about it, Dani."

"Neither do I." That was the truth. "You hungry?"

"Nope."

"How about some TV?" Dani picked up the remote control from a side table and noticed Liam's cell phone was lying beside it, turned off.

"Not in the mood," he said.

Cheering people up was not one of Dani's areas of expertise. But then, cheering up was not what Liam needed. There was no point in pretending the day's events hadn't happened.

"Let's go to the lake," Dani said.

He grimaced. "That's more your thing than mine."

"It's a lake," she said. "Maybe you remember we have some property there."

"I haven't been to the cabin in years."

"I know."

"Too rustic for my tastes."

"Then lucky for you, I'm not inviting you in. But you can't sit here and stare at four walls."

"Yes I can."

"But you shouldn't. You've seen a whole lot of ugly the last few days. Your soul needs something beautiful."

"If I have a soul, it's toast."

Theology was also not one of Dani's areas of expertise, at least not the arguing variety, but leaving Liam alone right now seemed like the worst idea in the world. She also was certain she couldn't make herself sit still in his apartment no matter how hard she tried. She opened the closet beside the apartment door, pulled a leather jacket off a hanger, and tossed it at Liam.

He caught the jacket reflexively.

"Come on. I'll drive." She opened the door and stood, waiting, until Liam relented and put his arms into the sleeves and straightened the jacket over his shoulders.

Dani drove, without speaking, to her cabin on the edge of Whisper Lake and turned off the ignition. Darkness had not yet overtaken the sky. Dani estimated they had another thirty minutes before sunset, plenty of time to savor the oozing orange hues fading into the horizon. She had no more need of words than Liam. To stand on the pier, where Ethan had interrupted her morning with news of his sighting of Quinn, was all Dani wanted.

Liam followed her lead and got out of the Jeep. Dani could see him looking around, as if scraping for memories of outings with their grandfather or identifying vague recognitions of what seemed different. Dani offered no explanations. That could come another day if Liam was ever genuinely interested. For now she led him along the path to the short pier and positioned herself at its farthest edge, listening for Liam's footsteps behind her. Silent and motionless, Dani gave herself over to the sensations.

The water lapping against the slender pilings of the pier.

The slight breeze rustling what was left of the leaves on the trees.

The almost imperceptible drop in temperature as evening eased its way in.

The disc of light dissolving into dusk and shadow.

They stood in full darkness when Liam finally spoke.

"I'm not sure how I can fit in here now. Maybe I should leave Hidden Falls."

Dani felt a pebble caught between planks of the pier under her feet and bent to dislodge it.

"I'd miss you," she said.

"You and Cooper," he said. "That would be it."

"There may be one or two others. Quinn, for instance."

"Quinn likes everybody. That's hardly a recommendation for popularity."

Dani threw the pebble out into the lake, listening for its *plink*. "As you know, I'm not an expert in popularity. But moving away is not going to change things."

"I'd get a fresh start."

"A fresh start to do what, Liam?"

"Make something of myself, obviously. If I stay here, I'll just be the laughingstock of Hidden Falls. Nobody will ever trust me with their money again, either."

He had a point. Liam's career might never be the same. Maybe his company wouldn't even want to keep him on if they thought he had anything to do with how the accounts were compromised.

"You did the right thing, Liam."

"Yeah, well, I'm relieved it's all over, but I still feel kicked in the gut."

"And a new town and a new job is going to change that?"

Liam had no response.

"Your soul is not toast," Dani said. "That's not what we learned in Sunday school."

"You think about Sunday school?" Liam said.

"Don't sound so shocked."

"Sorry."

"You know, Cooper would have helped me find whoever put a hole in my boat if I'd given him half a chance."

"Are we changing topics of conversation?"

Dani sighed. "No. Tackling Bobby Doerr wasn't one of my finest moments, and I was wrong to get angry at Cooper for doing his job. At least you did the right thing."

"Just barely," he muttered, "and only because I was afraid for my own skin."

"But you did it. Give yourself credit."

Beside Dani, Liam cleared his throat.

"I've been thinking about how old we are," Dani said.

"Not *that* old," Liam said.

"Old enough to stop thinking I can outrun God. Your soul is not toast."

6:29 p.m.

Jack's theory was that if he didn't look at Dominick, the old man couldn't be sure Jack had seen him and therefore would not be offended by his guest's intrusion into the dinner hour. Casually scratching the side of his nose, Jack angled his head away from the doorway where Old Dom lurked.

The muffled cough Dom managed was the most fake and least subtle expulsion of air Jack had ever heard.

"I'll just be a minute," Jack said, turning another thick page in the dusty ledger book from the mid-1930s. It had taken him a long time to adjust to decoding the slender flowery handwriting without feeling as if he was mentally translating word by word into a typeface he could recognize. Now that he was reading more fluidly, he was out of time.

Dom flicked the lights off and on a couple of times.

"You've been so helpful," Jack said. "Please bear with me."

"You're welcome to come back," Dom said, "but I've got to go. I don't normally drive after dark."

"I can take you home."

"Don't want to leave my car here."

Reluctantly, Jack closed the book without being sure what he'd accomplished by spending the last couple of hours with Dom. He still had no idea who was buried in the grave marked simply *Infant.* Here and there in the book, Jack noticed the dots and dashes Nicole had referred to, but he didn't know Morse code. Whatever conclusion Nicole had come to, she'd had the advantage of Quinn's secretive trail of hours of poring through the records and chatting with Old Dom about what he remembered. Jack was depending on his instinct, and it was falling short.

Jack's phone rang. He didn't have to look to know it was his wife.

"Dinner is on track for seven," Gianna said. "Are you?"

"I should come pretty close." Jack stepped across the room into Dom's office area. The groundskeeper turned off the lights and pulled the door closed before turning a key in the lock.

"If you're not here by 7:15, I'll keep a plate warm."

"Thank you," Jack said. "I won't be long." He heard no scolding in Gianna's tone. She didn't even ask where he was or what he was doing. Perhaps the last few days had moved them out of the tunnel they'd been stuck in for so long.

He walked out with Old Dom.

"Do you figure you'll be back?" Dom asked.

"I'm not sure." Jack pulled his keys from his pocket. "Tell me, Dom. If you had to say who was buried in that infant grave, what would be your guess?"

"I don't suppose I'd have a guess."

"No? Your father seemed to have opinions."

"Hard to say he was always right, though. I long ago gave up trying to ferret out what was in his mind."

"Oh?" Jack raised his brows. "I thought you believed he had his ways of knowing things."

"There's knowing, and there's *knowing,* if you get my gist."

Dom's words cast a blanket of doubt over what Jack thought he knew. If the cemetery records couldn't answer his questions about the mysterious grave, he would have to dig deeper into other sources of information — birth records, family histories, law enforcement records, missing children's reports. He could investigate multiple avenues before he gave up on isolating what kind of crime — or crimes — might have been committed and for what reasons. The main question was what consequences resulted. Who benefited?

"You heard a baby cry that day," Jack said. "Even then you thought something was funny. Wouldn't you like to know what really happened?"

Dom shuffled toward his car. "People have their reasons. I think that's what my daddy believed."

"There could have been a crime."

Dom nodded. "True. Or maybe it was just the best way out of a hard time."

Jack didn't want to let go. He would have to tell Ethan he was going to get to the bottom of whatever happened. He could promise to try to minimize the impact of the investigation on the Jordans, but there was no getting around the fact that the baby presumed to be in that grave had in fact not died for more than another twenty years.

"Good night, Dom. Thanks again." Jack got in his car. The hospital wasn't far from the cemetery and it wasn't large. How long could it take to determine whether Ethan was there? Jack could get this settled now and still make it home for dinner only slightly late.

At the hospital, Jack inquired about Ethan at the information desk and fingered the coins in his pocket while the volunteer on duty made a couple of calls. She hung up the phone and smiled at him.

"Looks like you just caught him," she said. "Our new doctor is checking on patients on the second floor. You should be able to catch him at the nurses' station."

Patients? Our new doctor? Jack withheld his opinion that the gray-haired woman had overstated Ethan's relationship with the Hidden Falls hospital, instead thanking her and moving down the hall toward the elevators. And the plural *patients* was a curious word choice, considering Ethan had only one patient.

Jack went up to the second floor and down the hall. Ethan was making notes on a small computer and looked up.

"Hello, Jack."

"Hello, Ethan. Got a minute?"

Ethan leaned his head away from the nurses' station, and Jack followed Ethan down the hall and a few feet into an unoccupied room.

"I've been thinking about our conversation yesterday," Jack said.

"Good," Ethan said. "I hope you've come to see how it would be best for my family if we left well enough alone at this stage."

"I understand how you feel." Jack hadn't thought through the words he would use at this moment.

"Thank you. I don't want to muck things up more than they already are. Let's just give history a fresh start."

Jack cleared his throat. This wasn't the conversation he'd intended to have.

Hidden Falls was supposed to be his fresh start, a chance not to muck things up further. Gianna would never understand if Jack held on to this against all odds — and no billable client. The truce between them held the promise of affection again, but it was fragile.

If Jack left now, he could still be on time for dinner with his family.

"I'm going to put the will and the contract right back where I found them," Jack said. "They'll be there if you ever decide you want them. In the meantime, I wish your family well."

"Thank you, Jack."

Out in his car again, Jack exhaled. He wasn't very experienced at letting go of a case that wormed its way into his mind, but he felt an odd sense of relief.

7:22 p.m.

Across the table at Fall Shadows Café, four eyes stared at Nicole. She cringed.

"Cooper, I was really hoping Ethan would have spoken to you by now," she said. Sylvia and Ethan both had said they would talk to Cooper.

Cooper didn't speak. Around them, tableware clinked and conversations rose and fell. Gavin zipped by with two platters of food.

"Say something," Nicole said.

Cooper turned his head to look at Sylvia. "Mayor, you don't seem surprised."

"I tried to talk to you this morning," Sylvia said. "It wasn't a good time for you."

"It wasn't the easiest day I've ever had." Cooper pulled his phone out of its holster on his hip. "I don't see any missed calls from either of you. Or Ethan."

Nicole and Sylvia exchanged glances.

Cooper cocked his head. "Is this where you tell me you've been out looking for Quinn on your own?"

"Well, I haven't," Nicole said. "Ethan wouldn't take me with him. I would have slowed him down."

"And you, Mayor?"

"I did what I could this afternoon, but I didn't come up with anything."

"I wish you had called me," Cooper said.

"You had your hands full." Sylvia laid her knife and fork across the top of her plate. "Liam needed you, and your staff has two people in custody."

"I could have called in more officers from Birch Bend," Cooper said. "Now it's been twenty-four hours."

"It's *Quinn*," Nicole said. "Of course Ethan and Sylvia are going to look for him."

"If there is foul play, interference could make it worse." Cooper tossed his napkin on the table.

Nicole didn't know Cooper until ten days earlier, but in that time she hadn't seen him this close to the edge. She pressed her lips together, giving him time to think.

"So what has Ethan been doing all day?" Cooper finally asked.

"Knocking on doors, stopping hikers, showing the picture he took last night." The process was nearly identical to what Nicole and Ethan had done together the day after Quinn disappeared — and with equal result. "Nobody saw Quinn."

"Maybe it wasn't him," Cooper said.

Sylvia tapped the table nervously. "But what if it was?"

"I saw the photo. It was Quinn." Nicole nudged her plate away. "Cooper, let's rehash what we should or shouldn't have done later. Right now what matters is looking for Quinn."

Cooper pulled a few bills from his pocket and dropped them on the table. "I've got to get to the station. I'm going to pull officers from Birch Bend, but we've lost the advantage of daylight now."

Nicole watched him stride out of the café and turned to face Sylvia. "He's angry."

"It'll be all right," Sylvia said. "He keeps his cool most of the time, but it had to be hard to watch his brother go through what happened this morning."

"You and Ethan covered a lot of ground today," Nicole said. "I'm not sure Cooper's team could have done much better — not with the arrest going on and Bobby Doerr in custody."

At least Ethan and Sylvia had been focused. Ethan combed the woods around the falls and the cabins along the lake for hours without being distracted by everything that would have been on Cooper's mind.

"We're going to find Quinn," Sylvia said. "And he'd better have a good reason for coming back to town and not letting us know he's here, or I'll throttle him."

Nicole puffed her cheeks and blew out her breath. Cooper was frazzled. Sylvia was frazzled. Ethan was frazzled.

And Nicole wished she could go for a long run to loosen the tension in her muscles.

"I have to get going." Sylvia scooted her chair back. "I want to see my mother before she goes to bed and then go make sure Lauren doesn't need anything."

Nicole's phone rang. "It's Ethan," she muttered as she answered.

"I'm leaving the hospital now," Ethan said. "Have you eaten?"

"Just finished, at the café. Ethan?"

"Yes?"

"Cooper knows." Nicole glanced up at Sylvia.

"Good. I wanted to tell him a couple of hours ago, but I didn't want to get into it in front of Lauren. She still needs her rest."

"Well, he knows now. You should probably call him."

"I will. Will you wait for me there?"

"I'll be out front. We can go see Cooper together."

"I should be there in fifteen or twenty minutes."

Nicole ended the call. "Ethan's coming."

"Good," Sylvia said. "I didn't want to leave you on your own."

"I'm fine," Nicole said. "Lauren's apartment is just down the street."

"It's far enough you should have a ride."

"Go," Nicole said. "Tell Lauren I'll see her tomorrow."

Sylvia paced swiftly through the restaurant. Nicole moved more slowly behind her. Outside, Nicole bypassed the wooden bench in front of the café, once again aching to go for a run, to let her body free and clear her mind. But she couldn't run. The best she could do was try to hop with more speed. On a clear sidewalk she could set her crutches down firmly and swing between them with more vigor than indoor maneuverings allowed. The motion felt good, and with plenty of time before Ethan would show up, Nicole moved farther down the street. At the end of the block, she paused and went a few feet around the corner before turning around to retrace her path.

When a hand clamped over Nicole's mouth, she nearly lost her balance. Pressure on her shoulders compelled her to hop in a half circle. In the stillness that followed, the tune fell on Nicole's ears.

Quinn's tune.

Nicole focused on the eyes twelve inches from her face. They were not Quinn's.

13
DISTINGUISHING MARKS

Wednesday
7:30 a.m.

Quinn tucked a throw pillow under Nicole's ankle propped up on a footstool. "I have orange juice concentrate in the freezer. Oh, and some sausage links."

Nicole looked into his yellow-brown eyes and gave herself once again to the sensation of relief and gratitude.

Quinn was home. Quinn was safe.

"You don't have to wait on me," Nicole said.

"My house, my rules," Quinn quipped. "I threw out all the fresh food because it was, well, not so fresh anymore. But we'll find enough odds and ends for a breakfast feast."

Nicole didn't care about the food. She only wanted to feast on Quinn. He picked up three large coffee mugs and a plate of cookie crumbs, evidence of the casual sustenance that had punctuated the last twelve hours, pausing to smile at her for the hundredth time. And for the hundredth time, Nicole grinned back.

"When you were a girl, you were never allowed to stay up all night gabbing with me," Quinn said.

"Now I am." It was the best all-nighter Nicole remembered with anyone.

"Sorry we had to nab you the way we did last night."

"I'll admit you scared me half to death."

"I should have told my minion to be less thug-like in his approach."

Nicole laughed. Quinn's minion — the man Ethan caught in the photo on Monday evening — turned out to be more of a teddy bear than a thug. Her heart rate had shot up when his hand sealed off the protest springing from her throat, and his humming of Quinn's tune launched a host of scenarios spinning through her mind. Only seconds later, though, with his hand still on her mouth, he'd shifted his position to allow her to see past him.

And Nicole saw Quinn's head tilted out of the shadowed window of a parked car across the quiet side street.

Her eyes flashed to the man, who whispered, "He doesn't want a fuss yet. Don't scream or call his name. Just get in the car, okay?"

Whether the stranger accurately reflected Quinn's wishes, Nicole wasn't about to dispute the conditions of a reunion with

Quinn. She nodded agreement — she would have done nearly anything to get to Quinn — and the stranger released his hold before gesturing that she should feel free to walk in front of him.

He could have a gun, Nicole thought at the time. But she didn't care. Quinn was in that car. She scrambled into the backseat, and Quinn twisted to smile at her.

It was all right.

The stranger got behind the wheel and asked directions. Quinn described the first couple of turns, and Nicole knew they were headed for his house.

And now she sat in Quinn's living room, beside the low-burning fire Quinn had tended in the hours approaching dawn. Safe. And he was safe — and had been safe all along.

In the kitchen, Quinn opened cabinets and drawers and the refrigerator. Nicole heard the plop of frozen concentrate dropping into a pitcher, the rush of water at the tap, and the rhythmic clunk of Quinn's stirring motion. The smell of a fresh pot of coffee wafted through the house as sunlight wiggled between curtains that were not quite closed. All of it was so wondrously normal.

Nicole couldn't stand not to be in the same room with Quinn. She let the booted foot down to the floor carefully and picked up her crutches. The carpet absorbed the sounds of her movement, and at the threshold to the kitchen, Nicole paused to watch Quinn in action. He'd pulled bread from the freezer and was now intent on separating frozen slices for the toaster. On the stove, sausage links sizzled in a frying pan.

He looked up. "I was going to bring you breakfast on a tray. I have a cloth napkin and everything."

"I should be making *you* breakfast, to welcome you home."

"Nonsense."

"I feel positively naughty and absolutely lucky to have you to myself for the whole night." Nicole's phone was full of frantic messages from Ethan, but Quinn had pleaded for a few more hours before the inevitable blitz of attention. She wouldn't deny him anything he asked, not under these circumstances after all this time.

"It's been an unexpected treat, though I suppose it will come to an end soon." Quinn pointed at the kitchen table with a wooden spoon. "You'd make me a lot less nervous if you'd sit down."

Nicole obliged. "Quinn, thank you."

"It's just breakfast and not a very good one."

Her throat thickened. Right now she would eat sand if Quinn put it in front of her. "I was so glad to see you at the banquet. Then when you disappeared —"

"I just went away for a while."

"Right. When you went away — and no one knew where you were — I was afraid I would never get to tell you how grateful I am for the presence you were in my life growing up." Words Nicole had kneaded smooth for a week tumbled together as they came out of her mouth. It wasn't quite the speech she'd prepared, but this was the right moment. "A broken ankle suddenly gives a person a lot of time to think, and I kept thinking about how much you loved me, how often you were there when I needed someone, how no matter how confused I got, you straightened me out. Thank you."

Quinn stirred the juice. "You're welcome."

"You saved me," she said, her voice hushed. "After my mother died, my life could have gone badly a dozen different ways. You were the one who made me believe I could still have a good life."

He looked at her, his eyes full of examination. "Are you happy?"

"Yes. Very."

"And your father?"

"He's well. I'm sure you know he moved away and started fresh, finally. We're in touch often now."

"I'm glad to hear that. I always hoped you would someday forgive him his grief."

Nicole supposed that was exactly what happened. Quinn held her up when her own father couldn't, buying them both time to find their way out of trauma and toward each other.

Footsteps thudded down the stairs. When the man from last night entered the room, freshly showered and his hair still wet, Nicole marveled again. She had watched one resemblance after another unfold in the late evening hours before Andrew — or was she supposed to call him Scott? — went to bed and left Nicole and Quinn to catch up on missing years. Their eyes were different colors but the same shape. Their noses sloped at the same angle. Their speech lilted with the same cadence. Even the way their shoulders and elbows were hinged was the same.

Brothers.

Quinn had a brother. And Nicole had nearly met him months ago in St. Louis. She might have, if the story she worked on about a doctor who caused disfigurement with his treatments for port-wine birthmarks hadn't settled out of court before her story hit the papers — and before she met the man who had been willing to see the doctor undercover if necessary to expose him. Instead, she had filed her story without a quote from Scott Wilson.

Or Andrew Kreske.

Nicole still couldn't believe she was right about the witness protection program — almost. She still hadn't pieced everything together. Quinn promised he would tell her everything, but last night he was much more interested in hearing about her life than explaining the reasons he entered the witness protection program just shy of his college graduation.

Scott Wilson was Andrew Kreske.

And Ted Quinn was Adam Kreske, Andrew's older brother.

He would always be Quinn to Nicole, but if he wanted her to learn to call him by the name on an obliterated birth certificate, she would do it.

"Good morning," Nicole said, when Scott — Andrew — peered at the coffeepot hopefully.

"Good morning. Did you two ever go to bed?"

Quinn and Nicole both laughed.

"Nope," Nicole said.

"I had a feeling you wouldn't." Scott took a mug from the cupboard. "Imagine how I felt when he turned up on my doorstep."

"Did you recognize him?"

"Immediately. I didn't want to go to sleep for two days."

"Make yourself useful," Quinn said, "and set the table."

Scott cocked his head at Nicole. "A bossy big brother is always a bossy big brother."

She chuckled. "He does have a way of getting people to do what he wants them to do."

Quinn removed two slices of bread from

the toaster, dropped two more into the slots, and then took the sausage off the stove.

"Adam, what are you going to do today?" Scott took three plates from a shelf.

Quinn sighed. "I wish I could just slip back into my life, but I suppose now there will be even more fuss than the night I left."

Nicole smiled. If Quinn thought the banquet was too much attention, no wonder he didn't want to face the extreme commotion ahead of him now.

"Will you go back to your real names?" Nicole asked.

"I guess we could." Scott glanced at his brother. "I admit it felt awfully good to hear someone call me Andrew."

"Are you certain there's no more reason to stay protected?" Nicole said.

"None whatsoever," Quinn said. "But what is a 'real name'? I've lived with the name Ted Quinn for more years than I was Adam Kreske. Even if I went through the legal hoops, can you imagine trying to get the people of Hidden Falls to call me by another name?"

"So you plan to stay in Hidden Falls?" Relief warmed Nicole.

"It's my home."

Nicole went soft at her core. Hidden Falls wasn't just a hiding place for Quinn.

"Of course, I'll feel free to leave the county now," Quinn said. "And have my picture taken. So I'll lose my charming quirkiness."

Nicole chuckled. "Marv Stanford is going to have a field day with this story in next week's *Dispatch.*"

"I may have to reel him in a bit," Quinn said. "I just want things to get back to normal. If I don't return to my classes soon, I'll be off track for the rest of the school year. There's no telling what the sub has been doing all this time without lesson plans."

"How long will you stay in Hidden Falls, Scott — Andrew?" Nicole said.

"Scott's fine. We'll see. I've got plenty of vacation time in the bank, and Oklahoma isn't going anywhere."

In her back pocket, Nicole's phone buzzed. She pulled it out. "It's another text message from Ethan." She scrolled through a long string of messages that had come through the night.

WHAT HAPPENED?

WHERE ARE YOU?

I'M WORRIED. CALL ME.

I'VE LOOKED EVERYWHERE FOR YOU.

ARE YOU HURT?

WHAT'S GOING ON?

WHY AREN'T YOU ANSWERING?

NICOLE, YOU'RE SCARING ME.

"You should respond," Scott said.

Nicole glanced at Quinn.

"Seriously," Scott said. "Quinn, there's no telling what Ethan will do if he doesn't hear from Nicole soon. Hidden Falls has been frantic about you for ten days. Why add worry about Nicole to the list?"

Quinn set the platter of sausages and toast on the table. "Call Ethan. But only Ethan. I want to do this on my terms."

8:03 a.m.

At first Ethan was unconcerned that Nicole wasn't waiting for him outside the café on Tuesday evening. He took a little longer to get there than he'd estimated, and she could have run into somebody she knew or decided to duck into a nearby shop while she waited.

By the time he'd been up and down Main Street, though, he was worried. Even people who didn't know Nicole should remember whether a woman matching her description had come into a store in the last few minutes. In his experience, something like a knee-high boot cast would catch people's eyes, especially when the cast was combined with crutches. But he'd been in every shop up and down Main Street twice — first expecting to spot her in a store, and then when he didn't, to ask if anyone had seen her. Gavin remembered what Nicole ordered for dinner, and that Cooper hadn't looked happy when he left, but no one else seemed to have noticed what happened to Nicole once she stepped outside the café.

She couldn't have gone running on a broken ankle. She couldn't drive, either — and her car was parked at her empty family home where she'd left it on the day of her injury. Nicole couldn't have just disappeared on her own.

Ethan had been up to Lauren's apartment twice, banging hard enough on the door to attract the stares of neighbors sticking their heads out of their apartments, but Nicole wasn't there, and no one had seen her since long before dinnertime.

Ethan worried.

Then he fumed. He sent her text after text and left her a string of voice mails. Why didn't she at least let him know where she was?

When his phone finally rang on Tuesday night, Ethan grabbed it, but it was a slightly irritable Cooper insisting that they had to talk immediately. Ethan had taken Cooper a copy of the photograph of Quinn, apologized for not calling Cooper sooner, relayed everything he'd done all day, and then headed out to look for Nicole again.

In his room at the motel, he hadn't slept. If Nicole didn't contact him soon, Ethan intended to go back to Cooper's office and report another missing person.

Ethan was almost at the hospital to check on Lauren and — he hoped — write her discharge orders if her drain was still clear and the latest scan showed nothing of concern.

When his phone rang and he saw it was Nicole's number, Ethan swerved to the side of the road and braked hard.

"Nicole, are you all right?"

"Yes. Are you alone?"

"In my car. Where are you?"

"You sound angry."

Ethan took a deep breath. "I'm worried about you."

"I'm all right. I'm sorry for not being where I was supposed to be last night."

"I've lost count of how many times I called you."

"Thirteen. And nineteen text messages. I think you'll understand why I couldn't answer them, though."

"Are you sure you're all right?"

"Positive. Can you come to Quinn's house?"

"That's where you are?"

"Please come," Nicole said. "As soon as you can."

"Who is with you? How did you get out there?" What would Ethan walk into?

"Just come." Her voice cradled promise. "It'll all make sense when you get here."

"I'll be right there."

Ethan glanced at the time in the dash. He'd been seeing Lauren every morning since the surgery. If the Hidden Falls hospital was like every other hospital in the country, discharge could take hours after a doctor's orders. The sooner he got the process going, the better, but it would have to wait. Ethan's heart pounded with relief that Nicole was all right tangled with curiosity about what awaited him at Quinn's.

It clicked.

Quinn was at Quinn's.

He dropped his phone into the passenger seat and mentally calculated the fastest route to his old neighborhood.

When Ethan approached Quinn's house, he could see the difference immediately. Wispy smoke rose from the chimney. While the curtains were still drawn, he could see lights on inside. A sedan with Oklahoma license plates sat in the driveway.

Oklahoma. The phone number that kept calling Lauren came from Oklahoma, whistling or playing the tune Quinn had made up to reassure Nicole when she was a girl.

Ethan pulled in behind the sedan, got out, and let his driver's door slam behind him. By the time he got to the door, Nicole had pulled it open and leaned on her crutches to greet him. When he kissed her, he tasted breakfast sausage.

Nicole reached one arm up around Ethan's neck. "He's here. He's really here."

"You scared the daylights out of me." If Ethan had any lingering doubts how he felt about Nicole, the terror of the night and the relief of the morning resolved them. He squeezed her to him.

"I'm okay. He's okay. Wait until you hear the whole story."

Quinn stepped into the foyer. "I'm afraid it was my idea for Nicole not to call you last night, but I'm glad to see you so concerned. It's just like the old days."

Ethan let Nicole loose but held her hand. Yes, just like the old days — if she would have him again.

"Quinn." Ethan offered a handshake, but Quinn opened his arms and wrapped Ethan in a bear hug.

"I'm delighted to find you still in town," Quinn said. "I had imagined you'd gone back to Ohio."

Ethan fell into the genuineness of Quinn's embrace and made no move to shorten it. Finally, Quinn released him.

"Come into the living room," Quinn said. "We have some catching up to do."

Nicole led the way in. Ethan sat next to her on the sofa. Quinn paused to put a log on the fire before taking a seat opposite them.

"Thank you for looking after Lauren," Quinn said. "Nicole told me what you did."

"Her aunt was the one who was alert enough to realize something was wrong." Ethan soaked up Quinn's relaxed countenance. Wherever he'd been, and whatever the circumstances, Quinn had come home happy.

At the mention of Sylvia, emotion flushed

through Quinn's face. "She'll be the next call, but I'll make that one myself."

"Call now," Nicole said.

"She would have been my first call," Quinn said, "if I hadn't seen you hobbling around on those crutches. I was surprised to find you still in Hidden Falls and had to know what happened."

"I wasn't *hobbling,*" Nicole said. "I was doing quite well, as I recall, until you came along."

"Yes, you were." Quinn chuckled. "I'll call Sylvia, but we may not have another time for just the three of us. I want to breathe it in for a few more minutes."

Ethan squeezed Nicole's hand.

"I'm so glad to see the two of you together." Quinn raised his hands, palms out. "I know, I know. Your relationship is not my business, and I'll stay out of the way while you sort things out. But when I think of how many times the three of us sat in this room together, well, it warms me from the inside out."

Ethan looked at Nicole. As if she felt his gaze, she returned it.

"When I asked you to come for the banquet," Quinn said, "I had no idea all this was going to happen. Nicole tells me you have jeopardized your career by staying in Hidden Falls."

"Well," Ethan said, "it has taken a turn."

"I'm sorry for that. But I'm glad you met

Dr. Glass. If he had any sense, he would snatch you up as soon as your residency is over."

A smile escaped Ethan's lips. "As a matter of fact, he made a persuasive argument that my services are needed in Hidden Falls."

Nicole leaned away from Ethan. "What are you talking about?"

"Persuasive." Quinn raised his eyebrows. "Did you hear that, Nicole? Persuasive. That implies success."

"Well, yes," Ethan said, "he was successful. We sealed the deal yesterday afternoon."

"Does this mean Gonzalez won't throw you out of your residency?" Nicole said.

"It would seem Dr. Glass was persuasive with Dr. Gonzalez as well. He pointed out that despite all his threats, when it comes down to it, Gonzalez doesn't want an incomplete residency in his stellar statistics. He offered to take me off Gonzalez's hands and supervise the last few months of my residency. Sort of a final medical rotation in rural medicine. That way Gonzalez can graduate me from his program."

"Like a proctored exam," Quinn said.

"Yes, something like that."

Quinn rubbed his palms together. "This is delightful news."

"Shocking news." Nicole's jaw went slack.

Ethan offered her a sheepish grin. "I was going to tell you last night."

"Now about my note," Quinn said. "I understand a certain photo came into your possession in a — *ahem* — creative manner."

"That was all Nicole's idea." Ethan pointed at her.

"I have no doubt," Quinn said. "She always was the instigator. However, Lauren's convincing Sylvia to open my box surprises me more than Nicole deciding to break into my house."

"Would you two like me to leave the room?" Nicole said. "Wouldn't that make it easier to disparage me?"

"I think we're doing quite well in your presence." Quinn grinned. "However it came about, I'm glad you know the truth now. Do with it what you will."

"Excuse me," Ethan said, "I realize you and Nicole had all night to catch up, but my curiosity is about to split me open. Where have you been all this time? And who were you with two nights ago when I took your picture?"

"Ah, yes, the photo at the falls."

"Shall I go get him?" Nicole asked Quinn.

He nodded. Nicole got up, stabilized herself, and swung herself on the crutches to the kitchen. Ethan realized he heard water running and movement from the other room. He'd been so absorbed in the pleasure of seeing Quinn and relief at Nicole's well-being that he hadn't noticed the obvious. Someone else was in the house. He squirmed on the sofa to see who would come through the door.

Quinn stood up. "Ethan, I'd like you to meet my brother, Scott Wilson."

Ethan was on his feet, ready to accept the proffered handshake. "You're the man in the photo."

Scott laughed. "We thought we were being so careful, staying off the main trails. It was almost dark. Nobody else would be starting a hike at that hour."

"I had a telephoto lens," Ethan said.

"So I hear."

Ethan reeled toward Quinn. "If you'd ever told me you had a brother, I would have remembered it."

"I didn't," Quinn said. "I couldn't."

"Witness protection," Nicole said.

Ethan couldn't keep his eyes from widening. "Seriously?"

"I'll fill you in on the details later," Quinn said. "But it was Nicole's comment on the night of the banquet that set me off. She talked about someone with a birthmark that looked like a peeling red onion on his lower back. It was such a specific description. My mother used to use it. What were the odds someone else would describe a birthmark that way, in that same spot?"

Ethan looked at Scott. "You mean?"

Scott yanked up his shirt and angled his

back toward Ethan.

"When I arrived at the banquet hall," Quinn said, "I had every intention of going through with the evening. I was glad to see you there and have the chance to ask you to stay a few more days. But the longer I thought about it, especially when I was alone behind the curtain, the more I realized I had to go. After more than thirty years, a clue about my brother's whereabouts that fell into my lap. I couldn't ignore it."

"But Nicole would have helped you," Ethan said. "If your brother was in St. Louis, and he was going to be part of a story, she would have known how to find him."

"We went all through that last night," Nicole said. "I'd never actually met Scott, or even spoken to him. But the main thing is that under the rules of protection, Quinn couldn't tell me why he would want to find this supposed stranger."

"I wasn't even supposed to be looking for him."

"But you have been," Ethan said. "The envelope Liam found from Santorelli in Pennsylvania."

"I'm very anxious to see the letter," Quinn said, "but until now, they haven't had much to encourage me. After all, I had no leads to give them, not even Scott's name. Over the last few years, Santorelli investigated cities up and down the eastern seaboard, but none of the scraps of information we started with went anywhere."

Ethan started to pace in front of the fire. "I still have questions."

"Shoot," Quinn said.

"How did you get out of town?"

"Imagine my surprise when I went out to the lot and my car was missing," Quinn said. "If I reported it, I'd miss my chance, so I walked up to the highway and stuck out my thumb. It was astonishingly easy."

"It must not have been anyone you knew." Even casual acquaintances would have heard about the search for Quinn and reported seeing him.

Quinn shook his head. "A very nice young man from Louisiana passing through on his way to Chicago. A person can get lost in Chicago, but they do have trains to St. Louis."

"When you came back, why didn't you come here, to your house?" Ethan said. "Where did you spend that night you were on the trail?"

"In the hollow behind the falls," Quinn said.

Ethan slapped his forehead. "I never went all the way down there to look behind the water."

"Hardly anybody does, especially in the dark. I haven't been there in years myself. I'd forgotten how cold it gets." Quinn's eyes seemed to drift off to another time and place. "I have to call Sylvia now."

9:17 a.m.

Her mother so seldom asked anything of Sylvia that when she did, Sylvia hated to say no.

This is why she was in the center aisle of the grocery store on a Wednesday morning when she ought to have been at Town Hall, or on the phone with Cooper, or visiting Lauren at the hospital, or ferreting out whether Ethan ever found Nicole last night, or checking in with Lizzie at Waterfall Books and Gifts before the store opened.

During their regular phone call at seven in the morning, Emma asked her daughter to take her to the grocery store. Their usual system was for Emma to keep a list on the kitchen counter, and Sylvia would pick it up every few days and bring the items by a day or two later. Sylvia suspected that lately Sammie Dunavant had been doing the same thing, because Emma's lists became shorter and less frequent, yet her cupboards remained stocked.

But today Emma had insisted she needed to go to the store and get ready for winter. Sylvia wasn't entirely sure what that meant. When she picked up Emma, Sylvia looked for the list, but there wasn't one. In any event, the likelihood of severe weather was still a few weeks away, and a quick look in the refrigerator showed plenty of fresh food, a pot of soup, and three kinds of cheese. The cupboards had crackers, pastas, and canned goods. Still Emma pressed to go to the store.

Sylvia had called Town Hall to let Marianne know she would be late, and here she was in the grocery store, pushing the cart at Emma's painstaking pace.

"How about some yogurt-covered raisins?" Sylvia suggested. Maybe her mother was looking for snack foods.

"How much are they?"

"Not too much." If Sylvia was more specific, her mother would recoil in horror at the cost of the item. She'd already done so at least six times. After forty-five minutes, only seven items lay in the cart, and Sylvia intended to distract her mother when the cashier rang up the total even if Emma found nothing else she wanted. Sylvia tossed the raisins in the cart, certain her mother would enjoy them.

"I can't decide what I'm in the mood for," Emma said. "There's so much to choose from. Has the grocery store always been so confusing?"

The store had remodeled five years ago, but its selections had not changed substantially, and even a year ago Emma shopped fairly well if Sylvia left her alone in the store. Emma's slide away from independence was slow but steady.

"I'm going to look at pudding. Where's the pudding?" Emma said.

Fortunately, they were in the correct aisle.

"Take your time." Sylvia pulled her phone out of her purse and dialed first Ethan's number and then Nicole's, as she had already done several times that morning. Neither of them answered. It was bad enough when Ethan said he couldn't find Nicole last night. Now it seemed that he'd gone AWOL as well.

What was happening to this town? Was she living in an episode of *The Twilight Zone*?

Her phone rang in her hand, making Sylvia jump.

Quinn's home number. *Quinn's number.*

"Quinn?" Sylvia said.

"Yes, it's me."

His cheerful voice made Sylvia go weak in the knees. *Quinn.* "Where are you? How are you?"

"I'm at home and I'm just dandy. Can you take a few minutes out of your busy day to drop over?"

Quinn was a master of understatement. His voice dripped over her spirit like honey. *Oh, Lord, thank You!*

"Sylvia? Are you there?"

She recovered her voice. "Yes, I'm here. Are you really all right?"

"Positively."

Tears heated her eyes, the first time Sylvia had allowed them to take full form since discovering Quinn was not standing on his mark behind the curtain at the banquet hall.

Quinn's voice dropped. "I really am all

right, and I want to see you. Please come."

"Of course I'll come. I'm at the grocery store with my mother, but if I have to I'll pick her up, put her in the cart, and roll her out to the car like a squalling toddler."

He chuckled. "Give Emma a kiss for me."

Sylvia's grip on the phone trembled even after Quinn's voice was gone. "Mom, we have to go."

"Are we finished shopping?" Emma said.

"As soon as we get your pudding." Sylvia took chocolate, butterscotch, and tapioca off the shelf and dropped them into the cart. "Let's get them all. That way you can decide what you're in the mood for later."

"I like to mix peanut butter in my chocolate pudding," Emma said.

"You have peanut butter at home." Emma had been doing that since Sylvia was a little girl. The day would come when Emma could not operate a microwave to warm up the pudding the way she liked it, but today was not that day.

Today was the day Quinn was home.

Sylvia aimed the cart toward the checkout counters, knowing full well that Emma could still keep up if she decided to.

"You can start a list," Sylvia said. "If you forgot anything, I'll get it later."

"You're a good daughter." Emma spoke matter-of-factly.

Sylvia's brimming tears threatened a deluge. "Thank you, Mom. Let's get home and put these things away."

Sylvia handed the checker in the express lane two canvas bags, swiftly unloaded the cart, and swiped her debit card before her mother could ask any more questions about what the items cost. Still, it was another thirty minutes before she got Emma home, offered her a snack, put the groceries away, and started for Quinn's house.

She parked on the street and took in the scene. Ethan's car in the driveway assured her he and Nicole hadn't disappeared. The other vehicle was unknown to Sylvia. Had Quinn rented it and driven home? When he asked her to come, Sylvia had imagined a more private reunion. Realizing others were present, she stood on the front step for an extra minute to compose her face and mood. When the curtains in the front window parted, Sylvia startled. Nicole grinned out at her. The front door opened before she knocked, and Ethan hustled her into Quinn's home.

In the living room, Quinn knelt on one knee beside the fire, rearranging logs. Sylvia realized how chilled she felt. Whether it was from the coolish September morning or the anticipation of seeing Quinn, she wasn't sure. Either way, she was grateful for the warmth in the room. Tending the fire was so characteristic of Quinn. He could have been kneeling before the flames on any ordinary morning, arranging the precise draft of air to feed the fire and keep it crackling with the perfection of a holiday movie.

"Quinn," Ethan said, "she's here."

Quinn's head rotated toward her, and Sylvia soaked up his face. The shape of it. The color of it. The crinkling features when he smiled. Even his balding head. Sylvia loved it all.

He stood and turned his entire body toward her and held out a hand. "Sylvia, come here."

She dropped her purse in a chair on the way to him, freeing up her arms to wrap around him. Quinn's heart beat against her at the core of the embrace.

"I'm so glad you're all right," Sylvia whispered in Quinn's ear. She knew Nicole and Ethan were in the room, but their presence faded away in the grip of Quinn's arms around her.

"I would have called if I could have," Quinn murmured. He kissed her ear as he finished speaking into it and then took her face in his hands.

Sylvia held her breath. Quinn hadn't touched her this way in years — decades — but she had never stopped wishing he would. When he leaned his face toward hers, she offered her lips.

Quinn kissed her full on the mouth — and lingered. Even when the clapping started behind her, Sylvia felt only Quinn's nearness.

"So this is the one," a strange male voice said.

Quinn broke the kiss and smiled into Sylvia's eyes. "This is the one. The only one."

Sylvia looked over Quinn's shoulder, wondering if the man had been there all along and she'd only seen Quinn, only wanted to see Quinn.

Quinn took one of Sylvia's hands. "Sylvia, this is my brother, Scott Wilson."

She fumbled for words as Scott shook her hand. "I didn't know Quinn had a brother." And why was his brother's last name Wilson?

"I couldn't tell you before now," Quinn said. "I didn't want to put you in danger."

"Danger?"

"Do you remember the day we hiked down to the back of the falls and stood for hours in that hollowed space?"

Sylvia remembered. When Quinn kissed her there and said how much he loved her, Sylvia had hoped he'd gone back to the jeweler for the ring they'd looked at. It was the perfect place to propose, an exquisite moment. He kissed her repeatedly that afternoon, but he never reached into his pocket for a little velvet-covered box. They never again talked of marrying, and only later did Sylvia look back and realize his kisses had been good-bye kisses — good-bye to the future they had both allowed themselves to dream of.

She remembered every detail and nodded now.

"In those early years," Quinn said, "my reasons for coming to Hidden Falls were raw. I had nightmares that my old identity would collide with my new identity and people I cared about would get hurt. I couldn't put you at risk by confiding."

What old identity was he talking about?

Nicole sat in the chair closest to Sylvia. "Quinn was in the witness protection program."

"We both were," Scott said. "We weren't allowed contact even with each other."

Sylvia had read enough novels and seen enough movies to know that if Quinn was in witness protection, he knew something terrible or had seen an awful crime.

"I would have kept your secret," she said.

"I wasn't worried about what *you* would do," Quinn said.

He didn't have to say more. Sylvia understood. Whoever Quinn witnessed against was well connected. But here Quinn was, standing in his home in Hidden Falls with his long-lost brother. What changed?

"Are you safe now?" she asked.

Quinn nodded. "After I found Scott, I had to make sure it was safe to come back."

"What happened?"

Quinn smiled. "It's a long story, and it involves a surreptitious meeting at the San

Francisco airport with a US marshal on his way to Paris. But there's plenty of time for it later." He moved to the end of the mantel and reached for a small box.

A jeweler's box. Sylvia's heart kicked into high gear.

"I love you, Sylvia." Quinn went down on a knee and opened the box. "If I haven't missed my chance by taking so long, I hope you'll still have me."

He had gone back to the jeweler in Birch Bend all those years ago after all.

11:30 a.m.

Dani shook her head at Liam's feeble effort with the fishing rod. How was it possible that they had the same grandfather, who took all his grandchildren out on the water, and yet Liam couldn't get the hook in the water without tangling the line? And of course, once he'd created the mess, he was useless at untangling. Dani sighed and traded rods, giving Liam the line that was already in the water.

"This was your idea," Liam reminded her. "I said we should go back to civilization when we got up."

In the end, after dangling their feet off the end of the pier until eleven o'clock the night before, they stayed the night in the cabin. They hadn't talked much. Dani's capacity to listen to the night sounds of the lake was nearly infinite. As long as Liam wasn't restless, Dani saw no reason to disrupt the peace that settled into the silence between them. A cloudless day slid into a cloudless night, and the longer they stayed out, the more stars they saw. Eventually Liam stretched out with his back on the pier and his hands locked behind his head, staring into endlessness.

It was Liam's stomach rumbling audibly that reminded them both that they hadn't had dinner, and Liam admitted he hadn't eaten lunch, either. Dani still kept their grandmother's old air-tight tins filled with crackers and dried fruit. Liam ate his fill and fell asleep in front of the fire Dani stoked from time to time. By its light, she watched her cousin's slumber. His business troubles were not over, and though Dani had never experienced a broken heart in the romantic sense, she didn't imagine Liam would get over Jessica anytime soon.

It was true that when he woke well after the sun was up, Liam suggested they go back to town. Dani countered by saying they might as well take some fresh fish with them. She knew now that she would have to catch anything they took home because Liam didn't have a clue what he was doing with a rod and reel. A cooler on the pier held two good-sized trout. Dani was hoping for one more.

When her phone rang, Dani ignored it.

Whoever it was could wait. She still had the entire afternoon available to answer calls and decide whether anything was the emergency a caller made it out to be.

Three or four minutes later, Liam's phone rang.

"Ignore it," Dani said.

Liam had both hands wrapped around the end of his pole. If he tried to answer his phone, he was likely to drop their grandfather's best rod into the lake. It was bad enough Dani had lost her brand-new reel when her rowboat went over the falls. But she could replace that one eventually — especially if she would answer her phone a little more often and come out to the lake a little less often. Losing her grandfather's old equipment was a different story. To Dani's relief, Liam made no move to answer his phone.

Less than five minutes later, Dani's phone rang again. "I knew I should have left my phone in the Jeep."

"Somebody's trying to reach us," Liam said. "Maybe it's Cooper."

Liam put one hand in his pocket, and Dani grabbed his pole. She wasn't taking any chances. Her phone rang four times, went silent, and immediately rang again. Dani answered it this time.

"Dani?" It was Nicole's voice.

"What's up?" Dani said.

"Are you at the lake?"

"That's right."

"By any chance is Liam with you?"

"Yes." Dani glanced at Liam, who was punching buttons on his own phone.

"Grab some of your famous fish and come to Quinn's house," Nicole said. "There's someone here who would love to see you."

"He showed up, did he?"

"Yep. Get over here before you miss the whole story."

Dani handed one rod back to Liam. "Do you think you can reel this in without falling into the lake?"

"Give me a little credit." Liam began to crank the handle on the reel.

"We're going to Quinn's," Dani said. "He's there."

Liam's gaze snapped toward Dani. "Quinn's back?"

"Didn't I just say that?" Dani had her line in. "I told everybody he'd come back when he was good and ready."

"Are you sure he wants to see me?" Liam asked.

"Why wouldn't he?"

Liam finally got his line reeled in. Dani secured the cooler in the back of the Jeep and drove straight to Quinn's.

"Looks like the party started without us," Liam said when they saw the cars parked outside Quinn's house.

Dani knocked on the front door but didn't wait for an answer before trying the knob and finding it unlocked. While she had never been as seriously concerned that something was wrong with Quinn as some of the people around town, Dani admitted — at least to herself — that she was curious to hear Quinn's explanation of his actions.

And she hadn't expected the news that Nicole's suspicions were not so far-fetched or that Quinn had a younger brother. Sylvia kept coffee cups filled as Quinn's account unfolded.

"I was fifteen," Quinn said, "and Andrew — Scott — was twelve when it all started. Our parents died within a few months of each other from unrelated causes."

"It was as if lightning struck twice," Scott said. "You don't expect it the first time, and you certainly don't think it will happen again."

Nicole took in air audibly. "No wonder you understood how I felt when my mother died."

"What happened to you after that?" Sylvia asked. "You were both underage."

"We had an uncle," Quinn said, "my father's brother. He and his wife had lost their only child when she was very young. They weren't quite sure what to do with a pair of adolescent boys, but they took us in. Scott and I were together, and it was all working, though we knew we'd be on our own once we finished school."

"So what happened?" Ethan asked.

Dani wished everyone would quit asking questions and let Quinn tell the story in his own time.

"We were almost there," Scott said. "Quinn was in college. I was in high school — still underage."

"This was all in New York City," Quinn said. "I had a scholarship, but to save on expenses, I was living at home. I planned to help Scott through school next. Then one night my uncle asked me to run a fairly routine errand for him."

"Swatches," Scott said. "He had a modest interior design business and had promised to get some swatches to an impatient client."

"It was on my way to a night class," Quinn said. "I just had to get off the subway one stop early and walk a few blocks."

Dani scanned the room to see how the story was sinking in.

Quinn got out of his chair and paced slowly in front of the fireplace. "I'm not going to tell you every sordid detail. If I had just walked away when no one answered the door, I would never have come to Hidden Falls or missed out on my brother's life. But my uncle had been emphatic that the swatches had to be delivered that night, so I tried the door and it opened. I walked in on a gruesome crime and it wasn't quite over. But I'm not going to put those images in your heads, like an episode of *Law and Order.* I care about all of you too much."

The silence was breathless, vacant. Sylvia's eyes leaked tears. Nicole clutched Ethan's hand. Liam paled. Dani ransacked her memory for any reference Quinn might have made, even years ago, that would point to this rendering of events.

"I dropped the swatches and ran," Quinn said. "It turned out someone had already called the police because of strange noises. An officer thought my behavior was suspicious and stopped me. Spending forty-eight hours in custody because they thought I was an accessory to the crime probably saved my life."

Scott cleared his throat. "Then one morning a note arrived threatening *my* life if Quinn testified about what he'd seen."

Whether he was Adam Kreske or Ted Quinn, this man in whose living room Dani sat now would have done the right thing. Of course he testified.

"The police did everything they could to keep us safe while we waited for the trial," Quinn said. "We stayed in school but otherwise kept to ourselves. We got so we could spot the plain-clothed officers watching us. But even when the trial was over the next year — with a guilty verdict — the danger wasn't. The police found the continuing threats to be credible and suggested protection. I was old enough to be responsible for my brother, and anyway, by now he was only months away from being a legal adult. My only requirement was that we both go into the program — together."

Dani realized now that the man she'd seen come to visit Quinn every year must have been a US marshal, Quinn's one contact with his past.

"Then what happened?" Nicole asked.

"It was all set," Quinn said. "I went with a marshal for some orientation about where they were sending us, and they only gave me documents for one new identity."

"You became Ted Quinn," Sylvia said.

He nodded. "I created a fuss that would make you all proud and refused to go without Andrew. But by the time I got back to our uncle's home, Andrew was gone."

"They broke their deal with you?" Dani finally gave in to the urge to ask her own question.

"Something glitched," Scott said. "My uncle said I should go with the marshals who came for me, that everything would be all right. Adam would sort it out. But somehow the arrangements had been made for us separately instead of together."

"I never saw Andrew again," Quinn said.

"And then Nicole told you the birthmark story," Ethan said.

Quinn nodded. "I'd been looking for years, on my own and through several private agencies."

"Santorelli," Liam said. "The envelope that went to my box by mistake."

"But it was the birthmark," Quinn said. "I had no reason to think anyone knew about it, but what if they did? What if Andrew was exposing himself by being willing to do that newspaper story?"

"My big brother still wanted to protect me," Scott said.

"What about never leaving the county?" Liam asked. "Wasn't Scott under the same restriction?"

"That was my personal rule," Quinn said. "At first I was afraid and wanted a controlled existence. Then I was . . . well, happy."

"But you couldn't give up on your little brother," Nicole said.

"That's right. So I went to St. Louis." Quinn stopped his pacing and pointed at Nicole. "That newspaper you work for is in complete disarray. It's a wonder they get an edition out at all. It took me three days before I could even get someone to talk to me. A woman named Terry came up with the name of the lawyer you worked with. I had the feeling she was thumbing her nose on her way out the door."

Nicole sighed. "That sounds right. She quit when the reorganization was announced."

"I staged a sit-in at the attorney's office." Quinn's eyes gleamed. "He'd found Scott through a multistate network of doctors he was working with and had been ecstatic Scott was willing to go to St. Louis."

"I had business there from time to time anyway." Scott positioned an ankle on the opposite knee. "A couple of meetings weren't a big deal."

"The attorney wasn't very forthcoming, though," Quinn said. "I finally drew a sketch of the birthmark. Since no photos of it had appeared in the paper — or even a description — that convinced him I did know the person with the birthmark."

"Probably spooked him," Nicole said.

"The lawyer called me," Scott said. "It was sort of a heads-up. If I didn't want to see the nutcase from Illinois, I didn't have to, but I was duly warned he was on his way to Oklahoma. I looked at him through the peephole, and the rest is history."

"But the danger," Sylvia said. "How are you sure you're safe?"

The brothers looked at each other.

"People get old," Scott said. "We insisted the authorities tell us what they knew. The man the marshals were watching most carefully all these years died seven weeks ago from pancreatic cancer at age fifty-seven. The last known associate of the man who threatened Adam — Ted — or me is serving life in prison for an unrelated crime. He stabbed another inmate and now has no possibility of parole."

Around the room, breath flowed out of lungs.

"If you'll all excuse me for a moment," Quinn said as he left the room.

"It was too much," Sylvia said. "We should have kept our questions to ourselves."

"He's all right," Scott said.

Dani cocked an ear and heard Quinn moving around in his den. She looked at Nicole. "Do you still have his computer?"

"Yes, but he knows the whole story."

Quinn returned with a folded check in his hand and held it out to Liam. "This probably isn't for nearly as much as you were hoping, but you'd do me a great service if you would invest it in the fund we talked about."

Liam stared at the check, unmoving. Dani nudged his elbow, and he finally reached to take the thin paper from Quinn's hand.

Dani rolled her eyes. If Liam was going to salvage his business, he would have to get over the notion that nobody wanted anything to do with him.

1:14 p.m.

When the phone on his desk rang, Jack kept his eyes on the real estate contract in front of him as he hit the speaker button and answered the call. "Jack Parker."

"This is Liam Elliott."

Jack pushed the contract away from the center of his desk and set a fresh legal pad in front of him. "How are you?"

"Better than you might think," Liam said.

"How so?" Jack put the point of a pen down on the paper, ready to begin writing. Maybe Liam was calling on behalf of Jessica McCarthy — or perhaps he had been mixed up in the financial violations himself. Everybody deserved a strong defense.

"Do you think you could come down to the corner?" Liam asked.

Jack heard a snicker in the background and laid down his pen. He was not in a mood to be the butt of a prank.

"Where are you, Liam?" Jack stood up and tapped his desk.

"About two minutes away."

"Why don't you just come up to the office? I'll be happy to speak to you."

"Come on, Jack. Loosen up."

Liam Elliott was telling Jack to loosen up? They weren't pals. Until the last week or so, they'd barely said more than good morning to each other as they passed on the stairs. Had Liam been drinking in the middle of the day? Jack could think of no reason not to end the call.

"Stop in," Jack said, his finger poised over the button that would cut off the call. "I'll see what I can do for you."

"Oh, I don't need a lawyer," Liam said. "Well, at least not today. Tomorrow could be a different story. Just come to the corner. We'll be there in one minute."

"Who's 'we'?"

"You'll see."

Liam's voice dropped away, and Jack realized the call had ended. He took his suit jacket off the back of his office door and pushed his arms into the sleeves as he left the suite. By the time he reached the corner at the end of the block, three cars had parked and the doors flew open.

Ethan raced around his black Lexus to get to the passenger door before Nicole emerged unassisted.

Liam and his cousin got out of her muddied Jeep.

The third vehicle was the mayor's red Ford Taurus. She got out of one side, and a man Jack didn't recognize got out of the other.

And Ted Quinn unfolded himself from the backseat. What in the world?

Jack buttoned his suit jacket.

"I don't remember if you've met Quinn." Liam strode toward Jack.

"In passing a couple of times," Jack said. Though he didn't know Quinn beyond his reputation in Hidden Falls and the affection his daughters felt toward him, Jack felt as if he'd been racing Quinn toward the goal of unraveling the mystery of the Pease and

Tabor babies — and Quinn had a considerable head start.

"He wants to talk to you."

The sidewalk was uncharacteristically crowded, but then most afternoons did not herald the return of the town's favorite personality. Quinn raised his head toward Jack and winked one eye, but at least a dozen people filled the space between them with others trailing behind Quinn's steps. Quinn patiently accepted embraces and offered handshakes.

Sylvia stepped in and spoke with mayoral authority, asking people to step back and assuring them there would be plenty of time to greet Quinn. With outstretched arms, she cleared a path for Quinn to walk toward Jack.

"Hello, Jack." Quinn extended a warm handshake. "I seem to be quite the celebrity today."

"People have been very worried about you," Jack said. "I know my girls have."

"How are your girls?" Quinn raised his eyebrows and looked sincerely interested.

"They're well — and they'll be delighted to hear that you're back."

"I'm looking forward to reading Eva's family history project," Quinn said. "She's the first Parker to come through my tenth-grade class, so it'll be a fresh family history to dive into. We've had some good conversations about it."

Jack looked around as more people came out of office buildings and around the corner from Main Street.

"I wanted to invite you for a cup of coffee," Quinn said. "I suppose that's not realistic now."

"Not unless you want to have coffee in the school gymnasium," Jack said. "I'm glad to see you are safe and sound."

Quinn waved away the concern. "I have a feeling the next few days are going to be out of my control. Before the whirlwind starts, I wanted to express my thanks for your help."

"My help?"

"With Nicole and Ethan. I understand you helped piece together some of the information about Ethan's history. It's a very different story than the one he wrote when he was in the tenth grade."

Jack shrugged. "You were the one who started that line of inquiry."

"Give yourself credit," Quinn said. "You did some good sleuthing. Ethan tells me you declined to destroy the old will and the contract between Pease and Tabor."

"That's right," Jack said. "They may yet come in useful."

"I would very much like to see them."

Jack's gaze bounced around the growing crowd. Sylvia, Ethan, and Liam were all fully engaged in encouraging people to allow Quinn to have this conversation. Nicole sat in Ethan's car with the door open watching the scene, and Dani leaned against her Jeep talking with the man Jack didn't recognize.

"I think the mayor has this in hand," Quinn said. "Let's give them all the slip."

Jack chuckled. "I believe you already tried that trick."

Quinn grinned. "And I was quite successful!"

Jack caught Liam's eye before leading Quinn into the office building and up the stairs. They were halfway to the second story when Jack's cell phone pinged, and out of reflex he looked at it.

"A text message from my daughter," he said.

"Which one?"

"Brooke. She says, 'Is it true that Quinn came home?' "

"Well, news gets around quickly in Hidden Falls," Quinn said, "but I didn't expect it to hit the schools quite yet. Tell her I look forward to seeing her at church on Sunday."

Jack typed while they walked. By the time he hit SEND, they had reached Jack's suite.

"I suppose you've got a few files on me," Quinn said. "The younger Mr. Morris handled my interests when I bought my home thirty years ago."

"Then the papers are here somewhere," Jack said. "Morris and Morris did not seem to believe in throwing anything away."

"A fortunate habit for us, or you would never have found that contract between Mr. Tabor and Mr. Pease, and we might have all sorts of notions about why Ethan Jordan looks so much like Harold Tabor."

Jack turned the key in the lock and opened the door. As he did so, his phone rang.

"Sorry," he said. "This time it's Eva calling."

"She should be in her sixth-period English class," Quinn said. "Let's hope Principal Devon doesn't discover she's been using her phone during class."

Jack debated about ignoring the call.

Quinn turned up one corner of his mouth. "May I answer your phone?"

"Help yourself." Jack turned on the phone's speaker and slapped it into Quinn's open palm.

"Good afternoon, Miss Parker," Quinn said.

Jack heard his daughter's gasp.

"Mr. Quinn?" she said.

"Yes, it's me."

The girl squealed. "Everybody, it's true. He's back."

"I'm delighted by your enthusiasm," Quinn said, "but your teacher may have other ideas."

Eva laughed. "She's the one who suggested we find out if the rumor was true."

"And what exactly was the rumor?"

"Zeke Plainfield's mom sent him a text

message and said she saw you on the street and it's a mob scene."

"The street is rather abuzz."

"When are you coming back to school?"

"Soon. So when you see your history classmates, tell them to get those projects in shipshape."

Eva giggled. "What are you doing with my dad's phone?"

"I'm at his office. I couldn't resist."

"Tell my dad to call me later, please."

"Will do." Quinn handed the phone back to Jack. "You heard the lady. Now about those documents."

"I'll be right back." Jack went into the file room, where he had created a new file folder with Ethan's name on it and placed it among his current files in a locked cabinet. When he sealed the envelope containing the originals of the relevant documents just a few hours ago, Jack hadn't expected he would break the seal so soon. He had intended only that he would be able to produce the files if Ethan wanted them at some point in the future. Now he laid the papers in a straight row on his desk and stepped aside so Quinn could inspect them.

Jack looked down on the scene in the street while Quinn read the tattered, yellowed papers.

After a few minutes, Quinn sighed. "It looks like we got to the same destination by separate routes, but I admit I'm glad to have this confirmation."

"From a legal standpoint, it's still largely speculation," Jack said. The contract didn't specify that the families were exchanging children, after all.

"Of course," Quinn said, "and if Ethan hadn't inherited the particular set of genes he did, we wouldn't even have had reason to speculate. Or if that crate of old Tabor belongings hadn't made its way to the historical society, we would never have known there was anything to speculate about."

"I suppose not," Jack murmured.

"A moment can change your whole life. Maybe someday I'll tell you about the one that changed mine."

Jack didn't know if he would have another private opportunity with Quinn. If he wanted to ask, he had to do it now. "About the grave?"

Quinn nodded as he stacked the documents and slid them back into the envelope. "I haven't quite got that part figured out, either. I finally decided I had to tell Ethan what I knew so far, even if not all the questions were answered."

Jack took the envelope from him and set it aside. Later he would again seal the past against the future. "Are you giving up on the final question, then?"

Quinn stepped away from the desk. "We

should probably go back down to the others."

"You've come this far," Jack pressed. "Don't you want to know?" Between the two of them, perhaps they could still figure out the mystery of who was buried in the infant grave only a few feet from the Pease markers without causing distress to the Jordan family.

"It's hard to know what to do when you're staring into the dark." Quinn tilted his head. "Sometimes you only go as far as you can see and then wait for the light again."

2:28 p.m.

"What's going on out there?" Lauren was sitting up in a chair in her hospital room and now leaned toward the closed door. Cooper sat in another chair borrowed from an empty room. He'd only come in about six minutes ago. "Did you see any ruckus when you came in?"

Cooper shook his head. "Just the usual frenzy of overworked hospital staff."

Lauren cocked her head. Something was definitely happening out there. She'd been in the hospital long enough to know what sounds were normal at mealtimes and shift changes and peak visiting hours. What she heard now wasn't normal. The door opened, and footsteps and voices rose, but Lauren couldn't make out any words.

Nurse Wacker came in. "How's the patient?"

"Not very patient." Cooper laughed at his own pun.

Lauren scowled at him.

"Your CNA seems to have gone AWOL," Nurse Wacker said. "I'm just going to get some quick vitals since you're off the monitor."

"Is something happening out in the hall?" Lauren asked.

"Like what?" The nurse put fingers on Lauren's wrist to feel for her pulse.

"Some kind of commotion. It seems noisy."

"Nothing for you to worry about."

Lauren held her retort. She wasn't worried. She was curious. What was wrong with asking a simple question?

"Your pulse is a little fast," the nurse said as she pushed up Lauren's sleeve and wrapped a blood pressure cuff around her arm. "Keep in mind that Dr. Jordan doesn't want you to be stressed."

"I feel fine." Lauren offered a smile as proof and took a deep breath, determined that the nurse would not find her blood pressure elevated as well.

A minute later Nurse Wacker rubbed Lauren's shoulder. "You look good. Just try to relax for a little while longer."

Once again when the door opened, the hall sounds rose for a few seconds. Lauren heard muffled laughter this time.

Cooper's phone emitted a sound Lauren had come to recognize as the signal that he had a text message. A smile spread across his face as he looked at his phone.

"Good news?" Lauren said.

"Yes, from my brother."

"Have you seen him today?"

"No, but he seems to be having a good day."

"I'm glad."

Lauren waited for Cooper to say more, but he didn't.

"I don't understand why Ethan didn't come to see me this morning," she said. "I was hoping he would spring me by now. My aunt was in and out of here in such a hurry last night, and I haven't heard a word from her all day, either."

"Give Sylvia a break. She's the mayor, runs a local business, and looks after her mother."

Cooper looked at his phone again, still smiling. If he wasn't going to tell her what he found so amusing, Lauren wouldn't press the question. She was more interested in what was happening outside the room.

She stood up. "I don't think there's any reason I can't take a short walk. I did it this morning."

That silly grin was still stuck on Cooper's face. It was starting to annoy Lauren.

"Do you want to come?" Lauren asked as she moved toward the door. With or without

Cooper, she was going to find out what the commotion in the hall was about.

"Maybe you should take it easy," Cooper said.

Lauren cinched her robe tighter. "I feel fine." She walked at an unhurried but determined pace toward the door and pulled on the handle.

It gave too easily, and Lauren stumbled back a couple of steps. Ethan appeared, pushing on the other side of the door.

"Hello, Lauren."

"Hello." Lauren lifted herself to her toes to look over Ethan's shoulder. How was it possible that the few square feet of the hall she could see were vacant at that moment? The buzz was still there, though, distinctly floating in one direction.

Ethan applied slight pressure to Lauren's shoulder, turning her around. "Why don't you sit down?"

"What's going on out there, Ethan?"

He shrugged. "You can never tell in a hospital hall. Maybe somebody got good news."

Lauren huffed, but she sat on the side of the bed. She was used to the paces Ethan would put her through, even though her responses had been normal ever since the procedure he'd done early Monday morning. She pushed against his hand, followed his finger in the path through the air, and winced when he drew his pen across the bottom of her foot.

"Has anything odd happened today?" Ethan said.

"You mean in addition to the funny stuff in the hall?"

He tilted his head and smiled. "Just wondering how you're feeling. No trouble with words or memory?"

"I feel fine, Ethan. When can I go home?"

"I think we can get discharge under way. I'll leave orders at the nurses' station."

"Good!" Lauren glanced at Cooper, wondering if he would want to take her home. First she'd have to ask Aunt Sylvia to bring her some clothes.

"Put your slippers back on," Ethan said. "I'd like Cooper to take you for a short walk."

"I told you it was okay." Lauren threw Cooper a glance.

"Why don't you go down to the waiting room?" Ethan said. "Get some new scenery."

Cooper stood and offered an arm. Lauren slid her hand into the crook of his elbow. His arm was solid muscle. Lauren wasn't sure why she'd expected anything else.

Ethan went first into the hall, letting Cooper hold the door for Lauren. She heard him murmur something to Nurse Wacker, who gave a sly smile. Lauren looked down the hall in both directions. Had the activity passed with such swiftness? It didn't seem possible the medley of voices she'd heard could have dispersed so quickly. She blew out her breath.

"Are you all right?" Cooper asked.

"I'm fine." Why did everyone keep asking her how she was? The crisis was long past. As she turned toward the waiting room, Lauren glanced over one shoulder at Ethan making notes at the nurses' station.

The farther down the hall they went, the more convinced Lauren became that the blanket of hushed noise she'd heard outside her room had transferred to the waiting room. She clutched Cooper's arm, wondering what she was about to encounter.

The room was full — of people, of laughter, of hugs, of light, of grins.

Of sheer joy.

"There have to be at least forty people here," Lauren said. She looked for a thread to connect the faces she saw, but the group was too varied. Some were from Our Savior Community Church, some from shops along Main Street, some from the hospital in their scrubs, some from neighborhoods all over town. Some she didn't even know. Lauren could connect one person to another, and then the second to a third, but by the time she got to the fourth or fifth, the direct connection faltered.

She could think of only one thing that would unite this diversity.

Quinn.

He stepped out of a huddle in the middle of the room. Lauren felt Cooper's grip on her elbow tighten as she gasped.

"You knew about this, didn't you?" she said.

"Guilty as charged."

Quinn moved toward her. Lauren was only briefly self-conscious about walking into a room full of people in her bathrobe and slippers.

"I hear you had a run-in with a sidewalk," Quinn said as he embraced Lauren.

"Could have been worse. Could have been the tree." Lauren remained in his arms. Quinn had never been one to hurry a hug.

"Congratulations on a wonderful job on the health fair," Quinn said. "My sources tell me it was a rousing success."

"I wish you'd been there."

"Me, too."

Lauren looked around at the crowded room, a medley of chattering voices and punctuating laughter.

"I have so many questions," she said, "but I guess I can't ask them right now."

"All in due time." Quinn waved at someone across the room.

"How about just one question?" Lauren said. "The calls to my phone — and the tune. I don't understand." This was one tiny piece of a giant puzzle that Lauren didn't understand, but it was the piece that had rattled her past enough to unnerve her.

"You do deserve an explanation of that. Come with me. I'd like to introduce you to someone." Quinn took Lauren's hand and led her around the outskirts of the mingling mass of townspeople. Cooper followed.

A man looked up at them. He reminded Lauren of somebody in a vague way. Then the sensation snapped into place. The man reminded her of Quinn.

"This is my brother, Scott," Quinn said. "This is Lauren, the young woman you pestered with your mysterious phone calls behind my back."

Scott shook Lauren's hand. "I suppose you'd like an explanation."

"Well, yes, if you have a short version." Lauren would press for the details later.

"Ted kept whistling the same simple tune — even picked it out on the tinny old piano at my house. One day I picked up his phone and noticed he'd called a certain number multiple times."

"Mine," Lauren said. Although Quinn did most of the organizing work for the health fair, he'd called Lauren with questions several times. Did she want him to make the announcements in church? Did she have a printer in mind for the flyer he had ready? Lauren had been at the fringe of the arrangements, but Quinn had called her more often than usual.

"My brother built a life here in Hidden

Falls," Scott said. "He told me enough about it that I knew people would be worried, but he refused to call anyone until he was certain the danger was past."

What danger? Lauren would have to ask later.

"I thought the tune might mean something, so I called and whistled it," Scott said.

"Only the tune didn't mean anything to me," Lauren said. How was a stranger to know she'd been bullied with a phone when she was a teenager?

"It was a long shot," Scott said. "I didn't know what the tune meant or whose number I was calling. I just hoped it would somehow be a message that my brother was all right."

"Scott tries hard," Quinn said, "but he's not very good at playing the spy."

Quinn had played the spy himself lately, Lauren thought. A secret box in Sylvia's attic, a curious photo in his file cabinet, Morse code in Old Dom's books at the cemetery, a sudden disappearance.

Cooper nudged Lauren and put his phone in front of her. "Now you can see this."

Quinn looked over her shoulder. "My goodness."

The image was so unexpected that Lauren had difficulty fitting it into a sense of reality.

In the picture on Cooper's phone, Quinn was kissing her aunt — and not on the cheek.

Cooper pointed. "She's over there."

Sylvia waved at Lauren with her left hand. The diamond on her ring finger caught the light perfectly and sent a dazzling greeting.

4:47 p.m.

Ethan shook Quinn's hand in the hospital hallway. There was still so much to talk about, so many questions about how Quinn had tracked down documents and connected the dots leading to the revelations of the last few days. For the moment, though, what mattered was getting Lauren out of the hospital. Ethan had done what he could to keep the administrative process moving.

Quinn tapped the cell phone in his shirt pocket. "I have your number now. I have a feeling there will be dinner plans that include you and Nicole. I'll call you."

"We all have to eat." Ethan doubted anyone who had welcomed Quinn home so far would decline if offered the chance to have dinner with Quinn. Certainly Ethan wouldn't.

"You'll be back in Hidden Falls before the wedding, won't you?" Quinn asked.

"Don't worry," Ethan said, "I'll be at your wedding." He hadn't heard Quinn or Sylvia mention a date yet, but Ethan anticipated tying up loose ends in Columbus and moving back to Hidden Falls fairly soon. Without an obligation to Dr. Gonzalez, Ethan had nothing to hold him in Ohio for longer than it took to organize the details of a move. Most of his furniture wasn't worth the expense of transporting it. He would divest himself easily enough and pull a small trailer to Hidden Falls.

Sylvia stepped toward them in the brisk, focused pace Ethan had come to expect from her. She moved physically in the same manner with which she discharged her varied responsibilities around town.

"She's ready," Sylvia said.

"Wheelchair?" Quinn said.

"In the room."

"I want to push it," Quinn said.

Ethan's lips turned up in amusement. He imagined hospital policy would specify an employee had to handle the wheelchair. Then there was the reality Lauren wouldn't want to ride in it at all. He would let them all sort it out.

When Quinn started for Lauren's room, Sylvia hung back.

"Come to Our Savior," she said.

Ethan tripped over the words, a tug toward his abandoned early faith pulling him out of the moment. *Come to our Savior,* he had heard. *Believe as you once did,* the voice continued, though Sylvia had paused. Ethan realized Sylvia meant the church, and the invitation he'd sensed came from deep within.

"Six o'clock," Sylvia said. "We might not be on a schedule, but there's a plan afoot."

"What sort of plan?" Ethan asked.

"A plan to finish what we started ten days ago." Sylvia radiated the pleasure of the day, her eyes shining, her features creased in a smile. "Make sure Nicole gets there."

Ethan nodded. Nicole was moving toward him now, coming from Lauren's room as a small mass of well-wishers nearly smothered Lauren. Quinn had his hands on the handles of the wheelchair, but the hospital transport employee had not given up the fight for control. Cooper walked alongside, holding her hand. At the rear — but closing in — were Sylvia and Quinn's brother.

An urge to call his own brother shot through Ethan. He couldn't remember the last time they'd spoken. They hadn't had a falling out, just a fading away, each of them finding his own path away from their father's disinterest in their lives. And whatever happened with his brother, Ethan would try harder to find something in common with his father. Richard might not be able to make an effort, but Ethan could, if for no other reason than the happiness it would bring his mother. All these years he'd thought only of himself, his own scars. Moving back to Hidden Falls might cut into the wounds again, but perhaps that's what it would take to keep them from seeping for the rest of his life.

Ethan stepped toward Nicole, wishing again he could take her hand as they walked and instead making sure his feet stayed out of the way of her crutches with an artificial distance between them.

"What a day," Nicole said.

Yes, what a day. What a week. They paused, and Ethan moved the hair off the left side of Nicole's face, exposing the mole she always tried to hide. He kissed her cheek.

"Sylvia said I should bring you to the church later," he said.

"She's up to something."

Ethan followed Nicole's gaze as the gaggle around Lauren crammed into the elevator, no one willing to be left behind.

"I'm going to get my father to come to Quinn's wedding," Nicole said. "I want Quinn to see that Dad is doing well, that at last he has found a new life for himself."

Ethan and Nicole drifted slowly toward the elevators themselves.

"Let's not do what Quinn did," Ethan said, pausing and turning toward Nicole.

She raised her eyebrows in question.

"Once I move back here," Ethan said, "I'll only be two hours from St. Louis. We can see each other frequently and figure things out." Ten years ago Ethan had let circumstances make decisions for him. He'd had more of his father's passivity in him than he thought, he realized now. Despite his ambition, he hadn't known how to get past his own fearful inertia when it came to Nicole. This time

Ethan wasn't going to hesitate about what he wanted.

He wanted Nicole.

"I won't be in St. Louis," Nicole said. "I've made other plans."

Ethan's stomach burned.

"While you were chasing after Quinn yesterday," Nicole said, "I was chasing down the truth at the paper in St. Louis. I was ready to resign, but they offered a separation package, and I took it."

"Did you get an offer from another newspaper already?"

"Well, I suppose Marvin Stanford would always take me back at the *Dispatch.*"

Ethan let out his breath. "You're going to be in Hidden Falls?"

"I'll pick up some freelance projects. Mostly I've decided to go into the home rehab business. A particular house I know needs a lot of work, but it might someday be a decent place to live again."

"I know the place." Ethan smiled. "I hear the neighbor over the back fence is an extraordinary guy."

"The people next door might not be so bad either," Nicole said. "They have an eligible bachelor son. A hotshot brain surgeon."

Ethan put his arms on Nicole's elbows to steady her. He intended to kiss her hard.

6:17 p.m.

Sylvia leaned over the open oven door, pulled back a corner of foil, and stuck a fork into the tray of lasagna. The escaping steam encouraged her.

"It shouldn't be too much longer," she said.

"I wish you'd let me help." Sitting in a chair in the corner of the church kitchen, Lauren pouted.

"You will sit right there until instructed to do otherwise."

Sylvia calculated — again — how many servings of lasagna now occupied the church ovens. Gavin had assembled ingredients at Fall Shadows Café with speed Sylvia had not thought possible and delivered the trays to the church. It looked like the food would be hot enough to serve before too much longer. The challenge was estimating how many people were coming. Sylvia would wait until she saw how much of the town's population caught wind of the impromptu event and how many potluck salads and bread baskets showed up before deciding whether she would reduce the recommended portion size of lasagna in order to feed everyone. Someone from Eat Right Here was supposed to bring over assorted dessert trays at any minute.

"I could at least go sit out in the fellowship hall," Lauren said.

Sylvia hesitated. She'd parked Lauren where she could see her for a reason, but the work in the kitchen was under control, and Sylvia herself would need to go out into the fellowship hall soon to make sure setting up was progressing satisfactorily.

"Well, all right," Sylvia said, "but I'm going to put Cooper in charge of you, and you know he's a stickler for the rules."

Together they left the kitchen and went into the main hall. Sylvia delivered Lauren into Cooper's willing custody and found Scott Wilson sitting in a folding chair against a side wall. Already Quinn was surrounded by people who had come to help set up.

"You okay?" Sylvia asked.

"I can't tell you how often I wondered about stuff like this," Scott said. "Where my brother was. Whether he had people who loved him. Whether he was happy after our whole lives changed in a split second."

A lump threatened to fill Sylvia's throat. "He is loved. Well loved."

"I can see that for myself now," Scott said. "After years — decades — of imagining what his life might be like, now I feel like I'm looking in from the outside."

Sylvia hoped Scott was as well loved as his brother. The last few hours hadn't allowed much opportunity to find out about Scott. Or maybe she should be thinking of him as Andrew. She could tell Quinn was making an effort to call his brother Scott, and Scott referred to Quinn as Ted, but she could also see the remembrance in both of them of when they were Adam and Andrew Kreske. Their safety all these years had come at a high price.

"I look forward to lots of visits back and forth between here and Oklahoma," Sylvia said.

Scott smiled. "I'm glad he has you. And I always wanted a sister."

Henry and Patricia Healy paced across the old tile floor. "Tell us what to do," Patricia said after Sylvia made the introductions.

Sylvia inventoried her mental list. "How about setting up the portable sound system?"

"I can do that," Henry said.

Scott stood up. "I'll help."

"Can you make sure the coffee urns are heating?" Sylvia said to Patricia. "Then we need tablecloths and dishes and silverware."

"Are we setting the tables?" Patricia said.

That would take a small brigade and more time than they had available.

"We'll just set up the long serving tables," Sylvia said decisively. "But let's use the real dishes, not the Styrofoam stuff."

Quinn would fuss about causing extra work, but Sylvia didn't care. She wanted the evening to be something solid even if it was last minute. Sylvia would stay all night in the church kitchen washing dishes, if she had to. While Patricia went off to check on the four large coffee urns Sylvia had set up forty-five minutes ago, Sylvia opened a cupboard and was relieved to find ample clean, folded tablecloths in various colors. She took two stacks out and set them on a nearby table. When she looked up, Sylvia saw Sammie Dunavant enter with Emma on her arm. She walked over to greet them.

"Thank you, Sammie," Sylvia said. She'd wanted to give her mother the option to attend, but if she'd gone herself to pick up Emma, preparations would have been substantially behind their current status.

"No problem," Sammie said. "As soon as I heard about this, I wanted to come anyway."

"How are you, Mom?" Sylvia looked for clues in Emma's face for how lucid she was.

"I don't usually like to go out at night," Emma said, "but I had to see for myself that the rumor is true that Quinn is here."

Sylvia was relieved to see the twinkle in her mother's eye.

"He's come home, Mom."

Sammie drew in a rapid breath. "Is that what I think it is on your finger?"

Sylvia nodded. There would be plenty of time for that story later. She'd like to tell it where her mother had fewer distractions to filter out than in the large church hall where each moment brought more activity.

"I'll be so glad to put Quinn back on my cleaning schedule," Sammie said. "Come on, Emma, let's go say hello to Quinn."

"He'll be happy to see you," Sylvia said. So far Quinn had been pleased to greet dozens of people today, but Sylvia had no doubt that he could greet five hundred more with the same untarnished warmth.

The number *five hundred* had popped into her head randomly. Neither the table space nor the lasagna would stretch that far, but Sylvia decided not to worry. Whatever the evening lacked in logistics, joy and delight would cap it off.

Sylvia was glad to see Nicole and Ethan enter next.

"It's coming together." Nicole smiled widely. "It'll be a great night."

"I hope so." Sylvia touched Ethan's arm. "We could use some help getting more chairs out. I have a feeling we should squeeze in ten to a table rather than eight."

"I'm on it," Ethan said.

Sylvia was delighted to see that Ethan still remembered right where the closet was that held the chairs the church used for overflowing events.

"Do you want to sit with Lauren?" Sylvia asked Nicole.

They both looked across the hall, where Cooper and Lauren tilted their heads toward each other from their chairs.

Nicole chuckled. "She looks well cared for, don't you think?"

Sylvia smiled in agreement.

"I want to help." Nicole crutched toward the stack of tablecloths. "I may not be the speediest assistant around, but I think I can manage this task."

"Thank you." Sylvia would send someone over to help as soon as she could politely interrupt a cluster of conversation. For now, she laid four folded tablecloths over one of Nicole's shoulders and spread a fifth over a table while Nicole balanced on her crutches and moved to a nearby table.

"There's Dani and Liam." Nicole flapped open a tablecloth.

Behind Dani and Liam were Eva Parker and Zeke Plainfield.

"We brought something to help with decorations," Eva said.

Zeke unfurled a banner. Sylvia recognized it immediately. THANK YOU, QUINN, it said. The planning committee had it made for the banquet ten days ago. She'd last seen it still on the wall of the dinner hall and amid the consuming events since that night had not wondered what became of it. As she was about to ask how the two teenagers gained possession of it, Sylvia remembered Zeke had been one of the servers for the event.

"Can we hang it?" Eva looked at Sylvia with wide, pleading eyes.

"Of course," Sylvia said. "Do you know where the ladder is, Zeke?"

"Yep."

"Have at it. Just don't put any new holes in the wall." Sylvia glanced at Dani.

"We'll make sure it's done right," Dani said, pulling on Liam's arm.

Sylvia couldn't think of a time in recent history that Liam had been inside the church building — or Dani. But here they were. Zeke and Eva would know where everything was, and Dani and Liam would keep them from doing anything careless.

The doors were opening and closing at a steady pace now as people brought in salads, breads, and vegetable dishes. They set the contributions on four long serving tables arranged end to end, where Patricia Healy made sure there was some organization to the fare and Scott transferred stacks of dishes from a rolling cart. Sylvia nodded in satisfaction as she saw Patricia was planning to serve from both sides of the tables. As soon as they relieved themselves of their food dishes, most visitors beelined for Quinn. He shook hands and kissed cheeks and dispensed hugs and grinned. He was as much himself as Sylvia had ever seen him.

Already it was clear they would have a good crowd. Sylvia had reckoned correctly that phones would be ringing all over Hidden Falls with the informal invitation to anyone who could come on short notice. They wouldn't have all the out-of-town guests who had held tickets to the original occasion, but the room would fill, and every person there would be glad to see that Quinn was home safe.

Sylvia watched Quinn, in gray cotton trousers and his signature plaid shirt, this one with a touch of yellow running through the pattern. He didn't need a tux to look dashing. He never had.

Quinn lifted his eyes out of the swelling huddle and found Sylvia's gaze. She moved slowly toward him, no longer mindful of the preparations and people. Quinn was all she wanted to see. He patted a few shoulders and emerged from the mingling to take her elbow in his gentle touch. Everything around her fell away.

"You did all this, didn't you?" he said.

"I had some coconspirators." Sylvia remembered his touch that morning when he'd wrapped his fingers around her hand after giving her the ring. His skin had been cool and smooth, and Sylvia would never forget the soft pressure and his reluctance to let go.

"How much time would you need to plan the wedding you'd like?" Quinn looked into Sylvia's eyes, unblinking.

Sylvia smiled. "I don't imagine it would take too long."

"I want it to be everything you want," he said.

"You'll be there," she said. "What else do I need?" Thirty years ago, Sylvia probably would have worn a puffy dress and mailed dozens of invitations. Her mother would have pressed for a stylish reception, arguing that Sylvia would only marry once. The flowers and the cake would have brought a minor economic boon to Hidden Falls. Now Sylvia wanted a simple ceremony, an intimate gathering of the man she had loved so long and the people closest to them.

"You pick the time and place and I'll be there." Quinn kissed Sylvia's cheek. "Now what am I supposed to do tonight?"

"Nothing you haven't already been doing. Enjoy your friends. Be glad you're home. Eat some good food."

Cooper approached them. "Sorry to interrupt, but the word from the kitchen is that everything is ready."

Sylvia glanced toward the kitchen and saw Patricia sticking her head out the door. Lizzie, Sylvia's assistant from the shop, and Marianne, her assistant from her office, were there, too, all of them with cockeyed grins on their faces.

"Is the sound system ready?" Sylvia asked.

"Henry says it is," Cooper answered.

"Then let's do this."

Quinn cleared his throat. "I don't have to stand on an X, do I?"

Sylvia laughed. "I am not taking the risk of putting a curtain between the two of us this time. Cooper, don't let him out of your sight."

She strode to the microphone. "Ladies and gentlemen, thank you for coming. Please find your seats while we cover the preliminaries."

The buzz of conversation subsided in exchange for the shuffling of chairs.

"This time," Sylvia said, "we don't have fancy menus and name tags and programs. We're not even going to have flowery speeches. But we have what matters most. We have friendship. We have hearts full of gratitude. We have the pride in Hidden Falls that binds us together. We have an abundance of food to share and an abundance of love that gathers us around these tables tonight. And we have Quinn, whose life of service has touched all of us at some time or another."

Sylvia swept one arm wide toward Quinn. "Before we begin the meal, let's welcome the guest of honor."

Applause thundered as every person in the room stood. Palpable joy rose from hands and faces. Nicole leaned on Ethan. Cooper had an arm around Lauren's shoulder. Dani and Liam gave each other playful punches. Jack and Gianna Parker smiled at their daughters. Even Colin was there. Emma. Henry and Patricia. The Gallaghers with their wiggly little girls. Gavin. Sammie. Benita. Pastor Matt. Lizzie. Marianne. And so many more — hundreds more. Sylvia knew the name of every person in the room and was certain Quinn did also. Stories crisscrossed through decades and neighborhoods and joys and sorrows.

Such love. Such richness of life.

Such beauty in the fullness that was Hidden Falls.

ABOUT THE AUTHOR

Olivia Newport's novels twist through time to find where faith and passions meet. Her husband and two twentysomething children provide welcome distraction from the people stomping through her head on their way into her books. She chases joy in stunning Colorado at the foot of the Rockies, where daylilies grow as tall as she is.

The employees of Thorndike Press hope you have enjoyed this Large Print book. All our Thorndike, Wheeler, and Kennebec Large Print titles are designed for easy reading, and all our books are made to last. Other Thorndike Press Large Print books are available at your library, through selected bookstores, or directly from us.

For information about titles, please call:
(800) 223-1244

or visit our Web site at:
http://gale.cengage.com/thorndike

To share your comments, please write:

Publisher
Thorndike Press
10 Water St., Suite 310
Waterville, ME 04901